DETROIT PUBLIC LIBRARY

P9-DNM-410

CHASE BRANCH LIBRARY
17731 W. SEVEN MILE ROAD
DETROIT, MI 48235
313-481-1580

MAY - - 2016

HIDE AWAY

ALSO BY IRIS JOHANSEN

Shadow Play

The Naked Eye (with Roy Johansen)

Your Next Breath

Sight Unseen (with Roy Johansen)

Live to See Tomorrow

Silencing Eve

Hunting Eve

Taking Eve

Sleep No More

Close Your Eyes (with Roy Johansen)

What Doesn't Kill You

Bonnie

Quinn

Eve

Chasing the Night

Shadow Zone (with Roy Johansen)

Eight Days to Live

Deadlock

Dark Summer

Quicksand

Silent Thunder (with Roy Johansen)

Pandora's Daughter

Stalemate

An Unexpected Song

Killer Dreams

On the Run

Countdown

Blind Alley

Firestorm

Fatal Tide

Dead Aim

No One to Trust

Body of Lies

Final Target

The Search

The Killing Game

The Face of Deception

And Then You Die

Long After Midnight

The Ugly Duckling

Lion's Bride

Dark Rider

Midnight Warrior

The Beloved Scoundrel

The Magnificent Rogue

The Tiger Prince

Last Bridge Home

The Golden Barbarian

Reap the Wind

Storm Winds

The Wind Dancer

HIDE AWAY

IRIS JOHANSEN

ST. MARTIN'S PRESS ☙ NEW YORK

This is a work of fiction. All of the characters, organizations, and events portrayed in this novel are either products of the author's imagination or are used fictitiously.

HIDE AWAY. Copyright © 2016 by Johansen Publishing LLLP. All rights reserved. Printed in the United States of America. For information, address St. Martin's Press, 175 Fifth Avenue, New York, N.Y. 10010.

www.stmartins.com

Designed by Omar Chapa

The Library of Congress Cataloging-in-Publication Data is available upon request.

ISBN 978-1-250-07582-6 (hardcover)
ISBN 978-1-4668-8720-6 (e-book)

Our books may be purchased in bulk for promotional, educational, or business use. Please contact your local bookseller or the Macmillan Corporate and Premium Sales Department at 1-800-221-7945, extension 5442, or by e-mail at MacmillanSpecialMarkets@macmillan.com.

First Edition: April 2016

10 9 8 7 6 5 4 3 2 1

HIDE AWAY

CHAPTER

1

S he was alone.

She mustn't panic. After all, she was eleven years old and had been taught to take care of herself. She had always been told that someday she might have to face this.

Cara Delaney leaned back against the door after leaving Eve Duncan's hospital room and tried to smother the fear that was surging through her. Her heart was beating hard and her throat was tight. They were going to send her away. It was all very well to tell herself she had known that it might happen someday, but it still came as a shock. She wasn't ready to face it yet.

But she'd better get ready. She'd been on the run most of her life and should have been prepared for the day that there would be no one here to help her. Her sister, Jenny, had been killed; Elena, who had cared for Cara since she was born, had been killed. Now Cara was the only one left, and if Eve had decided she didn't want her, she'd have to find a way to face the loneliness and protect herself.

What was she thinking? Cara thought in sudden disgust. She had been feeling so sorry for herself that she had forgotten that it was Eve that she was supposed to be worrying about. It was Eve who had to be taken care of as Cara had promised. Jenny had died so that Cara could live and so had Elena. Now it was Cara's turn to give back.

She drew a deep breath and opened her hands, which had been clenched into fists. She could work through this, she just couldn't give up. There had to be a way . . .

"Cara?"

Margaret Douglas was walking down the corridor toward her, a concerned look on her face. Margaret was Eve's friend, and she had taken over Cara's supervision to keep her out of the hands of Child Services. She had been kind to Cara since Eve had been in the hospital, and Cara liked her. But Cara didn't want kindness now.

She wanted to go back into that room from which Joe Quinn had sent her and start the battle to keep her place at Eve's side.

What on earth had happened to Cara, Margaret thought. Her gaze was fixed worriedly on the child's face as she came down the hall toward her. Cara's lips were tight, and there was a tension about the muscles of her shoulders. Maybe it was just the accumulated trauma of the last days that had finally hit home. What wouldn't be wrong with an eleven-year-old child who had gone through what Cara had suffered in the last few days, much less her short life, Margaret thought bitterly. She and her sister, Jenny, were the daughters of Juan Castino, the kingpin of a drug cartel in Mexico City, and they had been kidnapped as an act of vengeance by Salazar, the leader of a rival drug cartel. Jenny had been killed, and Cara had been taken on the run by her nurse, Elena, for eight long years. Just a few days ago, Elena had been murdered by a hit man, James Walsh, hired by Salazar to find them. Cara had later been cornered by Walsh, who had come close to killing her. Only Eve's intervention had prevented it, but it had landed her in this hospital with a concussion. Yes, Cara had every reason to look tense.

"Hey, what's the problem?" Margaret stopped in front of Cara and smiled gently. "Anything I can do to help?"

Cara shook her head. "I don't think so. I think it has to be me. Something has gone wrong. I could tell when Joe Quinn came into Eve's room and sent me out here. It's probably about me. He said it wasn't and that I didn't do anything wrong. But what else could it be?" Her hazel eyes were glittering with moisture. "Eve said they were going to take me home with them for a while. But Joe probably thinks that the reason Eve was hurt was because of me. He's right, you know."

Margaret reached out and gently touched the child's dark hair. "You don't know that he's upset with you, Cara. Joe is very fair. He knows that Eve does what she thinks is right, and nothing stops her. Yes, she was hurt trying to save your life. But Joe was there almost immediately afterward, and he was concerned for you as well as Eve." She cupped Cara's thin shoulders in her hands. "We were all concerned. It was a nightmare finding you and trying to keep you safe from that horrible man. There was no way Eve was going to stop."

"I know," Cara whispered. "Jenny said to trust Eve, that she would never stop until I was safe."

Margaret stiffened. "Jenny? Cara, your sister, Jenny is—" She hesitated. There was no other way to put it. "Jenny isn't with us. She died eight years ago."

Cara nodded. "I know that, but she . . . I dream about her." She looked at Margaret defiantly. "And she doesn't seem . . . Do you think I'm crazy?"

"Who, me?" She brushed the hair back from Cara's face. So much intensity in that small face, those wide-set hazel eyes that were more green than brown. The winged brows and pointed chin. In the few days since she'd come to know the child, she'd become aware of how much emotion and intensity lay behind that usually reserved expression. Intensity and strength. Strange to think of a child as being strong, but Cara's life had been different from that of other children. She'd had to be strong and enduring to bear the constant change and terror of being on the run. Even now when Walsh, the man who'd been hunting her had been killed, she knew she wasn't safe, that there might be another killer on the horizon. That life had made Cara mature beyond her years, and Margaret was constantly finding out new and different facets to her character. "I'm the last one to think anyone is crazy because of a few dreams. A lot of people think I'm a little weird because I don't march to their drummers."

"You don't seem weird," Cara said. "You seem . . . nice."

"One doesn't exclude the other. You seem nice, too." She stepped back. "And a dream can just be a memory."

"Yeah," Cara nodded. "But it seems like more." She paused. "I think Eve dreams about Jenny, too."

"It wouldn't surprise me. Eve has a kind of sensitivity to people like us. That's why I get along so well with her." She added gently, "I know this is all strange to you, Cara. *We're* strange to you. It's only been a couple days since you met all of us. We blew into your life at a time when everything was terrible and scary. You even lost your best friend, Elena, to that monster who was hunting you. You probably don't know whom to trust or how to react to all of us. You don't know where you're going next."

"You're wrong. I know where I'm going." Cara looked over her shoulder at the door of Eve's room. "I'm going with her. I have to take care of her. She needs me."

Margaret's brows rose. "Really? Everyone needs affection. But other than that, Eve's pretty strong, Cara."

"I have to take care of her," she repeated. "I promised Jenny."

"In that dream you had?"

She didn't answer directly. "I promised her." She went on in a rush, "And, like I said, Eve was going to let me stay with her and Joe for a while. She said so." She was frowning. "But when Joe came into the room a few minutes ago, I could tell that he was upset. Maybe he changed his mind."

"I doubt it." She tilted her head curiously. "What would you do if he did?"

"I'd go with her anyway. I'd find a way." Her gaze was still fixed on the door. "I have to take care of her."

Determination, intensity, and total commitment. Margaret shook her head with amazement. All of them had been so focused on finding and saving Cara during these last weeks that they had been thinking of her as helpless. She might have been in danger, but there was nothing helpless about this child. "Well, soon she'll be out of the hospital and on her way home. She won't need taking care of." She smiled. "Though I'm sure that she'll still want your company, Cara. You're jumping to conclusions. Come on, let's go to the waiting room and I'll buy you a soda."

She thought Cara was going to refuse, but then the girl turned away from Eve's door. "Okay. I can't do anything right now anyway."

"Very sensible," Margaret said, as they strolled down the hall. "There's probably not going to be anything to do anyway. Maybe it's your imagination."

"No," Cara said soberly. "It's not imagination." She glanced back over her shoulder at Eve's door. "Joe was . . . tense. Something *is* wrong . . ."

MEXICO CITY, MEXICO

Something was wrong, Alfredo Salazar thought impatiently. In his last report, Walsh had told him that he had located Castino's kid and that bitch, Elena Pasquez, who had hidden her all these years, and that they'd be dead within days.

Why the hell hadn't he heard from him? It was making him damn uneasy. He'd been losing faith in James Walsh lately, but there was no doubt he was an expert once he set his sights on a victim. What could have gotten in his way?

Or who?

He reached in his desk drawer and pulled out the dossiers he'd compiled from the reports Walsh had given him.

Eve Duncan. Joe Quinn. Cara Delaney.

There were other dossiers but none as important as those three.

Eve Duncan, forensic sculptor who had restored the skull of Jenny Castino after her bones had been recently unearthed. He glanced at her photo. Not to his taste. Slim, red-brown hair with hazel eyes. An attractive, interesting face, but he preferred exotic and voluptuous. Evidently she was brilliant because she was considered one of the world's most gifted forensic sculptors.

Also very determined and stubborn. He'd warned Walsh that he should get rid of her before she got in his way. But she was an artist, a sculptor, and not equipped to go up against an enforcer of Walsh's capabilities.

He glanced at the Joe Quinn dossier. Brown hair, brown eyes, strong jaw. Detective with the ATLPD, ex-FBI, ex-SEAL. He had lived with Eve Duncan for a number of years and was said to be extremely loyal to her. He was undoubtedly deadly and capable of interfering with Walsh.

He glanced at the photo of the child. Cara had only been three when Walsh had taken her from the Castino home. Her sister Jenny had been nine, but they'd had the same high cheekbones and winged brows. That damn Eve Duncan had reproduced Jenny's features almost exactly when she'd been sent that skull of the skeleton buried in northern California and found by the Sheriff's Department. Now Walsh was sure that she was trying to locate Jenny's sister, Cara.

Which could mean disaster for Salazar.

And he wasn't about to sit here and wait any longer for word from Walsh. If he hadn't completed the kill, it was time he was taken out himself.

He reached for his phone.

It rang before he could dial.

Ramon Franco.

Which did not bode well. When Salazar had begun to have his doubts about Walsh's efficiency, Franco was the young man Salazar had sent to shadow him and make certain he was performing effectively.

"Walsh is dead," Ramon Franco said harshly as soon as Salazar picked up the call. "Killed. I just found out last night, and I've been scrambling to get information. I told you that you should have sent me to take care of that kid. He bungled the kill, and now there are police all over the place. We'll be lucky if they don't trace anything back to you."

Son of a bitch!

Salazar's hand tightened on the phone as the fury tore through him. "That can't happen. I've spent eight years covering Walsh's incompetence. I won't let that bastard's death toss me into Castino's jaws for him to chew up. Who killed him?"

"Eve Duncan."

So he had been wrong. Evidently the artist had a few more lethal skills than her credentials suggested. He had warned Walsh that she was a possible problem when the woman had gone on the hunt for him after he had stolen her reconstruction of Castino's daughter's skull. Now she was no longer a problem; she was a major pain in the ass. "For God's sake, Duncan is only a forensic sculptor, and she managed to put down Walsh? How many people has Walsh killed over the years? He should have been able to squash her like a bug. How did it happen?"

"It could have been an accident. Her statement to the police claimed they were fighting on the high ledge of a cave, and he backed off and fell to his death." He added, "Or she might have outsmarted him. Castino's other daughter, Cara, was in the cave, and you told me she was the target."

"The last target," Salazar said bitterly. "And Walsh couldn't even manage to find and kill an eleven-year-old kid."

"He found her in that cave, but he couldn't finish the job. Eve

Duncan got in the way. He managed to kill her nursemaid, Elena Pasquez, but no one else. I would never have let that happen."

"And when the police start digging into who that kid really is, they'll toss her back to her father, Castino, and he'll go after me. He's just waiting for a chance to break the coalition agreement."

"Then we have to make sure he doesn't have a reason to do it until we're strong enough to bury him and all the rest of the men in his damn cartel. Give me the word and I'll erase Walsh's death and that little girl as if they'd never existed." His voice was suddenly impassioned. "You haven't been fair to me. Haven't I always been loyal to you? From the time I was twelve, I did everything you told me to do. No kill was too hard. Yet you sent me here to Carmel to watch that bumbler, Walsh, just to make sure he was going to be able to finish the kill on the Castino kid. It was a job for a beginner. I may be young, but I'm no beginner."

"No, I know you're not." He tried to make his tone soothing. Franco's tone bordered on insolence, and he was tempted to cut him down to size, but he might need him. He was the man on the spot, with all contacts in place. Better to handle Ramon Franco with kid gloves. The young recruits always lacked discipline, but they were also the ones most eager to prove themselves in blood. He was only nineteen, but his kill record with the cartel was impressive. He was quick, lethal, and totally vicious. "That's why I trusted you to watch Walsh. I never knew when I would have to have someone good enough to take over. Walsh had the experience, but he was going downhill, and I couldn't trust him." He paused. "Not like you, Franco. I see myself in you."

"You do?" Franco was silent, then said haltingly, "I'm honored, sir. It's just that I don't understand. You told me so little about what was going on with Walsh. I felt . . . like an errand boy."

Which was exactly how Salazar saw him. But circumstances dictated the errand boy be promoted until Salazar could take charge himself. "I don't want any of my other men to be jealous of you.

Particularly not now. I'd rather you concentrate on getting me out of the mess Walsh made up there in Carmel. You're going to have to dance a fine dance to save the situation. But you're a smart boy, and I know that you can do it for me."

"I'm a man, not a boy."

"Of course you are. But it's not a bad thing that others believe you to be a boy, so they won't suspect how very deadly you can be. I've seen you use that ploy before."

"Sometimes."

"Often. Do you think I haven't been watching you? Use your brains and that smile the ladies like so much."

"Then tell me what I need to know. Tell me what Walsh knew, what I should have known from the beginning."

A definite touch of arrogance, Salazar noticed. "You know the beginning. You grew up with it. The drugs, the vice, that son of a bitch, Juan Castino, constantly moving into my territory. He acted as if his cartel was the only one in Mexico, and every time anyone came close to taking him down, he managed to come out on top. I had the brains and the plans but Castino had the contacts and was always just ahead of me. If I hadn't managed to form a mutual coalition of all the cartels in Mexico, he would have eaten me alive. I can rein him in as long as he knows I have the backing of the coalition behind me."

"Until we find a way to kill him. That's the best way. Don't worry. I'll do it for you."

So simple, so incredibly naïve. "I know you will. But it has to be staged very carefully. I can't let any of the other cartels know that I'm getting ready to jump Castino." He paused. "Or that I yielded to temptation eight years ago to twist the knife and make him hurt. They might turn against me."

"Because you arranged with James Walsh to kidnap Castino's two little girls and their nanny and kill them? They all probably wish they'd had the balls to do it."

"They'd chop me up and serve me to Castino. And then move into my territory and split it up." His voice was laden with frustration. "It was going to be so simple. Walsh would kill them, and there would be no bodies or anything to connect me to it. I'd be able to sit back and watch Castino suffer, then, when the time was right, I'd make sure he joined his little girls in the graveyard. But Walsh screwed it up. He left me hanging and vulnerable if Castino finds out I paid Walsh to kill them. We have to fix it, Franco."

"I can do it if I work fast. I don't think that Castino knows anything yet. The kid's name on the police report is Cara Delaney, and Walsh is only suspected of being a serial killer. Nothing about Castino."

Hope and relief shot through Salazar. "You're certain?"

"I paid a good deal of your money to bribe a look at those reports. No mention of Castino . . . or you."

"Yet."

"As you say. But there may be a way to keep you safe if we work fast. Eve Duncan hasn't made a statement yet. She's in a local hospital being checked out for concussion, and her lover, Joe Quinn, isn't letting her be interviewed."

"Where's the kid?"

"She's being taken care of by a friend of Duncan's, Margaret Douglas."

"Not at Child Services? They're big on Welfare shit in the U.S."

"No, I'm sure. I knew you'd want to know where you could put your hands on her."

"Oh, yes." His hands around her throat to end this nightmare. "Then it appears you may have a multitude of targets in the near future. You need to find out how much Duncan knows about Cara Castino . . . and me. I have to know I'm safe from Duncan before I move forward again."

"You'll be safe. It's only a question which target I hit first." His voice was suddenly eager. "You tell me and it will be done. Duncan? Quinn? The kid?"

"You're moving too fast. I want you to go to that hospital and report back to me. Do you understand?"

"If I took out Duncan, it would stop the—"

"Report back to me," Salazar repeated. "Is that clear?"

"Yes, sir." He was silent. "I didn't mean to argue. You're the *Pez Gordo*, the big boss. I'm just concerned."

He was concerned because if Salazar and his cartel fell, he could be part of the collateral damage, Salazar thought cynically. It was obvious Franco was very ambitious. "Then it's time to use that concern in the way I told you."

"I'll leave for the hospital right away. I won't disappoint you." He hung up.

Franco was moving fast and was eager to please but Salazar still wasn't sure that he would obey instructions if an opportunity presented itself.

Oh well, Franco was a superb assassin, and Salazar was just angry enough with the way Eve Duncan had spoiled his plans that he was willing to take a chance that Franco wouldn't pay her a fatal visit in her hospital room without taking appropriate precautions. Salazar rather liked the idea of Duncan's lying helplessly in that bed in her room while Franco moved around that hospital like a lethal buzz saw.

But if Franco decided to do it, he'd damn well better do it right.

COMMUNITY HOSPITAL OF THE MONTEREY

"Cara has good instincts," Eve Duncan said as she turned back to Joe after watching the child walk out of her hospital room. "You're not easy to read, Joe. I'm glad that whatever you're upset about wasn't about her. Though I'm not sure she believed you. It would have been difficult explaining a sudden change of heart. Do you know, I'm starting to look forward to having Cara staying with us for a while?" She shook her head. "Remember, we were talking on the day Jane left for London about how my life may be changing? Then all of this happened. Do you suppose Cara is the change?"

"Not necessarily."

Eve went still. She couldn't miss that jerky roughness in his tone. "What are you talking about? What *is* wrong?"

"Not wrong. Strange. Bizarre." He shook his head. "I don't know what else."

"Stop playing around with words. Talk to me."

"I don't know how to say it."

"Just tell me."

"The hospital has the results from all the tests they've been running on you. The doctor stopped me in the hall to go over them."

"The results? Joe, I know you've been ramrodding everything connected to my treatment since you brought me to this hospital, but that's going a little too far. Why go over them with you and not with me?" She tried to smile. "Some terrible disease popped up that he thought you should break to me?"

"God, I'm not doing this right. No terrible disease. You're very healthy and ready to go home. He just didn't want you to leave the hospital without knowing."

"Joe, what are you trying to tell me?"

"In my completely clumsy and inadequate fashion." He reached out and took her hand. "I'm trying to tell you that you're going to have a child, Eve."

"You're joking," Eve said dazedly. **"It's some kind of mistake?"**

"No." Joe's hand tightened around her own. "And no. To both questions. I wouldn't have dared come in here if I hadn't made sure the doctor had checked and double-checked. You're pregnant." His teeth bit his lower lip. "And that goes to show how upset I am. *We're* pregnant. I can't quite take it in either. I went into shock when the doctor told me."

"Tell me about it," she said weakly as she sat up in the bed. "It wasn't supposed to happen. I thought it couldn't happen. It wasn't as if we weren't careful."

"I didn't think so either," Joe said. "We did everything right. Or maybe we didn't. But I don't know how we could have done anything different." He shook his head. "I'm a little confused on that point at the moment."

"Me, too." She met his gaze. "I . . . feel lost. I can't quite grasp it." She reached up and ran a hand through her hair. "How . . . long?"

"Barely. A few weeks. You must have conceived before we left the Lake Cottage to come out here to California."

"I remember when I was pregnant with Bonnie, I didn't know for months."

"Things have changed since you were sixteen. They can tell within five or six days now."

She nodded. "The whole world has changed. My whole life has changed. I'm not the same person."

"Yes, you are. You've just been tempered by experience." He lifted her palm to his lips. "And this particular experience may do some more very intricate tempering. Just don't let it throw you. We'll think about it, then make decisions."

"Decisions." No, she couldn't make decisions right now. Her head was whirling, and all she could think about was the fact that in nine months she would bear a child. It was impossible. No, it was going to happen. "How do you feel about it?"

"As dazed as you." He grinned. "Kind of . . . primitive. I've never fathered a child of my own. I suppose that's a natural reaction. I . . . like it." His smile faded. "I never suggested it to you. After all you've gone through, I thought that it had to come from you. I know what you went through when you lost your Bonnie; when she was killed. After we adopted Jane, I believed that might be the way we should go."

"So did I." She moistened her lips. "And now I'm wondering why we never talked about having a child of our own. Did I just bury my head in the sand? My God, Joe, I must have sensed you'd feel like this. Was I so afraid that I avoided facing it?"

He didn't answer.

Because he knew it was true, she realized. She was his center, and he wouldn't allow her to be hurt even if it meant being cheated himself. "You should have spoken to me about it."

He shook his head. "I have you. That's enough, more than enough." He leaned forward and kissed her. "Now stop fretting about me, you have thinking to do."

"Thinking," she repeated. "You said decision. You know I won't have an abortion. I couldn't do that."

"That's not what I meant. You told me once that you'd intended to adopt Bonnie out to a good home before she was born. Then, when you saw her, you changed your mind."

Eve stared at him in shock. "You'd consent to me doing that?"

"I have no idea. I doubt it. Every instinct is shouting no, but I just had to bring it up because you'd once considered it. You were a teenager then, poor, virtually alone, and Bonnie was illegitimate. Now you're older, but you have a career that obsesses you, and family would get in the way." He met her gaze. "Whatever your decision, it has to be made with your whole heart. After that, we'll work out what we need to do individually to meet both our own goals. We'll find a way to blend them together."

"Joe . . ."

"Hush." He squeezed her hand before releasing it. "I'm going to go and see about your release papers. You rest awhile, then I'll send Margaret in to help you dress." He paused. "Do you want me to tell her?"

She shook her head. "It's not real to me yet. How can I make it real to anyone else?"

"What about Cara? Do you still want to take her into our home for a while?"

"Of course I do. What are we supposed to do? Let her go back to Mexico and be torn apart in all those cartel wars? She's just a child, and she's already lost her sister and Elena, her best friend. You know that Salazar won't stop hunting her because Walsh is dead. We've got to keep her safe until we can find a way to get rid of Salazar."

"And Juan Castino, her loving father," Joe said grimly. "You're right, she's a pawn. She wouldn't stand a chance if immigration sends her back to Mexico." He turned toward the door. "I just thought that you might want me to handle it myself. You may be a little busy for a while."

"I believe the word is occupied," Eve said dryly.

"Whatever." He glanced back at her. "I wasn't sure that you'd be prepared for the hassle. We're going to have to whisk Cara away from here, keep her real identity from the authorities, and get her to Atlanta. Then I'll get to work on bringing down Salazar's cartel. That should keep him too busy to pay attention to Cara in the near future."

"I agree. But most of those arrangements are in your court."

"It will overflow."

She nodded. "Then I'll face it then." She smiled. "And a challenge will be good for me. It will keep me from . . . It will distract me."

"I doubt it."

The next moment, he was gone.

He was probably right, she thought. Nothing was going to distract her from this news that had shaken her world. But she had always found that hard work and putting her own problems at the end of the agenda could be a salvation.

But did she need salvation? Why had the word even occurred to her?

All she needed was to adjust to a situation that happened to millions of women every year.

So adjust.

She closed her eyes and leaned her head back on the pillow. Sort out what she really felt and examine it.

Shock.

A natural reaction.

Disbelief.

Also natural.

Fear.

A pregnancy was never easy when you were older.

Of course, there was an element of—

No, don't hide behind that easy answer. There was something else behind it.

Bonnie. Her little girl who had been her entire life during those seven short years before her death. Bonnie. The pain and agony that had almost killed Eve after she'd been taken.

The fear that agony could come back if she allowed herself to love another baby as she had Bonnie. She dearly loved her adopted daughter, Jane, but that was another relationship entirely. Jane had been ten when they'd found each other, and with a maturity that had made them more best friends than mother and daughter. So different from Bonnie. She had been responsible for her from the instant of her birth, and she had lost her. Could she bear the constant worry that another child would be taken from her?

Coward. She was a coward. Mothers faced that threat every single day.

Did you know what a coward I am, Joe? Is that why you never asked?

Well, there was no asking now. It was a fact. Stunning. Life-changing. Inevitable.

Magical.

The word had come out of nowhere.

Because that was the final emotion she had felt when Joe had told her she was going to have a child.

Magic. Joyous, rich, heady, magic.

She slowly looked down at her abdomen. Flat. No sign that someone was growing, taking on more life with every second. She reached
out tentatively and touched the skin of her stomach.

*What's happening? It's a crazy world out here, are you sure you want to
trust me to take you through it?*

Was she expecting an answer from this baby, who had just barely
been conceived? Of course not, the question was really for herself.
She had lost Bonnie. She would have to do better to prove herself to
this child.

Her hand dropped away from her abdomen.

*Later. We'll have to work on this. We're just starting out. We have a
long way to go.*

She sat up in bed and swung her legs to the floor. Time to start
living life and not trying to avoid it. She went to the closet and started
to take down her clothes.

"Hey, I'm supposed to do all that." Margaret had come into the
room. "Joe said I should give you a little while to rest, and here you
are ready to jump into your clothes."

Eve smiled affectionately at her. Margaret had been a tower of
strength during the last days when they had been hunting for Cara,
then Eve's time in the hospital. But then Margaret had shown remark-
able strength from the moment Eve had met her. She was young and
full of life and possessed instincts and a knowledge of animals that
was as unusual as her ability to deal with people.

"I want to get out of here." Eve headed for the bathroom. "And
I've done nothing but rest since I got here. I had a mild concussion,
and Joe insisted on having those doctors run every test under the sun
to make sure I was okay."

"Typical Joe Quinn," Margaret said. "He was a trifle . . . brief
when he was talking to me. Is everything okay?"

"Everything's fine."

"Then you might tell Cara. She's not too sure."

Eve stopped at the bathroom door. "She thinks I'm abandoning her?"

"No, it's not gotten that far yet. But who could blame her? She doesn't really know any of us. She's known since she was three years old and her sister, Jenny, was killed almost in front of her eyes, that she had to run and keep on running just to stay alive. Her nurse, Elena, taught her she mustn't trust anyone." She added grimly, "And with good reason. Elena died trying to protect her. Now Cara is alone, and she's trying to come to terms with taking care of herself." She shrugged. "Though she seems more concerned with taking care of you. Do you know she dreams about Jenny?"

"Yes."

"And she told me she thinks you dream about her, too. Do you?"

"Not exactly."

Margaret gazed at her, waiting. When Eve didn't go on, she said, "Okay, you don't want to talk about it. I understand. Well, I don't really, but I would if you'd trust me. I thought that those reports from 'confidential sources' you told our Sheriff Nalchek you received were a trifle suspect when we were hunting down Walsh." She suddenly chuckled. "Though he'd think what I'm guessing now is far more weird than suspect." She took Eve's suitcase out of the closet. "Go on, get dressed. Call if you need me. I'll pack you up, and we'll be set to go as soon as you're ready."

"Thanks, Margaret," Eve said quietly. "Thanks for everything. We would never have found Cara if you hadn't helped. You've been there for me since the beginning of this nightmare."

"Not quite." She tilted her head. "And that sounds remarkably like good-bye. Is it?"

"I prefer *au revoir.*" She hesitated. "What Joe and I are doing isn't exactly legal in taking Cara back to Atlanta with us. It's morally right, but you could still get in trouble. You and the Immigration Department aren't on the best of terms."

"We're fine with each other as long as I'm smart enough to avoid them."

And Eve knew Margaret had made a science of avoiding them and keeping under the radar. Eve had never been told why Margaret felt that was necessary and could only be grateful that she occasionally dropped into their lives. "And you might be caught in the cross fire if they find out that we're keeping Cara from her legal father."

"Who is a murderer, drug lord, and general scumbag."

"Joe and I will be working on clearing up her situation, but it will take time. In the meantime, Salazar will be a danger."

"Then I should be there to—"

"No, Margaret," Eve said firmly. "You have too much to lose. I won't have you stuck in a jail while they decide whether or not to deport you." She made a face. "Though I don't even know where they'd send you. You haven't been very forthcoming on that score."

"It's my life, my problems." Margaret shook her head. "I can't convince you, can I?" She shrugged. "Then I won't try. If you need me, get in touch." She started packing Eve's bag. "Do you need to know where to get phony documents for Cara? I know a few good places and some people who will—"

"No," Eve said. "You're out of this. Joe has managed to block any investigation on Cara's background, but there are still problems. It will be a very tentative fix, but as long as they think Cara is an orphan after the death of her supposed Aunt Elena, we may get away with it. We're hoping that Sheriff Nalchek will smooth things over with Child Services and persuade them to let us have temporary custody. He's well thought of in this area."

"He'll do it. He's like you. He won't want a child in danger."

"I believe you're right. We'll have to see. Everything is a little bewildering right now."

"Eve." Margaret was studying her face. "You're sure everything is okay? You look a little . . . unusual."

"Do I?" Trust Margaret to sense a truth that had only just been revealed to Eve. Unusual? The world was shaking. Everything was changing. She didn't know how she was going to cope. But she would do it.

She had to do it.

She smiled at Margaret. "I'm sure it's *going* to be okay. But you're right, I feel a little unusual. Nothing physical. Just a new challenge on the horizon."

"Cara?"

"She's definitely a part of it." She was closing the bathroom door. "I'll be right out, Margaret."

Margaret shook her head as she gazed at the closed door. Eve was going to prove obstinate, but that's what she had expected. She had tried to push her away earlier when she had been afraid to involve her beyond what she considered safe. She would have to find a way to—

Her cell phone rang, and she glanced down at the ID. Kendra Michaels.

It wasn't the first time she had phoned in the past week. Margaret had been too busy to take her calls and had put her off. She was tempted to do that now.

No, Kendra was her friend, and she was the one who had called to ask Margaret to get in touch with Eve when she'd been unable to reach her. She deserved to know what had happened.

"Hello, Kendra. I don't have much time. I have to help get Eve sprung out of this hospital."

"Hospital? And why is Eve in a hospital? And what the hell is going on?"

"I'm going to tell you. I just have to keep it brief, okay?"

"It's not okay, but I clearly have to put up with it. Eve told me practically nothing when she came out here to California except that she needed someone who was woods savvy and wanted you. Since I'm definitely not woods savvy, I had to find you."

"You sound distinctly grumpy."

"I couldn't see why I couldn't help," she said impatiently. "I still don't. Tell me."

"Eve came out here because Sheriff Nalchek had discovered the grave of a nine-year-old little girl at Sonderville, California. He sent Eve the skull to reconstruct. She did a great job and FedExed the reconstruction back to him. But the FedEx truck was hijacked, the driver killed, and the reconstruction stolen. Eve's computer and notes were also stolen that same day. Someone had no intention of letting that little girl's identity be discovered."

"And that pissed Eve off."

"Big-time. She had become very involved emotionally with that little girl, who she called Jenny, while she was reconstructing her skull. She and Joe Quinn came out here to try to find a clue to who that little girl was." She added, "And to catch her killer. That's why she wanted me to go to that grave in the forest and see what I could find."

"And what did you find?"

"Not as much as I would have liked, but I was helpful. Joe and Eve discovered that the name of her killer was James Walsh and started to try to track him. It became very convoluted because Walsh was on the hunt himself. He was an enforcer for a Mexican drug cartel, very nasty character, and had been hired by the head of a rival cartel to kidnap and kill Juan Castino's two daughters. They were supposed to just disappear, but something happened. The older girl was killed, but the younger child, Cara, and Elena, the nurse who cared for the girls, escaped. Walsh searched for them for years."

"Bastard."

"Oh, yes. It was a very bloody hunt. But we managed to find Cara almost at the same time as Walsh."

"Tell me he's dead."

"Yes, a very painful demise. Eve has only a minor concussion."

"And the child?"

"Cara is alive, but there are still problems. Eve is sure she can work them out."

"And are you sure?"

"Reasonably. As long as she's willing to accept help from her friends."

Kendra laughed. "You?"

"Well, I do like to see things through to the very end."

"I've noticed. An iron will occasionally peeks out from behind all that sunny sweetness."

"Sweetness? How cloying. I feel ill. And in dire need of an apology."

"You'll not get it." She was suddenly serious. "You're okay, Margaret?"

"Sure, I was just drifting along with the current."

"Never."

"Well, sometimes. Now the current is persistently reminding me I have to get Eve out of this hospital."

"Okay, okay. I'll talk to you later. But that explanation was very sketchy. I'll want details." She hung up.

And Kendra would keep at Margaret until she got all those details, Margaret thought ruefully. She was not only brilliant, she had boundless curiosity and fantastic instincts.

And she hadn't liked being passed over for Margaret when Eve needed help. She always liked being in control.

But then, so did Margaret.

So finish packing Eve up, then try to think of a way to get Eve to let her trail along and help put a period to this nightmare that was haunting both her and Cara.

CHAPTER

2

Will you be all right here?" Joe asked Cara. He gestured to the long bench outside the administration office. "I shouldn't be long. Just signing papers and giving them a credit card. Five minutes, no more."

She nodded as she opened her computer. "Unless you want me to go help Eve."

He shook his head. "Margaret will take care of her." He smiled. "And Eve usually prefers to take care of herself. You'll find that out if you choose to stay with us for a while."

"I'll stay with you." She gazed gravely at him. "And I think that you take care of Eve whether she wants it or not. Let me help."

He studied her face. "It should work the other way around, you know. You're just a kid. You have a right to have people look after you."

"You did look after me. Eve saved my life. You saved my life. Elena always said that I had to look after myself." She moistened her lips. "And now she's gone, and I can't expect any more help from any-one. I have to earn it."

"And you think you should earn your way by helping Eve?"

She nodded. "If she'll let me. If you'll let me. Will you?"

"I believe that can be arranged." He touched her cheek with his forefinger. "I think you'd be a good person to have on her side. She may need it soon."

"I know. I won't disappoint you."

"Just what do you know?" he asked curiously.

She shook her head. "I won't disappoint you," she repeated.

His hand dropped away from her face. "Stop worrying about responsibility and concentrate on healing. You've had a bad couple days." His lips twisted. "No, you've had a bad several years."

"Not so bad. Not all the time." Her eyes stung with tears. "Elena made them good because we were together."

"I'm sure you made them good for her, too," he said gently. He turned away and pushed open the door. "Five minutes. You can even see me through this glass door. If you need me, come and get me."

Her eyes were swimming with tears as she looked down at her computer.

Elena.

Don't cry. Tears never did any good. Elena had always told her that you just had to forget and go on.

But how was she going to forget Elena?

She wouldn't forget. She would lose her if she forgot all the years they'd—

"Would you like a tissue?"

She looked up to see an older boy in jeans and a white shirt who had dropped down on the bench next to her. She could barely see through the tears, but she was aware of dark hair, dark eyes. Her friend, Heather, would have said he was cute, and his hair was cut like one of the members in Heather's favorite rock band.

He handed her the tissue. "You look like you could use it." He took another tissue out of the same pack and dabbed at his own eyes. "Me, too. Life can be crap, can't it?"

"Yeah." She wiped her eyes. "Thanks."

He nodded. "Welcome." He leaned his dark head back against

the wall. "I hate this. My dad is in there paying the bill and for what? They couldn't get her well. My mom died anyway."

"I'm sorry." She took a deep, shaky breath. "It seems to be a good hospital. They're doing everything they can for Eve."

"Your sister?"

"No. Not my sister." She wiped her eyes again. "My sister died a long time ago. Do you have a sister?"

"Yes, Nella. She's in the chapel, praying for my mother's soul." His eyes filled again. "That's where I was when my dad called me and said he needed me. I didn't want to come. There didn't seem much I could do, and I felt helpless. I never liked to go to church, but my mother taught me that prayers help. I felt like maybe I was doing something in that chapel, that maybe she could hear me. Stupid, huh?"

She shook her head. "I don't think so. Elena always told me that when you couldn't trust anyone else that you should pray."

"Elena? You said Eve."

"No, my friend, Elena. She . . . died."

"Seems like everyone is dying," he said thickly. "Did it help you to go to church, like it did me?"

"I haven't been able to do that yet."

"You ought to try it. It can't hurt."

"Maybe later."

"That's what I thought when my mom died. All the things I was going to do and say. Sometimes I wasn't even nice to her. It's bad to put off things." He suddenly jumped to his feet. "Come on, let's go to the chapel. Neither of us is doing any good sitting on this bench. Who knows how long it's going to take for them to pay those blood-suckers?"

"What?" Cara's eyes widened in surprise. "I can't leave now."

"Sure you can." He pulled her to her feet. "The chapel's only three floors up. You can call down to say where you're going when we get there."

"What about your father?"

"He didn't really need me, or he wouldn't have parked me on this bench and left me to twiddle my thumbs." He was gazing down at her, his dark eyes glittering, his voice soft, persuasive. "Come on. Nella will like you to be there. I'm just a guy, and she's missing Mom so bad."

"I don't know if I—"

"Cara."

Joe was standing in the doorway. "And who is this?" His soft voice had a definite edge.

The boy smiled politely. "Kevin Roper, sir." He dropped Cara's hand and turned away. "I guess you won't want to go to the chapel now." He was heading toward the elevator. "It was nice to meet you, Cara."

"Good-bye, Kevin. Tell your sister I'm so sorry."

"I'll do that." He got on the elevator. "She would have liked to meet you." He nodded at Joe and Cara as the door started to slide shut. "Hope all goes well for Eve."

Joe was still staring at the door as the elevator started down. "It sounds as if you two had a cozy chat."

"His mom just died."

"And you were going to the chapel with him?"

"No. Yes. I don't know. I thought it might not—" She made a face. "I was confused."

"And this Kevin Roper is very persuasive. I caught that from the body language the minute I walked out of the office."

"He'd been in the chapel today with his sister, Nella, praying for his mother's soul. He said his sister needed someone to—"

"And you were in pain and could sympathize." He was taking out his phone as he spoke. "You say he was in the chapel today?"

"Yes."

He dialed quickly, then was speaking into the phone. "Connect me to the chapel." He waited and then spoke again, "I need to talk to Nella Roper. Is she there? Yes, I'll wait." He covered the phone and spoke to Cara. "It's a social-service volunteer. Everyone has to sign in when they arrive. She's checking." He went back to his conversation. "No? What about her brother, Kevin? They were supposed to both be there earlier today. Not at all? Thank you, sorry to bother you." He hung up. "And I would bet that Roper had no mother who died in this hospital. At least, not recently."

"Lies," she whispered.

"Very beautifully executed lies. A handsome young boy who had lost his mother, sits down beside a grieving young girl who needs someone near her own age who might understand what she's going through. Very clever."

"Why would he want me to go to the chapel? I don't—" She stopped. "He took the elevator down, not up. He told me the chapel was three flights up. He wasn't going to the chapel, was he?"

Joe shook his head. "I don't think you'd have made it out of the elevator alive. I imagine he has a few more skills other than being an expert liar."

"Salazar. Salazar sent him?"

"That would be my guess. I can't prove it yet. There's a possibility he might be a child molester or some other kind of creep who planted himself in a hospital where a victim is most vulnerable."

"If he was sent by Salazar, he was going to kill me?"

Joe was silent. "Do you think I like to tell you that? But I have to lay it on the line. If I'd come out of that office a few minutes later, I might have missed you. I'd like to say trust everyone, and you don't have to worry any longer. I'm not going to do that. I don't know how long you'll have to be careful, but you're not safe now. Do you understand?"

"He . . . was nice."

"He was probably deadly."

She nodded jerkily. "I was used to the idea of a monster, I wasn't expecting someone who looked like one of the guys I'd see around school." She drew a deep breath. "But I'll know better next time." She headed for the elevator. "We have to get back to Eve. I mentioned her name. He might try to—"

Joe was already ahead of her, his finger pressing the button. "I doubt if he could bounce back that fast, but we won't take a chance. We have to get out of here."

"I shouldn't have mentioned her. He just seemed—Hurry!"

Two minutes later they were at the door of Eve's hospital room. No Eve.

Cara stopped short, her gaze on the rumpled bed. "No," she whispered.

"I didn't expect you this soon. All done with the paperwork?"

Cara turned to see Eve standing in the doorway of the bathroom. She felt limp with relief. "Hi. I thought—" She swallowed. "I was scared. I did something stupid."

Eve's gaze narrowed on her face. "I can see you're scared." She looked at Joe. "What happened?"

"She ran into a wolf in sheep's clothing," Joe said. "I left her for a minute in the hall outside the administration office, and he pounced."

"Salazar?"

Joe nodded. "He recruited a young kid who was very good. Smooth as silk and very believable."

"A kid?" Margaret came out of the bathroom carrying three plastic bags filled with Eve's personal items. "That doesn't sound like a recruit to replace Walsh."

"He was good," Joe repeated. "And clever. Salazar might be trying something new. Walsh had to have been a miserable failure in his eyes."

"He was a miserable failure in anyone's eyes." Eve shivered. "But I didn't think that Salazar would have found out that Walsh was dead yet. Much less send a killer to replace him."

"He probably had someone watching Walsh and reporting back to him. I doubt if he would have trusted him after he'd failed him all these years."

"Do you know his name?"

"Kevin Roper. At least, that's what he told us. I'll check with Manez, my contact in Mexico who deals with the cartels, to see if I can verify." Joe glanced quickly around the room. "Have you got everything? We need to get out of here."

"These were the last items." Margaret went to Eve's bag, which she'd set on the floor on the other side of the bed. "She's ready to go." She looked back at him. "Where are you going to take her?"

"We're going home," Eve said. "I told you, Margaret."

"I thought there might be a change of plan." She fastened the suitcase. "Since I'm sure Salazar knows where you live."

"So am I," Joe said. "But it's my home territory. Easier to defend. We can't hide out here with Cara like she did with Elena. I know the police there, and I have friends."

"You won't be hiding at all," Margaret said soberly. "I know something about hiding. It seems like I've done it all my life. You should disappear until you're ready to make your move against Salazar." She glanced at Cara. "You know all about disappearing, don't you? They don't want to make you feel unsafe, they want to put you in a nice, cozy place. But sometimes those cozy places can be traps, and you have to leave them. There's no choice. Your Elena knew that, didn't she?"

Cara nodded. "She knew. She was trying to take me away again when Walsh . . . killed her."

"We'll take care of her, Margaret," Eve said quietly. "I know you mean well, but she's our responsibility."

"And I should butt out?" Margaret shrugged. "I take it that you haven't changed your mind about letting me come with you?" She didn't wait for an answer but turned back to Cara. "You'll get through this and come out on top. Eve and Joe are good people, and they're very smart." She grinned. "So smart that I know they'll call me to help as soon as they realize what a mistake they're making not to let me run this operation."

"We'll keep that in mind," Joe said dryly. He crossed the room and shook Margaret's hand. "And you may be right about cozy traps. I'll have to think about it. But there are elements in play of which you have no knowledge. All I want to do right now is to get Eve home. She may need that cozy trap for a little while."

"Really?" Margaret's tone was speculative. "Interesting." She turned to Eve. "I'd like to go into this, but we should get you and Cara away from here. Come on, I'll walk you down to your car." She linked her arm through Cara's and headed for the door. "Don't worry, we'll find a way around this."

"What way?" Eve asked warily as she followed Margaret from the room. "It's not like you to give up so easily."

"Maybe I'm getting resigned to being pushed to the side." She winked. "Or maybe I'm trying to keep you off guard while I figure out a way to get my own way."

There are elements in play you don't know about.

Margaret stood watching as Joe drove out of the hospital parking lot.

What elements, Joe?

She turned and walked slowly back toward the hospital, thinking. She'd been aware of something odd in Eve's behavior earlier. Joe's words just confirmed it.

Eve may need that cozy trap for a little while.

She went over the events of the last day and tried to put together a reasonable answer.

Nothing.

Forget reasonable. Try reaching out beyond reason.

A few possibilities, some actually interesting.

One or two that were fascinating.

She stopped short in the parking lot.

Yes, incredibly fascinating . . .

But if there was even a chance of its being true, there was no way she could let Eve go off without her help.

Help she'd refused already with great firmness. How to get around it?

She couldn't act herself, so pull the strings. Find someone Eve wouldn't be able to refuse. Not that easy. Eve was a workaholic, and that dictated a fairly solitary life. She had Joe Quinn, her half sister, Beth Avery, a few close friends, Catherine Ling, Kendra Michaels.

And her adoptive daughter, Jane MacGuire.

Margaret would have chosen Jane first except for the fact that she had been suffering from the tragic loss of her fiancé and was only now recovering.

Jane . . .

Margaret and Jane had grown very close during the past year. She knew Jane would not think twice about jumping into the situation no matter how risky to help Eve.

She also knew that Eve would not want Jane to know about that danger.

She thought about it.

. . . *elements in play you don't know about.*

What the hell? Why was she being so hesitant? She always ended up going by instinct anyway.

She reached for her phone and dialed quickly. It rang four times before it was picked up. "Jane? It's Margaret, do you have a few minutes? No, that's not right, maybe longer than that. I'm in Carmel, California. I need to fill you in on something that's been going on out here and then ask you to—"

"I almost had her," Ramon Franco's voice was tense with excitement. "A minute more, and I'd have had her in the elevator, then one needle, and she'd—"

"I told you not to make a move yet."

"I wasn't going to do it, but you wanted her dead. Wasn't that the primary goal? There she was, and Quinn had ducked into the administration office. I could tell by the way she looked that she'd be easy if I took her right then. I was right. I was that close to—"

"You didn't do what I said, Franco."

"You said you wanted her dead." He tried to keep the impatience out of his voice. Salazar had once been a man to respect, but he was getting old, and he'd forgotten you had to take advantage of the opportunities when you were on the hunt. "It would have been over almost before it began if I'd taken her out today."

"And it would have roused an inquiry that might have led to Castino. It has to be done quietly. All I wanted was information. Did you get it?"

"Didn't I say I would?" He could tell by the silence on the other end that he'd gone too far. "If I made a mistake, I'm sorry. I only thought to please you." He went on hurriedly, "Eve Duncan was admitted to the ER with a concussion. Not serious. She was released today. The kid is still going by the name of Cara Delaney and has been at the hospital visiting Duncan. After I left the hospital today, I called my contact at the police department, and there's been no interest in Cara. They're leaving her in the hands of Child Services." He paused. "And Child Services has been requested to leave her in the hands of Eve Duncan and Joe Quinn by a Sheriff John Nalchek, who was one of the lead investigators."

"And no doubt the request was granted." Salazar was silent. "We may be lucky, Franco. It appears that Duncan has no desire for the child to be returned to the loving arms of her father. It may buy us time." He amended. "Buy you time. Find out where they're taking the girl and follow them. But don't touch her until you're sure you can take Duncan down at the same time. And I want a clean kill, with no bodies."

"The kill would have been clean if I'd put the kid down at the hospital. I had it all planned the minute I saw her on that bench. It was just—"

"You were in the middle of a hospital with people all around you. You were taking a chance."

"I would have pulled it off."

"Forget it. You made a mistake. Admit it."

It hadn't been a mistake, Franco thought furiously. It had been bad luck, but he had been superb. He had almost gotten away with it, and this old fool couldn't see it. He had played that kid perfectly. He drew a deep breath and forced his voice to be contrite. "Of course, I made a mistake. I guess I was just too eager to please. I'll handle it the way you want me to handle it. I'll call you as soon as I know what's happening with them."

"Be sure you do that. I wouldn't want to have to replace you. As I said, you have great promise."

"Thank you, that means a great deal to me, sir." He hung up.

He sat there for a moment, fighting the hatred and the anger. How dare that fool humiliate him like this.

Keep calm.

His time would come.

But first he would have to disarm Salazar by giving him what he wanted. Duncan, the kid, and he might throw in Joe Quinn.

SAN FRANCISCO INTERNATIONAL AIRPORT

It took Joe five minutes to get in touch with Manez at Mexican Federal Police after he, Eve, and Cara arrived at the boarding gate and were waiting for the flight to be called. He quickly gave Manez the information about Kevin Roper and a complete description. "Nice-looking kid and no accent. I need the verification that he's one of Salazar's men. Will you get it for me?"

"I will do all I can. We need to talk, Quinn."

"I'll be glad to do it later. Right now I have a limited time before I'm boarding a flight to Atlanta. I need you to go over everything you know about Salazar and Castino and any details about those kids Walsh kidnapped."

"I already briefed you on my take on the matter."

"It was all piecemeal. That was okay as long as I was only concerned with finding Walsh and keeping him from killing Cara. Now I need to know everything so that I can find a way to take Salazar and Castino down, so they can't tear Cara into pieces."

"May I remind you I've been trying to do that for years?" Manez asked dryly. "Where do you want me to start?"

"Tell me about Salazar."

"Grew up in the gangs on the streets. Worked his way up through murder and killing off everyone in his way. Finally killed off the head of the Mulez Cartel and took power. Since then he's been fighting off other cartels and threats from within. Castino has been a constant headache to him. He hates his guts. Castino was starting to take over his territories, and Salazar scrambled to organize a coalition of other cartels in the area. Castino was forced to join or face a gang war that would have been very expensive. Salazar could never show publicly how he felt about Castino." He paused. "But he was my first suspect when Castino's daughters disappeared."

"Salazar's personal life?"

"He has a wife, Manuela, he married when he was seventeen. He has three sons and a daughter. He appears to be a devoted family man. His father was a small-time drug runner and was killed and decapitated when Salazar was starting to run drugs himself. His mother died two years ago."

"Any weakness?"

"Ambition. Other than that, you'll have to tell me."

"What about Castino?"

"He inherited the cartel from his father, Jorge Castino, but he learned well from the bastard. He's more vicious than his father ever dreamed of being. He grew up believing he should own the world, and he's been trying to take it over since his father was killed. He's got a gigantic ego that makes it impossible for him to admit he's not perfect in every way. He hated the idea of the coalition, but he was smart enough not to try to fight it. The moment anyone tried to break it, the others would pounce like ravening wolves."

"Personal?"

"Quintessential macho. Something of a womanizer in his early years. He married Natalie Kaskov several years ago. She's the daughter of Sergai Kaskov, one of the heads of the Russian Mafia. It might have been a marriage to meld the two Mafias or it might not. She's a beautiful woman, and I can see Castino going a little crazy about her. They seem to be very compatible, and she appears to like the good life as much as he does. She gave birth to the two girls, and the word was that Castino was disappointed not to have a boy. Not that he would admit it, that would have been a failure. So he went to the other extreme and made much of them whenever they appeared in public with him or Natalie."

"And made them targets to all the people who hated him. Send me photos of everyone we've talked about. I want to be able to know them when I see them."

"Hold on a minute." He was gone from the phone and when he came back, he said, "The photos are on their way. I'm curious to know just when you intend to formally make Salazar's and Castino's acquaintance."

"I have no idea yet. I'm just looking for a hook. I want to see what Salazar saw that would lead him to take a chance that could get him gutted. He must have hated Castino big-time to kill his kids."

"Salazar didn't look too closely at the situation, or he would have noticed that neither Castino nor Natalie paid the girls any attention when they weren't on display. Of course, after the girls were kidnapped, they were both supposedly heartbroken. Natalie in constant tears and Castino threatening vengeance if his girls were not returned to him."

"Just the effect Salazar wanted."

"He didn't let it show," Manez said. "Salazar's been very understated for the last few years. No one suspected him."

"He was walking a tightrope with his hired killer, Walsh. I imagine every minute they were afraid of being butchered by Castino if he found out Salazar had paid for the kidnapping."

"No one could prove it."

"The situation is changed now. We have Cara." Joe looked across the jetway at Cara and Eve standing in front of the huge windows. "And as long as Cara is alive, she's more of a threat than she's ever been to Salazar. Find out who this Kevin Roper really is, so I can identify that particular threat."

"I'll work on it. But I'm not going to be your clerk, Quinn. You and Eve Duncan are the smallest pieces in my puzzle of how to control these cartels. But I'll ask around." He hung up.

A moment later, Joe's phone pinged, and the e-mail photos arrived.

Just two photos but Manez must have thought they were enough.

The Salazar photo showed a tall, handsome, heavyset man in his forties with a thick head of black hair and dark eyes beneath a beach umbrella beside a swimming pool. He was wearing slacks, his white shirt open to the sun. He was sitting next to an attractive plump blond woman in a bikini with her hair tied back in a ponytail. They were both smiling at a young boy sunning himself on the tiles beside the water. Salazar and his wife, Manuela; presumably the boy was his son. A warm family picture. No one would dream that the man was a murderer who would kill a child without compunction.

He scrolled down to the next photo. It was taken on the street outside an outdoor restaurant. Castino was a dark-haired, slim, athletic-looking man who wore an elegant white suit that made his obviously good body appear excellent. He had fine features and a long nose that managed to look almost Roman. He was walking beside a tall, curvaceous, young woman with gleaming dark hair worn in a chignon. Natalie was dressed even more elegantly than Castino and was smiling and clearly talking vivaciously to him. Joe could see a faint resemblance to Cara in that face. Beautiful. Joe agreed with Manez that a man might go a little crazy over her. They were a perfect couple, assured, powerful, striding through life and paying no attention to anything in their path.

Joe could see why Salazar might have wanted to destroy that arrogance with one swift blow.

Yes, Manez had given him a capsule of the two men and their motivations with these two pictures. Joe needed more, but he couldn't push any more right now. Manez and his men were strained to the breaking point with trying to keep order and sanity in this madness of vice and drugs he was facing. He'd help Joe if it wasn't too taxing on his resources. And informants could be expensive and difficult to handle.

He could only hope that Manez would be able to hit it lucky.

"You look absolutely fascinated." Eve's gaze was on Cara's face as the girl stood at the tall windows overlooking the runways. "That's our plane at the gate. We should be boarding soon."

"I know. I heard them announce it." Cara's gaze never left the plane that was taking off on the far runway. "Look at them. Aren't they beautiful? I've seen lots of planes on TV, but I've never been as close to them as this. Elena and I never had enough money to travel by plane. We always took her car or a bus. But jets have so much power . . . They seem to sing as they lift off, a deep roar and then the higher notes that follow . . ."

"Only you would hear music in that sound," Eve said. "I'm certain that the neighborhoods surrounding the airport aren't appreciating them as you are." Yet it was entirely natural Cara would be able to hear music where others did not. Eve had been told by Cara's teacher that she was an extraordinary violinist though Eve had never heard her play. "And I don't hear anything as delicate as a string instrument in that roar."

"I do. It's a secondary theme, but it's there." She glanced at Eve. "Though it's more for a piano. Jenny would be able to hear it. She always liked the thunder. She'd play for me sometimes . . ."

Before Jenny had been killed when she was nine years old, before Cara and her nurse, Elena, had been forced to start the long run that had dominated Cara's young life. "You had to be only about three at that time. I'm surprised you remember."

"I remember. I remember everything about her. I didn't start playing the violin until I started school, but then I understood . . ."

"You loved it?"

"It was . . . everything," she said simply.

"I'll get you another violin as soon as we get to Atlanta."

"Thank you." A brilliant smile lit her face. "It will be . . . I won't feel as . . . alone."

"You're not alone, Cara." She reached out and gently touched her shoulder. "I know you probably feel that way right now, but you have Joe and me. Soon you'll have friends your own age. We just have to get through this patch."

She nodded. "And there always seems to be another patch just ahead. But that's the way it is. Elena always told me that we had to ignore the bad times and just enjoy the good times."

"She sounds like a very wise woman."

"She was great." Her voice was unsteady. "I miss her."

"I know you do."

"It shouldn't have happened. Sometimes I thought she was being too careful, but I was wrong." She moistened her lips. "I used to ask her why we couldn't just go to the police and tell everyone that Walsh had killed Jenny. But she said that it was too complicated. That my father was almost as bad as Walsh, and I mustn't get near either one."

"She was right. It wouldn't be safe. And you'd be in the middle of an international incident that could end very badly for you."

"I don't remember my father or mother. Elena said they hardly ever wanted to see Jenny or me. I didn't understand it. You see all those TV shows where the father and mother act all sloppy about their kids." She frowned. "And my father must have kind of liked us if that other guy, Salazar, thought he'd be sad if he killed us."

"I don't know what he felt. I've heard he's a very bad man. I do know that environment would be totally wrong for you. That's why we want you to stay with us until we can sort this mess out."

Cara nodded. "I promised Elena I wouldn't try to go back to see him or my mother. It's just hard to understand. I know Walsh was a terrible man. I know Salazar, who hired him, is bad. But it's not easy to think of your father as being just as bad and maybe hurting you." She spoke haltingly, trying to work it out. "But there are so many bad people out there. How can you tell who you'd be safe with?"

"You can't. Be careful and watch your back," Eve said. "I'd love to tell you that you have to have faith, and everything will work out fine. But I can't tell you that, Cara. It's not the world you live in right now."

"I know. That's kind of what Joe said."

"But you still came close to real danger when you trusted that boy at the hospital. I would have thought that you'd be more cautious."

"He wasn't like . . . I thought he'd lost someone like me. I wanted to help him."

"And he caught you off guard."

She nodded. "It won't happen again. I'll know better next time."

"Let's hope there won't be a next time," Eve said grimly. "Maybe Joe scared that slimeball away."

Cara gravely shook her head. "I don't think so." She turned back to the window again. "He didn't act scared. I believe I'll see him again."

Eve's brows rose. "You don't appear frightened."

"I know him now. I'm scared, but I know who I'm facing." She added, "It's all part of this business of not understanding. Nothing is what it seems. All the time that Walsh was hunting us, he was just a faceless monster. It was almost a relief when I actually saw him. Now he's dead, and there's someone else. I have to learn what I'm facing. I guess I was expecting someone who was like Walsh."

"And he wasn't."

"No, I think he might be even worse. He made me . . . care. But now I know the face of this monster," she said quietly. "And I'll never forget it."

LAKE COTTAGE

ATLANTA, GEORGIA

"It's beautiful here," Cara said softly as she climbed the steps to the front porch. "I love the lake. Elena took me to a motel in the hills that had a lake for a weekend last year. But it wasn't like this. I'll like being here until you send me away."

"Who said we were going to send you away?" Eve asked as they watched Joe unlock the front door. "I told you that this was a time of exploration while you decided what was best for you. You might like the lake, but you might not like the life Joe and I lead. We're pretty boring most of the time."

"I'm used to boring," Cara said. "Unless Elena wasn't working, I had to stay by myself in the apartment and not invite any of the kids over to visit."

"Pretty lonely?"

"I didn't mind. I had the music." She wrinkled her nose. "Well, sometimes I did mind, but I knew she was only doing what she thought best. She wanted to keep me safe."

"And she did," Eve said. "She gave up her life to do it."

Cara nodded. "One minute she was there, and then she was gone. I still feel as if she's out there somewhere, waiting for me."

Eve could see how that was possible. Cara had only been told that her friend Elena was dead, and it would have been difficult for her to accept the reality. Eve had avoided going into any details, hoping to spare the child. Now she could see that it had not been a kindness. "You know Elena was murdered. The police had to do an autopsy, and they haven't released the body for burial. After that happens, we'll arrange a suitable service for her." She hesitated. "But we may wait for the service until we're certain you're safe. I'm sure you understand why."

"You think they'll use her as a trap," Cara said flatly.

Eve nodded.

"Anywhere can be a trap." Cara looked around the lake and woods. "Even this beautiful place."

And it was incredibly sad that Cara had found that out, Eve thought. "I won't deny that's true. Our friend Margaret was trying to persuade us that Elena was right to run and hide and not settle in any one place. We may decide that they're both on the right track." She started up the steps. "But while we're here, Joe will make sure we're safe. That's why he insisted on going into the house first to check it out. Stop frowning, you don't have to worry."

"That wasn't what I was thinking about," Cara said as she followed her. "I was thinking that he was right."

"He?"

"That guy at the hospital. Kevin Roper."

Eve's gaze flew to her face. "That kid?"

"That monster." She added soberly, "He told me so many lies but there was truth in some of them. He said that I should go to church and pray for Elena's soul. He only meant to lure me away from Joe, and I would have gone. Because it seemed right. I tried to pray for her, but I— It wasn't what— I want to go to a church. Could I do that?"

"Of course. After we get you settled, I'll arrange for it. You choose the church, and I'll see that you get there tomorrow."

"Thank you." She looked out at the lake. "Though this is so peaceful, it's kind of like a church, isn't it? I just think that Elena would like me to go to church to pray for her. No matter where we settled, she made sure that she took me to confession and Mass."

"Whatever you like," Eve said gently. "A prayer is a prayer. It's the thought and the love behind it that matters." She opened the front door. "Now come in and let's get you settled. Joe is going to want to take you around and show you the property."

CHAPTER

3

Eve smiled as she watched Joe and Cara stroll down the path that led around the lake. It reminded her of the many times she had watched Joe and Jane over the years. Cara wasn't speaking, and her attitude was reticent, but that was how Jane had been in the beginning, defensive, wary. It had taken months for her to accept Joe after they had taken her off the streets. She and Eve had an instant rapport, but Joe was different. Jane had been in so many foster homes that she didn't trust anyone. But Joe had changed that, Joe always managed to change everything.

She turned away and went back into the house. It was good to be home, but she had things to do. She had to check her messages and see if there was anything pressing. She had put her other assignments on hold to do the reconstruction of Cara's sister, Jenny. There were probably several impatient messages asking when she was going to complete their projects.

She got a cup of coffee and picked up her phone to start going through them.

She'd just begun to scroll down when her phone rang.

Jane.

She hadn't heard from her since before she left for California, when Jane had arrived back in London.

A little odd that she was calling her the minute Eve returned?

"Hi, Jane. What's been happening? Have you been settling into—"

"Why didn't you tell me you were in the hospital?"

Apparently not odd at all. "It wasn't important. A little knock on the head. I'd have been in and out of the ER except Joe overreacted."

"Joe tends to do that with you. That doesn't mean you shouldn't have called me."

"I was hoping you would never know about it. For heaven's sake, you're in London. Why worry you about nothing?" She added grimly, "However, someone evidently saw fit to do that. Should I guess?"

"Margaret."

"That was my first guess."

"She thought I should know. She said that you'd sent her on her way, and she didn't think that you and Joe should be left without reinforcements. Good God, what have you gotten yourself into?"

"I'm certain Margaret told you in detail."

"Of course she did. I wouldn't have it any other way." She paused. "What about this little girl? How is she doing?"

"As well as can be expected. Cara's very strong, she reminds me a little of you."

"I haven't been very strong lately. No wonder you didn't trust me. I practically fell apart on you before I left Atlanta."

"You had a right. Trevor was shot and killed before your eyes. And you knew it was because he was trying to save you. It takes a long time to get over a trauma like that. I don't believe you ever really get over it. You just learn to live with it."

"Yes, and it's a tough lesson. But I didn't have to worry you as I did." She changed the subject. "But that's my problem. We're talking about yours. How do you want to handle this? Do you want me to come back there? Or do you want to come here?"

"Neither."

"It's one or the other. I'm not leaving you to face this without me."

"Back off, Jane. We'll handle it."

"Like you always back off when I'm in trouble? We're family, and you know I can't do that. Choose."

"Jane."

"I'll go along with whatever you say, but I really think you'd be better off coming across the pond. I agree with Margaret that you should be running and hiding rather than staked out for Salazar in a cave where he can corner you."

"It's a very nice cave, and you spent a number of years holed up here."

"I loved it. If I didn't think I'd cling too much to you and Joe, I'd be back there right now." She went on brusquely, "But as I said, you'd be safer here. Well, not here in London, but I'm planning on meeting MacDuff and Jock in Edinburgh in a few days, then we'll go directly to the Highlands."

"Oh, yes, the great treasure hunt. Your friend, Lord MacDuff has been trying to talk you into looking for Cira's gold for years." Cira was the ancestress who had come to Scotland from Herculaneum centuries ago and had founded the MacDuff dynasty. There had been legends that she had brought with her a chest of gold coins that would have astronomical value today, but it had never been found. MacDuff and his best friend, Jock Gavin, had been searching for it for years, and MacDuff had reasons to believe that Jane might be able to help them. But Jane had only agreed in the past weeks because she needed the distraction to cope with the depression, Eve knew. "And I believe it's a great idea. Is Seth Caleb going along?"

"No, I haven't seen him since I got back to London from Atlanta." She added flatly, "And I certainly didn't invite him."

Jane's tone was distinctly cool, Eve noticed. But that didn't surprise her. Caleb and Jane's relationship had been volatile since the moment they had met years ago. Caleb was an enigma, and Eve never knew which way he was going to turn. She did know that he probably felt something for Jane that he didn't feel for anyone else on earth. "Since when did Caleb require an invitation?"

"I'm trying to change the status quo in that regard. Look, that's not important. This whole idiotic treasure hunt isn't important. I'll put it off if you want me to come back. Otherwise, you come here, and we'll get lost in the Highlands while Joe is trying to set up a way to make Cara permanently safe from Salazar."

"And I'm supposed to involve you in this mess? No way."

"I'm already involved. The minute Margaret told me what was going on, I was involved. Accept it."

"I won't accept it."

"Yes, you will, maybe not this minute, but it will happen. I'll hang up, and you'll think about it. And you'll realize that we're family, and what happens to one happens to all of us. That's what you taught me when I was growing up, and nothing has changed."

"A lot has changed. You're grown-up, you have a career, you have a life outside—"

"We're family. Make a choice. Call me tomorrow. Or I'll be on the next plane back to Atlanta." She hung up.

She sounded totally determined, Eve thought in frustration. Once Jane made up her mind, there was no changing it. She listened, she looked at the problem from all sides, then she came to a conclusion and forged ahead. This time she had not indulged in the usual analyzing but jumped in with both feet when she'd heard Eve might be in danger.

Which was exactly what Eve would have done.

Family. Because family was everything.

Eve wanted to strangle Margaret. She had probably known exactly what effect recounting what had happened would have on Jane. Eve had known that, too, which was the reason she hadn't been in contact with her since she had left here for California.

And now she had to find a way to deal with Jane as well as everything else that was going on in her life.

Her hand instinctively went to her abdomen.

See, I told you it was crazy out here. And sometimes the craziness comes from the people you love the most. And if Jane knew about you, she'd be more difficult than ever.

But she didn't know, and Eve wasn't about to tell her. She had a better chance of dealing with the situation the fewer disturbing elements that were present. The presence of this child in her life was definitely disturbing.

Disturbing and yet comforting in a strange way. It was a sign that there were wonderful things in a world where darkness always seemed to be present.

But she still had to fight that darkness, so stop standing here and brooding about what Jane might or might not do. She had until tomorrow to make a decision, and she'd have to talk to Joe anyway.

She sat down on the couch and started to go through her messages.

"You two were gone a long time." Eve looked up from the Hamburger Helper she was stirring on the burner when Joe and Cara came into the cottage. "I hope you worked up an appetite."

"She had a lot of questions," Joe said. "And yes, I'm hungry. What about you, Cara?"

She smiled and nodded. "What are you fixing?"

"Just Hamburger Helper." She made a face. "I'm not much of a cook. Joe and I are working most of the time. We do a lot of take-out." She smiled at Joe. "But Joe is great on the barbecue grill. He'll have to demonstrate soon."

"My pleasure," Joe said. "But we may be a little too busy in the near future." He looked at the simmering skillet. "How soon will that be done?"

"Thirty minutes or so. As usual, I tossed everything in it to make it more palatable. I'm letting it simmer."

"It usually turns out pretty good." Joe turned toward the door. "I have an errand to run. I should be back by then."

"Where are you going?"

"I have something to pick up." He opened the door. "Lock up behind me and don't go out on the porch. Okay?"

Her gaze flew to his face. "Was everything all right out there?"

He nodded. "No signs. But it doesn't hurt to be careful." The door closed behind him.

"You're afraid someone would be here waiting for us?" Cara asked.

"No." She shrugged. "But Joe is right, it doesn't hurt to be careful." She moved toward the door and locked it. "Are you tired from that long walk?"

"You're trying to distract me." She was smiling. "I'm used to locked doors. It was a rule at the apartment." She moved over to the stove. "I sometimes put cheese in the Hamburger Helper. Did you try that?"

"Not this time." She looked curiously at her. "You cook?"

"I did most of the cleaning and cooking at the apartment. We divided up the jobs. It was only fair. Elena was working most of the time just to pay the bills." She looked in the refrigerator and got out some Brie cheese. "Okay, if I put some of this in it?"

"Be my guest." Eve watched her as she carefully cut up some cheese, then blended it in the mixture. "What else did you cook?"

"Oh, hamburgers, lasagna, stew, spaghetti, mostly easy stuff." She put down the ladle. "But I learn fast. If you want anything else, I'll make it for you."

She chuckled. "We didn't bring you here because we wanted a chef."

"I don't expect you to keep me unless I make myself useful. Why would you? You don't owe me anything." She said soberly, "And I have to stay with you. You might need me."

"Because you had a dream, and Jenny told you that you had to do it? I know you told me that." Eve shook her head. "We want you to stay with us but not because you think you have to do it. Jenny isn't with us any longer. She died a long time ago."

"But I still love her," she whispered. "I'll always love her." Her gaze was clinging desperately to Eve's. "And I think she loves you, too, Eve. I told Margaret I thought you dream about Jenny, too. Do you?"

"No." What could she tell her? Certainly not that she actually had experienced the spiritual presence of her sister, that she'd seen her, talked to her. It would be too much for her to handle. She was only eleven years old. "But I became very close to Jenny while I was working on her reconstruction. I felt as if I knew her very well." She paused. "I still do."

"The reconstruction," Cara repeated. "Margaret told me about what you do. It sounds . . . strange."

"I thought so, too, before I started to learn about it. Then I realized it wasn't strange at all. It was a way that I could bring the lost ones home to the ones who loved them. I just had to be taught that everything was there waiting to be brought out and how to do it." She met Cara's eyes. "And that's what I did with Jenny. In the end, I brought her home to you, Cara."

"Yes, you did." She smiled. "And Margaret told me how wonderfully it turned out. May I see it?"

"I don't have it. It's still being held by the Sheriff's Department in California." And actually seeing the skull from which she'd sculpted the reconstruction might still possibly have a negative effect. She thought that Cara understood but she preferred to introduce her slowly to her work and not on such a personal level. She shook her head. "And I don't think you should see it anyway. Memory is always better."

"You worked on it here?"

Eve nodded at the worktable across the room. "Over there."

Cara walked over to the worktable and touched it with her finger-tips. "I think you're right. I don't need to see that reconstruction. She'll always be with me." She looked across the room at Eve. "She saved me, you know. Elena had managed to get Jenny and me away from Walsh, but he almost found us in that forest. We heard him coming. Jenny told me to be quiet, and everything would be okay. Then she ran away from Elena and me toward Walsh. I didn't know what was happening. But Elena did and grabbed my hand and made me run and run and run. She was crying . . ." She swallowed. "Did you know that?"

"Yes," Eve said gently. "But I didn't know that you did."

"Sometimes I did. Sometimes I didn't. I didn't want it to be true. So I tried not to remember." She moistened her lips. "But then the nightmares came, and it would all be there again."

"Do you still have the nightmares?"

She shook her head. "No. For the past few weeks, I've just seen Jenny in my dreams and not that night in the forest. She talks to me and smiles, and I'm not afraid anymore."

"That's wonderful. She wouldn't want you to be afraid. She was very brave herself."

"It seems as if I've been afraid all my life. But I have to get over it. Being afraid didn't keep Elena from being killed. It won't keep Salazar from trying to kill me. I have to be like Jenny."

"No, fear never helps, but it's hard to fight. We'll work on it to-gether." She paused. "You remember that night when Jenny died. Do you remember anything else? Did Elena tell you anything about who kidnapped you? Or why you couldn't go to the police?"

"Elena didn't know what happened that night. She thought maybe we'd been given something in the food we had for supper, and when she woke up, we were in a truck with a group of workers . . . and Walsh."

"Did she recognize Walsh?"

Cara shook her head. "Elena worked and lived in our house. She didn't know anything about any of the men who belonged to the Castino or any other cartels. But she could tell Walsh was in charge and that he was . . . bad." She moistened her lips. "Her only thought was to find a way for us to escape. But her family had raised her to know that going to the police was an automatic death sentence. She wouldn't risk it. Any more than she'd risk taking me back to Mexico. She said that if my father's enemies had been able to reach me once, they could do it again."

"And how do you feel about your mother and father?"

"I don't remember them. Sometimes I have a vague memory of a woman with dark hair and a lovely smile. But she smiled more at Jenny, than at me." She added simply, "And Elena was my family. I didn't need anyone else."

"You were lucky to have her." She added gently, "I hope you can be as happy with us."

Cara nodded. "If you'll let me stay with you." She turned and moved back across the room toward the kitchen. She stopped as she saw a painting on the wall of the living room. "That's a painting of you." She gazed at the portrait of Eve in her blue work shirt. "I like it. It looks . . . warm."

"It was done by my daughter, Jane. She's an artist and very, very good. She gave the portrait to Joe as a gift."

"Is she very famous?"

"No, she's young and just starting out, but people are beginning to know her name." She started to stir the hamburger again. "She lives in London because that's where her agent and gallery are located."

She went closer to the portrait and peered down at the scrawled signature. "It's signed, but it's not—"

"Not mine or Joe's last name? Jane MacGuire. She's adopted. She was ten when she came to us."

"You must have loved her very much to have chosen her."

"Yes. But we kind of chose each other." She tasted the hamburger and put the lid on it. "The cheese definitely helped. Good job, Cara."

She smiled. "We did it together." She came toward her. "What else can I do?"

"Get some rolls out of the freezer and put them in the oven. I'll get down the plates." She shook her head. "I should have put those rolls in before. This Hamburger Helper is almost done."

"I kept you too busy," Cara said as she opened the freezer. "I asked a lot of questions."

"Yes, you did. And I asked you a few, too." She added, "It's a process called getting to know each other. How do you think we did?"

"Pretty good."

"Me, too. Dinner can wait a little while. Joe isn't—"

Even as she spoke she heard the key in the lock, and Joe came into the house.

"Hi. Just in time," she said. "Cara and I did a joint experiment, and it's very close to—" She stopped as she saw what Joe was carrying. "Is that what I think it is?"

"I called the music store from the airport and asked them to choose the best one they had in stock and have it ready for me." Joe came toward Cara and handed her the black-leather case. "I hope it will do. I don't know anything about musical instruments. I had to trust them."

"I don't care. It will be wonderful." Cara's eyes were glittering with excitement as she took the case and ran to the couch to open it. She carefully took out the violin and ran her fingers caressingly down the glossy surface. "It's beautiful." She began to tune it. "Beautiful . . ."

"I think we've lost her," Eve said to Joe. "I believe I'll even wait to put in those rolls." She took a step closer to him. "You constantly surprise me."

"I just thought it was better she had it sooner than later. She's had a lonely life. Her music was probably a closer friend to her than any-one but her Elena." He smiled as his gaze lingered on Cara's absorbed face. "Until she regards us as good friends, the violin will have to do for now." He glanced back at Cara. "I think we'll give her an hour to become acquainted with it. I'm going to take a look around out-side."

Eve walked him to the door. "Have you heard anything from Mexico City?"

"Not yet."

"Kevin Roper might not be connected to Salazar. You said there was a chance."

"A chance." He shrugged. "I have a hunch he is. He was too cool, too bold."

"I hope you're wrong. We need time."

"We may not get it." He paused. "And how are you feeling?"

"Fine. Why shouldn't I be? Joe, I'm barely a few weeks—" She shook her head. "I'm fine."

"Mentally as well as physically?"

She glanced back at Cara, then gave him a quick kiss. "Later." She pushed him out the door. "Be careful."

She drew a deep breath and moved back toward Cara. She'd wanted her discussion with Joe to be private but they could probably have had an in-depth conversation and Cara would not have heard a word. She was totally absorbed, and she might have been on another planet. Eve didn't want to take that chance. What she had learned this morning about having a child was only between the two of them and not to be touched by all the other madness that was going on in her life.

Only this morning. It seemed incredible that such a short time had passed since that moment when her entire life had been turned up-side down.

But that time had been filled with worry and adjustment and Cara. And that adjustment was still going on.

I had the music, she had told Eve. She'd had loneliness and fear and death, but she'd also been given the gift that had made all that tolerable. Now she had it again, and it was all there in her face and the loving delicacy of her fingers on the strings.

Joe was a very wise man.

She took her coffee and dropped down on the easy chair across from the couch where Cara sat. She was silent, watching her.

She'd get up soon and put away the food. Supper could wait. Cara needed this nourishment more than any food.

No sign of any intruders, Joe thought as he knelt to examine the grass beside the trail. It was still early in the game. They had moved fast and left the hospital only earlier today. Salazar or his man would have had to move equally quickly to track them down and position themselves for any assault. But Joe had no doubt that assault would come, and he would have to be ready for it.

He wanted it over.

He had anticipated that this nightmare that had tormented them would extend past the killing of Walsh. He had fully expected it. Walsh had only been a hired killer, and Salazar was still hovering on the horizon. Joe had been planning on parking Eve and Cara somewhere safe and going after Salazar himself. But that had been put on hold by the news that Eve was with child. He had been caught off guard, and he had to think and look at all the options.

Just as he had told her she had to look at her options. He knew her, and he knew how she would—

His phone rang. Detective Juan Manez, Mexico City.

"It's about time," he said when he picked up. "I thought you'd contact me sooner. What did you find out?"

"That you should be more respectful of both our friendship and the fact that my sources are not limitless. It should have taken me days, not hours. You're fortunate that I have a forgiving nature."

"And that you want to bring Salazar down with a solid crash."

"I'd prefer Castino, but Salazar will do. If you can't arrange a double event."

"Right now, I need you to focus on Salazar's group. Did you find a Kevin Roper."

"No." He paused. "But I found a Ramon Franco. You would find him interesting."

"One and the same?"

"You tell me. I'm sending you a photo."

"So tell me about him."

"A very nasty predator who pretends to be a follower, but I'd bet we'll have to contend with him in the upper echelons of the cartel in a very short time. The word out is he's very ambitious and willing to take out anyone who gets in his way."

"He's just a kid."

"Nineteen, almost twenty. Did that make you less lethal when you were his age?"

"Good point. Give me his history."

"Grew up on the streets of San Diego, father a drug runner, mother a prostitute. Ramon was acting as her pimp by the time he was ten. But he had a temper, and he caught his mother stashing some of the money for herself. He pushed her down a flight of stairs and broke her neck."

"Charming," Joe said dryly.

"He lost a meal ticket, but he learned from it. No more whores and no more losing his temper. Instead, he ran across the border and started trailing after the drug runners from Salazar's cartel, doing errands, making himself generally useful. By the time he was twelve, he'd graduated to collecting debts for Salazar. He became a sort of protégé of the mob. From then on it was straight up the chain. He dedicated himself to learning everything a good assassin should know, from explosives to poison, to his favorite, the machete. At last report, he'd killed at least fourteen, and that was business. He's smart and not shy of showing muscle to anyone in the cartel who causes him trouble or might get in the way of his rise to the top."

"Faults?"

"Temper, he likes to torture his victims if it doesn't get in the way of completing the job, and vanity, he believes he can talk anyone into doing what he wants."

"He may be right about that. Very smooth." He heard a ping and accessed the photo. Ramon Franco was gazing up at him, smiling recklessly. "You hit it," he told Manez. "It seems Salazar turned loose his pet tarantula on Cara."

"God help her."

"He has so far. Eve and I are attempting to offer a little assistance in that direction."

"She'll need it." He paused. "You've verified through that reconstruction that the child found in that grave was Jenny Castino?"

"If I said yes, you'd be obligated to tell your superiors and they'd be obligated to take action about returning her sister, Cara, to her native country."

"True. But it might also cause Castino to take down Salazar. Or Salazar to take down Castino. Either would be beneficial for us."

"I'm not prepared to sacrifice Cara to do that. We've already lost Jenny."

"I sympathize." He was silent a moment. "But we have a war down here. I don't know how long I'll be able to keep silent."

"You're warning me."

"I'm telling you that unless you can figure out a way to give me the result I want without bringing back Cara, I'll have to reconsider going to California and officially verifying Jenny's identity myself."

"How much time are you going to give me?"

"A week should give ample time to someone of your capabilities."

"Hardly ample."

"All I can afford. The only reason I'm giving you that much is because I remember how Castino and his wife treated those two children before Salazar kidnapped them. They were cared for by nurses, and I had reports they rarely saw them. Castino's wife, Natalie, would trot out the older girl, Jenny, to play the piano at her parties. But other than that, they scarcely had anything to do with them. Natalie was only interested in her parties and shopping. Castino never wanted to admit that anything he owned wasn't the best even though he wanted a son."

"You know a lot about them."

"I know a lot about all of the cartel bosses down here. That's why I'm on the hit list of practically every one of them. It's not only that I wish to break their power, it's sheer self-preservation. Get a plan together. One week." He hung up.

Succinct and to the point, Joe thought as he shoved his phone into his pocket. Manez would do exactly as he said he'd do. He was a good cop, and he'd do the best job he could to protect his people. He had no problem with that, he'd do the same under like circumstances. But it left him less time than he'd hoped to keep Immigration away from Cara.

Get a plan together.

And he would. He just had to line up the enemy and see how to take them down.

In one week.

Not impossible, just difficult. And he had to make sure there was no threat to Eve or Cara.

And no smiling tarantula hovering around them to take his bite.

Well, he was almost sure the tarantula wasn't on the move here and now. There was no way of being certain, but that was what instinct was all about. Joe had checked the cars, boats, exterior of the house. If Franco was on the property, he was keeping a safe distance and only observing. There was no telling about tomorrow but tonight was—

Music.

He stopped on the trail, his gaze on the lights of the cottage just ahead.

Exquisite, diamond-sharp, velvet-soft. Intricate and complex and yet simple enough to stop the heart. The music wasn't being played, it was being newly created with every note.

"My God," he murmured.

He stood there and let the music flow over him. The composition was familiar, but he wasn't sure what it was. He didn't care. It was enough that it existed. It was enough that the little girl who was playing it existed.

Oh, Cara, what the hell have Eve and I brought into our lives?

Eve was in bed but not asleep when Joe came into their bedroom. Cara was still playing in the living room but they could hear it only faintly back here in the bedroom. "I was beginning to worry."

"I stayed outside for a while listening. I didn't want to disturb— No, that's not true. I just wanted it to go on." He started to take off his shirt. "Is she as brilliant as I think she is?"

"Yes, I don't know about brilliant, but if that's the ability to tear the heartstrings, I think that's Cara. I finally came back here to the bedroom because I thought she might want to be alone with it. She's intensely personal with her music."

"Isn't that the way it is with any artist?"

"I don't know. But I've been lying here thinking about her sister, Jenny. She loved her music, too. I wish I could have heard her play the piano."

"I was talking to Manez, and he was saying that Jenny's mother always made her perform to entertain her guests. Jenny must have been a prodigy as talented as Cara." He'd finished undressing and got into bed and pulled her close. "And I'm sure Cara would be designated the same role if she was sent back to Castino."

"No!"

"Just a comment. It's something we have to face."

"No, we don't. Not if she doesn't go back."

"I thought that was the way you were heading."

"There's no other way to go. We both agreed that it would be both dangerous and cruel to submit Cara to what she'd go through if she had to be shipped back there. We'll keep her with us until we can work something out."

"That's short-term; if it goes long-term, we'd have to deal with a girl who is quite possibly going to turn out a prodigy. That could be a headache for people as busy as we are. Are you prepared for that?"

"No, I'm not prepared for anything. How could I be? We don't even know if she'd want to stay with us. All she knows is that she had a dream about Jenny, and she wanted her to stay with me."

"A dream? She didn't actually see Jenny as you've been doing?"

She shook her head. "If she did, she prefers to think of it as a dream. Kids these days are bombarded by television shows about ghosts and supernatural stuff. I'm sure that Cara thinks that Jenny's coming to her is like one of those stories, only more real."

"Maybe. Did you tell her that Jenny actually appeared to you?"

"No. The last thing I want is to encourage the fantasy. She needs to face the real world and get on with her life. She's gone through enough tragedy." She paused. "The violin was a master stroke, Joe."

"We promised it to her."

"And you fulfilled the promise." She moved closer to him. "We have another problem. Jane called me while you were gone."

"Why is that a problem?"

"Because Margaret got in touch with her and filled her in on what was going on."

"Yes, that makes it a problem. Reaction?"

"What do you think? She was upset. She pulled the family card."

"Uh-oh. And that means?"

"Ultimatum. One way or another, she's going to be with us. She'll either come here, or we'll go there."

"London?"

"No, Edinburgh. And then the Highlands. She's going on that treasure hunt for Cira's gold that MacDuff has been nagging her about. Remember? I told you she might when she left here."

"The Highlands . . . wild country. Who's going with her? MacDuff and who else?"

"Jock Gavin. You know how close he and MacDuff are. Jock grew up in MacDuff's castle, and they're like brothers. She said that Seth Caleb was not coming, but I imagine he'll show up whether she likes it or not. I don't know who else."

"Quite an entourage . . ."

"Why are you so interested?"

"She offered us an ultimatum. I'm exploring the possibilities."

"We need to get her to stay out of this."

"Yes. What do you think the odds are?"

Eve sighed. "She gave us until tomorrow."

"Then we'll have to think about it." He paused. "I heard from Manez. He identified the kid who accosted Cara at the hospital. Ramon Franco, nineteen, a very ugly customer who very likely killed his own parents and certainly murdered fourteen other people. He works for Salazar."

"You thought that he did," she said. "That means that they're moving very close to Cara."

"And to you. Salazar regards you as a problem he has to remove, or he wouldn't have given Walsh the order to kill you when you were hunting for Cara."

"But it's Cara who is the important one."

"The hell it is." Joe's voice was suddenly rough. "*You're* the important one." He was on one elbow looking down at her. "I'll do my damnedest to save Cara, but *you* have to live. So stop talking bullshit. I'm barely holding on by a thread right now."

She could see that as she looked up at him. His jaw was tight, and a muscle was jerking in his cheek. "Okay. I only meant a child is always more vulnerable."

"Yes." He reached down and touched her belly. "A child is very vulnerable and you should pay attention to your own words. There's a dual reason why you should be working hard to take care of yourself." He rolled away from her and put his arm beneath his head. He added jerkily, "Though we haven't had a chance to even discuss that minor event, have we?"

"It's not minor," Eve said.

"No? It appears to be far down on the agenda."

"It's not minor," she repeated.

"Then what is it?"

"A miracle."

He was still. Then he rolled over to face her. "Is that your conclusion?"

She nodded. "I don't know how it happened or why, but it can't be anything else. I'm confused and scared, but I was lying there in the hospital thinking, and it came to me that you can't argue or reject a miracle. You just have to accept it." She said hesitantly, "At least, I do. You have to make your own decision."

"Oh, do I?" He chuckled, his hand caressing her cheek. "I believe I made my decision the instant I gave you that seed. In case you haven't noticed, I have a thing about responsibility."

"It has to be more than that, Joe. When Bonnie was born, I would have given anything to have someone beside me sharing responsibility. But now I can handle it." Her lips were trembling. "I have to handle it, or I won't deserve to have this child. But you'll have to learn to love—you have to feel the miracle—it has to be more."

"It will be more." He drew her close and cradled her in the

hollow of his shoulder. "Just give me some time. I'm going to have a few problems refocusing some of the emotion I give you somewhere else. Okay?"

"Okay," she said huskily. She could feel the tears sting as she nestled her cheek against him. He felt warm and strong, and the musk and spice scent of him surrounded her. "I don't know any woman who would object to a request like that. We'll make it through this, Joe."

"I don't have any doubt. We just have a few obstacles in our path."

"Like murder and drug dealers and keeping that little girl alive," she said. "I'll probably be worried tomorrow but I'm not right now."

Right now, she was close to Joe, with his love surrounding her, the knowledge of the miracle to come, and the faint sound of the music of Cara's violin drifting to them.

It was enough. Tomorrow could wait.

It was after eight when Eve woke.

No Joe.

No sound of the violin.

She jumped up, slipped on her robe and left the bedroom.

"Good morning." Cara was in the kitchen and looked up as Eve came into the room. "I was just going to call you." She gestured to the bacon simmering in the pan. "This is about done. How do you like your eggs?"

"Scrambled." She shook her head. "But you didn't have to do this. I thought we had a discussion about—"

"We did." She made a face as she put bread in the toaster. "But maybe I was feeling guilty about playing my violin so late last night. I didn't even ask permission." Her brilliant smile lit her face. "Thank you, Eve."

"Thank Joe. He's the one who ran out of here to get it for you."

"I've already thanked him. Before he left to check out the woods again." Her smile faded. "He told me that boy at the hospital was one of Salazar's men. Ramon Franco. He said he was very bad." She turned back to beat eggs in a small bowl. "He wanted to make sure I wouldn't trust him again. But that wouldn't happen."

"No, I don't think it would." She sat down at the breakfast bar. "But Joe never takes chances."

She nodded. "I like that. It makes me feel safe about you."

"About us."

She smiled as she transferred the eggs to the frying pan. "But he doesn't really know me. I can tell how he feels about you."

"Feeling takes time to build." Joe had said something like that last night. "But you can trust him."

She nodded. "And he doesn't mind me playing my violin."

"Which evidently means more to you than all his protective instincts."

"Yes. I have to learn to take care of myself now, but if I couldn't play my violin . . ."

"I don't imagine you have any problem with anyone's objecting to your playing."

"You'd be surprised. Not everyone likes the violin. Not everyone likes music."

"Then I pity them."

"So do I." She scooped the eggs on a plate and added bacon and toast. "I think they must be empty inside." She put the plate in front of Eve. "But that's just me. And I have to be polite if I run across someone like that. Elena said it's rude to intrude on someone's space. Do you want some orange juice?"

"I can get—"

"I'm right here." Cara headed for the refrigerator. "Anything else?"

Eve's lips turned up at the corners. "No, you've met all my desires."

"I hope so." That brilliant smile was back. "Because you've met mine." She poured the orange juice. "And I cheated you out of dinner last night after Joe came in with my violin. Joe and I were starved this morning, so we ate before he went out hunting for any bad guys wandering around."

"I'm a little hungry myself." She started to eat. "Good heavens, these eggs are delicious. What did you do to them?"

"Mushrooms and a dash of chili powder. And I crumbled up a little bacon, too."

"They're absolutely wonderful." She supposed she should start thinking more about diet. "And healthy, too. Lots of protein. Thank you."

"You're welcome. I'll just wash up these dishes and . . ."

"Just toss them in the dishwasher," Eve said. "But you might go and clean up. When I went back to the bedroom last night, I looked up the nearest church. It's St. Michael's, and they have an eleven o'clock Mass. Do you think you can make it?"

"I can make it." She was putting dishes into the dishwasher with the speed of light. "I have to go take a shower. And I don't have a dress I can wear. I guess I'll just have to wear my jeans. Elena always liked me to dress up a little when we went to church. She said that it showed respect to God, and it was a kind of celebration."

"We'll go shopping and make sure you have one next time," Eve said. "And I think both Elena and God will forgive you for a lack of respect this time."

"I do, too." Cara was flying down the hall. "I'll be out in thirty minutes, okay?"

"Very much okay." She watched the door slam behind Cara.

Slamming doors, excitement, and the wonder of the young. So much better than the intensity, the sadness, the wariness that she had seen in Cara before. A foreshadowing of the Cara who could be. It warmed the heart.

But that sadness was still with Cara, and going to pray for her Elena would help. Thirty minutes, Cara had said, and Eve wasn't dressed either. She hurriedly finished her breakfast and started back toward her bedroom.

Joe still wasn't back when Eve and Cara got into the Toyota forty minutes later. She called him as she was backing out of the driveway. "Everything all right?"

"Yes. Just being thorough. The clock is ticking. They've had over a day to start moving. I should be back at the cottage in ten minutes."

"We're not there. I just got on the road. I'm taking Cara to St. Michael's for Mass."

"St. Michael's," he repeated sharply. "I don't like that."

"Special request. She wanted to pray for Elena."

"I still don't like it. Do you have your gun?"

"In the glove box." She felt a ripple of shocked distaste at the thought of having to take a gun to church in order to protect a child. "I'll take it in with me. But I doubt if even Salazar's pet killer would risk a public attempt in a church. Too many people around."

"Franco tried to lure Cara into that elevator at the hospital. We don't know what he'd risk. He's an unknown quantity."

Yes, that was true. The entire situation was unknown and fraught with risk. "You think I should turn around and go back?"

Joe was silent. "No sign of any surveillance. It may be safe. The alternative is keeping Cara locked up like a prisoner. Hell, and it may end up that way. But if this means that much to her, we'll try to give it to her. Go straight to the church. I'll follow you and wait outside." He hung up.

"He didn't like us going?" Cara asked quietly, her gaze fixed on Eve's face. "Is something wrong?"

"Not as far as we know. Joe is just careful."

She nodded. "But I don't want to be a bother to either one of you. If he doesn't want us to—"

"It's okay . . . this time." She reached out and took Cara's hand. "It may change."

"Whatever you say." Her hand tightened around Eve's. "I have to keep you safe."

"Because Jenny said you had to do it? I'm sure that she'd be equally concerned about you, Cara. We'll just concentrate on keeping each other safe." She squeezed her hand and released it. "Now stop worrying and just do what you told me you wanted to do. Think about your Elena and pray for her soul. We should be at the church in ten minutes."

CHAPTER

4

Cara was very quiet as they left the church and walked toward the parking lot after the service.

"Okay?" Eve asked gently.

"No." Cara's eyes were glittering with tears. "She shouldn't have died."

The eternal protest, Eve thought. There was nothing to say, so she just gave her arm a comforting squeeze. "I'm sorry, Cara. She was a good woman."

She nodded jerkily. "And God would be smart if he gave her some kind of special place or job to do. I told him so when I was praying for Elena."

"And I'm sure he'll pay attention."

"I don't know. He took Jenny *and* Elena. If he was paying attention, he'd know that was too much." She shook her head. "Elena would say that's not respectful. But . . . I loved them, Eve."

"I know. But their memory will be with you forever. You'll never lose that."

"No, I'll never lose that." She moistened her lips. "I was kneeling there and trying just to think of Elena and pray for her. But I kept thinking of Walsh and what he did to Elena and Jenny, and that

Franco, who smiled at me and wanted to kill me. Elena believed in Satan as well as God. They had to be sent by Satan. There's so much evil in the world, and maybe God can't keep up with it. Maybe we should help him."

"Joe's a detective, he goes after the bad guys every day. We all have to try in our own way." She added gently, "But you have a few years before you have to find your way, Cara." She had stopped beside her Toyota. "Give it time."

"Things happen. Sometimes there is no time." She got into the car. "So I'll hope and I'll pray, but, just in case, I'll fight, not run. I won't let anyone else be taken from me."

"Do me a favor? Run to Joe or me before you decide to take on the devil?" She was negotiating her way toward the exit. "A little help doesn't hurt."

Cara suddenly smiled. "No, it doesn't. Did I sound silly?"

"No, you sounded like someone who has been hurt and didn't want to be hurt again. And we have to concentrate on doing that." They had reached the exit and she waved at Joe, who was parked in a spot near the street. "And there's Joe waiting to make sure that doesn't happen. Now let's go home and talk about how we're going to go forward . . ."

"Wait!" Cara's hand suddenly gripped Eve's arm. "I think . . . Near the steps to the sanctuary . . ." Her gaze was on someone striding down the street. "No, he's gone."

Eve tensed, her eyes flying to the steps. "Who?"

"I think . . ." She was breathing hard. "I only had a glimpse, but I think it was the man you told me was Ramon Franco. No, I *know* it was." Her voice was fierce. "I told you I'd know him if I saw him again. It wasn't only his face. He had a way of moving, of cocking his head to the side."

"All of that in a few seconds? No mistake? You were talking about him and Walsh only a minute before. You're sure that it wasn't—"

"It was *him*." Her gaze was frantically searching the street. "He was in a hurry. He went down that side street. Believe me, Eve."

She did believe her, and a chill was running through her. "I was just making certain." She reached for her phone and dialed Joe. "Cara is sure that she caught sight of Ramon Franco a few minutes ago. What should I do?"

"Where was he?" Joe fired.

"He was coming from the church or maybe the parking lot. He went down a side street on the other side of the church."

Joe cursed. "He'll be gone by the time I get back there and chase him down. It might be what he wants me to do anyway. I'm not leaving you alone. Turn left and park on the street. I'll be right behind you."

Eve hung up and turned left on Danforth Avenue, and a block later, she found a place to park. A moment later, Joe parked and jumped out of the jeep.

He was beside the Toyota in seconds. "Get out. Go get in my Jeep. Keep off the street."

Eve settled Cara in the Jeep, then ran back to him. "What are you going to do?"

"I'm checking the car. Franco was on foot when Cara saw him. He didn't attack. He wasn't positioned for a shot. He had business to do. And after he completed the business, he took off." He carefully lifted the hood. "Nothing here. I didn't think there would be. It wouldn't be easy to rig anything in the engine without someone's seeing him. I would have noticed him myself. I was watching everything going on while you were in the church. I just had to be sure." He closed the hood. "But I didn't see Franco, and there had to be a reason."

"Rig?" Eve repeated. "Are you talking about a bomb?"

"It would make sense. It's a pretty common method of disposal among the gangs in Mexico City. Manez mentioned Franco was good at all kinds of methods for putting down Salazar's enemies. And a bomb would blow both of you to Kingdom Come with no trace evidence. Salazar would have been pleased with Franco."

"Shit."

"I didn't see him." He started for the rear of the car. "He would have had to stay low and out of my line of vision. Back of the car . . ." He knelt on his hands and knees and looked at the undercarriage beneath the car. "Nothing here." He crawled to the side. "I don't see— There it is!"

"What?" She knelt beside him. "I don't see—" Then she saw it. Near the left rear wheel, small, fastened with duct tape, with a blinking light. She gasped. "We should call the bomb squad."

"Maybe." He was wriggling beneath the car. "Give me a minute."

"Joe." Her throat was so tight, she could barely speak. She knew he'd been trained to both set and deactivate bombs when he was in the SEALs, but that didn't mean he wouldn't blow himself up. "Get out of there. You are *not* going to disarm that bomb yourself."

"I'm only looking at it. Very powerful but basic design. No remote-control switch. Just a timer." His hands were on the bomb, doing something to it.

"Joe, you'll set the damn thing off."

"No, I told you, it's basic. No problem. If I'd been worried, I would have made you go back in the Jeep with Cara when I first caught sight of it."

"Well, *I'm* worried. Get out of there."

He crawled from beneath the car. There was a streak of oil on his cheek and on the collar of his shirt. "It was set to go off in thirty minutes, about the time you'd get back to the house."

"You turned it off?"

"No, I reset it to allow for the time I spent here examining it."

"What?"

"We're going to let the bomb go off," Joe said. He handed her the keys to the Jeep. "You drive the Jeep. I'll meet you when you get off the freeway. I'll need you and Cara to be seen driving the Toyota as far as the property. Don't worry, the bomb's set for fifteen minutes leeway."

"What are you up to?"

"I'll explain later. No time now." He got into the driver's seat of the Toyota. "Trust me."

Trust him to drive home with a ticking bomb on the undercarriage of that car?

Trust his word that she and Cara would be safe for that last stretch in the Toyota?

No question.

But she was going to kill him later for scaring her like this.

She turned and jumped into the Jeep beside Cara.

"Don't ask. I don't know all the answers yet."

The Toyota was parked in a layby off Quinn Road a mile from the freeway when Eve exited and stopped beside it.

Joe rolled out from beneath it. "Get in. Quick. We lost five minutes."

"What were you doing?" Eve asked as she gestured for Cara to get into the Toyota. "Something wrong?"

What was she asking? The whole situation of a ticking bomb was wrong.

"No, I just wanted to check the undercarriage for any other explosive I might have missed before I let you drive it." He ran to the Jeep and jumped into the driver's seat. "Get out of the Toyota the minute you're on our property and the road is surrounded by trees. Jump out, and you and Cara hit the closest ditch. Don't wait until you get to the house."

"Why?"

"The house and driveway are open and can be viewed easily by a telescope. That's where the bomb was set to go off, and Franco will want to see it. The road in the woods when you first enter the property can't be clearly viewed or accessed. When the bomb blows, he'll think he just miscalculated by a few minutes."

"A *few* minutes?"

"Three, tops. Move!"

She moved. Her foot stomped on the accelerator, and the Toyota jumped forward.

She could see Joe in the Jeep in the rearview mirror. She was passing cars and houses as she drove through the neighborhoods bordering the lake property.

Three minutes.

"Eve?" Cara said softly.

"It's okay." She didn't take her eyes from the road. "We're handling it. Just move when I say move."

Cara nodded and fell silent.

Trees.

In a minute, they'd be on the lake property.

It was a long, long minute.

Trees. Shadows. Lake in the distance.

She braked, hard. A screech of metal. The Toyota turned sideways as it halted.

"Out, Cara!" She threw open the door. "Run for that ditch on the other side of the road."

Cara didn't question. She was already running. She was at the deep ditch before Eve, sliding down the muddy side.

Eve followed her.

One more minute.

"Crawl." Joe was in the ditch beside them. "Get as far away from the car as possible."

Eve nudged Cara ahead of her. "Hurry!"

Thirty seconds.

Eve was panting as she moved through the mud and rocks of the ditch. She could feel Joe behind her.

"Head down!" Joe shouted.

Kaboom!

Deafening noise. Glare of fire. Flying metal hurled into the air.

She was vaguely aware of heavy weight. Joe had sprung forward and covered Cara and Eve with his body.

She struggled to move, to sit up.

"Be still. Not yet. There's still flying metal."

A minute later, Joe moved off her. "Okay?"

She nodded as she sat up and looked at Cara. The girl appeared unscratched but her eyes were wide with disbelief as she stared at the fiery inferno just yards from them. Eve glanced at Joe. "You?"

Joe didn't answer as he reached for his phone. "Get in the woods and hike toward the far end of the lake. Wipe out your footprints as you go. *Now*. Franco may turn up any minute. I'm calling the police and fire department and bringing them on the scene so he won't be eager to do any in-depth search."

Eve grabbed Cara's hand and pulled her into the woods. She called over her shoulder. "You're not coming?"

"I'm going to stay here and appear properly devastated by the tragedy. I'll find you after midnight tonight. Get going."

She was already running. She grabbed a branch from beneath a tree, then another for Cara. "You heard him. Erase the footprints."

Cara didn't question but set about brushing the leaves over the faint indentations on the earth.

The air smelled of oil and smoke and burning rubber. It was hard to breathe.

Joe was alone. Would Franco get there before the fire trucks and police? No, she could hear the sirens now.

And Cara was now by her side, her expression intent, and Eve could almost feel the aura of protectiveness she was emitting. It's not supposed to be like that, she wanted to tell her. It should work the other way around. But she still felt the warmth and companionship of that protectiveness, and she would take that gift. She was feeling bewildered and had no idea why Joe had staged this explosion. All she could do was be patient and take one thing at a time.

Protect Cara from all dangers.

Get to the far end of the lake.

Erase all signs of their passing.

And wait for Joe to tell her what the hell was happening.

"It's kind of cold, isn't it?" Cara huddled closer to Eve beneath the shelter of a boulder beside the lake. "I think the fire from the Toyota has finally gone out. I don't see the glare any longer."

Eve nodded. "It's been hours since the explosion." She drew the girl closer to the warmth of her body and leaned back against the boulder. "It shouldn't be long until Joe gets here. You've been very patient, Cara. Not one question."

"I didn't think you'd be able to answer them." She wrinkled her nose. "You seemed very frustrated with Joe. And there wasn't much time for explanations."

"You're right there," she said ruefully. "On both counts."

"But you're not angry with him?"

"I'll let you know that when the explanations start coming in."

Cara looked up at Eve thoughtfully. "But I don't think you'll be angry with him then either. You wouldn't have done what he wanted if you thought he was wrong."

"Right and wrong is often a question of opinion. Joe and I aren't always on the same page."

"But most of the time?"

She nodded. "Most of the time."

"And you trusted him to do what was right for us."

"Yes, and I always will. It just may not be the way I would do it. Joe has great instincts, and he's sometimes way ahead of the curve." She paused. "And you can trust him, too. If the time comes when he wants you to do something crazy like blow up a Toyota, you go ahead and do it. He'll have a reason."

She chuckled. "But you still thought it was crazy to blow up the car?"

She sighed. "I loved that Toyota. It was like an old friend."

"But you know he'll be able to convince you it was the right thing to do."

"We'll see when he—" She broke off, her head lifting. "Shh, I heard something . . ."

Cara stiffened. "Maybe I should—"

"It's Joe."

Joe had moved out of the shadows behind them. He pulled her to her feet, and his arms went around her. "Everything okay?"

"You tell me." She gave him a quick kiss. "We didn't run into any trouble, did we, Cara?"

"No." Cara scrambled to her feet. "Hello, Joe."

"Hello, Cara." He took off the backpack he was wearing. "I want you to know getting your violin into this backpack posed major difficulties. Everything else had to go around it." He set it on the ground. "But I figured I might not be able to get you to budge unless it went with you."

"Went with her where?" Eve asked.

"Edinburgh."

"What?"

"I called Jane and told her you'd made your decision, and you'd be flying out tonight."

"Wait a minute. *My* decision?"

"Well, I let her believe that you were in agreement. And when she heard what was going on, she was in agreement, too. All you have to do is say no, but it would spoil all my plans."

"Which involved blowing up the Toyota," she said grimly. "And causing me to almost have a heart attack while you were driving all the way back here with that bomb underneath it. Not to mention sending Cara and me into the woods while you did your fancy staging for Franco."

"Guilty of all of the above."

"Then tell me why."

"I decided that Margaret was right, hiding in plain sight was too dangerous. I could do all the scouting and take all the safety precautions, and there still might be a slip. You and Cara would be squarely in the bull's-eye. I checked those cars for possible explosives when they were sitting in front of the cottage. When Franco couldn't safely get near them, he waited until you left the property and went to a place where he could access them." His lips tightened. "That can't happen again. You won't be safe, and I won't be able to concentrate on getting Salazar or Franco because I'll have to be standing guard."

"So you staged that bonfire to make Franco think he'd managed to kill Cara and me." Eve shook her head. "But they'll find out that there were no bodies in that car."

"Not for a while. That bomb was very powerful and meant to make it very difficult to obtain either dental records or DNA. In short, there would be a possibility of vaporization, or at least huge difficulty finding body parts. You can be safely in the Highlands before anyone realizes you're alive and gone."

"And where will you be?"

"Wherever Salazar is. He controls Franco. I need one to get the other."

"Mexico City."

"Maybe."

"Dammit, we're going to be at opposite ends of the world from each other."

"Not quite. And only if Franco and Salazar stay on my side. The minute one of them steps toward you, I'll be there."

"I don't like it."

"Neither do I. But it's how it has to be right now." He said roughly,

"Do you think I like the thought of sending you over there without me? It's the safest thing for you and Cara. Why do you think that I was asking who was on that hunt? MacDuff was in the 45 Commando of the Royal Marines and won a hell of a lot of medals. He's something of a folk hero in Scotland. Jock Gavin is young, but he might be the deadliest man I've ever met. Caleb is bound to show up, and you know what he is."

Yes, she knew. She had seen Seth Caleb in action and still had nightmares about it. "You've been thinking about this since last night."

"I was searching for a way out for you. This is it. It's the best I can do. It will be like having a Special Forces unit to protect you."

"And who is going to protect you?"

He didn't answer directly. "Manez and the Federales want that coalition of cartels broken up. He wants Salazar and Castino dead. He'll help all he can."

"If you ask him. Not if you think he's going to get in your way."

"I've already started to use him."

"For the time being. But you want Salazar and Castino put down regardless if you get the Mexican police to go along with you."

He glanced at Cara. "So do you, Eve."

"I don't want you dead."

"Neither do I." He smiled. "I'll see that doesn't happen. I have something very special to live for at the moment."

She wasn't going to be able to talk him out of it, she realized in despair. "I didn't want Jane involved in this, Joe. She's just beginning to be able to cope with her life again."

"We have no choice. *She* gave us no choice. I told her all the dangers. I'm calling MacDuff and Jock before I put you on that plane and make sure they're on board with this."

She made a face. "You really meant it when you said that you're forming a Special Forces unit."

"It's already in place. You have to be safe. Don't give me a hard time, Eve."

"Why not? As usual, it seems like it's all for me and nothing for you."

"Look, you have to protect Cara. I have to deal with Salazar. We both have our jobs to do. We can't do them together."

She knew he was right, she just didn't want him to be right. She drew a shaky breath. "You call me. You keep me informed. I want to know what's happening to you. Do you hear me?"

"I hear you loud and clear." He kissed her. "Under the circumstances, I'm not likely to let you run around those hills without my knowing what's happening." He turned to Cara. "You take care of her."

"I will," she said gravely. "Don't worry, I know that's what I have to do."

He reached out and gripped her shoulder. "And you might take care of yourself, too. Make it a package deal." He turned back to Eve. "I rented a jet, and you'll board it out of the Gainesville Airport." He checked his watch. "It should be ready for takeoff in an hour. I've arranged a rental car to meet us about a mile from here, and I'll drive there and see you on board."

"That's not necessary. I can get there myself."

"It's necessary. I waited until most of the hubbub about the explosion was over before slipping out of the house and coming here. I don't believe that Franco is still hanging around but I have to be sure you're safely away." He grabbed the backpack he'd set down earlier. "And I'll call MacDuff and ask him to set up the arrival in an airport where you can be under the radar."

"Illegal," Eve translated dryly. "Margaret would approve."

"There are times when Margaret and I agree on the basics of self-preservation. I don't want Salazar to tap his contacts and find that an Eve Duncan arrived anywhere in the United Kingdom. We'd have to do a cover for Cara anyway. She has no documents." He took Eve's elbow. "Come on, Cara. We need to go."

Eve hesitated, then started with them down the trail. It wasn't a foolproof plan, and some aspects scared the hell out of her. But it was the only game in town, and Joe had made it as safe as he could under the circumstances.

Except for himself.

She knew how he operated. He was clever and he could function in conditions that were intricate and complex . . . and dangerous as hell. He'd done it as a SEAL, and he thrived on it. Some of it was planned, other parts were pure instinct. All of it caused Eve to be afraid every minute that she knew what was happening.

But she wouldn't know, unless he told her.

And that scared her more than anything else.

"Relax. It's not going to be easy, but this is the way to handle it," Joe murmured, sensing that disturbance. "It's only the start of the game. Franco moved forward, and we checked him. That means we're ahead."

She nodded. "Just let me know what you're doing," she repeated unsteadily. "I don't want you to be alone."

"I'm not alone. That ended a long time ago. You're always with me . . ."

The pilot, Jeff Brandel, smiled down at Eve and Cara as Joe turned and walked away from the steps of the jet and headed back toward the rental car. "It should be a smooth flight. Is the little girl a nervous flyer?"

Eve shook her head. "She hasn't done much flying, but she'll handle it well. Right, Cara?"

"It's very interesting. And all the statistics say it's safe." She looked back down at her laptop. "And Joe wouldn't have chosen you if you weren't a good pilot, sir."

"Smart," Brandel said. "Yep, I'm pretty good at my job." He turned toward the cockpit. "And you're right, Quinn is tough. No excuses." He grinned. "A little like my wife. I just got married, and she's making me toe the line." He glanced over his shoulder at Cara.

"But having a sweet kid like that one might be worth it." He closed the cockpit door.

Eve watched from the window as Joe got into the car. He sat there, and she knew he wouldn't drive away until the plane was in the air. Joe was nothing if not thorough.

She didn't want to go, dammit.

But the plane was already taxiing down the runway, then lifting off. She could see Joe start the car and drive away.

Cara's hand was suddenly covering her own. "If you don't want to go, tell the pilot to turn around and take us back. You're both doing this for me, aren't you? I don't want you to be unhappy. It hurts me. Go back."

"It's partly for you." Eve squeezed her hand. "But Salazar would go after me anyway. I know too much. The minute I finished that reconstruction of Jenny and started to try to find her killer, I was on his hit list."

"But it's mostly for me."

"Or Jenny. She gave her life for you, Cara. She wouldn't want it to be in vain." Her lips tightened. "I won't let it be in vain. You're going to live and be happy. And we're going to punish all the people who are trying to take that away from you as they did Jenny."

"But you're scared about Joe. I *feel* it."

Eve gazed at her curiously. "Do you?"

She nodded. "Jenny said that I'd feel what you feel just as she did. It's happening." She paused. "Why, Eve? I don't understand it."

"I don't understand it, either." She had been trying to avoid confronting this subject with Cara. But she would not lie to her. "I can only guess."

"She's . . . not a dream?"

"Not for me. I don't know about you," she said. "I never felt a connection like that before with one of my reconstructions. I knew Jenny, I saw her. We had a . . . bond. I don't know why. We both thought it might be because she was sent to me because she needed help to save you." She added quietly, "But I grew to love her as you do. I was sad when she said she was leaving me."

Cara was silent. "It sounds kind of— Do things like that really happen?"

"You'll have to decide for yourself. It took me a long time to admit to myself that I wasn't having hallucinations when my daughter, Bonnie, came to me several years ago. She had been killed when she was only seven, and it almost destroyed me as well." She smiled gently. "And does it really matter as long as the love is there? Dreams or spirits or hallucinations. Whatever brings you peace and love. I like to think that Jenny and I are better for the time we spent together."

Cara nodded slowly. "She loved you, too."

"In your dream?"

She didn't answer directly. "She loves you. That's why I have to keep you safe." She leaned back in the seat. "But I'll go anywhere with you, do anything. We don't have to go to this Edinburgh."

"I'm afraid we do." She made a face. "Joe has set it up and he's probably right that it's the safest way to handle it. If there is a safe way. I just wish we didn't have to bring Jane into it."

"The daughter you adopted. She's the one who painted the picture of you. Will she be angry that I'm causing you trouble?"

"No, she'd never blame the innocent. You'll like Jane."

"But will she like me?"

"Count on it. I'm only worried because Jane has had such a rough life lately. She was engaged to be married, and Trevor, her fiancé, was killed. It was . . . difficult." Understatement for the heartbreak that had almost destroyed Jane. "But Jane is coming back to us now. I was glad when she decided to go on this treasure hunt."

"Treasure hunt," Cara repeated with a smile. "It sounds like pirates and that *National Treasure* movie. Sort of fun."

Eve nodded. "It does, doesn't it? But it's been on the horizon for Jane since she was seventeen. She's just been putting it off."

"Why?"

"I almost hate to tell you." Eve's eyes were twinkling. "Dreams again."

Cara's eyes widened. "What?"

"When Jane was seventeen, she was having dreams about a young actress, Cira, who lived in Herculaneum in ancient Italy at the time of the eruption of Vesuvius. I won't go into detail, but the dreams were so real that Jane became obsessed. She thought she must have seen something on the Internet or read something somewhere that might have triggered those dreams. She started to do research and found there actually was a Cira who had survived the eruption and fled to Britain, taking with her a chest of gold coins that in today's market would be astronomical in value. Cira settled there in the Highlands of Achavid, what they used to call Scotland, and founded a new dynasty. But after she arrived there, there were no tales, nothing written, about what happened to the treasure chest. It was as if it vanished once Cira reached Scotland."

"But Jane won't admit it?"

"Jane couldn't care less about the treasure. All she wanted was to have the dreams stop and find out the end of Cira's story."

Cara's eyes were fixed in fascination on Eve's face. "And the dreams about her did stop?"

Eve nodded. "But she wasn't happy about the end of the story."

"Why not?"

"It turned out the dynasty that Cira founded was the MacDuff family. And the current Lord of MacDuff has wanted to find that treasure for many years. He's tried to persuade Jane to go treasure hunting with him."

"Because of the dreams she had?"

"Partly. But also because a statue of Cira was found in the ruins of the theater in Herculaneum, and she resembled Jane. Also, there was a portrait of an ancestress, Fiona, in his family art gallery who looked identical to Jane. MacDuff tried to convince Jane she was a member of his family who had emigrated to the U.S. He even wanted to investigate and try to prove it." She shook her head. "Jane didn't want any part of it. She told him she was happy with who she was, and she didn't want to be a MacDuff, thank you."

Cara laughed. "Because she was your daughter. I can see why she'd feel like that."

"Well, anyway, MacDuff has been trying to get her to go on that treasure hunt for Cira's gold ever since. Maybe he thought because of her connection with Cira it would bring him luck. Jane finally gave in."

"Cira . . . I wonder what she was like."

"According to what Jane found out about her when she was researching, Cira was unique. Born a slave and fought her way from the gutters to fame and fortune. Loyal to her friends, tough to her enemies, honest when she could be."

"It's like a wonderful story," Cara said softly.

Eve could see how she might think so without knowing the harsher details. "Not really. Jane met her Trevor while going through it, and they fell in love. But it wasn't a happy ending. Trevor was killed recently trying to protect Jane."

Cara was silent. "Dreams or nightmare . . ."

Eve nodded. "Perhaps a little of both. If you accept them, you have to accept the risk."

"As you did with your Bonnie?"

"It wasn't risk with Bonnie, it was my salvation."

Cara was silent. "Dreams . . . You and me and now Jane. It's strange, isn't it?"

"Only because we're talking about it. I imagine everyone has their secret dreams. We just have to be sure we don't let them get in the way of living our lives. Mother Teresa once said, 'Life is a dream . . . realize it.'" She reached out and touched the silky hair at Cara's temple. "And that's enough talk, period, for the time being. It's going to be a long flight, why don't you try to sleep?"

"Okay. Will you be able to sleep? You're not going to worry about Joe?"

She probably would, but there was no use troubling Cara. "It's early days. If Joe managed to fool Franco, he'll give it a little time before he starts after him and Salazar." She hoped she was telling the truth. "We may be in a holding pattern."

"You didn't answer me. You'll sleep?"

"Little nag." Eve closed her eyes. "I'll sleep."

CHAPTER

5

"It's done," Franco said. "I told you I'd be able to take care of it, Salazar. A bomb on the undercarriage of Duncan's car. It took out Duncan and the kid in one explosion." He laughed. "And you should have seen Quinn standing there on the road staring at the fire while the fire trucks tried to put it out. He looked sick. I showed him he can't get the best of me. I've been waiting for that since he stopped me from taking the girl at the hospital."

"But he did get the best of you there. Are you sure that he didn't do the same thing this time?"

"The cops questioned the neighbors and two separate women saw Duncan and the kid drive by their houses only a few minutes before the car blew."

"You didn't see it yourself?"

He was silent. "I was waiting for them to get to the house. The car blew a couple miles down the road. But I was there within two minutes, and the bomb did its work. I put enough C-4 to practically vaporize the car and anyone in it. I did a quick check in the woods before the police got there, and there were no bodies or footprints. They were definitely in that Toyota."

"Proof?"

"I'll have it in a few days. It will take that long to scrape together what's left of them and attempt an ID. Which they'll have real trouble getting, especially in the kid's case. But they may be able to tell if it's a woman and a child. I'll let you know as soon as the report comes in." He paused, waiting for the praise he knew wouldn't come. "You said you wanted both of them dead, bodies destroyed, no way to connect you with the kid. I did everything right. Everything that Walsh screwed up on. Admit it."

"I'll admit it when you show me proof," Salazar said. He was silent a moment. "But you may have done a sufficient job. A little showy. Officials in the U.S. don't take kindly to car bombs. It makes them feel threatened. All that terrorist stuff. And Quinn is a detective, and he particularly wouldn't appreciate having his lover blown up in that manner."

"It was perfect. The lack of identification was just what you wanted."

"And you think Quinn is going to take it without acting like a raging bull? I don't believe that's true."

"Then let me take him out."

"I was just going to suggest that, but wait until you have the ID on Duncan and the kid. And don't do anything as attention catching as that explosion. Something quiet, perhaps even appearing accidental? Or maybe suicide. Give him a day or two after he finds out about Duncan, then take care of it." He laughed. "If he doesn't take care of you first."

Franco felt rage sear through him. "He's no threat to me. Naturally, I'll do what you want me to do. I'll tell you when it's done." He hung up.

Salazar had been taunting him. He probably realized that he was on his way up and might become a threat to him. He wanted the job done, but he didn't want him to feel that he was superior in any way.

He almost wished that he hadn't killed that kid. It might have been a way for him to insinuate himself into the power struggle of the coalition that was going to come when he got back to Mexico. Now Salazar was feeling safer, and he might move against him if he decided he knew too much.

But there were other ways to rise to power.

And it was best to do what Salazar wished for the time being and keep an eye on him for the possibility of betrayal. It was almost sure to come. His life had been a series of betrayals, and he knew how to deal with them.

Just as he knew how to deal with Joe Quinn. He had already taken his woman from him. He had shown him the cost of interfering with him. In a couple days, he would kill the son of a bitch in the discreet way Salazar had decreed.

In the meantime, he would wait and dwell pleasurably on the memory of Quinn standing before that blazing car while Eve Duncan turned to ashes before his eyes.

"They're on their way," Joe said when Jane picked up the phone. "You'll meet them at the airport?"

"I told you I would, Joe. I'm in my car now heading for Scotland." Her hand tightened on the phone. "No chance of your coming now, too?"

"Not now. Take care of them, Jane."

"I will. You take care of yourself."

"No doubt about that. I've never had more reason. I'll be in touch." He hung up.

Take care of them.

Damn right she'd do it, Jane thought. Eve had always been there for her since the moment she'd taken her in after a life on the streets and in foster homes. As she'd told Eve, family was everything, and Eve and Joe had created that family for her. There was no question she'd not let it be destroyed by the scum who had planted that bomb.

She could almost see that blast in her mind's eye. When Joe had told her what had happened earlier today, it had shaken her to the core.

So close to a fiery death.

If that child had not seen and recognized the killer.

If Joe had not suspected what was going on.

Too many ifs. Even one would have been fatal, and she couldn't lose Eve.

Not after she had lost Trevor.

Pain.

But not the terrible agony that had attacked her previously. She was beginning to be able to embrace the good memories and let the memory of the horrible night of his death start to fade. It wasn't a question of forgetting him, that would never happen. But she was alive, and she had to face the responsibilities of being alive.

And the biggest responsibilities were to the people she loved.

Her cell phone rang, and she glanced at the ID.

Seth Caleb.

Shit.

Not now.

Face it.

She pressed the access button.

"What do you want, Caleb?"

"I have a long list, and all of them mutually entertaining," he said mockingly. "Where do you want me to start?"

"I can't talk very long. What do you want?"

"At the moment, I want to know where I should meet you after you pick up Eve and that little girl."

She stiffened. "How do you know about my picking up Eve?"

"Not from you, obviously. I received a call from Joe Quinn, and he filled me in on what was going on. He appears to value my services far more than you do. And he must be very upset if he deliberately set out to bring me back into your life. He prefers I stay as far away from you as possible."

It was true. Caleb had saved Joe's life at one time, but the manner in which he'd done it had instilled a permanent guardedness in Joe. Eve had shared that distrust, but she had overcome it when Caleb had been there for Jane on a number of occasions.

"I didn't ask for you to come. I'm not asking now. We don't need you."

"It sounded to me as if you did," he said. "And I called MacDuff, and he wouldn't admit that he needed me. But he didn't object to my presence on your little sojourn into the wilderness. He thought I might add amusement."

"I don't agree."

"But you and MacDuff are looking at it from two different points of view. You've always been afraid of me."

"I have *not*."

"Let's say, that you've had moments of apprehension."

"Let's say, anyone with any self-preservation instincts would have moments of apprehension being with a man who has a talent for controlling the blood flow of anyone close to him," she said sarcastically. "That doesn't mean I'm afraid of dealing with you."

"Then deal with me," he said softly. "You're going to do it sometime. Why not now?"

"Because I don't choose to do it. You don't run my life, Caleb."

"But I could do such a magnificent job. You'd have such a good time." He suddenly laughed. "I can almost feel the sparks flying. I'll back away and let you go back in your shell for a while. Are you going to tell me where I should meet you?"

"No."

"Then I'll handle it myself. I'll see you soon." He hung up.

She drew a deep breath. She had no doubt she would see Caleb soon. He moved in and out of her life like a constant shadow outlined in fire, disturbing and bewildering her.

"Then deal with me."

He had meant on the most basic and sexual level. What else could it mean? The sexual chemistry between them had always been there though she'd tried to banish it. Caleb was nothing that she wanted. He was highly sexual, unpredictable, primitive, with questionable morals, and she would never know what he would do next. The ultimate fascinating bad boy.

And Trevor had been everything that she wanted. He had been the opposite of Caleb, honorable, trustworthy, humorous, gentle, loving, understanding. He had even tried to understand Caleb on those last days before he had been killed.

Why was she even comparing the two men? Caleb was a law unto himself, and Trevor was gone now.

Because Caleb was not gone, and she had to remind herself that she mustn't be drawn into that emotional vortex that he knew how to weave. It would be so easy to be swept away, and that could not happen. She had come back to London to devote herself to her work. It had been simpler when Caleb had seemed to vanish from her life after she had returned. She had started painting again, and met with her agent, and become totally engrossed in life as she meant to live it.

Until she had been torn away from it by the phone call from Margaret.

And then Caleb had stepped in as he usually did when she would be most vulnerable.

Not fair. Caleb liked Eve, and Jane knew he would help when she was in trouble whether or not Jane was involved. He would just take advantage of any weakness along the way.

And if Caleb could help Eve, then Jane had to accept it and let him do it. It was Eve who was important, not her relationship with Caleb. She would use him just as he tended to manipulate everyone else he encountered.

She would just have to be careful not to let her guard down while she was doing it.

ARDLAND AIRPORT
SCOTLAND

Jane was standing underneath the harsh pole lights by the hangar when the jet rolled up.

"There she is," Eve said to Cara as she unbuckled her seat belt and stood up. "That's my Jane."

Cara peered eagerly out the window. "She looks a little like you. I didn't expect it since she's adopted."

"She has the same coloring, red-brown hair, hazel eyes." She chuckled as she got the backpack down from the overhead compartment. "Big differences, though. I'm just interesting looking, she's positively beautiful."

"Yes." Cara was studying her. "Is that why you chose her?"

"Heavens, no. I told you, we chose each other." She was still smiling as she nudged Cara before her toward the door. "And your next question is probably did I choose her because she might have looked like Bonnie? Yes, Bonnie had the same coloring, too. But that had nothing to do with it either. We just bonded."

"Do you think I'm nosy? Elena said that it's rude to ask personal questions."

"I think you're curious, but most kids are curious. However, you have to realize it's not considered polite in most circles. But you're entering into a new life, and it's natural for you to be curious about the new people surrounding you. So we'll give you a little slack where manners are concerned." She was starting down the stairs. "But don't expect a permanent exception. Privacy is very important. Now come and meet Jane."

She'd gone only a few yards across the tarmac when Jane ran forward and enveloped her in a hug. "Hi, are you okay? You look fine."

"I told you I was fine. It was just a mild concussion." She gave her another hug and released her. "Joe just wanted to take advantage of a temporary weakness to have them give me a physical. He's always nagging, and I'm always forgetting."

"I remember." She linked hands with her and gazed searchingly at her face. "But that bastard's blowing up the car must have been a shock. It must have shaken you."

"I was too busy obeying Joe's orders to feel much of anything." She wrinkled her nose. "Which was probably one of Joe's strategies." She dropped Jane's hands and pushed Cara forward. "And Cara was so cool that I had to hold myself together to compete. Cara Delaney, Jane MacGuire."

"How do you do," Cara said politely. "Thank you for helping me, Ms. MacGuire. I'm sorry to trouble you."

"Jane." Jane held out her hand and solemnly shook Cara's. "And you're very welcome, Cara. Any friend of Eve's is a friend of mine."

Cara's lips turned up in the hint of a smile. "That's the way I feel, too."

"I suspected you might from what Margaret told me about you." She turned back to Eve. "Do you have any other luggage? We should get going."

"No, we're definitely traveling light." She chuckled. "Cara's violin took up most of the space."

Cara looked stricken. "I'm sorry."

"I'm not," Eve said. "I imagine Jane can fit us out with something for this grand treasure hunt. But we may have you work for it."

"Anything."

"You'll play for your supper," she said with a mock scowl. "And no complaints."

Cara smiled. "I promise. No complaints."

"Where are we meeting MacDuff and Jock?" Eve asked Jane, as they moved toward the car.

"We were supposed to meet in Edinburgh, but after Joe called MacDuff, he decided it would be smarter to avoid being seen together there if possible. We're going to Hazlet Castle, about a hundred miles north of here."

"Castles," Cara repeated. "And Eve said MacDuff is an earl? It's strange . . . and kind of neat. Should I be extra polite to him or something?"

"No way," Jane said. "He's arrogant enough as it is without pandering to his vanity. Be courteous because he's your host, but don't take any guff from him."

"I never found him arrogant," Eve said.

"You never tried to keep him from getting something he wanted," Jane said dryly. "I've been fighting him over this blasted treasure hunt for years. He'll probably drive us like Simon Legree while we're on the hunt."

"Why does he want it so badly?"

"One, it's horribly expensive to keep up a family property like MacDuff's Run. Most of the great homes have been forced to be turned over to the government because of taxes and maintenance. The money would be a godsend. Two, he's heard about Cira, the matriarch of the family, ever since he was born. He's curious about her."

"And you aren't?"

"Of course I am." She started the car. "But not enough to devote this much time to the relics of the past. I want to move forward."

"Even if it's your past, too? Is MacDuff still insisting you're some kind of distant cousin or something?"

"No, I was firm enough so that he won't make that mistake again. He knew that if he tried to gather me into all that nobility folderol, he'd lose any chance of getting me to search for Cira's gold."

"But why does he think you could find it?" Cara asked curiously.

"He's just playing a hunch." She glanced at Eve. "Did you tell her about those crazy dreams I had about Cira?"

Eve nodded. "Not crazy, just strange. You put together a story with those dreams that had a lot of factual content. I can see why MacDuff might think you'll find a way to provide a very satisfying ending."

She shook her head. "I stopped having dreams about Cira years ago. If there was a purpose, it must have been fulfilled. My chances of helping to find that treasure aren't any greater than yours or Cara's."

"And, if you don't find it, then you'll know you tried. I hate might-have-beens, don't you?"

"Yes." Jane's lips were suddenly tight. "I do. There's nothing worse."

She was thinking of Trevor, Eve realized. She quickly changed the subject. "Who owns this Hazlet Castle?"

"It's one of MacDuff's properties. More of a glorified hunting lodge than a castle, I hear. We won't be staying there long. I think he said we'd be leaving on the search tomorrow."

"That's good." She added slyly, "Off into the wilds of the Highlands. I wouldn't want to trade one cave for another, even one that looks like a glorified hunting lodge. Someone told me that's not a smart thing to do."

"Ouch," Jane grinned. "But that someone was right, as proved by current events."

"Perhaps. Joe certainly thought so." She pulled out her phone. "And I promised to call him when we arrived in Scotland. I'd better do it now."

Joe picked up the phone at two rings. "You're there?"

"Safe and sound. We're on our way to Hazlet Castle to meet with MacDuff. I'll text you when we reach there. Are you still at the lake?"

"Yes, I'm doing more research on Castino and Salazar and buying time for you." He paused. "How was the trip? How do you feel?"

"Fine. For heaven's sake, how else should I feel, Joe? It's not as if—" She broke off as she glanced at Jane, who was looking at her with raised brows. The last thing she wanted to do was to start worrying Jane unnecessarily. "No problem. What kind of research?"

"A fishing expedition. I'm trying to find a hook to spear Castino or Salazar or both. I turned Manez loose on going in-depth about everything connected with either one . . . and the kidnapping of the girls."

"We know about the kidnapping. Salazar wanted to cause Castino as much agony as possible without endangering himself or his status in the cartel coalition."

"And that may be the sole reason. When Manez finishes his investigation, we'll be sure."

"No sign of Franco?"

"Not yet." He added, "But I'm sure I'm being watched to see if I'm writhing in pain. I'll go out on the porch occasionally and let him see what he wants to see while I'm waiting on the release of the forensic reports. He's probably got a bribe in place and will find out there was no one in that car about the same time as I do."

"Then what?"

"He'll come after me and try to force me to tell him where you and Cara are."

"And you're looking forward to it."

"It will signal the opening of the game. And give me a chance to pay him back for trying to kill you. Then I move on to the next piece on the table."

Salazar. Eve's hand tightened on the phone. "You're so damn casual. Franco is dangerous. You said so yourself."

"I'm not casual. I'll be very careful. You do the same." He said, "Call me when you're on the trail. I'll keep in touch." He hung up.

"Not wonderfully reassuring?" Jane asked Eve.

"As good as can be expected when it's Joe." She slipped her phone back in her pocket. "He's being very patient, but I can never tell when he'll take off like a rocket."

"He won't do it if he believes it will hurt you or Cara."

"Unless he gets an idea he thinks will move the play along." She shrugged. "But maybe that won't happen. We may have at least until Franco finds out that Cara and I aren't dead." She looked in the backseat. "How are you doing?"

Cara nodded. "I'm okay. Sorry you're so worried about Joe."

"Hey, it's not your fault. Joe's certainly not worried." She smiled back at her. "I'll make a deal with you. You concentrate on having a good time chasing after Cira's gold and doing kid-type things, and I'll try to do the same thing."

Cara studied her, then she slowly smiled. "I think that would be fun. I've never searched for treasure or anything like that before. Elena didn't like me to play with other kids."

"Well, this time you'll be playing with the big boys," Jane said dryly. "MacDuff and Jock will be quite an experience for you."

It sounded to Eve as if any play or association of any sort would have been an experience for Cara. Always in danger, always having to be careful, always having to accept adult responsibilities while she was still a child. She smiled gently but her voice was determined. "And we'll make it a good experience."

He was out there somewhere.

Joe could feel it.

He moved across the porch to stare out at the lake. It wasn't like that first night when he'd been uncertain that Franco was in the vicinity. Franco was not only out there, he was probably getting ready for a move. It was logical that Joe be eliminated to make the cleanup complete.

But that move wouldn't come until Franco was sure that his initial kill was a success. Joe wasn't sure that Franco would make that decision, but Salazar was seasoned and wouldn't be hasty.

But this waiting was making Joe edgy. He almost wished Franco would get overeager and make his try.

No, give Eve her chance to become lost in those barren Highlands. He could wait. As long as he knew he was accomplishing—

His phone rang. Manez.

"That was fairly quick," he said when he picked up. "You've got something for me?"

"You could say that. I don't have details, but I heard a rumor from a prisoner, one of Salazar's men we picked up on a murder charge. It was secondhand from another prisoner in the same cellblock. He's trying to make a deal."

"Rumor? What the hell good will a rumor do us?"

"I'll leave that up to you to decide," Manez said. "Do you want to hear it or not?"

"I want to hear it. Spit it out."

Manez did just that, in one single sentence.

Joe inhaled sharply. "Holy shit!"

HAZLET CASTLE

Hazlet Castle was a small, two-story, stone structure built around a courtyard and set in rolling hills and surrounded by deep forests.

"It's pretty," Cara said as she got out of the car in the stone courtyard. "But not what I'd expect of a castle. Not like the history books, or fairy tales, or Disneyland."

"As I said, there are castles, and then there are castles," Jane said. "MacDuff's primary residence, MacDuff's Run, on the coast, is more what you'd imagine." She got out of the car. "But you still might like to explore it. I don't believe MacDuff would object."

"Object to what?" A tall, muscular man in black trousers and a herringbone jacket was coming toward them across the courtyard. He looked to be in his late thirties, with dark hair pulled back from his face, olive skin, a lean, interesting face, and eyes that sparkled with intelligence and vitality. He moved with swift, springy strength and he was smiling as he took Jane's hand. "A favor, is it?" The words were spoken with a definite Scottish accent. "I always like the idea of your owing me, Jane."

"I think it's a question of your owing me, MacDuff." She smiled back at him. "Why else am I here?"

"According to Joe Quinn, that's questionable." He turned to Eve. "Hello, Eve, I'm glad to see you. I understand you may make our project more interesting than I anticipated."

"And you're still glad to see me?"

"Quinn was very persuasive. He appealed to my sense of noble purpose." His face creased in a smile. "However, as Jane will tell you, my family earned our title as bands of renegades and cutthroats. But that's not a bad thing as far as you're concerned. I'm much more likely to find your situation interesting." He turned to Cara. "And you're Cara? I'm delighted to meet you."

Jane stepped forward. "Cara, this is the Earl of Cannaught, Lord of MacDuff's Run and sundry other properties here in Scotland and Wales. Known by all his subjects as the Laird." She smiled. "He's John Angus Brodie Niall Colin—"

"Stop." MacDuff held up his hand. "I'm sure that you don't intend this girl to remember any of that so you must be doing it to annoy me."

"Just giving you your due measure of respect, MacDuff."

"It's about time." He turned back to Cara. "Are you going to follow her example?"

"How do you do, sir," she said gravely. "You have a very pretty place here."

"But you find it small and unlike a Disney castle."

"I didn't know you heard me. Was I rude?"

"Honest. But I don't take offense. I completely agree with you. It's small and gradually crumbling into the earth. That's one of the reasons we're going to find Cira's gold and invest in a multitude of renovations on this and my other properties."

"You're certain you can find it?"

"Life is never certain, but I believe with Jane I have an excellent chance." He glanced at Jane. "Now all I have to do is convince her." He turned and gestured to the huge oak door. "Please, come in, and I'll ask Jock to show you your rooms while I finish making the soup I put on when we arrived a few hours ago. Nothing fancy. There aren't any servants here, a circumstance of which I'm sure that Quinn would approve. So you'll have to tolerate dust and the most basic of food."

He threw open the door. "Jock," he called. "Come and see Jane and Eve and meet our young guest."

A fair-haired young man with light eyes and a brilliant smile came across the paneled foyer toward them. "At last. Saved from boredom and kitchen duties."

Cara stopped, gazing at him, dazzled. She had never seen a more beautiful person or a warmer smile. Beautiful, yes that was the word. She would no more call him handsome than she would call a concerto handsome. His shock of blond hair framed a face with perfect features and gray eyes that seemed to glow against the tan of his skin. And that smile seemed to hold all the warmth and understanding in the world. He was now embracing Jane, and Cara couldn't stop looking at him.

"Hello, Jane. It's been a long time. I heard about Trevor." His voice was gentle. "Is there anything I can do . . ."

"No." She hugged him, then turned away. "Nothing. Thank you."

"You're staring, Cara," Eve whispered with amusement.

Cara couldn't take her eyes from Jock's face. "He's wonderful," she whispered back. "It's not only that he's so—there's something else . . . inside."

Eve nodded. "You're right. I'll tell you about him later."

MacDuff suddenly chuckled, his gaze on Cara's face. "Jock, I believe that you've managed to redeem my humble estate in her eyes. This is Cara Delaney. Jock Gavin. Tell me, Cara, is he Disney-land enough for you?"

"MacDuff," Jane said with a frown.

Jock's gaze swung to Cara. With one swift look he saw, analyzed, and stepped in to heal any hurt. "Don't pay any attention to him." His tone was light, teasing. "MacDuff is just jealous that I fill his shoes better than he does. You're perfectly right, I should have been the earl and he the housekeeper's son. Now tell the lass you're sorry, MacDuff."

"He doesn't have to do that." Cara looked MacDuff in the eye. "Yes, I do think he's like a prince from a Disney fairy tale. But life isn't a fairy tale, and people aren't always what they seem. I'm sure you do have some qualities that people admire."

"Ah, no backing down yet no overt rudeness that might be detrimental to Eve or Jane. Extraordinary." MacDuff tilted his head. "And I appreciate your trying to spare my feelings when I was so impolite as to poke fun at you." He bowed. "Shall we start again, Cara?"

She smiled. "You do seem more like an earl now. Though I've never met one."

"And you'll never meet another one like him." Jock laughed. "He passes muster every so often." He turned and headed for the staircase. "I've been ordered by MacDuff to find you rooms. Would you like to come with me?"

"By all means." MacDuff turned and went down the hall. "I'll be in the kitchen. We'll have a bite to eat in an hour or so. Then we'll go over the maps I have of Cira's castle, Gaelkar. I believe that's the place we have to start . . ."

There were several bedrooms on the second floor, and the three that Jock showed them were furnished comfortably. But all the rooms were dusty, and Jane gazed ruefully around the last bedroom. "I feel like getting a broom and starting in to work." She turned to Jock. "But it would take too long. I'll just open the windows and freshen it up. I hope there's decent plumbing?"

"Sufficient." He shrugged. "And MacDuff did the best he could when he realized that it might be up to us to offer protection to Eve and Cara. He decided it would be best to disappear and not leave any trace, so he whisked everyone out here."

"And I appreciate it," Eve said quietly as she crossed to the window and gazed out at the hills. "Though I hope we won't need that protection."

"It will be what it is." He turned to Cara. "You couldn't ask for a finer man or a better defender than MacDuff. He can be impatient, and he's not always gentle, but he's been my friend since I was a boy, and I could not ask for anyone more loyal."

"Were you really the son of his housekeeper?" she asked curiously.

"Aye. From the time I was a toddler, I was in and out of his castle, MacDuff's Run."

"You were his friend?"

"As much as a wild lad could be a friend to anyone. He was the Laird, and sometimes I fought it. He was a better friend to me than I was to him. I tried to make that up to him later." He changed the subject. "Do you have many friends?"

She shook her head. "I had a friend, Heather, but she wasn't . . ." She stopped. "I couldn't spend much time with her. So I don't really know if she was my friend at all. I guess my only real friend was Elena." She moistened her lips. "But she was enough. I didn't need anyone else."

Time to step in, Eve thought. She could see Cara was on the edge, and she didn't need the trauma of explaining the loss of the woman who had cared for her all these years. Cara was in a strange new world and surrounded by people who meant her well but were also alien to everything she knew. "I think it's time to wash up and go down to have supper with MacDuff, Cara." She made a shooing motion with her hands. "Use that first bathroom down the hall. It looked fairly clean. Jane and I will try to freshen up these bedrooms."

"I can do it," Cara said.

"Yes, you can, but I prefer to do it myself. We'll take turns in the bathroom." She was opening the windows. "Jock, is it safe in the courtyard?"

His brows rose. "Yes, I went over the entire castle and made sure it was all safe when we first got here. I didn't expect anything else. MacDuff alerted the guards that watch over this property to go through it when he knew we were coming. They're some of his old Marine buddies and very sharp. And there was no way anyone not authorized could get close to it after that without our knowing it. They'd report everything to MacDuff. Why?"

"There's no use making Cara stay around when we're going over MacDuff's plans. It will only bore her. After supper, we'll let her go outside in the courtyard and amuse herself." She turned back to Cara. "Be sure to take your violin when we go down to supper."

"My violin?" Her face suddenly lit. "I won't bother anyone? Is it okay?"

"More than okay. I doubt if anyone will even hear you through these thick walls. If they do, they'll receive a gift. Now get going."

Cara whirled toward the door. "I'll hurry, then I'll come back and help you." She suddenly looked back at Jock. "I do have another friend. I have Eve." Then she was gone.

Jane gave a low whistle. "Now that's a responsibility. She reminds me a little of myself at that age."

Eve shook her head. "No, you were much tougher. She had her Elena to remind her that the entire world wasn't garbage."

"She seems pretty tough to me," Jane said. "Most kids would have fallen apart after what she's gone through."

"You're probably right. It's just that she seems to quietly endure while you were such a fighter. Though I believe that leaf may be turning. I'm seeing signs that there's a change in the offing."

Jane was smiling. "And, however like or unlike we are, we have one thing in common. We managed to seek out one Eve Duncan and chose her as our friend." She came across the room to where Eve was standing. "And we thank God that she took us into her life."

"This may be only temporary as far as Cara is concerned. We may not be able to give her the life she needs."

Jane leaned forward and kissed her cheek. "Let's take one day at a time. I have a hunch that new things are going to happen in your world."

"Do you?" Eve smiled curiously. "You may be right. We'll have to see." She turned to Jock, who was staring at them with a quizzical expression. "What do you think, Jock? Are there new things on the horizon for all of us?"

"That would be interesting." He turned toward the door. "And now I'd better go down and help MacDuff prepare us supper. He's fairly competent, but you can't trust these upper-crust types with the basics." He glanced back and smiled. "I'm glad to see you both again. It's been too long." He had a sudden thought. "And, Jane, Seth Caleb phoned and asked me to tell you that he'd see you tonight."

"I can hardly wait," she said without expression.

"Did I detect a hint of sarcasm?" He paused. "Do you wish me to get rid of Caleb for you? MacDuff thought he might prove helpful in an emergency, but if you want him gone, just say the word."

"I didn't say that," Jane said. "I doubt if we'll need him, but I won't cheat Eve and Cara of his help if you think he's valuable."

"Whew," Jock said with mock relief. "I really didn't want to have to make the attempt of disposing of Caleb. I can handle most skills but that blood thing freaks me out a bit." He lifted his hand. "Remember, supper in an hour."

He closed the door behind him.

"You didn't tell me Caleb was coming," Eve said. "Though I suspected he would."

"If Joe hadn't called him, he would have known nothing about it. He announced he was coming along when he phoned me when I was driving up from London."

"I'd bet that he would have known about it regardless," Eve said. "He keeps an eagle eye on you."

"And that used to make you uneasy."

"It still does, but I've learned to accept the fact that I have to let you handle Caleb. If I find that you're wibble-wobbling, I'll step into the picture."

"Wibble-wobble. I wouldn't do that. Caleb would run right over me."

"Probably. But I've occasionally noticed that he allows you to escape punishment when I thought he'd pounce. He definitely has a weakness where you're concerned."

"Not that I noticed."

"You didn't watch him in that hospital in Atlanta when you were in a coma. He was driven." She paused. "And I was grateful to him. He saved your life. Jock may make fun of that 'blood thing,' but you wouldn't have lived if Caleb hadn't gone in and strengthened those arteries."

"I told him I was grateful, too."

"But he disturbs you, so you want to push him away. I understand, and it might be best for you. But you'd better learn how to cope with him or he might . . . Just learn how to cope." She turned away. "Now let's see if we can make a dent in this dust in the next half hour. We might smother if we have to inhale this stuff during the night."

CHAPTER

6

After a meal of beef soup, cheese crackers, and fruit, that turned out to be surprisingly good, MacDuff took them immediately to his study. A fire crackled in the huge fireplace, and the room smelled of pine and the leather of the oversized furniture.

"I'll get the plans." MacDuff went to the shelf in the bookcase behind his desk and drew out a large rolled paper. "I had a new schematic of the castle drawn eighteen months ago, so this should be fairly current. The one before was done in 1994. Still not too old when you remember that the castle is ancient. It was difficult to get anything but a basic map of the ruins." He unrolled the paper on his desk and anchored it on all four corners. "Here it is. As you can see, there's nothing much left. A dungeon, one wall, a staircase, and a few bedchambers, the courtyard. The first floor is a maze of rooms, some blocked by fallen walls."

Jane reached out and one finger traced the curving staircase. "I'm surprised that there's that much left."

"I'm not," MacDuff said. "Cira came from a culture that knew how to build to last. Look at the Coliseum." He pointed to the wall encircling the castle. "And she would have made sure that no invaders would get in and destroy what was hers." He met Jane's gaze. "You're the authority. Isn't that right?"

"How do I know? I'm not an expert on Cira."

"Close as it comes," MacDuff said. "Those dreams you had about her panned out historically." He paused. "And since you're almost certainly her descendant, there's something to say for ancestral and racial memory."

"You're the only one who believes that."

"Because you're too stubborn to let me prove it." He shrugged. "But maybe it will prove itself." He tapped the wall again. "Would you 'guess' that Cira would build those walls strong enough to repel an army?"

"It's logical considering what we've discovered about her character. She was intelligent, strong, and superdetermined or she would never have survived. I was always amazed that she was able to remain a decent human being along with it."

Eve laughed. "You're being so cautious, Jane. Play his game, it won't hurt. I know from what you went through during that time that you felt you knew Cira. Just go with the flow."

"Thank you." MacDuff inclined his head toward Eve. "I realize your opinion carries more weight than mine."

"I don't want anyone to assume that what I went through with those dreams of Cira had any basis in truth," Jane said. "Imagination, maybe. Perhaps something freaky that has nothing to do with your precious ancestral memory."

"Why are you objecting so strongly?" Jock asked curiously.

"Because I'm a realist," Jane said. "What happened to me when I was seventeen has all kinds of explanations, and I may never know which one is true. I had a weird experience, then it was over as if it had never begun. I forgot it, and I'm only revisiting it because MacDuff asked me to do it."

"And I'm very grateful," MacDuff said. He looked down at the schematic again. "Do you suppose this wall was Cira's idea? She wed her Antonio, and he was very strong-willed, too."

"It was Cira," Jane said. "She was an ex-slave and she was nearly fanatical about being free. She wanted her family to be safe at all costs." She smiled. "At least that's my opinion."

"It's on a hill," Eve said. "And it's rough country. Will we be spending all our time at Gaelkar?"

"Presumably. Unless the search leads somewhere else," MacDuff answered. "Why?"

"I have a different agenda than you. I have to protect Cara. I'll have to check out the surrounding countryside. I need to know what kind of problems I might have if Franco shows up."

"I'll help you," Jock said quietly. "We'll do it together. You'll find me very competent."

She didn't doubt it. More than competent. Superb in hunting, absolutely unstoppable when he went in for the kill. When Jock was in his wild teen years, he had run away from home to see the world. Tragically, that journey had led him to be kidnapped by a man who was conducting experiments on a group of chemically brainwashed boys and training them as assassins. It was incredible that Jock had managed to survive and become the person he was today. "I don't want to take you away from the search."

"I can do both." He grinned. "I'm a man of many talents, aren't I, MacDuff?"

"And some of them X-rated," MacDuff said dryly. "And often very annoying. He'll do exactly what he wishes to do and leave Jane and me to do the actual work."

"I do what's important." He dropped into a chair and stretched out his legs. "But I don't have to pay attention at the moment. Continue while I sit here and enjoy the fire . . ."

"You will tell us if we disturb you?" MacDuff asked. "We wouldn't want to let our planning get in the way of your relaxation." He bent over the schematic. "I was thinking about looking into the dungeons first. They're at the lowest point, and there might be passages that lead beneath the—"

The meeting lasted more than a full hour longer before MacDuff tied up the last details and dismissed them to go to their beds.

"At last," Jock said as he opened the library door for Eve and Jane. "Very boring, MacDuff," he said over his shoulder. "You could have made it more entertaining."

"I'll try to do better next time."

"I didn't find it boring," Jane said, as they moved down the hall. "He was very thorough. He's obviously spent a lot of time and work on it. He's made an in-depth investigation into that castle."

"I didn't find it boring either." His eyes were twinkling. "But you have to keep MacDuff in line. He's far too used to everyone kow-towing to him." He looked at Eve as she went past the staircase toward the front door. "You're going out to the courtyard to gather your chick and bring her in from the cold?"

Eve nodded. "Cara would probably stay out there all night if I didn't go get her. She has a tendency to become obsessed." She smiled. "And I dare you to refer to her in such a flip manner after you hear what that chick is creating out there."

"Really." He looked intrigued. "Then by all means let's go and see. I'm always ready to take a dare."

Jane was already opening the door. "I'll go with you. I've been curious about—" She stopped as the strains of Cara's violin flowed over them in a wild, passionate, flood of sound. "Dear God." She turned and gazed at Cara sitting on the edge of the fountain, the violin tucked beneath her chin. "That's coming from her?"

"The chick." Eve went down the steps toward the courtyard.

Jock was right behind her, his gaze on Cara. "Does she know how good she is?" he asked quietly.

"Maybe. But she doesn't care, it's all about the music."

He was silent, listening. "And do these bastards who want to kill her realize what they're taking away? To kill any child is a sin beyond belief, but they also want to rob all of us."

"They don't care. She's only a chess piece."

"Is she?" His face was hard in the moonlight. "Then I believe I should enter the game. I don't like being cheated of anything. Not her life, and certainly not that talent."

"Not a chick?" Eve asked.

"It was said in the most affectionate way." He smiled. "And I still might use it if she suddenly discovers how extraordinary she is, and I have to take her down a peg."

"Like MacDuff? I don't believe we have to worry. As I said, it's all about the music." She was only a few yards away from Cara, and she deliberately moved into her field of vision and stopped.

It still took Cara a few minutes to notice she was there. And a moment more to reluctantly lift the bow and stop the music. "Is it time to go in?"

"I'm afraid it is," Eve said. "It's been a long day. Time to get to bed."

She nodded and got to her feet. "I like it here, Eve. The music is stronger here than I've ever felt it. Even when I'm not playing, I can hear it."

"I know what you mean." Jane came closer to her and sat down on the edge of the fountain. "I'm no musician, and I can almost hear it. Some places seem to make their own music. The Highlands are like that. I think you'll like Gaelkar."

Jock nodded. "Aye, wild and wonderful things have happened there, haven't they, Jane?"

She met his eyes. "And how would I know? I've never been there. But it's deep in the Highlands."

"Well, we should be there by tomorrow night and she can judge for herself." He took Cara's hand. "May I escort you inside, mademoiselle?"

"Much better than chick," Eve murmured.

She watched as Jock and Cara walked back to the front door. The beautiful, strong young man and the small, fragile young girl. There was something very touching and old-world about the protectiveness that Jock was showing the child. She glanced at Jane as she started after them. "Coming?"

"In a moment." Jane dipped her hand into the water of the fountain and let the drops slowly fall back into the water. "I'll be in soon."

Eve stopped. "Okay?"

"I should be asking you that," Jane said. "I just want some quiet time."

Eve nodded and started up the steps. "I'll see you upstairs."

"Eve."

She looked back at her.

"I'm glad you came to me. I'm glad you trusted me to help." She smiled. "We'll get that little girl through this."

"Yes, we will. We can get through anything together." She blew her a kiss. "Family."

Jane watched Eve disappear into the castle and close the front door.

She stayed there, her eyes on the door.

Waiting.

One minute passed.

Two minutes passed.

"Dammit, what are you doing, Caleb?" she said impatiently as she turned to glare at the shadows of the stable across the courtyard. "What game are you playing?"

"No game." Seth Caleb strolled out of the shadows toward her. He was wearing a black turtleneck sweater and khakis, and the moonlight glimmered on the white thread in his dark hair and lit his high cheekbones, deep-set dark eyes, and full lips. "I was just admiring you in the moonlight. I don't often get a chance to observe you without your getting nervous. How long ago did you realize I was here?"

"I don't know. Not right away. Maybe I saw a movement."

"Then why didn't you sound the alarm?"

"Because I knew it was you."

"How?"

"You sent me a message you'd be coming tonight."

"Yes, I did." He stopped before her. "So it was entirely reasonable that you'd come to that conclusion." He smiled. "But reason had nothing to do with it, did it? You *felt* me here."

"Think what you like, Caleb."

"Oh, I will. I just want you to admit it to yourself, if not to me. We have a connection. It's been there from the beginning. Electricity?" He tilted his head. "Yes, along with something, deeper, less civilized. I sense you all the time when you're anywhere around me."

"I don't want to talk about this."

"Then be honest, Jane."

"It . . . might be possible. You gave me blood when I was hurt and you have that . . . thing with blood."

His brows rose. "Thing?"

"Hell, what else can I call it? What are we supposed to call it? I'm sure it doesn't have any technical name. I don't know anyone else who's able to manipulate the blood flow of anyone he's close to. It's too weird." And dangerous, she thought. It wasn't only healing that he could control if he chose to use that talent as a weapon. She had seen him do it, and that power frightened her. "And you have to admit it's hard to describe."

He nodded. "Unique, as far as I can determine, outside my family. A small gift, but my own."

"Well, it evidently worked for me at the time. And, since I don't have any idea how it works, I might still be subject to some kind of residual—but it doesn't mean anything." She stared him in the eye.

"Can we talk about something else? Like what you were doing lurking in the shadows while Cara was playing?"

"I wasn't lurking. Is it too much to believe that I didn't want her to stop when I arrived here tonight? I heard her playing while I was still driving down the road, and I parked outside the gate and walked up to the courtyard. I thought I'd take a few minutes for myself before I went in and became what you thought me to be." His lips twisted. "Haven't you heard that music soothes the savage beast."

"I believe the quote refers to 'savage breast'."

"I've always thought that my way was more appropriate. And you probably do, too. We've been together during many occasions when my true nature came to the forefront. Isn't that what you see when you look at me, Jane?"

It was true. They had known each other for a few years, and Caleb had seemed to appear whenever she was involved in a situation that was threatening. She had a sudden memory of a time when they had been together in the Alps and Caleb's throwing a body down before her like a savage giving a gift to his mate. The man he had killed had been attacking them, but all she had been able to remember was the savagery and pleasure in Caleb's face.

He laughed. "You're having to think about it. Are you afraid you're going to hurt my feelings? You're not usually so diplomatic."

"You're not a beast. You do have your primitive side. I don't know what you are, Caleb. I don't believe you want me to know. I do know you're intelligent, complex, and can be amusing. I know I owe you my life when you came to me in the hospital."

"And you may never forgive me for that." His smile was gone, his tone fierce. "You wanted me to let you die so that you could join your lover in the great beyond? I wasn't about to let that happen. I won't let you go, Jane."

"You gave me an invaluable gift. It doesn't matter whether I wanted it or not. I still have to be grateful for what you did." She smiled faintly. "And I'm sure that you're arrogant enough to believe that you have control of my life, but forget that. I'll run my own life. I have no intention of dying. I was wrong. There are people who need me. And two of them are in that castle." She got to her feet. "I didn't want you to come because you're always disturbing. But you're here, so make yourself useful. The only thing I want from you is for you to keep Eve and Cara safe." She added deliberately, "And not to get in my way while I'm trying to do it. Do you understand?"

"Of course. You're always very clear with me. Much more clear than you are with anyone else. It's as if you think I'll step outside bounds if given the excuse." He was smiling again. "I'll be very careful not to do that. I'll let you ignore me as much as you're capable. I'll be wonderfully helpful and make certain that all goes well with your world."

"And what are you going to get out of all this, Caleb?"

"Opportunity." He headed for the front door. "It's all I need . . ."

Eve had thought she would be tired enough to sleep, but she realized after an hour of tossing and turning that wasn't going to happen. Not surprising. She was still charged from the flight from Atlanta, and it seemed that every moment since then had been full of renewing relationships, making sure that Jane was okay with what was happening, and Cara was comfortable in this new environment. It was like a new and different life from the one she had left behind her in Atlanta.

And she should be grateful that life appeared to be so different. Talk of ancient ruins and treasures instead of bombs and threats of death at every turn. She *was* grateful. She just wanted to be back with Joe and working to have this nightmare over. It might be safer for her, but what about Joe?

Don't think about it. Do her job as Joe was doing his.

Cara.

She got out of the huge bed and padded across the room to the adjoining room, where Cara was sleeping. She quietly opened the door and peeked at the girl in the bed across the room.

She was fast asleep. It was clear Cara had not had the same problem as Eve. But then children usually slept well. She remembered Jane had no problems until she was in her teens, and Bonnie had been able to curl up anywhere and drop off. Eve had found her so many times in the hammock in the yard with her hand tucked beneath her cheek and her red curls mussed from play.

Bonnie . . .

Eve quietly closed the door and went over to the casement window that she had left thrown wide when she went to bed. She looked out at the forests and the hills beyond.

"I haven't heard from you, and it's beginning to scare me, Bonnie. You told me once that you might not be able to come to me anymore," she whispered. "Is it because you don't think I'll need you? I'll always need you. I want this child. It's a miracle. But I can't let you go. We've been together too long. It would be like losing you all over again."

Silence.

She touched her abdomen.

Hey, tell Bonnie we need her. I don't know if she had anything to do with making you come into our lives, but she might have. She's pretty special, and it wouldn't surprise me if she has influence. But we have to make sure that she sticks around for us, okay?

No answer there, either.

Of course not. What did she expect? The baby was trying to survive and become the child it was meant to be. It was Eve's job to handle everything else. She was being ridiculous, and she should go to bed and try to sleep.

She got as far as settling down in bed again. Then she was reaching for her phone and dialing.

Joe answered immediately. "What's wrong?"

"Nothing," she said. "Everything. I just wanted to hear your voice and know that you were all right. We're going to start off tomorrow trekking through some castle in the Highlands. I feel a million miles away from you right now."

"Me, too." He paused. "You're feeling okay?"

"Strong. Very strong. I could lift mountains."

"Exaggerating a bit?"

"A bit. But not that much. I remember I felt like this when I was pregnant with Bonnie. It was as if she was giving me her strength, too. The only problem was a few weeks when I couldn't keep anything down. So stop worrying. Everything's working out well with Manez?"

"Hell, yes. He's giving me more than I expected. Perhaps more than he expected. It may be a break for us."

"What are you talking about?"

"Just rumors right now. I'll let you know when I can confirm them." He paused. "I got a call from Les Carmody at the Forensics Department a couple hours ago. They wanted to assure me that they were making progress and should be able to tell me something fairly soon."

Not good. "I thought you said that it might be another day."

"I'm a cop." He grimaced. "They're trying their best to help me out. There's a good chance they're already suspecting the truth since they can't have recovered any trace of body parts yet. They just don't want to raise my hopes."

"And Salazar will probably know almost as soon as you do that there was no one in that car."

"I'd bet on it. And I'll be glad when you manage to lose yourself in those Highlands." He changed the subject. "How is Jane doing?"

"Better. Not as good as I'd like to see her, but she's healing. We can't ask for more than that right now."

"Does she know about the baby?"

"Not yet. I'm waiting. She's already trying to protect me. I don't want her worrying any more than she is already." She added teasingly,

"And have her ask every time she talks to me if I'm surviving this pregnancy."

"Was that aimed at me?"

"Gently. Lovingly."

"I'll accept both with thanks. On that note, I'll let you go so that you can get some sleep. Don't overdo it tomorrow while you're trekking over that ruin, even if you think you can lift mountains."

"Joe."

He laughed and hung up.

She was smiling as she put her phone on the nightstand and turned over in bed. The news had not been all good, but merely talking to Joe made her feel a sense that they were on the move . . . and together.

Don't think that any minute Salazar and Franco might find out that they had been fooled.

They would still have to find out where she and Cara had gone. That would take time.

Lord, she hoped it would take enough time.

Joe hung up from talking to Eve and stared down at his phone. She had sounded good, but she would not have phoned if she hadn't needed to touch base with him. Eve's career as a forensic sculptor dominated her life, and she was used to working nonstop. She would never have chosen to uproot herself and go on this outlandish treasure hunt in the wilds of Scotland.

But he had chosen for her, and she was trying to adjust and make it work for them.

At possibly one of the most crucial points of her life.

He wanted to be *with* her, dammit.

Calm down. They were already involved and had involved Jane and Cara. It had to work.

But push it along, make it happen sooner.

He picked up his phone again and quickly dialed Manez.

"Don't you ever sleep?" Manez asked sourly when he picked up the phone. "You may be driven, but I need my rest after a day of dealing with this scum."

"You promised me an address."

"That was less than twelve hours ago. Nothing moves fast down here unless you want to end up hanging from a bridge without a head."

"Bullshit. You're just as driven as I am. I'd bet you dove into squeezing all available informants the minute you hung up from me."

"That doesn't mean I was able to tap into information that was accurate."

"Were you?"

"Maybe. I'm still exploring the—"

"Give me an address."

"I'd prefer to verify first."

"We may be running out of time. I need to get a handle on this."

"I don't want you jetting down here and causing a blowup before I'm ready."

"I need that address."

Manez was silent. "Very well, but you don't move without me."

"As long as you don't drag your feet."

Manez sighed. "You're a very difficult man, Quinn. The address is one forty-five El Camino Road."

GAELKAR CASTLE
SCOTLAND

"Good God, MacDuff. It's magnificent." Eve was gazing out the window of the Land Rover at the staggering beauty of the amethyst-slate mountains in the distance as they neared the castle. The dramatic towering starkness of the peaks, the barrenness that was the vast glens took her breath away. The sun was shining, and yet these Highlands still retained their moody, almost stormy, grandeur. "You didn't tell me."

"It's always best to be surprised." He smiled at her. "You think Cira chose well for her new kingdom?"

"You'd have to ask Jane. I think it probably suited her. There's a wildness here that I can see her appreciating."

"I refuse to ask Jane. She won't want to commit herself."

Eve looked back at Cara, who was sitting beside Jane. "Do you like it, Cara?"

She nodded, her eyes fixed dreamily on the mountains. "So much music . . . And did you see the eagles?"

"I'm afraid I didn't notice either of those things. I was just taking in the general impact." She turned back to MacDuff. "How long before we get to the castle?"

"It's just around the curve up ahead. It may disappoint you."

"It's ruins, for goodness sake. Low expectations."

But she still found herself eager to see that castle built so long ago at the dawn of this land.

"There it is." MacDuff pulled to the side of the road and got out of the Land Rover. He looked up the hill at the ruins of the castle while they waited for Caleb and Jock, who had opted to come in Caleb's car. "It's not very large, but it's in better shape than you would imagine for the lack of repair. That one wall of the battlements is as strong as when they built it. The dungeons are still entirely intact. Once the family left, they abandoned it. They were moving up in the world and concentrated all their energies on building their new home on the coast."

"MacDuff's Run, the castle where you grew up?" Eve asked, as she and Cara got out to stand beside him. "I'm certain that anyone would agree it's much more impressive than this one."

"I like it." Cara's gaze was fastened on the broken walls and tumbled stone of the castle. "It's . . . nice."

MacDuff chuckled. "You constantly amaze me. You criticize my humble hunting lodge, which granted is not in wonderful condition, but you're besotted with this ruin."

"I just think it feels like home," Cara said simply.

"Providing your home has a dungeon." He turned to Jane. "What do you think? Does it feel like home?"

"That's a leading question." She smiled at Cara. "But a castle can be a home as well as a fortress. When I was still trying to find out everything about Cira, I went on archaeological digs in Herculaneum. We had to be very careful not to destroy anything that would indicate how the people lived or died. We worked with spoons, carefully sifting."

"Is that what you're going to do here?" Cara asked eagerly.

Jane glanced at MacDuff. "It's how I'd prefer to do it. It's surprising what secrets can be revealed by using a spoon instead of a shovel. Since we have no idea where we're going with this, it might be a good idea to see if we can get a clue." She added, "But then, I'm not in charge."

"And you think I'm going to use a battering ram because I'm too impatient?"

"I know about impatience," Jane said. "I've been there. Ask Eve. It's your show, MacDuff."

He nodded. "And maybe we'll try a spoon . . . for a little while."

"Good." Jane turned to Cara. "Then would you like to grovel in the dirt with me? Warning. You'll have an aching back and bruised knees unless we can find someplace that sells knee pads."

"Could I do that?" Cara's face was lit with excitement. "I saw a show on *National Geo* that had one of those college digs. It looked like fun."

"Like I said, sore knees. But I found it worth it. There's no guarantee that we'll find anything, but there's always a chance." She looked at Eve. "You're invited, too."

"I didn't expect you'd leave me out. It will give me something to do. I'm not accustomed to sitting around twiddling my thumbs." Eve stood looking up at the hill. "Those people who built that castle didn't know the meaning of twiddling their thumbs. You can almost sense the energy and determination. I wonder how much was done by hand."

"It was Cira's home," Jane said. "Her first taste of real freedom and power after being born a slave. She would have gotten down on her knees and laid those tiles herself. She would have rigged a pulley like the Egyptians to drag those stones in place. She probably loved this castle."

"Then why would she have left it?" Eve asked.

"She didn't, it was her descendants who finally decided they needed to take the next step. She built this place as a kingdom, but I'm sure that she instilled that thirst for power in those who came after her. She grew up in Herculaneum realizing how weak a woman could be if she didn't have wealth and influence. She did the best she was able, became a famous actress, and gathered what wealth she could. Then, when the volcano erupted, she fled with everything she owned." Jane smiled. "And some things she didn't own. She probably hid out in the Highlands for a long time after she first arrived here until she thought she was safe. Then she decided it was time to start to build."

"Well, after her descendants decided to abandon this place, they apparently never looked back on what she'd built," MacDuff said dryly. "We have no record of any of her family returning here after they reached the coast, where they built MacDuff's Run."

"They might have looked back," Jane said. "They liked money; you say the family earned their title by raiding and robbing along the border. If they didn't take those coins with them, then I can see them going back to get them. Unless there was a reason not to do it."

"Can we find out?" Cara asked.

"Maybe," Jane said. "If they left us a clue one way or the other."

"The spoon?" Cara grinned.

"The spoon," Jane said solemnly. She turned back to the Land Rover. "Let's start unloading our bags and supplies and get them up to the castle. I assume you didn't arrange for help here either, MacDuff?"

He nodded. "Jock and I will come back for the tents and camping supplies. Privacy appeared to be everything when Quinn called and asked me to take you. And it's a good rule to follow when you're going after a treasure trove, too."

"I can see that," Eve said. "But that hill looks like a climb." She was grabbing for her backpack. "Let's get to it."

"I'll do it." Cara was already helping Jane with her backpack. She was moving with alacrity, and her expression was eager. Eve was glad to see it. There was nothing better than purpose to make time pass quickly and give one a sense of worth.

"There's Caleb," Jane said as she watched his car come down the road toward them.

Eve was aware that Jane's easy casualness was abruptly gone. All she needed was to have Caleb show up on the scene, and she was charged, wary.

Jane looked at Eve and shrugged. "What can I say?"

"Nothing. I was just thinking that tutoring Cara in the art of the dig might be good for you, too." She started up the road, letting the barren beauty and austerity of the hills around her reach out and touch her, take her into the misty earth and blue sky. For this instant she could almost believe she belonged here.

Work.

Distraction.

It could be a solution for all of them.

Son of a bitch!

"It's not possible," Franco said through his teeth. "It's not true." He hung up, breathing hard as the fury tore through him. But it was true and he knew it. Jessup, that greedy bastard in Forensics, wouldn't lie to him. He knew what would happen to him if he did.

So what did he do now?

No choice.

He dialed Salazar. "We have a problem. Forensics found no body parts in the Toyota."

Silence. Then Salazar began to swear.

"You fool. How could you make a mistake like that?"

"I'm not a fool."

"You're worse, you stupid prick. You're worse than Walsh ever was. Quinn played you. You lost the kid *and* Duncan."

He had no defense. He was humiliated. But he was going to kill Salazar for talking to him like that. "Not for long. I'll go after Quinn and find out where he sent them. I won't let him do this to me."

"He's already done it." Salazar's voice was harsh. "You've been keeping track of Quinn?"

"Of course, you wanted him dead."

"It's good that you didn't kill him yet. He's the only one who knows where the kid is. Is he at the Lake Cottage?"

"He left there to go to the precinct where he works. I followed him, but he didn't come out. He'll probably be back this evening."

"Probably? Find out for sure. I'll cut your heart out if you lose him, too." He hung up.

He meant it, Franco knew. This last mistake had made his position impossible. Salazar might cut his heart out anyway no matter what he did. He would try to make amends by butchering Quinn, but he had to prepare for the worst-case scenario. Salazar would more than likely send one of his primo killers to make sure that everyone knew he was a failure and what was done with a man who failed him.

Get ahead of the game. He was smart. He could find out where Quinn had sent Duncan and the girl for safety. Then he could either tell Salazar or go ahead and take care of them himself.

Then he would dispose of Quinn in the most brutal way possible, a true *rematar,* a bloodbath.

And then he would start planning how he would rid himself of

Salazar without having to contend with the other members of the cartel. He was in a better position to do that than ever before.

He had an ace in the hole.

It would all come together. He just had to move fast. First, find Eve Duncan and Castino's brat.

"I need to talk to you," Salazar said. **"Tonight at ten."** He hung up.

He hadn't wanted to do this. This meeting was a risk when he didn't need any more risks.

He had no choice. Franco's failure had put him in a corner. He might need help, and he wasn't going to go through this alone.

It would be all right, they'd work it out.

All this hell would be worth it.

He got to his feet and moved out onto the patio where his children were swimming in the pool. Beautiful children, he thought with satisfaction as he watched his son, Carlos, race across the pool. Three fine sons.

Castino had never been able to produce sons, just those two puny daughters, who had caused him such a headache during these last years.

But one child was dead and the other would soon be totally out of the picture, too. And then he would have his reward.

Yes, and the meeting tonight would be worth the risk.

MEXICO CITY

One forty-five El Camino Road was an elegant creamy-tan stucco hacienda surrounded by trees behind a tall wrought-iron fence.

And the fence wasn't electrified, thank God, Joe realized, as he pulled himself up and over. He jumped to the ground, then darted behind the trees and made his way toward the house.

A soft glow issued from the windows at the rear of the house. Salazar?

There was no telling if Salazar would come to this house tonight, but, if what Manez said was true, there would never be a more likely time for him to show up. That was why Joe had jumped on a plane to fly down here when he'd been told the results from the Forensics Department.

He crouched behind a bank of large shrubs near the driveway, every sense alert.

Be patient, he told himself.

When you're playing a hunch, you have to be prepared for it not to pan out.

But that hunch was strong and burning bright. He needed a break, and this might be the one.

No one seemed to be moving around inside. There were no cars in the driveway.

But they could be parked in the back. The trees were so thick that any vehicles wouldn't be seen unless you were right on top of them.

So stake out the house.

And wait for lightning to strike.

Headlights from the sleek black Mercedes entering the gates, not surreptitiously as Joe would have thought, but boldly, recklessly.

The car was coming fast and was approaching the driveway in seconds.

A screech of brakes as the car stopped, and the driver's door flew open.

Come on, Joe thought, let me see you. Is it true?

Then the driver jumped out of the car and was striding toward the front door, every step emotion-charged and full of explosive anger.

Joe stiffened. Oh yes, it was true.

Moonlight fell on sleek dark hair.

And the beautiful face and winged brows that were so very like her daughter, Cara's.

Natalie Castino.

CHAPTER

7

Salazar flinched as the door slammed after Natalie came into the house.

"I see you're in fine temper," he said as he strolled out of the bedroom. "And you drove right up to the house instead of parking in the trees. Not smart, Natalie. The only way we've survived so far is to be careful. Do you want to get us killed?"

"I'd see that I wasn't the one killed." Natalie threw her handbag on the couch. "I'd just tell everyone that you lured me here to offer me information about the kidnapping of my little girls. A mother is always desperate and willing to take chances when it concerns a child. Of course, I'd have to shoot you so that it would make the story stick." Her eyes were glittering with anger as she strode toward him. "But I'm not desperate, I'm furious, because I think that you're going to tell me that you've made another mistake. Isn't that right?"

"Duncan and Cara weren't in the car. Franco doesn't know where they are."

"I knew it," she said through clenched teeth. "I could see it coming when you told me that Duncan had taken Cara to Atlanta. What are you doing about it? You're not relying on that stupid prick to find them?"

"I haven't taken him out of the action. I may be able to use him."

"What are you doing?" she asked again.

"I've tapped Jose Domingo, my distributor in Atlanta and told him to check out airline manifests on commercial airlines for the last two days. He's checking out train and bus, too. But I'd think that Quinn would want Duncan and the kid to go far and fast to get them to safety. So far, no records of them have surfaced. So Domingo is checking private and charter flights."

"How long before you'll know?"

"Only a few days. I have to be careful about pushing Domingo. His contacts are valuable to me. He doesn't want to make waves with ATLPD by any overt moves. After all, he could deal with any of the other cartels."

"Then go after Quinn," she said impatiently.

"We're getting there. He's been off the radar for the last several hours since we've heard about the forensic report. But Franco will locate him."

"Maybe he's gone to join Duncan and Cara."

"He went to the trouble of staging that elaborate red herring. He won't chance being followed and giving their hiding place away. He knows we're watching him. Franco will gather him up if he doesn't get another lead before that." He held up his hand as she opened her lips. "I know, an incompetent fool."

"You seem to hire no one else, first Walsh, now Franco. This entire thing has been bungled. You *promised* me. I trusted you." Her hands clenched into fists. "I gave you my daughters. You said that it would be over in a heartbeat, and no one would ever know."

"We've gone over this before. It didn't work out." He was sick to death of her attacking him. He just wished he was sick of her. He'd thought in the beginning that he'd grow tired of her and would be able to find a way to dispose of her and make his position more secure. It hadn't happened. He only had to see her, touch her, and he had to have her. Just thinking about her, and he got hard. He wanted her now. "And you wanted those girls dead as much as I did. I did you a favor."

"No, I told you I wanted them kidnapped. I didn't say you had to kill them."

"You knew that was the only safe way to handle it. You just closed your eyes. Why else were you so angry when I told you that Cara and that nurse got away?"

"Because at that point there was nothing else to do. I couldn't go back. I had to go on with it."

He slowly shook his head. "You wanted it." He moved closer to her. She smelled of vanilla and that exotic Russian perfume she'd worn since the day he'd met her. She'd told him her father sent it to her every year. Whether he screwed her or not, before he left her he always had to shower and get her scent off him before he went home to Manuela. His wife knew he had other women, but she couldn't know about Natalie, and that perfume was too distinctive. "And you wanted me. You still want me."

"Not now," she said impatiently.

"Now." He put his hand on her breast. "You're not sleeping with Castino. You need it. I can feel your nipples hardening." He rubbed at the sensitive tips through her silk shirt. "I'm doing everything you'd want me to do about the kid. It won't be long and you'll be safe." He unbuttoned her shirt. "But I need encouragement . . ." His tongue touched her nipple. "Give it to me."

"I don't need you." She was starting to breathe hard. "There are other men."

"None that I wouldn't kill if I caught you with them." He bit down hard and felt the shudder that went through her. "Like I did when I heard you were screwing that chauffeur you hired to take you around to your fancy parties. Do you remember what I did to him?"

"Yes. It was . . . bloody."

"You liked it. You liked knowing that you'd caused it. That you had the power. It was difficult for me to do it in a way Castino wouldn't suspect had a connection with you." He pushed her away and took off her blouse and bra. "So I set him up to be caught in a Federales raid near the border. I protected you then, too, didn't I?"

"And yourself."

"It's the same thing."

She looked at him challengingly. "You only want me because I belong to Castino."

"Not only. You know better. It might have started out that way, but we're both caught now."

"Not me." She stared fiercely up at him. "I'll let you have me only as long as you amuse me. When I get bored, I'll walk away."

"I haven't bored you yet." His hands tightened on her breasts. "Get in bed."

She didn't move. "That's not why I came here."

"It's why I came here. Sometimes you're so concerned someone will find out about this place that I can't get you to come. But you came tonight, didn't you?"

"Let me go."

"Get in bed. Why not? We're here now. You're hot, you need it." He added thickly, "And I need you. I'll make you scream, Natalie."

She smiled. "Perhaps."

"Are you teasing me? That's very dangerous."

"I've heard nothing but what you want." She took off the rest of her clothes and stood there naked. "I want to hear what you want to give me." She took down her chignon and her hair flowed around her shoulders. "Oh, I'll scream for you." She came toward him. "And I'll make you scream. But I came here for a purpose, and you'll give me what I want."

"I told you that I was working on it. I have to be careful."

She rubbed against him like a cat. "Not good enough. I don't care about being careful any longer. I want a promise that you'll keep." She reached down, caressing him. "And you'll give it to me."

Her breasts brushing against him. The scent of her . . . "Shit."

"I need it to happen. You either give it to me, or I'll find some-one who will."

"I'll kill you."

"No, you'll give me Duncan and Cara, and it won't be in a few days. You'll know where they are tomorrow. I don't care if it causes problems with your distributor in Atlanta. You'll do what you have to do." She went to the bed and lay down. "And before you leave here tonight, you're going to promise me that no matter what you have to do, I'll know where to find them."

"You?" He was over her, tearing off his clothes.

"Me. I can't leave it to you any longer." She gazed up at him as he came into her. "I have to make sure it's done." She whispered as she started to move, "Now promise me . . ."

3:15 A.M.

"Come back to bed," Salazar said thickly as he watched Natalie dress. "I'm not done with you."

"I'm done with you." She slipped on her shoes and went over to the mirror on the far wall. "You were right, I needed it. You were very entertaining." She ran her fingers through her hair. "We may have to arrange things so that we can do this more often. Would you like that?"

"I'd like to stay alive more," he said dryly. "Too dangerous."

"That's what I always say, but I'm beginning to think we should explore the possibilities. We need a change." She touched up her lip-stick. "If you find me exciting enough?"

She knew damn well the effect she had on him. "Stop playing games and come back here."

"You don't have time. You have calls to make, don't you?" Her smile was brilliant as she turned back to him. "And I have arrange-ments to take care of, too. Changes . . . Salazar." She headed for the door. "I can hardly wait."

He watched the door close behind her and cursed low and vehemently. He was still horny as hell, and that wasn't his only frustration. He didn't like it that Natalie was being so demanding, but he knew it had been coming. He had barely been able to restrain her for the last few years.

He looked at his phone on the bedside table. Those calls Natalie had spoken about were against his better judgment. Not good business. It was clever to stay beneath the radar and not do anything to disturb either the Feds or the police department and make them pay too much attention to his operations. But if he didn't meet Natalie's deadline, she would be even more likely to become difficult.

What the hell, he thought recklessly. He was ready for a change, too. He was tired of being careful. How many years had it been since he had been like Franco and taken what he wanted and made everyone around him fear him? He wanted that heady feeling again.

He picked up the phone and dialed Franco.

"I need to know where Duncan and the kid are by tomorrow night. Do you have any possibilities?"

Franco hesitated. "Your man here in town said that he'd discounted all the commercial airlines and narrowed it down to four or five private airlines. Three Quinn has used in the past nine years. I thought I'd check those out. I'll be careful. Domingo said you wanted us to be discreet."

"I want to know tomorrow night. Screw being discreet." He hung up.

3:35 A.M.

Joe watched Natalie Castino drive out of the gates and waited another fifteen minutes for Salazar to leave. He didn't come out of the house. The lights in the bedroom went off after another five minutes. He probably felt safe as long as Natalie wasn't with him.

You're not safe, you bastard.

He moved quickly toward the wrought-iron fence, and, a few minutes later, he was over the top and dropping to the grass.

A shadow in the bushes to his left!

He whirled and gave a roundhouse kick that hit the man in the throat, then moved in for the kill as he was falling.

"No!" Manez moved out of the bushes. "*Madre de Dios,* you've caused enough trouble, Quinn. I won't have you killing my men."

Joe stopped, breathing hard, trying to calm the rush of adrenaline. "Then you shouldn't have men who set themselves up to be taken out. I saw him the minute I hit the ground."

"Pedro is a very good man." Manez helped the man to his feet. "You're obviously just better. Go back to the car, Pedro. I'll take it from here."

Pedro gave Joe a glowering glance and turned and walked away.

"And you shouldn't expect me not to react if you don't tell me you're going to be on stakeout, Manez." Joe gazed after Pedro. "How much does he know about this house?"

"Why? Would you go after him and finish the job?" Manez said sourly. "He knows nothing. No one knows about this house but you and me and the prisoner who gave me the information. I just thought I might need backup."

"Against me?"

"Against Salazar. I'd be an even greater target than usual if he saw me here. Though I had an idea you might be popping in and causing trouble." He turned. "I need to get you off the street. I'll walk with you back to your car."

"I checked it out before I went to the house. Are you trying to protect me, Manez?"

"Only because I don't need you blowing the only lead I've had since—"

"I'm not blowing it," Joe interrupted. "I just had to verify so that I knew where I could go with it. I had to see what was happening."

"You should have left it up to me. I was going to bug the place and make sure that I had all I needed."

"This is Salazar and a woman he's been screwing for years. They both know the consequences. Do you think that he wouldn't take precautions? I had a listening device, and I should have been able to hear through the glass of the window and couldn't do it."

"So you found out nothing?"

"I found out that she went in angry and came out looking very sleek and satisfied. I don't know the dynamics, but they're definitely lovers." He stopped at his rental car. "And presumably have been lovers for a number of years according to your informant. The question is if she's his accomplice. I'd bet that she is."

"I'd . . . hesitate. A mother doesn't kill her children."

"We both know that's not true. It depends on what the stakes are and the personality of the mother." He paused. "It's the most unnatural crime imaginable, so the personality would have to be twisted beyond belief."

"Perhaps . . . she doesn't know?"

Joe looked at him.

Manez shrugged. "The idea offends me. What can I say?"

"You can say that you'll give me all the information possible on Natalie Castino. I suppose you got photos of her going through the gate?"

"I thought it might be useful."

"To stage an uproar between Salazar and Castino that would put the coalition in chaos? Not yet, Manez."

"I'll be the judge of that."

"No, not until Eve and Cara are safe." His lips tightened. "Salazar will have put precautions in place to make sure he's not connected to this place or Natalie Castino. That photo will mean nothing. Even if

Castino makes a move on Salazar and takes him out, it won't be good for me. Then he won't be able to give the order to stop Franco and whoever else he's put on tracking Eve down. Let me take care of him myself."

Manez shook his head.

"You gave me a week."

"That was before Natalie Castino appeared on the scene. I can use her, Quinn."

"A week."

Manez shrugged. "Five days. Subject to change if I find it necessary."

"Done." Joe got in the car. "You won't find it necessary. I believe Salazar's attention is going to be focused away from anything to do with the cartels for the time being. He's going to be doing everything he can to find Eve and Cara."

"And what are you going to do?"

He pulled away from the curb. "Get back to Atlanta and make sure he comes up against a stone wall."

"I like this." Cara dug her spoon into the stony dirt of the courtyard and smiled at Eve. "I kind of thought Jane was joking about it, but she really gave me a spoon."

Eve chuckled. "I believe it's more of a way of teaching patience and care than necessity. I remember when she was digging at the site in Herculaneum, she was very impatient. She must have learned an important lesson."

"But MacDuff hasn't learned it." Cara's gaze went to the area where the Laird was working with Jock. "I didn't think I'd see an earl with his sleeves rolled up and sweating. And he has a shovel."

"It's his idea of a compromise. He let us have spoons and he's going for the big stuff. He believes that the chest might be in the dungeon area. It would take a long time for him to get down there with a spoon. We're only looking for possible clues, keys, boxes, scrolls, or anything else written by family members. They're looking for the chest itself." She put her spoon aside. "But I'll have to leave you to it by yourself for a while. I have to go and take a look around the surrounding area and get my bearings."

Cara nodded. "It's a new place. Elena always used to look around the neighborhood when we moved to a different place. She said it made it safer for us."

Eve nodded as she got to her feet. She should have known Cara would not be alarmed. Her life had been one long flight for survival. "Stay close to Jane."

"You're going alone?"

"Jock was going to go with me, but he appears to be busy with MacDuff. I'll be fine."

"Yes, you will." Caleb was suddenly beside her. "But Jock thought that you'd be even better if you had someone to keep you company. He asked me to take his place." He grimaced. "A great compliment since he really doesn't trust anyone but MacDuff. I don't think he trusts me either, but he knows I can take care of you, and he knows where he can find me if he has to go after me."

Cara laughed. "But Jock wouldn't hurt you."

"Not if I could help it." He smiled at Cara. "You like him?"

She nodded. "He wouldn't hurt anyone."

Caleb looked at Eve. "I believe that's our cue to leave." He took her elbow to help her over the rocky terrain toward his car parked on the road. "I'll keep her safe, I promise, Cara."

Cara nodded and went back to her digging.

"Jock has her completely fooled," he said quietly. "She thinks he's some kind of Boy Scout. Are you going to tell her about him?"

"Not if I don't have to do it."

"Because she's a child?"

She shook her head. "She's not really a child. Because she's half-right, he wouldn't hurt anyone he didn't have to hurt. He is what she believes him to be. He didn't try to fool her, he was just being himself. I don't want her to think everyone she reaches out to is a threat."

"Well, I don't have that problem with Cara." He opened the car door for her. "If you've noticed, she regards me with the same wariness that everyone else does. I'm surprised that she permitted me to take her Eve away without her."

Eve glanced at him, her eyes twinkling. "But you were vouched for by Jock. That makes you totally acceptable."

He started the car. "Until she reaches the age of intimidation. Then I'd have my work cut out for me." He glanced at Jane sitting on a rock and going through a box of papers. "Wouldn't I, Eve?"

"Yes," she said bluntly. "But even Jane allowed me to go off with you without protest. She either trusts me to take care of myself, or you've made inroads on her trusting you."

"Which do you think?"

"I have no idea. I know you usually don't give a damn about anyone's trusting you. But Jane may be different." Her gaze narrowed on his face. "Is she different for you, Caleb?"

"She's a beautiful woman."

"Are you going to answer me?"

"So that you can rush to protect her?"

"I'll always do that."

"She's . . . different. I won't hurt her . . . if I can help it."

"That's not good enough."

He suddenly smiled recklessly. "It's all you'll get from me. It's more than I've ever given before. She fights me, and that makes me . . . angry."

"That's not what you were going to say." Her gaze was still reading him. "I think you were going to say it hurts. Were you?"

"Me?" He shook his head mockingly. "Why would you think I would succumb to that particular weakness? No one else believes that I would ever be that soft."

"I know you would never admit it. I don't know why I asked."

"Neither do I." He took out a folded paper from his pocket and handed it to her. "Jock gave me this map. He thought you might want to look it over. He told me to take you to the lake. It's the only area that has access from the north. From the south, anyone coming would be easily spotted."

She unfolded the map and checked it out. "By all means, let's go to the lake."

Gaelkar Loch was large, deep, crystal blue, and surrounded by craggy hills that fell steeply to its green banks. The north bank was bathed in thick gray mist that not only shadowed the lake itself but obscured a good fourth of the massive hills that hovered over it.

Eve felt suddenly small and overwhelmed as she stood on the edge of the steep slope nearest the road and looked out at the blue water and that ghostly mist. "What is it?" she murmured. "I've been to the Alps and I never felt . . ."

Caleb nodded. "It's principally that heavy fog. MacDuff tells me that it never goes away. Most unusual. It makes the place seem a bit menacing. It's easy to imagine that anything could happen in those mists. There are all kinds of legends about it. The locals say that it could hide the beginning or the end of the world." He shrugged. "Some people feel it, some people don't. It does manage to capture the imagination. These Highlands have been battlegrounds and full of pain and savagery for centuries. I'm sure that Cira was a part of those battles."

"But you feel it? You weren't born here either, were you?"

"No, my family settled in Italy centuries ago." He grimaced. "Much to the dismay of the villagers who were there before them. It seems my ancestors were far more intimidating than I am, and the villagers didn't understand the gift that was passed down through the family."

"Imagine that," Eve murmured.

"But I do have a home a few hundred miles from here now. I

like the wildness of the Highlands." He smiled. "I think I would have bonded with Cira."

"I believe you would, too." She looked back at the lake. "MacDuff believes Cira is Jane's ancestor."

He nodded. "But that means nothing to me. I want Jane exactly what she is, what she's made of herself." He inclined his head mockingly at Eve. "What you've made her." His smile faded. "As usual, I have a number of purely selfish interests in coming here, but one of them is to help you, Eve. I won't let anything happen to you or Cara." Then the smile was back. "Jane would have my head, and that's not the part of my anatomy I'm interested in giving her."

Outrageous. Totally outrageous. But she still had trouble smothering a smile. "It depends on how you look at it. But I do thank you for any help. There are many reasons why I need everything to go smoothly while we're here."

"Smoothly. What a curious word to use in this case." He looked at her speculatively. "And you're usually very clear and concise."

"It's just a word, Caleb." She could have bitten her tongue. The word had come out of nowhere. Everything had to be smooth. She had to take every care so that the child would be able to survive these next weeks. But Caleb was sharp and intuitive, and he had caught that subtle inference. "Stop reading something into—" Her phone rang, and she breathed a sigh of relief. She took the cell out of her pocket and her relief was gone in an instant.

Joe.

"I've got to take this." She walked a few yards away from Caleb as she punched the access. "Is there a problem, Joe?"

"The forensic report came back yesterday. Salazar knows that you and Cara weren't in the car."

She drew a shaky breath. "We knew that was coming. Yesterday? Why didn't you call me when it first came in?"

"I was a little busy."

She stiffened. "I don't like the sound of that. Did Franco come after you?"

"He didn't get a chance. I made myself unavailable. Something else popped up, and I had to check it out."

"Joe."

"I'm going to tell you. That's why I'm calling. It may be a way we can manipulate the situation to keep Cara in the U.S. I was in Mexico City checking out a lead one of Manez's informants handed him." He paused. "For at least the past six years, Natalie Castino has been sleeping with Salazar. Probably longer than that, but that's the only time span Manez's informant knew for sure."

"What?" Eve was stunned. "There's got to be a mistake."

"I was at their little love nest in the hills outside Mexico City. I saw her. She was angry with Salazar. She'd probably just heard about the forensic report."

"Joe, that doesn't make sense. It had to be dangerous for her to conduct a liaison with Salazar. If her husband found out, she'd be killed."

"Maybe she thought it was worth it." He paused. "Or maybe she was caught in a trap and couldn't get out."

"You think that she helped him kidnap the girls," she whispered. It was almost too horrible to say the words. There was no child more helpless and vulnerable than when a parent was involved. They were automatically thought to be the protector, not the aggressor. "Why, Joe?"

"Manez is trying to find out. He's digging for more information about her." He added ruefully, "He didn't want to believe it. He's a tough guy, but he probably loves his own mom, and it's hard for him to make the connection."

"It's hard for anyone." She was having trouble herself. Though she had done a few reconstructions on children who she had later found out had been killed by their parents, it had almost always been an accidental blow. Or by the father to hide proof of molestation. She could remember only two murders committed by a child's mother, and the women had both been declared by the court to be insane. But then, maybe judges had the same problem as Manez about accepting that a mother could kill her own child. "I don't understand. It's not as if she had much to do with Jenny and Cara. You told me that nurses took care of the children, and she and Castino didn't see that much of them. I've seen photos of them while they were with their parents and . . . they were damn adorable." She had to steady her voice. "Why would she do it? Was it because she was so obsessed with her lover, Salazar, that she'd do anything he wanted?"

"It's a possibility, but I don't believe that's true. The woman I caught sight of outside that house last night was no weakling. She exuded power, lots of power. What she was doing with Salazar was what she wanted to do." He added, "And I'd bet that if she was involved in the children's kidnapping, she wanted that, too."

"Did Manez give you anything more to go on?"

"He came back with a bare-bones report by the time I got back here to Atlanta. I'll forward it to you. Not much. She married Castino when she was eighteen and had Jenny only a year later. In Russia, she was Daddy's little girl and lived the life of a princess. Sergai Kaskov is a Mafia boss, but he evidently adored her and gave her everything she wanted. But maybe she didn't want to be a princess, she preferred being a queen. When Castino came to Moscow and she heard how powerful his cartel was, he seemed to be what she needed. For the first few years, her life in Mexico was ideal, parties, a husband who was crazy about her, designer clothes, the power she'd never had in Russia."

"It changed?"

"Not on the surface. She had another child, Cara, a few years after Jenny. The word was that she hadn't wanted to have another child, but Castino was insisting. He wanted a boy."

"And he didn't get one that time either."

"No. So he wanted to try again. Natalie suddenly became ill and flew home to Moscow to visit her father. She came back eight months later, and she was in fine form and absolutely radiant. Manez said that everyone who saw Natalie and Castino together during that period remarked on how she managed to dazzle Castino again. He wasn't pleased about her long visit to her father and had taken a mistress. But within a few weeks, he'd sent her away, and Natalie was queen again. She kept him so busy, in bed and out, that he wasn't pushing about her getting pregnant immediately."

"If she was that busy with her husband, she wouldn't have had time to seduce or be seduced by Salazar."

"I don't know, it depends on what spurred them to get together. Manez didn't give me any more details about that period."

"What about the girls? Would she have had an opportunity to help with the kidnapping?"

"The afternoon before Jenny and Cara disappeared, Natalie had taken Jenny to perform at the garden party at a friend's house in the hills. Cara stayed home, taken care of by Elena. Natalie said she and Jenny returned to the house at about six, and she sent Jenny and Cara to bed about nine. No one discovered they were missing until the next morning."

"She sent them to bed at nine," Eve repeated. "Her nurse would have put their nightgowns on them, wouldn't she?"

"Presumably."

"But Jenny wasn't found in a nightgown when they took her out of that grave. She was wearing a white eyelet dress and a black-velvet ribbon in her hair." She moistened her lips. "As if she'd gone to a party."

"You're saying you think that the girls were taken immediately after Jenny was brought back from that garden party?"

"It would give Salazar almost twelve hours more to whisk them out of Mexico before the search started." She felt sick. "Natalie gave him that time."

"But you still don't want to believe it." He said wearily, "Neither do I."

"I can't think why she would—"

"We'll find out eventually. We just have to accept that's almost certainly what happened." He was silent. "And be on guard against her."

"On guard?"

"Manez told me that she boarded a flight for Moscow this morning. It seems her father is ill and wants to see her. Convenient?"

"Perhaps she's panicking and going to him for protection."

"Or perhaps she'll surface somewhere other than Moscow. I just wanted to warn you that she may be a factor." He paused. "How are you? Everything okay with Cara?"

"She's digging in the dirt at the castle. She's smiling a lot and having a good time." She drew a shaky breath. "And how the hell do I tell her that her mother might have been responsible for killing her sister and Elena?"

"You don't tell her, not yet. Let it play itself out. You didn't answer me. How are you?"

"I'm digging in the dirt, too. And right now I'm with Caleb, gazing out at a lake that the Highlanders say might have been created to hide the beginning of the world or maybe the end of it."

"Caleb? If he showed it to you, then I'd bet on the end."

"Maybe. I can never tell about him. But Caleb's been more accommodating than usual." She changed the subject. "What are you doing?"

"Trying to keep Franco and Salazar from tracing you. I got behind when I flew down to Mexico. I'm on my way to Gainesville now to contact Jeff Brandel, the pilot who flew you to Scotland. I'm going to give him enough money to go out of the country for a while. He should have arrived back in Gainesville by now." He was silent for an instant. "Look, yes, the idea of Natalie Castino's killing her own child is horrible, but look at the good side that we found out about it. How likely is it that Immigration would send Cara back to a mother who's suspected of murdering her sister?"

"But how long would it take to prove that Natalie did that? It's hard to believe, people push it away. She might persuade everyone that she's a victim."

"The glass half-empty?"

"I want hope for Cara, Joe. I just don't want to take chances. Not with her, not with you. I love you." She added unsteadily, "Take care of yourself." She hung up.

She gazed blindly out at the lake that had so intrigued her before. The beginning of the world, the end of the world. Mist and swirling waters and no one knew what was happening beneath that mist.

And no one knew what had happened to twist the heart of Natalie Castino, who should have loved and cared for her children and instead had tried to destroy them.

"Bad news?" Caleb was studying her expression. "Quinn?"

She nodded. "It looks as if Salazar will be on the move soon, if he's not now. I guess that's actually not bad news. We knew it was going to happen."

He shrugged. "You looked stunned."

"Joe just found out that Jenny and Cara's mother was probably involved in their kidnapping." She made a face. "I suppose stunned is the word, and sick, and bewildered. I can't understand it. A child's life is so precious. I can't see how any mother could do that."

"You're saying kidnapping, do you mean killing?" he asked bluntly.

"I'm having trouble saying the word when connected to Jenny and Cara." She deliberately said, "Killing. Because that was where it was going to end, and Natalie Castino must have realized that."

"I'm just being very clear." Caleb's lips turned up in a half smile. "No one minces words about me, and I generally return the favor." He tilted his head. "This is really disturbing you."

"You're damn right it does. I'm a mother. I instinctively want to protect any child." She added fiercely, "And I want to punish anyone who would try to hurt a child."

"Back to the primitive. I understand that concept though I generally operate from a different standpoint." Caleb looked out at the lake. "Have you seen enough? Would you like me to take you anywhere else?"

"No, we should probably go back to the castle." She started to turn away, and then realized he was studying her again. Why? Had she been too passionate about the idea of Natalie Castino's crime and betrayal? She couldn't have been anything else. Perhaps that wasn't why he was staring at her so curiously. He might not have even noticed how upset she'd been.

Though he probably had noticed and would analyze and bring it up at his leisure. Not that she couldn't just laugh it off. But she seldom laughed at whatever Caleb deduced about anything. He always came too close.

Face it now. She turned to look at him. "What? You're staring at me."

"I like looking at you. I like *you,* Eve." He took her arm and led her back toward the car. "I can see why you and Jane are so close. You're both painfully honest . . . most of the time. I find that infinitely refreshing." As they reached the car, his hands slipped down and he grasped her hands as he stood looking down at her. "Though it's usually not in the least complimentary to me. But even that's forgiven, I always know where I stand." He stared directly down into her eyes. "And here's where *you* stand. Don't worry, I'll make sure that you'll be safe. You have Jock and MacDuff, who are the soul of everything bold and noble, but every little while you need someone who's not at all noble. That's me." He was smiling as he opened the car door for her. "I have an incredible number of dirty tricks at my disposal. And I'm putting them all at your disposal."

She stared at him in surprise. "What brought this on?"

He shrugged. "Occasionally something touches me, and I have

to respond." He got in the driver's seat. "You seem to have hit it to-day." He started the car. "Don't tell Jane, she'll say I'm conning you."

"No she won't. She knows you better than you think."

He nodded. "But she'd still put up barriers and have me jump through hoops. She doesn't like the idea that I might do something that's not totally on the dark side. It confuses her."

"It confuses me, too." She paused. "What . . . touched you today, Caleb?"

His smile was mocking. "Now that would be a revelation. There's always a price for a revelation of my unique personality. You wouldn't want to pay it."

Would Jane want to pay it? Eve wondered.

"In time," he said as if he had read her thoughts. "If I prepared the way." He changed the subject. "Now tell me about Cara and that music that was luring me like a Lorelei the other evening. What do you intend to do about her when this is all over?"

GAINESVILLE, GEORGIA

Still no answer.

Joe frowned as he hung up the cell.

It was the third attempt to reach Jeff Brandel he'd made since he'd gotten on the road today. Straight to voicemail on the first two calls, this time no connection at all.

He didn't like it.

Fifteen more minutes, and he'd be at the airport.

Nothing might be wrong.

But, dammit, he didn't like it.

CHAPTER

8

I need to see Brandel," Joe said as he strode into the small terminal that was more like an office. "Where is he?"

"In hangar Twelve E." A lanky young brunette woman in jeans and a plaid shirt looked up from the paperwork in front of her. "He's been there since this morning working on his plane. Should I call him for you?"

"I've been calling him." He left the terminal and strode out on the tarmac.

Hangar 12E.

And the metal door was pulled down.

It was a nice day, why the hell pull down the door?

Three minutes later he found out the answer.

Blood.

He stood there gazing at the man tied to the chair, who must be Jeff Brandel. It was impossible to tell because his face was cut and burned, and one eye was gouged out. His mouth was duct-taped shut.

"My God."

He moved closer and saw the drill beside the chair and the cuts on Brandel's body. The death wound was from the machete piercing his chest, and the blood was still flowing from it. He had gone through hideous torture, and had obviously tried to withstand it. He was a good guy and had probably not wanted to break and endanger Eve and Cara.

But there was no sign of the man who had done this so there was every chance that he had gotten the information he needed before he had killed Brandel.

He felt the anger rise as he looked again at the pilot. Anger and fear.

"Shit." He took out his phone and dialed Eve. "Brandel is dead. By the look of the body, he probably told them everything he knew."

"Dear God, no . . ." She was silent, trying to cope. "He had a wife. He told me he'd just gotten married two months ago. I . . . liked him."

"Yeah, so did I." He turned away from Brandel and walked to the open door. "But that's not important right now. Brandel talked. How much did he know? I only told him where he was to take you. Nothing else. Did you tell him anything?"

"No. He just said something about Cara and how he wanted kids and then about his wife."

"He couldn't hear anything you talked about with Cara?"

"No. The cockpit door was closed." She paused. "But he had to have seen Jane pick us up at the hangar. He was still sitting on the runway and hadn't pulled away yet."

Joe muttered a curse. "Even if he had no idea who she was, they'll be able to dig into our background and make a good guess fairly quickly."

"But that's all they'll know. MacDuff wouldn't have broadcast info about the hunt because he wouldn't want to have to deal with any other treasure hunters. Jane certainly wouldn't have talked about it. We arrived at the airport here in Scotland, then just vanished. It's not that bad."

"The hell it's not. They'll still be closer to you than I ever intended."

"But not closer than you thought might happen. I remember that remark you made about a Special Forces unit to protect us."

"*Might* happen. It wasn't supposed to happen." He looked back at Brandel. That wasn't supposed to happen either, a good man had suffered and died. "I'm going to call MacDuff and warn him what's going down. I wanted to tell you first."

"I can tell him. I'm almost back to the castle."

"Then go ahead and do it. I'll call him later. I need to phone the precinct and report Brandel's murder." He paused. "And break the news to his wife."

"I'm sorry. It's not going to be easy."

"None of it is easy," he said roughly. "And I don't want to stay here trying to heal wounds. I want to catch the next flight to you. I can't even do that because it's a sure thing I'm being followed. I can't risk leading anyone to you."

"Salazar and Franco," she reminded him. "I know you're feeling frustrated, but you might still be able to find them and take them down. Look how much you've already found out about Natalie Castino. We're safe for now, Joe."

"For now." He was gazing down at Brandel's bloody face. "I'll do what I can here. I don't know how long I'll be able to keep from saying to hell with it and just taking off. Watch everything that's going on around you. Take care." He hung up.

Only he should be the one taking care of her, he thought in frustration. He shouldn't be thousands of miles away. He couldn't stand it.

He had to stand it.

He punched in the number for the precinct. "Joe Quinn. I need a forensic team and the medical examiner out here right away. I'll give you the address . . ."

"Nasty. Real nasty." Detective Pete Jalkown shook his head as he gazed at the covered gurney as it was wheeled out of the hangar. "You knew him?"

"Slightly. I hired him for a job."

"It wouldn't have anything to do with Eve?" Pete asked. "You know, the captain is very curious about that explosion. She was happy that Eve wasn't in that car but definitely curious."

"She'll have to stay that way," Joe said. "I'll talk to her as soon as I'm free to do it."

"If it were anyone but you, Quinn, you'd be in that interrogation room on general principle." His glance shifted back to the medical examiner's van. "And this isn't going to make it any better. Serial killers are a big headache when the captain has to deal with the press."

"Serial killer?"

"Possible," Pete said. "Three hours ago we got a call from Travel-Rite Charter Service. They found one of their pilots, Zeke Dalkway, in the alley behind the terminal building. Worse condition than Brandel."

"Torture?"

"Four fingers missing and someone spent a long time on him before they killed him."

Because he hadn't been able to give them the information as Brandel had, Joe thought bitterly.

"The captain is going to jump on those cases with both feet," Pete said. "Much too visible and gory to ignore. It's like waving a red flag in front of a bull. Not smart."

Neither smart, nor discreet. Salazar had also jumped in with guns blazing. Nothing subtle about his attack mode. Patient for eight years of searching for Cara, but that patience had vanished overnight. He had gone for the jugular.

After he had spent the night with an angry Natalie Castino. Connection?

Blood and agony.

Two men ruthlessly tortured and dead because Joe had hired a pilot to help Eve and Cara escape. No more patience, no more careful planning to avoid confrontation. A complete change of modus operandi.

Yes, he could see a connection.

"I've got it!" Franco said as soon as Salazar picked up the phone. "You wanted it by tonight, I'm hours ahead of you."

"Where are they?"

"Scotland. Brandel delivered them to Ardland Airport outside Edinburgh."

"And where did they go from there?"

"He didn't know. If he'd known, he would have told me."

"I'm sure he would," Salazar said. "But I need more than you've told me. You've given me a city and country. I need an address. I need *them*."

"I have the description of the woman who met them at the hangar. I think it might be Jane MacGuire. She's Duncan's adopted daughter and lives in London. That's pretty close."

"An address."

"I'm on it. I'm taking the next flight to Scotland. I'll find them."

"If I don't find them first. I'll see you in Scotland, Franco."

Silence. "You're going to Scotland? You don't have to bother. I'll take care of it."

"That hasn't been my experience so far. I'm allowing you the opportunity to convince me. Don't disappoint me." He added with a touch of cool menace, "In the meantime, I'll be on the spot and making sure that doesn't happen."

Music, Eve thought drowsily. Faint, far away . . . beautiful . . .

Cara.

Far away?

Her eyes flew open.

Cara wasn't in her bedroll a few yards away!

Easy. If she was playing her violin, then there was nothing seriously wrong.

She drew a deep breath. Her pulse was gradually steadying. Okay,
find Cara.

She crawled out of the tent and knelt there, trying to locate the
sound.

The stone wall near the top of the ruin.

Cara was sitting there, her violin tucked under her chin.

And the magic coming out of that instrument was breathtaking.

Eve should tell her to come back to the tent. Cara shouldn't be
out there by herself. It was all very well for Eve to tell Joe that they
had a window of safety, but she wanted to keep that window guarded
and close to her. She'd have to go and disturb that magic and bring
Cara back to the tent.

Or maybe not.

There was a familiar figure climbing up the stone blocks toward
the top of the wall. Moonlight poured over his fair hair and slim,
powerful body.

Jock.

She felt a surge of relief and sat back down outside the tent.

Jock would handle it.

Cara was safe with Jock.

There was someone there in the darkness, Cara realized vaguely.
Someone was below her, climbing the stones. The presence was
friendly, warm, and comforting.

Eve?

Instant guilt.

She probably shouldn't be doing this. She had thought if she
got far enough away from the tent area that she wouldn't disturb
anyone. Darn it, that must not be true if Eve had to get up and come
after her.

She sighed and stopped playing. "I'm sorry. I didn't mean to bother anyone. I'll go back to—"

"As far as I know, you didn't bother anyone. I just thought you might want company." Jock Gavin climbed the last two stones and was standing there. He dropped down on the wall beside her. "Having trouble sleeping?"

She stared at him in shock. She hadn't spoken to him since that night in the courtyard, but it wasn't as if she hadn't thought about him. He always seemed to be somewhere near, working with MacDuff, talking to Jane or Caleb. He was like the music, beautiful, warm, moving in and out, simple, complicated . . . stirring. Even when she wasn't looking at him, she was aware of where he was, what he was doing.

"Cara?"

He was gazing at her inquiringly. What had he asked?

Sleep.

"Usually, I sleep fine." She looked out at the hills. "But like I told you, there's music all around us here. Sometimes I wake up . . ."

"And have to go join the music?"

She nodded. "Crazy, huh?"

"Not at all. I envy you. How does it feel?"

"It . . . fills me. Whenever anything goes wrong, it makes me able to take it and go on."

"Everything?" he asked gently.

Elena. Jenny. Her index finger pressed hard on the violin string. "My sister and my friend were . . . killed. I didn't think anything would help. But the music was still there." She moistened her lips. "And somehow it became . . . part of them."

"That's a wonderful thing."

She nodded. "I was so angry. I wanted to reach out and hurt. I still do. I went to church and prayed, but it didn't help. But the music helps. Eve helps." She looked at him. "You help, Jock."

"Me?" His brows rose in surprise. "I'm happy to be of service, but I don't see how that ever came to be."

"You're beautiful," she said simply. "Like that Tchaikovsky I was just playing."

He threw back his head and laughed. "I wasn't expecting that."

"Why not? You know what you are. Lots of people must have told you." She made a face. "MacDuff even made fun of me because he knew I was sort of dazzled. But it wasn't because you were like one of those princes in Disney movies, it was because of what you are inside. It kind of . . . shines."

"Really?" He was silent. "I'm flattered, but I'm not sure what you mean. And what you call my 'shine' could never come close to what I heard tonight."

"It does for me." But she didn't know how to put it in words. She didn't know why it had tumbled out. Yet it was strange that she didn't regret it or feel embarrassed. Not with him. "There are so many bad people in the world who kill and do terrible things. But you wouldn't do anything like that. Inside, you're clean and bright and warm. Just being around you makes me feel like that, too. Like Eve. Like the music."

He went still. "Cara. I'm not at all like Eve. The only similarity I have to your music is that I truly love it. I'm not what you think I am."

"Yes, you are." Her gaze went back to the violin she was holding. "Seth Caleb said something like that about you, but I don't believe it."

"Believe it," he said quietly. "Look at me, Cara."

Her gaze lifted to his face. It was hard, intense, and unsmiling. "I don't know what you're seeing, but it's not the man you want me to be. I've been every bit as terrible and violent as the people who have hurt you in the past. I try to tell myself that I had excuses, and I was a victim, too." His lips twisted. "But in the end we all have to accept responsibility for our own sins and try to come to terms and maybe change. There's nothing beautiful about me, Cara."

She gazed at him for a moment and shook her head. "You're wrong."

"You're not listening to me."

"Because I'd be afraid of you if you were bad. I had to learn that bad doesn't always look like bad. I did learn that, so now I have to rely on what I feel. I'm not afraid of you, Jock."

"Good. I would never do anything to hurt you. But you're too young to be able to judge the entire picture. I've done terrible things, Cara."

"But you wouldn't do them now."

He sighed. "How can I convince you? Yes, I would do them. It's difficult to stop once you've had that taste on your tongue. But I hope I would only do it to protect. But that's not a certainty, Cara."

But how she was feeling was a certainty. She was trying to frantically adjust that certainty to what he was telling her. "Protect. That's like the police or the FBI or the army or even those knights who lived here in this castle. They all did bad and bloody things, but it was for a good reason. Right?"

"Wrong. You're talking about heroes. I'm no hero. But if I could be anyone's hero, I'd want to be yours. I'd like to be your big brother, your knight, anything you want." He added gently, "I wish I could tell you that I'd qualify. I'd like the idea of you finding someone in this world to trust besides Eve and your music." He smiled. "Try MacDuff. He has some heroic qualities."

She shook her head.

"Then you're on your own. Caleb would be insulted if I tried to tell you that he's a hero." He snapped his fingers. "But you have Joe Quinn. He should be more than sufficient."

"I'm not looking for a hero. Don't be silly. All I said was that I know you're a good man."

"Shining."

She smiled. "Now you're making fun of me."

He smiled back at her. "Because you took me by surprise, and I'm on the defensive." He dropped to the stones at her feet and linked his arms around his knees. "And I need soothing. Play me that Tchai-kovsky that reminds you of me."

"I thought you were coming up to tell me to go back to my tent."

"Do you want to stop playing and go back down to reality?"

"No."

"Then play me that Tchaikovsky." He leaned his head back against the stones. "When you're ready, we'll go back."

She tucked her violin beneath her chin, then stopped. "You're not staying with me to protect me?"

"Why would I do that? That would be counter to everything I've been telling you. It would set me up to be a bloody hero." He airily waved his hand. "So let me be selfish and completely self-absorbed. Soothe me, Cara . . ."

She looked down at him and slowly lifted her bow. Not a hero? She still thought he was wrong about that. But she wouldn't argue with him anymore. He'd been so busy telling her all the things he couldn't be to her that he wanted to be. Big brother, knight, surely somewhere in that mix was . . . friend.

She started to play.

"You're awake," Cara whispered as she settled down in her bedroll an hour later. "Is that my fault, Eve? Did you hear me?"

"I heard you," Eve said. "You shouldn't have gone without tell-ing me. It might not be safe. The only reason I let you go alone when we were at the hunting lodge was that I knew it was safe. I can't be sure of that here. I was going to come after you, but I saw Jock climb-ing the stones. I knew you'd be okay."

"It seemed safe," Cara said. "There wasn't anyone around. It was beautiful. This is a wonderful place. Do you know, sometimes I look out at the hills and mountains and I see something, a rock, a tree . . . and then an hour later it's gone. I know it's probably shadows, but it seems kind of . . . mystical. And when I'm up there on the wall, I can see forever."

"But would you be watching while you were playing? I've seen your face, and you're not aware of anything but the music."

"You're right." Cara stared into the darkness. "I guess I was stupid. I'm sorry to worry you. I won't do it again."

"Not without telling me. But you didn't worry me. I told you that I knew Jock was with you." She paused. "You couldn't sleep? Dreams?"

"No, I just needed to play. Sometimes everything gets all tight inside, and I have to let it out."

"And did you? You played for a long time."

"Yes, I was going to come back sooner, but Jock wanted the Tchaikovsky again." She smiled. "Or maybe he didn't. He knew I wasn't ready and wanted to give me the extra time. He . . . understood."

"I'm sure he did," Eve said quietly. "Jock is nothing if not empathetic. And I could tell he likes you very much."

"I like him, too."

"That's pretty obvious," Eve said dryly. "You were very definite about what a great guy he is when Caleb was mildly critical."

"Because it's true. Or you wouldn't trust him."

Eve hesitated. "That doesn't mean he was always trustworthy, Cara. When he was just a little older than you, he fell into the hands of Thomas Reilly, a terrible man who was chemically and psychologically experimenting with mind control. Reilly was involved in all kinds of criminal and terrorist projects. Jock became his prime subject. While he was with Reilly, he did . . . things."

"I know that. He told me."

"He did?"

"Oh, not about that mind-control stuff, he just told me that he'd been very bad. He said that I shouldn't think that he was anything good." She was silent a moment. "But he *is* good. That wasn't his fault, and it was a long time ago. He's changed now, hasn't he?"

"Yes, it took a long time and Jane and MacDuff working with him, but he's changed."

"Jane helped him?"

Eve nodded. "She wouldn't stop until he was on his way back."

"That was good." She was silent again. "But he's not all the way back, or he wouldn't think he's so bad."

"Sometimes you can't return to what you were, you just have to go on," Eve said gently. "Jock is doing fine, Cara."

"He's wonderful," she said with sudden fierceness. "No one should have hurt him. No one should have made him think he was—" She broke off. "You're laughing at me."

"Yes, I was just thinking that you may have your first crush. You're getting toward that age."

"No, you have crushes on movie stars and rockers. Heather had them all the time. That's not like this."

"What is it like?"

She frowned. "I don't like the idea of the bad guys always winning. Elena . . . Jenny . . ." She paused, trying to work it out. "Jock. He still doesn't believe he's one of the good guys. He doesn't know about the shine."

"Shine?"

"Never mind. But he's still hurting, Eve."

"He'll work it out. It may take time." She added, "You can't do it for him, Cara."

She was silent.

What more could she say? Eve wondered. Cara had been surrounded by pain and loss since she was very young. Instead of growing callous, she had grown more sensitive to it. She had not been able to save the two people she loved most in the world, and now she couldn't bear to face Jock's being hurt. He had managed to reach out and touch her in a special way. Eve had known that when she had seen them together in the courtyard. "He won't appreciate your interfering in his life."

"I could try," Cara said stubbornly.

"Cara."

"Jane helped him before, but she's too busy now."

"Cara, he's a grown man, you're eleven years old. It should work the other way around. There's something wrong with this picture."

"That doesn't matter." She turned on her side and burrowed under the cover. "Jenny didn't think it was strange to tell me that I should take care of you."

"And one more doesn't make a difference?" Eve asked ruefully. "You're setting yourself up to take care of Jock Gavin?"

"Yes," she said drowsily as she rubbed her cheek on the pillow. "I'm going to take care of Jock . . ."

EDINBURGH, SCOTLAND

Salazar was walking toward the exit at the airport when he received a call from Franco.

"I'm in London," Franco said. "I've been scouting around Jane MacGuire's apartment and gallery, and she's definitely not here. She didn't leave any information with her agent about where she was going. Her landlord said he saw her leave in her car about the time that would coincide with an arrival at that airport in Scotland."

"Now you've told me about where she's not. Can you tell me where she is?"

"Not yet. But I think I've verified that she was the woman who picked up Duncan and the kid. I'm doing a complete background check on Jane MacGuire and her known contacts in London and Scotland now. I should have something for you soon."

"See that you do. My patience is gone. It's time we cleared this mess up." He hung up.

It wasn't only his patience that was gone. He hadn't heard from Natalie since he'd texted her the message about Duncan's arrival in Scotland. But he knew that he would soon.

That was fine with him. His adrenaline was pumping, and he felt more alive than he had in years. He was on the hunt. He could smell the blood.

He stepped outside the terminal and headed for the taxi line.

A sleek black Mercedes slid to the curb in front of him and a chauffeur jumped out and opened the passenger door. "Mr. Salazar."

Salazar stepped closer to the car and he was immediately enveloped in the familiar scent of vanilla and Russian perfume wafting from the backseat.

Natalie.

He hadn't expected to see her this soon.

It seemed she was smelling the blood, too.

He stepped forward and got into the car.

2:24 A.M.
GAELKAR CASTLE

Jane closed the ledger after she'd finished cataloging the afternoon's finds and leaned back in the chair. She should really go to bed. She had deliberately stayed up and worked in the research tent so that she'd be tired enough to sleep. She wasn't sure if it had done any good. She had trouble sleeping anyway, and the news that Eve had told them after she had talked to Joe was too disturbing. Working in this castle surrounded by the hills and winds and silences that whispered of the past had taken Jane away from the thought of the ugliness and violence of monsters who killed.

As they had killed Trevor.

As they might kill Eve and Cara.

"You're working late."

She looked over her shoulder to see Caleb standing in the doorway of the tent. He was dressed in black jeans and white shirt, with the sleeves rolled to the elbow. The night breeze was lifting his dark hair away from his face, which was, as usual, slightly mocking.

Darkness, flames, pure sensuality.

Her hand tightened on the ledger.

More disturbance that she didn't need.

"I'm done now." She forced herself to release the ledger and push it aside. "Or as done as I can be. What are you doing here? You startled me." Her lips twisted. "Which completely belies your claim that we can always sense each other."

He smiled. "I said I can sense you. You might possibly miss a tick occasionally with me. Though I don't see how considering how wary you are." He moved into the tent. "Why the burning of midnight oil? Are you getting close to something?"

"We've hardly scratched the surface. Though MacDuff has discovered a possible opening beneath the dungeons that might lead somewhere. Or not. It's all too vague to even guess." She got to her feet. "A wild-goose chase. If there's a treasure, I don't believe it's here."

"Why?"

"It's not the first time that the family has searched these ruins. The first expedition was in 1927, and there was another in 1969. Surely someone would have found a clue, something . . ."

"MacDuff's not stupid. Why is he here?"

She shrugged. "Because he's MacDuff and he thinks that he has a destiny. Hell, he was almost more involved with tracking down the Cira story than I was all those years ago. That's probably why he wanted me along. He's got this idea I'm part of his destiny, too. It's bullshit."

"No sudden psychic flashes from Cira?"

"I never had psychic flashes. Stop making fun of me, Caleb."

"I wouldn't think of it. But I've been watching you since we've been here. You're feeling something." He suddenly chuckled. "But then so am I. It's the Highlands, after all. In the courtyard, you told Cara that you could feel the music. Did you hear her playing tonight?"

"Yes, I went and stood outside the tent for a minute. I was worried. But then I saw Jock with her, and I knew it was okay."

"Because, in spite of Jock's wicked past, he has an honorable soul?" His tone was mocking. "Like Trevor."

"No, not like Trevor. Trevor didn't have an easy life, but he didn't go through the hell that Jock did." She met his eyes. "And Trevor did have an honorable soul. Even you could see that."

"Crystal clear. I even liked him except when he was getting in my way." He added deliberately, "But I don't have to worry about that now. I thought when Trevor died that he might pose an even greater threat than when he was alive. But I'm working my way through it." His gaze narrowed on her face. "And so are you. Every time we come together, I can see it happening."

She could feel her heart start to pound just looking at his face, that sensual mouth. No, she wouldn't let him do this to her. She forced herself to look away. "I'm going to my tent. I have to get up and start working in a few hours." She turned off the lanterns and started for the door. "You might not understand that, since you're not sweating and digging in the dirt like the rest of us."

"I understand, but I see no reason why I should join you in your misery. That's not why I came on this hunt. My job is to watch and listen and, if necessary, to act." He stepped aside to let her pass. "You'll find me much more valuable in that capacity."

"And is that why you dropped in on me at this hour tonight? Are you watching, listening?"

"All the time. And the hour didn't matter, I function better at night. But that's not why I came by when I saw the light streaming out of the tent. I've been debating all day if I should talk to you. Very unusual for me." He was strolling beside her toward her tent at the end of the row. "As you know, I seldom hesitate about anything. But this may be something sensitive that I should stay out of." He shrugged. "But since when am I sensitive? So I decided to go for it."

"I wouldn't expect anything else," she said dryly. They had reached her tent, and she stopped and turned to face him. Bright moonlight. She could see him almost as well as in the tent, and it was having just as powerful an effect on her.

Don't let him see it.

Get it over with and go into the tent.

"What is it, Caleb?" she asked impatiently. "It's been an upsetting day. I want to put a period to it."

"I know. You're upset about what Eve told you about Salazar closing in and finding out she's in Scotland."

"Dammit, of course I am. Aren't you?"

"Not as much as you. I knew it was going to happen. It was only a matter of time. I'll just make adjustments."

"I'm not that philosophical. I love Eve."

"Do you think I don't know that? But that love can be complicated, that's why I hesitated."

She stiffened. "It's more dangerous than she told us?"

"Not as far as I know. But she might want to save you worry. You'll have to make up your mind about that."

"I'm going into this tent in ten seconds."

"That's enough time." He smiled down at her. "Eve was upset when Joe told her about Salazar and Natalie Castino. Very upset. Particularly when she told me that Natalie might have killed her own children."

"Of course, she was. Anyone would be upset."

"That's what Eve said, particularly anyone who'd had children, a mother who would never understand how anyone could do that to her own daughters. She was near tears, very passionate about it."

"What's your point, Caleb?"

"That Eve was so upset when she said those words that she reached down . . ." His hand moved to Jane's belly and put his hand on it. "Like this. Just for a second." His hand dropped away from her. "I'm sure that she didn't even realize she'd done it. Pure instinct."

Jane went rigid. "What are you saying?"

"It made me curious. It could have been nothing. Or it could have been something very important."

"It was nothing."

He shook his head. "As I said, I was curious. So when I took her back to the car I stood there and took both her hands while I talked to her. Like this." His hands grasped Jane's, his thumbs on her wrists. "Blood is powerful, it controls so many things. You can feel it pound through your body, can't you?"

"Yes." Her breathing was shallow. She felt his thumbs on her wrists, her pulse leaping more every second. Her skin hot, burning where he was holding her. "Let . . . me . . . go, Caleb."

"Soon. Only a demonstration. I made sure that Eve didn't feel any discomfort at all. But it's not really discomfort, is it, Jane?"

"Let me go."

"Reluctantly." He dropped her wrists. "I just wanted to remind you that I can do a few things with blood that other people can't." He grimaced. "Not entirely true. I wanted to touch you. I used it as an excuse."

She drew a deep, quivering breath. "What a surprise." She moistened her lips. "And why did you reach out and hold Eve's hands?"

"I believe you've already guessed. The blood flow in all of us is very powerful, it can tell so much." He reached out again and ran his index finger across the vein of her left wrist. "But at certain times, it becomes even stronger and more definitive. It's incredible during that time."

Her pulse was leaping beneath that finger. Her mind was leaping even more frantically. "During what time?"

He lifted her wrist and pressed his lips to the pulse point. "Eve's pregnant, Jane."

"No!" She jerked her wrist away from him. "That's not true."

He sighed. "I was afraid that you'd be shocked."

"You can't be sure. You just touched her."

"I just touched you. Blood responds. In different ways, of course, depending on the demand. I was analyzing with Eve. If I'd had a little more time, I could have determined how far along she is, but that wasn't important. You can ask her."

"Yes, I can ask her," she repeated numbly. She shook her head to clear it. "If I decide I believe you. Which I'm not at all sure I do."

"Entirely your choice. I thought I'd give you the option. You've taken Eve under your wing, I thought you should know you're responsible for more than you counted on."

"She would have told me."

"Would she?"

No, she might not, Jane thought. She and Eve were so much alike. Jane would not have wanted to lay an additional burden on her, and neither would Eve. "It might not be true. For God's sake, you're not a doctor."

Caleb was silent.

But he had saved Jane's life in that hospital only a few weeks ago when all the doctors had given up on her.

"How certain are you?"

"Very. Some of her blood is being directed to a different place. It's very interesting."

"Interesting?" She rubbed her temple. "Yes, I'd say that it's interesting. However, I'm not in any shape to examine or comment on it. I think . . . I'm scared, Caleb."

"You? Our brave, bold Jane? Nonsense."

"Screw you. This is Eve. It's important. I don't know what she's feeling. She's got to be . . . I don't know."

"Which is why I told you. I could have kept it to myself and let Eve play her own game as she wanted. But that would have cheated you." His lips tightened. "She wouldn't have meant to do it, but in the end, you would have been cheated. I won't allow that, even from Eve."

"It's not your call. You have nothing to do with this."

"But I appear to be very much involved, don't I? It comes from that habit of inserting myself whether I'm wanted or not." He reached up and stroked her cheek. "I find I can't do anything else with you. Now, go to bed and try to sleep. Though I've probably robbed you of that option."

"Almost certainly," she said unsteadily.

"I just want you to remember while you're tossing and turning that there's nothing to be afraid of. I told Eve that I'll be there, and I meant it." He made a face. "That sounds sickeningly noble. Forget I said it. Just remember that I hate to lose. I won't lose this either." He turned and strode away from her.

Leaving Jane staring after him with clenched hands and a chaotic collection of feelings. Trust Caleb to destroy any possibility of serenity this trip might hold.

She wasn't being fair. She wouldn't have wanted him to hold that information back. His presentation had been quintessential Caleb, a combination of sex and charged emotion, but he had given her what he thought she needed to hear. But it didn't alter the fact that he had thrown her a curve that had taken her breath away.

She went into her tent and dropped to her bedroll. She would get ready for bed later, now she had to sit and let that stunning news sink in. There were all kinds of ramifications of Eve's being with child. She wanted to solve them, help her, but how could she when she didn't even know how Eve felt about it?

Or how she felt about it.

This wasn't Eve taking in a lost child as she had with Cara. This was Eve with a baby that might dominate her life as her Bonnie had done.

That had the potential to hurt her as Bonnie's death had done.

No! She felt an instant rejection at the thought.

But she wanted above all for Eve to be happy.

She sighed and laid her head back on the pillow. She obviously would have to work her way through this bewilderment before she talked to Eve . . .

"Are you sure you want to do this, Cira?" Antonio moved to stand behind her. He put his hands gently on her shoulders, and whispered in her ear. "You don't have to say farewell to him here. We can go back to the castle and have the priest give the Gods' blessings and bury him near us."

"No." She looked down at the small casket she'd had the carpenters craft with such care. "I want it to be here by the lake. Marcus liked it here." She could feel the tears sting her eyes. "He told me someday he was going to go into that mist and bring me gifts of gold and jewels fit for a queen. I told him not to be foolish, that I had all the riches I could possibly want already." She looked over her shoulder at Antonio. "It's true, you know. This is a hard, wild land, but we've made it our own. I have everything I ever dreamed about in those days when I was a slave in Herculaneum. I have a husband I love who gave me five strong sons and two daughters who may be even stronger."

"You would think that." He kissed her temple. "You did not feel love for me when you were going through those birth pains."

"It just seemed unfair that a woman has to bear all that pain. But I can see why the Gods didn't trust having children to men. We do it so much better."

"Whatever you say, love."

She could feel his tears on her temple and knew he would not argue with her at this moment. He was feeling her pain at the loss of Marcus as well as his own. Marcus, eight years old, beautiful as the sun, who had been ravaged by the fever and fallen into darkness.

She couldn't stand here, looking down at that small casket any longer. It was time to say farewell and send her son to take his final journey.

She stepped away from Antonio and gazed into the mist. "We're lucky, you know. To have had him this long, to have him the only one of our children that the Gods wanted with them."

"It doesn't seem lucky to me."

"No. At first, I wanted to rage and beat my head on the stones. But then I started to think of Marcus, and I was still angry, but there's a kind of comfort in knowing that he'll be here where he wanted to be. I can ride down here and imagine him running out of the mist and telling me how he'd just been hiding and playing in the caves and had great adventures to tell me." The tears were running down her cheeks. *"And now I believe we'd better go take him into that mist so that he can begin those adventures. Then we can go back to the castle and tell our other children that they must stop grieving and start living. Does that not sound like a good plan?"*

"A fine plan," Antonio said thickly as he touched her damp cheek. *"A magnificent plan, my own Cira . . ."*

A dream, Jane thought drowsily as she came out of the heavy mists of sleep. Mists? Strange that she had seized on that word. A dream. Only a dream.

But she had not dreamed about Cira for years. Why now? Why tonight?

She was suddenly wide-awake. Her eyes flicked open and she stared into the darkness.

For God's sake, why was she even surprised that she'd had a Cira dream? She was at the castle Cira had built, MacDuff was constantly making comments about his belief that Jane was a descendant of Cira's. Pure power of suggestion. It didn't mean that Jane was back on that roller coaster of Cira dreams that had plagued her when she was seventeen.

And this dream had involved a child, a dead child, and that could have been triggered by her worry about Eve and her child. Or even her worry about Cara. She mustn't believe it had anything to do with Cira. She would not walk down that path again.

Now go back to sleep, she told herself. She could see the faintest hint of gray in the sky, and she didn't have long before she would have to get up and start to work.

Don't think of Cira and her Antonio.

Don't feel the pain that they'd felt when they'd carried their son into that mist.

It was all a dream.

And the tears that were running down her own cheeks had nothing to do with that little boy who had wanted to bring his mother gold and jewels fit for a queen . . .

CHAPTER
9

I was right," Manez said when Joe answered. "Natalie Castino got off the plane in Moscow but immediately took a flight to Paris. From there she disappeared off the radar. I don't know where she went."

"Scotland," Joe said grimly. "I'd bet on it."

"Is that where you sent your Eve and Cara? You could have told me."

"You're in cartel heaven down there. You have too many leaks. Hell, we have too many leaks here, too. I actually counted on them when I was waiting for that report on the bomb." He paused. "I'm not going to tell you more than that they're in Scotland for that same reason. Salazar and Franco know that's where Eve and Cara have been taken. I hope that's all they know. They're probably scrambling like crazy to find out exactly where they are right now." He added, "But I don't know. I called a buddy at Scotland Yard to try to track them, but no luck yet. Who do you know over there?"

"I do have a few contacts."

"A few? You know every narcotics cop here and in Europe on a first-name basis. I met several of them when I went down to the cartel seminar you gave last year. All I need is one who is smart and has the informants who can find out what Salazar is doing and if he's getting close to finding out where Eve is."

"But then I'll owe him."

"And I'll owe you."

"That's right, it might be worth it," he said. "And what are you doing, Quinn?"

"Trying to keep myself from going over there and doing a major cleanup before Salazar even gets close to knowing where they are." He paused. "But I'm being watched."

"Salazar's men?"

"Yes, I spotted one of his men and ID'd him as Pauly Lomarto, who works for one of Salazar's local distributors. There's someone else, but I haven't been able to ID him yet. He's much better than Lomarto."

There was a silence. "He might not be working for Salazar."

Joe stiffened. There was something in Manez's tone. "What the hell do you mean? What do you know?"

"I don't know anything. I only suspect. That's my job, right?" He paused. "But you should know that I've heard rumors that your Justice Department has been making inquiries in the past few days of several of our government departments about the kidnapping of the two Castino children."

"What?"

"In particular, the older child, Jenny. Inquiries about the possibility of a body being found on American soil and if we knew anything about it. Nothing on an official level yet, but it's heading in that direction. I found it curious that no inquiry was addressed to my attention. You were talking about leaks. There might possibly be a leak in the Sheriff's Department, it was suspected that the skeleton in that grave in California was really Jenny Castino."

"And you weren't going to tell me?"

"It's only rumors so far."

"And you thought I wouldn't be interested? You didn't, by any chance, leak it yourself?"

"That would have been self-destructive. Why would I do that when I might have used the information myself to manipulate you? But I don't want you putting down a state department investigator by mistake. It might be awkward for you. If the information was leaked about the skeleton, then it was probably also leaked regarding both yours and Eve Duncan's involvement in the removal of Cara Castino from Child Services."

He was right, Joe thought. "And they probably know by now about the explosion that was supposed to have killed Eve and Cara and my sending them out of the country. None of which was legal." He muttered a curse. "They're probably gathering evidence against me and just waiting to step in."

"Do you have any idea who leaked the information?"

"It could be Sheriff Nalchek, but I wouldn't think so. Maybe someone in his department." His hand tightened on the phone. "It doesn't matter, I have to concentrate on damage control. Who did your 'rumors' say was heading the investigation?"

"Agent Jason Toller. What are you going to do?"

"Move on Toller before he can move on me." He hung up. He drew a deep breath and sat there thinking. Direct attack or try to stave off Toller until he could better control the situation?

God, he wanted to go in now.

That was emotion and impatience. He knew what the right way was to handle it. He reached for his phone and called the FBI Headquarters at Quantico.

Thirty minutes later, he hung up and sat back in his chair to wait.

It was close to three hours later that there was a knock on the front door.

"Detective Quinn?" The man at the door was lanky, tall, with short, graying hair and a Southern drawl. "Agent Jason Toller. I understand that you wish to talk to me." His voice never lost the pleasant intonation as he continued, "But I should tell you that I do resent your pulling strings to bring me here. You could have called me and invited me."

"That would have taken time, and I don't know how much time I have at any given point." He gestured for Toller to come in. "I need to know where I stand with you. Are you going to cause me trouble, Agent Toller?"

"It's possible." He looked around the house. "Nice. Very nice." He looked at Eve's work area. "Is that where Ms. Duncan works? I've heard great things about her. I'm sure she's a fine woman. I was very upset when I thought you'd blown her up."

"Is that supposed to be a shock tactic?"

"No, I honestly thought you might have murdered her. I'm a suspicious man, and I usually believe the worst until I find out otherwise." He smiled. "It was at the beginning of my investigation and the facts were a little confused. I was very happy to discover that you probably weren't a murderer. Would you care to tell me where Eve Duncan and Cara Castino are now?"

"No."

His brows rose. "May I ask why not?"

"What would you do with Cara?"

"Child Services, and then we'd have to start negotiations with the Mexican government. Considering the identity of her father, the situation is very delicate."

"And she would probably be murdered before all the red tape had been cut."

Toller nodded. "It might happen. But it's not my job to make judgments. I'm only a lowly agent who is trying to do what's right and still keep my pension."

"Bullshit."

Toller shrugged. "I can understand why you might be upset. But you might be a little more tolerant. I could have caused you a good deal of trouble. In fact, I was planning on it until I did my research on you." He smiled faintly. "You're respected by your captain and the other detectives. You do favors, but you don't demand a return. It was the same when I investigated your years with the FBI and the SEALs. In fact, you were the golden boy at Quantico until you resigned and came to live here in Atlanta. You kept strong ties with them, even though you were dedicated to your job here." He grimaced. "But you did ask a return favor from the Director of the FBI today. I'm flattered. It must mean a lot to you."

"I can't have you getting in my way."

"But I will get in your way. It's inevitable." He tilted his head. "I believe you're an honest man and trying to do the right thing, but unfortunately the right thing isn't always the way the world works. So shall I tell you how this will play out?"

"I can hardly wait."

"Since you're clearly the key to our finding Cara Delaney, we'll continue surveillance. The moment we get a clue as to where to find her, we'll act immediately. At that point, we'll proceed as I've outlined. And no strings you can pull will stop us from doing it. Understand?"

"Absolutely."

"On the other hand, there will be no incarceration of the popular and influential Joe Quinn unless you do something that will cause me problems. At that point, I won't give a damn if you rot in jail." He turned to leave. "I'm glad that we had this chat. I was going to initiate a meeting anyway. I hope you're equally satisfied?"

"Not quite. I expected you to be more of a hard-ass toward me. Why weren't you?"

"You don't understand. My job is to investigate and, if possible, to smooth troubled waters. It's my particular specialty. This situation has the potential to cause the U.S. government headaches for the next ten years even if Cara Delaney isn't killed. She'll be an international incident that will attract all kinds of fringe groups until her case is settled."

"And I'm part of those troubled waters."

"You could be. You certainly *will* be if you do anything that will make me look inefficient to my superiors. We have to maintain control of the situation. Don't try to avoid surveillance, Detective."

Joe didn't answer.

Toller shrugged. "Have a nice day."

The next moment, he was gone.

Son of a bitch.

Joe's fists knotted at his sides. Toller had drawn the lines clearly, and it was going to be difficult as hell to work around him. He couldn't afford to be tossed in jail, and there was no way he could risk leading Toller to Eve and Cara. Now he had to deal not only with Salazar's men but Toller.

He called Manez. "I may be stuck here for a while, and it's going to drive me crazy. When I do get out of here, I'm going to have to move fast. I need you to get me that help to locate Salazar."

"You sound angry. A problem with Agent Toller?"

"He's going to try to block me. He's good, and he may be looking for a reason to throw me into jail. I'll have to be careful with him and not take him down. Which means I can't risk taking a chance on going to Eve yet unless I know Salazar's already found out where they are. Then I'll do what's necessary no matter what the consequences. But there won't be a risk to her if I go over and take care of business with Salazar. You can help me do that."

"There's a risk of an officer of the law breaking that law," Manez said quietly. "You're a hunter, and I recognize that you want to defend what is yours by going after the prey. But I can't condone your being an executioner, Quinn."

"Then don't condone it, but will you tap your man in Scotland to get me information? I need to know where Salazar is and what he's doing."

Manez was silent. "I'll ask Burbank at the Yard. He might be able to help." He hung up.

Joe knew he had pushed him too far. Manez was torn between an obsession to take the cartels down at any cost and his ingrained respect for the law. Hell, Joe had the same respect, but he was also driven by the primitive desire to protect the good against the scum of the world.

And that good in his eyes was embodied by Eve.

So try to hold back if he could, but get ready.

Salazar. Franco. Natalie Castino.

They were probably all in a position to strike.

Well, so would Joe be as soon as Manez gave him the information he needed.

GAELKAR CASTLE

"You're very quiet, Jane." Eve looked up from the dirt she was shifting and studied her as Jane gave her a bottle of water from the tray she was distributing. "And you have circles under your eyes. Did you have a bad night?"

"Not good," Jane said. "I was up late cataloging the day's finds, then Caleb dropped by, and he's never soothing." She opened the bottle and took a drink of water. "But we've come to expect that, haven't we?"

"Yes." Eve's eyes narrowed on Jane's face. "And that's all? Tell me that you didn't hear Cara playing."

"I heard her. She didn't keep me awake."

"It seems the whole camp heard her. The only one I haven't heard from yet is MacDuff." She made a face. "I promise you it won't happen again. I've had a talk with her. She'll be mortified that she might have disturbed you."

"Then don't tell her." Jane looked away from her. "It was beautiful, I was only worried that she was out there alone. But then I saw Jock, and I knew it was all right."

"That was my thought, too." Her gaze went to Cara, who was working on the other side of the ruins near Jock and MacDuff. "Though I'm not certain now. I think Cara has adopted Jock."

"What?"

"She thinks that he needs taking care of." Her eyes were twinkling. "And you're too busy."

Jane looked at Cara. "She's really extraordinary, isn't she? I don't know how Jock will take that."

"I don't either, but I don't intend to interfere. I'll leave it up to the two of them. It may be good for both of them." She took another drink of water. "This tastes good. It's cool here at night, but it heats up during the day. For the last half hour, I've been thinking wistfully about that lake Caleb took me to yesterday. All that cool mist."

Jane went still. "Lake? You didn't mention a lake when you came back yesterday."

"You can appreciate it wasn't my top priority," Eve said dryly. "Joe blew everything out of my mind when he told me about Natalie Castino and that Salazar might soon be breathing down our necks."

"It did the same thing to me," Jane said. "You could have told me you went to Timbuktu, and I would have accepted it." Her gaze slid away from Eve to the wall overlooking the hills. "Where is this lake?"

"Maybe ten miles north. Caleb showed it to me because he said the castle was vulnerable from that direction." She took another drink. "Beautiful place. But weird, lots of mist. Caleb and I agreed it looked like either the beginning or the end of the world."

"Interesting." She looked back at Eve. "I'd like to see it."

"Maybe after we finish for the day?"

"I'd like to go now."

Eve paused in raising the bottle to her lips to look at her. "Why?"

"You said it was the one place that was vulnerable, didn't you?" She smiled. "I should see it. I'll go tell MacDuff to keep an eye on Cara while we're gone. Why don't you go wash your hands and face and meet me at the Land Rover in five minutes?"

Eve frowned as she gazed after Jane as she crossed the courtyard. That smile had been forced, and Jane was definitely not herself. It was just as well she'd have the opportunity to get Jane alone to probe a bit.

But it appeared they were not to be alone. Caleb was sitting in the driver's seat of the Land Rover when she and Jane reached the road where it was parked.

"Good afternoon, ladies." He smiled at Jane. "You should have gone with us yesterday. It would have saved us this trip."

"I was busy." Jane shook her head. "And we don't need you, Caleb. Eve and I will do just fine on our own."

"I'm sure you would." He met Jane's eyes. "But I assure you I won't get in the way. Once we're there, I'll just sit in the car and keep an eye on you. I got a call from MacDuff the minute you left after telling him you were taking Eve back to the lake. He told me that since I was a total handicap on the dig, I might just as well make myself useful by acting as guard dog to make sure the two of you were safe." He shrugged. "I told him that it was a pleasant place, and I'd be accommodating this time. Get in."

Jane hesitated.

"Get in," he said softly. "I won't interfere."

"That would be a first." She got in the backseat. "Get in, Eve. I guess we'll be accommodating, too. I should have known that MacDuff would bring in the Marines."

"I appreciate the compliment," Caleb said as he started the car. "But I don't have the same philosophy. I'm of a more solitary nature."

"I hadn't noticed that," Eve murmured. "Who knows? You may be changing, Caleb. There seems to be something in the air."

"Here we are," Caleb said as he brought the Land Rover to a stop. "I'll stay here as I promised and commune with nature."

"There's a lot of nature to commune with," Eve said as she got out of the car and started down the steep slope toward the lake. "What do you think, Jane? The beginning or the end?" She looked over her shoulder when Jane didn't answer. "Jane?"

The same.

The mist.

The hills running down into the deep blue of the lake. The north shore that was completely obscured by the mist.

The mist.

I'll see him running out of the mist and telling me he'd only been playing in the caves . . .

"Jane!"

Eve. She sounded concerned, Jane thought vaguely. She had to answer her. She shook her head to clear it. She couldn't remember what Eve had asked her. Say something. Anything. "It's as beautiful as you said." She followed Eve down to the shore. "Do you know, when we were in the study with MacDuff looking at all those schematics, I didn't even pay any attention to any landscape features. Did MacDuff mention it? Was this lake on the map?"

"I don't remember." Eve's gaze was focused on Jane's face. "What does it matter?"

"It doesn't. I just wonder why I wasn't aware that it was here. I thought maybe MacDuff had mentioned it, and I'd just forgotten."

"You wouldn't have forgotten it."

"I might have. I might have been tired from the drive, and it just escaped me."

"It's no big thing. Why are you behaving like this?"

It was a big thing to Jane, but she was acting weird, and Eve had noticed.

Straighten out.

She smiled and looked back at the lake. "The beginning or the end? I guess it depends on what happens to you here. Or maybe it might not even happen here but it becomes a part of—" She stopped and turned toward the car. "I've seen enough. We can go back now."

"No, we can't," Eve said quietly. "Not yet. Something is wrong, and it has something to do with this place. What is it?"

"Why should it have anything to do with this lake? I've never seen it before."

"This conversation is so familiar. You said words like that a long time ago in the very same way," Eve said gently. "Do you think I'd ever forget? You were seventeen, and you were trying to convince yourself that those dreams of Cira were just made up of scraps you'd read on the Internet or stumbled on somewhere. But they didn't turn out that way, did they?"

"A temporary mental aberration."

"That came back, Jane?"

Eve wasn't going to give up. Jane still tried to distract her. "I just wanted to see the lake."

"Why?"

She gave a deep sigh, then surrendered. "Because I saw it last night, and Cira was there on that north bank."

She went still. "Another Cira dream?"

"Yes, I haven't had one for years. I didn't want this one."

"But it happened."

"Yes, I tried to tell myself it was MacDuff's pressuring me about Cira and the treasure. We were at the castle she built all those centuries ago. I told myself it was the power of all that suggestion going on in my head." Her eyes were stinging as she turned back to Eve. "I don't want dreams or knowing about someone else's life or how they're hurting. I've been hurting enough myself lately. I want to live in the real world and deal with real problems. It's the only way I can survive."

"You do yourself an injustice, you're very strong. You can take anything, do anything." Eve took a step closer. "I've never known why Cira was woven into your life during those years, but I know the experience didn't hurt you. I know that you only grew stronger and more compassionate. I was glad when the dreams stopped, but if they're back, then you'll accept them and make the best of it." She smiled. "And, if you like, share them with someone you love. I'll always be here for you."

"I know you will." She was filled with so much love that the words were unsteady. "You always have been." She took a step forward and slipped her arms around Eve and held her close. "I should be saying that to you. I don't say it enough."

"Because it's not necessary, we both know it's there." She hugged her once more, then pushed her away. "And we're both getting all weepy and emotional." She dropped down on the ground. "Sit down and talk it out. Like you did when you were a kid." She grinned. "Though you never acted like you were a kid." She waved at the mist-shrouded lake. "And this isn't the front porch, and that isn't our lake, but it will do. Right?"

"Right." Jane sat down beside her and linked her arms around her knees. "And you thought the lake was a little weird, but I don't believe it is. I think the mist is friendly. I think it must be full of love."

"Why?"

She hesitated. "Because my dream was about Cira and her lover, Antonio, and her son, Marcus." She stared out at the mist. "Cira loved her son so much, and he loved her. He must have been a very special little boy."

"Yes. But then Cira was special, too. She created a world to suit herself."

They were both silent, gazing at the mist for a long time.

Then Jane said quietly, "There's another reason why I was trying to tell myself that the dream was all power of suggestion."

"Why is that?"

"The dream was all about a child."

"It reminded you of Cara?"

Jane turned and looked her in the eye. "Not Cara."

Eve's eyes widened. She opened her lips to speak, then closed them again. She drew a deep breath. "Oh, shit."

Jane had to chuckle. "I suppose that's an affirmation?"

"How did you know? Joe?"

"Not Joe. Do you think he'd ever tell me anything as important as that if you didn't want him to?" She nodded at Caleb sitting in the car. "You let it slip to him."

"I did not," she said indignantly. "How?"

"He was curious. He held your hands. He said some of the blood was being directed to another place. He found it interesting."

"Nosy bastard." Then she had to laugh. "I didn't have a chance of keeping it to myself, did I?"

"If Caleb hadn't been around, you might have. When he told me, I was stunned."

"So was I." She was silent. "You're not angry or hurt I didn't tell you?"

"No, I considered the source. The source is remarkably like me. You didn't want to burden me any more than you had to. I don't like it, but I understand. How far along are you?"

"Not even a month. I wouldn't have even known about it except Joe authorized a complete physical and tests when I was in the hospital with that concussion."

"And how do you feel about it?"

"I don't know. Scared, happy, bewildered . . . euphoric. Every time I think about having this child, it changes."

"But do you want it?" she persisted.

"Oh, yes," Eve said softly. "That's not even a question." Her smile was luminous. "I want to have this baby. I'm already beginning to feel . . . a presence. It's wonderful." The smile faded. "What's not wonderful is wondering if I'll be able to keep it safe. Or if I'll be so worried about trying to make sure nothing happens that I'll smother the poor kid."

"You'll muddle through," Jane said. "You did pretty well with me."

"You raised yourself, I was just there for support." She shook her head. "And I lost my Bonnie."

"Through no fault of your own." She reached over and touched Eve's hand. "And I'll be around to remind you of that the minute the baby makes an appearance." She gave a relieved sigh. "Though I'm glad we have a little time to prepare ourselves. I need it."

"I do, too. Another child after all these years . . ." She looked out at the lake. "Do you think this is a mistake, Jane?"

"Would you pay any attention to me if I said yes?"

"No. Well, I'd pay attention to you, but I'd seriously doubt your judgment." She looked back at her. "I know all the drawbacks. I'm not sixteen as I was when I had Bonnie. I'll have to be careful during the pregnancy. I have a career, and I'm set in my ways. You say I was a good mother, but I only remember my mistakes."

"What mistakes? I only remember the love," she said. "And, if there were mistakes, this isn't one of them. I think sometimes you were a little worried that I'd feel cheated because you loved Bonnie so much." She shook her head. "I understood. She was gone a long time before I came to you, but I could tell what she meant to you. She was the passion and tragedy of your life. I was your best friend. We were good together. But now you have a chance to bring someone else into your world." She added unsteadily, "It's going to be phenomenal, Eve. It will open doors. It will be different from me or Bonnie, but it will be like a new sunrise for you. And I'll fight like hell for that sunrise to come to you."

Eve was silent because she couldn't speak. "I can tell you're an artist. You're painting very beautiful pictures." She cleared her throat. "But that's down the road, and we just need to get through the next months so that it will be only clear sailing."

"I'll second that." Jane grinned and got to her feet. She reached down and offered a hand to Eve and pulled her to her feet. "And that means taking care of yourself while you're on the run from Salazar. Maybe you shouldn't be working on your knees in that courtyard."

"Don't start that," Eve said. "You sound like Joe. Exercise is good for me. I'm strong as a horse. Do *not* start pampering me."

"I'll try to remember," Jane said. "I'll do my best to forget you're pregnant and let you work yourself to the bone for the glory of MacDuff and Cira." She started up the hill. "I'll even refrain from telling MacDuff and Jock. I don't believe Caleb will discuss it. He just thinks it's interesting."

"Good," Eve said. "All I'd need is all those protective males giving me the same treatment as Joe is doing."

"Yeah, you're too tough for that."

"I can but try."

"And come off very effectively in that area." She smiled. "Don't be too tough, Eve. I owe you too much. Let me pay back a little."

"I know. I know. You've already expressed your feelings on that score. I knew I didn't have a chance of convincing you." She waved at Caleb as he got out of the car to greet them. "Particularly not now. You invoked the mantra. Family, Jane. Family."

GAELKAR CASTLE

Jane waited until after they'd eaten supper and all started to scatter before she followed MacDuff to his tent.

She poked her head through the entrance. "May I come in?"

MacDuff's brows rose, and he gestured for her to enter. "By all means, step into my parlor. I've been trying to convince you for years that's where you belonged."

"You are not a spider, and I detest flies. I have no ambitions to be one. You could have at least personified me as a butterfly. They have artistic value." She stepped inside. "I wanted to ask you a question."

"In the privacy of my tent. I can hardly wait. Personal, I hope?"

"Only as far as it's the present love of your life." She gazed around the tent to the portable desk piled high with scrolled plans and loose papers. "Is there anything in that mess that has anything to do with the terrain of the countryside around the castle?"

His eyes narrowed. "Why do you ask?"

"Is there?"

"One. I didn't regard it as important since we're concentrating on the castle."

"May I see it?"

"Why? You and Eve left the dig this afternoon to go traipsing back to the lake where Caleb took her yesterday. She was exploring the area to gauge the threat it posed to her and Cara. Were you doing the same thing?"

"I want to keep Eve safe."

"That's noncommittal. I think there's more to it." He smiled. "But I'll accept it for the time being." He turned and went to the desk and searched through the scrolled maps and plans until he found one with a thin blue border. He spread it on the desk and adjusted the lantern so that the light fell upon it. "It's just a basic map of the area."

That's exactly what it was. But Jane would take what she could get. Her gaze went quickly over the trails and roads and hills and then up to the huge lake. It was strange gazing at those simple lines on paper when she remembered the dark blue water, the pale mist, the trees, the hills.

"You wanted to look at the lake again," MacDuff murmured, gazing at her face. "It appears to have a fascination for you."

"It is fascinating. I'd like to paint it sometime." She didn't take her gaze off the map. "I suppose you've seen it?"

"Of course. This isn't the first time I've been to this castle. Everything about the place is absolutely riveting for me. I know every legend, every myth. It's the place my clan originated, where we all began. I'm very passionate about it."

Is it the beginning of the world, or the end?

"You hide it very well."

"I'm a Scot." He smiled. "And I've learned not to let my emotions rule me. I'm the Laird, and many people look to me. It's a complicated world I live in, and I can't let my guard down." He paused. "But I've let my guard down with you, Jane. Because you're one of mine. You belong to Cira and to me."

"Bullshit."

He chuckled. "I knew that would cause you to bristle." He looked down at the map. "Is there anything you'd like to ask me? I may know a few things more than this map will tell you."

"Because, after all, you are the Laird," she said dryly.

"Exactly."

She pointed to a line that appeared to wind from the castle to the lake. "What is this?"

"It's a dirt trail that leads down to the lake. I'm told as far as anyone knows that it's been there since the castle was built. The road was only built by my orders about ten years ago. I thought it was time it was accessible."

"Why?" She tilted her head. "Don't tell me you're thinking of rebuilding this castle?"

"Anything is possible if I find that chest of coins." He grinned. "After all, it's mine."

"So would be the entire world if you had your way." She looked back at the map. "What about the lake itself. It's very . . . unusual."

"The mists?" He nodded. "For decades, we've had forestry and environmental experts from the universities wanting to come in and make their tests. They want to find out why those mists never disperse. Sunlight or storm, the mists remain. They have all their theories, but it's frustrating them to hell that they can't come here and get confirmation."

"And you won't let them do it?"

"I don't want to know." He gazed at her. "Do you?"

"It's none of my concern."

"Do you?" he repeated softly.

He would come running out of the mist and tell me he'd been playing in the caves.

"No." She asked before he could reply, "In the past, haven't any of your family gone on that north shore and explored beyond those mists?"

"No, it would take a full-scale expedition, those mists are very thick. You can't see more than a few feet in front of you. My grandfather tried and fell and broke his leg when the bank gave way. He almost drowned before he got back to the south bank."

"And no one else?"

"Ah, you are curious." His finger traced the north curve of the lake. "As a matter of fact, one of those very pushy professors from Oxford sent a few of his prize students up here to get answers in hopes that I wouldn't prosecute them. One of my caretakers, Ned Colin, saw the cars on the road and went after them."

She had seen his "caretakers," who were old Marine buddies, and she felt an instant of sympathy for those college kids. "He wasn't afraid of getting lost in the mists?"

"Colin only went a few feet and shouted for them to come out. He said they seemed relieved to come stumbling toward him. He confiscated all equipment, cameras, and notes, and sent the kids on their way."

She went still. "They took photos?"

"That caught your interest. It caught mine as well. But you'd be disappointed. They're only a white blur. The sketches weren't much better."

"Sketches?"

"I knew that would pique your interest. Yes, one of the students had a sketchbook. But, as I said, nothing much more revealing than the photos."

"And the notes?"

"They didn't have much time to take notes. Only maybe four, five hours. Nothing interesting."

She looked back down at the map. "Any mention of the topography? Rocks, caves, mud, sinkholes, cleared areas?"

"They couldn't see, they didn't have time to set up their lighting equipment." He added, "Of course, I'm not an expert at examining that kind of data. Would you like to look at them yourself?"

"Yes."

"That was instant and vehement. You clearly don't trust me to have noticed whatever you're looking for. Would you care to tell me what that is?"

"I don't know." She would not lie to him, but to tell the entire truth would immediately set off that very active mind. "I have no logical reason."

"And it has nothing to do with why I brought you here?"

"That's definitely not why I'm interested in those reports."

And now I believe it's time to take our son into that mist so that he can begin his great adventures.

A search for a dream, some small proof that it didn't really exist.

She met his eyes. "I don't want to discuss it, MacDuff. Do I have to do it to have you get those reports for me?"

"Oh, the temptation." He shook his head. "No, I'll have my assistant, MacTavish, dig out the originals and clarify them as much as possible and e-mail them to me. They'll be in your hands by tomorrow sometime."

"Thank you." She turned to leave.

"But you do know I'll be making guesses, and my imagination will run free?"

"I wouldn't expect anything else of you."

"By the way, what do you think of our progress here at the castle?"

She had half expected that question. "I don't see any progress, but something could happen at any moment. What do you think?"

"I think that it's worthwhile exploring the dungeon for a day or two more, then we'll reassess." He smiled at her. "I wouldn't want to waste the time you've so generously given me."

"It's good to be appreciated." She left the tent and drew a deep breath of the cool night air. She had found what information she could but she'd probably given up as much as she'd received. MacDuff was ultrasharp, and he'd been processing and analyzing every bit of what she'd said. He would weave scenarios, then come back to her and wouldn't stop until she told him what he wanted to know. And what he wanted to know was if the dreams of Cira had come back as he thought they might. It would only confirm to him how right he'd been to bulldoze her into coming on this hunt.

Okay, back off from that burst of annoyance. He'd also taken Eve and Cara under his wing at a danger to himself. You had to accept the bad with the good with MacDuff, and most of the time that good came out on top. He had his agendas, but he was loyal and you could count—"

"What were you doing in MacDuff's tent?"

She turned to see Caleb standing a few yards away. He was standing at ease, but there was a faint tension to the muscles of his shoulders and stomach. She could feel the edge of heat and darkness surrounding him. She instinctively stiffened defensively. "That's really none of your business."

He was silent, then the tension was suddenly gone, and he was smiling. "Of course it's not. Forget I asked. Or tell me, and then you'll know I'm not storing it away and letting it fester. Being the sexual creature I am, I immediately jumped to a conclusion that's probably totally wrong."

"Yes, but you shouldn't be lurking around like some peeping Tom anyway."

"I wasn't lurking, not that I'm not capable of lurking if it suits me. But I wanted to speak to you before you went to bed. It didn't make me happy to see you duck into MacDuff's tent. It was fortunate that you didn't spend more time than you did with him. That would have made me feel dangerously unhappy."

"Is that supposed to mean something to me? It's still none of your business."

"That's where we have a problem. It depends on the viewpoint. You see I have a small problem with MacDuff. Ordinarily, I think you have too many frictions to decide to go to bed with him, but he's one of the good guys. Not as good as Trevor was, but still in the same ballpark. And you have a tendency to lean that way."

She turned and walked toward her tent.

He caught up and strolled with her. "But all that indignation can't be directed toward my interference. Your time with MacDuff must have been squeaky clean."

"I believe this conversation is over."

"Almost." He stopped outside her tent. "I wanted to tell you that I was glad that you told Eve you knew about the child and that it came out all right."

"I didn't have any doubt. You see complications where they don't exist. We love each other. That makes all the difference."

"Does it? I'll have to bow to your superior knowledge." He paused. "I like to see the two of you together. It . . . warms me."

She gazed at him. The words had been almost . . . she didn't know what. But then she often didn't understand Caleb. "She told me that you said you would protect her. Now, that warms *me,* Caleb."

He smiled. "You see, I can please you occasionally. I just never know when or where. But give me a chance, and I'll show you how."

That instant of rapport was gone, and she turned to go into her tent. "Good night, Caleb."

She heard him laugh as she entered the tent and turned on her lantern.

As usual, those few minutes had put Jane on edge and made her vibrantly, sensually, aware of Caleb. And this time she had thought she had sensed a vulnerability beneath the mockery.

Vulnerability? Not Caleb. There was no one tougher or more impervious to the forces around him. She had to keep thinking that way. If she softened, he would swoop down, and she might be lost.

Forget about Caleb. Think about Cira and that dream that had come out of the night after all these years. She had thought she had beaten it down and dismissed the idea that those dreams had any basis in reality. She had reluctantly accepted the idea of racial or ancestral memory being a vague possibility. But she had been grateful when those dreams had ceased, and she didn't want them to return. She wanted to deny them in any way she could.

But that lake of mists had definitely been the lake of her dream. The only way to disprove that it had nothing to do with Cira was to find out that the content was totally false.

No casket with the carnelian and copper inlays. No sign or clearing of a grave site where Marcus had been taken to start his final adventure. The small boy's body must have disintegrated to nothing in the centuries since he had died, but there might be pieces of that casket still intact.

Good Lord, she was playing a long shot. One she fervently wished to lose.

Because if the dreams were back, it might mean Cira was trying to tell her something.

And, with Eve pregnant and Cara in constant danger, the knowledge that the dream had been about a dead child gave Jane a feeling of chilling foreboding.

CHAPTER

10

A ren't you done yet?" Salazar was standing in the doorway of the hotel bedroom, watching Natalie rub her vanilla body oil over her naked body. It was a lazy, sensual movement that was an act of pure seduction. "You've been in here an hour. Manuela never takes this long."

"Perhaps that's why you prefer me to your wife." She turned to face him and lifted her naked breasts and offered them to him. "I take time in everything I do. Haven't you noticed?"

"Yes," he said hoarsely, his gaze on her breasts. "Sometimes you drive me crazy. Why don't we just go back to bed and start over?"

"Because I have things to do." She pulled on her red-silk robe and came toward him. "And so do you. Before we leave Scotland, we're going to have this problem resolved." She gave him a kiss as she passed him and went into the bedroom–sitting room. "And then we have to make other decisions." She sat down on the couch and reached for her phone. "But first, I have to call my father and prepare him."

"You think that Castino may call your father and check up to make sure that you flew to see him?"

"Perhaps, but that's not what I meant. I'll let you listen if you like." She started to dial. "Call room service and order breakfast, will you?"

Salazar shrugged and picked up the room phone. "That's not what I have an appetite for right now."

"Perhaps I'll concoct something wonderfully exotic for you after—" Her father had picked up, and she spoke into the phone, "Natalie, Daddy, I had to speak to you. Are you too busy to talk? I don't want to bother—"

"Hush," her father said impatiently. "When am I ever too busy to speak to you? What do you need?"

"Nothing. I just wanted to hear your voice, speak to you. I've been feeling so alone . . . without my girls." She cleared her voice. "It will be Cara's birthday in a few days. I don't even know if she's alive, Daddy. Sometimes it gets to be too much."

"You should come home to me."

"It's my duty to stand by my husband. We've been through so much together. Jenny, Cara . . . You know he's been very good to me."

"And so he should be. You're the mother of his children and he should have kept them safe for you. I remember when you brought them to Moscow the summer before they were taken." His voice was hoarse. "It was like having you again when you were little and happy . . ."

"It was a great summer," she said unsteadily. "I never dreamed this could happen to my little girls. If I hadn't had you to talk to, I don't know what I'd have done." She paused. "I have to tell you something. I know you probably won't like it, but I'm desperate."

"Natalie."

"Just listen. I've had a telephone call from a man who says he has my daughters. He's promised to return them to me if I give him money."

Her father was cursing. "It's a scam, Natalie. After all this time? How much money?"

"Four million dollars."

"What does your husband say?"

"He says he won't pay it. He says it's a scam, like you. But what if it isn't? What if I could have my girls back?" Her voice lowered. "Or what if they kill them because I don't pay?"

"Then I'll search them down and tear them apart."

"Too late . . ."

"I'll give you the money, Natalie."

"I know you will." Her voice was shaking. "But I can't ask that of you yet. I have to be sure they have my girls. I just wanted to tell you what was happening. I'll call you later after I hear from them again. Good-bye, Daddy." She hung up.

"Quite a performance," Salazar said. "Daddy's little girl. How long have you been playing him like this?"

"Don't be disrespectful of my father."

"How long?"

"We've understood each other from the time I was a teenager."

"And he's never caught you in a lie?"

"He never looked too deep. Everyone else lied to him. He needed to believe I wouldn't do it." She smiled. "So I made him happy, and he gave me what I wanted."

"What was all that business about ransom?"

"Preparation. What happens if you don't pay ransom? The kids end up dead. And I'm not under suspicion."

"It would be tricky."

"I don't know if I'll do it. I just want to be prepared. I think I could work it out." She got up and wandered over to the table and took a piece of toast from the tray. "I've gotten this far, haven't I?"

"You've had me."

She nodded. "We've had each other." She sat down and lifted the dome off her plate. "Though you've been close to failing me, Salazar." She started to eat her eggs. "I did everything to make it easy for you, and you couldn't even follow through for me."

"It wasn't my fault. Walsh screwed up."

"We won't argue." She gave him a brilliant smile. "Just so it ends well."

He watched her eat with voracious yet delicate hunger. "You set it up to end well with your father."

"It's more complicated than that. He's very important in anything I plan. He has power, he has money. I just had to make sure he would believe me if the time came."

"Everyone believes you." He shook his head as he sat down opposite her. "They have from the beginning. No one thinks that a mother would have anything to do with the death of her children."

"Kidnapping. I have to keep correcting you."

"When you came to me and asked if I wanted to do something that would hurt Castino, you never mentioned kidnapping. You just said get rid of them. No specification."

"I assumed you'd know what I meant. But I left it up to you." She smiled serenely. "After all, I'm only a woman."

It wasn't the first time that he'd heard that from her. But she'd known that if she turned him loose on her children exactly what the result would be. "Manuela would never have thought about doing anything like that."

"Manuela was not married to Juan Castino. It was a completely different situation." She looked up at Salazar. "And she was a wimp who would never argue with you or hunt for a way to better her-self."

"Is that what you did? Better yourself?"

"I defended myself." Her voice was suddenly fierce. "I'd had two girls, and Juan wanted sons. He blamed me. He'd started taking mistresses. It was only a matter of time before one of those whores gave him his damn boy. His current whore, Gracia, already had a son by another man."

"So?"

"He would have discarded me. He would have put that slut,

Gracia, in my place. That would never happen. I liked being Castino's wife and having everyone bow down before me." She wrinkled her nose. "Even your dear Manuela. She came to my parties and applauded when my Jenny played the piano." Her lips tightened. "She told me about her boys. She even showed me photos. She was a little too pleased with herself." She poured coffee into her cup. "And that's when I decided we had to meet, Salazar."

"Why, Natalie? You've only told me you wanted to get rid of them, that they were in your way. But weren't you afraid that getting rid of the children would do exactly what you were trying to avoid? That Castino would leave you and go try to find some woman to give him a son?"

"Not if I handled it the right way. And I always handle my affairs in the right way." She leaned back and smiled at him. "I was never meant to be a mother. Can't you see that it would get in my way? But I tried, when that bastard, Juan, insisted. It wasn't my fault that he couldn't produce a son. He even tried to blame me. Did he think I was a breeding animal? I was ready to be done with him when he took that Gracia as his mistress."

"But you weren't ready to be done with being Queen of Mexico City," Salazar said softly.

"No, that would have been unfortunate." She took a sip of coffee. "And completely unfair to me after all I'd done. So I decided to go another way."

"Get rid of the children."

She nodded. "In such a way that I would be a tragic figure for the rest of my marriage to Juan." She smiled. "And everyone would think Juan was a monster if he even thought of divorcing me and going to another woman. Particularly my father. My father was the key to it all." She took another sip of coffee. "Did I mention that my father had a great fondness for Jenny and Cara? He didn't have Juan's foolish prejudice that a man must have sons. I saw to that. Did you know that I had a brother, Salazar?"

"No."

"Alex was a great disappointment to my father. He finally betrayed him on a drug deal and had to be disposed of. My father was very sad." She met Salazar's eyes. "But I comforted him. He learned once again how valuable a daughter could be."

"And you had nothing to do with his 'disappointment' in your brother?" Salazar asked sarcastically.

"Why, I don't know why you would think such a thing. My father certainly didn't." She leaned back in her chair. "He believes I'm close to perfect. He's correct in many ways. But Juan always knew that he'd better step lightly with me, or all his deals with the Russian Mafia could go right down the drain. He even pretended to be besotted with the girls to please my father." Her lips twisted. "But his obsession with having a son was growing all the time. I knew he'd take the risk of tossing me out soon."

"And what would your father have done then?"

"Cut off dealings with Juan, but my father is a practical man. He was making a good deal of money using Juan's connections in the U.S. He would have eventually resumed dealing, then tried to make it up to me in other ways." Her eyes were suddenly glittering in her taut face. "There would have been *no* other way that would have satisfied me. But I might have lost the power I had over both of them if I'd had to go to battle."

"So you used the children."

"Why shouldn't I? They were mine. I brought them into this world, and I had the right to do what I wished with them. I was the one who was important, they were nothing."

"And your father would have had a completely different viewpoint if Castino had broken up with you after the kids disappeared."

"Yes, I was a mother who'd had a tragic, life-changing experience. My father wouldn't have tolerated me being hurt more after that blow." She looked at him over the edge of her cup. "Would you like me to tell you how he would have retaliated? First, he would have broken off the deals, then he would have started undermining the cartel, then, after a discrete time had passed, Juan would have suddenly been terminated in a very painful manner. Juan is not stupid, he knew what would happen. So he became a very sympathetic husband, and I kept my position intact. It *will* remain intact, Salazar. I may have to shift strategies a bit, but I won't let your carelessness destroy me."

He was silent, gazing at her. "Why did you tell me all this?"

"You asked me."

"I've asked you before, and you've only put me off." He smiled grimly. "Which usually involved sex."

"Which you enjoyed enormously."

"Why did you tell me?" he repeated.

"We've reached a crossroads. You like to screw me, you regard me as an accomplice, but you don't have the respect for me that you must have."

"I respect you."

"Not enough. But after you think about what I've told you, it will get better. You'll think twice about acting without me."

"Not necessarily; all your future plans involve keeping Castino powerful. That's not going to happen. I'm bringing your husband down and his cartel with him."

"I said I might have to make adjustments." She shrugged. "If you succeed, and Juan is destroyed, I'll look at the situation and decide what's best for me to do." She put her cup down and leaned her arms on the table, smiling at him. "It may include you getting rid of your sweet Manuela."

He stiffened. "I like my life. I like my family. I'm not going to let what's between us interfere."

She chuckled. "Like all men, you want it all. We'll have to see how it all plays out. The only thing you can be sure about is that I will come out on top. With or without you." She got to her feet. "Now I have to go dress. Why don't you call Franco and see what he's found out about Jane MacGuire?" She headed for the bedroom. "Just a suggestion . . ." She closed the door behind her.

EDINBURGH

TWENTY–FOUR HOURS LATER

"Wake up, Natalie." Salazar came into the bedroom and started to dress. "I just heard from Franco."

"It's about time." It had annoyed her when Franco hadn't answered Salazar's call yesterday. She hated waiting for anything. "If I'd have had to stay in this hotel one more day . . ." She threw the coverlet aside and swung her feet to the carpet. "I told you that you should have put someone else on finding—" She stopped. Men were very touchy about I–told–you–so's, and she needed to know what was going on. "Anything happening?"

"Maybe. Franco was nosing around the gallery and talking to MacGuire's agent and other personnel. He found out that she was pretty much of a loner, but there were a few people she knew who occasionally dropped into the gallery." He looked down at the list on his phone. "A Seth Caleb, John MacDuff, he's an earl and Lord of MacDuff's Run, Michael Trevor. Scratch Trevor. He died recently. So we're left with Caleb and MacDuff who she might have turned to for help."

"Does Franco have addresses?"

"I've got them. But Franco is already on his way to MacDuff's Run, where MacDuff lives most of the time. He tried to call him, but MacDuff wasn't picking up on the number the gallery gave Franco."

"Face-to-face is always better anyway from what you told me about Franco's success with that pilot," Natalie said. "Though he may have trouble using the same methods with an earl. Perhaps it would be better if we went to see him. I might have a better chance with him."

Salazar shook his head. "We'll go to Caleb's place. MacDuff might be a waste of time, and we have to hedge our bets." He got to his feet. "I told Franco to keep in touch. If he needs me, he'll let me know."

"Whatever you say." She got to her feet and headed for the bathroom. "I was only trying to help."

"And taking control of the action," Salazar added as he followed. "I'm not going to let that happen."

She smiled. "You sound defensive. I didn't mean to intimidate you." She opened the door. "Naturally, we'll work to do this together. Why else am I here with you?"

GAELKAR CASTLE

"I asked MacTavish to rush those notes and photos, and he said that he'd get right on it," MacDuff said the next morning as he paused to talk to Jane at the site where she was working next to Eve. "It may be awhile. He's trying to clarify the prints."

"Thank you." She sat back on her heels and looked up at him. "I suppose you're anxious to look through them again yourself? Do you think you'll find anything more at second glance?"

He shook his head. "Maybe. Perhaps I didn't know what I was looking for. What do you think?"

"You probably know as much as I do."

"Do I?" he murmured. "I'm not at all sure about that." He turned away. "I'd better get back to work. Though I'm not certain that we're getting anywhere. I'm having a few second thoughts."

Eve watched him walk away before turning to Jane. "What was that all about?"

"I asked him to have his assistant, MacTavish, send copies of notes and photos some college kids managed to get when they went exploring at that lake we went to yesterday."

"Why?"

"Just curious. It intrigued me." She looked away. "You're the one who was telling me all about it before I asked to see it. It must have intrigued you, too."

Eve nodded. "But evidently not as much as it did you. I forgot it once Joe brought me back to the real world." She was silent. "But you were really fascinated when you were there yesterday." She added deliberately, "Almost as if you were in another world yourself."

Jane turned and looked directly at her. "Ask it."

"No, you tell me."

"The Cira dream," she said briefly. "It concerned the lake. As I told you, it might have been triggered by all kinds of influences to which we're being subjected here. I just wanted to get some proof that would discount any validity." She paused. "I didn't mean to be elusive. I just didn't want to worry you."

"I lived with those Cira dreams for years, we worked our way through them. Why should I worry about this one?"

Because there was a dead child that made me cry, Jane thought, and I didn't want you to take it as some kind of foreboding.

"I don't know," she said. "Maybe because pregnant ladies are supposed to be high-strung."

"High-strung? Me?"

"No, you're sturdy as a rock." She went back to work. "I'll let you see those photos after I pick them up if you like."

"If you wouldn't mind. Caleb said that area was vulnerable, and I'd like to know everything I can about it."

"I don't mind. I just don't know if those photos and sketches will help."

Eve shrugged. "They might." She was silent a moment, digging in the earth. Then she said, "Things aren't the . . . same with me. It bothers me. I should have paid more attention when you told me about the Cira dream yesterday, but then you blew me away when I realized you knew I was pregnant. It was all I could think about. Nothing seemed as important as the fact that you knew about my child."

"Perfectly natural, Eve," she said gently.

"Is it? Maybe I can't afford to be so absorbed. I have to be aware of everything around me." She looked out at the hills. "It's so beautiful out there, yet there's a . . . waiting, isn't there?"

"Waiting?"

"It seems as if this place has been here forever, but it's still waiting for something. You can almost feel it, can't you?"

"Maybe." Jane's gaze followed Eve's. Then she moved her shoulders in a half shake. "Hey, I'm the one MacDuff is sure has a connection to this place. You're supposed to be practical and keep my feet planted firmly on the ground."

"Sorry." Eve was grinning. "Maybe it's just me that's waiting." She glanced down at her flat abdomen. "Waiting for the baby to change and grow. Waiting for Joe to come, so that we can be together." Her glance went across the courtyard, where Cara was sitting cross-legged on the stones, drinking a bottle of water and watching Jock shovel down at the dungeon level. "Waiting for her to be safe."

"Did Joe call you last night?"

Eve nodded. "He's very frustrated. I don't think he's going to last much longer." She made a face. "Which probably means an explosion. I guess I should be sensible and worry about it, but I'm feeling very primitive. I want Joe here with me." She sighed. "And I'm getting tired of digging with these damn spoons; I'm yearning for a shovel."

"So am I. I'm beginning to think it's a waste of time." Jane chuckled as she started back to work. "We'll have to do something about that soon. Jock and MacDuff may have to share."

Eve nodded. "Yes," she said absently. Her gaze had returned to those green hills bathed in shadows and mists.

Waiting.

Waiting for something.

And it was almost here . . .

"You look hot and thirsty." MacDuff had stopped by the upper courtyard, where Jane was working. "I believe I'm feeling guilty about working you so hard."

"And pigs do fly," she said. "Where is this going, MacDuff?"

"Such a cynic." He smiled. "I just thought I'd ask if you wanted to come to my tent and take a break and have a bottle of water."

She looked at him.

"And maybe take a look at those e-mails that I just got in from MacTavish? I printed them out for you."

She sat back on her heels. "You're a devious man, MacDuff. You know I want to see them." She got to her feet and dusted the dirt from her hands. "He was quicker than I thought he'd be from what you told me. You must have stressed a certain importance."

"Of which I have no idea of the nature. But I'm always willing to try to please you, Jane."

"For a price."

"On occasion." He turned and started across the courtyard. "I assume you'll want to wash up a bit before you handle those papers. Ten minutes?"

"Would you mind if I bring Eve along to look at them?"

"I would actually. This is a private viewing." The next moment he'd moved out of hearing.

She shook her head as she brushed the hair away from her brow. Private viewing? That didn't bode well. And he had gone to the trouble of getting those copies at top speed, and it wasn't to please her. It didn't matter, they were here.

She entered MacDuff's tent five minutes later.

"Ah, just as eager as I thought you'd be." He handed her a bottle of water. "Take a deep breath and relax."

"I want to see the prints."

"And you will, but the timing is questionable. I think you're aware of that, Jane."

Yes, she had known it would come to this. She had only postponed the inevitability. "Blackmail, MacDuff?"

"Not at all. An exchange of information between two partners who are after the same prize." His voice hardened. "But I did you a service, and it's time for you to reciprocate. Why did you want these notes and photos, Jane? I want to know."

She didn't answer.

"You're not being fair, Jane."

No, she was protecting herself and the delicate balance that she'd always maintained about those damned dreams. But she wasn't going to get what she wanted unless she gave MacDuff what he wanted.

"Okay. I had a dream," she said flatly. "It was about Cira and the lake."

He went still. "Ah, I thought maybe it might be that." He grinned. "No, I hoped it might be that."

"Don't get your hopes up. It was a dream, and there were all kinds of reasons that might have caused me to have it."

"But my hopes are up," he said simply. "Don't dash them now. Tell me about it, Jane."

She looked at him for a moment, then briefly and concisely told him about the Cira dream. "I just wanted to—"

"I know what you wanted to do," he interrupted. "I thought it was something like that. I was going to give you the chance to tell me yourself. But it seems time's run out. Look at those photos and sketches, scan those notes. Let's see if we see anything that collates."

"You don't have to ask me twice." She looked at the photos. "They're blurry, nothing here."

"That was quick. You're looking for something."

"For something I don't think is there." She scanned the notes. "No mention here."

"What are you looking for, Jane?" he asked.

"Caves." She picked up the prints of the three sketches the students had made. "I thought I'd have a better chance with these sketches. It's what the artist saw, not a camera. I'm looking for some sign of caves on that north bank. There didn't seem to be any sign of them anywhere on the other banks of the lake. It would be reasonable that the north end wouldn't have them either."

"Except you said that Cira mentioned them repeatedly in your dream when she was talking about her son," he said. "He played in them, ran out of them to greet her."

"It wouldn't be reasonable." Jane was gazing at the first sketch, tossed it aside, looked at the second sketch. "See, I told you that there wouldn't be any—" She stopped, as her gaze was caught by something on the upper corner of the second sketch. "It could be anything. It's just a few scrawled lines, the artist was obviously in a hurry. It doesn't have to be . . ." She moistened her lips. "It's no proof."

MacDuff was looking down at the sketch. As Jane had said, it was only a few lines, shrubs, a boulder . . . that appeared to be blocking the front of an opening of some sort. "But it could be."

Jane glanced at the third sketch. "Nothing here." She tossed it on the desk. "No proof," she repeated.

"Stop struggling against it, Jane," MacDuff said gently. "Not proof, but definitely a reason to explore beyond those mists."

"You want to believe in that dream. It's what you've always wanted."

"I won't deny it. I'm a desperate man. Hunting for Cira's gold has always been an impossible dream on its own. I searched every practical avenue I can find and came up empty. Then I came across you, Jane MacGuire, and I knew that you could help me. I wanted a clue, a path, and I always knew you could give it to me."

She shook her head. "None of this helps you."

"Stubborn. Yet you clearly realized that those caves were important. I recognized the significance immediately."

"I . . . thought that Cira might have buried her son in one of them."

"And she very well might have done that." He met her eyes. "But she might also have buried that chest with the coins in one of them. Cira liked caves, remember? That chest was hidden in a cave in Herculaneum before she took it away with her when she escaped the volcano. She obviously thought they were safe."

"And she would have liked the idea of her son caring for it," Jane whispered. "It would have been a way of keeping him as part of the family."

"You *were* thinking about it," MacDuff said. "Fighting against accepting it but thinking about it."

He was right. It had been in her mind all along though she had tried to block it out. "So what are you going to do about it?"

"What do you think?" He smiled recklessly. "We're going to go down to the lake and see what Cira hid in those mists."

"Gently. Respectfully."

"Cira is my family. She's one of mine. Would I do anything else?"

"No." She smiled faintly. "But you've been searching for that treasure for a long time."

"She wants me to have it," he said. "Why else would you have had that dream to help me along?" He shrugged. "And you know I was getting discouraged with searching here at the castle anyway."

"It's only been a few days."

"But you've been feeling that it's a waste of time, haven't you?"

"I didn't say that."

"No, you were very careful not to say it. Because you didn't want to lead me away from everything reasonable toward Cira and her son." He looked her directly in the eye. "But you wanted to go and see if she'd sent you a magnificent lifeline to save us all from having her legacy and everything she'd built tumble down around us."

"Saving *you*, MacDuff."

"I beg to differ. You're one of mine. Family is family."

Jane felt a ripple of shock. Family. How many times had that word come into play in the last days? She had used it, Eve had used it. Now MacDuff was throwing it at her.

And Cira had been involved in the most tragic of family duties in her dream.

"Strike a note?" MacDuff's gaze was fixed on her face. "You knew what this was about all along. It's not about the money, it's about saving what Cira created." He paused, then said, persuasively, "Let's go do that, Jane."

"It may be a red herring."

"Let's go see," he challenged softly. "I dare you."

She could feel a surge of the same recklessness she sensed in him. Why not? It was what she had wanted to do. Why else had she been so insistent about being proved wrong.

Because she had wanted desperately to be proved right.

"I don't take dares." She smiled at him. "But I have a boundless curiosity. When do we go?"

"*Yes.*" He threw back his head and laughed. "Now. A few hours. The sooner the better."

"A few hours? You're going to move camp?"

"That's what I said. Go back to your tent and pack up. I'll call Caleb and Jock and tell them to do the same." He turned toward the desk and rolled up the papers. "Then I'll call MacTavish and tell him to arrange to send special cameras and powerful floodlights that will let us pierce that thick mist."

"Those students didn't have those lights?"

"They were trespassers. They didn't know what they were getting into." He smiled. "Neither do we. Isn't it exciting?"

She wanted to back off, to say no. But she did feel the excitement. She felt as she had when she was a very young girl, reaching out for adventure, wanting to see what was around the next curve in the road. She turned to leave. "Make sure MacTavish does his research and gets us the right equipment."

"I'll convey your concern." He was dialing his phone. "Go tell Eve and Cara to get moving. I want to have our tents set up at the lake by nightfall."

"By all means." She headed for the entrance. "We all have to do as the Laird decrees."

"As is right and proper." He chuckled. "I'm glad you understand that concept at last, Jane."

"I was joking." She looked back over her shoulder. "This is what I want, what I decree. Or I wouldn't be doing it." She smiled. "I'm just using you, MacDuff."

She heard him laughing as she left the tent. She was still feeling that charge of energy and adrenaline, but her smile was fading. She had started MacDuff on a new phase of his hunt for Cira's gold. She could have lied, she could have not said anything, but she had been infected with MacDuff's recklessness. How was she to explain the sudden move to Eve?

By telling her the truth. By telling her all the details of the dream. By telling her that Cira had emerged from the past, and she had to go with her one last time . . .

"Why didn't you tell me all this before?" Eve asked quietly. "You didn't give me any details. You just sort of brushed it off."

"I was fighting against believing that it had any significance. I'm still fighting."

"But not too hard." Her gaze was on Jane's face. "I'm seeing something in you that I haven't seen in a long time. So many things have happened to you . . . You've been hurt, and life hasn't been easy. You've lost a lover and discovered that you can still survive. I think one of the reasons you were fighting so hard to not let Cira back into your life was that was the time you met your Trevor. Another painful memory linked to Cira."

"None of the memories of Trevor were painful until the last one, when he was shot." Her lips were tight. "Cira was just a part of a grand adventure we played out together. He was like MacDuff and was after the treasure."

"And now the adventure is back." She added shrewdly, "And you've discovered that you want to see it through. You want to do what Cira would want you to do."

She thought about it. "I guess that's true."

"But that still leaves the question, why didn't you tell me all the details of that dream before this?" She was silent, then said, "Never mind. I can figure it out. It's the child. You were afraid I'd read something into the fact that the dream was about a dead child. You mentioned a child, but not that the child was dead." She shook her head. "But that dream was also about hope and love and family. It was about life. And it may have been about how Cira intended to preserve the family fortunes far beyond what even she could imagine. You thought that I'd zero in on the little boy?"

"It occurred to me."

"Of course, it did. Because you're loving and protective, and there was something that could possibly hurt me."

"And it doesn't?"

"Look, if Cira is a fantasy, then the dream is a fantasy. If Cira is somehow reaching out and trying to tell you something, it wouldn't be to warn me that children sometimes die. I know that." She added fiercely, "And there's one way that Cira and I are very much alike. We take care of our own. I'm not going to let anything happen to my baby. I'll fight and I'll claw and I'll do anything I have to do. Cira would think it ridiculous that she would have to tell me that. No, any message she has is for you, not me, Jane."

"Well, I'm glad that's settled. I guess I was pretty foolish to worry about—"

"No." Eve took a step closer and gave her a warm hug. "Not foolish. Loving." She released her and stepped back. "And now I'd better go and tear Cara away from Jock and get her started on packing if you think MacDuff was serious about the camp being set up at the lake by nightfall?"

"He was serious." She gazed at Cara. "Are you going to tell her about the Cira dream?"

"If you don't mind." She smiled. "Cara and I had a discussion about dreams when we were flying over here. She's had some experiences with them. I think she regards your Cira dreams as a kind of wonderful fairy tale." She glanced at Jock. "And maybe Jock is part of a fairy tale, too. I've tried to gently disillusion her about both, but I don't have the heart to take all the fairy-tale ambience away. I'm not sure that she's ever believed in fairy tales unless they were full of beasts and monsters. Your Cira had a hard life, but she worked her way through to a happy ending." She motioned toward Jock. "And I don't know about the happy ending for him, but he's grown very strong, and he's actually quite wonderful. So yes, I don't mind letting Cara believe in those kinds of fairy tales."

"Neither do I," Jane said as she turned away and started for her tent. "Both Cira and Jock learned to defeat all the beasts and monsters. I'd say as role models they put Cinderella in the shade."

CHAPTER

11

I'm at MacDuff's Run," Franco said when he called Salazar late that afternoon. "All I've found out so far is that the Laird is officially not in residence. It's not going to be easy to track him down. Hell, he may be there, and those guards are lying to me. Maybe Duncan and the kid are there, too. I'll have to find out what palms I have to grease to find out. I know that MacDuff has sentries guarding the perimeter of the castle. The people in the village seem to be a closemouthed bunch. The old woman I started to question looked at me as if I'd insulted her when I asked if she'd seen any visitors at the Run. She told me to go ask at the castle and walked away from me. All of these people seem to be protecting MacDuff."

"Then you'd better use your boyish charm and get answers," Salazar said. "Sometimes, bribes don't work."

"I know that," Franco said. "I'm just telling you that it may take a few days to get those answers here. MacDuff is protected. Have you found out anything about Seth Caleb? He could be easier."

"He's not easier," Salazar said sourly. "Caleb's house is closed up, and no one is trying to protect it or him. But everyone in town just fades away when I try to ask questions."

"That sounds like protection to me."

"Because you wouldn't recognize the difference between loyalty and fear. I've seen it. It would take longer to get past whatever they feel about Caleb. He doesn't need sentries to protect this place. I'll keep trying here, but work on finding everything you can from MacDuff."

"As soon as I can." Franco hung up.

"Aren't there any other leads we can follow?" Natalie asked impatiently.

"We're probing. These are the best we've got so far."

"What about Eve Duncan?" Natalie asked. "I've been thinking that she may be the key to the whole business. She's soft, and soft people can be manipulated. She was the one who took Cara into her home to keep her safe. Give me the chance, and I'll find a way to get what we want from her."

"In case you haven't noticed, we're searching for Duncan and Cara right now, dammit."

"Then go through Joe Quinn to get her. Press him harder. Make him hurt. If Duncan's soft about Cara, she'll be soft about Quinn."

"I'm handling Quinn. I'll do what I have to do. I don't need you to tell me." He looked at her. "Now, would you care to go to the pub and see if you can charm any of the locals into talking about Seth Caleb?"

"Why not?" She smiled. "I've got to do better than you have. I'm beginning to be interested in Seth Caleb. I want to see why everyone is so terrified of him. I might find him fascinating." She added slyly, "I don't believe anyone is that afraid of you, are they, Salazar? What a pity."

The sun was going down when Jane parked the Land Rover on the road above the lake. "Here we are." She jumped out of the car and started to unload. "What do you think about it, Cara?"

The red light of the setting sun was casting a glow over the mists and gave the scene a surreal, almost otherworldly air. Eve wasn't surprised when Cara instantly picked up on that aspect.

"Another planet," Cara said. "I saw a movie about this spaceship full of people who had to settle on another planet, and it looked something like this. Elena said that it was a little too convenient that the planet was that beautiful. She said it was pure Hollywood." She jumped out of the Land Rover and stood there looking down at the lake. "But this isn't Hollywood."

Eve got out of the car and came to stand beside her. "I told you it was a little strange. And I didn't see it at sunset."

"It's gorgeous." She took a step closer to the slope. "I love it, Eve. That mist . . ." She drew a deep breath. "Is that where we're going to be searching?"

"I don't know how much we'll be doing. It depends on how well we can light that area. I don't want either one of us blundering around in that heavy mist and falling into the lake."

"Or falling into a cave." Her gaze was fixed on the mist. "It's kind of weird, isn't it? Caves. I almost died in a cave not so long ago. I *would* have died if you and Joe hadn't saved me. Yet here we are again."

"It won't be a cave like that one. MacDuff thinks if the caves exist, they would probably be small, not huge caverns. But they may not exist. We don't know, Cara."

"But Jane thinks they do exist, doesn't she?"

"Maybe. Jane is a little confused, too."

"But she's excited, I can tell."

"Yes, she's excited," Eve said. "And no matter how this turns out, I'm glad to see it. She's more enthusiastic than I've seen her in a long time."

"And she's not afraid, is she?" Cara had not taken her eyes off the mist. "I think she's . . . welcoming it."

Eve stiffened, her gaze flying to Cara's face. "You think she should be afraid? You said you loved it. Are you afraid, Cara?"

"A little. I do love it. But it's kind of scary. In that other cave, where you saved me, I could see everything, the bad and the good. But I don't know what's in that mist."

"You don't have to know. You don't have to go near it. You can stay on the south side of the lake."

She shook her head. "I want to go." She smiled. "I'm like Jane, I want to see what's waiting for me there."

Eve nodded. "Okay, if you change your mind, just tell me." She made a face. "You're not the only one who had mixed feelings about that mist. Caleb was comparing it to the beginning or the end of the world. I much prefer your simplification." She turned back to the vehicle. "But, in the meantime, we're letting Jane unload our tents. We'd better stop looking and start working." She could see Caleb's car bringing him and Jock coming down the road, followed by MacDuff driving the equipment truck. "Or maybe we'll just let MacDuff and Jock take care of it. MacDuff's the one who was in such a big hurry to get us out here."

"I'll help them." Cara had already reached the Land Rover. "Jock would probably be the one to do most of the work. I'm not sure why, but he thinks he owes the Laird."

"He probably does, but I'm sure he wants to pay his own debts."

"I'll help him." Cara was pulling the tents and bedrolls out of the back of the Land Rover.

Eve noticed that the plural had become singular. She shook her head as she went to the other side of the vehicle to help Jane unload the Coleman lanterns. She was not sure if Cara was going to help Jock with the unpacking or if she had a more long-range goal in mind. At any rate, there was no battling that determination. "As Jock would say, it was just a wee joke, Cara. Of course, we'll do our share to help *them*."

"I'll take that." Caleb took the bedroll Jane was carrying and slung it by its strap on his back, then took the two lanterns. "You just had surgery a few weeks ago. You probably shouldn't be doing all this lifting and carrying yet."

"I'm fine, Caleb." She tried to take the two lanterns back, then gave it up. "And since when are you acting the pack mule? You didn't help set up at Gaelkar Castle."

"You weren't climbing up and down hills, and MacDuff was trying to make it as easy as possible on you so that you wouldn't get pissed off and leave the hunt." He reached in the Land Rover and took out her sketchbook and computer bag and handed it to her. "These aren't too heavy." He smiled. "So stop wasting time arguing. You'll notice that I waited until everyone else was halfway down to the lake before I stepped in to rescue you. Now no one will think you're shirking."

"I'll just come back up here and help with the rest of the equipment."

He shook his head. "You'll make yourself busy setting up tents and helping Eve and Cara. Because you will have done the impossible and convinced me that I should waste my valuable time and energy helping MacDuff and Jock do the rest of the setting up. Everyone will be amazed and applaud you." He started down the hill. "Come on. It's getting dark, and that will make it more difficult."

She hesitated, then started down the hill after him. "This is a total waste of your 'valuable energy.' I'm almost entirely well now."

"Almost. But when you were climbing this hill with Eve the other day, I noticed you were short of breath when you reached the top, your cheeks were flushed, and your pulse was pounding in your temple. You're not there yet, Jane."

She couldn't deny it. "You didn't mention it then."

"It wasn't the time. This is the time."

"It's my responsibility to take care of myself. I do a pretty good job of it. So go back to being concerned only about Seth Caleb."

"I'm having a good deal of trouble doing that. It's a matter of great alarm to me." He glanced down at MacDuff, Jock, Eve, and Cara, who had all reached the bank of the lake. The light was almost gone, but it appeared they were sorting the bedding and equipment. "I'm not like them, Jane. I don't want to be like them. Yet at times, you make me want to do what they would do. I felt like that with Trevor. Very dangerous."

"Then save yourself, I've no desire to change you. It's not my business."

"I'm not sure that I can save myself." He suddenly chuckled. "Unless I find a way to change you. Maybe that's what I've been trying to do all along. Care to walk on the dark side, Jane? I promise I'll make it entertaining."

"You couldn't do that for—" She glanced at him and suddenly lost track of what she'd been saying. He was framed against the mist, and darkness was all around him. But it wasn't the darkness that held her. Heat. Intensity.

His eyes were . . .

She couldn't breathe. She could feel her pulse racing.

"Don't do that," he said thickly. "*Now* it hits you? I've got my hands full of this damn equipment, and all those people down there might see anything I'd do to you. I wouldn't care, but in the end, you'd blame me." His eyes were suddenly glowing recklessly. "What the hell?" He dropped the lanterns on the ground and took a step closer. "So blame me already."

His thumbs were on the hollow of her throat, and he was tilting her head back. His mouth was on hers, his tongue playing wildly.

Her pulse was pounding crazily beneath the pressure of his thumbs. Crazy. Crazy. She had to move back.

But she was moving closer, her mouth opening wider, taking more of him.

"We can go back to the car," he whispered. "Or we can stop. But it has to happen now. Go? Stop?"

How could she say stop? It was too late. She *needed* him.

Needed him enough to act like a bitch in heat? This wasn't the way she behaved. This wasn't—

"You're stiffening," Caleb said between his teeth. "Second thoughts?" He pushed her back. "Then get away from me. Or I'll be damned if I let you go." He bent down and picked up the lanterns from the ground where he'd thrown them. "I'm not Trevor or Jock or MacDuff. I've wanted you for a long time, and this time, I almost had you." His voice was rough as he started back down the hill. "And you *wanted* it. You've wanted me as long as I've wanted you."

She was gazing at him, trying to get her breath, trying to think. "I didn't mean . . . I've never denied there's a certain chemistry between—"

"Certain chemistry? It's enough to blow us up if we ever come together. But you're too wary to let that happen, aren't you? Well, it's going to happen. You almost lowered your guard enough tonight. Hell, but it came out of the blue. I wasn't expecting it."

"Neither was I," she said unsteadily. "One minute I was annoyed with you, then I—" She shrugged. "I must have gone a little crazy. It's not like me."

"Or is it? How do you know? Maybe it's exactly how you'll be with me. No analyzing, just feeling."

Feeling. Oh, yes, every cell of her mind and body had been feeling. She could still feel the throbbing of the pulse in her throat, his thumbs rubbing, pressing. Her breasts were still taut, aching.

Don't think about it.

It had been a moment that was completely wrong and shouldn't be repeated. "It's not how I want to be. And I'll fight not to be that way in the future." She moistened her lips. "This was my fault. I'd like to blame you, but I can't do it. I don't know why, but I must have been very vulnerable . . . and it happened. It won't happen again."

"The hell it won't." He looked back at her. "And you don't know why you suddenly wanted to screw me? Well, I do, Jane. I could see it, sense it. You're alive again. It's what I've been waiting for, and I'm not going to let the opportunity escape me." He smiled mockingly. "Would you like to bet how long it will take us to end up in bed?"

"You're totally outrageous."

"It's my modus operandi." He looked down at the lake. "They're lighting the lanterns. It was dark enough so that they might not have seen what was going on up here. But you'd better compose yourself by the time we get down there. You're all loose and warm and passionate. I can hardly stand to look at you."

That's exactly how she felt, but the fact that he had put it into words annoyed her. "And what about you?"

"I'm going to disappear for a while. No hiding what I'm feeling."

No, and he was giving out sexual vibrations so strong that she was beginning to feel that same stirring just looking at him.

"It's okay." The anger was suddenly gone from his tone. "You'll work your way through it. Now you know how I feel about 90 percent of the time I'm with you. Being alive has its disadvantages."

"Staying away from you would also have advantages."

"But how can you do it? I've suddenly developed a fascination for this lake. I believe I'll have to offer my services to MacDuff at every turn." He waved at Eve as they neared the campground. "Don't you think that everyone will think I've turned over a new and noble leaf?"

"I think that I'm going to work like hell to get MacDuff what he wants and get out of here."

"I thought that would be your reaction." He wasn't looking at her but at the mist that floated ghostlike in the darkness of the far bank. "But it's a strange place, a strange time. I felt it the first time I saw it. I wasn't surprised that you had dreamed about it." He added softly, "Will you ever be able to get out, Jane?"

"Don't be ridiculous."

He chuckled. "Don't slap me down when I'm being mystical. Of course you'll get free because I'll be there to pull you out. I wouldn't let that mist take you any more than I would anyone or anything. I've devoted far too much effort to you. But I had you for a minute, didn't I?"

"No, you did not." It was the mist and the night and the thought of what lay beyond them that had shaken her for that long moment. "But you obviously need something to distract you." And she had to find a way to get rid of him until her defenses were back in place.

She quickened her pace and passed him as she reached the bank. She called, "Sorry to be so long. Caleb is inclined to dawdle. But he says he's willing to be taught, so maybe you and Jock can do the job, MacDuff. He's bored, and he volunteered to go bring the rest of the equipment down himself." She gave Caleb a glance over her shoulder. "He said it was the least he could do. Isn't that right, Caleb?"

"I did mention something like that." He was discarding the bedroll and lanterns, dropping them on the ground. "I'd almost forgotten." He smiled at MacDuff. "I'm at your disposal. Anything you want, and I'm there for you and the rest of the team." He didn't look at Jane, but the next words were aimed at her and held a hint of mockery. "It will be interesting for me to work shoulder to shoulder, so to speak."

When Eve woke the next morning, it was to see Cara sitting cross-legged beside her. She was fully dressed, with a steaming cup in her hand. "Hi." She smiled. "I went out to the campfire and got a cup of coffee for you." She carefully handed her the cup as Eve scooted up to a sitting position in her sleeping bag. "Jock is cooking bacon. Doesn't it smell good?"

"Delicious." She sipped the coffee. "And so is this coffee. Thank you."

"You're welcome. If you want to wash up and brush your teeth, I'll go get you some bottled water."

"I believe I can do that for myself."

"But you shouldn't have to do it when I can do it for you. I should be taking care of you."

Eve gazed at her warily. "Has Jane been talking to you?"

Cara looked bewildered. "What?"

"Just a thought." She should have known that Jane wouldn't tell Cara about the baby. It would have just worried the child. "Don't tell me you dreamed about Jenny again."

"No. But I promised I'd take care of you, and I haven't been keeping my promise. I played the violin the other night when I shouldn't, and I've been spending too much time with Jock. I should have been doing stuff for you."

"No, you should not. You would have driven me crazy if you insisted on fetching and carrying for me. We discussed the playing and came to an agreement. And Jock would have sent you packing if you'd gotten into his way."

"I'm not sure he would," she said gravely. "He . . . likes me. He wouldn't want to hurt me. So I have to watch out to make sure that I don't do anything that would be bad for him."

"So you're carrying the whole responsibility on your shoulders?" She shook her head. "For heaven's sake, Cara, be a kid for a change. Let yourself enjoy every minute you can. There's sure not many of those. Anything I do for you, I want to do. You don't owe me."

"Yes, I do." She suddenly smiled. "But I won't fetch and carry if you don't want me to do it. But was it all right that I brought you coffee?"

"Extremely all right." She took another sip of coffee and sighed blissfully. "As long as you let me do something for you in return."

"But that wouldn't be—" She stopped. "There is something that—" She stopped again.

"You want to play your violin? I never meant to keep you from doing that, Cara."

"I know." She moistened her lips. "It's not that, I was just thinking I'd like to—I couldn't sleep, so I opened the door and sat there for a while looking out at the lake." She added quickly, "I didn't go outside. I just sat there. I was just wondering if I could—"

"Cara."

"You said not to go beyond the mists on that north bank without you," she said in a rush. "I really would like to go there, Eve."

"I don't see why that wouldn't be possible. It's probably going to be fairly safe once MacDuff gets those lights he ordered."

Cara was shaking her head. "I want to go now. MacDuff and Jock were talking about the shipment of lights while Jock was cooking, and they should be here later in the day. Could we go before they get here?"

"You're that impatient?" Eve asked, puzzled.

She shook her head. "I started getting scared last night while I was looking at it. First, I was sitting there, and I felt . . . good. It was beautiful, like I said when I first saw it. And I thought whatever was behind that mist must be beautiful, too. But then I began to think of the forest, where Jenny died. That was beautiful, too, but it hid ugly things."

"That didn't change the beauty," Eve said gently. "Sometimes ugliness exists side by side with beauty. Jenny gave her life for you in that forest and that was beautiful, too."

"I know," she whispered. "But it still hurts me to think of it. I remember how scared I was when she ran away from Elena and me. I began to get scared again last night when I was thinking of it. It sort of got mixed up in my head with the mist." She shook her head. "I can't be scared any longer, Eve. All my life I've been afraid, and I can't live like—" She reached out and touched Eve's hand. "I have to face it, Eve. I can't hide away from it. Will you help me?"

Help her? Eve felt a melting inside her as she gazed at this child who had lived a life of fear and death since she was a toddler. She wanted to take away that fear, shoulder the pain of those memories. But that wasn't what Cara was asking of her. She was asking her to show her how to handle the fear without flinching. And that would be a much harder task. "I'll help you. Of course I'll help you."

"Thank you." Cara suddenly launched herself at Eve and her arms closed tightly around her. "Thank you."

Eve froze in shock. Cara was not given to physical demonstrations, and Eve had told herself that it might be a long time before she was comfortable with any kind of affectionate gestures.

Don't question.

Accept.

She carefully put her coffee down and held Cara close. She was aware of the slightest stiffening but ignored it. Cara had made the first move. "You're welcome." She brushed a kiss on her temple. "I consider it a family obligation. But you'll have to let me know what I have to do. I'm a little confused about what you need from me."

Enough. Don't push it. Back away.

She let Cara go and picked up her coffee cup again. "So you need to go to the north bank? Why can't we wait for MacDuff's super-duper lights?"

"Because it would change what's there. It would be like wearing a bulletproof vest. I wouldn't be facing what I'm afraid of at all. Do you see what I mean?"

"I think I do. Though a bulletproof vest doesn't sound that bad to me." But she suddenly realized that Jane would understand what Cara was saying. "Without the mist it loses . . . integrity?"

Cara nodded eagerly. "I know MacDuff has to have those lights to find what he's looking for, but he'd be losing something, too." Her smile faded. "Right now there's a music to it. When you shine the lights, and the mist vanishes, will the music go, too?"

What could she tell her? Eve couldn't hear the music. "I don't know, Cara."

"I think it might. I want to face it all now." She paused. "With you, Eve. I don't want anyone else along."

Face the fear, face the beauty, with no protection, no raising of barriers. Wasn't that what Cira had done all those centuries ago when she had challenged a new land, a new life?

"Eve?" Cara was gazing at her.

Eve nodded. "Okay, no bulletproof vests," she said brusquely. "But it's not going to be easy pulling this off." She finished her coffee and got to her feet. "And we'd better get busy before MacTavish's truckload of lights and batteries comes rumbling down that road."

Cara eagerly jumped to her feet. "What are we going to do?"

"Finish getting dressed, eat breakfast, then go face MacDuff, Jock, and Caleb."

"I didn't see Caleb."

"Not surprising. He's not into hobnobbing. Jane?"

"She's still in her tent." Cara's eyes widened as she saw Eve reach into her suitcase and draw out her .38 revolver. "Why are you taking that? I was joking about the bulletproof vests. I meant—"

"I know what you meant." She tucked the gun into the pocket of her jacket but didn't put it on. "But if I can persuade MacDuff to let us go into that mist without them trailing after us, I want all the protection I can get. He told me that he has five of his Marine buddies in those hills near the north bank keeping an eye out for trespassers, but I don't want to have to count on them." She grinned at Cara. "And I may need it to shoot off a distress signal if we get lost in that mist. Though I hope not. It would be most humiliating."

Cara's gaze was still on the pocket into which the gun had disappeared. "I don't want to cause trouble. Am I being stupid, Eve?"

"No. There's no sign of anyone's knowing where we are, and MacDuff has given us adequate protection. The only danger is the mist, and, if we're careful, we can handle that." She grabbed her toothbrush and comb and headed for the portable canvas table against the tent wall. "But first I need to wash my face and brush my teeth. Go get us a plate of that bacon Jock is cooking and whatever else is available. Okay?"

"Okay." Cara's cheeks were flushed and her eyes shining with excitement. "Shall I tell them that—"

"No, leave it to me." She didn't want Cara to face the uproar alone. "After we have some hearty sustenance. We may need it. But first, I want you to go to Jane and tell her what we're doing. In a very real way, this is her lake, her territory. She has the right to know."

She shook her head ruefully after Cara ran out of the tent. It was true that there appeared to be no obvious danger, but that didn't mean that it was the safest thing on the planet to do. But Cara's problem was that she'd had to be careful, hide, always look behind her all her short life. How could Eve not understand and let her stop running if there didn't appear to be danger?

Appear was the key word, she thought dryly. She didn't know what was behind those mists.

With her luck, that north end of the lake was probably inhabited by a creature on the scale of the Loch Ness Monster.

When Eve and Cara left their tent fifteen minutes later, Jane was standing alone at the clearing, where only the embers of the campfire were still flickering.

"Let's go," she said quietly. "We don't have too much time. It took me quite a battle with MacDuff and Jock to get them to back off. They gave us ninety minutes; and then we can expect an invasion. Less if that truck with the power lights shows up while we're stumbling around out there." She gave flashlights to Eve and Cara and turned on her heel. "Come on, Cara. It's your show, you lead the way."

"Right." Cara started at a trot along the bank.

Eve fell into step with Jane as they hurried after her. "I didn't want to force you into coming with us. But you had a right to know."

"Yes, I did." She smiled faintly. "And you didn't force me to do anything. I don't know how I feel about this little foray into Marcus's kingdom, but I think there must be some reason Cara feels so strongly about it."

"It's not about Cira or Marcus or the treasure as far as she's concerned. It's about facing her devils."

"She's very young to have to confront them," Jane said. "And, who knows, maybe it's more about Cira and Marcus than she thinks. You told her the details about the dream?"

"Yes. I don't know, maybe she's somehow connecting Marcus's death with her sister's, Jenny's. She said something about Jenny's dying in a beautiful forest, too. She said she was too afraid that night, and she couldn't be afraid again." She glanced at Jane. "And you were close to her age when you had devils of your own to battle. So Cara isn't all that young."

"Young enough to be very fast. She's getting too far ahead of us to be safe." Jane's pace quickened. "She's entering the mist zone."

"Cara," Eve called. "Wait." She could barely see her in the mist, but at least Cara had halted and turned on her flashlight. Not that it was doing much good. Even though they were on the outer edge of the fogbank, the light was very weak.

But Cara's expression was glowing with eagerness as they reached her. "Isn't it awesome?" She held up her arm cloaked in mist. "I feel as if I could fly." She turned and started deeper into the mist. "Come on."

"Stay close," Eve said. "And don't drop your flashlight."

"I won't." Cara's voice was bright, excited in the smothering gray of the mist as she moved ahead. "I was wrong, Eve. There's nothing to be afraid of here. Oops." She laughed. "I almost slid into the lake. It's all muddy here on the bank. You warned me about that."

"Yes, I did. The bank probably never gets enough sunlight to dry out. Be careful, the farther in we go, the denser the mist. These flashlights aren't doing much good. I can't see more than a foot in front of me."

"Neither can I," Cara said. "But that's okay; as long as I watch the bank, I'll be safe. Isn't it neat? It's like exploring our own private planet. I think there are some big rocks up ahead." She stopped. "I think we can go around them, then come back to the lake."

"How do you know there are rocks?"

"I hear the sound of the lake lapping against them, don't you? And the mist blows against them in a different way . . ."

"No, I can't say I hear that," Eve said. "I don't think those college students got much farther than this. This is a heavier mist than I've ever gone through. And I don't see how they sketched as much as they did. Jane?"

"No, I don't hear what she hears," Jane said softly. "But I'm not afraid either, Eve. It's . . . good here. I believe it's okay to go a little farther."

Eve hesitated, then started forward again.

There *were* boulders ahead, and they felt their way around them and were once more making their way around the lake.

Total grayness, no hint of light, the flashlights totally useless now.

"The hills come straight down to the lake up ahead," Cara said. "But I think the path around the lake widens there."

"How do you know?"

"It just seems like it should," Jane said simply. "Doesn't it, Cara?"

Cara looked back at her. "Yes."

"What's going on?" Eve asked.

"I have no idea," Jane said. "Tell us, Cara."

"It's the music. The music is so strong here. And it gets stronger up ahead." She looked at Jane. "And you hear it, too, don't you?"

"Not like you do. But I hear something. Words. Cira's words." She quoted softly, "I can ride down here from the castle and imagine him running out of the mist and telling me how he'd just been hiding and playing in the caves and had great adventures to tell me." She added, "That has a music all its own, doesn't it?"

Cara nodded slowly.

"And do you want to go farther and search out that other music right now? We could do it. Or do you think that you've been given what you were meant to have when you led us into this mist?"

Cara didn't answer for a moment. "I want to go on."

"Now?"

Cara was silent again. "No, not now. It's enough." She turned and headed back toward the boulders. "Let's go back to the camp."

"But not because you're afraid," Jane said. "That's all gone?"

"Yes." Cara's voice drifted back to them. "That's all gone . . ."

The truckload of power lamps and batteries that MacTavish had promised MacDuff didn't arrive until late in the afternoon. By the time they were unloaded and taken down to the encampment, it was almost dark.

Eve sat down in front of the fire beside Jock and watched MacDuff and Caleb checking over two huge power bulbs. "You're going out tonight?"

"Why not?" Jock lifted his cup of coffee to his lips. "We've got to experiment with the equipment. We might have to order something different. Though MacTavish seemed to think that it would be enough."

"What do you think?"

Jock shrugged. "I'm no expert. I have to yield to MacTavish."

"But MacTavish was never out in that mist, like you were, was he?"

He gazed at her face and smiled. "No, he wasn't. How did you know I'd followed you?"

"Your boots. They were coated in mud when I caught sight of you right after we got back to camp. But you disappeared, and they were clean later."

"Very observant."

"Did you flip a coin to see who was going to follow us?"

"No, I was the logical choice. I didn't give anyone else an opportunity to argue." He took another drink of coffee. "It might have been blundered, and I never blunder."

"No, we had no idea you were anywhere near." She made a face. "Though I doubt if we would have known anyway. That mist is horrendous."

"Yes. It's . . . unusual. I was barely able to track you."

"I don't see how you could do it at all. We couldn't see anything."

"I've been trained to track in all situations and weather conditions." His lips twisted bitterly. "It was part of my schooling as a superassassin. That was why I was the logical choice. What's a little mist to someone like me?"

"You didn't have to follow us. We made it just fine."

"Correction. I did have to do it. I could see how Cara felt bound to stretch her limits, but I had to be there to make sure that exercise didn't hurt her."

"It was all about Cara?"

"No, don't be foolish. You and Jane are important. I would have gone anyway. But Cara is . . . she's too young to know— She'll get in trouble if someone doesn't watch out for her."

"Jane and I managed to bring her back in one piece," Eve said dryly.

"No insult intended," Jock said. "You did fine."

"Thank you. But you'll still be there to keep us from screwing things up for her." She shrugged. "It's to be expected. She appears to feel the same about you." She got to her feet. "And I believe I'll go check on Cara now and see if she's okay. She was a little quiet after she came back from the north bank."

Jock looked down at his coffee. "I noticed."

"Yes, of course you did." She hesitated. "No matter what you think, that little trip into the mist was good for her. She learned . . . something."

"I'm not arguing." He got to his feet and threw the remainder of the coffee in his cup into the fire. "Learning is necessary. You just have to live through it." He started toward Caleb and MacDuff. "Now I have to go and see if MacTavish's equipment is going to work."

"You didn't answer me. Do you think it will?"

"No." He didn't look at her. "I've never seen a mist like that one. The light will bounce off that fog like a ball against a wall. We'll need something better. But MacDuff wants to give it a try."

Eve watched him join the other two men, then went into the tent to talk to Cara.

No questions.

No urging for confidences.

Just a silent affirmation that she was there if Cara wanted to talk.

She had no idea exactly what had gone on between Cara and Jane in that mist. She wasn't sure if Cara knew. So it was best for Eve to be silent and wait to be told.

"Hey. I just talked to Jock." She smiled as she stood looking at Cara, curled up in her bedroll. "They're going to try to see what those superlights are going to do tonight. Want to come out and sit by the fire and wait until they come back?"

Eve waited until the camp had quieted down and Cara was asleep that night before she called Joe. She was tired and bewildered and wanted to touch base. She wanted to hear his voice.

"Things are fairly crazy here," she said when he picked up. "Don't say anything. We're all safe. It's just that we took our first journey into woo-woo land and I have no idea where I'm fitting into this."

He chuckled. "Some would say that you should be an expert in that area. I take it you meant you went into the mist. Accomplish anything?"

"No, Cara heard music. Jane had a flashback to a Cira dream. I was merely stumbling along in that mist and trying to keep everyone from tumbling into the lake. The three of us had flashlights, but they were useless. That mist is crazy."

Silence. "Three? The three of you were alone out there?"

She knew that would be his reaction, but there was no way that she would have kept it from him. "Cara wanted it that way. It was kind of a rite of passage for her. Or something like that. It was fine."

"It's not fine."

"It was my decision. I thought it was worth it. I still think it was." She changed the subject. "And it turned out we weren't alone. Jock shadowed us all the while we were on that north bank. Amazing. How do you shadow anyone when you can't even see them?"

"Don't do it again," he said sharply.

It struck her the wrong way. "My decision," she repeated. "MacDuff had guards in the hills, and there was no report of Salazar or his crew anywhere in this part of the Highlands. I have to do what I think is right, Joe. I didn't call you to listen to you tell me what I should do."

"Then why did you call me?"

"I don't remember. Something about love and missing you. Maybe about talking about where we're going to send our kid to college? That seemed to be important at the time."

Silence. "That is important."

"Then can we skip the lectures and concentrate on that?"

"In a minute." He added roughly, "I have to know what's going on. It's driving me crazy not to know what's happening with you. I'm sitting over here and not able to—"

"I try to let you know what's happening. It's all fairly run-of-the-mill and pretty boring. Nothing to do with Salazar or Franco. We went for a walk in the mist. Then MacDuff, Caleb, and Jock went for a walk in the mist. They were experimenting with some high-powered lights, which turned out to be a complete failure. MacDuff is contacting some lab in London to explore using infrared technology. He thinks he can get some kind of apparatus up here by late tomorrow and—"

"Okay. Okay." Joe said. "I don't want to hear about that damn mist. I just want to know that you're not going into it alone. I don't like the idea of Jock's being able to creep behind you without your knowing it."

"I'll take it under consideration." She added, "But your nerves are pretty ragged, or you wouldn't have gone on the attack. What's happening with you, Joe?"

"Not a damn thing. Toller's man is being discreet but letting me know that he's ever-present. I saw Salazar's guy staking me out when I went to the precinct this morning." He added with leashed ferocity, "I feel like I'm in a box. I've got to get *out*." He drew a harsh breath. "I'm in touch with Burbank, Manez's contact at Scotland Yard. He says that the word is that Salazar is on the hunt and gathering a team together from the local Mafia." He paused. "He's going to be ready once he finds out where you and Cara are. I can't wait for that to happen."

"You'll do what you think is best," she said. "Just as I am, Joe." She tried to laugh. "But I really don't want to have to come back there and bail you out of jail. It would be really difficult keeping Cara under wraps if that happened."

"I just wanted to let you know. I'm trying to hold back. I won't do anything rash, but the situation is becoming . . . volatile." He suddenly changed the subject. "What about Harvard?"

"What?"

"You asked what school we should send the kid to. Harvard is good."

She was glad that he had chosen to switch gears. The conversation had gotten too heavy. "Too snooty."

"I went to Harvard."

"The defense rests. Your parents were snooty, and you just managed to escape the curse. If you'd grown up in the slums like me, you'd have a better perspective on education. But you still insisted on Jane's going to Harvard."

"Only because she wanted to go." He paused. "I believe we have a little time in which to make up our minds, don't you? What made you think of it anyway?"

"I don't know." She sighed. "Yes, I do. I was thinking of Cira's little boy and how he'd not had a chance to chase his dreams. Thinking about the future is important even though sometimes that future never comes to be. I guess I'm feeling the need to plan for Cara, plan for our child. Maybe it's the nesting instinct."

"Cira's son . . ." Joe's voice was thoughtful. "A little boy . . . Do you know, I never even thought that we might be having a son. Somehow, I thought the child might be a girl."

"Why?"

"Didn't you? You lost your Bonnie. Maybe some kind of cosmic justice?"

"I haven't had time to think about the sex, cosmic justice, or anything else." But she was thinking about it now. "And I think that you're going down the wrong road. This isn't my child, it's our child. It will be what it will be."

"You don't want to know whether it's a boy or a girl?"

"No. Do you?"

"Maybe."

"Then maybe we'll find out. We'll talk about it. It's your child, Joe. Our child."

"Yeah." Silence. "But first we've got to make sure that our child is safe. So take care of yourself. No stumbling around in the fog and falling into the lake. It's not good for the kid."

"Point taken. I'll remember."

"I mean it, Eve. It's been too quiet. I've got a hunch that everything is going to explode."

"You included," she said dryly.

"Probably." He paused. "I want to be there to take care of you, take care of my child. I love you, Eve."

"Likewise." She cleared her throat. "I'll call you tomorrow, and I promise it won't be to tell you that I went strolling in the mist." She hung up.

Everything is going to explode.

She had felt a chill when he'd said that. It might be a hunch, but she believed in Joe's hunches. His instincts were infallible most of the time.

Everything is going to explode . . .

CHAPTER

12

MACDUFF'S RUN

The blood gushed onto Franco's wrists as his knife sliced across the guard's throat. More a sentry than a guard, Franco thought, as he wiped his hands on the man's shirt. He'd had a soldier mentality and endurance, too. He hadn't told Franco what he'd wanted to know until he'd cut off both his thumbs.

He pulled the guard's body into the bushes and carefully hid it. Then he started across the courtyard to the small side door facing the ocean. MacDuff's castle towered over the surf, and Franco had verified there were sentries on that side, too. But he could avoid them if he moved fast enough. And then all he had to do was get inside and find the target.

It was about time. It had taken too long, and Salazar was growing more impatient. None of MacDuff's people would talk, and it wasn't until he'd concentrated on the local village pub that he had hit pay dirt.

He'd spent a few hours schmoozing the employees, telling them he was a tourist who had been told about this castle and had come to see for himself. It had not been easy, but he'd finally found a young waitress who had told him enough to get him started.

It was true that MacDuff was not at the castle at present.

But his assistant, Rob MacTavish, was there and was an old and trusted employee.

He had known that he would have to make do with MacTavish. He only hoped he was as trusted by MacDuff as he'd been told. No problem getting to him. Franco had studied the positions of the sentries on that first day and could use one of them to get him to MacTavish.

It had all gone smoothly. Now Franco had the security alarm code from the sentry to get him into the castle.

And he knew where to find MacTavish.

Ten minutes later, he was moving quietly through the halls toward the study. Someday he'd have a place like this, he thought as he looked up at the high-arched ceilings. Only his castle would be new and lush, and there would a pool where all the women would be—

He reached the study, and paused outside the oak door. It was so thick and well made he couldn't see any light around the edges. But he could hear the sound of music. MacTavish evidently liked Madonna.

He braced himself. Move fast. Be prepared for anything.

Take him down.

He exploded through the door. He was across the room in seconds.

MacTavish jumped to his feet, his blue eyes wide and alarmed behind wire-rimmed spectacles. "What are you—" He whirled and was reaching into a top drawer in the desk.

Franco's machete sliced into his hand as he reached for the gun.

MacTavish screamed.

It was done. He *had* him.

Franco was behind him, freeing the knife from his hand and pressing it to MacTavish's stomach. "Don't move. Do exactly what I say." He pushed him back into the chair. "We're going to talk. I'm going to ask you questions, and you're going to answer."

"Who are you?"

He stuck the knife into his shoulder.

MacTavish screamed again.

"You aren't listening," Franco told him. "You don't ask the questions, old man. I ask the questions." He turned the knife in the wound. "Does that hurt?" MacTavish was groaning, biting his lip in agony. Franco felt the familiar surge of power and pleasure. "We've just started. Now let's have a talk about MacDuff and Jane MacGuire."

"I know where Jane MaGuire is," Franco said triumphantly when Salazar answered the phone five hours later. "I wasn't able to talk to MacDuff. He wasn't at the castle. But he had an assistant, Rob MacTavish, who had everything at his fingertips."

"And what is that?" Salazar put his phone on speaker, so that Natalie could hear. He pulled the rental car over to the curb. "What's everything, Franco?"

"MacGuire is with MacDuff and some friend, a Jock Gavin."

"What about Eve Duncan?"

"MacTavish didn't know anything about Duncan. I don't think MacDuff told him about her."

"Then he didn't have everything at his fingertips, did he?" Salazar asked sarcastically.

"He had enough. MacDuff has been planning a hunt for some kind of treasure for the last few weeks. Jane MacGuire was scheduled to go along. MacTavish ordered all the equipment for him and made arrangements with his property caretakers at all his properties."

"You're sure MacGuire didn't cancel at the last minute?"

"No, MacTavish e-mailed MacDuff some notes and photos that Jane MacGuire wanted to see just last night."

"What notes?"

"Something about a lake on the property where they're searching." He paused. "MacTavish said that he didn't think anyone would cancel out on a chance of getting a share of that treasure MacDuff was hunting. MacDuff has been gathering information and making

plans for years, and he told MacTavish when he asked for the information that he thought he was very close, that this time he was going
to find it."

"Eve Duncan," Salazar said impatiently, to bring him back to the
subject at hand.

"I know. I'm sure she's with Jane MacGuire," he said hurriedly.
"But you should listen to me. MacTavish thinks MacDuff is close
to finding that treasure. It could be worth millions, maybe billions."

"Billions?" Salazar repeated. "Treasure hunt? It sounds like some
kid's game."

"That's what I told MacTavish. He said that they're searching for
a chest full of ancient coins brought over from Herculaneum." He
paused. "One of them was said to be one of the pieces of silver Judas
was paid to betray Christ. It was supposed to have been found by
some professor a couple years ago, but the Vatican refused to accept
it as authentic. That means it could still be part of the treasure. That
could be very big money."

"Maybe," Salazar said. "But we can't deal with that right now.
We're going after Eve Duncan and the kid."

"Don't be impatient," Natalie suddenly spoke up. "Franco is
right, we shouldn't discount the possibility of raking in that kind of
money. You did very well, Franco."

Silence. "A woman?" Franco said warily. "You have a woman
there? Even if she's your wife, you shouldn't involve her in—"

"I'm not his wife," Natalie said softly. "I'm Natalie Castino. Do
you know who I am?"

An instant of shocked silence. "Yes. I've never met you, but I've
seen you."

"I want you to know that I appreciate your hard work. I look forward to meeting you. I think with a little thought and planning, we
might be able to snatch that chest of coins right from under MacDuff's
nose."

"It will get in the way," Salazar said flatly.

"Not if we work it right." She smiled at him. "You have power and a good deal of money in all your Grand Cayman accounts. But Franco and I have to think of the future, don't we, Franco?"

"It's . . . a lot of money."

"Of course, it is. And we should take a little time to see if MacDuff is as close as MacTavish said. You made sure that he wouldn't have lied to you?"

"He didn't lie."

She chuckled. "And you have a reputation for making it impossible for anyone to do that. Even my husband was impressed when he heard about you."

"Was he?"

"Absolutely. Now where is this hunt going on?"

"Gaelkar. It's in the Highlands."

"And that must be where we can find Duncan and Cara. Suppose you set out right away, and we'll meet together and talk."

"Salazar?" Franco asked.

"Come ahead," he said shortly. "I'll talk to you on the road." He hung up and glared at Natalie. "What the hell are you doing?"

"Exploring possibilities. There's a possibility that I won't be able to use you or my husband to give me what I need. You both have your own agendas. It would be very convenient to have a fortune of my own."

"A share of a fortune," he corrected sourly.

"It appears as if there might be plenty to share." She took out her computer and opened it. "You go ahead and GPS this Gaelkar. I'll see if I can Google any information about MacDuff and this chest of coins . . .

"Something's wrong, Jane," Eve murmured as she watched MacDuff stride toward them down the bank. His expression was more grim than she'd ever seen it. "And I don't think it has anything to do with that damn mist."

"Come to my tent," MacDuff said curtly as he stopped before them. "Both of you. Right now."

"Can you wait until we clean the mud off our shoes and wash our hands?" Eve asked. "We ran into a spot of—"

"No, right now." He turned on his heel. "I don't give a damn about that shit." The next instant, Eve and Jane were watching him stride down the bank. "I don't think you're going to give a damn either, Eve."

Eve felt a surge of fear and automatically looked toward Cara. As usual, she was with Jock and appeared perfectly okay. Whatever had happened hadn't touched her yet. "I don't like this."

She quickly followed Jane around the bank toward the tent area.

Not Cara.

Joe?

Possible. Danger was always possible where Joe was concerned.

Stop worrying. She'd know in a few minutes.

But, dear God, MacDuff had looked grim.

MacDuff still looked grim as they entered his tent. He had poured a shot of whiskey and was lifting the glass to his lips. He glanced at them. "Sorry to be rude. Would you like a drink? I felt the need of one."

"Why?" Jane asked as she came toward the desk. "What's happened, MacDuff?"

"I'm drinking to an old friend." He lifted his glass in a half toast. "Who was recently butchered by an acquaintance of yours, Eve."

Eve felt a ripple of shock. "What?"

"Rob MacTavish, my assistant." He took a drink of whiskey. "MacTavish has been with me for years and my father before me. He was a good man. He was planning on retiring soon. He was training his grandson to take over for him."

"What happened, MacDuff?" Jane repeated quietly.

"I received a call from Sean Donlachen, head of security at MacDuff's Run. He was abjectly apologetic." He took another drink.

"Because he'd failed in his duty to me. Last night, the courtyard sentry was taken, tortured, and killed. But not before he'd given the alarm code to get into the castle. Early this morning, they found both the sentry and MacTavish. It appeared that MacTavish had received even harsher treatment than the sentry." His lips were tight. "Because he was a tough, loyal old man, and it must have taken a long time to break him."

"I'm so sorry, MacDuff," Jane said. "It was MacTavish you asked to send me those notes and sketches. Did that have anything to do with it?"

"No," Eve said unsteadily. She couldn't stop shivering. "I don't believe that what happened had anything to do with Cira's treasure. It sounds too much like what happened to those pilots in Atlanta. They were tracking you down to find Jane, Cara, and me, MacDuff. Isn't that what you're figuring?"

"That's what I'm thinking," MacDuff said. "I'm betting it was that Franco Quinn told me about. And they found a nice old man who knew where I was." He tossed back his whiskey. "And butchered him."

"Do you want Cara and me to leave?" Eve asked. "If we go, even if Salazar and Franco came, they might leave you alone if they see that we aren't here."

"You may have to leave. Since they know where you are, I won't risk you and the child. But not right away. I have to find a place for you that I consider safe." His lips twisted. "And by that time, they could be right on top of us." He turned back to Jane. "But they'll be coming from the north, over the hills to the lake. It would be the safest route for them. They wouldn't realize what they'd run into if they try to go through that mist." He paused. "I don't want anyone to go near that mist at the north end until I tell you it's safe."

"And when will that be?" Jane asked. "Because I don't think you're including yourself in that order, are you?"

"It occurred to me that it might be more efficient to get rid of the threat after I'm sure that Eve and Cara are safe." He poured himself another drink. "Picking Franco and Salazar off in that mist would be so much cleaner than having to keep those bastards from hunting Eve and Cara down. I'm sure MacTavish would approve."

"They might not even to try to go through that mist," Eve said. "They might just go over the hills and hit us from the northwest."

"Maybe. But then they might decide that they should explore other lucrative goals while they're at it." His lips twisted. "And I won't let Cira's gold be taken by those sons of bitches who killed MacTavish."

"Is that a possibility?" Eve asked.

"The office was ransacked, and the file with the photos was taken. MacTavish must have told Franco everything concerning the hunt as well as where we are. Hell, he probably told him anything and everything to stop the pain. I even told MacTavish during that last call that I thought I was coming very close to finding Cira's gold. Yes, I'd say that it's a possibility Salazar might have an interest." He added through set teeth, "I almost hope they do. I'd like to repay a little in kind."

"I can see how you would," Eve said. "And I regret what happened to your friend MacTavish, but you can settle scores after I get Cara safe. Right now, I don't care about Cira's gold or preserving your estates or the fact that you want revenge." She turned to leave. "Now I'm going to call Joe and tell him that Salazar probably knows where we are and is moving fast." She looked over her shoulder. "And if you can find a safe house for Cara, do it. Or I'll do it myself."

She walked out of the tent.

She stood there for a moment, struggling against the anger and panic coursing through her. Two more deaths as Salazar and Franco moved nearer. Two strangers whom she had never seen had died for her and Cara. How many more would there be before this was over?

Get a grip. She drew a deep breath and straightened her shoulders. Cara. She had to find Cara. She headed back toward the bank.

She saw Cara immediately. She was still with Jock, and he was smiling down at her. Was it Eve's imagination, or was the closeness growing, the bonding between them becoming more firm? A bonding that would probably be broken when she snatched Cara away from Jock, and they went on the run. She felt a pang as she thought how many friendships had been lost when Cara had been forced to run in her short life.

It couldn't be helped. Her pace quickened as she hurried toward Cara. Get Cara to her tent, prepare her for what was to come.

Then make the call to Joe.

"Go ahead. I'll be there in a few minutes, Eve," Cara said, trying to smile. She had to be very calm, she told herself. She must not let Eve know how upset she was. She could tell that Eve was already upset herself, and she mustn't make it harder for her. "It won't take me long to get ready. Go call Joe."

"Cara . . ." She gazed at her, then at Jock. Then she nodded. "Don't be too long. MacDuff is going to be working on finding a safe place to take us. I don't know how much time we're going to have." She turned and headed back toward the tent area.

Cara's hands knotted into fists as she watched Eve leave. "She wants to give me a chance to say good-bye to you. Isn't that nice of her? Eve's always thinking about other people. Did I tell you that she saved my life once? She didn't even know—"

"Shut up," Jock said roughly. He was suddenly beside her, turning her to face him. "Stop pretending. I know what this is doing to you. How many times has it happened before? That's what Eve is thinking, too. It's hurting her to make you go on the run again." He took her shoulders in his hands and looked down into her eyes. "It's hurting me. So don't pretend. It makes me feel lonely."

"Does it? Why?"

"Because I like the way you play the violin." He smiled. "Because I like the way you smile at me. Because I've never had a sister, and you make me think it might be kind of nice to have one. Do I have to have any other reason?"

"No." She cleared her throat. "You . . . make me feel as if I'm not alone either. I don't want to leave you."

"Shh. We can get around that."

She shook her head. "You might need me. I think sometimes you have . . . pain. I should be here."

"I'll be fine."

He was smiling and so radiant that she wanted to reach up and touch his face. She repeated, "You might need me."

He was silent, gazing down at her. "I think I might always need you. But that doesn't mean we have to be together. Friends stay friends even when they're far apart."

She shook her head. "But then I won't know when you need me." But maybe he was trying to say that she was clinging too tight. "You're right." She tried to back away from him. "That's the way you're friends with Jane. It's just not my way. I'll work on being more like Jane." She moistened her lips. "I'd better go. Eve told me not to—"

"Hush," he said. "Jane is fine. Jane is great. But you don't have to be anyone but yourself. That's quite enough. Too much sometimes."

"Too much?"

"I'm not going to go into that," he said. "And do you really think that I'd let you get away from me? That's not going to happen."

"We're friends?" she whispered. "Really friends?"

"It couldn't be any more real," he said gravely. "And I'm not ever going to let you walk away unless that's what you want to do. I'll be closer to you than your Elena, closer than Eve. But you have a long way to go, and we can't be together all the time. I'll have to make do without you."

"You're not . . . joking?"

"Heaven forbid. Now, run along to Eve. I have to go see MacDuff. I knew MacTavish, too, and MacDuff may need someone to talk to about his old friend."

She nodded. "I tried to talk to Eve about Elena, but sometimes the words didn't come."

"And MacDuff may not say anything. In that case, we'll only have a drink. But he'll know I'm there, and that can be important, too." He yanked his thumb toward the tents. "Go. Let me see you safe in your tent before I leave."

"It's only a little way, Jock." She smiled at him as she turned to leave. "I couldn't be safer. I'm not worried."

"Neither am I. Not as long as I'm watching over you. You don't ever have to worry about anything happening to you while I'm keeping an eye on you." He smiled back at her. "You'll never have to look over your shoulder again. No one will ever hurt you. I'll always be there for you."

He was smiling, but Cara could sense that he could not have been more serious. "I don't want anyone to have to take care of me. Elena, Eve, Joe, Jane. Now you and MacDuff. Elena always told me I had to take care of myself, and she was right. It's my turn to take care of people now."

"We'll discuss it later." He nodded at the tents. "Go see what Joe's decided for you and Eve. Move."

Cara stood there, staring at him.

He frowned. "What's wrong?"

"I just wanted to look at you for a minute. Things . . . happen. I tried to remember what Elena looked like that last morning, and I couldn't do it."

"Cara." A mixture of expressions chased across his face. "Oh, shit. What can I say to that?" He leaned closer and cupped her face in his hands. "Hey, it's going to be fine. I promise nothing is going to happen to me or Eve or Jane or . . . should I go down the list?"

"You promise?"

He nodded. "You know it." He brushed his lips across the bridge of her nose. "Now will you go?"

"Sure." She smiled. "Of course, I will." She turned and flew across the bank toward the tents. She had spoken without thinking. The words had tumbled out. She knew that there was no way that he could guarantee that he or anyone in this camp would live even another day. Her sister, Jenny, had died. Elena had died. Both of them had been young and with their entire lives before them. Death came, but life should be held close to fight him off.

Maybe by making Jock give her that promise, he would think, remember, when death came too near him.

"Get out of there, Eve," Joe said harshly. "Now!"

"We're packing up. MacDuff is only waiting until he locates a safe house he'll be satisfied with."

"I'll call Burbank and see if he can find one. He's with Scotland Yard and should know the area. It's probably better if you go back to the city anyway. You can get lost there."

"I could get lost here. You haven't seen those mists."

"Stay out of those mists. I told you I—"

"It was just a comment. I'll go where MacDuff tells me to go. Wherever I can keep Cara safe. I just wanted to call and tell you what had happened."

"I'll call MacDuff myself. And I'll get back to you as soon as I talk to Burbank."

"And then what?" she asked. "This is the explosion you thought would come. It's not all about me. What's your next move, Joe?"

"I think you know. I've made some advance plans. I have to get off this phone and get to work. I'll see you soon." He hung up.

She did know, Eve thought, as she hung up. Joe was in battle mode, and he'd be totally ruthless in execution. He had to extricate himself both from Salazar's tail and Toller's before he'd come to her, but he'd said soon, and he meant it.

Don't think of the danger and difficulties that he'd face. Just believe in him.

And concentrate on doing her part to keep Cara safe.

·   ·   ·

Joe's first call after hanging up from Eve was to Burbank at Scotland Yard. "I've just had word that Salazar is on the move, Burbank. See if you can find out what's happening?"

"I already know," Burbank said. "I've just had an informant tell me. Six men from Maitland's cartel in Liverpool, heading west on Salazar's orders. And not the usual run-of-the mill hired killers. The word is that Salazar requested specialists."

"What kind of specialists?"

"I don't know yet. I'm still checking."

Joe didn't like it. "I need to know, Burbank."

"I'll let you know when I do. I'd give you a destination, but Salazar hasn't told them anything but that he wanted them to rendezvous with him and Franco near Glasgow."

"Keep me informed." He paused. "I may send Eve and Cara to you if you can find a safe haven for them. Possible?"

"Possible. I'll ask around." He hung up.

Okay. Confirmation that Salazar was definitely heading toward the Highlands.

Now he had to get the hell out of here.

He made one more phone call.

Then he left the lake cottage and headed for the airport.

The airport was crowded, but Joe had only carry-on luggage, and he moved effortlessly through security. Then he took the train to the International concourse at Terminal E.

Lomoto, Salazar's man, was at the front of the car.

The tail Toller had assigned him was standing holding on to the iron bar by the sliding doors.

There was a dark amusement at seeing both of them caught on this train with him. If anything would have amused him right now.

He saw the boarding sign above the check-in counter the minute he got off the escalator that led from the train.

Geneva, Switzerland, with continuing service to Rome, Italy.

He checked in at the gate and went over to the window to watch the scurry of activity around the jet on the tarmac below.

His phone rang. Toller.

"Hello, Toller. I've been expecting you."

"What the hell are you doing, Quinn?"

"I thought I'd take a little trip to Switzerland. Does the agent you have following me ski? It would make it so much more pleasant for him."

"What are you up to? You know that there will be an agent waiting when you get off the plane in Geneva."

"And your agent here will make sure I board this plane. I don't doubt that you're handling my departure with efficiency. By the way, what's his name?"

"Dixon."

"Dixon looks to be a clean-cut young man. Maybe a little too much government-issue. Crew cut, nice suit and tie. Just what I'd expect of you. Much more presentable than that scumbag, Lomoto, who Salazar assigned to me. He's wearing jeans and a red jacket, and I'll bet he's missing the gun he had to give up to get past security."

"What's happening, Quinn?"

"Probably what you thought would happen. But you'll notice I'm obeying your instructions and not even trying to avoid surveillance. I would have even made an attempt to become more compatible with your agent, Dixon, but I didn't want to make Salazar's hit man jealous. Lomoto is looking a bit uptight at the moment. He's obviously not sure whether to try to take me out here or wait for instructions from Salazar."

"You could neutralize the threat by coming in and having a talk with me about Cara Castino."

"Yes, I could do that." He glanced at the boarding desk. "I believe they're starting to call my flight. It was nice talking to you, Toller." He hung up.

Time to rid himself of Lomoto.

He moved toward the restroom across the hall from the gates.

Lomoto followed only seconds later.

Good. The restroom was unoccupied except for someone in a stall at the far end.

Joe pressed back against the wall beside the entrance.

Waiting.

Not for long.

Joe saw a blur of jeans and red jacket.

He moved!

His arm encircled Lomoto's neck, and he jerked him into the urinal area. His leg swept out and brought him falling to the floor.

One savage and effective blow to the carotid artery.

Lomoto grunted and collapsed.

Joe caught him and dragged him into the nearest stall. He dumped him on the toilet, locked the door, and listened. The toilet flushed from the stall occupied down the long row. The sound of running water. No sound of anyone else's entering the restroom. Joe stepped on the toilet, and then pulled himself over the locked door and jumped to the floor. He had been lucky, any number of things could have gone wrong. But they hadn't gone wrong, and he had rid himself of Lomoto. Now it was time to rid himself of Toller's man. But this removal would be infinitely more difficult and complex. He straightened his clothes and left the restroom.

Just in time.

Toller's agent had evidently decided not just to monitor but to investigate. He was walking toward the restroom.

Joe smiled and nodded. "Nice of you to be concerned about me. But I wouldn't miss this flight." Then he moved toward the boarding line.

Toller's agent, Dixon, hesitated, then turned back to watch Joe give his boarding pass to the agent.

Joe hadn't thought that he'd go into the restroom and investigate the sudden absence of Lomoto. Dixon didn't give a damn what happened to Salazar's man, he was only worried about keeping Joe in view.

Joe waved at him as he was given back his boarding pass and headed for the jetway door. Joe knew that he would probably stay there, watching, until the plane took off.

Joe moved slowly down the curving jetway. He'd deliberately waited until almost everyone had boarded before he started. He'd counted on the fact that there would be a last-minute scramble, with the flight attendants scurrying around, finding places for carry-on luggage and serving drinks. It would be the best time to make his move.

"You cut it close," Rick Stacy growled as Joe rounded the last turn in the jetway. Stacy's face was almost as green as his baggage handler's uniform, and he nervously moistened his lips. "We've got about five minutes before they shut the baggage doors."

"Then let's get moving." Joe took the green airline jacket that Stacy handed him and put it on. "That should be enough time." He pulled on the matching cap. "You set up the car for me?"

"Yes. Hertz." Stacy opened the jetway door that led down to the tarmac and baggage compartment access. "Just get into the truck and keep low. I'll have you back at the parking lot in ten minutes. When do I get the other half of my money?"

"When I'm sure that you didn't double-cross me. Not that you would, Stacy. I can tell you're a fine, upstanding man." He moved quickly to the truck, opened the passenger door, and jumped in. He glanced up at the windows at the gate. He was on the other side of the plane, and even if Toller's man was watching, he wouldn't be able to see him. But his bet was that Dixon was still watching the boarding gate to make sure Joe didn't come back.

He heard the cargo doors slam, then Stacy was in the truck beside him.

"Down!" Stacy muttered.

Joe slid down in the seat.

A few minutes later, the truck was cruising by the wire-enclosed airline lot that adjoined the regular passenger parking lot.

"Slow down," Joe said. "I'll jump out and hide behind those machines until you get back to baggage."

"My money," Stacy reminded him.

"I'll wire it into your bank account once I'm sure of you. This is just the first step for all of us, Stacy."

But a crucial first step, he thought. Once he got safely away from the Atlanta Airport, he'd drive to Birmingham and board a private jet to Edinburgh.

Seven hours at most and he'd be with Eve.

HILLS OF GAELKAR

"I want to talk to Eve Duncan, Salazar," Natalie said. "What can it hurt? Just give me ten minutes. She has no way of knowing that I'm involved in the kidnapping. To her, I'd just be a grieving mother as I am to everyone else. I might be able to set a trap for her and Cara. Much better than trying to blunder in and take them."

"Not everyone is fool enough to believe that you're what you pretend to be, Natalie," Salazar said.

"If they don't, they feel so guilty at being heartless that the effect is the same." She turned to Franco. "Don't you think it's a good idea?"

"Maybe," he said cautiously. "I don't know that she would—"

"Never mind." She waved her hand dismissingly. "You're so afraid of offending Salazar that you wouldn't admit I'm right. I forgive you." She stared down at the mist-shrouded lake hundreds of feet below them. "But then I believe we do need an example to show those people we're sincere. Perhaps one of those guards we skirted around when we were climbing up this perfectly exhausting mountain?" She smiled at Franco. "Could you do that for me, Franco?"

"If you want me to." He smiled. "An example . . . I think you're right."

"Franco," Salazar said warningly.

"With your permission . . . sir."

Franco was back in line, Salazar thought sourly, but he was clearly dazzled by Natalie and had been since the moment they had met. And Natalie wasn't above using Franco if it suited her purpose. Hell, she wasn't above using the devil himself. "An example might be beneficial. It might shake them up to realize how easily we can reach out and touch them. Go see what you can do."

"Eve Duncan," Natalie reminded Salazar softly. "Why not see what I can do, too?"

"Joe is on his way," Eve said to MacDuff as she hung up the phone. "He just boarded a flight in Birmingham. He wants me out of here and in a safe house by the time he gets here."

"And what do you want, Eve?"

"I want Cara safe." She gazed out at the lake. It wasn't only the lake that was misty today. The hills were draped, covered, in a suffocatingly heavy fog that was increasing every minute. "And, yes, I want to be safe, too. It's important right now." She looked back at him. "Have you found us a place?"

"Possibly. I'm exploring options. There's a flat in the Old Town section of Edinburgh that should be safe."

"Your men haven't seen anything of Salazar yet?"

"I would have told you." He added grimly, "Or you would have heard it. I guarantee that no one would get near you without our knowing it. Ned Colin is one of my best men, and I told him to call in at least eight or nine men to patrol those hills. There are four men just guarding the camp." He turned away. "I've got one more place to check out near London. We should be able to get you on the road within a couple hours." He frowned. "I hope. The weather forecast says this fog isn't going to lift for hours. If it really socks in, it will be impossible to travel. I'll try to get you moving right away."

And she wasn't helping anything by standing talking to him, Eve thought. She turned and strode back to her tent, where Cara was waiting.

"Joe's on his way," she told her. She glanced around the tent. "Everything seems to be packed up and ready. You've been very efficient."

"There wasn't much to pack. Not like when Elena and I had to move to a different city." She went to stand by the door and looked out at the heavy fog. "It looks . . . strange, doesn't it."

"We're just not used to the entire valley being foggy. Yes, it does look different."

"Could I go outside for a little while? I won't go far. I thought I'd go sit by the fire. I feel . . . closed in."

"Sure. MacDuff says the camp is guarded. Want company?"

She shook her head. "I don't think so."

Because she was sad and maybe a little scared. Or maybe she wanted to go talk to Jock again. "I'll call you when MacDuff says we have to leave."

She watched Cara disappear into the fog. She wished MacDuff would make a decision so that they could get out of here. She was as on edge as Cara.

It would be better when Joe got here.

Everything would be better when Joe was here.

He had said six hours. It seemed a lifetime right—

Her cell phone rang.

No ID.

She hesitated. "Hello."

"Eve Duncan?" A woman's voice, rushed, broken. "Tell me they didn't lie to me again. You're the one who has my daughter?"

Eve stiffened. "This is Eve Duncan. Who are you?"

"Natalie Castino. You have my Cara?"

Shock jarred through Eve. "I don't know what you're talking about."

"Just tell me that she's safe. That those horrible men haven't hurt her." She was sobbing. "They told me that they killed my Jenny but that Cara is still alive. But that she won't be for very long if I don't do what they say. We've got to save her."

"What men are you talking about?" Eve asked cautiously.

"The people who kidnapped her. I think they have something to do with the leader of one of the rival cartels who hate my husband. But how could they do it? How could they hurt a child?"

The words and tone couldn't have sounded more genuine, Eve thought. If Joe hadn't told her about Natalie's meeting with Salazar, she might have even believed her. What was Natalie trying to do? Play it cautiously. "It's not a question of how, they obviously did kill Jenny. And you obviously have been told that there's a threat to Cara. Suppose you tell me what's happening?"

Natalie drew a shaky breath. "A few days ago, I received a telephone call and was told that my daughter Jenny had been killed and that Cara would also die unless I place four million dollars in an account in the Grand Cayman. My husband thought it was a scam and refused to pay, but my father agreed to transmit the funds if I could get them to prove they had Cara, and she could be safely extracted." Her voice broke. "He meant he thought they might kill her anyway. They sent me a school picture of her in some kind of choir robe . . . She looks like me. But she's so big now . . . My little girl is so big. My father said that photo didn't prove anything except that she'd still been alive sometime this year. He wanted a current photo and to set up a release." She drew a deep breath. "And then they told me that they didn't have her after all, that you'd stolen her away from them."

"If that's true, then you should have been relieved."

"Except they said that they would hunt her down and kill her. They said you'd taken her to Scotland, and they told me to come here and find a way to get them the money. Only they're angry now, and they want more. They said you'd found some kind of treasure or something, and they want that, too. Is that true?"

Eve was silent a moment. "It seems that they're well informed. What would they do if you refuse?"

"They told me it would only be days, maybe hours, before they either took Cara back or shot her. Please don't let them do that." She said in a rush, "My father looked you up, and he doesn't think you're part of this. You're some kind of sculptor or something, and you'd care if my daughter was hurt or killed. I hope he's right."

"Yes, I would care very much."

"Then help me, help us," she said. "I beg of you. You've been told my husband is a terrible man, and I suppose I have to say he can be terrible in many ways. I guess I'm a little bitter toward him because he doesn't seem to love our daughter as much as I do. But Cara shouldn't suffer because of his sins. I've already been forced to lose my Jenny."

So plausible. She was striking all the right notes. "We've been able to keep Cara safe so far. What makes you think we can't continue?"

"Because they hate my husband, and the only thing that would make them stop hunting for Cara is that money."

"And as soon as they had it, they'd kill her anyway."

"Do you think I'm not afraid of that? That's why I'm calling you. I want you to make a deal with Salazar. Tell him that you'll turn Cara over to my father if he gives him the money. Maybe give him that other treasure thing, too. My father will send a helicopter to pick her up with two of his most trusted men."

"And you?"

"Of course. I can't wait to see her. Did you know in a few days it will be her birthday?"

"No, I didn't."

"It's been so many years since I've been able to think of that day without tears. Has she ever spoken about me?"

"She doesn't remember much about you. All she remembers is her sister and her nurse, Elena."

"I guess I can't expect anything else. But I'm still bitter about the fact that Elena never brought her back to me."

"Bitter? She died saving Cara."

"And I'm grateful, but she should have known I'd have found a way to protect all of them." She paused. "But I have my chance now. I can save my Cara. If you'll help me. Will you do that?"

What to answer? Eve's mind was zooming, careening, as she tried to come up with the right thing to say. "I'm not certain if throwing my lot in with you is the right thing to do. One of the reasons that we took Cara away from the authorities in San Diego was that we didn't want to put her in a situation where she'd be sent back to Mexico to face danger from all sides. I'm still not sure that wouldn't happen. You say you love Cara, but you weren't able to prevent her kidnapping. How can you assure me that it wouldn't happen again?"

"Because my father would be involved. He loved his granddaughters. He wouldn't let anything happen to Cara now that he knows there is a danger."

Eve was silent. "Just what are you suggesting?"

"I contact Salazar and tell him that you've agreed to bring Cara to meet the helicopter my father will send with the ransom money. It will be your responsibility to get her to the helicopter safely, but once there, my father's men will take over. He'll whisk her away and you, too, if you wish. I understand that you've made yourself a target by interfering with Salazar."

"You could say that," she said dryly. "And we all fly away and live happily ever after?"

"Live is the key word," Natalie said quietly. "I've learned to value those words in the past eight years. Will I permit you to interfere with my relationship with my daughter once she's safe? I don't promise you that. What mother would give up her child because an outsider thinks she knows better than she does how to raise her? You'll have to do battle to get her back from me."

"I don't have to do battle, I still have Cara. The choice is mine."

"But you won't let her die, if you can help it. I can tell that you care about her . . . just as I do." She rattled off a phone number. "You'll make the right choice. Call me when you do." She hung up.

Natalie Castino was a force to be reckoned with, Eve thought as she slowly hung up. She had gone through that conversation, pressing all the buttons, changing tone, altering character, as she went along.

If she was a killer, then she was an exceptionally clever one. If she was a grieving mother, fighting to keep her daughter alive, then she might have come up with a plan to do it. Yet Joe thought that she had helped Salazar to take the girls, and he was seldom wrong.

Still, they had no concrete proof of her involvement . . . except for the fact that Jenny had been buried in that white eyelet dress instead of her nightclothes. No sign that Natalie had been involved in MacTavish's death. All those tears, the sobs, the agony, might be real, but in the end, Eve would have to make her own decision.

And that decision would not only concern Cara and her but everyone in this camp.

She got to her feet and left the tent and was immediately assaulted by waves of fog. She could dimly see Cara's hazy figure sitting by the fire with Jock. What would she say if Eve told her that she'd just spoken to her mother?

She wasn't ready to find out. She turned and headed for Jane's tent.

"Did she believe you?" Salazar asked Natalie, as she hung up from talking to Eve Duncan. "I told you it was a waste of time. You should have stayed out of it."

"It wasn't a waste of time." Natalie smiled. "I was plausible. I gave her something to think about. If you do your part and frighten her enough, she might run right toward me."

"Toward us."

"That's what I meant, of course."

"Of course. You mentioned that treasure MacDuff's supposed to be hunting."

"I just wanted to get a feel for her take on that chest. She didn't laugh or ridicule the idea. MacTavish might have had it right." She glanced at Franco. "You were very clever to dig that out of him."

Franco nodded and smiled.

"A waste of time," Salazar repeated.

"We'll see. I certainly wouldn't want to do that. I don't want to spend any more time than necessary in these hills with those rather odorous men you've imported." She glanced around the camp, then at the man tied and gagged across the fire from them. He was staring at her pleadingly. His face was bloody, and so was his throat. Franco had been playing with him after he'd captured him a few hours ago. She looked away from him and shrugged. "You gave me my chance. By all means, let me see what you can do, Salazar." She got to her feet. "In the meantime, I'll call my father and tell him how upset I am that I haven't heard any more about ransom for my Cara."

"You made two calls last night."

"How suspicious you are. One to my father, one to my husband. My father to reinforce the myth, my husband to tell him how much I missed him and that I couldn't wait to get home to him. One must always follow through with a lie and not let it just dangle in the wind." She tilted her head. "But you knew that, didn't you? You checked my phone after I went to sleep. One call to Moscow. One call to Mexico City. You just wanted to know why." She added softly, "You don't trust me, Salazar?"

"I'm not a fool. Our relationship is not based on trust."

She threw back her head and laughed. "True." She sauntered away from the fire. "It's based on getting my sweet daughter back to me. And perhaps acquiring a few other gifts along the way."

CHAPTER
13

Y ou don't actually think Natalie Castino is genuine?" Jane
asked quietly.

"No, but I'm trying to be unbiased," Eve said. "We don't know
enough about her. Most of it is hearsay, and who knows what a mother
would do to find her child."

"You're in a very vulnerable state where that concept is concerned," Jane said. "You might not be thinking straight." She shook
her head. "It could be a trap."

"That was my first thought." Eve grimaced. "I tend to trust Joe's
judgment more than I do Natalie Castino's motherly love. But if it is
a trap, can we turn it against them? I'm supposed to call her if I decide to help her whisk Cara away into the loving arms of her grandfather. There has to be some way we can use that."

"But we'd need help. You have to tell MacDuff, Eve."

She nodded. "I know that. I just wanted to talk it out and get it
straight in my head before I brought him into the picture. MacDuff
can be overwhelming once he makes up his mind."

"Tell me about it," Jane said dryly. "But that doesn't alter the fact
that he's the best game in town and certainly the one with the most
cards he can play. Do you want me to talk to him?"

"No, I'll do it." Eve gave her a hug. "I have to check on whether he's located a safe house yet and whether we can travel in this fog. My guess is a big negative. And I'm getting more and more nervous about having Cara out in this wilderness." She moved toward the door. "I'll get back to you."

Jane followed her and watched until she disappeared into MacDuff's tent. She stood outside surrounded by the fog, which didn't appear to have abated at all. Then she turned to stare out at the lake.

The beginning or the end.

Today the lake appeared much more ominous than the day she had first seen it.

"You're very tense. It's not all that bad."

She turned to see Seth Caleb coming toward her and automatically stiffened. "I have a right to be tense. I have more at stake than you do, Caleb." She was suddenly aware of something different, charged, electric, about him. Not so different. She had seen him like this before when there was a threat, but it always disturbed her. "Or perhaps you haven't heard that Salazar is on the move. You haven't been around very much lately."

"I was merely being sensitive to your feelings." He was smiling recklessly as he came closer to her. "You were pedaling backward at top speed the last time I saw you, and I thought I'd allow you time to regroup. And I knew about Salazar at the same time you did. Perhaps a little earlier."

"Earlier?"

"I feel things sometimes. A sort of primal instinct. And we all know how primitive I can be."

"And how much you enjoy it."

"I can't help it," he said simply. "And I won't lie to you. If you expected me to stay close to the home fires and circle the wagon train, that wasn't going to happen. It's not how I operate. I took off for those hills and started hunting."

She went still. "And did you find anything?"

"Maybe. I didn't locate Salazar's camp. They're probably moving it every three or four hours. But there are only a couple ways they could cause us problems, and perhaps they won't think of them. And I have the lay of the land now. I know where I'd strike."

"I don't want them to strike at all. I want Eve and Cara out of here."

"So do I." His lips twisted. "They'll get in my way. Plus robbing the situation of any hint of fun. After all, I promised Eve I'd take care of her, and responsibility tends to be exceptionally boring."

"How unfortunate," Jane said. "No one asked you to take responsibility, Caleb. Eve is my responsibility." She turned to go back into her tent. "And when she leaves here, I'm going with her."

"Which means I'll have to tag along." He shrugged. "But I'll try to make it interesting as well as worthwhile. In the meantime, I'll go back to those hills and see if I can discover anything else of importance."

Jane suddenly whirled on him. "Why," she asked fiercely. "Do you just like to take risks? You've already found out what you wanted to know. Those bastards could be out there just waiting for a chance to—" She broke off. Why ask when she knew the answers? "Do what you wish. What do I care if you want to behave like a self-indulgent child?"

"But you do care," he said softly, his gaze on her face. "Why, Jane? You try so hard not to give a damn about me, but it just keeps coming back, doesn't it? Why do you suppose that happens?"

Her hands clenched into fists at her sides. "I'll get over it."

"Oh, no, I can't allow that to come to pass." He smiled. "I've worked too hard. Every time we come together, I get a step closer. I get to know you a little better."

"And I don't really know you at all, Caleb."

His smile faded. "True. I've been very careful about that, but I might have to relinquish a bit of who I am to make you feel safer."

"And would I feel safer?"

"I don't know. It would be a risk." The brilliance of his smile came back full force. "But then I like risks. You might learn to like them, too." He turned and started back toward the path to the hills. "But not when it concerns your Eve." He looked back over his shoulder at her, and she was again aware of that charged electricity, the suppressed excitement that was just below the surface. Dear God, she was beginning to feel that same reckless disturbance she saw in him, she realized. She wanted to follow him into that mist. She wanted to find the thrill of danger and adventure she could sense in him.

And he could see it. "Never Eve," he repeated. "Never anyone you care about and protect. No risks there, I promise."

And then he was gone.

But who was going to protect Caleb? Who had ever protected him?

Just another thing that she didn't know about Seth Caleb.

And why was it hurting her to realize that he could have been vulnerable and in pain, and she would not have been able to help him?

Forget Caleb.

Go back into the tent. Finish packing, then go find Eve.

And keep all risk away from her and Cara and the child.

2:40 P.M.

SOUTHERN ATLANTIC CHARTER FLIGHT 1257
SOMEWHERE OVER THE ATLANTIC OCEAN

Three more hours, Joe told himself as he checked his watch. He'd land in Edinburgh in another two hours and catch a helicopter to Gaelkar.

Three more hours.

It was too long. He felt caught, helpless, in this plane above the Atlantic. He couldn't get to her.

His phone rang, and he glanced at the ID. Manez.

"I trust that you're winging your way across the Atlantic even as we speak," Manez said when Joe answered. "You caused something of an uproar, you know. Toller was most upset that you slipped away from his agent. He didn't find out that you weren't on that plane until he managed to get a head count from the flight attendants right before the flight reached Geneva."

"And how did you know?"

"I've been keeping my eye on you . . . and on Toller. Things are becoming . . . interesting. I assume you're finding it necessary to go and rescue your Eve. Salazar is on the move?"

"He's found out where Eve and Cara are."

"A very determined man. But Toller is also determined. He wants no interference. If he finds out where you are, he'll have you arrested, Quinn."

"Do you think I don't know that?" He paused. "And are you going to tell him where I'm headed?"

"I really should, in deference to international cooperation."

"Are you going to do it?"

"I don't actually know where you're going, do I? Of course you mentioned Scotland, but you were careful not to pin down a location." He was silent a moment. "And I don't like the way Toller is handling this. As I told you, he's not involving me in his investigations into Jenny Castino's death. This is my city. No one knows more about the cartel bosses than I do, including Castino. My conclusion was that Toller wanted to remain in control and manipulate events to suit himself. That made me very curious, so I decided to dig very hard into Toller's sources to discover who had given the tip that Jenny was Castino's daughter."

"And you found out?"

"It wasn't Sheriff Nalchek or anyone in his office."

"I didn't believe it was Nalchek."

"But you weren't sure that it wasn't one of his men. A reasonable conclusion. I looked there first."

"And where else did you look?"

"In places that weren't at all reasonable. I found an agent in Toller's department who was a bit careless, and I have excellent hackers on my team. Would you like to know who tipped Toller?"

"Stop playing games, Manez."

"I don't play games. But Toller may think he's going to do so," he said grimly. "But the U.S. government can stay out of my business." He paused. "James Walsh tipped off Toller that the body in the grave was Jenny Castino's."

"What?" His hand tightened in shock on the phone. "No way. Walsh killed Jenny. He wouldn't have done that."

"Unless he was trying to protect his ass if he thought Salazar was getting impatient and might try to take him out. Maybe he was trying to make a deal." Manez added, "I've seen stranger things happen. It's dog eat dog in the cartels down here. And there have been a lot of rumbles on the street lately. Something is going to happen. I can smell it."

"Look, there's no way I can concentrate on Toller or his plans that might be upsetting you right now. I owe you, and I'll get around to it once Eve and Cara are safe. Later, Manez."

"I'm not asking for help. I can handle my own problems. I just thought you should know that not everything is what it seems." He paused. "And that you probably have only five or six more hours before Toller manages to track you down. He's working hard, and he's very clever. Not as clever as I am, but he doesn't know that. Or he wouldn't have made the mistake of trying to ignore me. Good luck, Quinn." He hung up.

He might need good luck, Joe thought grimly. And he knew damn well that often nothing was as it seemed. But the information about Walsh had stunned him. But, as he'd told Manez, he couldn't

think about anything right now but getting to Eve and finding a way
to get rid of Salazar and Franco once and for all.

Three more hours.

4:45 P.M.

LOCH GAELKAR

"We leave for Edinburgh in thirty minutes, Eve." MacDuff had
suddenly appeared at the entrance of her tent, and his voice was curt.
"Get ready."

Eve scrambled to her feet. "I thought we were waiting for the fog
to lift. You said we couldn't even drive through this muck."

"We'll manage somehow. We can't wait any longer. I just got a
report from Caleb, and it wasn't good. He saw signs of Salazar's force
and activity in the hills. I don't like the idea of having you and Cara
stranded out here when we don't know exactly where Salazar is located."

"We could find out." Caleb was suddenly standing beside them.
"We know he's out there in the hills, and he's not alone. He's moving
fast, and I'd say he has at least nine or ten men with him. Hard to tell
in this fog. You'd better warn your guards that they may be out-
matched." He smiled. "Want to go hunting, MacDuff?"

"It appears you've already gone hunting," MacDuff said dryly.
"And I'm not going to do anything until I get Eve and Cara safe. I
checked with weather, and the fog is lighter in the valley beyond
Gaelkar. It's about seven miles, and we can hike there, and I'll have
a helicopter meet us. Where's Cara?"

"At the campfire with Jock. Where else? I'll go get her." Jane left
the tent and hurried toward the campfire.

"We all go. I promised Eve," Caleb said quietly. "Though I'd prefer to take Salazar's goons down ourselves. Between Jock and me, I

believe we'd have a good chance. And you're not too bad either, MacDuff."

"I'm flattered," MacDuff said dryly. "But I believe I'll call in Ned Colin and a few more of my men to accompany us until we get out of this fog. Not that I'd want to insult your—"

A shot shattered the words!

"What the hell!" MacDuff pushed Eve down to the ground and turned off the lantern.

Caleb was already out of the tent and zigzagging toward the campfire.

But Jock had already knocked Cara down and covered her with his body.

Another shot.

And a scream!

"Stay here." MacDuff was on his feet but crouching low as he ran out of the tent.

Eve rolled over and crawled toward the door. Let that scream not be Cara, she prayed. It had not sounded like a child, but it had been high-pitched.

Rat-a-tat-tat.

A rapid spate of bullets.

Another scream.

Not close. Somewhere in that gray mass of fog ahead.

She started to crawl across the ground toward the campfire. She caught up with MacDuff a moment later and rose to her feet.

"I told you to stay in the tent," MacDuff said, not looking at her. "You don't pay any more attention to orders than Jane." His gaze was raking the terrain. "Damn this fog." He took out his phone. "Don't worry, I'll call Colin and tell him to get down here."

Don't worry? "Do you see Cara or Jane?"

He was dialing rapidly. "Safe. Jock got them away from the fire and into those shrubs by the lake." He listened. "No answer. That's not good. I don't—"

"MacDuff?" The voice on the phone was so clear that Eve could hear it. "Alfredo Salazar. I'm afraid your man, Colin, is indisposed. Is Eve Duncan close by? I really need to talk to both of you."

MacDuff turned up the speaker. "I want to talk to Colin. What did you do to him?"

"I needed an example, and Franco ran across a prime candidate. He didn't want to cooperate, but we managed to convince him. Franco is very talented in that area. Are you listening, Eve Duncan? All of this is really for you and that annoying child."

"I'm listening."

"That's good. Then I can tell you that everything that happens from now on is on your head. Every scream, every death, is because you're here and causing me trouble. Do you hear that, MacDuff? All of this could end if you'd turn her and the kid over to us."

"Go to hell."

"Whatever you say," Salazar said. "And you Eve? You appear to be such a gentle person. Do you want to see MacDuff and your other friends die? And what about Jane MacGuire? You've managed to draw them all into something that wasn't your business in the first place."

"I'd be a fool to think that you'd let anyone live if I let Cara go to you," Eve said. "You'd never permit a witness to escape, Salazar."

"I might. If the price was high enough to make it worth my while. I understand that you and your friends might be able to pull something out of MacDuff's lake that would tempt me. Make me an offer."

"I'm not a fool."

"Oh well, first things first. Back to the example, MacDuff. We're taking your guard, Colin, to a place in the forest several hundred yards from your camp. He's still alive, but very frightened. Come and get him." He hung up.

Another shot.

An agonized groan from the depths of the fog.

"It's a trap," Eve said. "You won't be able to see them. They'll pick you off."

"I can't leave Colin out there," MacDuff said. "Salazar won't be able to see us either. I'll get Jock and Caleb to scout the area ahead, and I'll go in and get Colin. Go and stay with Cara and Jane. I'll call in the perimeter guards to protect you."

Before she could speak he was gone.

EDINBURGH AIRPORT

One more hour.

Joe strode across the tarmac toward the waiting helicopter. Providing he could get to Gaelkar in this pea soup of a fog, he thought bitterly. The weather forecast said that the fog wouldn't lift for that area for another eight to ten hours. Definitely not flying weather.

Screw it. He'd get there somehow. But first he'd check to see if MacDuff had managed to move Eve and Cara into a safe house here in Edinburgh.

His phone rang. Burbank. He'd asked Burbank to check on safe houses, too.

He accessed the call. "What's happening, Burbank?"

"Nothing," Burbank said. "Everything's at a standstill. We have a bit of a fog."

"So I've noticed. Why did you call?"

"You asked me to check on the specialities of the men Salazar hired from the Maitland Cartel. You seemed to think it important."

"It might be."

"Four of them are Afghani nationals and trained by the Taliban. Expert at explosives and setting *IEDs*."

"Shit!"

"I take it you do think that it's important."

"I should have guessed. Franco has a fondness for bombs, and he'd gravitate in that direction." And in this fog, you wouldn't be able to see a booby trap even if it wasn't set by an expert. "Thanks, Burbank." He hung up and called Eve.

She didn't answer.

He tried again.

She answered on the third ring. "Joe? I can't talk now. Things are bad. Salazar has shown up, and he's hurt one of MacDuff's men. MacDuff has gone after—"

"IEDs," he interrupted. "Tell MacDuff to be careful of IEDs. Salazar has imported some experts."

"I'll go and tell—"

She'd hung up.

He tried to get her back.

No answer.

And it scared him to death. The last thing he'd wanted was to have Eve running around in that fog after what he'd just found out.

He had to get to her.

He ran for the helicopter.

Eve was dialing MacDuff even as she ran toward the direction she'd seen him take.

No answer.

She hadn't expected one.

He wouldn't take time out to answer a phone when he was trying to save the man Salazar had shot.

Jock.

She dialed his number.

He answered. "Not a good time, Eve."

"IEDs. Joe said to be careful of IEDs. Tell MacDuff."

Jock muttered a curse. "No sign of anything yet. Caleb and I have been scouting all around, and I see MacDuff up ahead. And Salazar didn't move Colin to this area until after we heard the shots. We may only have to worry about snipers."

"Is that all?" Eve asked shakily. "That's enough. But Joe said that Salazar brought in some Taliban specialists they could be using. It might be—"

"Taliban?" Jock's voice was sharp. "Shit. No IEDs. That's not what they're doing. I was sent to one of their training camps, and they'd go another route. Hang up. I've got to get through to MacDuff. *Hell. No time.* I'll go after him. He should be getting near to Colin." He didn't bother to hang up, and she could tell he was running. He shouted, "MacDuff! Stop! Now! MacDuff! Get away from—"

Kaboom.

The earth shook, throwing Eve to the ground.

The thick fog ahead was lit by flames.

An explosion, she realized dazedly. Jock was wrong. There had been an IED . . .

She lifted herself on her elbow.

Or maybe not, she realized in horror.

MacDuff!

She jumped to her feet and ran toward the fire.

She had only gone several yards when Caleb appeared beside her. "No." He grabbed her arm. "You don't want to go there."

"Salazar strapped explosives to Colin's body, didn't he?" she asked shakily. "*He* was the trap."

"Yes, that way they didn't have to stay close and risk being attacked by MacDuff's men. They just pressed a button when their infrared showed MacDuff was close to the body."

"Dear God." Eve felt sick. She tried to shake off Caleb's hand. "Let me go."

Caleb's grip tightened. "No way. We can't be sure that Salazar didn't stash a sniper in those trees just in case he might get lucky if one of the targets showed. Go back to the camp."

"The hell I will. I have to get to MacDuff."

"No, you don't."

Her gaze suddenly flew to Caleb's face. "What do you mean? Is he dead?"

"I don't know. The blast got him, but I don't know how bad. Jock was examining him when I got there. He told me to secure the area and make sure you were all protected."

"Maybe I can help him."

"Not now. I promised you, I promised Jane, I promised Jock. You stay alive. No one touches you. I don't want to hurt you, but I will. We go back to camp."

He meant it.

"Then hurt me," she said fiercely. "Because I won't leave MacDuff without—"

"You don't have to leave him." Jock was coming out of the fog carrying MacDuff's limp figure. MacDuff was a strong, tall man, but Jock seemed no more aware of his weight than if he were a child. "I'm bringing him back to camp."

"Is he—"

"Dead? No, but I don't know if I can keep him alive. I don't know what's wrong with him yet." His eyes were glittering with unshed tears. He seemed to be in shock, the agony twisting his features was stunning to see. "I probably shouldn't have moved him, but I couldn't leave him there."

"No, of course not," Eve said gently. "Get him back to camp, and we'll take care of him."

"I will. They made a mistake hurting him. He's my friend, almost my brother. It was a bad mistake." He started toward the camp, then turned to look over his shoulder at Caleb. "There was someone in the trees when I got to MacDuff. He had a sniper rifle. After I was sure MacDuff wasn't dead, I decided I had time to take care of him. I broke him, but I didn't kill him. I thought that you might be able to get information out of him that might help."

"I'll do that."

"You don't have to hurry. I like the idea of his hurting." His tone was completely without expression. "If he doesn't talk, just leave him. He has to die anyway. They all have to die."

He disappeared into the fog.

Caleb gave a low whistle. "I believe Jock may be right. Salazar made a very bad mistake."

Eve called Joe the moment they got MacDuff back to his tent and settled.

"Thank God," he said when he heard her voice. "Are you safe?"

"I have no idea. Salazar is out there somewhere, and he's just blown up one of MacDuff's men. MacDuff was hit by the blast, and we still don't know if he's going to live. But right now I guess we're as safe as we can be. Salazar is trying threats and intimidation rather than going into attack mode."

"That sounds like attack mode to me," Joe said grimly.

"Where are you?"

"On my way. But I won't be able to land anywhere near Gaelkar. You're still fogged in. Can you get out?"

"I don't want to leave MacDuff, and I have no idea—" A call waiting buzzed on her cell. She stiffened as she looked down at the ID. "I'd better take this call. It's Salazar." She put Joe on hold and accessed the call. "You failed, Salazar. I know you'll be disappointed. You didn't kill MacDuff."

"I'm not sure I believe you. He must have been very close, or Franco would never have pressed the button to blow up Colin. It was a pity you didn't see it, Duncan. His remains were scattered all over the clearing."

"You're a monster."

"He wasn't important. MacDuff *was* important. Aren't you tempted to give yourself and that kid up and save anyone else you care about from being blown up? You're trapped, you know. If you try to go through the hills, we'll be on the lookout and catch you. If you try to take that road to escape, you'll end up like Colin."

"You're bluffing."

"Am I?" He spoke to someone over his shoulder, then was back on the phone. "Look up at the road. On the count of three. One. Two." He paused, then said softly, "Three."

A shot.

And an explosion at the side of the road at the top of the hill!

"Trapped," Salazar repeated. "IEDs. Think about saving the people who tried to save you." He hung up.

She drew a deep breath as she gazed at the fire burning the grass at the side of the road. Then she went back to Joe's call. "I guess we got an answer. No, we can't get out. Salazar has planted IEDs on the road that leads out of Gaelkar."

Joe muttered a curse. "How much time do you have before Salazar makes a move?"

She tried to think. "I have Jock. I have Caleb. I still have MacDuff's men who are in the hills. But I don't want to bring all of them here to make them sitting ducks. I'd rather they stay in the hills and be a constant threat to Salazar. I think maybe the reason Salazar hasn't come after us yet is that he doesn't have enough men to make it completely safe."

"Then I have to clear that road fast," Joe said. "I'll take the helicopter as close as I can, then hike the rest of the way. I'll be there as soon as I can."

"Joe . . ."

"Can you think of any other way?"

"No." But she didn't want Joe to have to fight to disarm those IEDs when it was impossible to see anything more than a couple feet in front of him. She felt sick at the very thought. "Damn this fog."

"Don't be too eager to condemn it. It may turn out to be a good friend to us." His voice was suddenly rough with feeling. "You take care of yourself. I'll call you when I get close to the lake."

"How is he, Jock?" Jane whispered as she came into MacDuff's tent two hours later. "Has he regained consciousness yet?"

Jock shook his head. "Not yet. He has a broken left forearm and at least two broken ribs. I don't how much internal damage. Blasts can—" He stopped. "It can be bad. I might have hurt him myself by moving him."

"You couldn't do anything else. He was helpless. You had to get him to safety, or those bastards might have decided to strap explosives on him, too."

"That wouldn't have happened. I wouldn't have left him." He gently touched MacDuff's temple. "He never left me. No matter what I did, he fought for me. I remember when I was in that mental hospital because I kept trying to commit suicide, he found me and he took me home. He was there for me until I healed." He shook his head. "No, I never really healed, but he was there until I was strong enough to face what I'd done and live with it."

"It wasn't you who did it," Jane said. "You were a victim. You were just a boy, not even twenty years old, and those brainwashing chemicals they fed you made you helpless to think. You had no idea what you were doing. How many times do MacDuff and I have to tell you that?"

"I was a victim? That bastard, Reilly, proudly counted my kills at over twenty-two. All executed perfectly. I was an assassin par excellence. What about those victims?"

"MacDuff wouldn't like to hear you talk like that."

"And I don't, when he's around. I keep it inside so that he won't feel that he's failed me in any way." His lips twisted. "He hasn't failed me, Jane. You haven't failed me. But I have to work my way through this hell, and no one else can help me at this point." He looked back at MacDuff. "I love him, you know. There's nothing I wouldn't do for him. I'd die for him. Every bit of sanity and humanity I have left, I owe to him."

"No, that's not true. You were born with a soul, and, somehow, you were robbed and hurt. Even if MacDuff hadn't been there, I think that, somehow, you would have survived."

"We disagree." He smiled without mirth. "Right now, I'm lean-ing toward the thought that without MacDuff, my soul would have vanished in a puff of smoke. So I have to keep him alive, don't I?"

"Will you trust me to sit with him?" Jane asked. "I'll call you the minute he stirs."

He shook his head. "I trust you, Jane. But what if he doesn't stir? I have the foolish idea that if he starts to fade away from me, I might be able to bring him back."

"That's not such a foolish idea." She cleared her throat to rid it of tightness. She had felt like that when her Trevor had been dying. It had seemed impossible that he could leave her when she had wanted so badly for him to stay. "I'll be outside. Call me, if you need me, okay?"

"Okay." His gaze shifted back to MacDuff. "Thank you, Jane."

She stood there, looking helplessly at him for an instant, then left the tent.

She didn't move for a moment, trying to rid herself of this feel-ing of discouragement and sadness. She had known MacDuff for years and Jock for almost as long. They were part of her past, part of her life, and she couldn't bear the thought of what was happening to them. There had to be something she could do.

"Is he still alive?"

She looked to her right and saw Cara sitting on the ground, lean-ing against the tent, her legs crossed, her face shimmering pale in the fog. "What are you doing here? I thought you were with Eve."

"She knows I'm here. She said it was okay. She wouldn't tell me, but I don't think she wanted to bother about me right now. She's wor-ried about Joe." She paused. "Is the Laird still alive?"

"Yes."

"But Jock thinks he might die."

"How did you know that?"

"I saw his face when he carried him into the tent. It . . . hurt me."

"And you've been sitting out here ever since?"

"You were with Jock. He didn't need me."

"Well, evidently he didn't need me either." She wearily rubbed the back of her neck. "He told me to go about my business."

"Then is it all right if I go in and sit with him?"

"It's not the time, Cara. He won't want you either."

"May I try?"

Jane gazed at her. What could she say? The strain she saw on Cara's face was almost an echo of Jock's. "He might say things you won't want to hear. He's in pain."

"I know." Her lips were trembling. "And it's my fault."

Jane looked at her, shocked. "No!"

Cara nodded. "Salazar and Franco wouldn't have come here except for me. The Laird wouldn't have been hurt. Jock wouldn't have lost . . . It's my fault."

"Nonsense." She tried to make her voice firm. "It's Salazar and Franco who did all this. MacDuff and Jock had a choice. Eve had a choice. I had a choice. Sometimes you just have to fight the bad guys when you run across them. It's the way the world works. None of this was your fault, Cara."

She didn't speak for a moment. "May I go in to Jock?"

Jane wasn't sure she had gotten through to her, but she didn't want Cara sitting out here by herself. "I guess. I'll be in my tent or Eve's if you need me."

Cara nodded, and the next moment, she was on her feet and running into MacDuff's tent.

Jane shook her head and turned to go to find Eve, who was probably in just as much pain as the two people she had just left.

"What are you doing here?" Jock asked Cara, without looking away from MacDuff. "This is no place for you. You shouldn't be here, Cara."

"Yes, I should." She came closer to his camp chair and sat down on the floor at his feet. "I have to stay with you."

He shook his head. "Why? Do you want to see him die? That's what might happen. Go away."

"No. You need me."

"I don't need anyone." He looked away from MacDuff and down at her. "You're just a kid. Why should I need you?"

"I don't know. But you said some things . . . I think you do." She moistened her lips. "And I have to be here if you do."

"You were upset. I wanted to make you feel better."

"And you want to make me feel better now. You don't want me to be here if the Laird dies." She paused. "But I remember what you said when you told me you had to go to the Laird after he heard that Mac-Tavish had been killed. You knew he needed you. If only to keep him company, or be someone to drink with to say good-bye to an old friend." She tried to smile. "I can be company, Jock. If you want, I'll even drink to the Laird if he doesn't make it. But I'd rather pray that he does."

He looked at her for a long moment. "I'd rather you pray, too," he said gruffly. "Eve would have my head if I contributed to the delinquency of a minor."

"I can stay?"

"God, yes." He closed his eyes for an instant, then opened them and looked back at MacDuff. "Maybe I do need you." His hand touched her head at his knee for the briefest instant. "Stranger things have happened in my life. Just don't blame me if things don't go the way we'd like them."

"You're not the one to blame," she whispered. "I tried to tell Jane that but she wouldn't—" She stopped. She had gotten what she wanted, and he would probably argue as Jane had done. None of them understood. Jenny and Elena dead. Salazar hovering over them, ready to pounce. "I'll be quiet now. You won't want me to talk." She leaned her head back against his chair. "Thank you for letting me be with you, Jock . . ."

CHAPTER

14

J oe?" Eve leaped for her cell when it rang. She had been on pins and needles worrying about him for the past three hours. "Where are you?"

"I've reached a point on the road that's two miles east of the lake where I've just located and removed two IEDs. I'll have to take it very slowly from now on. It appears as if these two were planted very hurriedly and hopefully so will the others. They'll be a lot easier to disarm. But hurry breeds carelessness. I can't let my guard down." He paused. "Is either Jock or Caleb available? I haven't seen any sign yet of Salazar's men, but I could use another set of eyes and ears to watch my back."

"I'll check it out. I'll find someone."

"Tell them to stop on the slope and avoid the edge of the road and call me when they get close. I'll guide them to a safe access where I've already removed the IEDs."

"Right. Be careful, Joe." She hung up and drew a deep breath. Her heart was beating rapidly, and her palms were damp. She ran out of the tent to look up the long, steep slope that led to the road. She could see nothing, of course, but she knew that Joe was somewhere in that thick gray fog. The knowledge was filling her with hope and joy and a terrible fear.

Because he was alone and needed help.

She ran to Jane's tent. "Joe's here. He could use some help clearing the road. Where's Caleb?"

"He's scouting the perimeter with three of MacDuff's men." She reached for her phone. "I'll call him."

"Wait." She tried to think. MacDuff was down and perhaps dying. Jock's care might be the only barrier between MacDuff and death. Caleb was the only protection Cara and Jane had, and he might be forced to extend that protection to MacDuff. She couldn't let that protection be taken away from them. "Call Caleb. Tell him once he's finished to come back and stay on guard here until we get those IEDs cleared."

"We?" Jane repeated. She shook her head. "I don't like the sound of that, Eve."

"Neither do I. But we're stretched too thin. Joe needs help. "

"Then let me go."

Eve shook her head. "Joe and I are a team. Sometimes he doesn't recognize that fact, but I'm not going to let him do that job alone. It's not as if I have to have a particular set of skills. I just have to do what Joe tells me to do. I watched him change the settings on that damn bomb Franco planted in our car, and I hated every minute of it. I won't let him push me out of the way now." She grabbed her flashlight and gun. "You'll keep Cara safe?"

"Of course, I will. But since she won't leave Jock, I may not have the opportunity for much interaction."

"Jock is more than enough protection. I'll be back as soon as I can, and we'll get the hell out of here." She gave Jane a quick hug and tore up the hill toward the road.

"Colin . . ."

The word was so weak that Cara barely heard it.

But she knew Jock had heard it because his entire body had stiffened, galvanized. He leaned toward MacDuff. "Don't talk. You've been—"

"Colin," MacDuff said, his voice stronger. "What happened to Colin?"

"Dead. The bastard strapped a bomb to him."

"Son of a bitch," MacDuff said. "Did you . . . get them?"

"Not yet. I've been busy."

"Just as well. I want to do it myself . . ."

"You might have to wait a bit. How do you feel?"

"Sore." He thought about it. "A bad headache. The blast?"

"Yes. You have a couple broken bones. I don't know about internal injuries. We need to get you to a doctor to check you out."

"I'll be fine." His glance fell on Cara. "What are you . . . doing here?"

"Praying." She smiled. "Jock said I shouldn't be allowed to drink with him. I'm glad you're back with us, sir."

"So am I. I guess that nonsense is supposed . . . to mean something. But I'm too tired to decode it at the moment." He closed his eyes. "Is everything okay, Jock? We can get out of here?"

"Everything is okay," Jock said. "We've got it under control. Quinn will be here any minute. We've just been waiting for you to come around so that we can start moving. But you can take a nap until we're ready."

"That sounds a little . . . condescending." His eyes were closing. "I'll have a word to say to you later . . ."

"You do that." Jock swallowed hard. "Later."

A moment later, Jock sat back in his chair as MacDuff's breathing steadied, then deepened.

"He's safe?" Cara whispered.

"I believe so. We'll have to see." He smiled down at her, that radiant smile that lit up his entire face. "He's complaining and trying to order me about. That's a good sign."

"Is it?" she asked eagerly. She was so happy to see that smile. "But he'll be angry when he wakes up and finds you've lied to him."

"Maybe when he wakes up, it won't be a lie." He reached down and helped her to her feet. "Now go and tell Jane that MacDuff has regained consciousness and everything that's happened. She'll want to know and come to check him out for herself."

Cara nodded. "I'll go right away." She flew toward the door. "I'll be right back."

"I know you will. You're very determined, Cara. And what a blessed quality that can be." He added gently, "Sometimes a mixed blessing, but in you it's pure gold."

Joe had said to call before she left the slope to go on the road, Eve thought. Well, he hadn't actually been referring to her, but she was here, and he'd have to deal with it. With the fog still as thick as it was, the fact that she had come instead of Caleb should be the least of his worries. Not that he would look at it that way.

She dialed Joe's number. "I'm on the slope about one yard down and closest to the west approach to the road. Can you get me safely on the road?"

Silence. "Eve?" Then he was swearing. "Get the hell back down to that camp."

"Get me safely on the road," she repeated. "You needed someone to watch your back. I've been doing that job for years. Things are dicey down there at the camp. I'm the only one really available."

"Then I can do it alone. All I wanted was—"

"Someone to keep anyone from shooting you while you concentrated on disarming those IEDs. I can watch. I can shoot. And no one cares more than I do that you come out of this alive."

"Eve, for God's sake, you're going to have a baby. If you won't be careful of yourself, think of the child."

"Do you think that I'm not thinking of my baby? I haven't been thinking of anything else since I started up here." Her voice was shaking. "No, that's not true. I was also thinking about you. I was thinking that you have to live. My child needs a father, and it has to be you. Because you'll always be there, you'll always protect and keep our baby safe. Just as you're going to do in the next couple hours. You'll keep us all safe. Because that's what you do." She started to move up the slope. "I'm coming, Joe. Tell me where to go, where to step."

Silence. "Hang up the damn phone. You're so close I can hear you without it." He drew a harsh breath. "I think you're about ten feet to the left from me. I haven't had a chance to disarm that far on the road yet." He repeated. "Ten feet, Eve. Count those feet aloud to me so I can track your voice."

"One. Two. Three. Four." She was moving slowly, trying to be precise. How could she be exact when she could barely see where she was going? And how had Joe managed to disarm any of those explosives? He must have had to be painstakingly careful. No wonder he'd needed someone else to keep watch for Salazar's men when he'd had to concentrate on just keeping from being blown up. "Five. Six. Seven." She could smell the burned grass on the side of the road from the explosion Salazar had ignited to show her how helpless they all were. Screw you, Salazar. Joe wasn't helpless, and neither was she. They'd get through this. "Eight. Nine—"

"That's far enough." Joe was suddenly in front of her, grabbing her wrist and jerking her up on the road. "Keep still for a minute. Get your balance. This isn't time for a misstep." He held her close, burying his face in her hair. "Damn you, Eve," he said hoarsely. "You shouldn't have done—"

"Hush." She held him closer. She could feel his heart pounding against her, the scent of him, the warmth of him. "And you shouldn't swear at me when you're so scared I'm going to die. Think how you'd regret it if I did." Then she pushed him away. She had needed that moment. But they needed to get off this road more than she needed comfort. "Now let's get to it." She took a step back away from him. "You said no sign of Salazar's men up here yet?"

"No, but that doesn't mean he won't send a man up to check to make sure that someone isn't trying to destroy his booby traps. And that's why I can't just explode the IEDs. I had to have Burbank send one of his men to meet my helicopter with a military Stingray water-blade device so I could scramble the IEDs' firepower."

Eve nodded. "Whatever. I don't know what the hell you're talking about. But Salazar's more likely to think that he has us cowed down at the camp. He has to know that he injured MacDuff and that Caleb has been scouting the hill area. He doesn't know about you. He believes he has us all contained. His focus will probably be on attack and conquer." She looked down the road. "And does he have us contained? Do you have any idea how far these explosives are planted on the road?"

"I'd have to have a crystal ball to know that. All I can do is try to clear enough of the road to make it safe for us to get two vehicles up from your base camp and safely on the way out of the Gaelkar area. We'll need at least two since MacDuff is injured." His lips twisted. "And it's not going very quickly, Eve. It might take at least another couple hours."

"I can see how it might."

"Of course, we could wait for the fog to lift and just take the fight to Salazar. But I'd rather get you, Jane, and Cara out of here and somewhere safe. I'll be as fast as I can."

"As fast as it's safe," she corrected. "No hurry." She tried to smile. "Take your time. You have a great backup."

"Yes, I do." He turned away. "Keep behind me and close. If I say jump, you don't question, you dive for the side of the road and roll down the slope. Promise me."

"I promise. What else?"

"Primarily, I need you to listen since you can't see a damn thing."

"How can you see the IEDs?"

"Very carefully." He took out a LED penlight. "I shaded the beam, and I'm focusing only on the ground and also blocking the light with my body. Hopefully, the fog is doing the rest."

"You said we might be grateful to this fog."

"At the moment. Up to now, it's been a royal pain in the ass."

He was crouching low, his gaze fixed intently on the ground, moving with extreme care. He was on task, fully focused on the job ahead.

Do your part, Eve told herself.

Keep close.

Listen, he had said.

Concentrate on everything around them so that Joe would not be forced to do it.

Listen . . .

"MacDuff's awake!" Cara burst into Jane's tent, her eyes shining with excitement. "Just now. He woke up and spoke to Jock. Well, me, too. But I think I just confused him, but he knew me, and he—"

"Slow down." Jane jumped to her feet. "What are you trying to tell me." She hoped it was what she thought Cara was trying to say. "MacDuff is better?"

"That's what I said." Cara drew a deep breath. "He woke up, and he spoke to Jock. He asked about Colin, and when Jock told him that he was dead, he asked if Jock had taken care of Salazar. He said he was glad Jock hadn't had the time because he wanted to do it himself."

"That sounds like MacDuff," Jane said. "He *is* better."

"Jock thinks he's going to be okay." Cara's face was glowing. "But then he fell asleep again, and Jock told me to run and get you. He told me to tell you everything. He said he knew that you'd want to come and see for yourself."

"Yes, I do." She felt as if an enormous burden had been lifted. MacDuff was going to live. "I'll go right away."

"I'll go with you." Cara was heading for the door. Then she stopped. "No, I'll go to Eve's tent and tell her. She'll want to know."

Jane suddenly remembered that Cara wasn't aware that Eve had gone to help Joe. She wasn't about to worry her about another potential danger when she was so happy about MacDuff. "No, come back with me. Joe showed up while you were with Jock, and Eve's helping him find a way to get us out of here."

"Joe's here?" Cara smiled eagerly. "Everything's going right, isn't it, Jane?"

"It appears to be on the right path." She took Cara's arm. "Come on, let's get back to Jock."

They were out in the dark, and the fog closed in on them once more.

It was only when they were almost to MacDuff's tent that a thought occurred to Jane that caused a chill to go through her that had nothing to do with the fog.

She hesitated, almost stopped.

No. It didn't have to be true.

"Jane?"

Cara had caught the hesitation and was staring at her.

"Coming." Jane started forward again.

The next moment they were in MacDuff's tent.

"I brought her, Jock," Cara said. "You were right, she wants to see MacDuff for—" She stopped.

Jock was not in the tent.

MacDuff was sleeping peacefully on the cot, but Jock was nowhere in sight.

"Where's Jock?" Cara whispered.

It's what Jane wanted to know. But she didn't want to alarm Cara. "Maybe he needed to take a break. He's been cooped up in here since he brought MacDuff back. He'll probably be back in a minute."

"Jane." MacDuff's eyes were open. "All hell is breaking loose. You need to get Eve and the girl out of here."

"Shh." She went to him and took his hand. "We're working on

it. Joe is here. That will be a big help. You just relax and let us handle it." She smiled. "This one time the Laird isn't going to give the orders."

"Then God help us." His eyes started to close again. "Maybe you should take over. After all, you're family. Cira might decide to give you a hand. It's not beyond the . . ." He was asleep again.

And Jane's hand tightened on his for a moment before she released it. God had already helped them, she thought gratefully. MacDuff was back with them. Like Jock, she was sure that he would be all right now.

Jock.

The chill returned as she turned away from MacDuff. "I think I'll go to Jock's tent and see what's keeping him, Cara. Will you stay with MacDuff while I'm—"

Cara was gone.

Panic.

"Shit!"

Jane ran out of the tent.

Fog. Darkness. Fear.

"Cara!"

Smother the panic. Maybe she'd gone to Jock's tent to look for him.

She ran down the row of tents.

Jock's tent was dark.

No Jock.

No Cara.

Jane's heart was beating hard, painfully.

But there was a note scrawled on a piece of paper pinned to the canvas beside the door.

It won't take long, Jane.

"Damn, damn, damn." She dialed Jock.

No answer.

She took a deep breath and phoned Caleb. "I need you to come back to the camp right away. Things are happening, and I need help."

"I'm already on my way," Caleb said. "Jock called me and told me that. I should be there soon."

"Jock called you? When?"

"About ten minutes ago. He said MacDuff was better but that you were going to need me."

"He must have called you right after he sent Cara to get me." Her hand tightened on the phone. "I was so damn happy about MacDuff that it didn't occur to me right away. Why would he have to send her to get me? Why not just phone me and tell me to come."

"He wanted to get rid of her." Caleb asked, "He's gone, Jane?"

"You're not surprised. Did he tell you?"

"No, but I knew it was bound to happen. Jock would have gone for Salazar after he found MacDuff if he hadn't had to try to save him. He cares about MacDuff. He wasn't going to let anyone who hurt him live. When he called to tell me that you'd need me, I thought that he judged it was time." He paused. "I wouldn't worry about him. From what I've heard about Jock, it's Salazar who should worry."

"I do worry about him. I know very well what Jock is capable of. Do you think I want him to start killing again?" Her voice was shaking. "And what about Cara? I suppose I shouldn't worry about her either?"

"Cara?"

"I turned away for a moment to talk to MacDuff, and she was gone. I'm sure she went after Jock. She's out there in the darkness and the fog looking for him. Hell, she wants to take *care* of him."

"We'll find her."

"Before Salazar finds her? Before Franco finds her?"

"I'll call Jock and tell him to locate her and bring her back."

"I tried. He's not answering. He obviously doesn't want anyone to interfere with what he's going to do. Which means Cara can't reach him either. She's alone out there."

"She won't be alone long. As soon as I assign some men to taking care of you and MacDuff, I'll start tracking her."

"I'm going with you. You assign men you can trust to care for MacDuff. I'm not going sit here and twiddle my thumbs while Cara is out there."

"I can travel faster without you."

"No, you can't. I'll do whatever I have to do. I promised Eve when she went to help Joe that I wouldn't let anything happen to Cara. I *promised* her. I'm not going to break that promise."

"Okay, calm down. We'll make it work. We already have a start."

"What start?"

"Jock took down a sniper on the scene where Colin was blown up. He told me he broke him but didn't kill him. He sent me to get information from him while he tended to MacDuff."

"You didn't tell me that."

"It wasn't pleasant, and what I did to get that information wasn't pleasant either. I didn't want to shock your delicate sensibilities."

"But you got the information? Will it help?"

"It will help." He hung up.

He was close, Jock thought as he moved silently through the forest. He could hear Salazar's men up ahead. No conversation, just breathing, and the sound of footsteps on the wet leaves. Salazar had probably told them to be quiet, so that the team Caleb had patrolling the perimeter wouldn't spot them.

But they were amateurs, Jock thought. Even Salazar and Franco would have been disposed of in a matter of moments if they'd been designated as prey by Reilly, the man who had trained Jock all those years ago.

He increased his pace. Get it over with. He didn't know how

many men Salazar had stationed around their camp. He might have to get back and help Caleb take them out.

He stopped and listened. At least six men moving single file through the forest.

Single file. That would make it easier.

Remove them one by one until he got to the head of the column.

And hope it was Salazar.

No, not six men. One stride was lighter, shorter-spanned, the rhythm different. Boots, but not like the others.

A woman.

Natalie Castino?

It didn't matter. It wasn't as if he hadn't killed women before. And, according to what Quinn had told Eve, this woman might have tried to kill Cara.

So just block out the ingrained hesitance and concentrate on being the assassin that Reilly had created. It would be no problem. He could feel the past training slipping effortlessly into place.

No joy. There had never been joy. Just a steel-like intensity and determination that was focused on the prey.

No, there was something more that was involved. Because this was not the usual prey.

Revenge.

"Done."

Joe turned to face Eve. "We've cleared enough of the road for the cars. Let's get the hell out of here."

Eve breathed a sigh of relief. It hadn't taken as long as she'd thought it would for Joe to disarm those IEDs, but every minute that had passed had been excruciating. "I'll second the motion." She looked down at the lake, and she could see a faint watery outline in the darkness. "And it appears to be just in time. Some of the fog is dispersing. It was going to be easier for them to see what we were doing soon."

"But we'll be able to see his men if they try to plant any more explosives, too." He took her arm, led her across the road to the slope, then carefully helped her start down the slippery incline. "Now let's get down to the camp and get you all packed and out of here."

"We've already packed up most of it. It's MacDuff we have to worry about. Lord, I hope we have to worry about him." She took out her phone and dialed Jane. "When I left, I wasn't sure if he was going to make it. I know Jane knew what we're doing and wouldn't have called and disturbed me, but I have to check on—" She broke off as Jane picked up. "Jane, we're through up here. Joe got the job done. We're coming down."

"Thank God," Jane said. "At least, that's one thing that's positive."

Eve stiffened. "MacDuff?"

"No, he's doing better. Which freed up Jock to go hunting." She paused. "And for Cara to get it into her head to follow him."

"What?"

"I know. I'm as afraid as you are. Caleb and I are searching the forest for Cara now. We haven't found any sign of her yet. We've just got to hope that Cara finds Jock before anyone else finds her."

"Yes," Eve said numbly. "We've got to hope. Joe and I will start searching as soon as we get down. We'll split up the territory." She hung up and told Joe, "Cara's gone. She followed Jock when he went after Salazar."

Joe muttered a curse. "Why in hell would she—"

"We both know why she'd do it," Eve said. "She's had too many people die trying to keep her alive. She can't help but blame herself. She cares about Jock. She couldn't bear the idea of not going with him, helping him, if he was going to be in danger." She started at a half run down the slope, slipping and sliding, catching herself. "We've got to find her, Joe. There has to be some way . . ."

•   •   •

Jock twisted hard, and the man's neck snapped.

His knees buckled and Jock lowered him carefully to the ground.

Three down.

Four men to go.

And the woman.

She was clumsier than the men, and occasionally someone in the party would try to steady her, help her.

Everything was going smoothly.

He'd soon have them all.

His phone was vibrating again. He'd been ignoring it since he left the camp. It was a rule that you never answered a call when you were on a mission. Particularly this mission. Too many people he cared about would be trying to interfere.

He prepared to ignore it again. He moved down the path, making no sound, listening. There was a curve up ahead. He could detect the swish of bodies on the shrubs as they took the turn. If Jock cut left into the trees, he should be able to bring down the next prey before he made that turn.

He moved swiftly into the trees.

His phone vibrated again.

Ignore it, as he'd done since the hunt began. He should have turned it off. But he couldn't do it while MacDuff was lying in that tent injured.

It vibrated again.

He impatiently glanced down at the screen.

A text.

I CAN'T FIND YOU. I'M ON THE HILL NEAREST THE LAKE. WHY DON'T YOU ANSWER ME? YOU SHOULDN'T HAVE GONE. WHERE ARE YOU, JOCK?

Oh, my God.

Cara.

He was standing in the woods on the hill nearest the lake at this moment.

And he'd just killed three of Salazar's men on this hill.

Don't call her. Don't make a sound that would draw anyone's attention to her. His fingers flew over the keys.

PUT YOUR PHONE ON VIBRATE. DON'T MOVE. STAY WHERE YOU ARE.

I AM ON VIBRATE. IT WOULD BE PRETTY STUPID NOT TO BE. JUST AS YOU'RE STUPID TO HAVE TRIED TO FOOL ME. I TRUSTED YOU. NOW YOU COME BACK WITH ME. YOU'RE NOT GOING TO BE HURT. I WON'T LET THAT HAPPEN. IF YOU DON'T CARE WHAT I THINK, DO IT FOR MACDUFF. NEVER MIND, HE PROBABLY LIKES THE IDEA OF EVERYBODY'S KILLING EACH OTHER, TOO. IT'S NOT WORTH IT. DO YOU HEAR ME? IT'S NOT WORTH IT. NOW WHERE CAN I FIND YOU?

CARA, WHY ON EARTH DID YOU FOLLOW ME?

YOU WERE ALONE. I DIDN'T WANT YOU TO BE ALONE.

Such a simple answer. An answer that had led her to risk everything. Dear God, an answer that he should have known would be triggered when he'd left MacDuff's tent tonight.

WHERE ARE YOU ON THE HILL? ARE THERE ANY LANDMARKS? WHAT DO YOU SEE?

FOG. THOUGH IT'S NOT NEARLY AS BAD AS IT WAS BEFORE. JUST TREES. LOTS OF TREES.

No help at all.

CARA, LISTEN TO ME. STOP LOOKING FOR ME. FIND A PLACE
WITH SOME COVER AND HIDE. I'M NOT SURE HOW CLOSE SALA-
ZAR IS TO YOU.

WHERE ARE YOU?

CLOSE. STOP LOOKING FOR ME. TRUST ME. I'LL COME TO YOU
RIGHT AWAY. WAIT FOR ME.

Silence.

I'LL WAIT FOR YOU.

Thank God. He had bought some time. But now he had to move
fast and try to neutralize any threats to her. He could no longer hear
Salazar and his men. They had passed out of his range while he was
texting Cara. He dashed off a text to Caleb.

CARA. ON THE FIRST HILL NEXT TO THE LAKE.

He stuffed his phone in his pocket and took off through the woods
in the direction he'd last tracked Salazar's men.

Find a place with cover and hide, Jock had said.
    Cara had no idea where that would be, she thought desperately.
As she had told Jock, there was no cover, no boulders. Just a few shrubs
along the path. Well, then use what there was available. She scavenged
around and found a few large branches on the ground, then dragged
them deeper into the woods and tried to rig a barrier among the
shrubs.

Hide.

She started to move behind her barrier.

She stopped.

A sound.

A footstep.

Jock?

Don't take a chance.

She had to take care of Jock.

Her fingers were flying over the keys.

STAY—

It was the only word she had time to type before the phone was knocked out of her hand.

Then an arm was around her neck, cutting off her breath.

"How nice to see you again, Cara." Ramon Franco's voice in her ear was the last thing she heard before a cloth was rammed over her mouth and nose. "I've been looking forward to this. You've been making me look very, very bad."

Chloroform.

Darkness.

STAY—

Jock gazed blindly down at the phone he'd just picked up from the ground where Cara had dropped it. Her phone and the single word that was tearing him apart.

A warning. Even at that moment when Cara knew she might be caught, lost, she was trying to save him. If she hadn't taken the time to type in that word, could she have saved herself?

He didn't know, he couldn't think. All he could do was look at that word.

She was the target. How long would they let her live? Maybe

they'd killed her already. Maybe he'd find her body within yards of this barrier she'd built.

Agony. So deep, so sharp, that he couldn't bear it.

He had to bear it. Because there was a chance. He couldn't let that chance vanish.

STAY—

Block it. Look at the scene. Look at the footprints that usually told the story.

He knelt on the ground and examined the prints of the man who had taken Cara. Concentrate. Tell yourself she's alive. Don't give up and fall apart.

STAY—

"They've got her," Jock said jerkily as he handed Eve Cara's phone over an hour later, when Eve and Joe met with him in the woods. "I found this on the ground in the woods. She was trying to text me a warning, but she didn't get the chance."

When had Cara ever had a chance, Eve thought numbly as she gazed down at the one word on the screen. "You didn't find her body?"

"No. I don't think they've killed her yet. It was a single man who captured her. Not Salazar. This man was smaller, lighter. Probably Ramon Franco. And his footprints were heavier when he left the scene than when he came. He was carrying something heavy enough to be Cara." He handed her a white towel. "And this was tossed into the shrubs where I found the phone."

Joe took the towel and sniffed it. "Chloroform."

"Which means we have a chance to negotiate," Jock said. "They took her captive, but she's not dead." His lips thinned. "She's not going to be dead. Stall. I'll get her back."

"We'll get her back," Joe said quietly. "But we may not have much time. The intent was always to kill Cara and remove the evidence of who had taken her from Castino. Like Eve, I expected to find only her body if Salazar got his hands on her. Unless they wanted to dispose of it as they tried to do with Jenny's body."

"Of course, that's what they'd want to do." Eve shivered. "And they have a deep lake and all of these hills to hide her." How could they be standing here talking about Cara's death? All she could think about was Cara's laugh, her wistful eyes, her absorbed, intent, expression when she was playing her violin.

And that's all she would think about, because she wouldn't accept that they could lose her.

Okay, then try to find a different outcome. There had to be some way. Her mind began racing frantically, weighing options, trying to recall her contacts with Salazar . . . and Natalie Castino.

Joe's gaze was fixed on her face. "Eve, she's alive. We have hope."

He probably thought she was in shock, she thought. He was only half-right. "They could have had another reason for not killing Cara right away. They want me, too. They believe I know too much. Maybe they want to find a way to get hold of us both."

"You mean use Cara as bait to trap you?" Jock asked.

"It's possible. And we might be able to turn it around to close the trap on them." Her lips tightened. "Or I'd be content just to get Cara out of their hands. No, I'd be ecstatic."

"No bait," Joe said flatly. "We'll try something else."

"We'll try whatever we think might work." Eve looked him in the eye. "Remember when we talked about a division of labor about keeping Cara safe? You stayed behind and worked behind the scenes to find out what was going on and put up a smoke screen. My job was to stay with Cara and keep her safe. You did your job. I didn't do mine. I didn't watch her close enough. Well, it's time I made that right."

"It was my fault," Jock said hoarsely. "I didn't think. I was just feeling, or I would have known what Cara would do."

"And it was Cara's fault for running after you because she was afraid that you'd be killed like her Jenny, like Elena," Eve said. "We can blame ourselves all night, and it's not going to bring her back. We have to stop it and get to work."

"You may be wrong," Joe said. "If we wait until Salazar puts out bait instead of going after him, Cara could be killed."

"No, we can't wait." She had a sudden thought. "But maybe we don't go to Salazar. Maybe we go around him."

"Around him?" Joe repeated. "What do you mean?"

"Natalie Castino. I told you about the fairy story she was handing me when she called me."

"She was trying to trap you."

"I don't doubt that for a minute. But she was wonderfully plausible, and I had to question my own instincts at the time. She's clever, and I'm sure she plays everyone around her as skillfully as Cara does her violin." She paused. "You got the impression that she was in control of everything she did. Was she in control of Salazar?"

"Possibly."

"Probably. She'd made the effort to keep him as a lover for all those years. But she wouldn't let him know that he was dispensable unless she was prepared to jettison him." She turned to Jock. "When you called us and told us to come here, you said that you'd been tracking Salazar's men. Was Natalie Castino with them?"

"There was a woman with them. I assumed that it was her. I never saw her."

"Then her story was definitely bogus. We have to work from there." She was thinking frantically, going over her conversation with Natalie sentence by sentence. "What are her priorities? She wants to be safe. She likes power and wants to maintain it. She doesn't want to be under her father's thumb or her husband's or Salazar's, but she's capable of using all of them. She wants to be queen and will do anything to—" She stopped. "But a queen needs a crown and a treasury, doesn't she? That may be the bait we need to tempt her."

"Treasury," Joe repeated. "As in treasure?"

She nodded. "She mentioned the treasure while she was talking to me. She asked if we'd found it yet. And Salazar said something about the possibility of a deal later. There was definitely an interest from both of them in Cira's gold."

"Then maybe we should deal with Salazar if he wants it, too," Joe said.

"You have nothing with which to deal," Jock said. "We haven't found it yet, dammit."

"But we know where it might be," Eve said. "If I have to, I'll use that to strike a deal."

"Salazar is desperate," Joe said. "He's not going to risk Cara's being found and talking about his arranging for that kidnapping on the chance that there might be a big payoff. He'll take the safe road."

And the safe road was to kill Cara. Eve knew he was right, and she was desperate herself, or she wouldn't be considering taking the risk. "Then we deal with Natalie Castino. She's not desperate. I'm sure she wants Cara dead to protect herself, but if you could have heard her talking to me, you'd realize that she thinks she rules the world. Why not? She's convinced everyone that she had nothing to do with her daughter's disappearance for the past eight years. She has a superb self-confidence. She'll think she can deal and get the best of me and have it all. We just have to make sure that she's wrong."

"What can I do?" Jock asked. A muscle in his cheek jerked as he bared his teeth from tension. "I have to *do* something. I'm not thinking very well right now. Tell me how to help. Tell me how to get her back."

"Any way you look at it, we have to remove Salazar's men and try to leave him defenseless," Joe said. "From what you said, you were on your way to doing that before you found out about Cara. But we can't risk making him edgy until we're sure we have a way to get Cara. We'll just plan and set up, then execute when she's safe." He added, "You found Salazar once. Can you find him again?"

"I'll find him," he said grimly.

"Cara will probably be with them. You'll want to step in and take her," Joe said. "Don't do it. Don't take the chance."

Jock was silent.

"Don't do it, Jock," Eve said. "Just let us know and keep watch over her."

He finally said, "I'll keep watch." He added, "And you won't have many men to take out by that time. But I don't promise anything." He turned to leave. "I'll let you know when I find them. It will be very soon."

Eve watched him walk away. She could almost feel his pain, which was making him as volatile as the IEDs Joe had disarmed tonight.

But nothing was going to disarm Jock but seeing Cara alive and free.

"I don't promise either," Joe said roughly. "I don't like any of this, and if I could see any other way, I'd take it. But I'm not going to let you sacrifice yourself to save Cara. That's not an option."

"Then let's hope that Natalie Castino can be persuaded that she can have it all." Eve turned to go back to the campsite. "I'm going to check with Jane about MacDuff, then I'm going to call Natalie. Time's running out."

He nodded curtly. "I'll get with Caleb, and we'll begin to throw together a plan." He strode away from her. "I meant what I said, Eve."

He always meant what he said, Eve thought wearily. But particularly when it came to her safety. She'd already stretched him to the limit tonight up on that road.

But sometimes there were no limits. Not when a child was concerned.

Jane.

She dialed her quickly. "Salazar has Cara. But she's alive. Franco, or whoever took her, used chloroform. We're moving to get her back."

"Oh, my God."

"We *will* get her back, Jane."

"How?"

"We have a few ideas. Where are you?"

"Right now I'm back at camp with MacDuff. I started thinking while I was searching for Cara about how vulnerable MacDuff is right now with only a couple guards to watch over him. Salazar wanted him dead. Who's to say he won't try again? Cara has you and everyone else looking for her, and I couldn't let MacDuff be pushed aside." She added, "So I told Caleb to go on without me, and I came back. That's what he wanted anyway." She paused, then said with frustration, "Though I admit it's driving me crazy. I want to be out there with the rest of you."

"I know how you feel. But you're right, MacDuff was hurt because he was trying to help us. He deserves all the care we can give him. How is he?"

"I think he's better. I can't be sure. He goes in and out. But when he comes around, he's pure MacDuff." She added brusquely, "But we have to get him to a hospital. I was thinking of loading him into a vehicle and using that road that Joe cleared of explosives earlier to get him away from here. But it would be pretty bumpy, and I'd run the risk of running off the road."

"Very risky."

"The fog is lifting. It's worse in the valleys than anywhere else. I called an air ambulance, and they said they'd try to get to us as soon as possible, but they weren't sure when that would be." She added dryly, "Needless to say, I told them not to land on that road."

"And you're probably not going to have to worry about Salazar's men interfering with them if they land in the camp," Eve said. "I guarantee that they're going to be kept very busy in the next few hours. I have to go, Jane. Take care of MacDuff."

"That's why I'm here," she said. "You didn't tell me what ideas you have to get Cara back."

"There are a couple brewing."

"And you don't intend to tell me." She paused. "You think it would scare me or worry me. You're right, that's the name of the game right now. I'm feeling helpless. I want to be with you. But I can't, so all I can do is tell you to be careful and remember that I can't do without you. Now, go do whatever you have to do." She hung up.

Eve drew a deep breath, then did what she had to do. She dialed the number Natalie Castino had given her.

Would she even answer?

If she didn't, there was little hope that they could keep Cara alive.

One ring.

Two.

Three.

Then Natalie Castino picked up the call. "Eve Duncan? I can't tell you how glad I am that you called me back. I was so afraid that you wouldn't. You've decided to help me?"

Her tone held the same heartbreaking agony that it had the first time she'd called Eve. She was still playing the same role she'd assumed before. Poor victimized mother just trying to get her child returned to her. It seemed incredible that Natalie would still think that ploy would work.

But in order to get anywhere with the woman, Eve would have to jar her out of that role. "I was hoping that we might be able to help each other. But that can't happen unless you're honest with me, Natalie. There is no ransom, is there? It's all a hoax. You and Salazar were in together on the kidnapping of the girls."

Silence. "How can you say that? I wouldn't harm my own daughters."

"I don't expect you to confess. You're entirely too clever to incriminate yourself on the phone. I just want you to know that I'm aware of who and what you are. Though God knows I don't understand how you could do it. Jenny and Cara were extraordinary human beings and very lovable."

"Who would know that better than me, Eve?" Natalie said gently. "That's why I'm trying to save my Cara. If I'm not mistaken, I believe that you're trying to do the same thing. Why else did you call me?"

"Not to play your old game. I want to offer you a new one that would have advantages to both of us. Are you with Salazar now?"

"How did you guess? He forced me to come to meet him. He thought I might be useful in negotiating the ransom. I had no choice."

No agony. Her voice was smooth and almost without expression. She was not going to say anything incriminating but she was clearly willing to talk around the subject.

"Can he hear you now?"

"No, I demanded some privacy."

"He has Cara. I want her back."

Silence. "But I'd know if he had her, wouldn't I?"

"I believe you do know. She was chloroformed and taken to Salazar. He's going to kill her if you don't step in."

"I don't know what you're talking about."

"I'm talking about your daughter. I'm talking about death. I'm talking about your saving her."

"Everyone knows I'd do anything to save her." She paused. "Are you begging me, Eve? You don't have to beg me. Just tell me about this new game you wanted to offer me. The one you said might help all of us."

"Cira's treasure. It's a game centuries old, and that makes it all the more precious. MacTavish told Franco that some of those coins in the chest are priceless, but I'm sure an enterprising woman like you would be able to find a buyer. I've heard you like power, and money like that could put the world at your feet."

"And you're offering to give me this treasure?"

"I'm offering a trade."

"You've . . . found this chest?"

Make it sound totally convincing. "Yes."

"And you'll give it to me for Cara?"

"I will."

"Why? She's just a child. She can't be of any value to you."

For the first time, Eve realized exactly what she was dealing with in Natalie Castino. That question was asked with complete sincerity. Cara had no value for Natalie, and, therefore, she couldn't see any value in her for anyone else. Natalie was clearly a complete sociopath. And, therefore, it would be difficult for Eve to explain her affection for Natalie's daughter and make her believe it. "I've never cared anything about the treasure. But I don't want Salazar to get what he wants. He's caused me a good deal of trouble. Not to mention that he's tried to kill me."

"You're foolish not to want the treasure. But I can understand how you'd want to get back at Salazar."

Yes, Natalie could identify with anyone not giving her what she wanted. "So you'll deal with me?"

"How can I? I don't have Cara."

Eve smothered her exasperation. It was clear Natalie would never do anything to incriminate herself unless she knew she was perfectly safe. Eve could see how she had been able to deceive everyone about her innocence all these years.

"If you had Cara, would you deal? Hypothetically?"

"I do like money. It might be an answer for many troubles in my life. And, of course, I'd always want my dear child safe. But Salazar is a very dangerous man, and he might kill me if I got in his way. It's a very difficult situation."

"Give me an answer."

"And you might spread lies about my part in these negotiations for my daughter."

"You don't think you can handle my 'lies'?"

"Oh, I could handle them. It would just be a bother."

"Give me an answer."

Silence. "When would I get this treasure?"

"You get Salazar to release Cara, and I'll take you to where we hid it on the lake."

"That's not exactly . . . safe for me."

"That's the only way we can handle it. Your child is not that important to me. I might decide I want the treasure after all. Take it or leave it."

Another silence. "Naturally, I'll do everything possible to save my daughter. But you've got to keep Salazar from hurting me. I'll call you and tell you when and where to come." She hung up.

It was done.

Eve drew a relieved breath as she hung up. It had been both harder and easier than she had anticipated. It was difficult trying to understand Natalie's thinking and make her believe that Eve was on the same page. It had been easier than she thought to make Natalie go for the deal itself. But Natalie was clever, and there might be all kinds of hidden agendas in her acceptance.

But the deal had been struck. Now all she had to do was tell Joe.

And to sit and wait for Natalie's call.

"She wanted a deal?" Salazar asked when Natalie hung up. "You look very pleased with yourself."

"I am very pleased with myself. They have the treasure and want to trade for Cara." She glanced at the girl slumped unconscious on the ground by a tree. "She may prove very valuable in more ways than the obvious." She smiled at him. "Unfortunately, you weren't included in the deal. Eve Duncan wants me to persuade you not to kill Cara, then set her free. Do you think I'm that persuasive, Salazar?"

"You made the deal?"

"It seemed the thing to do. We get Eve Duncan and the treasure. We already have Cara. A win–win situation." She glanced at Franco. "You've already come through for us by finding Cara. Do you think you can get Eve Duncan to tell us about the location of the treasure?"

"It won't be a problem. Women break easier than men."

"How very sexist. You just haven't been exposed to the right women, has he, Salazar?"

"When are you going to call her back?" Salazar asked. "I want this over. I've lost three men tonight. MacDuff's people must be better than we thought."

"I'll give it an hour. I want to make her sweat." She tilted her head. "Though she might not. I believe I'm beginning to have respect for Eve Duncan. How very strange. I don't remember ever respecting another woman before." She shrugged. "Oh, well, I'll still make her wait. I have to keep my word . . ."

CHAPTER

15

I've located Salazar's camp," Jock said when he called Eve and Joe thirty minutes later. "Salazar's here, and so is Franco. Cara is still alive. They're keeping her knocked out. Every time she rouses, someone is there with that damn chloroform." He paused. "And that damn bitch just sits and watches them do it."

"How many men does Salazar have in that camp?" Joe asked.

"Including Franco, six." He paused. "Caleb and I could take them down."

"Not without a risk to Cara," Eve said. "You know that Jock."

Silence. "I know that. It's the only reason I'm calling you and not doing it."

"Because it's the right thing to do." She added, "But they're probably all going to be on the move soon. If you can unobtrusively eliminate a few of them on the trail, it would help."

"Oh, I can do that." He paused. "That woman in the camp, the one who's laughing and talking and letting them drug Cara. She's Cara's mother?"

"Yes, Natalie Castino."

"Can she be one of the ones I take down?"

"No, we need her."

"I don't need her. Cara doesn't need her." He added harshly, "Okay, okay. Maybe later." He hung up.

"He appears to be upset with our Natalie," Joe murmured. "Let's hope she survives to show up at our meeting."

"She will. Jock's not going to do anything to jeopardize Cara. This is very difficult for him."

"It's difficult for all of us," Joe said. "And I'm not blaming Jock for wanting to rid us of Natalie. I'm feeling the same way right now."

"She's keeping Cara alive. That's all that's important. Look, he'll take out a few of Salazar's men on the trail. You can set up an ambush once we find out where Natalie is arranging the meeting. We agreed that was the best way."

"But not the only way. That way involves you in the middle of the action."

"Joe."

"I'm being honest with you. If I see another solution, I'm taking it." He turned and walked away from her.

"Six A.M. **Three hours from now. The top of that craggy hillside** that you can see from the lake. You show up alone and unarmed," Natalie Castino said when Eve picked up the phone an hour later. "I wasn't able to talk Salazar into releasing Cara, but I can guarantee we'll be there. I can guarantee that she'll be alive. After that, it's up to you. But I'll expect you to keep your part of our agreement regardless."

"You want Cira's gold."

"It will help. I'm a woman who has to make her way in a man's world," she said softly. "If I'd have been in control, I might never have lost my girls. I'm sure you can understand, Eve."

"Perfectly."

"I thought you would. We have some differences, but we're alike in many things."

God forbid, Eve thought. "You mean, we both want our own way."

"Exactly. I'll see you at six, Eve." She hung up.

"Alone and unarmed," Joe repeated. "She'd have to be crazy to expect you to go along with that."

"She doesn't expect me to go along with it. You heard her. She said it was up to me." She smiled without mirth. "Or up to you, Joe. You have a little over three hours. Work it out."

He was already heading to the clearing where he could look up at the hill. There was still a light fog wreathing the slopes that plunged toward the lake, but the rising sun was shining weakly through the clouds to light the craggy, sparsely vegetated glade near the top. "It will be hard as hell to stage an ambush up there." He tilted his head thoughtfully. "Unless . . ." He was silent for a moment. "Why not? He's supplied us with everything we need . . ." He took out his phone. "I've got to call Jock back. I have something for him to do."

Joe was already thinking, planning, analyzing, Eve realized. She just hoped he'd come up with something that was relatively risk-free.

Risk-free? There was nothing that was going to be without risk in the next few hours.

She could only hope that they'd all survive.

Eve and Joe didn't start out for the meeting with Natalie and Salazar until over two hours later. It took them close to an hour's climb before they reached the final approach to the glade where they were to meet them.

"You know what to do." Joe's voice was sharp with tension. "Don't deviate, Eve. I may not be able to avert at the last minute."

"You make this sound like a SEAL raid," she said. "I have every intention of following your orders, Joe. But I can't guarantee I won't have to 'deviate.'"

"I know." He stopped. "I can't go any farther with you. Jock says Salazar has planted sentries in those trees up ahead. Jock and Caleb should be somewhere up there, too. But they're in place. I can't chance being spotted and endangering you. When you go into those woods, you have to appear totally alone." He looked at her, his hands clenching. "You don't have to do this, dammit."

"I know I don't. But I have to do what I can to save her." She said quietly, "I left Cara with Jane when I went up to the road to help you. I don't know if it would have made any difference if I'd been there with her when she got so upset when Jock left to go after Salazar. I might not ever know. But I chose you, Joe. This time I have to choose Cara."

"Change your mind. We can find another plan to—"

"Too late." She gave him a quick kiss and started down the trail. "That would be deviating." Don't look back. She didn't want to see him standing there, or she'd want to run back to him. Just concentrate on what lay ahead.

And hope that Natalie's greed was greater than her obsession for protecting herself.

Because if it wasn't, Eve would probably be shot by one of the sentries Salazar had planted as she entered those trees ahead.

Joe watched Eve until she disappeared into the trees before he started to move. He'd go to the edge of the forest and wait for the action to start.

He *hated* it. Even Jock and Caleb were closer to Eve and might be able to see if there was trouble. But there shouldn't be trouble, he told himself. He'd spent two hours up here making preparations before he'd gone down to the camp to bring Eve. He'd briefed Caleb and Jock against what he'd thought was every possible thing that could go wrong.

But it was always the things you didn't think could go wrong that invariably did.

It was the unexpected that could get you killed.

Could get Eve killed.

His phone was vibrating.

A text.

He went still. Jock? Caleb?

Relief. Manez from Mexico City. Not what Joe had been worried about. Surely not the unexpected blow that could put Eve in greater danger.

He read the text.

Shit!

"Hello, Eve." Natalie Castino smiled brilliantly at her as Eve walked out of the stand of trees into the glade. She was dressed in a cream-colored silk blouse, khaki designer trousers, and fine leather boots. She looked beautiful but totally out of place. "Salazar wasn't sure that you'd come, but I told him that you were a woman who knew what you wanted. Have you actually met Salazar?"

"Only by reputation. We've chatted." She stared coolly at Salazar, who stood there with an AK-47 held casually in his arm. "And he hired Walsh to kill Cara and me. I understand he still has a price on my head." She looked at Franco. "You'd know about that?"

"Search her," Salazar told Franco.

She stiffened as Franco came toward her. But she stood still and unresisting as his hands ran over her. When he stepped away from her, she glanced quickly around the clearing to get her bearings. The glade was surrounded by trees except for the cliff to the west that was rocky and contained several large boulders. Then her attention turned to Natalie Castino. Salazar. Franco. She had only seen photographs of them, but they were so familiar to her, she knew so much about them, that she felt as if she had known them for years. The only true strangers were two dark-skinned men dressed in boots, camouflage pants, and jackets, and carrying rifles. According to Jock, there were two more of Salazar's men acting as sentries in the forest. Eve couldn't be concerned about them. They were the responsibility of

Caleb, Joe, and Jock. She had to focus on what was going to happen in this glade.

Cara. Where was Cara?

Cara was lying beside the trail, as if she'd been tossed there like some kind of garbage, Eve thought angrily. She looked smaller and more delicate than usual. Or maybe Eve was just more aware how fragile Cara's situation was at this moment. "Have you hurt her?" She strode over to Cara and fell to her knees beside her. "Cara." She gently brushed back Cara's dark hair away from her face. "Cara, it's Eve. Can you hear me?"

Cara didn't move.

"Cara."

"Eve?" Cara whispered. Her lids slowly opened. "So . . . sorry. Jock?"

"He's fine. So are you. Everything's going to be okay."

"No . . . Sorry . . ." Her eyes closed again.

"She's right, it's not going to be okay," Salazar said to Eve. "Not unless we get what we want. Maybe not then. You offered Natalie a deal. If it was true, there might be some reason to keep you alive for a while."

"She actually told you everything?"

"Are you surprised?"

"No, nothing she could do would surprise me." She glanced at Natalie. "But I thought there was a possibility that she might wish to surprise you."

"Why would I want to do that?" Natalie asked as she took a step closer to Salazar. "We're used to protecting each other, aren't we?"

"Yes." His gaze narrowed on Eve. "Why did you say that?"

"I was stating the obvious. She impresses me as a woman who doesn't like to be taken for granted." Don't challenge them. There were things to be done. She frowned as she gazed down at Cara. "She needs to be moved over on those rocks. The grass is too wet here. All this dampness has to be bad for Cara."

"She's fine here," Salazar said flatly.

Eve tried not to show panic. Cara was lying too close to Salazar. And he wasn't going to let her be moved. Try Natalie, the wild card. She turned to her. "Cara needs to be moved."

"Does she?" Natalie gazed at her curiously. "I think you really do care about her. How very odd." She turned to Franco. "It won't hurt to do as she asks. Take the girl over to those rocks."

Franco glanced at Salazar. He didn't move.

"Franco," Natalie said. "Do it. You heard me."

He hesitated, then shrugged and strode over to where Eve was kneeling beside Cara.

"What do you think you're doing, Franco," Salazar said angrily. "Do as I say."

"I'm sorry, he won't be doing anything you tell him to do," Natalie said as she turned and strolled away from Salazar across the glade. "He belongs to me. He has for a long time."

Salazar muttered a curse as he watched Franco lift Cara and take her to the rocks. "What's happening here, Natalie?"

"It's over, Salazar. Our association has become more trouble than it's worth. I've decided to terminate it." She turned and smiled at Eve. "Or I should say, I'm going to let Eve terminate it. I'm sure she's made all the necessary arrangements."

Salazar went still. "She has no weapon." He lifted his automatic rifle and pointed it at Eve. "Are you trying to get me to kill her?"

Eve was frozen as she stared into the barrel of the rifle. Natalie's move had stunned her. "I was wrong, Salazar. She did surprise me. But I have an idea she's trying to manipulate both of us. Are you going to let her do that?" She slowly got to her feet. "Now, I'm going to go over to Cara. This is between you and Natalie. All I want is to get the child out of here. Give me Cara, and I'll get you that treasure. I don't care who takes it as long as Cara and I come out of this alive."

She was moving toward the rocks. "But I'd keep my gun pointed at Natalie or Franco if I were you. As you said, you know I'm no threat." Three more steps, and she'd be at the rocks. Jock had told her the rocks would be safe. She had to reach the rocks. "It sounded to me as if that might not be the case—" She'd almost reached the rocks where Franco was standing over Cara's body. "With your errand boy here. Don't you think that you should—"

Now.

She dove on top of Cara! The next second she'd rolled off the rock, taking Cara with her. Two more rolls, and they were both behind the boulders.

She could hear Salazar cursing. "Get her! Get that bitch. I want her—"

A shot.

Jock's shot, aimed with deadly accuracy at the explosives Joe had taken from the IEDs on the road and planted a few hours earlier in the glade.

The glade exploded.

Screams. Smoke. Fire.

The rocks sheltering Eve and Cara were chipping, splintering. Eve held Cara closer, her arm over the child's head. She could hear Salazar screaming, moaning.

More explosions.

She couldn't hear Salazar anymore, but she heard Franco gasping, cursing, with pain. She lifted her head to see him beating at his pants to put out the flames. He looked up and met her eyes. She saw pure rage.

"I'm going to kill you." He started toward her.

Eve frantically looked around for something, anything, to defend herself. She reached for a rock.

"Get away from her, Franco." Natalie was suddenly beside them. Her face was streaked by smoke, and she had a tear in the sleeve of her silk shirt. "Now."

"I'm going to kill her."

"You'll do no such thing. She might be very valuable to me." She glanced at Cara. "She's alive, Eve?"

"Yes."

"Then she might stay that way if you cooperate." She pulled out a pearl-handled pistol and strode through the smoke, to where Salazar lay crumpled, bloody and torn apart by the explosion. "Dead. I knew he would be the first target. There had to be a reason why you wanted to get Cara as far away as possible from him. I thought it might be a sniper. I didn't expect you to blow everything up."

"Salazar conveniently supplied us with the explosives from the IEDs we disarmed on the road," Eve said. "Joe just grabbed them and came up here to give them back to him."

"It's a little messy, but I suppose it worked for you." She whirled and ran back toward them. "We have to move quickly, Franco. Grab the girl and let's get out of here. Eve's friends will probably be all over this place in minutes." She started running down the rocky slopes, away from the forest. "Coming, Eve?"

Eve had no choice.

Franco had lifted Cara in a fireman's lift over his shoulder and was running behind Natalie.

Eve couldn't let them out of her sight.

She ran after them.

This entire side of the hill was shale and loose stones.

Eve skidded, fell, got up, stumbled, and fell again. The smoke was drifting down, enveloping them as she ran. Her eyes were stinging, and she could just barely see Natalie ahead of her. She couldn't see Franco at all, and that frightened her. He had Cara, and he was a killer who was wounded and enraged. Her only hope was that he'd obey Natalie Castino. Which was a slim hope indeed. Since Natalie was proving to be more dangerous than Franco.

"Hurry," Natalie said over her shoulder. "We need to get out of here."

"Why? You're not going to get away. Joe will hunt you down, and he's got very lethal friends. Give it up and take your chances. You said that you weren't worried about anyone thinking you were guilty of having your girls kidnapped. You just called it a bother. Tell Franco to stop and put Cara down."

"Presently." Her brows lifted. "Do you really think that I'm just running blindly, that I have no plan? That's not the way I do things, Eve. We're almost there. Just around the next corner in the trail . . ."

Eve was already turning that next corner as she spoke.

She stopped short, her eyes widening as she gazed at the army-green helicopter tucked away and half-hidden by brush, rocks, and branches near the ledge of the slope. "What the hell?"

"I had to protect myself, didn't I?" Natalie waved at the pilot, and he started the engine. "Nikolai has been sitting in the valley below waiting for the weather to clear so that he could slip in here and wait for me. He managed to do it last night."

"Nikolai?"

"He's one of my father's men. My father put him at my disposal when I told him that I was trying to free my little girl. He was very worried about her. He'll be glad to know that Salazar didn't kill her, and I managed to take her away from him . . . and kill that terrible man in the process." She smiled. "My father believes in revenge. So do I. Salazar was enjoyable, but he didn't treat me with the respect I deserved." She called to Franco, "Put the girl in the helicopter. I have to get out of here."

Franco was opening the helicopter door and shoving Cara into the aircraft.

"He *does* belong to you," Eve murmured.

"Oh, yes. I've been planning this for a long time. When I saw how clumsily Walsh was handling the hunt for Cara, I decided to take matters into my own hands. I was tired of being Salazar's mistress and Castino's wife. I wanted something more." She smiled. "So I paid a visit to California. I found Franco, and I set him up to help me. He's ambitious, you know. All I had to do was convince him I'd be grateful, and he'd be rich if he went along with me. I had a long-term plan, but some of it had to be adjusted as I went along. But Franco didn't like Salazar, so that made it easier for me to keep him in line. He was very valuable when I was keeping so many balls in the air. When I decided that Salazar had to go down for taking the girls, Franco even pretended to be Walsh and alerted the U.S. Justice Department that the body in the grave was Jenny Castino."

"And was it your decision to let Franco go to that hospital and try to kill Cara?"

"It wouldn't have mattered in the long run. Salazar had the right idea for the most part. I just had to work it into my plans."

So cold. Absolutely no feeling in her tone.

"You're looking at me with horror. Not that I mind. There's a kind of respect connected with that emotion. I just thought you might understand." She shrugged. "But, as it turned out, I was glad that Salazar failed with Cara and you. When Franco told us about Cira's gold, I realized that you were holding the key to everything I'd ever wanted, everything I deserved."

"Dammit, I think I hear someone on the rocks on the hillside," Franco said. "Let's go."

"I'm going." She pulled out her gun. "It's time we left, Eve." She pointed it at her. "As I told Franco, I need you. You know where that treasure is located. It's going to be mine."

"What if I don't know? What if it was a bluff?"

"Not as good, but acceptable. Then I'd still need you. Franco said MacTavish was certain that you were going to find it. You'll find it for me."

"Natalie!" Franco's gaze was on the trail. "You don't have time for this."

"You're right." She motioned with her gun. "Why don't you stay and stop them for me, Franco?"

"What?"

"No, on second thought, I've decided to rid myself of you now instead of later."

"You bitch." His eyes were blazing. "I've done *everything* for you."

"And now you can do the ultimate."

She shot him in the heart.

She watched him fall to the ground. "What a pity. But he really knew too much, Eve. He might have thought he could blackmail me later. My relationship with my father has to remain solid. He's all I have now."

"Now that you've gotten rid of Salazar?"

"No, I've burned all my bridges." She added softly, "If all went as scheduled, at five thirty a.m. GMT, my dear husband will have been gunned down outside the apartment he keeps for his current mistress. There will be abundant evidence that the kill was financed by Salazar because of his fear that my husband would learn that he'd kidnapped and killed Jenny and Cara."

Eve gazed at her in shock.

"I told you, I was tired of Juan Castino. I was tired of being forced to be Salazar's lover, so I could control him. It was time I got rid of both of them and became my own woman. So I had Franco contact his sources in Mexico City and arrange it."

"I suppose that would be the obvious solution in your eyes."

"There were others, but I was impatient. I want to start a new life."

"With Cira's gold."

"Yes. The minute I heard about it, I knew it was meant for me." She opened the helicopter door. "Get in the helicopter, Eve."

"She's not going anywhere." Joe was standing by the trail with a gun pointed at Natalie. "Back away from the helicopter and put down your weapon."

Natalie stiffened. "You must be Joe Quinn? I've heard about you. Could we come to an agreement?"

"No way in hell."

"I didn't think so, but I could probably persuade you if I had the time."

"Put down that weapon."

"You're afraid for Eve?" She turned the gun on Eve. "Yes, I can see that you are."

"Put it down, Natalie," Eve said.

"That wouldn't be intelligent. He's not going to press the trigger because he knows that even if it was a great shot, I still could kill you." She backed toward the helicopter door. "But it appears that I'd be wise to cut my losses and avoid this confrontation. It's not as if I still won't win in the end."

"Get away from that helicopter," Joe said.

Natalie shook her head. "I'm getting on board, and Nikolai is taking off." She looked Eve in the eye. "I have Cara. We can still come to a deal. It will be a little complicated for me, but I can keep Cara alive until you give me what I want."

"Let her go, Natalie."

Natalie got in the helicopter. "Or I can do what I always do and look out for myself. It will be up to you. Now I'm going to point the gun away from you and on Cara. Will Quinn take the chance of killing her?" The helicopter was lifting. "I don't think so. Most men are so soft about children . . . It's always amazed me." She was suddenly looking out the window at Eve, and her eyes were cold. "I don't like to lose, Eve. I did very well, but this was only a partial victory for me. I want it all. I think I need to do something to impress you with that."

She was lifting her gun.

Aiming it.

Aiming it at Joe!

"No!"

Eve was running toward him.

Tackling him, bringing him down.

She could feel the bullet as it passed her cheek.

And as it struck Joe.

Then she could feel the blood.

"Eve."

Her arms tightened around him.

"Eve, it's okay."

How could it be okay? She had felt the bullet as it struck Joe. She could feel his blood on her arm . . .

He was pushing her away and sitting up. "It's only a flesh wound. My side . . ." He looked down at his left side. "I think you did more damage tackling me than she did with that bullet. She must be a lousy shot."

"You're wrong. I think she must be a very good shot." Eve was shaking with both fear and intense relief. "I watched her shoot Franco. She knew what she was doing. She probably was doing exactly what she told me she was going to do. Showing me that she had no intention of losing." She reached out and touched the blood on his shirt. "I guess we're both lucky that she didn't want to drive the point home." She turned and looked out at the horizon. The helicopter was still in view, but it was almost out of sight.

"She *will* lose, Joe. We can't let her win." She shook her head to clear it. She couldn't think of Natalie right now. She had to take care of Joe. She began to unbutton his shirt. "You're right, it's only a flesh wound. Hardly more than a scratch." She tore up his shirt and began to dab the wound. "She told me that she'd arranged for Castino to be assassinated. She said it was supposed to be done this morning."

"She was telling the truth. I got a text from Manez right after you left me. Castino is dead."

She nodded jerkily. "I didn't doubt her. She's capable of anything." She moistened her lips. "And she makes it work, Joe. She thinks she can get away with any atrocity, and she finds a way to do it."

"But we know her now. What we know, we can beat."

"She has Cara, Joe. We don't know what she'll do with—"

"That bitch got away?" Jock was striding down the rocky path. "I saw the helicopter from the top of the hill. She got away?"

"Yes." Eve gestured to Joe. "After taking a shot at Joe. It's not bad, thank God."

"Good," Jock said absently as he strode to the edge of the cliff and looked out at the horizon. "Cara? I didn't see Cara. Is she still alive?"

"Yes. She's with Natalie Castino." She'd finished bandaging Joe, and she rose to her feet and went to stand beside Jock. "But Natalie still wants Cira's gold. That means we can still save Cara."

"I thought we'd done that. Hell, we blew up Salazar and his men, and I thought she'd be safe." His voice was low but vibrating with agony. "I told her once I'd keep her safe, that she'd never have to look over her shoulder again. I didn't do enough. I should have done more."

"We didn't know that Natalie had an escape plan. You did all you could."

"If I'd done all I could, Cara would be here with us now. I'm going after her. I'll get her back."

"We think Natalie Castino is going to Moscow to be with her father."

"I don't care if she's going to hell. It's where I'll send her anyway." He turned and strode back up the trail.

"He's hurting." She went back to Joe. "But we can't let him move too fast. If Natalie gets spooked, she might decide that Cara's not worthwhile to her."

"We don't know what's fast or slow right now." Joe was getting slowly to his feet, and Eve moved closer to help him. "It's a whole new ball game, and Natalie is writing the rules." He began walking toward the trail. "But right now I'm just happy that she seems to believe she needs you. It will be good not to have you designated as a target."

Not at the moment, Eve thought. But Natalie had no compunctions about using people, then killing them. Salazar, Castino, Franco. It would be just as well not to bring that up to Joe right now.

And right now, Natalie also needed Cara. After she got what she wanted from holding her daughter hostage, would she hesitate about killing her?

Not for a minute.

Joe's arm slid around her waist. "It's going to be okay," he said quietly. His hand gently moved to her abdomen. "The three of us have gone through a hell of a lot in the past weeks. We can get through the rest."

She nodded and stepped closer to him. She needed to feel his warmth and strength. "I know that." She did know it, but she was tired and scared and wanted nothing more than to go home with Joe and Cara and this new, ever-changing life in her body.

But there was no Cara yet.

But there would be. There would be.

She had to believe it . . .

Jane watched the EMTs load MacDuff's stretcher into the air ambulance before turning to Jock. "The doctor examined MacDuff before they moved him from his tent. He believes that there won't be any serious consequences from his injury."

"I didn't think there would be once he regained consciousness. MacDuff is tough." Jock started toward the ambulance. "I'm going to the hospital with him just to make sure."

"But you're not going to stay there long."

"No." He looked back at her. His silver-gray eyes were ice cold and without expression. "Not long at all, Jane." He climbed into the helicopter and shut the door.

She was still feeling the chill as she watched the air ambulance take off. Chill and despair and helplessness. "I wasn't sure that he'd be going with him," Caleb said as he came toward her. "Jock isn't quite himself right now."

Jane shook her head. "I knew he'd want to be with him until he was positive of his condition. He loves MacDuff."

"But he's burning inside." Caleb smiled faintly. "I know a lot about that."

"I imagine you do." Jane glanced one last time at the helicopter before she turned away. "I expected Joe to be down here getting some first aid. When Eve called me, she said that he'd been wounded."

"Just a scratch. He's still up in the hills dealing with damage control because of several bodies that have to be dealt with. Not to mention, MacDuff's men. They were pretty upset about Colin's murder, then MacDuff's injury. And they didn't like it that they were left out of that blowup that took out Salazar." He shrugged. "I don't blame them. I would have felt the same if I'd missed all the fun."

"I won't even address that remark," she said. "Eve wouldn't tell me what was happening, but I guarantee I wouldn't have thought it was 'fun.'"

"You just did address it. In the way that was predictably your own." His smile faded. "And if anything had happened to Eve, I wouldn't be saying that. I don't believe I would have had the nerve to send her in to face Natalie Castino and Salazar. I know Quinn didn't want her to do it. It was her choice. She wanted to be sure that Cara would be protected."

"She still wants her to be protected."

"We all do." He lightly tapped his chest. "Even my callous, barbaric self." He turned away. "And now I've got to get back to Quinn and offer my help. I'm actually becoming accustomed to being a team player. No, that's not true, but it sounds good, and I thought you'd like to hear it." He met her eyes. "I just wanted to check to see how you were doing. I know it was harder for you to stay out of the action than it was for Colin's men."

"Yes, it was, but it was the right thing to do."

"Boring." He smiled. "I promise I'll never make you do the right thing, Jane." Before she could answer, he had turned away. "But I brought Eve down from the hills with me, and she might need someone to talk to about right and wrong. She's much more on your wavelength than I am." His voice drifted back to her. "She's down by the lake . . ."

Jane stood watching him for a moment. Why was it always so difficult to look away from Caleb? He seemed to gather all the light and darkness around him until it became a part of him. She forced herself to look away and down at the lake.

But Eve wasn't at the lake as Caleb had said. She was standing beside her tent, and she was looking down at Cara's violin, which she was holding.

Not good.

"Eve." Jane walked quickly toward her. "The air ambulance just took MacDuff and Jock to the hospital. Everything seems to be—"

"Easy." Eve looked up and met Jane's eyes. "I'm not going to fall apart. I've just been scared and having trouble remembering that Natalie Castino isn't infallible. She's just a smart woman who is evil beyond belief." She glanced back at the violin. "But Cara is smart, too. Smart and good and gifted. She's already survived more than anyone would think she could. She can survive this, too." She bent down and carefully put the violin back in its case. "All she needs is help from the people who love her. She's going to get that, Jane." She moved down the slope toward the lake. "And it's going to be enough to save her."

"Yes." Jane moved down to stand beside Eve on the bank. The fog was gone, but the heavy mist that always wreathed the north bank was still there. So much violence and killing had echoed through these

IRIS JOHANSEN

hills in the last days, but that eternal mist was still beckoning, calling, as it had for centuries. "We'll make it enough."

But, Cira, we could use a little help from you if you can see your way clear. This is about a child, too. Your Marcus would have liked her. You would have liked her. Don't let us lose her as you did Marcus. Please, don't let Eve lose her.

Eve was gazing out at the mist, too. "It seems . . . different today." She tried to smile. "What do you think? The beginning or the end?"

Jane moved a step closer and took her hand. "The beginning," she said. "Definitely, the beginning."

35674056831259

CHASE BRANCH LIBRARY
17731 W. SEVEN MILE ROAD
DETROIT, MI 48235
313-481-1580

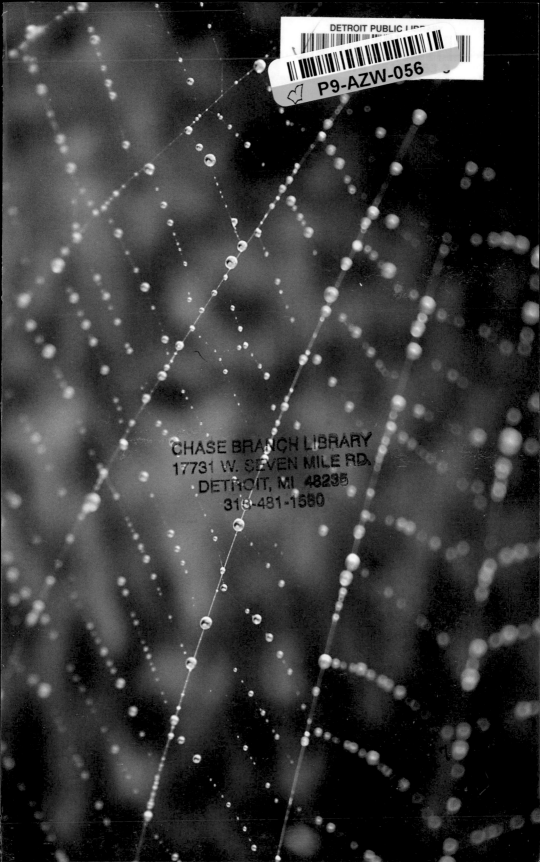
DETROIT PUBLIC LIBRARY

P9-AZW-056

CHASE BRANCH LIBRARY
17731 W. SEVEN MILE RD.
DETROIT, MI 48235
313-481-1580

THE
LIAR

CHASE BRANCH LIBRARY
17731 W. SEVEN MILE RD.
DETROIT, MI 48235
313-481-1580

FEB 17
CH

NORA ROBERTS

Hot Ice	*Montana Sky*	*Blue Smoke*
Sacred Sins	*Sanctuary*	*Angels Fall*
Brazen Virtue	*Homeport*	*High Noon*
Sweet Revenge	*The Reef*	*Tribute*
Public Secrets	*River's End*	*Black Hills*
Genuine Lies	*Carolina Moon*	*The Search*
Carnal Innocence	*The Villa*	*Chasing Fire*
Divine Evil	*Midnight Bayou*	*The Witness*
Honest Illusions	*Three Fates*	*Whiskey Beach*
Private Scandals	*Birthright*	*Tonight and Always*
Hidden Riches	*Northern Lights*	*The Collector*
True Betrayals		

SERIES

IRISH BORN TRILOGY
Born in Fire
Born in Ice
Born in Shame

DREAM TRILOGY
Daring to Dream
Holding the Dream
Finding the Dream

CHESAPEAKE BAY SAGA
Sea Swept
Rising Tides
Inner Harbor
Chesapeake Blue

**GALLAGHERS OF
ARDMORE TRILOGY**
Jewels of the Sun
Tears of the Moon
Heart of the Sea

**THREE SISTERS
ISLAND TRILOGY**
Dance Upon the Air
Heaven and Earth
Face the Fire

KEY TRILOGY
Key of Light
Key of Knowledge
Key of Valor

**IN THE GARDEN
TRILOGY**
Blue Dahlia
Black Rose
Red Lily

CIRCLE TRILOGY
Morrigan's Cross
Dance of the Gods
Valley of Silence

**SIGN OF SEVEN
TRILOGY**
Blood Brothers
The Hollow
The Pagan Stone

BRIDE QUARTET
Vision in White
Bed of Roses
Savor the Moment
Happy Ever After

**THE INN BOONSBORO
TRILOGY**
The Next Always
The Last Boyfriend
The Perfect Hope

**THE COUSINS
O'DWYER TRILOGY**
Dark Witch
Shadow Spell
Blood Magick

eBOOKS BY NORA ROBERTS

CORDINA'S ROYAL FAMILY
Affaire Royale
Command Performance
The Playboy Prince
Cordina's Crown Jewel

THE DONOVAN LEGACY
Captivated
Entranced
Charmed
Enchanted

THE O'HURLEYS
The Last Honest Woman
Dance to the Piper
Skin Deep
Without a Trace

NIGHT TALES
Night Shift
Night Shadow
Nightshade
Night Smoke
Night Shield

THE MACGREGORS
The Winning Hand
The Perfect Neighbor
All the Possibilities
One Man's Art

Tempting Fate
Playing the Odds
The MacGregor Brides
The MacGregor Grooms
Rebellion/In from the Cold
For Now, Forever

THE CALHOUNS
Suzanna's Surrender
Megan's Mate
Courting Catherine
A Man for Amanda
For the Love of Lilah

IRISH LEGACY
Irish Rose
Irish Rebel
Irish Thoroughbred

Best Laid Plans
Loving Jack
Lawless

Summer Love
Boundary Lines
Dual Image
First Impressions
The Law Is a Lady
Local Hero
This Magic Moment

The Name of the Game
Partners
Temptation
The Welcoming
Opposites Attract
Time Was
Times Change
Gabriel's Angel
Holiday Wishes
The Heart's Victory
The Right Path
Rules of the Game
Search for Love
Blithe Images
From This Day
Song of the West
Island of Flowers
Her Mother's Keeper
Untamed
Sullivan's Woman
Less of a Stranger
Reflections
Dance of Dreams
Storm Warning
Once More With Feeling
Endings and Beginnings
A Matter of Choice

NORA ROBERTS & J. D. ROBB

Remember When

Silent Night
(with Susan Plunkett, Dee Holmes, and Claire Cross)

Out of This World
(with Laurell K. Hamilton, Susan Krinard, and Maggie Shayne)

Bump in the Night
(with Mary Blayney, Ruth Ryan Langan, and Mary Kay McComas)

Dead of Night
(with Mary Blayney, Ruth Ryan Langan, and Mary Kay McComas)

Three in Death

Suite 606
(with Mary Blayney, Ruth Ryan Langan, and Mary Kay McComas)

In Death

The Lost
(with Patricia Gaffney, Mary Blayney, and Ruth Ryan Langan)

The Other Side
(with Mary Blayney, Patricia Gaffney, Ruth Ryan Langan, and Mary Kay McComas)

Time of Death

The Unquiet
(with Mary Blayney, Patricia Gaffney, Ruth Ryan Langan, and Mary Kay McComas)

Mirror, Mirror
(with Mary Blayney, Elaine Fox, Mary Kay McComas, and R. C. Ryan)

ALSO AVAILABLE . . .

The Official Nora Roberts Companion
(edited by Denise Little and Laura Hayden)

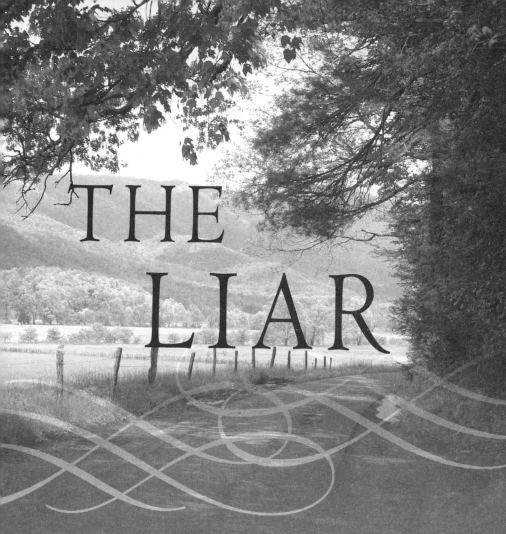

THE
LIAR

Nora Roberts

G. P. Putnam's Sons / New York

PUTNAM

G. P. PUTNAM'S SONS
Publishers Since 1838
Published by the Penguin Group
Penguin Group (USA) LLC
375 Hudson Street
New York, New York 10014

USA • Canada • UK • Ireland • Australia
New Zealand • India • South Africa • China

penguin.com
A Penguin Random House Company

Copyright © 2015 by Nora Roberts
Penguin supports copyright. Copyright fuels creativity, encourages diverse voices,
promotes free speech, and creates a vibrant culture. Thank you for buying an authorized
edition of this book and for complying with copyright laws by not reproducing, scanning,
or distributing any part of it in any form without permission. You are supporting writers
and allowing Penguin to continue to publish books for every reader.

Library of Congress Cataloging-in-Publication Data

Roberts, Nora.
  The liar / Nora Roberts.
    p.   cm.
  ISBN 978-0-399-17086-7
  I. Title.
  PS3568.O243L53   2015   2014040678
  813'.54—dc23

International edition ISBN: 978-0-399-17440-7

Printed in the United States of America
10 9 8 7 6 5 4 3 2 1

Book design by Meighan Cavanaugh

This is a work of fiction. Names, characters, places, and incidents either are the product
of the author's imagination or are used fictitiously, and any resemblance to actual persons,
living or dead, businesses, companies, events, or locales is entirely coincidental.

For JoAnne,

the amazing forever friend

PART I

THE FALSE

It is not the lie that passeth through the mind, but the lie that sinketh in, and settleth in it, that doth the hurt.

FRANCIS BACON

1

In the big house—and Shelby would always think of it as the big house—she sat in her husband's big leather chair at his big, important desk. The color of the chair was espresso. Not brown. Richard had been very exact about that sort of thing. The desk itself, so sleek and shiny, was African zebra wood, and custom-made for him in Italy.

When she'd said—just a joke—that she didn't know they had zebras in Italy, he'd given her *that* look. The look that told her despite the big house, the fancy clothes and the fat diamond on the fourth finger of her left hand, she'd always be Shelby Anne Pomeroy, two steps out of the bumpkin town in Tennessee where she was born and raised.

He'd have laughed once, she thought now, he'd have known she was joking and laughed as if she were the sparkle in his life. But oh God, she'd dulled in his eyes, and so fast, too.

The man she'd met nearly five years before on a starry summer night had swept her off her feet, away from everything she'd known, into worlds she'd barely imagined.

He'd treated her like a princess, shown her places she'd only read about in books or seen in movies. And he'd loved her once—hadn't he? It was important to remember that. He'd loved her, wanted her, given her all any woman could ask for.

Provided. That was a word he'd often used. He'd provided for her.

Maybe he'd been upset when she got pregnant, maybe she'd been afraid—just for a minute—of the look in his eyes when she told him. But he'd married her, hadn't he? Whisked her off to Las Vegas like they were having the adventure of a lifetime.

They'd been happy then. It was important to remember that now, too. She had to remember that, to hold tight the memories of the good times.

A woman widowed at twenty-four needed memories.

A woman who learned she'd been living a lie, was not only broke but in terrible, breathtaking debt, needed reminders of the good times.

The lawyers and accountants and tax people explained it all to her, but they might as well have been speaking Greek when they went on about leveraging and hedge funds and foreclosures. The big house, one that had intimidated her since she'd walked in the door, wasn't hers—or not enough hers to matter—but the mortgage company's. The cars, leased not bought, and with the payments overdue, not hers, either.

The furniture? Bought on credit, and those payments overdue.

And the taxes. She couldn't bear to think about the taxes. It terrified her to think of them.

In the two months and eight days since Richard's death, it seemed all she did was think about matters he'd told her not to worry about, matters that weren't her concern. Matters, when he'd give her *that* look, that were none of her business.

Now it was all her concern, and all her business, because she owed creditors, a mortgage company and the United States government so much money it paralyzed her.

She couldn't afford to be paralyzed. She had a child, she had a daughter. Callie was all that mattered now. She was only three, Shelby thought, and wanted to lay her head down on that slick, shiny desk and weep.

"But you won't. You're what she's got now, so you'll do whatever has to be done."

She opened one of the boxes, the one marked "Personal Papers." The lawyers and tax people had taken everything, gone through everything, copied everything, she supposed.

Now she would go through everything, and see what could be salvaged. For Callie.

She needed to find enough, somewhere, to provide for her child after she'd paid off all the debt. She'd get work, of course, but it wouldn't be enough.

She didn't care about the money, she thought as she began going through receipts for suits and shoes and restaurants and hotels. For private planes. She'd learned she didn't care about the money after the first whirlwind year, after Callie.

After Callie all she'd wanted was a home.

She stopped, looked around Richard's office. The harsh colors of the modern art he'd preferred, the stark white walls he said best showed off that art, and the dark woods and leathers.

This wouldn't be home, and hadn't been. Would never be, she thought, if she lived here eighty years instead of the scant three months since they'd moved in.

He'd bought it without consulting her, furnished it without asking what she'd like. A surprise, he'd said, throwing open the doors to this monster house in Villanova, this echoing building in what he'd claimed was the *best* of the Philadelphia suburbs.

And she'd pretended to love it, hadn't she? Grateful for a settled place, however much the hard colors and towering ceilings intimidated. Callie would have a home, go to good schools, play in a safe neighborhood.

Make friends. She'd make friends, too—that had been her hope.

But there hadn't been time.

Just as there wasn't a ten-million-dollar life insurance policy. He'd lied about that, too. Lied about the college fund for Callie.

Why?

She put that question aside. She'd never know the answer, so why ask why?

She could take his suits and shoes and ties and his sports equipment, the golf clubs and skis. Take all those to consignment shops. Take what she could get there.

Take whatever they didn't repossess and sell it. On damn eBay if she had to. Or Craigslist. Or a pawnshop, it didn't matter.

Plenty in her own closet to sell. And jewelry, too.

She looked at the diamond, the ring he'd slipped on her finger when they got to Vegas. The wedding ring, she'd keep, but the diamond, she'd sell. There was plenty of her own to sell.

For Callie.

She went through files, one by one. They'd taken all the computers, and those she didn't have back yet. But the actual paper was tangible.

She opened his medical file.

He'd taken good care of himself, she thought—which reminded her to cancel the memberships at the country club, at the fitness center. That had gone out of her mind. He'd been a healthy man, one who kept his body in tune, who never missed a checkup.

She needed to toss out all those vitamins and supplements he'd taken daily, she decided as she turned over another paper.

No reason to keep those, no reason to keep these records, either. The healthy man had drowned in the Atlantic, just a few miles off the South Carolina coast, at the age of thirty-three.

She should just shred all this. Richard had been big on shredding and had his own machine right there in the office. Creditors didn't need to see the results of his last routine blood work or the confirmation of his flu shot from two years ago, paperwork from the emergency room from when he'd dislocated his finger playing basketball.

For God's sake, that had been three years ago. For a man who'd shred enough paperwork to make a mountain range, he'd sure been possessive about his medical receipts.

She sighed, noting another, dated almost four years ago. She started to toss it aside, stopped and frowned. She didn't know this doctor. Of course, they'd been living in that big high-rise in Houston then, and who could keep track of doctors the way they'd moved every year—sometimes less than that. But this doctor was in New York City.

"That can't be right," she murmured. "Why would Richard go to a doctor in New York for a . . ."

Everything went cold. Her mind, her heart, her belly. Her fingers trembled as she lifted the paper, brought it closer as if the words would change with the distance.

But they stayed the same.

Richard Andrew Foxworth had elective surgery, performed by Dr. Dipok Haryana at Mount Sinai Medical Center, on July 12, 2011. A vasectomy.

He'd had a vasectomy, without telling her. Callie barely two months old and he'd fixed it so there could be no more children. He'd pretended to want more when she'd begun talking about another. He'd agreed to get checked, as she got checked, when, after a year of trying, she hadn't conceived.

She could hear him now.

You've just got to relax, Shelby, for God's sake. If you're worried and tense about it, it'll never happen.

"No, it'll never happen, because you fixed it so it couldn't. You lied to me, even about that. Lied when my heart broke every month.

"How could you? How could you?"

She pushed away from the desk, pressed her fingers to her eyes. July, mid-July, and Callie about eight weeks old. A business trip, he'd said, that's right, she remembered very well. To New York—hadn't lied about the where.

She hadn't wanted to take the baby to the city—he'd known she wouldn't. He'd made all the arrangements. Another surprise for her. He'd sent her back to Tennessee on a private plane, her and her baby.

So she could spend some time with her family, he'd said. Show off the baby, let her mother and grandmother spoil her and spoil Callie for a couple of weeks.

She'd been so happy, so *grateful*, she thought now. And all the while he'd just been getting her out of the way so he could make certain he didn't father another child.

She walked back to the desk, picked up the photo she'd had framed for him. One of her and Callie, taken by her brother Clay on that very trip. A thank-you gift he'd seemed to value as he'd kept it on his desk—wherever they'd been—ever since.

"Another lie. Just another lie. You never loved us. You couldn't have lied and lied and lied if you'd loved us."

On the rage of betrayal she nearly smashed the frame on the desk. Only the face of her baby stopped her. She set it down again, as carefully as she might priceless and fragile porcelain.

Then she lowered to the floor—she couldn't sit behind that desk, not now. She sat on the floor with harsh colors against hard white walls, rocking, weeping. Weeping not because the man she'd loved was dead, but because he never existed.

THERE WAS NO TIME TO SLEEP. Though she disliked coffee, she made herself an oversized mug from Richard's Italian machine—and hit it with a double shot of espresso.

Headachy from the crying jag, wired up on caffeine, she combed through every paper in the box, making piles.

Hotel and restaurant receipts when viewed with newly opened eyes told her he hadn't just lied, but had cheated.

Room service charges too high for a man alone. Add a receipt for a silver bangle from Tiffany's—which he'd never given to her—from the same trip, another five thousand at La Perla—the lingerie he preferred she wear—from another trip, a receipt for a weekend spent in a bed-and-breakfast in Vermont when he'd said he was going to finalize a deal in Chicago, and it began to solidify.

Why had he kept all this, all this proof of his lies and infidelity? Because, she realized, she'd trusted him.

Not even that, she thought, accepting. She'd suspected an affair, and he'd likely known she had. He kept it because he'd thought her too obedient to poke through his personal records.

And she had been.

The other lives he'd lived, he'd locked away. She hadn't known where to find the key, would never have questioned him—and he'd known it.

How many other women? she wondered. Did it matter? One was too many, and any of them would have been more sophisticated, more experienced and knowledgeable than the girl from the little mountain town in Tennessee he'd knocked up when she was nineteen, dazzled and foolish.

Why had he married her?

Maybe he'd loved her, at least a little. Wanted her. But she hadn't been enough, not enough to keep him happy, keep him true.

And did that matter, really? He was dead.

Yes, she thought. Yes, it mattered.

He'd made a fool of her, left her humiliated. Left her with a financial burden that could hound her for years and jeopardize their daughter's future.

It damn well mattered.

She spent another hour going systematically through the office. The safe had already been cleared. She'd known about it, though she hadn't had the combination. She'd given the lawyers permission to have it opened.

They'd taken most of the legal documents, but there was five thousand in cash. She took it out, set it aside. Callie's birth certificate, their passports.

She opened Richard's, studied his photo.

So handsome. Smooth and polished, like a movie star, with his rich

brown hair and tawny eyes. She'd so wished Callie had inherited his dimples. She'd been so charmed by those damn dimples.

She set the passports aside. However unlikely it was she'd use hers or
Callie's, she'd pack them up. She'd destroy Richard's. Or—maybe ask
the lawyers if that's what she should do.

She found nothing hidden away, but she'd go through everything
again before she shredded or filed it all away again in packing boxes.

Hyped on coffee and grief, she walked through the house, crossed the
big two-story foyer, took the curving stairs up, the thick socks she wore
soundless on the hardwood.

She checked on Callie first, went into the pretty room, leaned down to
kiss her daughter's cheek before tucking the blankets around her little
girl's favored butt-in-the-air sleeping position.

Leaving the door open, she walked down the hall to the master suite.

She hated the room, she thought now. Hated the gray walls, the black
leather headboard, the sharp lines of the black furniture.

She hated it more now, knowing she'd made love with him in that bed
after he'd made love with other women, in other beds.

As her belly twisted she realized she needed to go to the doctor herself.
She needed to be sure he hadn't passed anything on to her. Don't think
now, she told herself. Just make the appointment tomorrow, and don't
think now.

She went to his closet—one nearly as big as the whole of the bedroom
she'd had back in Rendezvous Ridge, back home.

Some of the suits had barely been worn, she thought. Armani, Versace,
Cucinelli. Richard had leaned toward Italian designers for suits. And
shoes, she thought, taking a pair of black Ferragamo loafers off the shoe
shelf, turning them over to study the soles.

Barely scuffed.

Moving through, she opened a cupboard, took out suit bags.

She'd take as many as she could manage to the consignment shop in
the morning.

"Should have done it already," she muttered.

But first there'd been shock and grief, then the lawyers, the accountants, the government agent.

She went through the pockets of a gray pinstripe to be certain they were empty, transferred it to the bag. Five a bag, she calculated. Four bags for the suits, then another five—maybe six—for jackets and coats. Then shirts, casual pants.

The mindless work kept her calm; the gradual clearing of space lightened her heart, a little.

She hesitated when she got to the dark bronze leather jacket. He'd favored it, had looked so good in the aviator style and the rich color. It was, she knew, one of the few gifts she'd given him that he'd really liked.

She stroked one of the sleeves, buttery soft, supple, and nearly gave in to the sentiment to set it aside, keep it, at least for a while.

Then she thought of the doctor's receipt and dug ruthlessly through the pockets.

Empty, of course, he'd been careful to empty his pockets every night, toss any loose change in the glass dish on his dresser. Phone in the charger, keys in the dish by the front door or hung in the cabinet in his office. Never left anything in pockets to weigh them down, spoil the line, be forgotten.

But as she gave the pockets a squeeze—a habit she'd picked up from her mother on washing day—she felt something. She checked the pocket again, found it empty. Pushed her fingers in again, turned the pocket inside out.

A little hole in the lining, she noted. Yes, he had favored the jacket.

She carried the jacket back into the bedroom, got her manicure scissors out of her kit. Carefully, she widened the hole, telling herself she'd stitch it up later, before she bagged it for sale.

Slipping her fingers in the opening, she drew out a key.

Not a door key, she thought, turning it in the light. Not a car key. A bank box.

But what bank? And what was in it? Why have a bank box when he had a safe right in his office?

She should probably tell the lawyers, she thought. But she wasn't going to. For all she knew, he had a ledger in there listing all the women he'd slept with in the past five years, and she'd had enough humiliation.

She'd find the bank, and the box, and see for herself.

They could take the house, the furniture, the cars—the stocks, bonds, money that hadn't been nearly what Richard had told her. They could take the art, the jewelry, the chinchilla jacket he'd given her for their first—and last—Christmas in Pennsylvania.

But she'd hold on to what was left of her pride.

SHE WOKE FROM SHIVERY, disturbing dreams to the insistent tugging on her hand.

"Mama, Mama, Mama. Wake up!"

"What?" She didn't even open her eyes, just reached down, pulled her little girl onto the bed with her. Snuggled right in.

"Morning time." Callie sang it. "Fifi's hungry."

"Mm." Fifi, Callie's desperately beloved stuffed dog, always woke hungry. "Okay." But she snuggled another minute.

At some point she'd stretched out, fully clothed, on top of the bed, pulled the black cashmere throw over herself and dropped off. She'd never convince Callie—or Fifi—to cuddle up for another hour, but she could stall for a few minutes.

"Your hair smells so good," Shelby murmured.

"Callie's hair. Mama's hair."

Shelby smiled at the tug on hers. "Just the same."

The deep golden red had passed down from her mother's side. From the MacNee side. As had the nearly unmanageable curls, which—as Richard preferred the sleek and smooth—she'd had blown out and straightened every week.

"Callie's eyes. Mama's eyes."

Callie pulled Shelby's eye open with her fingers—the same deep blue eyes that read almost purple in some lights.

"Just the same," Shelby began, then winced when Callie poked at her eye.

"Red."

"I bet. What does Fifi want for breakfast?" Five more minutes, Callie thought. Just five.

"Fifi wants . . . candy!"

The utter glee in her daughter's voice had Shelby opening her blood-shot blue eyes. "Is that so, Fifi?" Shelby turned the plush, cheerful face on the pink poodle in her direction. "Not a chance."

She rolled Callie over, tickled her ribs and. despite the headache, reveled in the joyful squeals.

"Breakfast it is." She scooped Callie up. "Then we've got places to go, my little fairy queen, and people to see."

"Marta? Is Marta coming?"

"No, baby." She thought of the nanny Richard had insisted on. "Remember how I told you Marta can't come anymore?"

"Like Daddy," Callie said as Shelby carried her downstairs.

"Not exactly. But I'm going to fix us a fabulous breakfast. You know what's almost as good as candy for breakfast?"

"Cake!"

Shelby laughed. "Close. Pancakes. Puppy dog pancakes."

With a giggle, Callie laid her head on Shelby's shoulder. "I love Mama."

"I love Callie," Shelby replied, and promised herself she'd do whatever she had to do to give Callie a good, secure life.

AFTER BREAKFAST, she helped her daughter dress, bundled them both up. She'd enjoyed the snow at Christmas, had barely noticed it in January, after Richard's accident.

But now it was March, and she was thoroughly sick of it, and the bitter air that showed no sign of thawing. But it was warm enough in the garage to settle Callie into her car seat, to haul all the heavy garment bags into the sleek-lined SUV she probably wouldn't have much longer.

She'd need to find enough money to buy a secondhand car. A good, safe, child-friendly car. A minivan, she thought, as she backed out of the garage.

She drove carefully. The roads here had been well plowed, but winter did its damage however exclusive the neighborhood, and there were potholes.

She didn't know anyone here. The winter had been so harsh, so cold, her circumstances so overwhelming, she'd stayed in more than going out. And Callie caught that nasty cold. The cold, Shelby remembered, that had kept them home when Richard took the trip to South Carolina. The trip that was supposed to be a family winter break.

They would've been with him on the boat, and hearing her daughter chattering to Fifi, it didn't bear thinking about. Instead she concentrated on negotiating traffic, and finding the consignment shop.

She transferred Callie to her stroller and, cursing the biting wind, dragged the top three bags out of the car. As she fought to open the shop door, keep the bags from sliding and block Callie from the worst of the wind, a woman pulled open the door.

"Oh, wow! Let me give you a hand."

"Thank you. They're a little heavy so I should—"

"I've got them. Macey! Treasure trove."

Another woman—this one very pregnant—stepped out from a back room. "Good morning. Well, hello, cutie," she said to Callie.

"You got a baby in your tummy."

"Yes, I do." Laying a hand over it, Macey smiled at Shelby. "Welcome to Second Chances. Do you have some things for us to consider?"

"I do." A quick glance around showed Shelby racks and shelves of clothes and accessories. And a very tiny area dedicated to men's clothes.

Her hopes sank.

"I haven't had a chance to come in before, so I wasn't sure what you . . . Most of what I brought in are suits. Men's suits and shirts and jackets."

"We don't get nearly enough menswear." The woman who'd let her in tapped the garment bags she'd laid on a wide counter. "Is it all right to take a look?"

"Yes, please."

"You're not from around here," Macey commented.

"Oh, no. I guess not."

"Are you visiting?"

"We— I live here in Villanova right now, just since December, but—"

"Oh my goodness! These are gorgeous suits. Pristine condition so far, Macey."

"Size, Cheryl?"

"Forty-two Regular. And there must be twenty of them."

"Twenty-two," Shelby said, and linked her fingers together. "I have more in the car."

"More?" both women said together.

"Shoes—men's size ten. And coats and jackets, and . . . My husband—"

"Daddy's clothes!" Callie announced when Cheryl hung another suit on a holding rack. "Don't touch Daddy's clothes with sticky hands."

"That's right, baby. Ah, you see," Shelby began, looking for the right way to explain. Callie solved it for her.

"My daddy went to heaven."

"I'm so sorry." One hand on her belly, Macey reached out, touched Callie's arm.

"Heaven's pretty," Callie told them. "Angels live there."

"That's absolutely right." Macey glanced at Cheryl, nodded. "Why don't you go out, get the rest?" she told Shelby. "You can leave— What's your name, cutie?"

"Callie Rose Foxworth. This is Fifi."

"Hello, Fifi. We'll watch Callie and Fifi while you bring the rest in."

"If you're sure . . ." She hesitated, then asked herself why two women—one of them about seven months along—would run off with Callie in the time it took her to get to the car and back. "I'll only be a minute. Callie, you be good. Mama's just getting something out of the car."

THEY WERE NICE, Shelby thought later as she drove off to try local banks. People were usually nice if you gave them the chance to be. They'd taken everything, and she knew they'd taken more than maybe they might have but Callie had charmed them.

"You're my lucky charm, Callie Rose."

Callie grinned around the straw of her juice box, but kept her eyes glued to the backseat DVD screen and her ten millionth viewing of *Shrek*.

2

⁂

ix banks later, Shelby decided the luck may have run out for the day. And her baby needed lunch and a nap.

Once she had Callie fed, washed and tucked in—and the tucking-in part always took twice as long as she hoped—she geared up to face the answering machine and the voice mail on her cell phone.

She'd worked out payment plans with the credit card companies, and felt they'd been as decent as she could expect. She'd done the same with the IRS. The mortgage lender had agreed to a short sale, and one of the messages was from the realtor wanting to set up the first showings.

She could've used a nap herself, but there was a lot she could get done in the hour—if God was kind—Callie slept.

Because it made the most sense, she used Richard's office. She'd closed up most of the rooms in the big house, cut the heat back wherever she could. She wished for a fire, glanced at the black and silver gas insert under the black marble mantel. The one thing she'd enjoyed in the overwhelming house was being able to have a fire—the warmth and cheer of it—at the flick of a switch.

But that flick cost money, and she wouldn't spend it just to have gas flames when the sweater and thick socks kept her warm enough. She got out the list she'd made—what had to be done—called the realtor back, agreed to the open house on Saturday and Sunday.

She'd take Callie off somewhere, get them both out and leave that business to the realtor. Meanwhile, she dug out the name of the company the lawyers had given her that might buy the furniture so she could avoid repossession.

If she couldn't sell it in a swoop, or at least a good chunk of it, she'd try doing pieces online—if she ever had access to a computer again.

If she couldn't get enough, she'd have to face the humiliation of having it repossessed.

She didn't think the neighborhood ran to yard sales, and it was too damn cold anyway.

Then she returned the calls from her mother, her grandmother, her sister-in-law—and asked them to tell the aunts and cousins who'd also called that she was fine, Callie was fine. She was just real busy getting everything in order.

She couldn't tell them, not all of it, not yet. They knew some, of course, and some was all she could share right that minute. Talking about it made her angry and weepy, and she had too much to do.

To keep busy, she went up to the bedroom, sorted through her jewelry. Her engagement ring, the diamond earrings Richard had given her for her twenty-first birthday. The emerald pendant he'd given her when Callie was born. Other pieces, other gifts. His watches—six of them—and his army of cuff links.

She made a careful list, as she had with the clothes she'd taken to the consignment shop. She bagged the jewelry with their appraisals and insurance information, then used her phone to search for a jewelry store, as local as she could manage, that bought as well as sold.

With the boxes she'd picked up while they'd been out, she began packing up what she considered hers, and important to her. Photographs, gifts to her from family. The realtor had advised her to "depersonalize" the house, so Shelby would do just that.

When Callie woke from her nap, Shelby kept her entertained by giving her little tasks. As she packed, she cleaned. No more housekeeping staff to scrub and polish the endless miles of tile, of hardwood, of chrome, of glass.

She made dinner, ate what she could. She dealt with bath time, story time, bedtime, then packed more, hauled boxes to the garage. Exhausted, she treated herself to a hot bath in the soaking tub with its soothing jets, then crawled into bed with her pad, intending to write out the next day's agenda.

And fell asleep with the lights on.

THE NEXT MORNING she headed out again, with Callie and Fifi and *Shrek*, and Richard's leather attaché case holding her jewelry and its paperwork, his watches and cuff links. She tried three more banks, widening her area, then, reminding herself that she had no room for pride, parked in front of the jewelry store.

She dealt with a three-year-old cranky at having her movie interrupted again, and bribed Callie into submission with the promise of a new DVD.

Telling herself it was business, just dollars and cents, she pushed Callie into the shop.

Everything shone, and seemed as hushed as a church between services. She wanted to turn around and go, just go, but made herself move forward to the woman wearing a sharp black suit and tasteful gold earrings.

"Excuse me, I'd like to talk to someone about selling some jewelry."

"You can speak to anyone here. Selling jewelry is what we do."

"No, ma'am, I mean to say I'm selling. I'd like to sell some pieces. It says you buy jewelry, too."

"Of course." The woman's eye was as sharp as the suit, and carved Shelby down, top to toe.

Maybe she wasn't looking her best, Shelby thought. Maybe she hadn't been able to camouflage the dark circles under her eyes, but if there was one thing her granny had taught her, it was that when a customer came into your place, you treated them with respect.

Shelby stiffened a spine that wanted to buckle, kept her eyes direct. "Is there someone I should speak to, or would you rather I take my business somewhere else?"

"Do you have the original receipts for the pieces you're interested in selling?"

"No, I don't, not for all, as some were gifts. But I have the appraisals and the insurance papers. Do I look like a thief, one hauling her daughter around fancy jewelry stores trying to sell stolen merchandise?"

She felt a scene rising up in her, a dam ready to burst and flood hot and wild over everything in its path. Perhaps the clerk sensed it as she stepped back.

"One moment, please."

"Mama, I wanna go home."

"Oh, baby, so do I. We will. We'll go home soon."

"May I help you?"

The man who stepped up looked like somebody's dignified grandfather, the sort in a Hollywood movie about rich people who'd been rich forever.

"Yes, sir, I hope so. It says you buy jewelry, and I have some jewelry I need to sell."

"Of course. Why don't we go over here? You can sit down, and I'll take a look."

"Thank you."

She struggled to keep that spine straight as she crossed the shop to an ornate desk. He pulled out a chair for her, and the gesture made her want to blubber like a fool.

"I have some pieces my—my husband gave me. I have the appraisals and all that, the paperwork." She fumbled open the attaché, took out pouches and jewelry boxes, the manila envelope holding the appraisals.

"I— He— We—" She broke off, closed her eyes, drew a couple of breaths. "I'm sorry, I've never done this."

"It's perfectly all right, Mrs. . . . ?"

"Foxworth. I'm Shelby Foxworth."

"Wilson Brown." He took her offered hand, shook it gently. "Why don't you show me what you have, Mrs. Foxworth?"

She decided to go with the biggest straight off, and opened the pouch that held her engagement ring.

He set it on a velvet cloth, and as he took out a jeweler's loupe, she opened the envelope.

"It says here it's three and a half carats, emerald cut, a D grade—that's supposed to be good, from what I read. And with six side stones in a platinum setting. Is that right?"

He looked up from the loupe. "Mrs. Foxworth, I'm afraid this is a man-made diamond."

"I'm sorry?"

"It's a lab diamond, as are the side stones."

She put her hands under the desk so he couldn't see them shake. "That means it's fake."

"It simply means it was created in a lab. It's a very nice example of a man-made diamond."

Callie began to whine. Shelby heard the sound through the throbbing in her head, automatically dug in her bag, pulled out the toy phone. "You call Granny, baby, tell her what you've been up to. It means," she continued, "this isn't a D-grade diamond, and this ring isn't worth what it says here on this paper? It isn't worth a hundred and fifty-five thousand dollars?"

"No, my dear, it's not." His voice was as gentle as a pat, and made it worse. "I can give you the names of other appraisers, so you can ask for other opinions."

"You're not lying to me. I know you're not lying to me." But Richard had, over and over and over. She wouldn't break down, she told herself. Not now, not here. "Would you look at the rest, Mr. Brown, tell me if they're fake, too?"

"Of course."

The diamond earrings were real, and that was all. She'd liked them because they were pretty, and they were simple. Just studs that didn't make her feel awkward in the wearing.

But she'd prized the emerald pendant because he'd given it to her the day they brought Callie home from the hospital. And it was as false as he'd been.

"I can give you five thousand for the diamond studs, if you'd still like to sell them."

"Yes, thank you. That'd be just fine. Can you tell me where I should take the rest? Is it best to go to a pawnshop? Do you know of a good one? I don't want to take Callie into someplace that's . . . you know what I mean. Sketchy. And maybe, if you don't mind, you could give me an idea what it's all really worth."

He sat back, studied her. "The engagement ring is good work, and as I said, a good example of a lab diamond. I could give you eight hundred for it."

Shelby studied him in turn as she pulled off the matching wedding ring. "How much for the set?"

She didn't break down, and she walked out with $15,600—Richard's cuff links weren't fake, and had given her what she thought of as a bonus. Fifteen thousand six hundred was more than she'd had. Not enough to pay off debts, but more than she'd had.

And he'd given her the name of another shop that would look at Richard's watches.

She stretched her luck with Callie, tried two more banks, then gave it up for another day.

Callie picked a *My Little Pony* DVD, and Shelby bought herself a laptop and a couple of flash drives. An investment, she justified. A tool she needed to keep everything straight.

Business, she reminded herself. She wouldn't think of the fake jewelry as another betrayal, but as something that gave her some breathing room.

She spent naptime creating a spreadsheet, entered the jewelry, the payment for it. Canceled the insurance policy—and that would help her expenses.

The utilities on the big house, even with rooms closed off, were a killer, but the money from the jewelry would help there.

She remembered the wine cellar Richard had been so proud of, hauled the laptop down and began to catalog the bottles.

Somebody would buy them.

And what the hell, she'd splurge on a bottle for herself, have a glass with her dinner. She selected a bottle of pinot grigio—she'd learned a little about wines in the last four and a half years, and at least knew what she liked. She thought it would go just fine with chicken and dumplings—a Callie favorite.

By the time the day was done, she felt more in control. Especially when she found five thousand dollars tucked into one of the cashmere socks in Richard's drawer.

Twenty thousand now in the fund for cleaning up the mess and starting over.

Lying in bed, she studied the key.

"Where do you fit, and what will I find? I'm not giving up."

She could maybe hire a private detective. It would likely take a good chunk of that cleaning-up fund, but might be the sensible thing to do.

She'd give it a few more days, try some banks closer to the city. Maybe go into the city.

The next day she added thirty-five thousand on the sale of Richard's collection of watches, and two thousand three hundred more for his golf clubs, skis and tennis racket. It so boosted her mood that she took Callie for pizza between banks.

Maybe she could afford that detective now—maybe that's what she'd do. But she needed to buy a minivan, and her research told her that purchase would take a deep chunk of her fifty-eight thousand. Plus, it was only right she use some of that to bump up the payments on the credit cards.

She'd work on selling the wine, that's what she'd do, and hire the detective that way. For now, she'd just check one more bank on the way home.

Rather than haul out the stroller, she propped Callie on her hip.

Callie got that look in her eye—half stubborn, half sulky. "Don't want to, Mama."

"Me either, but this is the last one. Then we're going to go home and play dress-up tea party. You and me, baby."

"I wanna be the princess."

"As you wish, Your Highness."

She carried her now giggling daughter into the bank.

Shelby knew the routine now, walked to the shortest line to wait her turn.

She couldn't keep hauling Callie around this way, every day, disrupting routine, in and out of the car. Hell, she felt pretty damn stubborn and sulky herself, and she wasn't three and a half years old.

She'd make this the last one after all. The very last altogether, and start seriously researching private investigators.

The furniture would sell, and the wine would sell. It was time for optimism instead of constant worry.

She shifted Callie on her hip, approached the teller, who glanced at her over the tops of red-framed cheaters.

"Can I help you?"

"Yes, ma'am. I need to speak with a manager. I'm Mrs. Richard Foxworth, and I have a power of attorney here. I lost my husband last December."

"I'm very sorry."

"Thank you. I believe he had a safe-deposit box in this bank. I have the key here, and the power of attorney."

Much quicker than fumbling around, she'd learned, telling bored bank people she'd found the key, didn't know what it went to.

"Mrs. Babbington's in her office, and should be able to help you. Straight across, to the left."

"Thanks." She went across, found the office, knocked on the open glass door. "I beg your pardon, ma'am. They said I should speak to you about getting into my husband's safe-deposit box."

She walked straight in—something else she'd learned—sat with Callie on her lap.

"I have the power of attorney here, and the key. I'm Mrs. Richard Foxworth."

"Let me check on this. You have such pretty red hair," she said to Callie.

"Mama's." Callie reached up to grab a hank of Shelby's.

"Yes, just like your mother's. You're not listed on Mr. Foxworth's box."

"I— I'm sorry?"

"I'm afraid we don't have a signature card for you."

"He has a box here?"

"Yes. Even with the POA, it would be best if Mr. Foxworth came in personally. He could add you on."

"He—he can't. He was—"

"Daddy had to go to heaven."

"Oh." Babbington's face radiated sympathy. "I'm very sorry."

"Angels sing in heaven. Mama, Fifi wants to go home now."

"Soon, baby. He— Richard— There was an accident. He was in a boat, and there was a squall. In December. December twenty-eighth. I have the documentation. They don't issue a death certificate when they can't find . . ."

"I understand. I need to see your paperwork, Mrs. Foxworth. And some photo ID."

"I brought my marriage license, too. Just so you'd have everything. And the police report on when it happened. And these letters from the lawyers." Shelby handed it all over, held her breath.

"You could get a court order for access."

"Is that what I should do? I could ask Richard's lawyers—well, my lawyers now, I guess, to do that."

"Give me a moment here."

Babbington read over the paperwork while Callie shifted restlessly in Shelby's lap. "I want my tea party, Mama. You said. I want my tea party."

"That's what we'll do, soon as we're done here. We'll have a princess tea party. You should think about what dolls you're going to invite."

Callie began to list them off, and Shelby realized the nerves of waiting gave her a sudden and urgent need to pee.

"The POA's in order, as is the rest of your documentation. I'll show you to the box."

"Now?"

"If you'd rather come back another time—"

"No, no, I appreciate it so much." So much that she felt breathless and a little giddy. "I've never done this before. I don't know what I should do."

"I'll walk you through it. I'll need your signature. Just let me print this out. It sounds like you'll have a lot of guests at your tea party," she said to Callie as she worked. "I have a granddaughter about your age. She loves tea parties."

"She can come."

"I bet she'd love to, but she lives in Richmond, Virginia, and that's pretty far away. If you'd sign this, Mrs. Foxworth."

She could barely read it the way her thoughts were racing around in her head.

Babbington used a swipe card and a passcode, accessed a kind of vault where the walls were filled with numbered drawers. Number 512.

"I'm going to step out, give you some privacy. If you need any help, just let me know."

"Thank you very much. Am I allowed to take what's in it?"

"You're authorized. Take your time," she added, and drew a curtain to block off the room.

"Well, I have to say holy . . . s-h-i-t." She set the big bag she used for Callie's things and her own, and Richard's attaché, on a table, then, clutching her daughter, stepped to the box.

"Too tight, Mama!"

"Sorry, sorry. God, I'm nervous. It's probably just a bunch of papers he didn't want in the house. It's probably nothing. It may even be empty."

So *open* it, for God's sake, she ordered herself.

With an unsteady hand, she slid the key into the lock, turned it. Even jumped a little when it clicked open.

"Here we go. Doesn't matter if it's empty. The important thing is I found it. On my own. I did it myself. I've got to set you down a minute, baby. You stay right here, you stay right here with me."

She set Callie on the floor, pulled out the box, put it on the table.

Then simply stared.

"Oh God. Holy shit."

"Shit, Mama!"

"Don't say that. I shouldn't have said that." She had to brace a hand on the table.

It wasn't empty. And the first thing that caught her eye was a stack of banded money. Hundred-dollar bills.

"Ten thousand each, and oh God, Callie, there's so many of them."

Now her hands weren't just unsteady, but shook as she counted the stacks. "There's twenty-five of them. There's two hundred and fifty thousand dollars, cash money in here."

Feeling like a thief, she flicked an anxious look at the curtain, then shoved the money into the attaché.

"I have to ask the lawyers what to do."

About the money, she thought, but what about the rest?

What about the three driver's licenses with Richard's photo? And someone else's name. And the passports.

And the .32 semiautomatic.

She started to reach for the gun, pulled her hand back. She wanted to leave it, couldn't say why she didn't want to touch it. But she made herself lift it, remove the magazine.

She'd grown up in the Tennessee mountains, with brothers—one who was now a cop. She knew how to handle a gun. But she wasn't carrying a loaded gun with Callie around.

She placed it and the two extra mags in the attaché. She took the passports, the licenses. Discovered Social Security cards under the same three names, American Express cards, Visas. All under those names.

Was any of it real?

Had any of it ever been real?

"Mama. Let's go, let's go." Callie tugged on her pants.

"In a second."

"Now! Mama, now!"

"In a second." The tone, sharp and firm, might have had Callie's lip quivering, but sometimes a child had to be reminded that she didn't run the show.

And a mama had to remember that a three-year-old had a right to get tired of being hauled all over creation and back every damn day.

She bent, kissed the top of Callie's head. "I'm almost done, I just have to put this back now."

Callie was real, Shelby thought. That's what mattered. The rest? She'd figure it out, or she wouldn't. But Callie was real, and over $200,000 would buy a decent minivan, pay off some of the debt, maybe squeeze out enough for a down payment on a little house once she got steady work.

Maybe Richard hadn't meant to, and she didn't know what it all meant, but he'd provided for his daughter's future after all. And he'd given her room to breathe, so she'd think about the rest later.

She hauled Callie up, shouldered the bag, gripped the attaché as if her life depended on it.

"Okay, baby girl. Let's go have a tea party."

3

S he opened up all the rooms, turned the heat back up, even switched
on the fireplaces—all seven of them.

She bought fresh flowers, baked cookies.

The time spent on her laptop researching the best way to sell a house,
and fast, had suggested cookies, flowers. And as the realtor had decreed,
depersonalizing.

Keep it all neutral.

As far as she was concerned, the place was as neutral as they came. She
didn't find the big house welcoming, but then she never had. Maybe with
softer furnishings, warmer colors—it might have felt like a home.

But that was her sensibility, and hers didn't matter.

The sooner she unloaded the damn place, the sooner that section of
the crushing debt lifted off her shoulders.

The realtor arrived armed with flowers and cookies, so Shelby figured
she could have saved her time and money there. She'd brought what she
called a staging team with her, and they swarmed around changing the
placement of furniture, displaying more flowers, lighting candles. Shelby

had picked up a dozen scented candles, but decided she'd keep that to herself, just return them or keep them, depending on what seemed best when this was all said and done.

"The place is immaculate." The realtor beamed at Shelby, gave her a congratulatory pat on the shoulder. "Your cleaning crew did a terrific job."

Shelby thought of her midnight scrubbings and polishings, and only smiled. "I want it to show well."

"Believe me, it does. Short sales can be tricky, and will put some potential buyers off, but I'm confident we're going to get offers, good ones, and quickly."

"I hope you're right. I wanted to say, I've got someone coming in Monday morning to see about the furniture, but if anyone who comes in is interested in buying it, any of it, I'm going to price it to sell."

"That's excellent! There are so many wonderful pieces. I'll make sure we let people know."

She took a last critical look around herself, thought of the gun, the papers, the cash she'd locked in the safe in Richard's office.

Then she hefted the big bag she habitually carried.

"Callie and I are going to get out of the way. I have errands to run."

And a minivan to buy.

HER DADDY MIGHT NOT have approved that she didn't buy American, but the five-year-old Toyota she'd found through CarMax got high ratings on safety and reliability. And the price was right.

The price got better when she made herself haggle—offering cash. Real cash.

Her hands wanted to shake as she counted it out—half now, the rest when she picked the car up the next afternoon—but she bore down hard.

Maybe she had to pull over three blocks away, rest her forehead on the wheel. She'd never in her life spent so much money in one place. Never in her life bought a car.

Now she let herself shake, but it wasn't from nerves, no, not now. It was from stunning delight.

Shelby Anne Pomeroy—because that's who she was down into it, whatever the legal papers said—had just bought a 2010 Toyota minivan in happy cherry red. By herself. On her own.

And had shaved a thousand dollars off the deal because she hadn't been afraid to ask for it.

"We're going to be fine, Callie," she said, though her daughter was deep in her *Shrek* zone. "We're going to be just fine."

She used her cell, called the leasing company and arranged for them to pick up the SUV. And bearing down again, made herself ask for a ride to pick up the minivan.

Might as well deal with the insurance while she was at it, and Callie was in her zone. She'd just consider the SUV her office, temporarily.

Once she arranged for the car insurance to be transferred, she checked the online site where she'd listed the wine for sale.

"Oh my goodness, Callie, we've got bids!"

Delighted, fascinated, she scrolled through, adding in her head, and found over a thousand dollars already bid.

"I'm going to put another twelve bottles up tonight, that's just what I'm going to do."

Since it seemed her luck was running hot, she geared herself up for the drive into Philadelphia. Even with the GPS she made three wrong turns, had her belly knotted by the traffic. But she found the fur shop, hauled the never-worn chinchilla and her daughter inside.

To her surprise, no one looked at her like she was pathetic, or made her feel small for returning the coat. And that carved away a major chunk from a credit card, knocking the principal down to not-quite-as-scary, and lowered the painful interest rate.

She'd sat frozen for too long, Shelby admitted, and treated her little girl to a Happy Meal. Way, way too long. She'd broken the ice now, and damn it, she intended to make a flood.

She waited until she was out of the city again, gassed up the car—cursed the cold and the price of gas—then drove aimlessly for a while as Callie had fallen asleep.

Twice she drove by her own house—or the lender's house—and kept going when she counted the cars out in front. That was good, of course that was good, anyone who came to look at the house could be the one to buy it. But God, she just wanted to take Callie back, settle in, work on her accounting spreadsheet.

She stalled long enough so just the realtor waited.

"Sorry, give me one minute," Shelby said on the run. "Callie really needs to pee."

They made it—just barely. When she went back out to the great room, the realtor sat working on her tablet.

"We had a *very* successful open house. Over fifty people, and this time of year that's excellent. We had a lot of interest, and two offers."

"Offers." Stunned, Shelby set Callie down.

"Low offers, and I don't think the lender's going to accept, but it's a good start. And we have a family of four very interested. I have a good feeling about them. They're going to talk it over and get back to me."

"That's terrific."

"I also have an offer on your master bedroom suite. One of the lookers brought her sister, and while the sister isn't in the market for a house, she is for furniture. The offer's a little low, in my opinion, and she'd want it right away. Monday at the latest."

"Sold."

The realtor laughed, then blinked in surprise when she realized Shelby meant it. "Shelby, I haven't even told you her offer."

"It doesn't matter. I hate that furniture. I hate every stick of furniture in this house. Except for Callie's room," she amended, pushing at her hair as her daughter pulled out the basket of toys Shelby kept in one of the base kitchen cabinets. "It's the only one where I picked everything out myself. She can come haul it away tonight, for all I care. There are plenty of other places to sleep in here."

"Can we sit down?"

"I'm sorry, of course. I'm sorry, Ms. Tinesdale, I'm a little wound up, is all."

"I told you to call me Donna."

"Donna. Do you want some coffee or something? I've forgotten every bit of my manners."

"Just sit. You're dealing with a lot. Frankly, I don't know how you're dealing with it all. I want to help you. That's my job. The offer for the furniture is too low. Let me make a counteroffer. There's nothing wrong with a bargain, Shelby, but I don't like feeling you're getting taken advantage of. Even though it's ugly furniture."

"Oh!" Something inside Shelby just lit up. Like vindication. "Do you think so, too? Really?"

"Just about every piece of it, except Callie's room."

Shelby let out a laugh that to her shock turned to weeping in a finger snap.

"I'm sorry. God, I'm sorry."

"Mama." Callie crawled into her lap. "Don't cry. Mama, don't cry."

"I'm all right." She clutched Callie, rocked. "I'm okay. I'm just tired."

"Mama needs a nap."

"I'm okay. I'm okay, baby. Don't worry."

"I'm going to pour you a glass of wine," Donna announced, and dug tissues from her pocket. "You sit. I saw a bottle in the fridge."

"It's kind of early."

"Not today it isn't. Now tell me," she continued as she went to get a glass. "What else do you want to sell? The art?"

"Oh my God, yes." Worn to the bone, she let Callie pat a tissue over her face. "It's on my list to see about. I don't understand paintings like all these."

"Rugs? Lamps?"

"I've packed up everything I want out of here, except for Callie's room and my clothes, and a few things I need to keep around while we're living here. I don't want any of it, Mrs.— Donna. Even the dishes aren't mine."

"There's quite a wine collection downstairs."

"I've put twenty-four bottles online, this site I found. People are already bidding. I'm going to put another dozen on tonight."

Donna angled her head, gave Shelby what Shelby thought of as an appraisal. "Aren't you clever?"

"If I was clever, I wouldn't be in this fix. Thank you," she added when Donna gave her the wine.

"I don't think that's true, but let's start where we are. Can you give me the name of the company you have coming in about the furniture?"

"It's Dolby and Sons, out of Philadelphia."

"Good. That's good, and exactly who I'd recommend." Sipping wine, Donna made notes on her tablet, spoke briskly. "I'll make a counteroffer, but this buyer is going to have to come up to reality if she's serious about the master bedroom furniture. Otherwise, Chad Dolby—that's the oldest son, and he's probably the one who'll come in to give you a price—will make a fair offer. I know someone who would give you another price on your dishes, glassware, barware. And there are two art dealers I'd recommend for purchasing your art."

"I don't know how to thank you."

"It's my job," Donna reminded her. "And it's a pleasure. I have a daughter just a couple years younger than you. I'd hope someone would help her out if she ever found herself in . . . this kind of fix. I noticed you'd cleaned out your husband's closet."

"I did. Mama's fine, baby." She kissed Callie's hair. "You go ahead and play now. I took most of it into Second Chances," she told Donna when Callie slid off her lap.

"Perfect. Macey and Cheryl are very good at what they do, and their store gets a lot of traffic."

"Do you know everyone?"

"That's part of the job. How about the books?"

"I packed up my books, the ones I like. Richard bought the ones left in the library. He just bought them—what was it?—in a lot."

"And we'll sell them the same way." Donna nodded, tapped on her tablet. "I'm going to add that to my notes. And if it's what you want, I'm going to put some of the contacts I have in touch with you. You can set up appointments."

"That would be wonderful. I would appreciate that so much. It feels like I've been stumbling around, trying to figure out what to do with what for so long now."

"From what I'm seeing, you've figured it out very well."

"Thank you, but it helps so much to have advice and direction. You're so nice. I don't know why you made me so nervous."

Now Donna laughed. "I can have that effect. Should I give the contacts your cell number or the landline?"

"Maybe you could give them both. I try to keep my cell phone with me, in a pocket, but sometimes I forget."

"Done. These are businesspeople, and they're looking to make a profit. But they won't lowball you. If you think of anything else, you just let me know." She smiled. "I really do know everybody. And, Shelby, I'm going to get you an offer on this house, a good one. It's a beautiful space in a prime location, and the right buyer's out there. I'll find the right buyer."

"I believe you will."

And because she did, Shelby slept better that night than she had in weeks.

THE ENTIRE NEXT WEEK her head never stopped spinning. She made the deal with Dolby and Sons, shipped off wine won through the online auction house, picked up a very nice check from the consignment shop for some of Richard's clothes—and hauled in three garment bags from her own closet.

She accepted the offer for the dishes and glassware, packed it all up—and bought a set of four colorful plastic plates, bowls, cups.

They'd make do.

Though it might have been more sensible to eke out payments, she paid off one of the credit cards in full.

One down, she thought, eleven to go.

The art—not originals, as Richard had claimed—wasn't worth as much as she'd hoped. But the quantity made up for some of that.

Every day she felt lighter. Even the storm that blew in fourteen inches of snow didn't throw her off. She bundled Callie up like an Eskimo, and together they built their first snowman.

Nothing to write home about, she thought, but she did just that, snapping pictures with her phone to send back to Tennessee.

And the adventure wore her little girl out so Callie and Fifi were tucked in by seven. That gave Shelby a long, solid evening with her spreadsheet, her bills and her to-do list.

Should she use this money here to pay off one of the smaller credit cards, just get it gone? Or should she apply that money to one of the big ones, cut the interest payment down?

As much as she wanted to say two down, ten to go, it made more sense to cut down the interest.

Carefully she made the payment online, the way she'd taught herself, logged it onto her spreadsheet.

Four hundred and eighty-six thousand, four hundred dollars down. Only two million, one hundred and eighty-four to go.

Not counting the next bill that came in from the lawyers, the accountants. But at the moment, hell, that seemed like chicken feed.

The phone rang, and seeing Donna's name on the display, she snatched it up.

Maybe.

"Hello."

"Hi, Shelby, it's Donna. I know it's a little late, but I wanted to let you know we got a good offer on the house."

"Oh! That's such good news."

"I think the lender's going to approve this. You know it can take weeks, even months, but I'm going to do everything I can to push it through. It's the family I told you about, from the first open house. They really love the house, and the location is just what they wanted. And one more thing—she hates the furniture."

Shelby let out a laugh, lifting her face to the ceiling, cutting loose. "She really does?"

"Absolutely hates it. She told me she had to look past it, pretend it wasn't there, to really *see* the house, the layout. He's nervous about the short-sale aspect, but she wants it, and he's willing to go that route. And I think if the lender counters, asking for closer to their asking price, this buyer will come up."

"Oh my God, Donna."

"I don't want to get ahead of ourselves, but you should celebrate, at least a little."

"I feel like stripping naked and dancing all over this damn house."

"Whatever works."

"Maybe just the dancing part. Thank you. Thank you so much."

"Fingers crossed, Shelby. I'll contact the lender first thing in the morning. You have a good night."

"You, too. Thanks again. Bye now."

She didn't strip naked, but she did bring up the satellite radio. She hit with Adele, danced around the office, picked up the lyrics, let her voice loose.

She'd had ambitions once, aspirations, dreams. She'd be a singer—a star. Her voice was a gift, and she'd tended it, used it, appreciated it.

She'd met Richard through her voice, when he came into the little club in Memphis where she was lead singer with a band they called Horizon.

Nineteen years old, she thought now. Not old enough to buy a legal beer in the club, though Ty, their drummer who'd been a little bit in love with her, used to sneak her a bottle of Corona when he could.

God, it felt good to sing again, to dance. Other than lullabies, she hadn't used her singing voice in months. She rolled through Adele, straight into Taylor Swift, then fumbled with the remote to mute the volume when her phone rang again.

Still smiling, still dancing, she answered.

"Hello."

"I'm looking for David Matherson."

"I'm sorry, you've got the wrong number."

"David Matherson," he repeated, and rattled off the phone number.

"Yes, that's this number but . . ." Something lodged in her throat. She had to clear it, grip the receiver tight. "No one by that name lives here. I'm sorry."

She hung up before he could say anything else, then hurried to the safe, carefully entered the combination.

She took the manila envelope to the desk, and with stiff and shaky fingers, opened it.

In the envelope she kept the identification she'd found in the bank box, the ones with Richard's face smiling out.

And one set of identification was in the name of David Allen Matherson.

She didn't feel like singing anymore, or dancing. For reasons she couldn't explain, she was compelled to check all the doors, check the alarm system.

Despite the waste of electricity, she left a light burning in the foyer, left the second-floor hall light on. Rather than go to her own bed, she slid in with Callie.

And lay awake a long time praying the phone didn't ring again.

. . .

THE FURNITURE COMPANY sent a crew who packed up two guest rooms, the foyer, and the dining room, where Shelby hadn't had a meal since Richard's accident. After some haggling, she'd agreed to sell the master bedroom suite to the private buyer.

She wiped out the time payment, paid off a second credit card.

Two down, ten to go.

The house felt even bigger and less friendly with so much of the furniture gone. She had a nagging itch at the base of her spine to get gone herself, but there were details yet, and they were her responsibility.

She had an appointment at one-thirty with the book buyer—made at that time so she'd have Callie down for her nap. She tied her hair back, put on the pretty aquamarine dangles her grandparents had given her for Christmas. Added some bronzer, some blush because she looked too pale. She changed the thick socks she liked to wear around the house for good black heels.

Her grandmother claimed heels might pinch the toes some, but they boosted a woman's confidence.

She jumped when the doorbell rang. The book man was a solid fifteen minutes early, time she'd counted on to put coffee and cookies out in the library.

She rushed down, hoping he didn't ring again. Callie slept light at naptime.

She opened the door to a man younger and better looking than she'd expected—which went to show, she supposed, about assumptions.

"Mr. Lauderdale, you're timely."

"Ms. Foxworth." Smoothly, he held out a hand to clasp hers.

"Come in out of the cold. I'll never get used to northern winters."

"You haven't been in the area long."

"No, just long enough to go through a winter. Let me take your coat."

"I appreciate that."

He had a strong-looking stocky build, a square-jawed face, cool hazel eyes. Nothing, she thought, like the thin, older, bespectacled bookworm of her imagination.

"Donna—Ms. Tinesdale—said you might be interested in the books I have." She hung the sturdy peacoat in the foyer closet. "Why don't I take you right into the library so you can have a look?"

"You have an impressive home."

"It's big, anyway," she said as she led him back, past a sitting room with a grand piano nobody played, a lounge area with a pool table she still had to sell, and to the library.

It would've been her favorite room, next to Callie's, if she could have made it cozier, warmer. But for now she had the fire going, had taken down the heavy drapes—also in the to-sell pile—so the winter sun, what there was of it, could leak through the windows.

The furniture here, the leather sofa in what she thought of as lemon-pie yellow and the dark brown chairs, the too-shiny tables would all be gone by the end of the week.

She hoped the cases full of leather-bound books no one had ever read would be gone, too.

"Like I told you on the phone, I'll be moving before much longer, so I'm inclined to sell the books. I've already packed up the ones I want myself, but these—well, to tell you the truth, my husband bought them because he thought they looked good in the room."

"They look impressive, like the house."

"I guess they do. I'm more interested in what's in a book than how it looks in a cabinet, I guess. If you'd like to take a look at them, I can make coffee."

He wandered over, took out a book at random. *"Faust."*

"I read how a lot of people buy books this way, by the foot? To decorate."

She wanted to clutch her hands together, had to order herself to relax. She should be used to this by now, she thought, it shouldn't still make her nervous.

"I guess I think it'd be nicer—more appealing to the eye, to my eye," she corrected, "if they weren't all the same. The bindings, the height. And I guess I have to say, I wouldn't be one to curl up in front of the fire and read *Faust*."

"You're not alone in that." He slipped the book back in place and turned those cool eyes on her. "Ms. Foxworth, I'm not Lauderdale. My name's Ted Privet."

"Oh, did Mr. Lauderdale send you to take a look?"

"I'm not a book dealer, I'm a private investigator. I spoke to you on the phone a couple nights ago. I asked about David Matherson."

She took a step back. Heels or not, she could and would outrun him. Get him outside, away from Callie.

"And I told you, you had the wrong number. You need to go now. I'm expecting someone any minute."

"I only need a minute." With a smile, he lifted his hands as if to show her he was harmless. "I'm just doing my job, Ms. Foxworth. I tracked David Matherson to this area, and my information . . . I've got a photo." He reached into his inside jacket pocket, holding his other hand out and up in a gesture of peace. "If you'd just take a look. Do you know this man?"

Her heart hammered. She'd let a stranger into the house. She'd gotten careless, having so many people going in and out, and she'd let him in. With her baby sleeping upstairs.

"You let me think you were someone else." She put a whip in her voice, hope it stung. "Is that how you do your job?"

"Yeah, actually. Some of the time."

"I don't much like you or your job." She snatched the photo out of his hand. Stared at it.

She'd known it would be Richard, but seeing him—the movie-star smile, the brown eyes with hints of gold—hit hard. His hair was darker, and he wore a trim goatee she thought made him look older, just like the identification from the bank box. But it was Richard.

The man in the photo had been her husband. Her husband had been a liar.

What was she?

"This is a picture of my late husband, Richard."

"Seven months ago, this man—going by the name of David Matherson—swindled a woman in Atlanta out of fifty thousand dollars."

"I don't know what you're talking about. I don't know any David Matherson. My husband was Richard Foxworth."

"Two months before that, David Matherson swindled a small group of investors in Jacksonville, Florida, out of twice that. I could go back, go on, including a major burglary in Miami about five years ago. Twenty-eight million in rare stamps and jewelry."

The swindling, after what she'd learned in the past weeks, didn't shock her. But the thievery, and the amount of it, had her stomach twisting, her head going light.

"I don't know what you're talking about. I want you to go."

While he tucked the photo away, he kept his eyes on hers. "Matherson was most recently based out of Atlanta, where he ran real estate scams. You lived in Atlanta before coming here, didn't you?"

"Richard was a financial consultant. And he's dead. Do you understand? He died right after Christmas, so he can't answer your questions. I don't know the answers to them. You've got no business coming in here this way, lying your way in and scaring me."

Once again, he held up his hands—but something in his eyes told Shelby he wasn't harmless at all.

"I'm not trying to scare you."

"Well, you have. I married Richard Foxworth in Las Vegas, Nevada, on October 18, 2010. I didn't marry anyone named David Matherson. I don't know anyone by that name."

His mouth twisted into a sneer. "You were married four years, but you claim you don't know how your husband really made his living? What he really did? Who he really was?"

"If you're trying to tell me I'm a fool, get in line. Made his living? What living?" Overcome, she threw out her arms. "This house? If I can't get it sold and fast, they'll foreclose. You want to claim Richard swindled people, stole from people? Almost thirty million dollars? Well, if it's true, whoever hired you to find him can get in line, too. I'm digging out from the three million dollars in debt he left me holding. You need to go, you go tell your client he's got the wrong man. Or if he doesn't, that man's dead. There's nothing I can do about it. If he wants to come after me for the money, well, like I said, there's a line, and it's long."

"Lady, you want me to believe you lived with him for four years but you never heard of Matherson? You don't know anything?"

Anger swallowed fear. She'd had enough. Just enough, and that temper lit her up like a flash fire. "I don't give a good damn what you believe, Mr. Privet. Not one single damn. And if you pushed your way in here expecting I'd just pull a bunch of damn stamps and jewelry out of my pocket, or hundreds of thousands in cash to send you on your way, *I* believe you're a stupid man as well as a rude one. Get out."

"I'm just looking for information about—"

"I don't *have* any information. I don't know anything about any of this. What I *know* is I'm stuck here in this place I don't know, with this house I don't want, because I . . ."

"Because?"

"I don't know anymore." Even the temper faded now. She was just tired. "I can't tell you what I don't know. If you have any questions, you can talk to Michael Spears or Jessica Broadway. Spears, Cannon, Fife and Hanover. They're the Philadelphia lawyers handling this mess I'm in. Now, you're going, or I'm calling the police."

"I'm going," he said, following her as she strode out and went directly to the closet for his coat.

He took out a business card, held it out to her. "You can contact me if you remember anything."

"I can't remember what I don't know." But she took the card. "If it was Richard who took your client's money, I'm sorry for it. Please don't come back here. I won't let you in a second time."

"It could be the cops at the door next time," he told her. "You keep that in mind. And keep that card."

"They don't throw you in jail for being stupid. That's my only crime."

She pulled open the door, let out a little yip at the man reaching for the doorbell.

"Ah, Mrs. Foxworth? I startled you. I'm Martin Lauderdale."

He was older, with eyes of faded blue behind wire-rimmed glasses and a trim beard of more salt than pepper.

"Thank you for coming, Mr. Lauderdale. Goodbye, Mr. Privet."

"Keep that card," Privet told her, and skirting around Lauderdale, walked down the cleared front walk to a gray compact.

She knew cars—after all, her granddaddy was a mechanic, and she took careful note of this one. A Honda Civic, in gray, Florida license plates.

If she saw it in the neighborhood again, she'd call the police.

"Let me take your coat," she said to Lauderdale.

By THE END OF THE WEEK the library and the master bedroom stood empty. She sold the pool table, the piano, Richard's workout equipment and countless odds and ends through Craigslist.

She had one of the ten remaining credit cards down so close to payoff she could taste it.

She stripped the remaining art from the walls, sold that as well, and the fancy coffeemaker, the fancy bar blender.

. . .

AND WHEN SHE WOKE UP on the morning of what should have been the first day of spring to six inches of snow and still falling, she wanted to crawl back into the Princess Fiona sleeping bag currently serving as her bed.

She was living in a damn near-empty house. Worse, her baby girl was living in a damn near-empty house, with no friends, with no one to talk to or play with but her mother.

Four and a half years before, on a simmering October evening out West, she bought a pretty blue dress—Richard had liked her in blue—spent an hour blowing out her hair because he liked it smooth, and walked down the aisle of the silly little chapel carrying a single white rose.

She'd thought it the happiest day of her life, but it hadn't been her life at all. Just an illusion, and worse, just a lie.

And every day after that, she'd done her very best to be a good wife, to learn to cook the way Richard liked, to pack up and move when Richard had the whim, to dress the way he liked. To make sure Callie was washed and fed and dressed pretty when he came home.

All that's done, she thought.

"All that's done," she murmured. "So why are we still here?"

She went into her old dressing area, where she'd started some half-hearted packing in the Louis Vuitton luggage Richard had bought her in New York to replace the duffel bag she'd stuffed with clothes when she'd run off with him.

She packed in earnest now, then breaking a hard-and-fast rule, she set Callie up with *Shrek* and cereal in the kitchen while she packed her daughter's things. Following one of her mother's hard-and-fast rules—never call anybody but the police, the fire department or a plumber before nine in the morning—she waited until nine on the dot to call Donna.

"Hi, Shelby, how are you?"

"It's snowing again."

"It's the winter that won't die. They're saying we'll get about eight inches, but it's supposed to go up to about fifty by Saturday. Let's hope this is the last gasp."

"I'm not counting on it. Donna, there's not much left in the house here but me and Callie. I want to take the TV in the kitchen, the under-the-counter one, home for my grandmother. She'd just love that. And the big flat-screen—any of them. There's nine in this house, I counted. I just want to take one home for my daddy. I don't know if maybe the buyers want the others? I know the deal's not final, but we could make the sale of the TVs contingent on it. Honestly, I don't care what they want to pay me for them."

"I can propose that to them, of course. Let them make you an offer."

"That would be just fine. If they don't want them, or only want some of them, I'll take care of it."

Somehow, she thought, rubbing at her aching temple.

"But . . . when I get off the phone with you, I'm calling a moving company. I can't get Callie's furniture in the van, not with the boxes I'm taking, and the suitcases and her toys. And, Donna, I'm going to ask you for an awful big favor."

"Of course, what can I do?"

"I need you to put one of those lockbox things on the house, and for us to do whatever the paperwork is that's coming if this goes through, by mail or e-mail or whatever it is. I need to go home, Donna."

Saying it, just saying it, eased the knots in her shoulders.

"I need to take Callie home. She hasn't had a chance with all that's going on to make a single friend her age. This house is empty. I think it always was, but now you can't pretend it isn't. I can't stay here anymore. If I can get everything arranged, we're leaving tomorrow. Saturday at the latest."

"That's no favor and no problem. I'll take care of the house, don't worry about that. You're going to drive all that way, alone?"

"I have Callie. I'm going to cancel this landline, but I'll have my cell if you need to reach me. And my laptop, so I'll have e-mail. If the sale doesn't go through, you'll just show it to somebody else. But I hope it does, I hope those people who want it get it, and make a home out of it. But we have to go."

"Will you shoot me an e-mail when you get there? I'm going to worry about you a little."

"I will, and we'll be fine. I wish I'd known how nice you are sooner. That sounded stupid."

"It didn't," Donna said with a laugh. "I wish the same about you. Don't worry about anything here. If you need something done after you're home, you just let me know. You've got a friend in Philadelphia, Shelby."

"You've got one in Tennessee."

After she hung up, Shelby took a deep breath. And she made a list, a careful one, of everything that needed doing. Once she'd crossed the last thing off, she was going home.

She was taking Callie back to Rendezvous Ridge.

4

It took most of the day, and some creative bribery, to keep Callie from interrupting her. Accounts to be closed, others to be transferred, the change of address, the forwarding. The cost of the moving company to break down Callie's furniture, ship it and set it up again made her wince. And she considered renting a U-Haul and doing it herself.

But she'd need help getting the bed and dresser downstairs and into a trailer anyway.

So she swallowed hard and went for it.

It paid off, to her way of thinking, as the next day, for a twenty-dollar tip, the movers took the big TV off the wall in the living room, wrapped it and carted it out to the van for her.

Donna, as good as her word, had the lockbox installed.

She packed what was left, stowed whatever she might need on the road in a big tote.

Maybe it was foolish to leave so late on a Friday. Smarter, more sensible to get a fresh start in the morning.

But she wasn't spending another night in a house that had never been hers.

She walked through, bottom to top, top back to bottom, then stood in the two-story foyer.

She could see now, with the stark art, the too sleek furnishings re-moved, how it might be. Warmer colors, softer tones, maybe some big old piece, something with character, a little bit of curve in the entranceway to hold flowers, candles.

A mix of old and new, she thought, aiming for casual elegance with touches of fun.

Antique mirrors—yes, she'd group old mirrors, different shapes, along that wall, jumble books with family photos and pretty little whatnots on those shelves. And . . .

Not hers now, she reminded herself. No longer her space, no longer her problem.

"I'm not going to say I hate this place. That doesn't seem fair to who-ever moves in after me. It's like putting a hex on it. So I'm just going to say I took care of it best I could while I could."

She left the keys on the kitchen counter with a thank-you note for Donna, then reached for Callie's hand.

"Come on, baby girl, we're going on our trip."

"We're gonna see Granny and Grandpa and Gamma and Granddaddy."

"You bet we are, and everybody else, too."

She walked out to the garage with Callie wheeling her little Cinderella—her once favorite princess, currently usurped by Fiona—overnight bag behind her.

"Let's get you and Fifi strapped in."

As she secured Callie in the car seat, Callie patted Shelby's cheek. Her signal for: Look at me, and pay attention.

"What is it, baby?"

"We're gonna be there soon?"

Uh-oh. Torn between amusement and resignation, Shelby patted Cal-lie's cheek in turn. If the versions of *Are we there yet?* began before they pulled out of the garage, they were in for a very long trip.

"It's all the way to Tennessee, remember? That's going to take some time, so it's not going to be real soon. But . . ." She widened her eyes to demonstrate the excitement to come. "We're going to get to stay the night in a motel. Like adventurers."

"'Venturers."

"That's right. You and me, Callie Rose. Fingers on noses," she added, and Callie giggled, put her fingers to her nose so Shelby could close the side door of the van.

She backed out of the garage, sat for a moment until the door came all the way down again.

"And that's that," she said.

She drove away without a backward glance.

TRAFFIC WAS A MISERY but she wasn't going to care about that. It would take as long as it took.

To save *Shrek* for when real boredom hit, she kept Callie entertained with songs, ones her little girl knew, and fresh ones she'd stored up to avoid the endless repetition and save her own sanity.

It mostly worked.

Crossing the state line into Maryland felt like a victory. She wanted to keep going, just keep going, but at the three-hour mark made herself get off the highway. The Happy Meal put a grin on Callie's face, and food in her tummy.

Another two hours, Shelby thought, then she'd be over halfway there. They'd stop for the night. She already had the motel picked out, the route in the GPS.

When she stopped in Virginia, she saw she'd made the right choice. Callie had had enough, and was getting her cranky on. The adventure of jumping on a motel room bed changed the mood.

Fresh pajamas, Fifi and a bedtime story did the trick. Though she doubted fireworks would wake her little girl now, Shelby went into the bathroom to call home.

"Mama. We've stopped for the night, like I said we would."

"Where are you, exactly where now?"

"At the Best Western around Wytheville, Virginia."

"Is it clean?"

"It is, Mama. I checked out the rating online before I headed here."

"You got the security lock on?" Ada Mae demanded.

"It's on, Mama."

"You put a chair under the doorknob, just for extra."

"Okay."

"How's that sweet angel?"

"She's sound asleep. She was so good on the drive."

"I can't wait to get my hands on her. And on you, sweetie pie. I wish you'd told us you were starting out today before you did. Clay Junior would've come up there, driven you down."

She was the only girl, Shelby reminded herself, and the baby of three. Her mother would fret.

"I'm fine, Mama, I promise. We're fine, and already halfway there. Clay's got work and family of his own."

"You're his family, too."

"I can't wait to see him. See all of you."

The faces, the voices, the hills, the green. It made her want to cry a little, so she worked to bump up the cheer in her voice.

"I'm going to try to get on the road by eight, but it may be a little later. But I should be there by two o'clock at the latest. I'll call you so you know for sure. Mama, I want to thank you again for letting us stay."

"I don't want to hear that from you. My own child, and her child. This is home. You come home, Shelby Anne."

"Tomorrow. Tell Daddy we're all safe for the night."

"Stay that way. And you get some rest. You sound tired."

"I am a little. 'Night, Mama."

Though it was barely eight, she crawled into bed, and was asleep in minutes like her little girl.

. . .

SHE WOKE IN THE DARK, shocked out of a dream she remembered in bits and pieces. A storm at sea, drowning waves swamping a boat—a rolling white dot in a thrashing sea of black. And she'd been at the wheel, fighting so hard to ride it out while waves lashed, lightning flashed. And Callie, somewhere Callie cried and called for her.

Then Richard? Yes, yes, Richard in one of his fine suits pulling her away from the controls because she didn't know how to handle a boat. She didn't know how to do anything.

Then falling, falling, falling into that drowning sea.

Cold, shaken, she sat up in the strange dark room, trying to get her breath back.

Because it was Richard who'd fallen into the water, not her. It was Richard who'd drowned.

Callie slept, her cute little butt hiked in the air. Warm and safe.

She slid down, lay for a while stroking Callie's back to comfort herself. But sleep was done, so she gave it up, walked quietly into the bathroom. She stood debating.

Did she leave the door open so if Callie woke in a strange place she'd know where her mama was? Or did she close the door so the light and the sound of the shower didn't wake her baby, which they were all but guaranteed to do?

She compromised, left the door open a crack.

She didn't think a motel shower had ever felt so good, warming away the last chills from the dream, washing away the dragging dregs of fatigue.

She'd brought her own shampoo, shower gel. She'd been spoiled on good products long before Richard. But then she'd been raised on them, as her grandmother ran Rendezvous Ridge's best salon.

And day spa now, Callie thought. There was just no stopping Granny.

She couldn't wait to see her, to see everyone. To just be home, breathe the mountain air, see the greens, the blues, hear the voices that didn't make hers sound somehow wrong.

She wrapped her hair in a towel, knowing it would take forever to dry, and did what her mother had taught her when she'd been hardly older than Callie.

She slicked on lotion everywhere. It felt good, that skin to skin, even if it was just her own hands. It had been so long since anyone had touched her.

She dressed, peeked out to check on Callie, and left the door open just a little wider as she started on her makeup. She wasn't going home pale and heavy-eyed.

She couldn't do anything about going home bony, but her appetite would come back once she got there, settled in, pushed some of the weights off the heavy end of the scale.

And the outfit was nice—black leggings, the grass-green shirt that made her think of spring. She added earrings, a spritz of perfume, because according to Ada Mae Pomeroy, a woman wasn't fully dressed without them.

Deciding she'd done her best, she went back into the bedroom, packed up everything but Callie's outfit for the homecoming. A pretty blue dress with white flowers and a white sweater. Then turning on one of the bedside lights, she climbed onto the bed to nuzzle her daughter awake.

"Callie Rose. Where is my Callie Rose? Is she still in Dreamland riding pink ponies?"

"I'm here, Mama!" Warm and soft as a baby rabbit, she turned into Shelby's arms. "We're on a 'venture."

"You bet we are." She cuddled for a moment because those moments were precious.

"I didn't wet the bed."

"I know. You're such a big girl. Let's go pee now, and get dressed."

Even with fussing Callie's hair into a braid tied with a blue bow to match the dress, cleaning her up again after a breakfast of waffles, gassing up the van, they were on the road by seven-thirty.

An early start, Shelby thought. She'd take it as a good sign of things to come.

She stopped at ten, another pee break, fueled her system with a Coke, filled Callie's sippy cup and texted her mother.

Got going early. Traffic's not bad. Should be there by twelve-thirty. Love you!

When she pulled back onto the highway, the gray compact slipped out three cars behind her. And kept pace.

So the young widow was heading home in her secondhand minivan. Every action she did reasonable, normal, ordinary.

But she knew something, Privet thought. And he'd find out just what that was.

When she caught sight of the mountains, the great green rise of them, Shelby's heart jumped to her throat until her eyes stung. She'd thought she knew how much she wanted this, needed this, but it was more.

It was everything safe and real.

"Look, Callie. Look out there. There's home out there. There's the Smokies."

"Gamma's in the 'mokies."

"Ssssssmokies," Shelby said with a grinning glance in the rearview.

"Sssssssmokies. Gamma and Granny and Grandpa and Granddaddy, and Unca Clay and Aunt Gilly and Unca Forrest."

She rattled off family names, and to Shelby's surprise got most of them, down to the dogs and cats.

Maybe, Shelby thought, she wasn't the only one who wanted and needed this.

By noon she was winding, winding up through the green with her window half down so she could smell the mountains. The pine, the rivers and streams. Here there was no snow. Instead wildflowers sprouted— little stars, drops of color—and the houses and cabins she passed had daffodils springing yellow as fresh butter. Here clothes flapped on lines so the sheets would carry that scent into bedrooms. Hawks circled above in the blue.

"I'm hungry. Mama, Fifi's hungry. Are we there? Are we there, Mama?"

"Almost, baby."

"Can we be there now?"

"Almost. You and Fifi can have something to eat at Gamma's."

"We want cookies."

"Maybe."

She crossed what the locals called Billy's Creek, named for the boy who'd drowned in it before her father was born, and the dirt road that led down to the holler and to some ramshackle houses and double-wides where hunting dogs bayed in their pens and the shotguns stayed loaded and handy.

And the sign for Mountain Spring Campground, where her brother Forrest had worked one long-ago summer, and where he'd gone skinny-dipping—and a little more—with Emma Kate Addison, a fact Shelby knew as Emma Kate had been her closest friend, diapers through high school.

Now the turn for the hotel/resort built when she was about ten. Her brother Clay worked there, taking tourists out for white-water rafting. He'd met his wife there as she worked as a dessert chef for the hotel. Now Gilly was pregnant with their second child.

But before the wives and the children, before jobs and careers, they'd run tame here.

She'd known the trails and the streams, the swimming holes and the places where the black bear lumbered along. She'd walked with her brothers, with Emma Kate, on hot summer days into town to buy Cokes at the general store, or to her grandmother's salon to beg for spending money.

She'd known places to sit and look out at forever. How the whippoorwill sounded when dusk fell in clouds of soft, soft gray after the sun died red behind the peaks.

She'd know it again, she thought. All of it. And more important, her daughter would know it. She'd know the giddy feeling of warm grass under her feet, or cold creek water lapping her ankles.

"Please, Mama, *please*! Can we be there?"

"We're really close now. See that house there? I knew a girl who lived there. Her name was Lorilee, and her mama, Miz Maybeline, worked for Granny. She still does, and I think Granny told me Lorilee works for her, too. And see, just up ahead, that fork in the road?"

"You eat with a fork."

"That's right." Almost as impatient as her daughter, Shelby laughed. "But it also means a split in the road—where you can go one way or the other? If we went to the right—the hand you color with? If we went that way, we'd be in Rendezvous Ridge in a spit. But we go left . . ."

Her own excitement rising, Shelby took the left fork—a little faster than maybe she should. "And we're heading home."

"Gamma's house."

"That's right."

A few houses, some of them new since she'd left, scattered around— and the road still winding and rising.

Emma Kate's house, with a big truck in the drive that had *The Fix-It Guys* painted on the side.

And there it was. Home.

Cars and trucks everywhere, she noted. Packed in the drive, ranged on the side of the road. Kids running around the front yard and dogs with them. And the spring flowers her parents tended like babies already a show at the hem of the pretty two-story house. The cedar shakes gleamed in the sun, and the pink dogwood her mother prized bloomed as pretty as Easter morning.

A banner hung between the front-porch posts.

WELCOME HOME, SHELBY AND CALLIE ROSE!

She might have laid her head on the steering wheel and wept in sheer gratitude, but Callie bounced in her car seat.

"Out! Out! Hurry, Mama."

She saw another sign propped on a sawhorse right in front of the house.

RESERVED FOR SHELBY

As she let out a laugh, two of the boys spotted her van, ran over cheering.

"We'll move it, Shelby!"

Her uncle Grady's boys, who looked to have sprung up another six inches since she'd seen them at Christmas.

"Somebody having a party?" she called out.

"It's for you. Hey, Callie, hey." The older of the two—Macon—tapped on Callie's window.

"Whozat, Mama? Who?"

"That's your cousin Macon."

"Cousin Macon!" Callie waved both hands. "Hi, hi!"

She eased the van off the road, and with intense relief, turned off the ignition. "We're here, Callie. At last."

"Out, out, out."

"I'm working on it."

Before she could get around the van, kids swarming her, to open the side door, her mother came running.

Nearly six feet, Ada Mae had long legs to cover the ground from house to van. Her yellow sundress billowed around those legs, set off her crown of red hair.

Before Shelby could take a breath she was caught in a bear hug and surrounded by the scent of L'Air du Temps, her mother's signature perfume.

"Here you are! Here's my girls! My God, Shelby Anne, you're skinny as a snake. We're going to fix that. For goodness' sake, you kids give us some room here. Look at you, just look!" She cupped Shelby's face, tilted it up. "Everything's going to be just fine," she said when Shelby's eyes teared. "Don't you go running your mascara. It's all fine now. How do you get this door open?"

Shelby pulled the handle so the side door slid open.

"Gamma! Gamma!" Callie reached out, arms stretched. "Out, out!"

"I'm going to get you out of there. How the hell do you get her out of there? Oh, just look at you!" Ada Mae covered Callie's face with kisses as Shelby released the harness, the seat belt. "You're pretty as a sunbeam in May. And what a pretty dress, too. Oh, give your Gamma a big hug."

In her yellow sling-back heels, Ada Mae turned circles in the road while Callie clung to her like a burr.

"We're all over the place." Tears slid down Ada Mae's cheeks as she circled.

"Don't cry, Gamma."

"That's just joy spilling out, and good thing I've got waterproof mascara. We're out here, in the house, out the backyard where they've got the big grill going already. We've got food to feed the army we are, and some champagne, too, to celebrate."

With Callie on her hip, Ada Mae pulled Shelby in for a three-generation hug. "Welcome home, baby."

"Thank you, Mama, more than I can say."

"Let's get you inside, get you some sweet tea. The moving van was here not two hours ago."

"Already?"

"Carted everything right up to Callie's room. We've got it all made up so sweet and pretty. Your room's right next to your mama's," she said as they walked to the house. "I put you in Clay's old room, Shelby, as it's bigger than the one you had. It's been fresh painted, and we got a new mattress. The old was worn out. Callie's in Forrest's old room, so you know you'll share that bath between them. We got some nice new towels in there for you. Got them from your granny's spa, so they're nice."

Shelby would've said she shouldn't have gone to so much trouble, but if Ada Mae wasn't fussing, she wasn't breathing.

"Gilly baked a cake, all fancy. She's about ready to pop, but that girl can bake like Betty Crocker."

Her brother Clay came out. He'd gotten his parents' height, and their father's coloring with his dark hair and eyes. Grinning, he plucked Shelby off her feet, spun her like a top.

"About time you got here," he murmured in her ear.

"Soon as I could."

"Give her over," he ordered his mother, and snatched Callie. "Hey there, sunshine. Remember me?"

"Unca Clay."

"Girls always remember the handsome ones. Let's go find some trouble."

"If anybody can," Ada Mae said, and wrapped an arm around Shelby's waist. "You need a cold drink and a chair."

"I feel like I've been sitting for days, but I'd take the cold drink."

Family spread around the house so there were more hugs and welcomes, more yet when they reached the kitchen. Gilly—and she did look ready to pop—stood with a boy just a year younger than Callie on her hip.

"I've got him." Clay transferred his son, Jackson, to his other hip. "Got me a set now." He took off running out the back door, letting out a war hoop that had both kids squealing.

"Born to be a daddy. And a good thing," Ada Mae added, giving Gilly's belly a gentle pat. "You get off your feet now."

"I'm feeling fine. Even better now." She wrapped her arms around Shelby, swayed with the hug. "It's so good to see you. We've got pitchers of tea outside, and plenty of beer. And four bottles of champagne—your mama has decreed it's for the ladies only, as none of the men here can appreciate it."

"Sounds about right. I'll start with the tea." Shelby hadn't caught her breath, not yet, but decided she'd catch it later. "Gilly, you just look wonderful."

Hair as sunny as Clay's was dark, slicked back in a pretty tail to leave her face—round with pregnancy—unframed. Eyes of cornflower blue sparkled.

"Really wonderful. Are you doing good?"

"I'm doing great. Five weeks and two days to go."

Shelby made her way outside, onto the wide back porch, looking over the big backyard with its vegetable patch already sprouting, kids clambering over a swing set, a grill smoking, picnic tables lined up like soldiers with balloons tied to chairs.

Her father stood at the grill—the general—in one of his silly aprons. This one suggested you kiss his grits.

She was in his arms in seconds. She wouldn't break down, she told herself. She just wouldn't spoil it. "Hey, Daddy."

"Hey, Shelby."

He bent from his six feet, two inches, kissed the top of her head. Handsome and fit, a marathon runner for pleasure, a country doctor by trade, he held her close.

"You're too thin."

"Mama said she'd fix that."

"Then she will." He drew her back. "The doctor says food, drink, plenty of sleep and pampering. That'll be twenty dollars."

"Put it on my bill."

"That's what they all say. Go, get that drink. I've got ribs to finish."

As she stepped back, she was caught in a round-the-back bear hug. She recognized the wonderful prickle of whiskers, wriggled around and hugged. "Grandpa."

"I was just saying to Vi the other day, 'Vi, something's missing around here. Can't quite put my finger on it.' Now I got it. It was you."

She reached up, rubbed her palm over the stone-gray whiskers, looked up into his merry blue eyes. "I'm glad you found me." She laid her head against his barrel of a chest. "It looks like a carnival here. Everything full of fun and color."

"It's time you came back to the carnival. You fixing to stay?"

"Jack," Clayton muttered.

"I've been ordered not to ask questions." Those merry eyes could turn pugnacious in a finger snap—and did. "But I'm damned if I won't ask my own granddaughter if she's fixing to stay home this time."

"It's all right, Daddy, and yeah, I'm fixing to stay."

"Good. Now Vi's giving me the hard eye 'cause I'm keeping you from her. At your six," he said, and turned her around.

There she was, Viola MacNee Donahue, in a bright blue dress, her Titan hair in a sassy curling wedge, big movie star sunglasses tipped down her nose, and her eyes bold and blue over them.

She didn't look like anyone's granny, Shelby thought, but called out to her as she flew over the lawn.

"Granny."

Viola dropped her hands from her hips, threw out her arms.

"About damn time, but I guess you saved the best for last."

"Granny. You're so beautiful."

"Aren't you lucky to look just like me? Or like I did some forty years back. It's the MacNee blood, and good skin care. That little angel of yours has the same."

Shelby turned her head, smiled as she saw Callie with cousins, rolling on the grass with a couple of young dogs. "She's my heart and soul."

"I know it."

"I should've—"

"Should'ves are a waste. We're going to take a little walk," she said when Shelby's eyes filled. "Take a look at your daddy's vegetable patch. Best tomatoes in the Ridge. You put the worry aside now. Just put it aside."

"There's too much of it, Granny. More than I can say right now."

"Worry doesn't get things done, it just gives a woman lines in her face. So you put the worry aside. What needs doing will get done. You're not alone now, Shelby."

"I . . . forgot what it feels like not to be, so all this seems like a dream."

"This is what's real and always has been. Come here, darling, hold on awhile." She drew Shelby close, rubbed her back. "You're home now."

Shelby looked out at the mountains, smoked with clouds, so strong, so enduring, so true.

She was home now.

5

Somebody brought out her grandfather's banjo, and in short order her uncle Grady's wife, Rosalee, had a fiddle, her brother Clay his guitar. They wanted bluegrass, the music of the mountains. Those high bright notes, the close harmony of strings plucked and sawed stirred memories in her, lit a light inside her. A kind of birth.

Here were her beginnings, in the music and the mountains, in the green and the gatherings.

Family, friends, neighbors swarmed the picnic tables. She watched her cousins dancing on the lawn, her mother in her yellow heels swinging little Jackson to the rhythm. And there, her father with Callie in his lap having what appeared to be a very serious conversation while they ate potato salad and barbecued ribs.

Her grandmother's laugh carried over the music as Viola sat cross-legged on the lawn, sipping champagne and grinning up at Gilly.

Her mother's younger sister Wynonna kept a hawk eye on her youngest girl, who seemed joined at the hip with a skinny guy in torn-up jeans her aunt referred to as "that Hallister boy."

As her cousin Lark was sixteen and as curvy as a mountain road, Shelby figured the hawk eye was warranted.

People kept pushing food on her, so she ate because she felt her mother's own hawk eye on her. She drank champagne even though it made her think of Richard.

And she sang because her grandfather asked her to. "Cotton-Eyed Joe" and "Salty Dog," "Lonesome Road Blues" and "Lost John." The lyrics came back to her like yesterday, and the simple fun of it, singing out in the yard, letting the music rise toward the big sunstruck blue bowl of the sky, soothed her battered heart.

She'd let this go, she thought, let all of it go for a man she'd never really known and a life she knew had been false from the first to the last.

Wasn't it a miracle that what was real and true was here waiting for her?

When she could get away, she slipped into the house, wandered upstairs. Her heart just flooded when she stepped into Callie's room.

Petal-pink walls and fussy white curtains framing the window that looked out on the backyard, and the mountains beyond it. All the pretty white furniture, and the bed with its pink-and-white canopy all set up. They'd even arranged some of the dolls and toys and books on the white bookcase, tucked some of the stuffed animals on the bed.

Maybe the room was half the size of the one in the big house, but it looked just exactly right. She moved through the Jack and Jill bathroom—sparkling, as her mother would have it no other way—and into what had been her brother's room. What was her room now.

Her old iron bed where she'd slept and dreamed through childhood faced the window, just as it had in the room down the hall. As she'd liked it best so she could wake to the mountains. A simple white duvet covered it now, but Ada Mae being Ada Mae had set pillows in lace-edged shams against the iron headboard, and more in shades of green and blue mounded with them. A throw—blues and greens again—crocheted by her great-grandmother, lay folded at the foot.

The walls were a warm smoky green, like the mountains. Two watercolors—her cousin Jesslyn's work—graced them. Soft dreamy colors, a spring meadow, a greening forest at dawn. A vase of white tulips—

her favorite—sat on her old dresser, along with the picture in its silver frame of her holding Callie at eight weeks.

They'd brought her suitcases up. She hadn't asked—hadn't had to. The boxes, well, they were probably already stacked in the garage waiting for her to figure out what to do with the things she'd felt obliged to keep from a life that no longer seemed her own.

Overcome, she sat on the side of the bed. She could hear the music, the voices through the window. That's how she felt, just a step apart, behind the glass, sitting in a room of her childhood, wondering what to do with what she'd carried with her. All she had to do was open the window and she'd be a part instead of apart.

But . . .

Right now, today, everyone said welcome home, and left all the rest unsaid. But the questions murmuring under the welcome would come. Part of what she carried with her were answers and still more questions.

How much should she tell, and how should she tell it?

What good would it do to tell anyone that her husband had been a liar, and a cheat—and she feared he might've been worse. She feared down deep in her bones he'd been a swindler and a thief. And yet whatever he'd been—even if it turned out to be worse—he was still the father of her child.

Dead, he couldn't defend or explain any of it.

And sitting here brooding about it wasn't solving a thing. She was wasting that welcome, that sunstruck day, the rising music. So she'd go down again, she'd have some cake—though she already felt a little queasy. Even as she ordered herself to get up, go down, she heard footsteps coming down the hall.

She got to her feet, put an easy smile on her face.

Forrest, her brother, the only one who hadn't been there to welcome her, stepped into the doorway.

He didn't have Clay's height, skimmed just shy of six feet, and with a more compact build. A brawler's build, their granny claimed (with some pride), and he'd done his share. He had his daddy's dark hair, but his eyes, like hers, were bold and blue. They held hers now. Coolly, she thought, and full of the questions no one asked.

Yet.

"Hey." She tried to boost up her smile. "Mama said you had to work today." As a deputy—her brother the cop—a job that seemed to suit him like his skin.

"That's right."

He had sharp cheekbones, like their father, and his mother's eyes. And right now he sported a faint purple bruise on his jaw.

"Been fighting?"

He looked blank for a moment, then flicked his fingers over his jaw. "In the line. Arlo Kattery—you'd remember him—got a little . . . rambunctious last night down at Shady's Bar. They're looking for you outside. I figured you'd be up here."

"Back a few steps from where I started."

He leaned on the jamb, doing his cool study of her face. "Looks like."

"Damn it, Forrest. Damn it." No one in the family could twist her up, wring her out and smooth her down again like Forrest. "When are you going to stop being mad at me? It's been four years. Almost five. You can't stay mad at me forever."

"I'm not mad at you. Was, but I'm more into the annoyed stage now."

"When are you going to stop being annoyed with me?"

"Can't say."

"You want me to say I was wrong, that I made a terrible mistake, running off with Richard like I did?"

He seemed to consider it. "That'd be a start."

"Well, I can't. I can't say that because—" She pointed to the picture on the dresser. "That makes Callie a mistake, and she's not. She's a gift and a glory, and the best thing that ever happened to me."

"You ran off with an asshole, Shelby."

Every muscle in her body went hot and tight. "I didn't think he was an asshole at the time or I wouldn't have run off with him. What makes you so righteous, Deputy Pomeroy?"

"Not righteous, just right. It's an annoyance to me that my sister took off with an asshole, and I've barely seen her or the niece who looks just like her in years."

"I came when I could. I brought Callie when I could. I did the best I knew how. You want me to say Richard was an asshole? There I can oblige you, as it turns out he was. I had the bad judgment to marry an asshole. Is that better?"

"Some." He kept his gaze level on hers. "Did he ever hit you?"

"No. God, no." Stunned, she lifted her hands. "He never touched me that way. I swear."

"You didn't come back for funerals, for births, for weddings. Clay's, you made Clay's, but barely. How'd he keep you away?"

"It's complicated, Forrest."

"Simplify it."

"He said no." Temper began to simmer and burn inside her. "Is that simple enough?"

He stirred himself to lift his shoulders, let them fall. "You didn't always take no for an answer so easy."

"If you think it was easy, you're wrong."

"I need to know why you looked so tired, so thin, so beaten when you came home for what seemed like ten minutes at Christmas."

"Maybe because I'd come to realize I'd married an asshole, and one who didn't even like me very much."

Temper hammered against guilt with guilt slapping against fatigue.

"Because I'd come to realize before I found myself a widow and my child without a father that I didn't love him, not even a little. And didn't like him much, either."

Tears clogged her throat, threatening to burst through the dam she'd so laboriously built to hold them back.

"But you didn't come home?"

"No, I didn't come home. Maybe I married an asshole because I was an asshole myself. Maybe I couldn't figure out how to pull myself and Callie out of the muddy mess I'd made. Can you leave it at that for now? Can that be enough for now? If I have to talk about all the rest of it now, I think I'll break into pieces."

He walked over, sat beside her. "Maybe I'll move annoyed down to mildly irked."

Tears swam and spilled; she couldn't help it. "Mildly irked's progress." She turned, pressed her face to the side of his shoulder. "I missed you so much. Missed you like an arm or a leg or half my heart."

"I know." He draped an arm around her. "I missed you the same. It's why it's taken close to five years to get down to mildly irked. I got questions."

"You always have questions."

"Like why you drove down from Philadelphia in a minivan that's older than Callie, and with a couple of suitcases and a bunch of packing boxes and what looks like a big-ass flat-screen TV."

"That's for Daddy."

"Huh. Show-off. I got more questions yet, but I'll wait on them. I'm hungry and I want a beer—I want a couple of beers. And if I don't get you down there shortly, Mama's bound to come looking, then she'll skin my ass for making you cry."

"I need some time to settle myself before the questions start. I need to breathe for a while."

"This is a good place for it. Come on, let's get down there."

"Okay." She got up with him. "I'm going to be mildly irked with you for being mildly irked with me."

"That's fair."

"You can work some of that off getting Clay to help you bring in that TV, and then help figure out where it needs to go."

"It needs to go in my apartment, but I'll just come over here and watch it, and eat all Daddy's food."

"That's fair, too," she decided.

"I'm working on fair." He kept an arm draped around her shoulders. "You know Emma Kate's back."

"What? She is? But I thought she was up in Baltimore."

"She was up until about six months ago. I guess more like seven now. Her daddy had that accident last year, fell off Clyde Barrow's roof, busted himself up pretty good."

"I know about that. I thought he was doing okay."

"Well, she came back to take care of him—you know how her mama is."

"Helpless as a baby duck with no feet."

"That's the truth. She stayed a couple months. He was in and out of the hospital, in physical therapy, and her being a nurse, she could help more than most. The guy she's hooked up with, he came down off and on. Nice guy. Shortening it up, the time off and budget cuts cost her her job at the Baltimore hospital—or made it hard for her to keep on. She and her guy, they moved on down as she got an offer to work at the clinic in the Ridge."

"Daddy."

"Yeah. He says she's a damn good nurse. Matt—that's her guy—he moved on down with her, started a business with his partner. Griff's out of Baltimore, too. Construction-type business. They're The Fix-It Guys."

"I saw a truck with that name on it at Emma Kate's house."

"Matt and Griff are doing a new kitchen for Miz Bitsy. What I hear is she changes her mind every five minutes on what she wants, so it's taking a while. Emma Kate and Matt got the apartment across from mine, and Griff's got the old Tripplehorn place out on Five Possum Road."

"That place was falling down when we were ten," she remembered.

And she'd loved it.

"He's fixing it up. Likely take him the rest of his life, but he's got it going."

"You're stock full of news, Forrest."

"That's only because you haven't been around to hear it. You should go see Emma Kate."

"I wish she'd come today."

"She's working, and she's likely still in the annoyed stage where you're concerned. You might have to work some to bring that down."

"It's hard knowing how many people I hurt."

"Then don't do it again. If you decide to leave, say goodbye proper."

She looked out the back door, saw Clay running around with his son on his shoulders, and her grandmother pushing Callie on the swings.

"I'm not going anywhere. I've already been gone too long."

SHE SLEPT IN HER childhood bed on a new mattress, and though the night was cool, kept the window open a crack so the night air could waft in. She woke to a quiet rain, snuggled right in with a smile on her face as the sound of it pattered so peacefully. She'd get up in just a minute, she told herself, check on Callie, fix her baby some breakfast.

She'd deal with the unpacking, and all the other chores that needed doing. In just five more minutes.

When she woke again, the rain had softened to a misty drizzle, a drip and plop from leaves and gutters. Around it she heard the birds singing. She couldn't remember the last time she'd woken to the song of birds.

Rolling over, she glanced at the pretty glass clock on the bedside table, then shot up like an arrow from a bow.

She scrambled up, dashed through the bath and into Callie's room to find the bed empty.

What kind of a mother was she, sleeping till after nine o'clock and not having a clue where her daughter might be? Barefoot, a little panicked, she raced downstairs. A fire burned in the living room hearth. Callie sat on the floor, the old mutt Clancy curled beside her.

Stuffed animals sat in a line while Callie busily poked and prodded at the pink elephant lying trunk up on a kitchen towel.

"He's very sick, Gamma."

"Oh, I can see that, baby." Curled in a chair, sipping coffee, Ada Mae smiled. "He's looking peaked, no doubt about it. It's lucky you're such a good doctor."

"He's going to be all better soon. But he has to be brave 'cause he needs a shot." Gently, she rolled him over, and used one of her fat crayons as a syringe. "Now we kiss it, kiss the hurt. Kisses make hurts feel better."

"Kisses make everything feel better. Morning, Shelby."

"I'm so sorry, Mama. I overslept."

"It's barely nine on a rainy morning," Ada Mae began as Callie leaped up, ran to Shelby.

"We're playing hospital, and all my animals are sick. I'm going to make them better. Come help, Mama."

"Your mama needs her breakfast."

"Oh, I'm fine, I'll just—"

"Breakfast is important, isn't it, Callie?"

"Uh-huh. Gamma made me breakfast after Granddaddy had to go help the sick person. I had slambled eggs and toast with jelly."

"Scrambled eggs." She lifted Callie for a kiss. "And you're all dressed so nice. What time did she get up?"

"About seven. And don't start. Why would you deny me a couple hours with my only granddaughter? Have we had fun, Callie Rose?"

"Lots and lots and *lots* of fun. I gave Clancy a dog cookie. He sat like a good boy, and he shook my hand, too. And Granddaddy gave me a piggy-back ride all the way downstairs because I was quiet and didn't wake you up. He had to go help the sick people. So I'm helping the sick animals."

"Why don't you bring your animals in the kitchen while I fix your mama some breakfast? She's going to eat it all up like you did."

"I don't want you to have to feel you need to— Yes'm," she finished, warned by the narrowed stare.

"You can have a Coke since you never did learn to be civilized and drink coffee. Callie, you can bring all the sick animals and fix them up right over there. You're going to have eggs with ham and cheese—get some protein in there. I've got the whole day. I took off work until middle of the week. I've got a connection with the boss."

"How will Granny run the place without you?"

"Oh, she'll manage. Get your Coke, sit down there while I get this going. She's fine, Shelby," Ada Mae added in an undertone. "She's busy and she's happy. And your daddy and I enjoyed her company this morning. Now, I don't have to ask how you slept. You look better already."

"I slept ten hours."

"New mattress." Ada Mae chopped some ham. "And the rain. Makes you want to sleep all day. Haven't been sleeping well, have you?"

"Not especially."

"Or eating much."

"It's been hard to work up an appetite."

"A little pampering might make that easier." She glanced over at Callie. "I'm going to tell you you've done a good job with that girl. Of course, some of it's just disposition, but she's well-mannered without being all prim about it—something that just makes my back itch in a child—and she's happy."

"She wakes up every day raring to go."

"She wanted you first thing, but all I had to do was take her to your bedroom door, show her you were there sleeping, and she was fine. That's a good thing, Shelby. A child who clings usually says more about the mother clinging. And I expect it's been hard not to cling, on both sides these past months, when it's just been the two of you."

"I never saw any kids her age around the neighborhood up North. But then it was so awful cold, and it seemed it was snowing every five minutes. Still, I was going to look for a good preschool, just so she could socialize, but . . . I just didn't after—you know. I didn't know if it was the right thing for her after. And you and Daddy came for a while, and Granny came, and that was good. It helped us both having y'all there."

"I hope it did. We all worried we'd left you alone too soon." Ada Mae poured whisked eggs in the skillet over the ham chunks, grated cheese into the mix. "I don't know if I could've left if you hadn't said you'd come home as soon as you could."

"I don't know how I'd've got through if I hadn't known I could come home. Mama, that's enough eggs for two people."

"You'll eat what you want, then one bite more." Over her shoulder she sent Shelby a narrow look. "They're wrong when they say you can't be too thin, because you are. We're going to plump your mama up, Callie, and put roses in her cheeks."

"Why?"

"'Cause she needs it." Ada Mae plated the eggs, added a slice of toast, passed it over the counter. "And one bite more."

"Yes, ma'am."

"Now." Ada Mae busied herself tidying the already tidy kitchen. "You've got a hot stone massage booked at two o'clock at Mama's."

"I do?"

"Could do with a facial, too, but I'll do that myself later in the week. A woman drives clear down from Philadelphia hauling a toddler's earned a good massage. And Callie and I have plans this afternoon."

"You do?"

"I'm taking her over to Suzannah's. You remember my good friend Suzannah Lee? She couldn't come yesterday as she had her sister's girl's wedding shower. That's Scarlet? Scarlet Lee? You went to school with Scarlet."

"Sure. Scarlet's engaged?"

"Got a May wedding planned, to a nice boy she met in college. They're getting married here as Scarlet's people are here, then moving clear up to Boston, where he's got a job in advertising. Scarlet got her teaching degree so that's what she'll be doing."

"A teacher?" Shelby had to laugh. "As I remember, Scarlet hated school like it was spinach soaked in arsenic."

"Goes to show. What it goes to show, I can't say, but it goes to show.

Anyway, I'm taking Callie over to Suzannah's, show her off some, and Suzannah's getting her granddaughter, Chelsea—she's three, like Callie—that's her son Robbie's daughter who married Tracey Lynn Bowran. I don't think you've met Tracey. Her people are from Pigeon Forge. She's a nice girl, a potter. That's one of her bowls there, with the lemons in it."

Shelby glanced at the rich brown bowl with its bold blue and green swirls. "It's beautiful."

"She's got herself a kiln, works out of her house. They carry some of her pieces in town, at The Artful Ridge, and up at the hotel gift shop, too. We'll be giving you and Tracey a day off as Suzannah and Chelsea and Callie and me, we're having us a playdate."

"She'll love that."

"So will I. I'm going to be greedy with her for a while, so I expect you to indulge me. I'm taking her over about eleven. They'll get acquainted, then we'll have lunch. If the weather lets up, we'll take them out awhile."

"Callie usually naps about an hour in the afternoon."

"Then they'll have a nap. You can stop fretting about it, as I can see you are." With her chin jutted up, Ada Mae fisted a hand on her hip. "I managed to raise you and two boys besides. I think I can handle a toddler."

"I know you can. It's just . . . she hasn't been out of my sight in . . . I can't think how long. And fretting because she will be says more about me."

"You were always a bright girl. I wouldn't have any other kind," Ada Mae added as she came around the island, laid her hands on Shelby's shoulders. "Sweet Jesus, girl, you're nothing but knots. I booked you with Vonnie—you remember Vonnie, she's a cousin on your daddy's side."

Vaguely, Shelby thought, as cousins were legion in her family.

"Vonnie Gates," Ada Mae continued. "Your daddy's cousin Jed's middle girl. She'll work these out of you."

Shelby reached her hand back, laid it over her mother's. "You don't have to feel you need to take care of me."

"Is that what you'd say to your daughter, under these circumstances?"

Shelby sighed. "No. I'd tell her it was my job and my wish to take care."

"Well then. One bite more," Ada Mae murmured, kissing the top of Shelby's head.

Shelby ate one bite more.

"After today, you'll clear your own dishes, but not today. What do you want to do this morning?"

"Oh. I should unpack."

"I didn't say should," Ada Mae reminded her as she cleared Shelby's plate. "I said want."

"It's both. I'll feel more settled once I get things put away."

"Callie and I'll help you with that. When's the rest of your stuff coming?"

"I've got everything. I brought everything."

"Everything." Ada Mae stopped and stared. "Honey, they only took up a couple of suitcases, well, and Callie's things since you had those boxes marked. Clay Junior didn't stack more than a half dozen boxes, if that, in the garage."

"What was I going to do with all those things, Mama? Even when I find a house—and I have to find a job first—I couldn't use all those things. Did you know there are companies that come in, look things over and buy furniture all at once, right out of the house?"

She said it conversationally, lightly, as she rose, bent to pick up Callie, who was dancing, holding her arms up. "The realtor helped me find them. She was such a help to me with that sort of thing. I should send her flowers when the sale's all done, shouldn't I?"

The question didn't distract her mother as Shelby had hoped.

"All that furniture? Why, Shelby, there were seven bedrooms in that house, and that big office, and I don't even know all the other rooms. It's as close to a mansion as I've ever been in without paying for the tour. And so new." Shock and worry clear on her face, Ada Mae rubbed the heel of her hand between her breasts. "Oh, I hope you got a good price for all that."

"I worked with a very reputable company, I promise. They've been in business over thirty years. I did a lot of research online on that kind of thing. I swear, I could get a job as a researcher with all I've done with it, if I didn't think I'd want to shoot myself before the first week was done.

"We're going to unpack, Callie. You gonna help before you and Gamma go?"

"I'll help! I like helping Mama."

"Best helper ever. Let's get started. Mama, do you know if Clay took up the box that had Callie's little hangers? I can't use regular ones for her things yet."

"He took up everything that had her name on it. I'll just go out and look, be sure."

"Thanks, Mama. Oh, I'll go out, change the car seat over to your car."

"I wasn't born yesterday." The edge in Ada Mae's voice told Shelby her mother was still reeling from the idea of selling all that furniture.

She didn't know the half of it yet.

"Your daddy and I got the same one you use," Ada Mae added. "It's all ready for her."

"Mama." Shelby stepped over and with her free arm pulled her mother into a hug. "Callie, you have the best Gamma in the whole world."

"My Gamma."

And that distracted Ada Mae—enough, Callie thought as she knew her mother would chew over the idea of selling all the furniture in a near-to-ten-thousand-square-foot house in one fell swoop.

IT WAS ODD not having Callie underfoot or playing in her eye line, but she'd been so excited about the playdate. And it was true enough she'd be done with the unpacking and sorting in half the time without Callie "helping."

By noon, with everything put away, the beds made, she wondered what in the hell to do with herself.

She glanced at her laptop with some dislike, but made herself boot it up. No notices from creditors—so that was good news. Nothing yet on the sale of the house, but she wasn't expecting it. She did read a short e-mail from the consignment shop, letting her know they'd sold two of Richard's leather jackets, his cashmere topcoat and two of her cocktail dresses.

She replied with a thank-you, telling them yes, it was fine to wait until the first of the month to send a check to the address she'd left with them.

With unpacking and business done, she showered, dressed. Still too early to go in for the massage—and wouldn't that be heaven? So she'd take a walk. She could use a good walk.

The thin drizzle persisted, a steady trickle of wet out of a sky soft and gray as smoke. But she liked walking in the rain. She pulled on a hoodie, short, soft leather boots, and reached for her big bag. Her Callie bag. And remembering she'd given it to her mother to take, pushed her wallet into the back pocket of her jeans.

She felt so light, so unencumbered, she didn't know what to do with her hands, so slipped them into the pockets of the hoodie, found the little pack of wet wipes she'd stuffed in there the last time she'd worn it—when she hadn't been so unencumbered.

She drew in a deep breath of the cool, damp air when she stepped outside. Just stood breathing in with her fingers around Callie's wet wipes and the empty afternoon stretching ahead of her.

Everything was greening and sprouting and blooming with the misty rain turning the green, the color, more vibrant. All those scents—wet grass, wet earth, the tender sweetness of hyacinths dancing purple among the yellow of daffodils—drifted to her as she walked the long, familiar road.

She could walk by the Lee house, just to check. It was getting on to nap time, and Callie wasn't a hundred percent on the potty training in her sleep. About ninety-eight, but she'd be so embarrassed if she had an accident because her grandmother didn't think to take her in to pee before her nap.

She could just walk by, just a quick peek to . . .

"Stop it. Just stop. She's fine. Everything's just fine."

She'd listen to her mother's advice, take the day to do what she wanted. A walk in the rain, taking her time, time enough to study the mountains in their smoky blanket, to appreciate the spring flowers and the quiet.

She glanced over at Emma Kate's house, noted the handyman truck in the drive, and the bright red car behind it. She wondered how she'd approach Emma Kate now that they were both back in the Ridge.

And her friend got out of the car.

She wore a hoodie, too, in a bold candy-pink Callie would have loved. She'd changed her hair, Shelby thought as Emma Kate pulled two market bags out of the backseat. She'd hacked off the long nut-brown braid Shelby remembered, wore it all cute and shaggy, with bangs.

She started to call out, then could think of nothing to say and felt stupid and awkward.

As she swung the door closed, Emma Kate spotted her. Her eyebrows lifted under the warm brown fringe of bangs as she hauled one strap onto her shoulder.

"Well, look who's standing out in the rain like a wet cat."

"It's just a drizzle."

"It's still wet." She stood hipshot a moment, bags hanging from her shoulders, her wide mouth unsmiling, her deep brown eyes critical even through the rain. "I heard you were back."

"I heard the same about you. I hope your daddy's doing okay."

"He is."

Feeling more stupid just standing there, Shelby walked up the short driveway. "I like your hair."

"Granny talked me into it. I'm sorry about your husband."

"Thanks."

"Where's your little girl?"

"With Mama. They have a playdate with Miz Suzannah's granddaughter."

"Chelsea. She's a pistol. You got a destination, Shelby, or are you just out wandering in the wet?"

"I'm going into Viola's, but I have all this time on my hands with Callie off with Mama, so . . . I'm wandering first."

"Then you'd better come inside, say hello to my mother or I won't hear the end of it. I've got to take her these groceries anyway."

"That'd be nice. Here, let me take one."

"I've got it."

Rebuffed, as she was meant to feel, Shelby hunched her shoulders as they walked to the door. "I . . . Forrest said you're with someone, and living in town."

"I am. Matt Baker. We've been together about two years now. He's at Viola's right now, fixing one of the sinks."

"I thought this was his truck."

"They have two. This is his partner's. Griffin Lott. Mama's redoing the kitchen, and driving us all insane."

Emma Kate opened the door, glanced back at Shelby. "You're the talk of Rendezvous Ridge, you know. That pretty Pomeroy girl who married rich, was widowed young, come back home again. What will she do?" Emma Kate smirked a little. "What will she do?" she said again, and walked inside with her market bags.

6

riff considered himself a patient man. He didn't fly off the handle as a rule. And when he did, all bets were off, but it took a lot
of pushing to get him off the ground.

But right at the moment he was seriously considering duct-taping
Emma Kate's pretty adorable mother's mouth closed.

He'd worked on getting the base cabinets in all morning, and she'd
been peppering him with questions all morning.

Breathing down his neck, hanging over his back, all but crawling up
his ass.

He knew damn well Matt had taken off to Miz Vi's place to spare
himself the headache of his girlfriend's sweet, chatty—and let's face it—
ditzy mother.

Worse, she was still dithering—"dithering" would be the word of the
day—about the cabinets even as he installed them. And if he had to take
them out because she changed her mind again, he might do worse than
duct tape.

He had bungee cords, and he knew how to use them.

"Oh now, Griff honey, maybe I shouldn't have gone with the white.
They're so plain, aren't they? And white's cold, it's just a cold color, isn't
it? Kitchens ought to be a warm place. Maybe I should've gone with the

cherrywood after all. It's so hard to know before you see them right there where they're going, isn't it? How do you know what it's going to look like until you see what it looks like?"

"Clean and fresh," he said, trying to sound cheerful when he wanted to grind his teeth. "Kitchens should be clean and fresh, and that's what you're going to have."

"Do you think so?" She stood, nearly at his elbow, twisted her linked fingers together. "Oh, I don't know. Henry finally just threw up his hands and said he didn't care either way. But he'll care if it isn't right."

"It's going to look great, Miz Bitsy." He felt like someone, possibly himself, was shooting a nail gun dead center of his forehead.

He and Matt had dealt with fussy clients back in Baltimore. The control freaks, the whiners, the demanders and the ditherers, but Louisa "Bitsy" Addison was the undisputed queen of the ditherers.

She made the previously reigning champs—John and Rhonda Turner, who'd had them tear out a wall in their row house in Baltimore, build it back in, then tear it out a second time—seem resolute, steady as a brick wall—in comparison.

What they'd estimated as a three-week job—with a three-day contingency built in—was currently in week five. And God knew when it would end.

"I don't know," she said for the millionth time, patting her hands together under her chin. "White's kind of stark, isn't it?"

He set the cabinet, pulled out his level, shoved one hand through his mop of dark blond hair. "Wedding gowns are white."

"Now, that's true, and . . ." Her already big brown eyes got bigger, and a giddy thrill shone out of them. "Wedding gowns? Oh now, Griffin Lott, do you know something I don't? Has Matt popped the question?"

He ought to throw his partner under the bus. He ought to throw him under, then back up and drive over him again. But . . . "I was just using an example, like . . ." He did a frantic mental search. "Magnolias, for instance. Or—" Sweet Jesus, give me one more. "Ah, baseballs."

Crap.

"The hardware's going to punch it all up," he continued, just a little desperately. "And the countertop. That warm gray's going to give you friendly and sophisticated at the same time."

"Maybe it's the wall color that's wrong. Maybe I should—"

"Mama, you're not having those walls repainted." Emma Kate marched in.

Griff could've kissed her, could have dropped down and kissed her feet. Then he lost track of her completely when the redhead stepped in behind her.

He actually thought, Holy shit—and hoped he hadn't said it out loud.

She was beautiful. A man didn't get to be just shy of his thirtieth birthday without seeing some beautiful women, even if it was just on a movie screen. But this one, in the flesh, was one quick *wow.*

Masses of curling hair the color of a sunrise all tumbling around a face that looked like it had been carved out of porcelain—if they carved from porcelain, how would he know? Soft, full lips with a perfect dip at the top, and big, deep, sad blue eyes.

His heart actually skipped a couple of beats, and his ears buzzed for a minute so he missed most of the argument between Emma Kate and her mother.

"The kitchen's the heart of a home, Emma Kate."

"The way you keep turning and twisting it, you're lucky to have a heart left. Let Griff work, Mama, and say hello to Shelby."

"Shelby? *Shelby!* Oh my God!"

She raced across the room, grabbed the redhead in a wide, swaying hug. Shelby, grabbed Shelby, Griff thought. Nice name, Shelby. Currently his favorite name ever.

Then it clicked. Shelby—or Shelby Anne Pomeroy, as Bitsy squealed as she gave the redhead another squeeze. His friend Forrest's sister.

Miz Vi—on whom he had a mad crush—Miz Viola's granddaughter.

You could see if you stopped being dazzled for two seconds, just how

Miz Vi had looked as a young woman. How Ada Mae might have looked twenty-some years back.

Miz Vi's granddaughter, he thought again. The widow.

No wonder she had sad eyes.

He immediately felt guilty for wanting to wrap her up the way Bitsy was—then reminded himself it wasn't his fault her husband was dead.

"Oh, I'm just sick about missing your welcome home yesterday, but Henry and I had to go to his cousin's daughter's wedding, clear to Memphis. And I don't even like his cousin. Just a snooty woman, puts on airs because she married a Memphis lawyer. But it was a beautiful wedding, with the reception at the Peabody Hotel."

"Mama, give Shelby a chance to breathe."

"Oh, I'm sorry! I'm just going on and on. I'm so excited to see you. Griff, Emma Kate and Shelby here were joined at the hip, I swear, before they were so much as a year old right up to . . ."

It seemed to occur to her just why Shelby was home.

"Oh, honey. Oh, honey, I'm so sorry. You're so young to have such a tragedy in your life. How are you holding up?"

"It's good to be home."

"Nothing like home. And here mine's all torn up, so I can't even fix you something nice. And you so thin, too. Honey, you're skinnier than a New York model. You always were tall enough to be one. Emma Kate, do we have any Coke? You always were fond of Coke, weren't you, Shelby?"

"Yes, ma'am, but don't trouble about it. I love your new cabinets, Miz Bitsy. They're so clean and fresh, and just so pretty against that blue-gray on the walls."

Widow or not, at that moment Griff wanted to kiss her. Everywhere.

"Why, that's just what Griff said. He said they were clean and fresh. Do you really think—"

"Mama, we haven't even introduced Shelby. Shelby, this is my boyfriend's partner, Griffin Lott. Griff, Shelby—it's Foxworth, isn't it?"

"Yes." She turned those amazing eyes on him, and yeah, hearts could skip a beat. "It's nice to meet you."

"Hi. I'm a friend of your brother's."

"Which one?"

"I guess both, but mostly Forrest. And I might as well tell you right off, I'm in love with your grandmother. I'm working on a way to get her away from Jackson so we can run off to Tahiti."

That wonderfully shaped mouth curved, those sad eyes lightened, just a little. "It's hard to blame you."

"Griff's living out at the old Tripplehorn place," Emma Kate added. "He's rehabbing it."

"So you work miracles?"

"As long as I can use tools. You should come by and see it sometime. It's coming along."

She smiled at him, but it didn't reach those big sad eyes this time. "You've got your work cut out for you. I need to get on. I'm due at my grandmother's place."

"Now, Shelby, you come back when this is all finished and we'll have a nice long talk." Bitsy fluttered around her. "I expect to see you in and out of here just like you used to be. You know you're same as family here."

"Thank you, Miz Bitsy. It was nice meeting you," she said to Griff again, turned to go.

"I'll walk you out." Emma Kate shoved the market bags at her mother. "There's cold cuts and made-up salads and plenty of ready-to-eat food. You don't have to worry about cooking until your new stove's in. I'll be right back."

Emma Kate said nothing on the way to the door. "Say hey to Granny," she said as she opened it.

"I will." Shelby stepped out, turned. Bitsy's open welcome made Emma Kate's reserve all the more painful. "I need you to forgive me."

"Why?"

"Because you're the best friend I've had in my life."

"That was then. People change." After shaking back her shaggy hair, Emma Kate stuck her hands in the pockets of her hoodie. "Look, Shelby, you've had a hard knock, and I'm sincerely sorry about it, but—"

"You have to forgive me." Pride demanded she walk away; love wouldn't allow it. "I didn't do right by our friendship. I didn't do right by you, and I'm sorry. I'll always be sorry. I need you to forgive me. I'm asking you to remember that friendship before I ruined it, and forgive me. At least enough to talk to me, to tell me what you've been doing and how you are. Just enough for that."

Emma Kate studied her face, her dark eyes thoughtful. "Tell me one thing. Why didn't you come back when my granddaddy died? He loved you. I needed you."

"I wanted to. I couldn't."

With a slow shake of her head, Emma Kate stepped back. "No, that's not enough for forgiveness. You tell me why you couldn't do something you had to know was important, just sent flowers and a card like that was enough. Tell me the straight truth on that one thing."

"He said no." The shame of it washed over Shelby's face, burned in her heart. "He said no, and I didn't have the money or the nerve to go against him on it."

"You always had nerve."

Shelby remembered the girl who'd always had nerve like she remembered her cousin Vonnie. Vaguely.

"I guess I used it up. It's taking all I've got left to stand here and ask you to forgive me."

Emma Kate took a long breath. "You remember Bootlegger's Bar and Grill?"

"Sure I do."

"You meet me there tomorrow. Seven-thirty should work for me. We'll talk some of this out."

"I need to ask Mama if she can watch Callie."

"Oh yeah." The chill came back, cooler and damper than the drizzling rain. "That would be your daughter, the one I've never laid eyes on."

That twisted—both shame and guilt. "I can keep saying I'm sorry, as many times as you need to hear it."

"I'll be there at seven-thirty. Come if you can make it."

Emma Kate went back inside, then leaned back against the door and let herself cry just a little.

GRIFF SET THE LAST base cabinet in blessed peace since Emma Kate fell on her sword and took her mother shopping. He gave himself a break, swigging Gatorade straight from the bottle and eyeing the progress.

He didn't doubt the champion waffler would love every square inch of the remodeled kitchen once it was done. And it would look clean and fresh—just like the redhead.

Something going on there, he mused, with Bitsy going on about how Emma Kate and Shelby had been friends practically in the womb, and Emma Kate standing there as stiff and cool as he'd ever seen her. And the redhead sad and awkward.

Girl fight, he supposed. He had a sister, so he knew girl fights could be long and bitter. He'd have to poke at Emma Kate. It was just a matter of finding the right spot, getting her to open up and spill.

He wanted to know.

And he wondered how long was a reasonable length of time before a guy asked a widow out.

He should probably be ashamed of himself for wondering, but he just couldn't drum it up. He hadn't had such a quick and strong reaction to a woman in . . . ever, he decided. And he liked women a lot.

He set the Gatorade down and decided since Matt was taking all damn day to fix a sink, he'd start on the upper cabinets. Plus it wouldn't be just the sink, he thought, as he hauled his stepladder over. There'd be conversation. Nothing got done in Rendezvous Ridge without considerable conversation.

And iced tea. And questions, and long, lazy pauses.

He was getting used to it, found he enjoyed the slower pace, and definitely appreciated the small-town vibe.

He'd had a choice to make when Matt decided to move to Tennessee with Emma Kate. Stay or go. Find a new partner, run the business himself. Or take the leap and start over, more or less, in a new place with new people.

He didn't regret taking the leap.

He heard the front door open. That took getting used to, the way people in the Ridge rarely locked a door.

"Did you have to make her a new sink?" Griff called out, then set the drill on the last screw of the first upper.

"Miss Vi found a few other things for me to do. Hey, you're moving along. This looks great."

Griff grunted, stepped down to eye the cabinet. "Word of the day is 'dithering,' which has a picture of Bitsy Addison beside it in every dictionary across the land."

"She has a little trouble sticking to decisions."

And there was Matt's gift for understatement.

"I don't know how she decides to get out of bed in the morning. I'd be further along if your woman had gotten here sooner and taken Bitsy away. She's thinking the white's too white, and maybe she picked the wrong countertop. Or the wrong paint color. Don't ask about the backsplash."

"Too late now to change her mind on any of it."

"You try telling her."

"You gotta love her."

"Yeah, you do. But Christ, Matt, can't we put her in a box for the next three days?"

Grinning, Matt took off his light jacket, tossed it aside.

Where Griff was long and lanky, Matt was tough and ripped. He wore his black hair neat and trim where Griff's strayed past his collar with a hint of curl. Matt kept his square-jawed face clean-shaven while Griff's narrow, hollow-cheeked one tended toward scruff.

Matt played chess and enjoyed wine tastings.

Griff liked poker and beer.

They'd been as close as brothers for nearly a decade.

"Got you a sub," Matt told him.

"Yeah, what kind of sub?"

"That fire-breather one you like. The one that burns off the stomach lining."

"Cool."

"How about we get a couple more up, take a break? A quick one? Who knows how long Emma Kate can keep Bitsy out of our hair."

"Deal."

As they got to work, Griff decided to start poking.

"Miz Vi's granddaughter stopped by. The one who just moved back. The widow."

"Yeah? Heard some buzz about that while I was in town. What's she like?"

"A heart-stopper. Seriously," he said, when Matt spared him a look. "She's got hair the color of her mom's and Miz Vi's. Like that painter used."

"Titian."

"Right. It's long and curly. And she got their eyes, too. That dark blue that's nearly purple. She looks like something poets write about, right down to the sad eyes."

"Well, her husband died, what, like right after Christmas. Happy freaking holidays."

About three months, Griff calculated, and that was probably too soon to ask her out on a date.

"So what's up with her and Emma Kate? Check the level."

"What do you mean, what's up? Take your end up a couple hairs. Stop there. Perfect."

"Bitsy went on about what good friends they were—are—whatever, and the body language said the opposite. I don't remember Emma Kate ever talking about her."

"Don't know," Matt said as Griff set the screws. "Something about how she left with the guy she married."

"It has to be more than that." Griff prodded again, wondered if he'd need his drill. Matt never hung onto the more subtle details when it came to people. "A lot of people move somewhere else when they get married."

"They lost touch or something." Matt just shrugged. "Emma Kate mentioned her a couple times, but didn't have much to say about her."

Griff could only shake his head. "Matt, what you know about women could fit in a thimble. When a woman brings something up, then doesn't have much to say about it, she's got a *lot* to say about it."

"Then why doesn't she say it?"

"Because she needs the right opening, the right angle. Forrest hasn't said much, either, but he knows how to keep things tucked away. I didn't think about giving him an opening on it before."

"Before you knew she was a heart-stopper."

"There's that."

Matt checked the level again, all sides, before they moved on to the next.

"You don't want to start sniffing around a widow with a kid who's a friend's baby sister."

Griff only smiled as they lined up the second cabinet. "You don't want to start sniffing around some sassy southern girl who keeps telling you she's too busy to start anything up."

"I wore her down, didn't I?"

"Best thing you ever did. Got it?"

"Got it."

Griff let go of the cabinet to attach it to the first. "You should ask Emma Kate what the deal is."

"Why?"

"Because after she walked the redhead out, *she* had sad eyes. Before she walked her out, she was a little bit pissed, and after, she looked sad."

"Really?"

"Yeah. So you should ask her."

"Why would I ask her about something like that? Why stir it up?"

"Matt, jeez. Something's in there. It'll just stay in there being pissed or sad until it's stirred up and let out."

"Like a wasps' nest," was Matt's opinion. "You want to know so much, you ask her."

"Wuss."

"About this kind of stuff? Oh yeah, and not ashamed." He checked the level. "Right on the mark. We do good work."

"We fix it."

"That we do. Let's get the rest of this line up, then have a sub."

"I'm with you, brother."

VIOLA STARTED OUT doing hair for fun, doing up her sisters' or her friends' hair in fancy dos like they saw in magazines. She told the story of how the first time she took the scissors—and her granddaddy's straight razor—to her sister Evalynn's hair, she escaped a hiding because it looked as fine as what Miz Brenda down at Brenda's Beauty Salon charged good money for.

She'd been twelve, and from that point on, in charge of cutting everybody's hair in the family, and styling the girls—her mama included—for special occasions.

When she'd been carrying her first, she'd worked for Miz Brenda, and had done some side business out of the tiny kitchen in the double-wide where she and Jackson had started out. When Grady had been born—with her still four months shy of her seventeenth birthday, she added on manicures, and worked exclusively out of the two-bedroom house they rented from Jack's uncle Bobby.

By the time her second followed close on Grady's heels, she squeezed in cosmetology school with her mother minding the babies.

Viola MacNee Donahue had been born ambitious, and wasn't afraid to give her husband a few prods in the same direction.

By the time she was twenty, with three children and the loss of one that had broken off a piece of her heart she would never get back, she had her own salon—buying Brenda's place when Brenda ran off on her own husband with a guitar player from up in Maryville.

It put them in debt, but while Viola wasn't one to agree with the preacher saying how God would provide, she believed He'd look kindly on those who worked themselves sweaty.

She did just that, spending often eighteen hours a day on her feet while Jack worked just as hard and long at Fester's Garage.

She had a fourth child, worked herself steadily out of debt, then dived right back into it when Jack started his own car repair and towing service. Jackson Donahue was the best mechanic in the county, and he'd been carrying most of Fester's business as Fester was stumbling drunk by noon five days out of seven.

They made their own, raised four children, and bought a good house.

And with the nest egg Viola tucked away, she bought the old dry goods, expanded, and had the town talking when she put in three fancy pedicure chairs.

Business stayed steady enough, but if you wanted more, you figured out how to get it. Tourists wandered through the Ridge here and there, looking for quaint or cheap, or picturesque in a quieter setting than Gatlinburg or Maryville.

They came to hike and fish and camp, and some to stay in the Rendezvous Hotel and ride the white water. Those on vacation tended to be looser with their money, and more apt to take a few indulgences.

So she took the leap, expanded yet again. And yet again.

The locals called her place Vi's, but the tourists came into Viola's Harmony House Salon and Day Spa.

She liked the sound of it.

The latest—and, Viola claimed, the last—expansion added on what she billed a Relaxation Room, which was a fancy name for waiting area, but fancy it was. Though she enjoyed bold, rich colors, she'd kept the tones soft, added a gas-burning fireplace, banned all electronic devices, and offered specialty teas made local, spring water, deep-cushioned chairs and plush robes with her logo embroidered on them.

Since the expansion, this latest and last, had been in the works while Shelby had been moving from Atlanta to Philadelphia, Shelby hadn't seen it all done.

She couldn't say it surprised her when her grandmother led her through a locker room/changing area and into the room that smelled lightly of lavender.

"Granny, this is amazing."

She kept her voice down as two women she didn't know sat in oatmeal-colored chairs paging through glossy magazines.

"You try some jasmine tea. It's made right here in the Ridge. And relax some before Vonnie comes to get you."

"This is as nice as any of the spas I've been to. Nicer."

Amenities included shallow dishes of sunflower seeds, a wooden bowl of sharp green apples, clear pitchers of water with inserts holding slices of lemon or cucumber, and hot pots for tea clients could drink out of pretty little cups.

"It's you who's amazing."

"It's not enough to have ideas if you just let them sit around. You come see me when Vonnie's done with you."

"I will. Would you . . . could you just check with Mama? I just want to be sure Callie's behaving."

"Don't you worry about a thing."

Easier said than done—or so Shelby thought, until Vonnie, who couldn't have been more than five-three, had her on a warm table in a dim room with soft music playing.

"Girl, you've got enough rocks in these shoulders to build a three-story house. Take a deep breath for me now. And another. That's the way. Let it go now."

She tried, then she didn't have to try. She drifted.

"How're you feeling now?"

"What?"

"That's a good answer. I want you to take your time getting up. I'm going to turn the lights up a little, and I've got your robe lying over your legs."

"Thank you, Vonnie."

"I'm going to tell Miz Vi you could use another next week. It's going to take a few times to get you smoothed out, Shelby."

"I feel smooth."

"That's good. Now, don't go getting up too fast, you hear? I'm going out and get you some nice spring water. You want to drink a lot of water now."

She drank the water, changed back into her street clothes and made her way out to the salon area.

Four of the six hair stations were working, and two of the four pedicure chairs were occupied. She saw two women getting manicures and glanced at her own nails. She hadn't had her nails done since right before Christmas.

While the Relaxation Room stood as a sanctuary of quiet, the salon rang with voices, the bubble of footbaths, the whirl of dryers. Five people called out to her—three beauticians, two customers—so she got caught up in conversations, acknowledged offers of sympathy and of welcome before she found her grandmother.

"Perfect timing. I just finished doing Dolly Wobuck's highlights, and my next appointment canceled, so I've got time to give you a facial. Go put a robe back on."

"Oh, but—"

"Callie's fine. She and Chelsea are having a tea party, with costumes. Ada Mae said they hooked together like two links in a chain and reminded her of you and Emma Kate."

"That's good to hear." Shelby tried not to think of that cool look in the eyes of her childhood friend.

"She'll have your baby home in a couple hours. That'll give you time for a facial, and us time to talk." Viola tipped her head, and the light through the front window tipped gold in the red. "Vonnie did you some good, didn't she?"

"She's wonderful. I don't remember her being such a little thing."

"Takes after her mama."

"She may be little, but she has wonderfully strong hands. She wouldn't let me tip her, Granny. She said Mama had seen to it, and anyway, we're family."

"You can tip me by giving me an hour of your time. Go on, get a robe on. The facial rooms are in the same place. We'll be in the first one. Get!"

She did as she was told. She wanted Callie to make friends, didn't she? To have someone to play with, to be with. It was healthy and right. And foolish to feel so anxious because she was spending the day at her grandmother's salon.

"I've got just the thing for you," Viola said when Callie came in. "It's my energizing facial. It'll give you and your skin a boost. Just hang that robe on the hook there, lie down here and we'll tuck you up."

"This is new, too. Not the room, but the chair, some of the machines here."

"If you want to be competitive, you've got to keep up." Viola took out a bib apron and tied it over her cropped pants and bold orange T-shirt.

"I've got a machine in the next room that works on lines with electrode pulses."

"Really?" Shelby slipped under the sheet onto the inclined chair.

"Only two of us trained to use it for now, that's me and your mama, but Maybeline—you remember Maybeline?"

"I do. I can't remember a time she didn't work for you."

"Been some years, and now her girl's working here, too. Lorilee's got the same good touch on nails as her mama. Maybeline's training on the new machine now, so we'll have three can use it. Not that you have to worry about lines for some time yet." She laid a light duvet over the sheet, then banded back Shelby's hair. "But let's have a look at things. Your skin's a little dehydrated, baby. Stress'll do that."

She started out with a cleanse, her hands soft as a child's on Shelby's face.

"There are things a girl can tell her granny she might not say right out to her mama. It's that safety zone. And Ada Mae, she looks at bright sides, she's blessed with that outlook. You've got trouble, and it's not grief. I know how grief looks."

"I'd stopped loving him." She could say it out loud, with her eyes closed and her grandmother's hands on her face. "Maybe I never really did love him. I know now he didn't love me. It's hard knowing that, hard knowing we didn't have what we should have and he's gone."

"You were young."

"Older than you were."

"I got awful lucky. So'd your grandpa."

"I was a good wife, Granny. I can say that and know it's true. And Callie—we made Callie, so that's something special. And I wanted another baby. I know maybe it's wrong wanting another when things aren't the way they should be, but I thought maybe it's just how it would be, and it was all right. It could be good if there was another baby for me to love. I had such a hunger for another baby, such a yearning in me."

"I know that hunger well."

"And he said that was fine. He said it'd be good for Callie to have a brother or sister. But it didn't happen, and it happened so easy and fast the first time. I had tests, and he said he had tests."

"Said he had?" Viola repeated as she worked a gentle exfoliant into Shelby's skin.

"I . . . I had to go through all his papers, and his files after. There were so many things to go through."

Lawyers and accountants and the tax people, the creditors, the bills and debt.

"And I found a doctor's receipt or invoice, whatever. Richard, he kept everything. It was from a few weeks after Callie was born, the time I brought her home, her first visit, and he said he had a business trip. He was so good about us coming home, he made all the arrangements. Private plane and a limo to get me to it. But he went to a doctor in New York and had a vasectomy."

Viola's hands paused. "He got himself snipped and let you think you were trying to make a baby?"

"I'm never going to be able to forgive him for that. Out of all of it, it's that I can't forgive."

"His right to decide if he wanted to make another baby, but not his right to get fixed and not tell you. It's a terrible lie. And a man who could tell that terrible lie, live with that terrible lie, had something missing inside him."

"There were so many lies, Granny, and finding them after he's dead?" There was an emptiness left there, Shelby thought, that could never be filled again. "I feel like a fool, I feel like I lived with a stranger. And I don't understand why he married me, why he lived with me."

Despite what churned up inside her, Viola kept her hands gentle, her voice calm. "You're a beautiful girl, Shelby Anne, and you said you were a good wife. And you're not to feel like a fool because you trusted your husband. What else did he lie about? Were there other women?"

"I don't know for certain, and can't ask. But I have to say yes, from things I found, yes, there were other women. And I find now I don't care. I can't even care how many—he took so many trips without us. And I went to the doctor a few weeks ago, got tested in case . . . He didn't give me anything, so if he had other women, he was careful. So I don't care if he had a hundred other women."

She worked up her nerve while Viola slathered on the energizing mask.

"The money, Granny. He lied about the money. I never paid much attention to it because he said that was his business, and mine was to run the house and Callie. He—he could lash out like a whip over that without raising his voice or his hand."

"Cold contempt can be a sharper blade than hot temper."

Comforted, Shelby opened her eyes, looked into her grandmother's. "He cowed me. I hate admitting it, and I don't even know how it happened. But I can look back and see it so clear. He didn't like me asking questions about money, so I didn't. We had so much—the clothes and the furniture and the restaurants and the travel. But he was cheating there, too, and running some sort of scam. I'm still not clear on all of it."

She closed her eyes again, not in shame—not with Granny—but in weariness. "Everything was on credit, and the house up North, he hadn't made even the first payment on the loan, and he bought it back in the summer. I didn't know a thing about it until he told me in November we were moving. And there were the cars, and the credit cards, and the time payments—and some debts in Atlanta he left behind. Taxes unpaid."

"He left you in debt?"

"I've been sorting it out, and setting up payment plans—and I sold a lot off in the last few weeks. There's an offer on the house, and if it goes through, it'll take a lot off."

"How much did he leave you owing?"

"As of right now?" She opened her eyes, looked into her grandmother's. "One million, nine hundred and ninety-six thousand dollars and eighty-nine cents."

"Well." Viola had to draw in breath, let it out slow. "Well. Jesus Christ in a rocking chair, Shelby Anne, that's a considerable sum of money."

"When the house sells, it'll cut it back. The offer's for one point eight million. I owe a hundred and fifty more than that on it, but they forgive that with this short-sale business. And it started out around three million. Some over that with the lawyers' bills, and accounting bills."

"You paid off a million dollars since January?" Viola shook her head. "That must've been one holy hell of a yard sale."

7

A massage, an energizing facial and coming home to find her little girl bubbling over with happiness, those went a long way toward lifting Shelby's mood.

But the biggest lift had been unburdening herself to her grandmother. She'd told her everything—about finding the safe-deposit box and what was in it, the private detective, the spreadsheet she'd created, and her need to find a paying job as soon as she could.

By the time she'd given Callie her supper, her bath, tucked her in for the night, she felt she knew all there was to know about Chelsea—and had made a promise to have Chelsea over as soon as she could.

She went back down, found her father stretched out in the La-Z-Boy recliner he loved, watching a basketball game on his new TV. And her mother sitting on the sofa crocheting.

"She go down all right?"

"Out like a light before I'd finished her bedtime story. You wore her out today, Mama."

"It sure was fun. The two girls were like tadpoles swimming in their own pond, hardly still a minute. Suzannah and I talked about taking turns, having Chelsea come here, then taking Callie there. And I've got

Tracey's number for you, right in on the kitchen board. You ought to call Chelsea's mama, honey, make a good bridge there."

"I will. You gave her a happy day. Can I ask you for a favor?"

"You know you can."

"I ran into Emma Kate today."

"I heard about that." Fingers still working yarn and needle, Ada Mae glanced up with a smile. "It's the Ridge, baby. If I don't hear about something ten minutes after it happened, I know I have to have your daddy check my hearing. Hattie Munson—you remember she lives across from Bitsy, though they're feuding about something half the time. They're feuding now because Bitsy's getting a new kitchen and didn't take Hattie's advice about the new appliances. Hattie's boy works for LG, but Bitsy bought Maytag, and Hattie took that as a personal insult. Of course, Hattie Munson takes offense if she sneezes in her own kitchen and you don't say *Gesundheit* from yours."

Amused at the way her mother found a way to wind through a story, and how her father cursed at the ballplayers, the referees, the coaches, Shelby eased a hip on the arm of the couch.

"So, they might be feuding, but Hattie doesn't miss any tricks and saw you and Emma Kate outside Bitsy's house, and saw you go on in. How's that kitchen coming? I haven't gotten over there in more than a week."

"They were putting cabinets in. Pretty ones."

"Emma Kate's young man—Matt—and Griffin. Cutie-pies, the pair of them—and they do fine work. I'm having them do me a master bath, an en suite, out of your old room."

"Now, Ada Mae." Clayton surfaced from the game long enough to hear about the bathroom.

"I'm doing it, Clayton, so you'd best climb on board. Griff said how they could take out that wall, and I could have me a spa-like en suite bathroom. I've been looking at magazines, getting ideas. And Griff, he's got whole books just on plumbing fixtures—I've never seen the like of some of them. He's done himself an en suite already. I went over to the old Tripplehorn place to see it, and it's like a magazine, even if he is still sleeping on an air mattress on the bedroom floor. He's finished the kitchen over there now, and it just makes me green with envy."

"Don't even start, Ada Mae."

"I like my kitchen just fine," she said to Clayton, then grinned at Shelby, mouthed, *For now.* "I bet you and Emma Kate picked up right where you left off."

Miles from that, Shelby thought. "That's the favor. She said she'd like to meet me tomorrow, at Bootlegger's, about seven-thirty, if I could. But—"

"You go right on and do that. Old friends are the bricks and mortar of your life. I don't know what I'd do without Suzannah. Your daddy and I will watch Callie, get her to bed. We'd love to."

"Finally something I can agree to." Clayton looked over at his daughter. "You take some time catching up with Emma Kate. We'll spoil Callie."

"Thank you." She leaned over, kissed her mother, got up, kissed her father. "I'm going on up because a day of pampering's made me sleepy. Thanks for that, too, Mama. And we'll need to eat at six tomorrow night. I'm cooking dinner."

"Oh, but—"

"I'm doing it, Ada Mae," she said in the same tone her mother had used to her father, and had Clayton snickering.

"I've gotten to be a pretty good cook, and you'll judge for yourself. I'm going to pull my weight while Callie and I are here, because I was raised right. 'Night."

"She was raised right," Clayton said when Shelby started upstairs. "So let's pat ourselves on the back there, and we'll see what's for dinner tomorrow."

"She wasn't so pale and tired-looking tonight."

"No, she wasn't. Let's see how it goes for the next few days, and be glad we've got them home."

"I am, and I'll be gladder when she makes things up with Emma Kate."

IT WASN'T HARD to keep busy. By mid-morning, she hauled out the stroller. Taking Callie on a stroll around town, picking up what she wanted for the chicken dinner she intended to make for her parents was an easy—casual—way to wander around the Ridge and see if anyone was hiring.

The clouds had lifted, and the air had the bright-edged sparkle of spring after a shower. She put Callie in her pink denim jacket with a light cap—and since she might find herself applying for a job, did her makeup before setting out.

"Are we going to see Chelsea, Mama?"

"We're walking to town, baby. To the grocery store, and I have to open up a bank account. Maybe we'll stop in and see Granny."

"See Granny! Chelsea, too."

"I'll call Chelsea's mama later, and we'll see."

She passed Emma Kate's house, noted the workman truck in the drive—and had to resist the urge to lift a hand in a wave across the street where she imagined Hattie Munson's eagle eye was trained on her.

People like Ms. Munson did plenty of talking, she knew. There was welcome in the Ridge, but there were those—and more than a few—who'd enjoy gossiping over the back fence and in the grocery store aisle, over lunch at Sid and Sadie, about the poor Pomeroy girl who'd come home a widow with a child. But what did you expect when she'd run off that way with a man nobody knew a thing about?

They'd talk about how she'd moved north, rarely came home, dropped out of college after her parents had worked hard to send her.

There'd be plenty to gossip about. And they didn't know the half of it.

The smart thing to do would be to keep her head down, be friendly and get steady work. Steady work would mean some sort of day care for Callie, so that had to be balanced.

Day care would be good for Callie. Just look how she'd latched onto this Chelsea. She needed to interact with other kids, even if it meant most of any paycheck coming in went out again.

While Callie talked to Fifi, Shelby took the fork into town. She kept her eyes peeled for houses for sale. When she moved out on her own, she wanted something close by. Close enough maybe Callie could walk to her grandmother's, or to Granny's. To friends, to town, just as she had.

A little house, two bedrooms, maybe with enough land for a small garden. She'd missed gardening in the condo, and hadn't had a chance in Philadelphia.

She let her mind drift, imagined the house in her head. Like a cottage, that's all they needed, and she'd plant flowers and have a vegetable patch, some herbs. She'd teach Callie how to plant and tend and harvest.

She could haunt yard sales and flea markets for furniture, for bargains she could refinish or paint or reupholster. Warm colors and sink-into chairs.

They'd have a good life here, whatever it took to make it.

She took the main road, with shops and a few old houses on each side of the winding street.

She could work in a gift shop, or wait tables, ring up sales at the drugstore or food at the market. Granny had told her she could come work at the salon, but she didn't have any real talent for hair—or a license. Whatever she did there would be make work, and her family was already making enough for her.

She could check at the hotel or the lodge just outside of town. Not today, not with Callie along, but they should go on her list.

She liked the way it all looked, freshening up for spring with storefronts shining in the sunlight, tubs and hanging baskets of flowers decking the buildings that climbed up or down the hilly road. She enjoyed seeing people stopping to talk, a few tourists wandering along the steep sidewalks, hikers with their big backpacks taking pictures of the town well, where legend had it star-crossed lovers, from feuding families, would meet at midnight.

Until the girl's father shot the boy dead, and the girl died of a broken heart.

Their rendezvous, so it was said, gave the town its name, and the well—haunted, of course—ended up on a lot of cameras and canvases.

Maybe she could get an office job since she had decent computer skills. But the truth was she had no experience there. Her work experience spread to helping out at the salon—filling shampoo bottles, sweeping the floor, working the register—babysitting, working in the college bookstore a couple of semesters.

And singing with the band.

She wasn't likely to form a band, and was beyond filling shampoo bottles. So retail maybe. Or maybe she could look into opening a day care. But the Ridge had one—and those who had family usually had a mother or cousin or sister who'd watch their kids when they worked.

Retail, she thought again. Retail or waitressing. There could be opportunities there, especially since summer was coming, and summer brought more tourists, more hikers, more families who rented cabins or stayed at the hotel.

The Artful Ridge—local artists mostly. Mountain Treasures, gifts and whatnots. The Hasty Market—selling staples and snacks for anyone who didn't want to go the half mile to Haggerty Food Market. There was the pharmacy, the ice cream shop, the bar and grill, the Pizzateria, Al's Liquors.

Farther down and around the corner sat Shady's Bar, which was just that. And her mama would have a heart attack if she took a job there.

Considering her options, she stopped in the salon first so her granny could show off Callie.

"I'm going to do your hair," Viola told Callie. "Crystal, get me one of those booster seats, would you? You can sit right here at Granny's station,

Callie Rose. I used to do your Gamma's hair, and your mama's. Now I get to do yours."

"Callie's hair." Callie lifted her arms to Viola, then brushed at Viola's hair. "Granny's hair."

"About the same, isn't it—though mine takes some doing these days."

"Some doing," Callie echoed, and made Viola laugh.

"Have a seat there, Shelby, Crystal doesn't have another head for a half hour. Look at this beautiful hair."

Callie, who could sometimes be fussy and impatient at hair-fixing time, sat happily staring at herself in the mirror.

"I wanna be a princess, Granny."

"You *are* a princess, but we'll give you hair worthy of your rank." She brushed through the curls, grabbed one of the big silver clips to hold some back, and began to do a fancy French braid on the side.

"I heard Bonnie Jo Farnsworth—that's a cousin of Gilly's sister's husband—is getting a divorce from her husband. That's Les Wickett, Shelby, who ran with Forrest some when they were boys. They haven't been married two years, and have a baby not six months old. Had a big wedding at the hotel cost her daddy two arms and his left leg."

"I remember Les a little. I'm sorry to hear he's having troubles."

"I heard trouble's been brewing since before they cut the wedding cake." Crystal, who owned a tumbling mane of streaky blond hair, gave a knowing wiggle of her eyebrows. "But I probably shouldn't say."

"Of course you should say." Viola tied off the first braid, started on the second. "And in considerable detail."

"Well, maybe you didn't know that Bonnie Jo used to go around with Boyd Kattery."

"Loretta Kattery's middle boy. Those Kattery boys are rough custom-ers. Forrest had a set-to with Arlo—the youngest of them—not long ago when Arlo got skunk drunk down to Shady's and started a fight over a pool game. Arlo took a swing at Forrest when Forrest went in to break it up. You know Arlo, Shelby. Bony boy with straw-colored hair and a bad attitude. Drove a motorcycle, and tried to catch your eye."

"I remember Arlo. He got suspended and sent off awhile for beating up on a boy half his size outside of school."

"Boyd's considerably worse, let me tell you." As she talked, Crystal readied her station for the next customer. "And he and Bonnie Jo were always sneaking off, then they broke up when he got arrested for . . ."

She glanced at Callie, who was too busy admiring herself in the mirror to pay attention.

"For, ah, having certain illegal substances in his possession. Then Bonnie Jo took up with Les, and before you can click your heels they're planning a wedding. You ask me, her daddy was so relieved she was marrying a nice boy and done with Boyd, he'd've paid double what that wedding cost. But Boyd got released right before the wedding, and there's been some talk down in the holler he and Bonnie Jo have, well, taken up again, and now the two of them are off down to Florida, where he has cousins—she left that baby behind like it was leftover pizza or something. And it's said the cousins make up some of the substances he was put away for."

It was nearly as good as a massage and facial, just sitting there for twenty minutes, watching her granny create a princess do for her girl while Callie preened in the mirror. And listening to gossip that wasn't about her.

Viola looped the braids into a crown, gathered the curls into a tail she fixed with a rose-trimmed band.

"Pretty. I'm pretty, Granny!"

"Yes, you are." Viola bent down so their faces reflected together. "A girl should know when she's pretty. But there's a couple things I can think of right off more important."

"What's more?"

"Being smart. Are you smart, Callie Rose?"

"Mama says."

"And she knows. Then there's being kind. If you can be pretty and smart and kind, well, that's what makes a real princess."

She kissed Callie's cheek, lifted her down. "If I didn't have somebody coming in, I'd take you two girls out to lunch. Next time we'll plan it."

"Next time we'll take you out to lunch." Shelby settled Callie in her stroller. "Crystal, I'm thinking I should find some work. Do you know anybody who's hiring?"

"Oh, let's see now. Spring and summer they hire on extra a lot of places. I didn't think you'd be after work, Shelby, not with the money you'd have from—"

She slapped a hand over her mouth, looked at Callie in distress. "I'm awful sorry. I don't know why my mouth just runs out without being hitched up to my brain."

"It's all right. I just want to keep busy. You know how it is."

"I know how it is to need to pay the bills, but if you want busy work, maybe over at The Artful Ridge. It's got some class, and they do good business, especially once the tourists start coming in. Might be they could use another hostess at the big restaurant. They want good-lookers there. Oh, and Rendezvous Gardens—you know the landscape place? They always need help this time of year. That could be fun if you like plants and such."

"Thanks. I'll think about it. We've got to get to the food market. I'm making dinner for Mama and Daddy tonight. Granny, you and Grandpa should come. I'd love to make dinner for you."

"I'd love to have you make dinner for me. I'll tell Jackson."

"It's at six, but you could come a little early because I have to leave by about twenty after seven and meet Emma Kate."

"Have you met Emma Kate's boyfriend?" Crystal asked.

"Not yet."

"She hooked a good one. Now the other—Griffin?" She patted a hand to her heart. "If I wasn't engaged to be married for the second time in my

life, I'd head straight in that direction. He's got a swagger to him. I just
love a man who's got a swagger to him."

"There's your eleven-thirty just come in, Crystal."

"I'll bring her right back. It was nice talking to you, Shelby." She gave
Shelby a good, hard squeeze. "It's really good to have you home."

"It's good to be home."

"Her first husband had a swagger to him," Viola said under her breath.
"And he swaggered off with anything female he could talk into it."

"I hope she does better this time."

"I like this one. No swagger, but a steady way about him, which she
needs to balance her out. I love that girl like I love raspberry sherbet, but
she needs that balance. What's for dinner?"

"I'm going to surprise you. And I'd better get to the market or we'll be
ordering from the Pizzateria."

She ran into Chelsea and her mother in the food market, which added
a half hour onto her time—and produced a deal to meet at the town park
the next day so the girls could play together.

Now that she was cooking a meal for six she fiddled with the menu as
she shopped. She made a good roast chicken with garlic and sage and
rosemary, and she could make some red potatoes in that zingy dressing
she cut out of a magazine, the carrots in butter and thyme Callie liked so
much, and some peas. And she'd make biscuits.

Richard hadn't cared for her biscuits, called them hick bread, she remembered.

Well, the hell with him.

Maybe she'd make some appetizers, really do it up. And profiteroles
for dessert. The cook they'd had three times a week in Atlanta had shown
her how to make them.

She loaded up ingredients, bribed Callie with animal crackers. And
tried not to swallow out loud when she checked out.

For family, she reminded herself as she counted out the money. Family was putting a roof over her head, and her daughter's. She could and would afford to pay for a good family dinner.

It wasn't until she wheeled the cart and stroller outside that she remembered she'd walked.

"Oh, for God's sake, how stupid am I?"

Three bags of groceries, a stroller and a mile-and-a-half walk.

Muttering to herself, she crammed two bags in the back of the stroller, slung the big Callie bag over one shoulder and hefted the last grocery bag.

She switched arms at the half-mile mark, seriously considered calling her mother, or poking into the sheriff's office to see if Forrest was there and could give her a ride.

"We'll make it. We'll make it fine."

She thought back to when she'd run the mile into town, and back again, as a child. Up and down those hills, around those curves.

Well, now she had a child, and three bags of groceries. And she might be working up a blister on her heel.

She made it to the fork, arms aching, and stopped to gather herself for the last leg.

The Fix-It Guys truck pulled up beside her. Griff leaned out the window.

"Hey. Did your car break down? Griff," he added, in case she'd forgotten. "Griffin Lott."

"I remember. No, my car didn't break down. I didn't take the damn car because I wasn't intending to buy so many groceries."

"Damn car," Callie said to Fifi, and had Shelby sighing.

"Okay. Want a ride home?"

"More, at this moment, than I want a long and happy life. But . . ."

"I get you only met me yesterday, but Emma Kate's known me for a couple years. I'd be in jail if I were an ax murderer. Hey, cutie. Is your name Callie?"

"Callie." The little girl angled her head, an accomplished flirt, and fluffed at her new hairdo. "I'm pretty."

"As pretty as they come. Look, I can't leave you by the side of the road with the pretty girl and three bags of groceries."

"I was going to say I want a ride, but you don't have a car seat."

"Oh. Right." He shoved a hand at his hair. "We'll break the law, but it's less than a mile, and I'll drive slow. I'll pull over anytime another car's coming, either direction."

Her heel burned, her arms ached and her legs felt like rubber stretched too hard and long. "I think driving slow's going to be enough."

"Hold on. Let me help you."

That made the second person who wasn't family in the last little while who'd offered to help her. It was hard to remember how long before that anyone had.

He got out of the truck, took the bag from her. Feeling came back into her arm in pins and needles.

"Thank you."

"No problem."

He stowed the groceries while she lifted Callie out. "You sit right there," Shelby told Callie. "Sit still while I fold up the stroller."

"How does it— Oh, I get it." Griff folded the stroller as if he'd been doing so for years.

She turned back to Callie as he stowed it, and saw her daughter had opened a takeout bag sitting on the seat beside her.

She was now eating french fries.

"Callie! Those aren't yours."

"I'm hungry, Mama."

"It's okay." Laughing, Griff got in the truck. "I wouldn't trust anybody who could resist fries. I had to pick up some stuff in town, grabbed lunch for me and Matt while I was at it. She can have some fries."

"It's past her lunchtime. I didn't expect to be gone so long."

"Didn't you grow up here?"

She took a deep breath as he drove—true to his word—at about twenty miles an hour. "I should've known better."

Now sitting on her lap, Callie held out a fry to Griff.

"Thanks. You look like your mother."

"Mama's hair."

"Yours is really pretty. Have you been to Miz Vi's?"

"That's Granny, Callie. Miz Vi's Granny."

"Granny did my hair like a princess. I'm pretty and smart and kind."

"I can see that. You're the first princess I've had in my truck, so this is a pretty big deal for me. Who's your friend?"

"This is Fifi. She likes french fries."

"I would hope so." He eased into the driveway. "Whew." He took a mock swipe at his forehead. "Made it. You get the princess and her carriage. I'll get the groceries."

"Oh, that's all right, I can—"

"Haul in three bags of groceries, a kid, a stroller and whatever's in that suitcase you've got there? Sure you can, but I'll get the groceries."

"You carry me!" Callie shoved out of Shelby's arms, threw herself at Griff.

"Callie, don't—"

"I've got my orders." He climbed out, crouched down, tapped his back. "Okay, princess, climb aboard."

Callie said, *"Whee,"* and hooked herself on for a piggyback while Shelby scrambled out the other door to try to heft whatever was left.

He beat her to it, pulled out two grocery bags, and with one in each arm, her daughter bouncing gleefully on his back, headed to the front door.

"Is it locked?"

"I don't think so. Mama may have . . ." She trailed off as he was already going inside, Callie clinging to his neck and chattering in his ear like he was her new best friend.

Flustered, Shelby pulled out the stroller, got the last bag, swung her Callie bag on her shoulder. She managed to get it all in the house, left the stroller by the door to deal with later.

He'd set the bags on the island. Before she could speak, he stopped her heart by swinging Callie off his back, dangling her upside down while she squealed in insane delight, then tossed her up in the air, catching her neatly. And settled her on his hip.

"I love you," Callie said, and kissed him enthusiastically on the mouth.

"Is that all it takes?" Grinning, he gave her hair a tug. "Obviously I've been going about my conquests the wrong way for a lot of years."

"You stay and play with me."

"Would if I could, but I've got to get back to work."

Callie took a hank of his hair, obviously finding it to her liking, and wound it around her finger. "You come back and play with me."

"Sure, sometime." He looked over at Shelby, smiled, and since she was staring, she saw he had eyes as green and clever as a cat's. "You've got a keeper here."

"She is. Thank you. Ah, do you have children?"

"Me? No." He set Callie down, gave her a friendly pat on the butt. "Gotta go, Little Red."

She wrapped her arms around his legs in a hug. "Bye, mister."

"Griff. Just Griff."

"Gwiff."

"Grrr-iff," Shelby corrected automatically.

"Grrr," Callie said, and giggled.

"Grrr-iff's gotta go," he said, glanced back at Shelby. "You set?"

"Yes. Yes, thank you so much."

"No problem." He started out. "Love this kitchen," he added, and strode to the door and out—he did have a swagger about him—before she could think of anything else.

"Grrr-iff," Callie told Fifi. "He's pretty, Mama, and he smells good. He's going to come back and play with me."

"I . . . umm. Huh."

"I'm hungry, Mama."

"What? Oh. Of course you are." Giving herself a shake, Shelby got back to reality.

8

By the time her mother got home, Shelby had the chicken in the oven, the potatoes and carrots scrubbed, and the dining room table—used only for important meals—set with the good dishes.

Not the *best* dishes, which were her father's grandmother's and worth more in sentiment than money, but the company dishes with the roses around the rims.

She'd added linen napkins, folding them into fussy standing fans, rearranged candles and flowers into a pretty centerpiece, and was finishing the last of the pastries for the profiteroles.

"Oh my goodness, Shelby! The table looks just beautiful, like for a high-class dinner party."

"We *are* high class."

"We're sure going to eat like we are—and it smells *wonderful* in here. You always were one to know just how things should go together to look pretty."

"It's fun, fussing a little. I hope it's all right I asked Granny and Grandpa to come."

"You know it is. Mama told me when I stopped into Vi's after my garden club meeting—and after Suzannah and I did a little shopping. I got Callie the *cutest* outfits for spring. I had the best time."

She set three shopping bags on the counter, began to pull things out. "I can't wait to see her wearing this—it's just precious, isn't it? The little skirt with the pink and white stripes, and the frilly shirt. And these pink Mary Janes! Now, I checked her size before I left, so they should fit. But if they don't, we'll just take them back."

"Mama, she'll love those. She'll just go crazy for those shoes."

"And I got this cute shirt with 'Princess' on it, and the sweetest little white cardigan sweater with ribbon trim." She pulled more out as she talked. "Where is she? Maybe she can try some on."

"She's napping. I'm sorry she's napping so late, but it all took me longer, and then I had to fix her lunch, and she was revved up, so I didn't get her down until almost three."

"Oh, we won't worry about that. So I stopped into Vi's, and there was Maxine Pinkett—you remember she moved to Arkansas a few years ago, but she was back visiting, and came into Vi's hoping I could give her a cut and color. I don't do hair anymore as a rule, but she's an old customer, and I know what she likes."

Shelby had a misty memory of Mrs. Pinkett, so made assenting noises as she began to fill the pastries with cream.

"She told me that she was disappointed when Crystal told her I was off, then I walked in, and she asked if I couldn't please see to her hair. She's not happy at all with the stylists she's tried in Little Rock. So I set her up. Turns out her daughter's husband may take a job in Ohio now, and this after she moved to Little Rock to be close by her daughter and three grandchildren. She's in a state, let me tell you. I know just how she feels, so I . . ."

Ada Mae shut her eyes, gave herself a shake. "I can't keep my mouth shut with a stapler."

"You don't have to. You didn't get to make many memories with Callie for more than three years. And more, I see now, she didn't get to make them with you. That's on me, Mama."

"It's all over and done now, and we're making plenty of memories all around. What are you making there? Little cream puffs? Oh, she's awake." Ada Mae looked toward the baby monitor on the counter. "I'm going to take her new things up, and we'll have some fun. You need help here, honey?"

"I don't, Mama, thanks. I don't want you to do a thing but sit down to this meal. You go have fun with Callie."

"Oh, I hope the pink Mary Janes fit, 'cause they couldn't be cuter."

She'd take pictures of Callie in the pink Mary Janes, Shelby thought. Callie might not remember them when she grew up, but she'd remember her grandmother loved her, enjoyed getting her pretty clothes. She'd remember her granny had fixed her hair like a princess.

That's what counted. Like a good family dinner at the dining room table, that's what counted.

She finished the pastries, basted the chicken, got the potatoes and carrots going.

She needed to change, not only for dinner, but to go out and meet Emma Kate. With a glance at the timer, she ran upstairs, tiptoed from the landing to her room so she didn't distract Callie and her mother and their fashion show.

And spent the next fifteen minutes agonizing over what to wear. She'd once had three, maybe even four times as many clothes, and had never agonized.

Maybe, she thought, because it had stopped being important.

It was the bar and grill, she reminded herself. People didn't dress up especially to go there. It was at least three giant steps up from Shady's, but about an equal amount down from the big restaurant at the hotel.

She settled on black jeans, a simple white shirt. And she'd put the leather jacket she'd kept—one she just loved—over it. The pewter gray went well with her hair, and wasn't as harsh as black.

Since the evenings ran cool yet, she chose heeled half boots.

Mindful of the meal, she slipped straight back down and into the kitchen, grabbed an apron this time to start on the biscuits.

It *was* fun to fuss, she thought, and after hunting up a pretty platter for the chicken, stood trying to imagine if it would look better if she laid the potatoes and carrots around the chicken or if she put them in bowls.

Forrest came in the back door.

"What's all this?" He sniffed the air. "What is that?"

"What's wrong with it?"

"I didn't say anything was wrong. It smells like . . . It smells like I'm hungry."

"You can stay for dinner if you want. Granny and Grandpa are coming. I'm cooking."

"You're cooking?"

"That's right, Forrest Jackson Pomeroy, so take it or leave it."

"Do you always get dressed up to cook dinner?"

"I'm not dressed up. Hell. Am I too dressed up to go to Bootlegger's?"

His eyes narrowed. "Why?"

"Because, you idiot, I'm going to Bootlegger's and I don't want to dress wrong."

"I meant why are you going to the bar and grill when you're fixing dinner?"

"I'm going after dinner, if you need every detail of it. I'm meeting Emma Kate."

His face cleared. "Oh."

"Am I too dressed up or not?"

"You're okay." He opened the top oven, peered in at the chicken. "That looks damn good."

"It will be damn good. Now stay out of the way. I need to set out the appetizers."

"Aren't we fancy?" He stepped around her, got himself a beer.

"I just want it to be nice. Mama's getting me massages, and Granny's fixing Callie's hair, and—you saw how they fixed the rooms upstairs for us. I just want it to be nice."

He gave her shoulder a rub. "It is nice. The table looks like a company meal. It's good you're meeting Emma Kate."

"We'll see how good when I do. She's still awful mad at me."

"Maybe you should fix her a chicken dinner."

It felt good to have her family around the table enjoying a meal she'd made. And made her realize it was the first time. There'd be a second time, she promised herself, and she'd make sure Clay and Gilly and little Jackson were around the table that next time.

She knew she'd done well when her grandfather had seconds of everything—and Granny asked for the recipes.

"I'll write them out for you, Granny."

"You'll want to do it twice." Ada Mae got up to help clear. "That chicken put mine to shame."

"You'd better've saved room for dessert."

"We've got room, don't we, Callie?" Jack patted his belly so Callie leaned back in her booster chair to pat hers.

The best was watching eyes go big when she came in carrying the tower of profiteroles she'd made, with their topping of melted chocolate.

"That's as pretty as anything you'd see in a restaurant," her father told her. "Is it as good as it looks?"

"You're going to find out. I need to go, so Mama, would you serve this up? I don't want to be late."

"You don't go till you've put on some lipstick." This was her grandmother's decree. "Something with a little pink it in. It's spring."

"All right. Make Forrest help with the dishes."

"I was going to," he said immediately. He grabbed her hand when she bent over to kiss Callie. "It was a real good meal, Shelby. Don't drink and drive."

"You're the one with a beer on the table. Callie, you be a good girl."

"Gamma said I get a bath with bubbles."

"Won't that be fun? I won't be late."

"Oh, be late." Ada Mae served up generous portions of pastry. "Go have some fun."

"I will. Don't—"

"Scat!"

"All right."

It felt odd going out at night, on her own. And then add in the nerves, the worry that Emma Kate wouldn't forgive her.

But she put on lipstick, added a little more blush for good measure. And drove to town hoping she'd find the right words, make the right penance to get her best friend back in her life.

The streetlights gleamed, and she caught a few lights glimmering in the mountains. Shops shut down by six, but she noted Pizzateria was doing good business, and a few people strolled along the sidewalk.

She found the stingy parking lot beside the bar and grill already jammed, started hunting up a place on the street. Maybe she had to give herself a mental push to get out of the car, but she did it, and walked the half block down, opened the door, stepped into the noise.

She didn't recall the place doing this level of business on weeknights. But then she hadn't reached legal drinking age when she left so had spent more time with pizza or at the ice cream parlor.

Still, most of the tables and booths were full, and the air smelled of beer and barbecue.

"How're you doing?" A waitress—hostess?—approached with an easy smile, and dark eyes that scanned the crowded room, probably looking for a free table. "I can seat you at the bar if you're . . . Shelby? Shelby Anne Pomeroy!"

Shelby found herself enveloped in a hug that smelled of peach blossoms.

She drew Shelby back, a good-looking woman with skin like polished walnut and thickly lashed dark eyes. "You don't remember me."

"I'm sorry, I—" It clicked, stunning her. "Tansy?"

"You do remember. Can't blame you for taking a few minutes. I've changed some."

"Some?" The Tansy Johnson she'd known had been gawky, gap-toothed, acne-prone and bespectacled. This one was admirably curvy with a gorgeous smile, clear skin and luminous eyes.

"My skin cleared up, I filled out, got my teeth fixed and wear contacts."

"You look just fantastic."

"It's nice to hear it. But then, you and Emma Kate never made fun of me like some of the girls did. I'm sorry about your husband, Shelby, but I'm glad you're home."

"Thanks. You work here now. It's busier than I remember, and nicer."

"That's good to hear, too, because I don't just work here, I'm the manager. And I happen to be married to the owner."

"Wow. Things have changed. When did you get married?"

"A year ago in June. I'm going to tell you all about my Derrick first chance, but Emma Kate's waiting for you."

"She's already here?"

"I'll take you over. I got you a corner booth—prime real estate, especially on Wing Night." She hooked her arm through Shelby's. "You've got a little girl, don't you?"

"Callie. She's three."

"I'm going to have one."

"Oh, that's great, Tansy." It called for another hug. "Congratulations."

"Just hit four weeks, and I know they always say wait until after the first trimester, but I can't wait. So I'm telling everybody, even complete strangers. Look who I found!"

Emma Kate looked up from her phone. "You made it."

"I did. I'm sorry if I'm late."

"You're not. I forgot it was Wing Night, so I had Tansy save us a table and got here a little early."

"Sit down." Tansy waved toward the booth. "And you two do your catching up. What'll you have, Shelby? First one's on the house."

"I'm driving, so . . . Well, I ought to be able to handle one glass of wine."

"We've got a nice selection by the glass." Tansy rattled off several choices.

"The pinot noir sounds perfect."

"I'll get that right out to you. You okay there, Emma Kate?"

Emma Kate lifted her beer. "I'm good, Tansy."

"So good seeing you." Tansy gave Shelby's shoulder a squeeze before she walked away.

"I didn't recognize her for a minute."

"She grew up. She's about the happiest person I know, but then she always had a sunny nature."

"Despite being bullied and picked on half the time. I remember in high school especially how Melody Bunker and Jolene Newton made deviling her a mission."

"Melody's as sour and snotty as she ever was. She was second runner-up in the Miss Tennessee pageant—something she tosses around like candy wrappers. You know she's never forgiven you for beating her out for Homecoming Queen."

"God, I haven't thought about that in years."

"Melody's existence is based on being the prettiest and most popular. She fell short. And Jolene hasn't evolved much, either." Emma Kate leaned back, settled into the corner of the booth, diagonal from Shelby. "She's engaged to the son of the hotel's owners, and likes to drive around town in the fancy car her daddy bought her."

A waitress brought over Shelby's wine. "Tansy says enjoy, and just let me know if you want anything else."

"Thank you. I don't care about Melody or Jolene," Shelby continued while she turned the wineglass around and around in small circles with her fingers. "I want to hear about you. You got your nursing degree just like you said you would. Did you like Baltimore?"

"I liked it well enough. I made some friends, had good work. Met Matt."

"It's serious, you and Matt?"

"Serious enough I dealt with my mama's shock and horror when I told her we were moving in together. She still gives me pushes toward marriage and babies."

"Don't you want that?"

"I'm not in a rush about it, like you were."

Shelby accepted the hit, took a sip of wine. "You like working at the clinic?"

"I'd have to be stupid not to like working for Doc Pomeroy. Your daddy's a good man, a fine doctor." After another sip of her beer, Emma Kate straightened a couple of inches. "What did you mean, you didn't have the money to come back? The word I got was you were rolling in it."

"Richard handled the money. As I wasn't working—"

"Didn't you want to work?"

"I had Callie to tend to, and the house. And I'm not qualified for any serious work. I didn't finish college or—"

"What about singing?"

It flustered her not to finish a sentence. There'd been a time when she and Emma Kate could finish each other's—but this was different.

"That was just a childish fantasy. It wasn't like I had any real skills or experience, and I had a child, and he married me, provided for me and Callie, gave us a good home."

Emma Kate sat back again. "And that's all you wanted? To be provided for?"

"With Callie, and having no skills or the education—"

"Did he tell you that you were stupid? You want my forgiveness, Shelby?" Emma Kate said when Shelby went silent. "You tell me the truth. You look me in the eye and you tell me the truth."

"All the time, one way or the other. How was he wrong? I didn't know how to do anything."

"That's a big bucket of bullshit." With her eyes fired up, Emma Kate set the beer down, shoved it aside and leaned across the table. "You didn't just sing in that band, you did most of the managing and marketing. You figured out how to do that. They made you assistant manager at the college bookstore after a month so you knew how to do that. You started writing songs, and they were good, Shelby, damn it, so you knew how to do that. You redecorated my bedroom when we were sixteen—and not only did it look beautiful, but you figured out how to get around Mama on it. Don't sit there and say you didn't know how to do anything. That's him talking. Speak for yourself."

The words, fast as machine-gun fire, left Shelby breathless.

"None of those things were practical or realistic. Emma Kate, things change when you have a child depending on you. I was a housewife and a stay-at-home mother. There's nothing wrong with that."

"There's not a thing wrong with that if it makes you happy, if it's appreciated. It doesn't sound like it was appreciated, and when you talk about it you don't look happy."

She shook her head in denial. "Being Callie's mama is the best thing in my life—it's the light in it. Richard worked so I could stay home with her. A lot of mothers who want to can't, so I should be grateful he provided for us."

"There's that word again."

She felt sick inside, with a thin layer of shame coating it. "Do we have to talk about this?"

"You want me to forgive you for running off—and that I could—but to forgive you for cutting me off, for staying away, for not being there for me when I most needed you. But you're skirting around the truth of it."

She was because the center was so dark and sticky. The noise of voices and dishes that had seemed festive and fun when she'd come in now pounded against her head.

Her throat felt so painfully dry she wished she'd asked for water. But she pushed the words out.

"I didn't have the money because if I managed to tuck a thousand dollars away, he'd find it, and he'd take it. To invest, he'd say, because I didn't have a head for money. I had charge accounts, didn't I, if I wanted to buy clothes or some other toy or outfit to spoil Callie with so I didn't need cash money. And what was I complaining about, I had someone to clean the place, someone to help with Callie, someone to cook because I didn't know anything but country cooking. I should be grateful. And I couldn't take off to Tennessee every time somebody died or got married or had a birthday. He needed his wife home."

"He cut you off from your family, your friends. He whittled your world right down, didn't he, and hammered at you to be grateful for it."

He had, of course he had. She hadn't seen it happening because it was so gradual—until it was just her life.

"Sometimes I thought he hated me, but he didn't. He didn't feel that much for me. The first few months, even the first year, it was exciting and full, and he made me feel so special. I let him run everything. I was along for the ride, and I was carrying Callie and so happy about it. After she came, he . . . it was different."

She took a breath, let herself settle into it.

"I thought it was different," she said slowly, "because a baby changes things. He never paid much attention to her, and if I said anything about that, he'd get angry or act insulted. He was making sure she had a good life, wasn't he? I didn't want to travel so much with the baby, and he didn't push. So he was gone a lot. Sometimes he'd come back and things would be good for a while, sometimes not so good. I never knew which it was going to be. I couldn't anticipate how it was going to be, so I tried to make sure everything was the way he liked it. I wanted my girl to have a peaceful, happy home. That was the most important thing."

"But you weren't happy."

"It was the life I'd made, Emma Kate. The choices I'd made."

"You chose to be abused."

Her spine went stiff and hard. "He never laid a hand on me or Callie in anger."

"You're smart enough to know that's not the only kind of abuse."

Though her tone was brisk, no-nonsense, she kept it low, under the other chatter. Even in a noisy restaurant people often heard what you'd rather they didn't.

"He made you feel less, feel small and stupid and obliged. And he cut you off as much as he could from people who'd make you feel whole and special and really happy. And from what I'm hearing, he used Callie to keep you in line."

"Maybe he did. He's dead now, so it's over with."

"Would you have stayed with him, just stayed living like that?"

Frowning, Shelby ran a finger around the rim of her glass. "I thought about divorce—I'd be the first in our family, and that was a weight. But I thought about it, especially when he went on this last trip. It was supposed to be the three of us, a family vacation. A few days in the warm, but when Callie got sick and we couldn't go, he went anyway. He left us in the awful house the day after Christmas, where I didn't know a soul, and our girl was running a fever."

Now she looked up, and some of the bottled rage gleamed out. "He didn't even say goodbye to her, in case she was contagious, he said. I thought, He doesn't love her. It's okay if he doesn't love me, but he doesn't love our daughter, and she deserves better. She damn well deserves better. I thought about a divorce, but I didn't have money for a lawyer, and I thought he had so much money he might go ahead and get the divorce, and what if he took Callie to spite me? I was thinking what to do, how I could do it, when they came to the house, the police. They said there'd been an accident down in South Carolina, the boat, and Richard was missing."

She picked up the wine now. "He'd called in an SOS, said he was taking on water, and the engine had gone out. They were talking to him, getting the—what do you call it?—bearings or headings or whatever it is, sending out a rescue boat, but they had lost contact.

"They found the boat, all wrecked, and they searched for him, for almost a week. They found some of his things. His windbreaker, all torn up, and one of his shoes. Just one. They found one of the life preservers.

They said the boat capsized, and he got washed away and likely drowned. So I didn't have to think about getting a divorce."

"If you feel guilty about that, you are stupid."

"I stopped being guilty about it."

"There's a lot more, isn't there?"

"There's more, but can this be enough for now? Just enough for right now?" Needing the contact, she reached over to grip Emma Kate's hand. "I'm sorry for hurting you, and I'm sorry for not being strong enough to stand up for what I knew was right and best. I just . . . God, I need some water." She glanced around for the waitress, then pushed out of the booth. "Wait!"

When she rushed off, skirting around tables, trying to get through the crowd at the bar, Emma Kate got up to follow.

"Are you sick? The bathrooms are the other way."

"No. I thought I saw somebody."

"A lot of somebodies in here on Wing Night."

"No, somebody from Philadelphia. This private detective who came looking for Richard."

"Private detective? That is more."

"Couldn't have been him. No reason for it. It's just talking so much about Richard, and thinking about all of it. I don't want to think about it anymore right now. I want it off my mind for right now."

"All right."

"Can we just talk about something else? Even Melody and Jolene, I don't care. Anything else."

"Bonnie Jo Farnsworth's getting a divorce. She married Les Wickett in a big, fancy wedding not two years ago."

"I heard about that. She's taken up with Boyd Kattery again, and they're in Florida maybe cooking meth with his cousins."

"So you're getting back in the loop. Let's go sit back down. I want another beer since I'm not driving."

Grateful, Shelby walked back with her. "You live close."

"We live in one of the apartments over Mountain Treasures so I left my car parked and walked over. Let me find the waitress and . . . oh hell."

"What?"

"Matt and Griff just came in. I got caught up. I was supposed to text Matt if I decided I didn't want him to come in and give me an excuse to ditch you. Since I didn't, we're going to have the boys around so I won't be able to pry any more out of you once you relax again."

"Is it enough that I've told you more than anyone but Granny?"

"It'll do for now." Emma Kate smiled, waved her hand.

"Your Matt's awful cute."

"He really is. And really good with his hands."

As Shelby choked out a laugh, Matt worked his way through. He hooked his really good hands under Emma Kate's elbows, lifted her off her feet, kissed her. "There's my girl." He set her on her feet, turned to Shelby. "And you're Shelby."

"It's nice to meet you."

"Really happy to meet you. You two weren't leaving, were you?"

"Just heading back to the table," Emma Kate told him. "I'm ready for another round."

"This one's on Griff."

"Two Black Bears. I think I'm going for a Bombardier. What'll you have, Shelby?"

"I was just after a glass of water."

"I don't know if I can afford that, but I'll dig deep since it's you."

"I'm driving," Shelby said as an explanation as they maneuvered back to the booth.

"We're not." Matt said it cheerfully, draped an arm around Emma Kate's shoulders when they sat. "And we had a really good day. Put in a little OT at your mother's, hon, and the countertop's done."

"How'd she like it?"

"She didn't like it. She *loved* it. Told you she would."

"You have more faith, and less experience, with Mama's waffling ways."

"I saw the kitchen the other day, when some of the cabinets were in," Shelby told Matt. "It already looked wonderful. You do nice work."

"I like your friend. She has excellent taste and a very good eye. How do you like being back home?"

"It feels good, and right. It's a big change for you from Baltimore."

"I couldn't let this one get away."

"That shows you have excellent taste and a very good eye."

"We'll drink to that when Griff gets back with the beer. He said your daughter's cute as they come."

"I think so."

"When did Griff see Callie?" Emma Kate wondered.

"Oh, he gave me a ride home this afternoon when I found myself carting three grocery bags and Callie on foot. I had a brain freeze in the market. She's smitten with him."

"Sounded like he was smitten with her. So . . ." Smiling, Matt twirled a lock of Emma Kate's hair around his finger. "Now that we're such good friends, tell me something embarrassing about Emma Kate her mother wouldn't know about. I think I've worked most of the embarrassing stories out of Bitsy."

"Oh, I couldn't do that. I couldn't tell you about the time she stole two cans of Budweiser out of her daddy's six-pack, and we sneaked out of the house and drank them until she got sick in her mother's hydrangeas."

"Sick? Hydrangea sick on one can of Bud?"

"We were fourteen." Emma Kate narrowed her eyes at Shelby, but there was a laugh in them. "And Shelby was sicker."

"I was. I chugged it down as fast as I could because the taste was so hard and sour to me, then I sicked it all back up again. I never did acquire a genuine taste for beer."

"She doesn't like beer?" Griff set the pilsners in front of his friends, a glass of water with a slice of lime in front of Shelby, then slid in beside her with his own drink. "That may affect my plans for playing up to you so I can enlist your help in running off with Viola."

"He's not altogether kidding." Matt lifted his glass. "Well, to friends, even when they don't have the good sense to drink beer."

PRIVET SAT OUT in his car making notes. He'd parked across the street from where Shelby had left her minivan. It seemed to him the young widow was enjoying herself, having a glass of wine with an old friend. She wasn't quite as oblivious as he'd thought, as she'd nearly spotted him.

Now it looked like she was having a double date in the local bar and grill.

And still she'd made no suspicious moves, was hardly tossing money around.

Maybe she'd had nothing to do with it, after all. Maybe she didn't know anything.

Or maybe she was smart enough to sit tight in Nowhere, Tennessee, until she thought the coast was clear. Considering what was at stake, he could give it a few more days.

For his cut of nearly thirty million, he could spare the time.

9

S he had fun, grown-up fun, normal-night-out-with-people fun. She saw glimmers of her old friendship with Emma Kate break through, and it gave her hope that it would beam bright again.

Seeing a man, and he seemed like a good man, besotted—that was the word that came to her mind—over her friend made her glow a little.

She liked the way they looked together, easy and comfortable but with some sparks over the familiarity. She'd seen her friend in love before, but with the teenage angst and drama and wonder that flamed like a comet over a night sky, and was as quickly lost from view. What she saw here struck her as real and grounded, a good, sturdy sapling sinking roots.

If the lost years came home to her not only in the way Emma Kate fit with Matt, but the connection between her and Griff, the obvious brotherhood between him and Matt, she could be grateful they opened that very tight unit to include her for an evening.

Maybe she had to work some to stay relaxed sitting next to Griff—pretty much hip to hip in the little booth. It had been so long since she'd been in close proximity with a man, which explained the occasional belly flutters. But he made conversation easy—they all did. And God it felt good not to talk about herself and her problems for an hour.

She nursed her water to make it all last.

"I don't think things have changed so much in the Ridge that it could've been easy to start up a new business, especially since you're not . . . local."

Matt grinned at Shelby across the table. "You mean for us Yankees."

"That would be a factor. But you do have the cutest accent," she said, and made him laugh.

"It helps we're good, and I mean damn good. Then there's the Emma Kate factor." He gave her shaggy hair a tug. "Some people were curious enough about the Yankee their own Emma Kate hooked up with to hire us for some odd jobs."

"Painting," Griff commented. "I thought we'd never stop painting. Then Emma Kate's father gave us a boost when a tree fell on the Hallister house. They called him in for the roof, and he nudged them to us for the rest. Their bad luck was our good."

"That Hallister boy's family?" Shelby wondered. "The one my cousin Lark's glued to?"

"That's the one," Emma Kate confirmed. "And Granny gave them another lift."

"Did she?"

"She hired Dewey Trake and his crew out of Maryville to do the Relaxation Room at the day spa, and finish off the little patio. Some this and that," Emma Kate continued.

"What about Mr. Curtis? He always did her work."

"He retired about two years back, and even Granny couldn't coax him out to take this one on. So she hired Trake, but that didn't last two weeks."

"Shoddy work." Griff tipped back his beer.

"Overpriced," Matt added.

"Granny thought so, and fired him."

"I happened to be in there at the time." Griff picked up the story, that easy rhythm. "Man, she lit into him. He'd had about four days on the job and was already running behind, making noises about overruns and delays. A lot of bullshit, basically. She handed him his ass, and told him not to let the door hit it on the way out."

"Sounds like Granny."

"That's when I fell for her." Griff let out a sigh, ending it on what Shelby would term a dreamy smile. "Something about a woman who can hand somebody their ass just does it for me. Anyway, not to let an opportunity slide—"

"Dewey Trake's bad luck being your good."

"Exactly. I asked her if she'd let me take a look."

"Griff's our community liaison," Matt said.

"And Matt handles the accounting. It works. I took a look, asked to see the plans, told her I could have an estimate for her by the next morning, but ballparked it for her on the spot."

"You were eleven hundred off," Matt reminded him.

"Ballpark, on the spot. She measured me up—you've probably been measured up by Miz Vi."

"Countless times," Shelby agreed.

"Fell a little deeper, but restrained myself from asking her to run away with me. Timing's everything. She said something like: 'Boy, I want this done before Christmas and I want it done right. You get me that estimate, written down proper, first thing in the morning, and if I like it, be prepared to start work then and there.'"

"I take it she liked it."

"She did, and the rest is history," Griff claimed. "Once you get the thumbs-up around here from Viola Donahue, you're pretty well set."

"It didn't hurt that Griff went out and snapped up that old house, and its four overgrown, trash-strewn acres," Matt put in. "It was just crying, 'Buy me, Griff, come on! I've got tremendous potential.'"

"It really does," Shelby agreed, and earned a quick, flashing grin from Griff that had those butterflies swarming again.

"You can't miss it if you know where to look. A lot of people thought— probably still think—I was crazy."

"That probably gave you another nice, hefty lift. We do prize our crazy in the South."

"Why, you know that young Lott boy from up to Baltimore?" Emma Kate began.

"He may be addled," Shelby finished, "but he's handy."

She saw Forrest wander in. Checking up on me, she thought. Some things didn't change.

"The law's coming," Griff commented as Forrest walked over to the booth. "Hey, Pomeroy. Is this a raid?"

"Off-duty. I'm here for the beer and wild women."

"This one's taken." Matt squeezed a little closer to Emma Kate. "But you can slide in and get the beer."

"Beer first." He nodded toward Shelby's glass. "Is that water?"

"Yes, Daddy. Did you come from home? Is Callie doing all right?"

"Yes, Mama. She had a bubble bath of epic proportions, talked her granddaddy into two stories, and was sleeping with Fifi when I left. You want another round of water?"

"I should probably get back."

"Relax. Another round?" he asked the rest of the table.

"I'd take a Diet Coke this time, Forrest," Emma Kate told him. "I've had my quota."

When her brother went off to order the drinks, Shelby looked around. "I know we didn't come in here all that much, but I don't remember it ever doing this kind of business."

"You should see it every other Saturday night." Since he had another coming, Matt drained his beer. "They have live entertainment. Griff and I are talking to Tansy—and she's talking to Derrick—about adding on— bigger stage, dance floor, second bar."

"They could use it for private parties." Now Griff scanned the room. "You keep it all in line with the original architecture, make sure you've got good acoustics, good traffic flow. They'd have something."

"Drinks are coming." Forrest slid in on the edge of the bench. "How's that kitchen going for Miz Bitsy?"

"A couple more days," Matt said, "we're out of there."

"You know, my mama's talking about doing a big master bath off the bedroom. With a steam shower." He narrowed his eyes at Griff. "You did know."

"Maybe we've had a few words about it."

"It's going to eat up Shelby's old room, and as she has Clay's now and Callie's got mine, that's all the bedrooms there are."

"Are you planning on moving back in with your parents?"

"No, but you never know." He shot Shelby a glance. "Do you? So if she gets her way—and she will—and my circumstances change, I'll be moving into your place."

"I've got the room. You still on for Sunday?"

"You still buying the beer?"

"I am."

"Then I'll be there."

"Griff's taking out another wall or two at the old Tripplehorn place," Emma Kate told Shelby.

"Do you think when I've lived there twenty years it'll be the old Lott place?"

"No," Forrest said flatly. "Hey, Lorna, how're you doing tonight?"

The waitress served the drinks. "I'm doing just fine, but I'd be doing better if I was sitting down here having a drink with all these handsome men."

She set Shelby's water in front of her, bussed the empties. "You watch out for this one, honey." She gave Griff a poke on the shoulder. "A man this charming can talk a woman into most anything."

"I'm safe enough. He's pining for my grandmother."

Lorna set the tray of empties on her hip. "You Vi's grandbaby? Of course you are, you look just like her, to the life. Well, she's sure on top of the world having you home. You and your little girl. I was in the salon today, and she showed me a picture she took with her phone of your baby after Vi did her hair up. She couldn't be prettier."

"Thank you."

"Just give a holler if you need something else. I heard you, Prentiss!" she called over her shoulder when another table hailed her. "Keep an eye on him anyway," she said to Shelby.

"I don't remember her. Should I remember her?"

"You remember Miss Clyde?"

"I had her for English literature, twelfth grade."

"So did we all. Lorna's her sister. She moved here from Nashville about three years ago. Her husband dropped stone dead from a heart attack at fifty."

"That's sad."

"They didn't have any kids, so she packed up, came here to live with her sister." Forrest took a sip of his beer. "Derrick says Tansy's his right hand around this place and Lorna's his left. Did you see Tansy?"

"I did. It took me more than a minute to recognize her. Matt said they're thinking about adding on here, putting in a dance floor and a stage and a second bar."

"Now you've done it," Emma Kate said as the talk turned to demolition and materials. "It'll be nothing but construction talk now."

She liked the construction talk, and the extra half hour she took to sit with her brother.

"This was nice, but I've got to get on."

"I'll walk you out to your car," Griff began as he slid over to let her out.

"Don't be silly. I think my brother keeps the streets of the Ridge safe enough. You can take my seat," she told Forrest, "spread out a little."

"I'll do just that. Why don't you text me when you get home?"

She started to laugh, saw he was serious. "How about I text you if I have any trouble getting home, all one and a half miles of it? 'Night, everybody. Thanks for the drink, Griff."

"It was water."

"I'll see if I can do more damage next time."

She walked out happy. Happy enough to roll the windows down despite the chill, turn the radio up and sing along. She didn't notice the car pulling out after her and following her that mile and a half.

Inside the bar, Forrest switched seats. "Walk her to her car?"

Griff studied his beer. "Your sister's hot."

"Don't make me punch you."

"You can punch me, but she'll still be hot."

Forrest decided to ignore him, shifted his focus to Emma Kate. "It looks like you two made things up."

"We got a start on it."

"How much did you get out of her?"

"Enough to be damn sure that dead husband of hers was a son of a bitch. You figured he was, Forrest."

"Yeah, I figured he was." Forrest's eyes chilled; his mouth thinned. "Couldn't do a goddamn thing about it."

"What kind of a son of a bitch?" Griff demanded.

"The kind that made her feel stupid and small and kept his money in a tight fist." The angry heat she'd banked down flashed out now. "The kind who likely had affairs while she was home taking care of the baby— the baby I got the clear impression he didn't pay much mind to. And there's more to it, I know there's more. She didn't let it all out tonight."

Emma Kate took a long breath. "I swear, if he hadn't gotten himself killed, I'd be holding your coat while you kicked his ass, Forrest, or you'd be holding mine."

"She should've done some ass-kicking herself."

"I bet nobody's ever made you feel stupid or small." Griff shook his head. He thought of those sad eyes, and the bright, flirtatious little girl.

His anger went on simmer. It could boil up—long, slow and rolling. If and when it boiled over, it scalded to the bone.

"My sister was hooked up with a guy for a while. Passive-aggressive, manipulative fucker. He twisted her up pretty good, and he only had a few months to do it. No kid involved. People like that, they start off making you feel like you're the most amazing thing on the planet, you're perfect, they're lucky to have you in their life. Then they start chipping away, a little at a time. Got on her to lose weight, and my sis is no pudge."

"She's not," Forrest agreed. "I've met her. Your sister's hot."

"Well played. This jerk was all over Jolie. Why didn't she do something with her hair? If she couldn't afford a better salon since she's stuck working in some dead-end job, he'd pay for it. His treat."

"Kick and kiss," Matt said. "I remember that guy. When Jolie finally broke it off, Griff baited him into taking a swing."

"I needed to get a punch in, and that way I could say he threw the first."

"It's still assault."

"Shut up, Deputy, it was worth it."

"Shelby was always so . . . what's the word?" Forrest muttered.

"Vibrant," Emma Kate supplied. "She went after things. She wouldn't walk over somebody to get it, but she'd go head-to-head with you. And if you tried walking over her or somebody else, especially somebody else?" She paused to glance at Griff. "You got your ass handed to you."

"She's still vibrant. You two don't see it maybe because you've known her all your lives. But I see it."

Emma Kate cocked her head at Griff. "Why, Griffin Lott. Shelby said her little girl was smitten with you. Are you smitten with the mama?"

"Her brother's sitting right here, and he's already threatened to punch me."

"She'd be your type," Matt put in.

"My type?"

"Because you don't have a type, as long as she's female."

"Her brother's sitting right here," Griff repeated, and applied himself to his beer.

SHELBY KEPT THE PLAYDATE in the park and enjoyed it nearly as much as Callie. Best of all, she and Chelsea's mother made an arrangement.

Tracey would watch the girls for a few hours while Shelby ran some errands the next day, and two days later, Shelby would do the same for her.

Everybody won a little something.

And maybe, she thought as she once again examined her wardrobe,
she'd net herself at least a part-time job.

She opted for a dress—simple lines in pale yellow for spring—and a
good pair of nude pumps, with a short white jacket to set it off.

She pulled her hair back into a tail, fastened on earrings with little
pearl drops. Costume, as she'd had them since college, but pretty and
right for the outfit.

With her mother back at work, she and Callie had the house to themselves, and she didn't have to explain she was gearing up for a job hunt. If
she got lucky and landed one, she'd present it all as a fait accompli.

If she got a job *and* sold the house? She'd do handsprings up and down
High Street in front of God and everybody.

"Mama's pretty."

"Callie's prettier." Shelby glanced over where Callie sat on the bed,
methodically stripping the clothes off two Barbie dolls.

"Baby, why are your Barbie dolls naked?"

"They need to change clothes for Chelsea's house. Chelsea has a kitty
named Snow White. Can I have a kitty?"

Now Shelby looked down at the old dog who snored at the foot of the
bed. "And how do you think Clancy would feel about that?"

"He could play with the kitty. My kitty's name's Fiona, like *Shrek*.
Can I have a kitty, please, Mama? And a puppy. I want a puppy most."

"I tell you what, when we get a house of our own, we'll see about getting a kitty."

"And a puppy, too! The puppy's name is Donkey, like *Shrek*."

"We'll see about that."

Richard had had a no-pet policy. Well, when she had a house for Callie, they'd have a dog and a cat.

"And a pony!"

"Now you're pushing it, Callie Rose." But she scooped her up, spun her around. "Is Mama really pretty today? I want to look my best today."

"Mama's beautiful."

She pressed her cheek to her daughter's. "Callie, you're my best thing in the world."

"Is it time to go to Chelsea's house?"

"Just about. You dress those dolls, then we can put them in the Callie bag and take them to Chelsea's house."

Once she'd dropped Callie off, chatted with Tracey, she headed straight into town.

She was capable, she told herself. She was smart enough to learn. She even knew a little about art, and she knew—or had known—some of the local artists and craftspeople. It made perfect sense to try to wrangle a part-time job at The Artful Ridge.

After she parked, she sat for a moment, gathering herself.

Don't act desperate. If worse comes to worst, buy something. She could do this.

Fixing a smile on her face, ignoring the churning in her belly, she got out of the car, strolled down the sidewalk, and into The Artful Ridge.

Oh, it was pretty—she'd love to spend time here. It smelled of scented candles and glowed with natural light. She saw half a dozen things at a glance she'd be happy to have in her own home, once she got one.

Wrought-iron candlesticks, pale blue blown-glass wineglasses, a painting of a mountain stream on a misty morning, a long, sinuous jar the color of top cream polished like glass.

Tracey's pottery, too—and she loved the tulip-shaped stacking bowls.

Glass shelves sparkled, and while the old wood floor creaked a little, it held a subtle gleam.

The girl who came around the counter couldn't have been more than twenty and wore a half dozen colorful studs around the curve of her ear.

Not in charge, Shelby thought, but maybe a gateway.

"Good morning. Anything I can help you with today?"

"It's just beautiful in here."

"Thank you! We carry local artists and artisans. There are so many talented people in the area."

"I know it. Oh, that's one of my cousin's paintings. A set of them." She stepped over to a grouping of four small watercolors.

"You're a cousin to Jesslyn Pomeroy?"

"I am, on my daddy's side. I'm Shelby Pomeroy. Foxworth now."

Who your people were mattered, Shelby knew, and could be another gateway. "She's my uncle Bartlet's middle daughter. We're all so proud of her."

"We sold one of her paintings just last Saturday to a man from Washington, D.C."

"Isn't that wonderful? Cousin Jessie's art on somebody's wall in Washington, D.C."

"Are you visiting the Ridge?"

"I was born and raised here, and while I've been away a few years, I've moved back home. Just a few days ago, actually. I've been settling in. The fact is, I'd like to find some part-time work. It would be just lovely to work in a shop like this, with my cousin's art right there."

"And Tracey Lee's," she added, as it never hurt to know people. "Her little girl and mine have become best friends already."

"We can't keep Tracey's coffee mugs on the shelf. They just fly out of here. My sister Tate's married to Robbie's—that's Tracey's husband—to Robbie's cousin Woody. They're living up in Knoxville."

"Would that be Tate Brown?"

"That's right. It's Bradshaw now, but that's my sister. You know Tate?"

"I do. She dated my brother Clay for a time when they were in high school. So she's married and living in Knoxville?"

Gateways, Shelby thought, as they chatted about family connections.

"We're just starting to look for some extra help, for the season. Would you like to talk to the manager about it?"

"I would, thank you."

"Just give me a minute. Browse around if you like."

"I will." In fact, as soon as the girl was out of sight, Shelby checked the price on the tall jar. Winced a little. A fair price, she imagined, but a little out of her reach right now.

She'd make it a goal.

When the girl came back moments later, the friendly had drained out of her eyes, and her tone was cool.

"You can go on up to the office. I'll show you."

"Thank you. It must be nice," Shelby continued as they walked to the back of the shop. Here rustic wooden cases and shelves held pottery and textiles. "Working around all these pretty things."

"You go right up the stairs here, it's the first door you come to. It's open."

"Thanks again."

She went up the sturdy stairs, turned into a room backed with three narrow windows that opened up to a view of the Ridge and the rise of the hills.

Here was art and pretty things as well, a sweet chair with curvy legs done in deep blue, and a wonderful old desk refinished so the oak shone gold. A vase of red roses and baby's breath stood on it, along with a computer and a phone.

It took her only a moment to focus in on the woman behind the desk—and understand the abrupt change in the clerk's demeanor.

"Why, hello, Melody. I had no idea you worked here."

"I manage the gallery. My grandmama bought it just about a year ago and asked me to get it in shape for her."

"Well, from what I see, you've done a wonderful job of it."

"Thank you. You have to do what you can for family, don't you? And look at you." She rose then, a curvy woman in a fitted dress of rosy pink. Her blond hair fell in a long, soft wave to her shoulders, sweeping around a heart-shaped face with poreless skin glowing from an expert hand with bronzer or a good self-tanner.

Shelby knew Melody would never expose her face to the sun and risk lines and spots.

Her eyes, a chilly blue, flicked over Shelby as she walked over, moved in for a cheek bump.

"You haven't changed a bit, have you! My goodness, this humidity that's moving in must play havoc with your hair."

"It helps to have easy access to good salon products." Yours could use a root touch-up, she thought, as no one made her hackles prickle faster than Melody Bunker.

"I'm sure it does. I heard you were back. It's just tragic about your husband, Shelby. Just tragic. You have all my sympathy."

"Thank you, Melody."

"And back where you started now, aren't you? Living back with your mama, aren't you? Oh, please, have a seat." Melody leaned a hip back on the desk, holding the higher ground, the position of power. "And how are you, Shelby?"

"I'm fine. I'm happy to be home again. How's your mama, Melody?"

"Oh, she's doing fine. We're going to Memphis in a couple weeks, having a few days, doing some shopping, staying at the Peabody, of course."

"Of course."

"You know how hard it is to find decent clothes around here, so we try to get into Memphis every season. I have to admit, I never thought to see you back in the Ridge, but being a widow, you must need the comfort of family."

"They are a comfort."

"But I sure was surprised when Kelly came up and said you were downstairs and asking about work, what with all the talk about how well off you were, landing yourself a rich husband. And you have a daughter, don't you?"

Those blue eyes sparkled now, but it wasn't with friendship or camaraderie. "Some say that helped with the landing."

"I'm sure they do, as some will say all manner of unattractive things just to hear their own voice. I'd like to work," Shelby said simply.

"I'd sure like to help you out, Shelby, but working here at The Artful Ridge takes certain requirements. I don't suppose you've ever worked a cash register in your life."

Melody knew very well she had, at the salon.

"I ran one since I was fourteen, weekends and summers at my grandmother's salon. I was assistant manager of the bookstore in college—University of Memphis, if you can't recall. That was a few years ago, but I'm sure I could get references if you need them. I know how to work a register, a computer, I know most of the basic softwares."

"A family beauty parlor and a college bookstore don't give you much of a foundation for an upscale showplace of arts and crafts. And do you know how to sell? Working a bookstore in college? Why, that sort of thing sells itself, doesn't it? We carry a superior range of art, a lot of it exclusive to us. We're a landmark in this town now. In the county, come to that. And we've got a reputation."

"I'm sure the reputation's earned, considering what you showcase here, and how you display it. Though I'd have taken those cane-back chairs from the front and put them at that burl wood table in the back, done something interesting on the table with the pottery dishes and some wineglasses, some of the textiles."

"Oh, would you?"

She only smiled at the frigid tone. "I would, but that's me. And I can say so because you don't have any intention of giving me a job."

"I wouldn't think of it."

With a nod, Shelby rose. "That's your loss, Melody, because I'd have been an asset to your grandmother's business here. I appreciate the time."

"Why don't you go over to Vi's? I'm sure your grandmother could find you work there, suited to your skills and experience. She has to need someone sweeping up and washing out the sinks."

"You think that's beneath me?" Shelby angled her head. "I'm not surprised, Melody, not at all surprised. You haven't changed since high school, and still holding a grudge because they put that Homecoming crown on my head instead of yours. That's awful sad. It's just awful sad your life hasn't gotten any richer or more satisfying since high school."

She walked out, head up, started down.

"I was second-runner-up Miss Tennessee!"

Shelby glanced back, smiled at Melody, who stood, hands on hips, at the top of the stairs. "Bless your heart," she said, and continued down, and straight out.

She wanted to shake. She wasn't sure if it was anger or humiliation, but she wanted to shake. Walk it off, she ordered herself, and crossed the street.

Her first instinct was to go to the salon, vent it all out, but she turned sharply, headed for the bar and grill.

Maybe Tansy could use another waitress at Bootlegger's.

Running on that anger and humiliation, she banged on the door. Maybe they didn't open for another half hour, but somebody, by God, was in there.

On her second series of bangings, the door opened. The tough-looking guy in a T-shirt with cut-off sleeves that showed off arms with muscles carved like a mountain range gave her one hard look out of eyes black as onyx.

"We're not open until eleven-thirty."

"I know that. It says so clear enough. I'm looking for Tansy."

"Why would that be?"

"That would be my business, so . . ." She broke off, bore down on herself. "I'm sorry—I apologize. I'm upset and I'm being rude. I'm Shelby, a friend of Tansy's. I'd like to talk to her a minute if she's around."

"Shelby. I'm Derrick."

"Oh, Tansy's husband. It's nice to meet you, Derrick, and I really am sorry for being rude. I've embarrassed myself."

"Bygones. It's clear you're upset. Come on in."

A couple of waitstaff did setups on the tables. In the relative quiet Shelby heard kitchen noises, raised voices.

"Why don't you have a seat at the bar? I'll get Tansy."

"Thank you. I won't take much time."

She sat, tried to fall back on the yoga breathing she'd practiced when she'd taken classes in Atlanta. It didn't help.

Tansy came in, all smiles. "I'm so glad you came by. We didn't really have time to talk last night."

"I was rude to your Derrick."

"She wasn't that rude, and she's already apologized twice. Want a drink?" he asked her.

"I—"

"How about a Coke?" Tansy said.

"God, yes. Thanks. I'm repeating myself, but I'm sorry. I just had a little altercation with Melody Bunker."

Tansy slid onto a stool. "Want something stronger than a Coke?"

"I'm tempted, but no thanks. I went over there to see if I could get a part-time job. I wish I didn't like the place so much. It's just wonderful, and has such a good feel about it. Until I went upstairs and talked to Melody. She was as biting as a nest of rattlers, I swear. Wouldn't you think she'd let go of high school?"

"Her type never lets go of anything. I'm the one who's sorry. I sent you over there. I didn't think about Melody—I try not to."

Tansy sent Derrick a smile when he put a ginger ale in front of her. "Thanks, baby. Melody's only in there two or three hours a day, and only a few days out of the week. Otherwise she's off to some club meeting or getting her nails done, or having lunch up at the big restaurant. It's Roseanne, the assistant manager, who really runs the place."

"Whoever runs it, Melody would burn it to the ground before she hired me on. Thank you," she said to Derrick when he set the Coke in front of her. "I'm sure I'm going to like you because you have such good taste in wives. And I love your place. I had the best time here last night. Oh, and congratulations on the baby."

"That about covers it. I already like you." He poured himself a fizzy water. "Tansy's told me about you, and how you'd take up for her when somebody like that bitch across the street picked on her."

"Derrick, you shouldn't call her that."

"She is a bitch," Shelby said, and drank. "At least I gave her some of her own back. It's been a while since I've given anybody some of their own back. And it felt damn good. Maybe a little too good."

"You were always good at it."

"Was I?" Calmer, Shelby smiled, sipped. "It sure came back to me. Smoke was spiraling out of her ears when I left, so that's something. So, I won't be working there in the foreseeable future. I wonder if you need any help here. Another waitress, maybe?"

"You want to wait tables?"

"I want a job. No, I need a job," Shelby amended. "That's the truth. I need a job. I'm making the rounds today while Tracey Lee's got my Callie with her Chelsea. If you're not hiring, that's all right. I've got a list I'm going down."

"Have you ever done any waitressing?" Derrick asked her.

"I've cleared plenty of tables, served plenty of food. I'm not afraid of hard work. I'm only looking for part-time now, but—"

"Waitressing isn't for you, Shelby," Tansy began.

"All right. Thanks for listening, and for the Coke."

"I'm not done. Derrick and I, we've been talking about adding some entertainment on Friday nights. We have," she insisted when Derrick frowned.

"Talked about it, some."

"Two Saturdays a month we have a live band, and we do good, strong business. We'd add to Friday night's till with some entertainment. I'll hire you right now, Shelby, to sing on Friday nights, eight to midnight."

"Tansy, I appreciate your offering, but I haven't done anything like that in years."

"Do you still have your voice?"

"It's not that . . ."

"We couldn't pay a lot, at least until we see how it goes. Forty-minute sets, and ten of the twenty between you'd work the crowd some. Go around the tables. What I want is to try a kind of weekly theme."

"She's got ideas," Derrick muttered, but with a spark of pride.

"I have good ideas." With the ginger ale in one hand, Tansy tapped a finger on the bar. "And this good idea is we'd start off with the forties. Songs from the forties, specialty drinks from then. What did they drink back then? Martinis or boilermakers. I'll figure that out," she said, waving it aside.

"Next week it's the fifties, and we work our way up. It's all nostalgia. We'll draw in a lot of people. I'll get it set up. We'll use a karaoke machine for now. Maybe if we do the expansion, we can get a piano, or we can hire a couple of musicians. For right now, to start, we'll get that karaoke machine, Derrick, because we're going to start doing Karaoke Mondays, too."

"She's got ideas," he said again.

"I got one says people just love hearing themselves sing whether they can't pipe out a single true note. They'll be flocking in here Monday nights. And now Fridays, too. That's what we'll call it—just 'Friday Nights.' I know it's only one night a week, Shelby, but that'll give you room to find some day work if you need it."

"Are you all right with all this?" Shelby asked Derrick.

"She manages the place. I just own it."

"Not this Friday," Tansy continued, steamrolling over them both. "It's too soon, and I have things to put together. Next Friday. You'll want to come in a couple times, rehearse, once I get it set up. We're going to need that expansion, Derrick, once we get this going. You'd better talk to Matt and Griff, get that nailed right soon."

"Yes, ma'am."

"So. Shelby?"

Shelby blew out a breath, drew in another. "All right. I'm in—and if it doesn't work out, no hard feelings. But I'm in, and grateful. I'll be your Friday Nights."

10

S he all but danced over to the salon.

"Why, don't you look a treat," Viola said the minute she stepped in. "Sissy, you remember my granddaughter, Shelby."

That started a winding conversation with the woman in Viola's chair while Viola removed a forest of enormous rollers and began the styling.

The minute she had an opening, Shelby announced her news.

"Won't that be something? Tansy and her Derrick, they're making something out of that place, and there you'll be. A headliner."

Shelby laughed, automatically shifting the basket of used rollers out of her grandmother's way. "It's only Friday nights, but—"

Sissy interrupted with a story about her daughter starring in the high school musical while Viola poofed her hair to twice its volume.

"I really should get on. I guess Mama's doing a treatment."

"Back-to-back facials. Tracey's got Callie for a while yet, doesn't she?" Viola asked. "I got a break coming up."

"I still have a couple of stops to make. I thought I'd see if Mountain Treasures is hiring part-time, or maybe The What-Not Place as Tansy says they do well with tourists and locals."

"I got some sweet Depression glass teacups there to go with my collection," Sissy told her.

"It's on my list. The Artful Ridge isn't as they're not hiring, at least not me as long as Melody Bunker has a say in it."

"Melody's been jealous of you since you were children." Knowing her client, Viola sprayed a fierce cloud of holding spray over the mountain of hair. "You be grateful she didn't hire you, baby girl. If you worked over there, she'd make your days a misery. There, Sissy. Big enough for you?"

"Oh now, Vi, you know I like to make a statement with my hair. God blessed me with plenty of it, so I like putting it to use. It looks just wonderful. Nobody does it up like you. I'm having lunch with my girlfriends," she told Shelby. "Doing it fancy, up at the hotel."

"Won't that be fun?"

It took a few minutes more to scoot Sissy along, then Viola blew out a breath, sat in the chair. "Next time, I swear, I'll just use a bicycle pump on that hair of hers. Now, how many days a week you thinking of working?"

"I could do three or four—maybe even five with shorter hours if I can work out a deal with Tracey, and maybe ask Mama to fill in with Callie otherwise. Any more than that, I'd have to see about taking her to day care."

"That'd eat up your paycheck."

"I was hoping to wait for the fall for it, give her time to settle in, but I may have to do it sooner. It'll be good for her to be around other kids."

"True enough. Here's what I'm going to say to you. I don't know why you're going over to Mountain Treasures and other places when I can use you right here. You could help with the phones, the book, the stock and supplies, and the customers. And you could help keep things organized as you've got an organized nature. You find something you like better, that's fine. But for right now, I could use you three days a week. Four when we're busy. You could bring Callie in here and there. You spent plenty of your time in the salon when you were her age."

"I did."

"Did it hurt you any?"

"No, I loved it. I've got good memories of playing here, listening to the ladies talk, getting my hair and nails done like a grown-up. I don't want to take advantage, Granny. I don't want you to make work for me."

"It's not taking advantage or making work when I can use you. I can't say you'd be doing me a favor as I'd have to pay you. It makes good sense, unless you just don't want to work here."

"I wish you would," Crystal called over from her station. "It would save the rest of us from having to answer the phone or check the book for walk-ins if Dottie's in the back or it's her time off."

"I could use you three days a week ten to three, and on Saturdays from nine to four when we're hopping." Viola paused, seeing the hesitation on Shelby's face. "If you don't take the job, I'll have to hire somebody else. That's a fact. Crystal?"

"That is a fact. We were just talking about looking for somebody to come in part-time." With the rat-tail comb in her hand, Crystal crossed her heart. "I swear on it."

"We'd need to go over some things as it's been some time since you did any filling in around here," Viola continued, "but you're a bright girl. I expect you'd catch on quick."

Shelby looked over at Crystal. "You're swearing she's not making busy-work for me?"

"She sure isn't. Dottie's doing a lot of running between the salon and the treatment rooms, back in the locker and relaxation areas. And Sasha hardly has time for that anymore since she got her license and she's doing face and body treatments. We keep up with it, but it would sure be nice to have somebody doing more of the running."

"All right." Shelby let out a surprised laugh. "I'd love to work here."

"Then you're hired. You can give me the hour you'd have spent going all around seeing about a job, and go in the back there. Towels should be dry by now. You could fold them and bring them out, put them at stations."

Shelby leaned down, pressed her cheek to Viola's. "Thank you, Granny."

"You'll be busy."

"That's just what I want," Shelby said, and got to work.

. . .

BY THE TIME she got home with Callie she'd worked out a doable sched-
ule. She'd barter one day a week with Tracey, pay her for two days when
Saturday was called for, and Ada Mae scooped up the other day as her
"Gamma and Callie Day."

Whenever it didn't work, she'd take Callie with her.

Friday nights her mother and grandmother would switch off—their
idea, she thought, as she pulled in the drive.

She could earn a decent enough living, her child would be well cared
for. She couldn't ask for more.

And as Callie got that glassy-eyed look on the short drive home, Shelby
calculated she could get her down for a nap right off, then spend some
time looking up songs from the forties, starting her playlist. With Callie
half asleep on her shoulder, she started straight upstairs.

She made the turn toward Callie's room, swaying and humming to
keep her daughter in the nap zone, then let out a short scream when Griff
stepped into the hallway.

Callie jumped in her arms, and rather than a short scream, blasted out
a wailing screech.

"Sorry!" Griff dragged the earbuds off. "I didn't hear you. Sorry. Your
mother said— Hey, Callie, I'm sorry I scared you."

Clutching Shelby, Callie stared at him, sobbing, then threw herself at
him. He had to scramble forward, grab hold. Callie clung, crying on his
shoulder.

"It's okay. It's all right." He rubbed her back as he smiled at Shelby.
"Your mother wants that new bathroom. I said I'd stop over first chance,
make sure on the measurements. Wow, you look really good."

"I'm just going to sit down a minute." She did so, right on the top step.
"I didn't see your truck."

"I walked over from Miz Bitsy's. We're just punching out there, so we
can start here next week."

"Next week?"

"Yeah." He patted and jiggled as Callie's tears dissolved into sniffles. "We've got a couple of little jobs, but we'll juggle this in. I had music in my ears, so I didn't hear you."

"That's okay. I probably didn't need those last ten years of my life. I'm just going to put her down for her nap."

"I've got it. Over in here, right?"

He stepped into Callie's room. By the time Shelby pushed up, walked across, he had her on the bed, under her light blanket, and was quietly answering the singsong questions she often came up with at nap or bed time.

"Kiss," Callie demanded.

"You got it." He kissed her cheek, stood up, glanced at Shelby. "Is that it?"

"That's it." But she did a come-away motion, and eased out. "It's only that easy because she wore herself out at Chelsea's."

"She smells like cherries."

"Juice box, I imagine."

And her mother smells like a mountain meadow—fresh and sweet and wild all at once. Maybe the word of the day should be "pheromones."

"You really do look good."

"Oh, I've been job hunting, tried to look presentable."

"You went way over presentable into"—he caught himself on "hot"— "excellent. How'd you do on the job hunt?"

"I did great, out of the park with bases loaded."

Jesus, baseball metaphor. He might have to marry her.

"I want a Coke," she decided. "Do you want a Coke?"

"I wouldn't turn one down." Especially since it meant he got a little more time with her. "So what's the job?"

"Now, that's much too direct for around here," she warned him as they started downstairs. "We have to work up to how I went about getting it."

"Sorry, still shedding the Yankee."

"Well, don't shed it all, it works for you. What were you listening to?" She tapped her ears.

"Oh, it's a pretty eclectic playlist, I guess. I think it was The Black Keys when I cut that ten years off your life. 'Fever.'"

"At least I lost a decade to a song I like. Now to your question. First, I got my butt kicked and my ego flattened when I tried for a job at The Artful Ridge as my high school rival, at least in her mind, manages it."

"Melody Bunker. I know her. She hit on me."

"She did not." Amazed, she stopped short, gaped up and gave him a chance to look close. Her eyes really were almost purple.

"Did she really?"

"She'd had a couple of drinks, and I was new in town."

"Are you going to tell me if you hit back?"

"I thought about it," he said as he walked to the kitchen with her. "She's great to look at, but there's that mean streak."

"Not everyone—particularly those who are male—notice that."

"I've got a pretty good eye for mean. She was with another girl, and there was a lot of . . . How do I put this without saying 'meow'?"

"You can say it, it fits her. She's always been catty. And she does have a mean streak, deep and wide. She tried her best to make me feel stupid and useless today, but she didn't manage it. She's following after a superior act in that area of mean, and fell short, well short."

She caught herself, shook her head as she got out Cokes, glasses. "Doesn't matter, and it was for the best. For more than the best."

"What did she say to you—or is that too direct?"

"Oh, she started with snide little comments about my hair."

"You have amazing hair. Magic mermaid hair."

She laughed. "That's a first. Magic mermaid hair. I'll have to use that with Callie. In any case, Mean Melody got in a few jabs about my current circumstance, which I tolerated as I wanted the damn job. She moved on, though, trying to scrape me down to the bone, how I wasn't qualified, didn't have enough class, basically, or intelligence, and it was clear I didn't have a cherry snow cone's chance in hell of working there, so I landed a few jabs of my own, with, I will say, more subtlety and style."

"I just bet."

With a cool, sharp smile, Shelby poured Cokes over ice. "She was so steamed up when I was leaving she shouted out how she'd been second-runner-up Miss Tennessee, which is her spotlight of fame. To that, I ended the encounter with the southern woman's sweetest and most pitying insult."

"I know that." He pointed a finger. "I know that one. You said 'Bless your heart.'"

"Haven't you caught on fast?" After topping off the glasses, she handed him one. "I knew that one landed, but I was so fired up, I marched over to the bar and grill. I was going to ask Tansy to hire me on as a waitress. I met Derrick—and doesn't he look like an action movie star."

"I hadn't thought of it."

"You'd be looking at him as a man does. From a woman's eyes?" She laughed again, waved a hand in front of her face. "Lucky Tansy—and lucky Derrick because she's a sweet, smart, sensible woman. So after I apologized for being rude to him, because I was fired up, they didn't want me for a waitress."

"Sounds like a rough day on the job hunt."

"Not at all. They wanted me for Friday nights, to sing. I'm going to be their Friday night entertainment. Or, as Tansy's calling it, I'm going to be Friday Nights."

"No kidding? That's great, Red, seriously great. Everybody says you can sing. Sing something."

"No."

"Come on, a couple of bars of anything."

"Come into Bootlegger's a week from Friday, and you'll hear plenty." After lifting her glass to him, she took a satisfied drink. "Then, because that's not all, I went in to tell Granny before I hit a couple other possible places for day jobs, and she cornered me into working part-time there. She made me believe she could really use me, so I'm hoping she meant it."

"In my shorter experience, Miz Vi usually means what she says."

"It's true enough, and Crystal swore to it they'd already talked about hiring someone part-time. So, I didn't just get a job, I got two. I'm employed, gainfully. God, it feels so good."

"Want to celebrate?" He watched her eyes go from sparkling happy to just a little wary. "Maybe we could get Matt and Emma Kate, go have dinner."

"Oh, that sounds like fun, it really does, but I need to buckle down, work out a playlist. Tansy wants to change it up every week, so I've got some research to do. And there's Callie, though it's likely to be more of a weight on me leaving her for hours at a time than for her leaving me."

"Does she like pizza?"

"Callie? Sure she does. It runs a close second to ice cream on her favorites list."

"Then I'll take you both out for pizza one night after work."

"That's awful nice of you, Griffin. She's already got a crush going on you."

"Mutual."

She smiled at him, topped off his Coke. "How long have you been in the Ridge now, Griffin?"

"Going on a year."

"And don't you have a girl by now? Somebody who looks like you ought to have the single girls flocking."

"Well, there was Melody for about ten minutes. And there's Miz Vi, if only she'd reciprocate."

"Grandpa'd fight you for her."

"I'd fight dirty."

"So would he, and he's very canny. I have to say, I'm surprised Emma Kate—or surely Miz Bitsy—hasn't tried fixing you up."

"Tried, didn't stick." He shrugged, downed some Coke. "I haven't been interested in anyone particularly. Up to now."

"I guess it just takes . . . Oh." It may have been a long while, but she supposed a woman didn't forget that look in a man's eyes, that tone in a man's voice. Flustered, and under the flustered she couldn't deny flattered, she took a careful drink. "Oh," she repeated. "I've got to say, Griff, I'm a complicated, twisted-up mess of a thing right now."

"I fix things, Red. It's what I do."

She managed a nervous laugh. "This is a complete overhaul—what you'd call a gut job, I think. And I come as a set."

"I like the set, and I know I'm hitting on you pretty quick considering. It just seems to me it's better to be straight-out. You knocked me flat when you walked into Bitsy's kitchen. I planned to be slow and a lot smoother about it, but hell, Shelby, why?"

That was straight-out and forthright, she thought, and as unnerving as it was flattering. "You really don't know me."

"I plan to."

This time she let out a laugh that was more stupefied. "Just like that."

"Unless you take a strong dislike to me, and I don't think you will. I'm likable. I want to take you out, when you're ready and want to go. Meanwhile, since I'm attached to Matt and he's attached to Emma Kate, we'll be seeing each other. Plus, I really like your kid."

"I can see that. If I thought different, if I thought she was a kind of conduit with you to me, this would be a different conversation. As it is, I don't know just what to say to you."

"Well, you can think about that. I've got to get back, and you've got things to do. Tell your mom I've got the measurements. Once she settles on the tile, the fixtures, we'll get them ordered."

"All right."

"Thanks for the Coke."

"You're welcome." She walked back with him, considering the nerves—

those interesting, fluttery nerves she hadn't felt in so long. A mistake, absolutely a mistake to act on them at this point in her life.

"I meant it about the pizza," he said at the door.

"Callie would be thrilled."

"Pick the day, let me know." He frowned outside a moment, his gaze following the car that passed. "Do you know somebody with a gray Honda? Looks like a 2012."

"Can't think of anyone. Why?"

"I keep seeing it. I've seen it around a lot the last few days."

"Well, people do live here."

"Florida plates."

"A tourist, I guess. There's good hiking now while it's still cool, and the wildflowers are popping out everywhere."

"Yeah, probably. Anyway, congratulations on scoring the jobs."

"Thank you."

She watched him walk away—that swagger really was damn appealing. And he'd gotten her blood moving in ways she'd forgotten it could move.

Still, it was best all around if she kept all her attention on Callie, her new work, and climbing her way out of the canyon of debt.

Thinking of debt, she started upstairs. She'd change, work out a new budget, check and see if there was any progress on the house sale, or if there was any more money coming from the consignment shop. Then she could think about a playlist.

That was work, true enough, but it was also fun—smarter to get the hard over with first.

She stopped dead in the doorway of her room.

A gray Honda with Florida plates. She scrambled for her dresser, pulled out the drawer where she'd put all the business cards from Philadelphia.

And there was Ted Privet, Private Investigator. Miami, Florida.

She *had* seen him in the bar and grill. He'd followed her all the way back to the Ridge. Why would he do that? What did it mean?

He was watching her.

She made herself go to the window, look out, search.

She had no choice about the debt coming home with her, but she wouldn't sit still, do nothing, when more of Richard's mess tried to push its way into her life now.

Instead of getting to work, she picked up her phone.

"Forrest? I'm sorry to bother you at work, but I think I have some trouble. I think I could use some help with it."

HE LISTENED TO HER, didn't interrupt, didn't ask any questions. That only made her more nervous, babbling it all out to her brother while he sat there cool as ice, his eyes on her face telling her nothing.

"Is that it?" he said when she ran down.

"I think so. Yes, that's it, that's all. I guess it's more than enough."

"Do you have the IDs, the ones you found in the bank box?"

"Yes."

"I'm going to need them."

"I'll go get them."

"Sit. I'm not done."

So she sat back down at the kitchen counter, knotted her hands together on it.

"Do you have the gun?"

"I . . . Yes. I made sure it wasn't loaded, and I have it in a box, top of my closet, where Callie can't get to it."

"And any of the cash—from the box?"

"I kept three thousand of it in cash—it's up in my closet, too. I used most of the rest, like I said, to pay off bills. And I put some in the bank here. I opened an account here in the Ridge."

"I want all of it. The IDs, the gun, the cash, the envelopes, anything you have that came out of the box."

"All right, Forrest."

"Now, I'm going to ask you why the fuck, why the fuck, Shelby, you're just telling me all this now?"

"The hole was so deep, and it got deep so fast. First Richard's dead, and I'm trying to think what to do, then the lawyers are telling me there's all this trouble. I start going through the bills. I just never did that, because he locked them up. They were his business—and don't slap at me for it. You weren't there, you didn't live that life, so don't slap at me for it. Then I found out about the house, and everything. I had to deal with it. I found the key, and I *had* to know. Then when I found the bank box, and what was in it . . . I don't know who I married, who I lived with, who fathered my child."

She took a long breath. "And I couldn't let that matter, couldn't let that take the rest over. What matters is now, and dealing with it until I'm clear of it. Keeping Callie clear of it. I don't know why this detective followed me here. I don't have anything. I don't know anything."

"I'll deal with that."

"I'll thank you for it."

"I might've slapped at you some, Shelby. But just to wake you up. You're my sister, goddamn it. We're your family."

She linked her fingers together again, to hold herself in. "You think I've forgotten that, and you're wrong. If you think I don't value that, you're stupid."

"What should I think?" he countered.

"That I did what I thought was right. I couldn't come back until I'd started climbing out of that hole, Forrest. I wouldn't. Maybe you think that's just pride, just stupid, but I couldn't come back and put all of it on my family."

"You couldn't ask for a hand, a hand to reach down and help you up out of it?"

"Well, Jesus God, Forrest, aren't I doing just that? But I had to get up far enough to reach a hand. That's what I'm doing now."

He pushed up, paced around the room, stopped at the window for a while, looking out in silence. "All right. Maybe I see your side of that. I don't have to say you're right to sée it. Go ahead, get me everything you have."

"What are you going to do? It's still my business, Forrest."

"I'm going to have a talk with this Florida PI, let him know I don't take kindly to him stalking my sister. Then I'm going to do what I can to find out who the hell you were married to."

"I think he stole that money he had stashed in the bank box, or he swindled it. Dear God, Forrest, if I have to pay all that back—"

"You won't. You took what you took legally. Whatever he did, it's pretty damn clear there's nothing left to pay anybody back. One more thing. You're going to tell all of this to the rest of the family. You're going to get this out."

"Gilly's about to have a baby."

"No excuses, Shelby. You're going to sit down tonight, after Callie's in bed, and tell everyone. I'll make sure they're all here. You want them to get word some private investigator from out of state's asking questions about their daughter, their sister?"

Because she saw the sense of it, she pressed her fingers to her eyes. "No. You're right. I'll tell them. You have to take my side, Forrest, when Mama and Daddy start talking about helping me pay off this debt. I won't have it."

"That's fair enough." He came over, put his hands on her shoulders. "I am on your side, you idiot."

She dipped her forehead to his chest. "I can't wish the years away without wishing Callie away, but I can wish I'd been stronger standing up to him. It feels like every time I found my footing, something changed and I lost it again."

"It sounds to me like he was good at making sure people didn't find their footing around him. Go on, get all the things from the box. Let me get going on this."

· · ·

IT DIDN'T TAKE LONG to track down the private investigator, not when the man had opted to hide in plain sight. He'd registered under his own name at the hotel—though he'd spread the word he was a freelance travel writer.

Forrest considered confronting him there, but he thought he'd give Privet a taste of his own medicine. Once he was off duty and in his own truck, he did some cruising until he spotted the Honda parked outside The Artful Ridge.

Forrest parked the truck, got out and strolled by the shop. Sure enough, the man he'd spent an hour or so running stood talking with Melody.

He'd get an earful about Shelby from that source, no question. With his target sighted, he went back to his truck, waited.

He watched Privet come out, cross over to the bar and grill. Doubtful he'd find the same well of information in there, but if he was any good— and from the run it seemed he wasn't bad—he'd pull out some.

Making the rounds, Forrest concluded as, fifteen minutes later, Privet came out of the bar and grill, walked down and into the salon.

Following Shelby's path from earlier in the day, which meant Privet had trailed her through the morning.

That put a knot in Forrest's craw.

This stop took longer, but when Forrest did another stroll by, he noted that Privet sat in a chair getting a haircut. At least he put some money in the local pot while trying to mine information.

Forrest settled back in his truck, patient, waited for Privet to come out, get back in his car.

He pulled out after him, paced him easily in the light town traffic. Privet took the fork toward Shelby and home. When the Honda drove straight by, Forrest calculated, turned off—did a three-quarter turn to face the road again.

He dug out his Kojak light, fixed it to the roof, and waited.

When Privet drove by a second time, eased to the side of the road a few yards down from the house, Forrest pulled out, hit the light so Privet would see it in his rearview.

He eased up behind the Honda, walked up to the passenger window—already rolled down.

Privet had a map out, and a frustrated expression on his face.

"I hope there's no problem, Officer, and that you can help me. I think I made a wrong turn somewhere. I'm looking for—"

"Don't waste my time. I believe you know who I am, and I sure as hell know who you are, Mr. Privet. I want your hands on the wheel where I can see them. Now," Forrest said, setting his hand on the butt of his weapon, "I know you're licensed to carry, and if I don't see both your hands on the wheel, we're going to have some trouble here."

"I'm not looking for trouble." Privet held his hands up, placed them carefully on the wheel. "I'm just doing my job."

"I'm doing mine. You went to see my sister up North, and entered her home on false pretenses."

"She asked me in."

"You cornered a woman with a small child in her home, then you followed her across several state lines where you've spied on her, followed her."

"I'm a private investigator, Deputy. My license is in my—"

"I said I know who you are."

"Deputy Pomeroy, I have a client who—"

"If Richard Foxworth swindled your client, that's nothing to do with my sister. Foxworth's dead, so your client's out of luck there. If you spent ten minutes with Shelby and think she had anything to do with it, you're a damn fool."

"Matherson. He used the name David Matherson."

"Whatever name he used, whatever name he came into this world with, he's dead. Personally, I hope the sharks had a good meal off him. Now, if it's true you're not looking for trouble, you're going to stop following my sister, stop asking about her around town. I expect I could go into The Artful Ridge, the bar and grill and my granny's place and they'd all tell me how when you were in there somehow the conversation came around to Shelby. That stops. I catch you at it again, I'm taking you in. Around here we call what you're doing stalking, and we got a law against it."

"In my business it's called doing the job."

Forrest leaned conversationally on the bottom of the window. "Let me ask you something, Mr. Privet. You think if I was to arrest you right here and now, and take you in, the judge around here is going to say there's no problem with you sitting here—with those binoculars on the seat beside you?"

"I'm an amateur ornithologist."

"Name me five birds indigenous to the Smokies." Forrest waited two beats while Privet scowled. "See, you could say that bird, it won't fly. I tell my boss, and we tell Judge Harris—who's a third cousin, twice removed—that you've been sitting here watching my family home and my sister, been following her and her little girl around town, been asking questions about my widowed sister with her fatherless child, you think he's going to say, 'Why, that's just fine. Live and let'? Or do you think you'll be spending the night on a jailhouse cot tonight instead of your hotel bed?"

"My client isn't the only one Matherson swindled. And there's a matter of nearly thirty million in jewelry he stole out of Miami."

"I believe you. I believe he was a fucking bastard, and I know he did a number on my sister I won't forget. I'm not going to let you do the same."

"Deputy, do you know what the finder's fee is on twenty-eight million?"

"It's going to be zero," Forrest said equably, "if you're looking for it through my sister. You stay away from her, Mr. Privet, or you'll have plenty of the trouble you don't want to have, because if I catch you at it, I'll make sure of that trouble. You can tell your client we're all sorry for his bad luck. If I were you, I'd head back to Florida and do just that. Tonight. But it's your choice."

Forrest straightened up again. "We clear on that?"

"We're clear on that. I've got one question."

"Ask it."

"How could your sister live with Matherson for years and not know what he was?"

"Let me ask one back. Is your client a reasonably intelligent individual?"

"I'd say he is."

"How did he manage to get himself swindled? You're going to want to move along now, and you don't want to drive back down this road again. That's literal and metaphorical."

Forrest walked back to his truck, waited until Privet drove away. Then he drove himself the short distance to his family home, parked so he'd be there when Shelby told the family her story.

PART II

THE ROOTS

We're too unseparate. And going home
From company means coming
to our senses.

ROBERT FROST

11

onfessions and truth telling exhausted the body and the brain.
When Shelby dragged herself out of bed in the morning, she realized she'd start her day already worn down.

It was hateful to disappoint the people who'd raised you. She thought
of Callie, wondered if one day she'd do something stupid and wake up
with this same dragging sensation.

Odds were pretty good on that, so Shelby vowed to remember this
morning, and to try to give her daughter a break when the time came.

She found Callie, still luckily too young to do something really stupid,
sitting in bed having a cheerful conversation with Fifi. So Shelby dived in
for a morning snuggle that pulled her mood up a notch or two.

She got them both dressed, then took Callie downstairs.

She put on the coffee, decided she'd make up some of the ground
she'd lost with her parents the night before by making French toast—and
the poached eggs her father favored.

By the time her mother came down, she had Callie settled in her
booster with some sliced banana and strawberries, with breakfast well on
the way.

"'Morning, Mama."

"'Morning. All bright and early, I see. 'Morning, my sunbeam," she said to Callie, and crossed over for a kiss.

"We get to have eggy bread, Gamma."

"Do we? Why, that's a special morning treat."

"Nearly done," Shelby told her. "I'm poaching some eggs for Daddy. Do you want any?"

"Not this morning, thank you."

When Ada Mae walked over to pour coffee, Shelby turned, wrapped her arms around her mother from behind. "You're still mad," she murmured.

"Of course I'm still mad. Mad doesn't turn off and on like a light."

"Still pretty mad at me."

Ada Mae sighed. "That part's on a dimmer switch. It's easing down some."

"I'm so sorry, Mama."

"I know you are." Ada Mae patted Shelby's hand. "I know. And I'm trying to come around to it being the situation you were in, and not that you didn't trust your family to help you."

"It was never that. Never. I just . . . I got myself into it, didn't I? Somebody raised me to face my own troubles and deal with them."

"Seems we did a fine job there. But not as fine a one on teaching you troubles shared are lessened."

"I was ashamed."

Now Ada Mae turned, took Shelby's face firmly in her hands. "You're never, *never* to be ashamed with me." She glanced over to where Callie was busy with her sliced fruit. "I could say a lot more, and likely will when there aren't little pitchers with big ears close by."

"Pitchers don't have ears, Gamma! That's silly."

"It is, isn't it? Why don't I fix you a piece of this eggy bread your mama's made up."

Clayton came down, dressed for the day in one of his habitual white shirts tucked tidily into his khakis. He walked to Shelby, gave her a knuckle rap on the head, then kissed it.

"Looks like a weekend breakfast in the middle of the week." He got out a mug. "Sucking up?" he asked Shelby.

"I am."

"Good job."

SHE DID HER BARTER DAY with Tracey and took the girls to the park so Emma Kate could come by, have a little picnic with them on her lunch hour and finally meet Callie.

"When I was a little girl, Emma Kate was my very best friend, like you and Chelsea."

"Did you have tea parties?" Callie asked Emma Kate.

"We did, and picnics just like this."

"You can come to Gamma's house for a tea party."

"I would absolutely love to."

"Gamma saved Mama's tea set so we can use it."

"Oh, the one with the violets and little pink roses?"

"Uh-huh." Callie's eyes rounded owlishly. "We have to be careful not to break it 'cause it's deliquit."

"Delicate," Shelby corrected.

"Okay. We're going to swing now. Let's go swing, Chelsea!"

"She's beautiful, Shelby. Beautiful and bright."

"She's all of that. She's my very best thing. Emma Kate, do you have some time after work? There's some things I still need to tell you. Just you."

"All right." Since she'd been expecting this—or hoping for it—Emma Kate already had a plan. "We could take a hike up to the Outlook like we used to. I'm off at four today, so I could meet you at the trailhead at maybe four-fifteen."

"That'd be perfect."

Emma Kate watched Callie run around the swings with Chelsea. "If I had somebody like that depending on me, there's a lot I'd do I wouldn't do otherwise."

"And a lot you don't do you would do otherwise."

"Mama! Mama! Push us. Push us, Mama! I want to go high!"

"Takes after you," Emma Kate commented. "You could never swing high enough."

With a laugh, Shelby stood up. "I'm sticking closer to ground level these days."

As she got up to help push the girls on the swing, Emma Kate thought that was a real shame.

SHE MANAGED TO SQUEEZE OUT some time to start a playlist, to pump a fist in the air when the consignment shop reported the sale of two cock-tail dresses, an evening gown and a handbag. She adjusted her spread-sheet, calculated that she might be able to pay off another credit card with one more good sale.

She organized herself for the next day, her first day working at the salon, then pulled out her old hiking boots—ones she'd kept tucked away in her closet so Richard couldn't insist she toss them out.

She dropped Callie off at Clay's for a visit with Jackson as arranged and watched her daughter happily exploring her cousin's little backyard fort before driving to the trailhead.

More she'd missed, she thought as she parked and got out. The quiet that let you hear birds calling and the breeze singing through the trees. The sharp smell of pine on air fresh and just cool enough. She hooked on her light pack—something else she'd tucked away from Richard.

She'd been taught from childhood to always carry water and some basics even on a short, easy hike. Cell service could be spotty—at least it had been the last time she'd taken this trail—but she'd tucked her phone in her pocket like always.

She didn't want to be more than a call or text away from her daughter.

She'd bring Callie here, she thought, take her along the trail, point out the wildflowers, the trees, maybe spot a deer or a scurrying rabbit.

Teach her how to identify bear scat, she thought, smiling as she calculated Callie was just the right age to find that idea thrillingly disgusting.

She looked up at the clouds that skimmed over the tops of the higher hills. She might take her daughter on an overnight. Pitch a tent, show her the pleasure of sleeping out under the stars on a good, clear night, and telling stories around a campfire.

This was the true legacy, wasn't it? The years traveling from place to place, the time in Atlanta, in Philadelphia, that was some other world altogether. If Callie chose one of those worlds, or another entirely, she'd have these roots to return to whenever she wanted.

She'd always have family in the Ridge, and a place to come home to.

Shelby turned when she heard the car, looked back, looked out to take in the view of the town rising and falling with the hills. And despite knowing she'd have to go through yet another painful confession, smiled when Emma Kate parked beside her.

"I almost forgot how beautiful it is here, just right here, with the town on one side, the trail on the other, so you can choose what you want and just go."

"Matt and I hiked up to Sweetwater Cave the first time he came back with me. I wanted to see what he was made of."

"That one's a quad killer. How'd he do?"

"I'm still keeping him around, aren't I? You've still got those hiking boots?"

"Broke in just right."

"So you always said. Finally traded mine in last year. I try to get in a hike once or twice a week. Matt, he joined the gym over in Gatlinburg as he's one for weights and machines. He's making noises about finding a place to build one in the Ridge so he doesn't have to drive all that way. Me, I'd rather just take the trail, and maybe fit in one of the yoga classes your granny's got going on Saturdays at the day spa."

"She didn't say anything about that."

"She's got a lot going. We'd better get going, too, if we're going to hike up to the Outlook."

"Our favorite spot to talk about boys and parents and what annoyed us."

"Is that what we're doing now?" Emma Kate asked as they began to walk.

"In a way, I guess. I've come clean, you could say, with my family. You always were my family, too, so I'm going to come clean with you."

"Are you running from the law?"

With a laugh, and because it felt right, Shelby took Emma Kate's hand, gave their arms a swing. "Not the law, but it feels like I've been running from everything else. I've stopped now."

"Glad to hear it."

"I've told you some. Now I'm going to tell you the rest. It started after Richard died. It all started before, but you could say it all fell on top of me after."

She filled in pieces she'd left out, backtracking when Emma Kate blurted out questions. The climb steepened, winding up, making her legs ache in a good way. She caught sight of the rich feathers of a bluebird winging through some wild dogwood with its buds just peeking open, waiting, just waiting, to burst out full white.

The air cooled as they climbed, and still she felt the good, light sweat of the physical challenge on her skin.

It was easier, she realized, to say it all here, out in the open, where the hills carried her words away.

"First, I'm still not used to having somebody I know millions of dollars in debt—and it's not your debt, damn it, Shelby."

"I signed the loan papers on the house, at least I guess I did."

"Guess?"

"I don't remember signing any loan, but he'd push papers in front of me now and then, 'Sign this, it's nothing.' I think half the time he just signed my name himself. I could maybe have gotten out of it if I'd gone through the court process or just tossed it all in and declared bankruptcy. I wasn't going to do that. When the house sells, and it will, that'll take the big weight off. And until it does, I'm chipping away."

"Selling clothes?"

"I've made nearly fifteen thousand on clothes so far—not counting the fur coat I took back with the tags still on it—and I might make that much again before it's done. He had a hell of a lot of suits, and I had things I never even wore. It was a different world, Emma Kate."

"But your engagement ring was a fake."

"I guess he didn't see the point in putting a real diamond on my finger. He never loved me, I see that now. I was useful to him. I'm not altogether sure how, but I must've been useful."

"Finding that safe-deposit box. That hardly seems possible."

Looking back, she could see she'd been tilting at windmills. But . . . "I was on a mission. You know how it is."

"I know how you are when you're on a mission." As the sun changed angles, Emma Kate adjusted the bill of her cap. "All that cash in there, and that doesn't even get to the other identification."

"He couldn't have come by it legal. I've had some moments over that, but I didn't steal it, or swindle it, and I've got Callie to consider. If it comes down to having to pay that back sometime, I'll deal with it. For now, I've got some tucked away in the bank, and when I can see my way clear, I'm going to use it to get us a little house."

"What about this private detective?"

"He's wasting his time with me. I have to figure he'll come to that on his own, or Forrest persuaded him."

"Forrest can be persuasive."

"He's still mad at me, at least a little. Are you still?"

"It's hard to be when I'm more fascinated."

They walked in silence, along the familiar trail.

"Was the furniture really that ugly?"

Amused her friend would zoom in on that, Shelby laughed. "Uglier. I wish I'd taken pictures. It was hard and slick, and dark and angular. I always felt like I was visiting in that house, and couldn't wait to get out of it. He never made the first payment, Emma Kate. By the time he died, the bank had already sent out notices I hadn't seen."

She paused to open her water bottle. "I'm thinking now he was in trouble. Something in Atlanta, maybe. So he wrangled that big house up North without telling me that, either. Set it all up, then told me we were moving, he had some business opportunities. I went along. I guess that's one way I was useful. I went along. Looking back, it's hard to imagine how many times I did.

"I don't even know who he was. I can't say for sure I even knew his name. I don't know now what he did, how he made the money he had. I just know none of it was real—not my marriage, not the life we lived."

She stopped at the Outlook, felt her heart lift.

"This is what's real."

She could see for miles, the roll and rise of that deep, secret green, the dips of the valleys cupped between the rises—delicate as her old tea set. And the carpeted peaks swimming into the clouds so full of mystery and silence.

The light had gone soft as the afternoon wound down. She thought of how it looked at sunset, all brushed with gold, little tips of fire red as the mountains went to gray.

"I know, too, I took this for granted. All of it. I never will again."

They sat on an outcropping of rock, as they had countless times over the years. Emma Kate pulled a bag of sunflower seeds out of her pack.

"It used to be gummy bears," Shelby commented.

"I used to be twelve. I could go for some gummy bears," she decided.

Smiling, Shelby opened her own pack, pulled out a bag. "I let Callie have them now and again. Whenever I'd open a bag of them, I'd think of you."

"Something about gummies." Emma Kate opened the bag, dived in. "You know, your family would help you with some of the debt—and I wouldn't do that, either," she said before Shelby could speak.

"Thanks. It helps you understand the why of that. I'm going to make a good life here. I know I can. Maybe I had to leave so I could come back, see what was real for me, and what wasn't."

"And you'll sing for your supper after all."

"That's the icing. I really like Tansy's Derrick."

"He's a winner. And what a face."

"He sure is pretty. But—"

"What a body," they said together, and laughed until they lost their breath.

"Now we're sitting here." Shelby let out a sigh, looked out over the spread of green. "Just like we used to and still talking about boys."

"A puzzle that can never be truly solved."

"So worth talking about. And both of us are doing—or for me about to do—what we used to wish for. Emma Kate Addison, RN. Do you love it?"

"I do. I really do. Hell, I never worked so hard in my life as I did to get that RN. I figured I'd work in a big hospital. And I did. I liked it, I liked it a lot."

She looked back at Shelby. "The thing I didn't know is I'd like working at the clinic even more, and I do. So maybe I had to go off awhile to see that."

"Is Matt your icing?"

"He's definitely icing." Emma Kate grinned as she popped another gummy bear in her mouth. "And at least one layer of cake."

"You going to marry him?"

"I don't plan on marrying anybody else. Not in a rush about it, even if

Mama wishes I would be. Things are really good as they are for now. I heard they're going to do that big master bath for your mama."

"She's got sample books and magazine pictures. Daddy pretends he thinks it's crazy, but he's getting a kick out of it."

Shelby took a sip of water, then took her time carefully screwing the cap back in place. "Griffin was over measuring the other day."

"They're looking forward to the demo. They're both like little boys about the demo stage."

"Hmm." Wondering if she should bring it up—and out—Shelby looked out, caught a glint of a curving stream in a splash of sunlight. Talking about boys here, she thought, was tradition, after all.

"The thing is, while he was over at Mama's, Griffin pretty much came straight out and said he was interested. In me."

On a snort, Emma Kate popped another gummy bear. "I saw that one coming."

"Because he makes moves on women a lot?"

"He makes moves like any normal guy, but no. Because he looked like he'd been struck by lightning when you walked into my mother's kitchen that first day."

"He did? I didn't notice that. Shouldn't I have noticed that?"

"You were too busy feeling guilty and awkward. What did you say to him?"

"I just fumbled around some. I can't really be thinking about things like that."

"But you are thinking about things like that."

"I shouldn't be. Richard just died. And that's not even official."

"Richard—or whatever the hell his name was—is gone." As even the thought of him pissed her off, Emma Kate mimed balling something up, flicked it out toward the drop. "You're here. Your marriage was unhappy, and basically a sham—you said so yourself. There's no required mourning period here, Shelby."

"I'm not mourning at all. It doesn't seem right."

"Aren't you tired of doing what you tell yourself seems right? You've done that for about four years now, and it looks like it landed you in a mess."

"I don't even know him. Griffin, I mean."

"I know who you meant, and that's why they invented this thing we call dating. You go out somewhere, have conversations, discover what interests you might share and if you're attracted to each other. What about sex?"

"Richard didn't seem interested the last few months before— Oh, you meant with Griffin. God, Emma Kate." Laughing, Shelby reached for gummy bears. "We haven't even gone on that invention called dating. I can't just have sex with him."

"I don't know why not. You're both free, healthy and of age."

"And look what jumping into sex with someone I barely knew got me last time."

"I can promise you, Griff's no Whatever-His-Name-Was."

"I don't think I know how to date anymore."

"You'll ease into it. The four of us can go out and do something."

"Maybe. Griff wants to take us out for pizza, and I made the mistake of saying something about it to Callie. She's asked me about it twice since."

"There you go." Problem solved to Emma Kate's mind, she slapped Shelby on the leg. "You let him take the two of you for pizza, the four of us will have dinner or something. Then you can try a solo."

"My life's a pure hot mess yet, Emma Kate. I shouldn't be dating anyone."

"Honey, when you're single, going out with a good-looking guy *is* living. Go have pizza," she advised, "and see where it goes from there."

"You're going to get sick of hearing it, but I missed you so much. I missed this right here. Sitting in this spot, talking to you about anything and everything, and eating gummy bears."

"It's the good life."

"It's the best." And caught up in it, she grabbed Emma Kate's hand. "Let's make a vow. When we're eighty or so, if we can't make the hike, we'll get a couple of young studs to cart us up here so we can sit, talk about anything and everything and eat gummy bears."

"Now, that's the Shelby Pomeroy I remember." Emma Kate swiped a finger over her heart. "That's a vow. But they have to be hot young studs."

"I thought that was understood."

SHE MOVED INTO A ROUTINE, a contented one, working on her song list, practicing, weaving herself back into the fabric of the Ridge with her work at the salon.

She found it strange and wonderful how quickly it all came back, the voices, the rhythm, the easy gossip, the sights of the town and the mountains coming to life with spring.

As promised, demolition began, so mornings before she left for work or errands, the house was filled with men's voices, hammering, drilling.

She got used to seeing Griff and Matt—and maybe she was thinking about it, a little. Off and on. It was hard not to think about a man when he showed up at your house every day with a tool belt slung around his hips, and that look in his eyes.

"Sounded good this morning."

She stopped on her way to get her Callie bag when Griff stepped out into the hallway from her old bedroom.

"Sorry, what?"

"You. You sounded good. Singing in the shower."

"Oh. It's a handy rehearsal hall."

"You've got pipes, Red. What was the song?"

"I . . ." She had to think back. "'Stormy Weather.' It's the forties."

"Sexy in any decade. Hey, Little Red."

He crouched down when Callie bolted up the stairs. "Mama's going to work at Granny's. I'm going to Chelsea's 'cause Gamma works to day, too."

"Sounds like fun all around."

"Can we have pizza?"

"Callie—"

"Deal's a deal," Griff interrupted. "I could go for some pizza tonight. Tonight work for you?" he asked Shelby.

"Well, I . . ."

"Mama, I want pizza with Grrr—iff." To seal it, Callie climbed into his arms, then turned her head toward her mother, smiled.

"Who could say no to all that? That would be nice, thanks."

"Six work for you?"

"Sure."

"I'll pick you up."

"Oh, well, car seat. It's easier if we meet you there."

"Right. Six o'clock. Have we got a date?" he asked Callie.

"We gotta date," she said, and kissed him. "Let's go, Mama. Let's go to Chelsea's."

"Right behind you. Thank you, really," Shelby said when Callie started down again. "You made her day."

"It's making mine. See you later."

When he walked back into the work space, Matt raised his eyebrows. "Moving in on the local talent?"

"One step at a time."

"She's a looker. Got herself a very complicated life, bro."

"Yeah. Good thing I've got tools." He picked up the nail gun. "And know how to use them."

He thought about her throughout the day. He couldn't think of a woman who'd intrigued him more—the contrast of the sad, cautious eyes and the quick smile when she forgot to be careful. The seamless way she handled the kid. The way she looked in snug jeans.

It all worked for him.

He almost thought it was too bad the job was moving along so smoothly. A few glitches and he'd have more time to see her for a few minutes every day.

But Ada Mae was no Bitsy. When she decided on a tile, on a color, on a fixture, she stuck.

He had time to go home, clean up, change. A man didn't take two pretty females out for pizza smelling of job sweat and sawdust. It would be an early evening, he calculated, with a three-year-old along. Which was probably for the best. He could put in a couple of hours on his own job.

In fact, he thought he might move his focus to the bedroom. A man didn't bring a pretty female home to bed when that bed was an air mattress on the floor.

He fully intended to bring Shelby home to bed. When she and the room were ready for it.

He drove into town, snagged a parking spot on the street just a few doors down from Pizzateria. And deemed his timing perfect when Shelby got out of her minivan two spots up.

He strolled up as she lifted Callie out of the car seat.

"Give you a hand?"

"Oh, I've got it. Thank you."

"Hey." He heard the tears in her voice even before she turned with Callie in her arms and he saw them welling in her eyes. "What's wrong? What happened?"

"Oh, it's just—"

"Mama's happy. She has happy tears," Callie explained.

"You're happy?"

"Yes. Very."

"The combination of me and pizza doesn't usually bring women to tears."

"It's not that. I was just on the phone. We were a little early as Callie was so anxious. And the realtor called. The house up North, it's sold." One of the tears spilled down her cheek before she could brush it away.

"Happy tears," Callie announced. "Hug Mama, Griff."

"Sure."

Before she could evade, he had both Shelby and Callie wrapped in a hug.

He felt her hold stiff for a moment, then just melt.

"It's just such a relief. It's like a mountain fell off my shoulders."

"Good." He pressed a kiss to the top of her head. "We're definitely celebrating. Right, Callie? Happy pizza."

"We don't like the house. We're glad it's not ours now."

"That's right. That's right." Shelby took a breath, leaned in just one more moment, then straightened. "We don't like the house, not for us. Now somebody who does like it has it. Very happy pizza. Thank you, Griffin."

"You need a minute?"

"No. No, I'm good."

"Then give me the girl." He hefted Callie into his arms. "And let's get this party started."

12

❧

The kid was a charmer, entertained and engaged him—and flattered him by insisting on sitting next to him in the booth.

He might have had a moment or two wishing the mother would flirt as overtly as the daughter, but a man couldn't have everything.

It was a nice break to his day, between the job and the project.

When the manager came out, pulled Shelby from her seat for a hug, he examined his reaction.

Not jealousy, not exactly, but a kind of inner "Careful there, buddy" as he waited to see just what was what.

"I kept missing you." Johnny Foster, a man with a sly smile and an easy manner, kept his hands on Shelby's shoulders to take a long look. "But here you are now. Didn't realize you knew Griff." Johnny slung an arm over Shelby's shoulders as he turned to Griff. "Shelby and I go back."

"My cousin Johnny, here, and my brother Clay used to look for trouble together."

"And found it as often as possible."

"You're cousins?"

"Third, fourth, what is it?" Johnny wondered.

"Third, I think, once or twice removed."

"Kissing cousins," he said, and gave her one, lightly. "And you're Callie, and aren't you as pretty as a strawberry float. It's nice meeting you, cousin."

"I'm on a date with Griff. We're going to have pizza."

"This is the place for it. We're going to find some time and catch up," he said to Shelby. "All right?"

"All right. Clay said you were manager here now."

"Yeah. Who'd have thought? Y'all get your order in?"

"Just a minute ago."

"You watch over there, Callie." He pointed to the counter where a man in a white apron ladled sauce on dough. "I'll be making your pizza myself, special. And I've got some tricks. Meant to tell you, Griff, whatever y'all did with the furnace worked like a charm. Hasn't given us any trouble since."

"Good to hear."

"Pizza coming up."

Shelby slid back into the booth. "It sounds like you and Matt are fixing something somewhere all over the Ridge."

"That's the plan. The guy who can fix your furnace when the temperatures dive, or your toilet on a Sunday morning when you've got people coming to dinner? He's a popular guy."

She laughed. "And who doesn't like being popular? Busy, too. How do you manage to make yourself popular and do all the work on the old Tripplehorn place?"

"Being popular's the job. The house is the project. I do better with the job when I've got a good project going."

"Mama, look!" Callie bounced in her seat. "The cousin man's doing tricks."

"And he's learned some new ones," Shelby commented as Johnny tossed up dough, did a quick spin, caught it.

"Looks like we're having magic pizza."

Wide-eyed, Callie turned to Griff. "Magic pizza?"

"Pretty sure. Don't you see that magic dust flying?"

With eyes like blue saucers now, she looked back at Johnny, gasped. "It sparkles!"

The power of a kid's imagination, Griff thought. "You bet. When you eat magic pizza, it turns you into a fairy princess in your dreams."

"It does?"

"That's what I've heard. Of course, you've got to eat it, then when your mother says it's bedtime, you've got to go right to bed, and wish for it."

"I will. But you can't be a fairy princess 'cause you're a boy. That's silly."

"That's why I'm the prince who slays the fangbeast."

"Princes slay dragons!"

"I don't get that." Playing it up, he let out a sad sigh, shook his head— caught Shelby smiling at him from across the table. "I like dragons. You might be able to squeeze in another wish and get yourself your own dragon. You could fly on him over your kingdom."

"I like dragons, too. I'm going to fly on mine. Her name's Lulu."

"Can't think of a better name for a dragon."

"You've got a way," Shelby murmured, and Griff grinned over at her.

"Oh, I've got lots of ways."

"I just bet you do."

He decided it was the best hour of his day, sitting in the noisy pizzeria, entertaining a little girl and making her mother laugh. He didn't see why it wasn't something he couldn't work into his regular schedule.

Everybody could use some magic pizza now and then.

"This was so nice," Shelby said when he walked them back to her car. "You sure made Callie's first date one to remember."

"We'll have to have a second. Are you going to go out with me again, Callie?"

"Okay. I like ice cream."

"That's a real coincidence—I'm starting to think we're made for each other. I like ice cream, too."

She gave him what he could only term a femme fatale smile from under her lashes. "You can take me on a date with ice cream."

"Now look what you started." Amused, Shelby hauled Callie up into the car seat.

"How about Saturday?"

Busy strapping Callie in, Shelby glanced back. "What?"

"How about an ice cream date on Saturday?"

"Okay!" Callie bounced in her seat.

"I have to work," Shelby began.

"Me, too. After work."

"Well, I . . . I guess. Are you sure?"

"I wouldn't have asked if I wasn't. Don't forget to make your wish, Callie."

"I'm going to be a fairy princess and ride my dragon."

"Callie, what do you say to Griffin?"

"Thank you for the date." In joyful innocence, she held out her arms. "Kiss."

"You got it."

He leaned in, kissed her. Laughing, she rubbed his cheek.

"I like your scratchies. They tickle. Kiss Mama now."

"Sure."

He figured she'd offer a cheek, and didn't see why he had to settle. A man could move fast without seeming to, especially when he'd thought it through.

He set his hands on her hips, glided them up her back with his eyes on hers. He watched hers widen in surprise—but not protest. So he went with it.

He dipped down, took her mouth with his as if they had all the time in the world. As if they weren't standing on the sidewalk of High Street, seen by anyone who passed by or glanced out a window.

It wasn't hard to forget where they were when her body melted against his, with her lips, warm and soft, yielding.

Her mind just emptied, every thought—past, present, future—
flooding away as sensation flooded in and swamped her. Her body went
limp even as it leaped to life. Her head spun in long, lazy circles as if she'd
had just a sip too much of good wine.

She smelled soap and skin and the hyacinths in the whiskey barrel
across the sidewalk. And heard what she realized later was the hum of
pleasure in her own throat.

He let her go as smoothly as he'd taken her. His eyes stayed on hers
again, watchful.

"I thought so," he murmured.

"I . . . just . . ." She realized she couldn't quite feel her feet, had to fight
the urge to look down to make sure they were still there. "Have to go."

"See you later."

"I . . . Fingers on noses, Callie."

Callie put her fingers on her nose. "Bye, Griff. Bye!"

He waved as Shelby closed the door, hooked his thumbs in his pockets
when she walked around to the driver's side. And couldn't stop the grin
when she staggered, just a little.

He waved again when, after some fumbling, she started the engine,
pulled away.

Yeah, definitely the best hour of his day. He couldn't wait to do it
again.

SHE DROVE HOME with extra care. She really did feel as if she'd had a
bottle of wine instead of a glass of Coke with her pizza. And that hum
kept wanting to come back to her throat, a kind of echo to the butterflies
dancing around in her belly.

Callie started nodding off on the short drive home, the excitement of
the day taking its toll. But she perked up again, a little on the hyper side,
when Shelby parked.

She'd let her daughter run down again, she thought. It wouldn't take

long. And she had to be coherent, put all this business aside. She didn't
have time for flutterings or hummings.

Shelby didn't have to do much more than listen as Callie frantically
relayed the details of her date to her grandparents.

"And we're gonna have an ice cream date on Saturday."

"Is that so? Well, this sounds pretty serious." Ada Mae shot Shelby
a speculative look. "Maybe your granddaddy should ask this boy his
intentions."

"And his prospects," Clayton added.

"I'm their chaperone," Shelby said cheerfully. "Oh, I saw Johnny Foster. Didn't have much time to talk to him as they were busy. He's the one
who tossed the dough. He made the magic pizza, right, Callie?"

"Uh-huh, and Griff said I can ride a dragon, and he's going to kill
the . . . what is it, Mama?"

"I think it was a fangbeast."

"He's gonna kill it dead, and then we'll get married."

"That must've been some pizza," Clayton commented.

"You can be the king, Granddaddy, and Gamma's the queen." She ran
in circles around the room, twirling, jumping. "And Clancy can come,
too." She threw her arms around the old dog. "And I'm going to wear a
beautiful dress, then it says kiss the bride. It tickles when Griff kisses,
doesn't it, Mama?"

"I—"

"Does it?" Now Ada Mae wore a smug smile.

"Uh-huh. When is it Saturday, Mama?"

"Soon enough." Shelby caught Callie on the fly, gave her a spin. "Now
we're going up. You need your bath before you go dreaming and getting
married to handsome princes."

"Okay."

"Go on up, put your clothes in your hamper. I'll be two seconds. She
had the best time," Shelby said when Callie ran for the stairs.

"How about you?"

"It was nice. He's so sweet with her. But what I wanted to tell you both is right before dinner, I got a call. The house sold."

"The house?" Ada Mae looked blank for a moment, then plopped down in a chair as her eyes filled. "Oh, Shelby, the house up North. I'm so glad. I'm so glad of that."

"Happy tears." Shelby pulled out one of the tissues always in her pocket. "I did the same. It's such a burden lifted." She turned into her father when he stepped over, folded her into his arms, rocked her side to side. "I thought I knew how much it weighed, since I've been carrying it. But now that it's lifted, it was heavier than I thought."

"We can help you with the rest of it. Your mama and I talked it over, and—"

"No, Daddy. No. Thank you so much. I love you." She laid her hands on his cheeks. "I'm doing it. It's going to take a while, but I'm doing it, and doing it feels good. It balances out, some, all the times I just let things go, stopped asking questions, let somebody else take care of everything."

She leaned against him, smiled at her mother. "And the worst of it's behind me now. I can deal with what's ahead. I'm so grateful to know if it gets too heavy again, I can ask."

"Don't ever forget that again."

"I swear it. I've got to get my baby in the tub. I had a good day," she said as she pulled back, hauled up her bag. "I had a real good day."

Once she'd tucked Callie in, she sat down with her spreadsheet. She should probably wait until settlement, but she thought she had every right to be optimistic. When she balanced the sheet with the sale, she shut her eyes, just breathed.

It was still a painful debt, but oh God, she'd cut it down to size.

The worst, she thought again, was over. And what was ahead?

She lay back on the bed, called Emma Kate.

"How was pizza?"

"It was magic, or so Griff convinced Callie, so she went to bed with a big smile and the anticipation of being a fairy princess riding a dragon. Before she and Griff get married with all due pomp and ceremony."

"He's got a way with kids. I think he's got a lot of little boy left in there."

"He kissed me."

"Was that magic, too?" Emma Kate asked without missing a beat.

"My brain's still soft. Don't tell Matt my brain went soft. He'll tell Griffin, and I'll feel like an idiot. I don't know if it's because it's been so long since I've had a serious kiss, or if he's just that damn good at it."

"I've heard he's damn good at it."

Shelby smiled, curled up. "Did your brain go soft the first time Matt kissed you?"

"It liquefied and leaked out of my ears. Which sounds disgusting, but was anything but."

"I feel so good, so good I'd forgotten how it feels to feel so good. I just had to call you. I sold the house, and got kissed brainless on High Street."

"You— Oh, Shelby, that's great! On both counts, but shedding that house. I'm so happy for you."

"I'm starting to see my way clear, Emma Kate. I'm really starting to see a clear path. Some more bumps to get over, but I see the clear."

And part of the clear was being curled up on her bed talking to her best friend.

THE GOOD DAY ROLLED into a good week. She could savor the sensation of being happy and productive, of earning her way.

She mopped floors, filled dispensers, booked appointments, rang up sales, listened to gossip. She commiserated when Crystal complained about her boyfriend, comforted Vonnie when the masseuse's grandmother passed peacefully in her sleep.

She set up chairs and tables in the little back garden area of the day spa, potted up some flowers.

After checking out the preschool where Chelsea would go come fall, she enrolled Callie. And felt the pride and the pang of what she knew would be the first of many layers of separation.

She had ice cream with Griff and discovered the second kiss could be as powerful as the first. But she hedged when he asked her out to dinner.

"It's just my time's so budgeted right now. I've got a routine going at the salon, so I'm easier there. But until I sing Friday night, see how that goes, I'm using up my free time rehearsing and planning for the next week."

"After Friday." He laid out the elements that would heat the tile floor of the new bathroom. "Because it's going to go great."

"I hope so. Maybe you could come by Bootlegger's on Friday for a set."

He sat back on his haunches. "Red, I wouldn't miss it. I like listening to you rehearse in the shower."

"I'm heading out right now to rehearse in place before the bar and grill opens. I hope Tansy's right about people wanting to hear somebody sing old songs while they're eating their pork chops or scooping up nachos."

She pressed a hand on her belly. "We're going to find out."

"Nervous?"

"About the singing? No. I don't get nervous about singing, it feels too good. About the draw not justifying what they pay me. I'm nervous about that. I've got to get on. It's looking good in here."

"It's coming along." He smiled at her. "Let's make the word of the day 'gradation.' One step at a time."

"Mmm," she said, understanding he wasn't just talking about a new bathroom.

SHE SQUEEZED IN A LAST REHEARSAL Friday morning, and ordered herself not to think about what she could do with the songs if she had a couple of live musicians.

Still, she thought she put a little of her own spin on the old classic "As Time Goes By."

"Play it, Sam," Derrick said from behind the bar.

"Of all the gin joints in all the world."

"Are you an old-movie fan?"

"My daddy is, so we had to be. And who doesn't love *Casablanca*? How'd that sound to you, Derrick?"

"It sounded like Tansy had it right. We're going to rack them, stack them and pack them on Friday Nights." Restacking glasses freshly cleaned from the night before, he cocked an eyebrow at her. "How do you feel about it?"

"Hopeful." She stepped down off the tiny stage. "I just want to say, if it doesn't pull in a big draw, if it just doesn't work, it's not a problem."

"Are you setting up to fail, Shelby?"

She cocked her head, walked toward the bar. "Forget what I just said. We're going to kick ass so high here tonight, butts'll be landing on the moon, and you're going to be obliged to give me a raise."

"Don't get carried away. Want a Coke?"

"Wish I had time for one, but I have to head over to the salon." To be sure she wasn't already late, she tipped her phone out of her pocket to check the time.

"Tonight should bring people in, just to see," she said. "There's me, the girl who wasn't there for a while, and all the hyping Tansy's done. Flyers everywhere, and I'm plastered all over your Facebook page. Hell, my family's big enough to be a crowd, and a lot of them will be here. That's something."

"Kick ass high."

"Kick ass high," she agreed. "I'll see you tonight."

She walked out, distracted, still rehearsing in her head. She barely noticed the woman who fell into step beside her until she spoke.

"Shelby Foxworth?"

"Sorry." She'd gotten used to "Pomeroy" again in such a short time she nearly said no. "Yes. Hello."

She stopped, smiled and searched her memory banks. But the stunning brunette with the cold brown eyes and the perfect red lips didn't ring any bells.

"I'm Shelby. I'm sorry, I don't recognize you. Who are you?"

"I'm Natalie Sinclair. I'm Jake Brimley's wife. You knew him as Richard Foxworth."

The half-smile stayed on Shelby's face as the words sounded like a foreign language to her ears. "What? What did you say?"

Something feline moved into the woman's eyes. "We really need to talk, somewhere more private. I saw a cute little park not far. Why don't we go there?"

"I don't understand. I don't know any Jake Brimley."

"Changing a name doesn't change who you are." Natalie reached into a pale blue handbag, drew out a photograph. "Look familiar?"

In the picture the brunette was cheek to cheek with Richard. His hair was longer than he'd worn it, a bit lighter. Something was different about his nose, Shelby thought.

But it was Richard smiling out at her.

"You—I'm sorry—are you saying you were married to Richard?"

"No. Wasn't I clear? Let me say it again, in case you have trouble understanding. I was, and am, married to Jake Brimley. Richard Foxworth never existed."

"But I—"

"It's taken me quite a while to track you down, Shelby. Let's have a chat."

Brimley was not one of the names she'd found in the bank box. My God, had he had another? Another name. Another wife.

"I need to make a call. I'm going to be late for work."

"Go right ahead. It's a quaint little town, isn't it? If you go for gun racks and camo."

And didn't she sound just like Richard? "There's also art." Shelby bit off the words. "Music, tradition, history."

"No call to get testy about it."

"People who consider us hicks are generally self-important snobs from somewhere else."

"Ouch." Looking amused, Natalie gave a quick shudder. "Struck a nerve."

Rather than try to explain what was going on in a call, Shelby texted her grandmother, apologized, let her know she'd be a little late.

"Some people like quaint. I'm a city girl." Natalie gestured toward the crosswalk, began to walk in gorgeous heeled sandals of pale gold. "So was Jake. But you didn't meet Jake here."

"I met Richard in Memphis." Everything seemed just a little blurry. "I was singing with a band during my summer break from college."

"And he just swept you away. He was good at that. Exciting, charming, sexy. I'll bet he took you to Paris, a little café on the Left Bank. You'd stay at the George Cinq. He bought you white roses."

A raw, ugly sickness roiled in her stomach—and must have shown on her face.

"Men like Jake have patterns." Natalie patted Shelby's arm.

"I don't understand. How can you be married to him? I mean, he's dead, but how could you have been married to him? We were together for over four years. We had a child together."

"Yes, that was a surprise. But I can see how the family unit could work for him. I had the poor judgment to marry him—whirlwind to Vegas. Sound familiar? And I had the good sense not to divorce him when he left me in the lurch."

It dropped on her, a single crushing weight. "I was never married to him. That's what this means. That's what you're saying."

"Since he was still legally married to me, no, you weren't ever married to him."

"And he knew."

"Of course he knew." Now she laughed. "What a bad boy! Of course, that's part of the appeal. Such a bad, bad boy, my Jake."

The park held quiet. No kids on the swings or teeter-totter, none running over the green, climbing on the jungle gym.

Natalie sat on a bench, crossed her legs, patted the space beside her.

"I wasn't sure if you realized that part and played along. It seems he duped you. But then, that's what he does." For an instant something that might have been sorrow flickered over Natalie's face. "Or did."

"I can't think." Shelby lowered to the bench. "Why would he do this? How could he do this? Oh my God, are there any more? Did he do this to another woman?"

"I couldn't say." Natalie gave an easy shrug. "But since he swung pretty quick from me to you, I don't think there's another wife in between. And that's the time I'm interested in."

"I don't understand." Suddenly breathless, Shelby sat back, pushed both hands through her hair, held it back a moment. "I can't understand any of this. I was never married," she said slowly. "It was all fake, just like the ring."

"You lived pretty well for a while, didn't you?" Natalie angled to her, aimed a look of contempt. "Paris, Prague, London, Aruba, Saint Bart's, Rome."

"How do you know all that? How do you know where I went with him?"

"I made it my business to know. You had a luxury condo in Atlanta, country clubs and Valentino dresses. Then the mansion in Villanova. You can't claim he didn't give you plenty. Seems to me you had a good deal."

"A good deal? A good *deal*?" Not breathless now, not when insult and fury rolled through. "He lied to me, right from the start. He made me his whore without my knowing. I thought I loved him. At first, I thought I loved him enough to leave my family and everything I knew and thought I'd wanted."

"Your mistake, but you were compensated. Plucked you out of this little hick town, didn't he? Oh, *excuse* me, this art-and-culture-ridden town. Dropped you right in the lap for a few years, so don't whine, Shelby. It's unattractive."

"What's the matter with you? You come here, tell me all this. Maybe you're the liar."

"Check it out, be my fucking guest. But you know I'm not lying. Jake had a way of making women fall for him, and do what he wanted."

"Did you love him?"

"I liked the hell out of him, and we had a damn good time. That was enough, would've been enough if he hadn't hung me out to dry. I made an investment in him, you could say. And I paid a high price. I want my payoff."

"What payoff?"

"Twenty-eight million."

"Twenty-eight million what? Dollars? Are you crazy? He didn't have anywhere near that kind of money."

"Oh, he had it. I know because I helped him get it. Just shy of thirty million in sparkly diamonds, emeralds, rubies, sapphires and rare stamps. Where is the take, Shelby? I'll settle for half."

"Do I look like I have diamonds and emeralds and all that? He left me in debt up to my eyeballs. That's the price I'm paying for believing him. What did you pay?"

"Four years, two months and twenty-three days in a cell in Dade County, Florida."

"You—you were in prison? For what?"

"For fraud, since I rolled like an acrobat on Jake and Mickey. That's Mickey O'Hara, the third member of our happy little band. Mickey's got twenty years to go, last I heard."

Smile sharp and derisive, she ticked her finger at Shelby. "You don't want Mickey O'Hara coming after you, Shelby. Take my word on that."

"You hired that private investigator to hound me."

"I can't say I did. I do my own investigating—it's one of my skills. Half, Shelby, and I'm gone. I earned every penny of it."

"I don't have half of *anything* to give you." Shelby lurched to her feet. "Are you saying Richard stole millions of dollars? That the detective from Florida was telling me the truth?"

"It's what we do, sweetheart. Or in his case, what he did. Find the mark. Rich, lonely widows worked best for Jake. He could turn them into putty in a matter of days. Easy to get them to 'invest' in a land deal—that was his specialty. But the big one, the biggest of our career, the one that went wrong, that was jewels and stamps, and she had some beauties. If you expect me to buy that you knew nothing about nothing, you're not selling it."

"I'm not selling a damn thing. If he had all that, why am I paying off his debts?"

"He always was a bit of a hoarder. And those jewels were hot. The stamps? You'd need to find just the right collector for them. When it went south, Jake could take off with them, but if he'd tried to sell them, even breaking the jewelry down to the stones, they'd have tracked him. Something like that, it's best to give it a few years, lay low."

"Lay low," Shelby murmured.

"That was the plan. Four or five years, we figured, before we could liquidate and retire. Or semi-retire, as who wants to give up all the fun? You were his cover, that's clear. But you're going to have to go a ways to convince me you're stupid enough to know nothing."

"I was stupid enough to believe him, and that's what I'm going to be living with."

"I'll give you some time to think about it. Even if you're the driven snow, Shelby, you lived with the man for more than four years. You think about it hard enough, you'll figure out something. Consider half of close to thirty million—maybe a little more now—motivation."

It was Shelby's turn for contempt. "I don't want half of anything you stole."

"Your choice. Turn your part in, take the finder's fee if you're delicate. It'd be fat enough to pay off some of the debt you're swimming in. Like I said, I get what's mine, I'm gone. If you want to stay in this little nowhere town, working in your grandmother's beauty parlor for peanuts, singing on Friday nights in a bar for rubes? Your choice. I get what's mine, you keep what's yours. You've got that pretty little girl to think about."

"You go near my daughter, you think about going near my daughter, I'll take you apart."

Natalie just looked over the side of her shoulder, lips curved. "Do you think you can?"

Shelby didn't think; she acted. She reached down, hauled Natalie to her feet by fisting a hand on the front of her blouse. "I can, and I will."

"That's what caught Jake's eye. He liked some fire, even in a mark. You can relax. I'm not interested in little girls or in going back in a cell. Fifty-fifty, Shelby. If I bring Mickey in on this, you'll get nothing but pain and heartache. He's not as civilized a negotiator as I am."

She shoved Shelby's hand off her blouse. "Think about it. I'll be in touch."

Because her legs wanted to shake, Shelby sat on the bench again when Natalie strolled away.

Twenty-eight million? Stolen jewelry and stamps? Bigamy? Who in God's name had she married? Or thought she married?

Maybe it was all a lie. But what would be the point?

But she'd check, check all of it.

She pushed to her feet, pulled out her phone as she walked to call Tracey and check on Callie.

By the time she got to the salon she was fired up again.

"I'm sorry, Granny."

"What kept you? And put the wrath of God in your eyes?"

Shelby shoved her purse under the front counter. "I need to talk to you and Mama, soon as you're both free. I'm sorry, Mrs. Hallister, how are you doing today?"

The woman in Viola's chair—that Hallister boy's grandmother—smiled. "I'm doing right well. I came in for a touch-up, and here Vi's talked me into highlights. Let's just see if Mr. Hallister notices."

"It's nice, brightening things up for spring. Granny, I've just got to make a quick call, then I'll check supplies."

"Towels should be ready to fold."

"I'll see to that."

Over the shop talk they exchanged a look. Viola nodded, and held up a hand behind the chair back. Five minutes.

Shelby went back into the laundry and supply room, and called her brother Forrest.

13

She couldn't think about it. Callie was safe, and Tracey would keep her that way. She didn't know one damn thing about any stolen jewelry, and wouldn't know a rare stamp if someone stuck it to her forehead. If this Natalie person thought she did, she'd just have to live with the disappointment.

But it upset her how easily she could believe Richard—or Jake, or whatever his name was—had been a thief, a liar.

But never her husband, she thought, as she folded and stacked towels. In a terrible way, now that the weight had settled in, she took comfort from that.

She'd do her work, smiling and chatting with customers, restocking supplies. Then she'd go home, have dinner with her little girl before heading to the bar and grill to give Tansy and Derrick their money's worth.

She wouldn't let anyone down again, including herself.

Forrest found her at the end of the day while she swept the little courtyard.

"Did you find her?" Shelby demanded.

"No. Nobody by that name or description in the hotel, the lodge, in any of the cabins, the B&Bs. She's not staying in the Ridge. And I've got nothing so far about a Natalie Sinclair doing time for fraud in Dade County."

"It's probably not her real name, either."

"Probably not, but a good-looking brunette's bound to stick in some-body's memory if she's staying in the Ridge, or poking around. We'll take a look further out if she comes back, if she bothers you again."

"I'm not worried about that."

"Then start. You tell Mama?"

"I told her, and Granny, and they'll tell the rest of the family. I'm not taking chances, Forrest, but I don't know anything about these jewels or stamps she says she's after."

"You may know more than you think. Don't get your claws out," he said as she whipped around to him. "Christ's sake, Shelby, I don't think you had anything to do with it. But along the way he might've said some-thing, done something, you overheard something that didn't click at the time. Now this is all planted in your head, maybe something will click. That's all."

Tired, she rubbed a spot between her eyebrows where a headache wanted to brew. "She put me on edge."

"Imagine that."

Shelby let out a short laugh. "Is it crazy for me to be glad somewhere down deep finding out I was never married to him?"

"I'd say it's about as sensible as it gets."

"Okay then, I'm going to be sensible. I'm finished up here, so I'm going home. Mama picked Callie up already from Chelsea's. I'm going to be with my girl awhile, make sure she has a good supper. Then I'm going to change and fix up so I look like somebody who should be singing on a Friday night."

"I'll follow you home. Safe's better than sorry every time," he said be-fore she could object.

"Okay, thanks."

Did she know something, something buried deep? Shelby wondered as she drove home with Forrest cruising behind her. It was true enough she could look back now, see little signs Richard was up to something. The phone calls that ended when she walked in or walked by, the locked doors and drawers. The dismissal of any question she had about what he did, where he went.

She'd thought affair, and more than once. But until now she'd never really considered thievery—not in a major sort of way, whatever that detective had claimed. And millions of dollars in jewelry?

That was about as major as it got.

And now that she knew? She shook her head as she pulled into the drive. She had nothing. Just nothing.

She gathered her things, waved to Forrest. And when the first thing she heard when she opened the front door was Callie's laughter, she let everything else go.

After hugs and kisses and an excited retelling of her day with Chelsea, Callie settled down with a coloring book while Shelby helped her mother in the kitchen.

"You've got pretty white tulips up in your room," Ada Mae said.

"Oh, Mama, my favorite! Thank you."

"Don't thank me. They came about an hour ago. From Griffin." Ada Mae slid her gaze and smile over. "I think you have a beau, Shelby Anne."

"No, I— That was awful nice of him. Sweet of him."

"He's got a sweetness, and not so sugary it makes your teeth ache. Such a nice young man."

"I'm not looking for a beau, Mama, or a young man."

"It's always seemed to me things are more exciting when you're not looking and you find them."

"Mama, I've not only got Callie to think about, and what's already in my lap, but what just fell into it this morning."

"Life's still got to be lived, baby girl. And a nice young man who thinks to send flowers adds a pretty touch."

IT DID. She couldn't deny it as she glanced over at the white tulips. Her favorite flower, she mused, so he'd obviously asked someone who knew her. She thought about it while she changed into a simple, classic-cut black dress.

Whether she looked for it or not, Griffin was giving her some romance, and it had been a very, very long time since anyone had.

And she bet he knew the flowers made her think of the way he'd kissed her—twice now. She couldn't blame him for that—and found she didn't blame herself for thinking she wouldn't mind being kissed again.

Soon.

She put on earrings. She'd thought to find something stage-flashy, but had opted for simple, like the dress, and pinned her hair back at the sides, let it fall in mad curls down her back.

"What do you think, Callie?" She did a model's turn for her daughter. "How do I look?"

"Bee-utiful Mama."

"Bee-utiful Callie."

"I wanna go with you. Please, please!"

"Oh, I wish you could." She crouched down, stroked Callie's hair as her daughter pouted. "But they don't let kids come."

"Why?"

"It's like the law."

"Uncle Forrest is a lawman."

Laughing, Shelby cuddled her girl. "A lawman."

"Uh-huh. He said. He can take me."

"Not tonight, baby, but I'll tell you what. I'll bring you with me to a rehearsal next week sometime. It'll be like a special show just for you."

"Can I wear my party dress?"

"I don't see why not. Tonight, Granny and Grandpa are coming to be with you, and won't you have fun?" And after the first set, her parents would come back, switch off.

It was good to know her family would be there.

"Let's go down now. I've got to get going."

The place was packed. She'd expected a crowd this first night as people were curious, or in the case of family and friends, supportive. Whatever brought them in, it felt good, damn good, to know she'd earned her keep this first time out.

She'd said hey and thanks for the good wishes countless times before she made it to the table, right in the front, where Griff sat.

"You look amazing."

"Thanks, that was the aim."

"Dead on."

"Thank you for the flowers, Griffin. They're just beautiful."

"Glad you liked them. Emma Kate and Matt are on their way, or nearly, and I had to fight off a dozen people to keep their chairs. That's close to literal with some giant Tansy called Big Bud."

"Big Bud? Is he here?" She did a quick scan, spotted him with his mighty bulk squeezed into a side booth chowing down on ribs while a skinny girl she didn't recognize sat across from him poking at whatever was on her plate and looking bored.

"We went to high school together. I heard he's a long-haul trucker these days, but . . ."

She trailed off as her gaze passed over Arlo Kattery, then backtracked to meet his eyes.

He hadn't changed much, she thought, and those pale eyes of his still had the power to give her the creeps when they stared.

He kicked back in a chair at a table shared with a couple of men she thought she recognized as the same two he'd always hung out with.

She hoped they wouldn't stay long, and take Arlo and his snake-stare around to Shady's, where they usually spent their beer money.

"What's the matter?" Griff asked.

"Oh, nothing, just somebody else from back some years. I expected some would come in tonight, curious to see if I rise or fall."

"Sensation," Griff said. "That's the word of the day, since you'll be one."

She turned back to him, forgetting Arlo. "Aren't you clever with your words?"

"The word of the day has to fit. This one does. I was supposed to let you know Tansy's got your parents, Clay and Gilly there." He gestured to a table at his right with a big RESERVED card on it. "Nobody argued with her on that one. Not even Big Bud."

"Oh, Big Bud always did idolize Clay. He's all right, Griff, just . . . insistent now and then. Daddy's just waiting on Mama to finish primping, so they'll be here soon. I'm really glad you're here now."

"Where else would I be?"

She hesitated, then sat. She had plenty of time. "Griffin, you're really not going to pay any mind to what I said about my life being a hot mess and all the rest?"

"It doesn't look like such a mess to me."

"You're not in it. And I found out more today, worse today. I can't talk about it right now, but it's twisted up something terrible."

He brushed a hand over the back of hers. "I'll help you straighten it out."

"Because that's what you do?"

"That, and because I've got a thing for you that just keeps getting bigger. And you've got one for me."

"You're sure of that?"

He only smiled. "I'm looking at you, Red."

"I've got no business having a thing for you," she muttered. Then as she had on Callie's laugh, she let it go. "But maybe I do." Her smile was pure temptation as she rose. "Just maybe I do." She trailed a fingertip down his arm, felt the low vibration. She'd forgotten how heady that small, simple power could be. "You enjoy the show now."

She went back into the kitchen, which was utter chaos, slipped into the broom closet of an office to take a breath.

Tansy rushed in. "Oh sweet God, Shelby, we're slammed. Derrick's pitching in behind the bar so we can keep up. How are you? Are you ready? I'm half sick with nerves." She pressed a hand to her belly. "And you look cucumber cool. You're not nervous?"

"Not about this. There's so much else I have to be nervous about, so this? It's like sliding into an old pair of slippers. I'll do good for you, Tansy."

"I know you will. I'm going out in just a few minutes, quiet them down and announce you."

She pulled a ragged strip of paper from her pocket. "My checklist. I do better with one. Okay. The machine's all set up just the way you wanted, and you know what to do there."

"I do."

"If anything goes wrong with it—"

"I'll wing it," Shelby assured her. "Thanks for saving that table for my parents."

"Are you kidding? Of course we saved them a front-row seat—absolutely top of the checklist. And it stays reserved when they leave until your grandparents get here. I've got to go check on a few things, then we'll go for it. You need anything?"

"I've got it all."

Since she wanted it to be easy, natural, she went out early, chatted with a few people she knew at the bar. Got herself a bottle of water.

She knew her mother tended to get worked up before she performed—or always had—so she didn't go to her parents' table but sent them a smile. And another for Matt and Emma Kate. One more for Griff as Tansy stepped onto the little stage.

When Tansy spoke into the mic the clattering, scraping and voices quieted some. "Welcome to our first Friday Nights. We're traveling on back to the forties tonight at Bootlegger's, so sit back and enjoy those martinis and highballs while we bring you tonight's entertainment. Most of y'all know Shelby, and most have heard her sing. Those who haven't are in for a treat. Derrick and I are pleased and proud to have her here, on our stage, tonight. Now y'all give a Rendezvous Ridge welcome to our own Shelby Pomeroy."

Shelby walked onto the stage, faced the room, the applause. "I want to thank y'all for coming out tonight. I'm so glad to be back in the Ridge, hearing familiar voices, breathing that good mountain air. This first number puts me in mind of what it was like to be away."

She started with "I'll Be Seeing You."

And here she felt like herself. Shelby Pomeroy doing her best thing.

"She's just great," Griff murmured. "Sensation."

"Always was. You've got stars in your eyes." Emma Kate patted his arm.

"That's okay, I can see fine through them. They just brighten things up."

She sailed through the first set, pleased to see people come in, crowd at the bar or at tables. When she took her break Clay walked straight up to her, lifted her off her feet.

"So proud of you," he whispered in her ear.

"It felt good. Really good."

"Wish we could stay, but I've got to get Gilly home."

"She okay?"

"Just tired. It's the first night in a month she's made it past nine." He laughed, squeezed Shelby again. "Come on over before we leave."

She glanced over, saw Matt and Griff pushing the tables together so her family, her friends made one unit.

Maybe she'd had a rough start to the day, she thought, but it was turning into a perfect night.

She spent some time with them, then went back to the bar for more
water.

It didn't hurt her feelings when she noticed Arlo and his friends leaving. She'd lose that mild discomfort from having him stare at her.

He'd often stared at her, just like that, when they were teenagers. And,
she recalled, had tried to get her to take a ride on his motorcycle or sneak
off for a beer.

She'd never done either.

And she found it downright creepy that years later, he'd still just stare
at her, unblinking as a lizard.

Griff slipped up to the bar beside her, and made her think of much
more pleasant companionship.

"Go out with me tomorrow night."

"Oh, I—"

"Give a guy a break, Shelby. I really want some time with you.
Just you."

She turned, looked straight into his eyes—bold, green, clever. Absolutely nothing about those eyes made her uncomfortable.

"I think I want that, too, but I don't feel right leaving Callie two nights
running, and asking my parents to sit her again."

"Okay. Pick a night next week. Any night, and anywhere you want
to go."

"Ah . . . Tuesday would probably be best."

"Tuesday. Where do you want to go?"

"I really want to see your house."

"You do?"

She broke out in a smile. "I really do, and I've been trying to figure
how to invite myself for a tour."

"Consider it done."

"I could bring dinner."

"I'll take care of it. Seven?"

"If we made it seven-thirty, I could give Callie her bath first."

"Seven-thirty."

"I need to check with Mama first, but I expect she'll be fine with it. And you should listen to what else has come out before we make any sort of date."

"It's already a date." He kissed her lightly before he walked away.

She thought that quick gesture had been a statement, a kind of stamp. And couldn't quite figure out if she minded that or not. She put it in the back of her mind as she went back on stage for her next set.

She saw Forrest come in with her grandparents, take the empty seats.

But she didn't notice the brunette until halfway through her set. Shelby's heart jumped, but she kept the song going when their eyes met.

Had she been there all along, tucked into a table at the back, barely visible in the shadows?

Shelby looked away, tried to catch Forrest's eye, but he'd gone up to the bar, wasn't looking in her direction.

The brunette rose, stood a moment, sipping from a martini glass. Then she set it down, put on a dark jacket. She added a smile, kissed her fingertip, flicked it in Shelby's direction, then strolled out.

She finished out her set—what else could she do? Then made a beeline for Forrest.

"She was here."

He didn't have to ask who. "Where?"

"In the back."

"Who?" Griff demanded.

"She left," Shelby continued. "Easy fifteen minutes ago. She's gone, but she was here."

"Who?" Griff demanded again.

"It's hard to explain." Shelby pasted on a smile, turned and waved when someone called her name. "I have to work. Maybe you could fill them in some, Forrest. I couldn't get your attention when I saw her, but I swear she was here."

"Who?" Griff demanded for the third time when Shelby walked over to another table.

"I'll tell you about it, but I'm going to take a little look around outside."

"I'll go with you." When Matt started to rise, Griff shook his head. "Keep the table. We'll be back."

"What's all this?" Viola leaned over.

"Nothing to worry about. I'll explain when I get back." Forrest gave her shoulder a rub, then made his way out with Griff.

"What the fuck, Forrest? What woman? And why did she put that look in Shelby's eyes?"

"What look?"

"Half scared, half pissed."

Forrest paused at the door. "You read her pretty well."

"I'm making a study of it. Get used to it."

"Is that so?"

"That's down-to-the-ground so."

Forrest's eyes narrowed as he nodded. "I have to think about that. Meanwhile, we're looking for a hot brunette, about thirty, round about five-six, brown eyes."

"Why?"

"Because it's looking like she was married to the guy Shelby thought she was married to."

"What? Thought? What?"

"And she's bad business—so was the asshole Shelby likely wasn't married to after all. A lot worse than I figured, and I figured bad enough."

"Was Shelby married or not?"

"It's hard to say."

"How can it be hard to say?" Frustrated, and temper building under it, Griff threw up his hands. "It's yes or no."

Forrest scanned the street, the cars parked along the curb, the light traffic passing by. "Why are people from the North always in such a damn hurry? A story takes time to tell properly. I'll do that while we walk around back, see what we see. Have you put your hands on my sister?"

"Not so much. Not yet. But I'm going to, so get used to that, too."

"Does she want your hands on her?"

"You should know me well enough by now, damn it, Forrest. They don't go on her unless she wants them on her."

"I know you well enough by now, Griff, but it's my sister here, so that takes more. And it's my sister who's been fucked over right, left, sideways. So that's more yet."

He told the story as they walked around the side of the building, made their way toward the back and the parking lot.

"And you think this woman's telling it straight?"

"She's telling enough of it straight so I know the bastard Shelby was with was a liar and a thief. I'll be doing some looking for something on this millions in jewelry and stamps she claims they stole or conned somebody out of."

His eyes, shadowed in the dim light, scanned the cars. "If they hadn't bussed the brunette's table, I could've gotten prints off it, gotten her name, her real one."

"If she's telling the truth about being married to Foxworth, he was using Shelby all along." Griff stuffed his hands in his pockets, paced away. "And Callie . . ."

"Callie's going to be fine either way. Shelby will see to that. But I'd like to have a conversation with this woman who's dogging her."

"Brunette, right? Hot, brown-eyed brunette."

"That's right."

"I don't think you're going to have any conversations with her. Better come over here." Griff took a deep breath as Forrest hurried toward him. "Looks like we found her."

She sat, slumped in the driver's seat of a silver BMW, eyes wide and staring. Blood still seeped from the tiny black hole in her forehead.

"Well, shit. Well, shit," Forrest repeated. "Don't touch the car."

"I'm not touching a goddamn thing," he said as Forrest pulled out his phone. "I didn't hear a shot."

Forrest took a picture from the side, one from the front. "Small caliber, and see how it's burned around the entry wound? Held it right against her. Right up against her forehead, pulled the trigger. Somebody might've heard a pop, but it wouldn't be all that loud. I've got to call my boss."

"Shelby?"

Like Griff, Forrest looked back toward the bar and grill. "Let's just wait on that a little bit. Just wait on it. We need to secure this area. And shit, we're going to have to start talking to people inside the bar and grill. Sheriff?"

Forrest adjusted his stance, re-angled the phone. "Yes, sir. I got a body here in the parking lot of Bootlegger's Bar and Grill. Yes, sir, that sure would be a dead one." He glanced at Griff as he spoke, nearly smiled. "I'm certain of that as I'm looking right at her and the small-caliber bullet wound, close-contact, in her forehead. I got that."

On a sigh, Forrest shoved his phone in his pocket. "Sure wish I'd finished that beer because it's going to be a long, dry night now." He studied the body another moment, then turned to Griff. "I'm deputizing you."

"What?"

"You're a competent individual, Griff, and you sure keep your head when you find a dead body, as you've just proven. Don't shake easy, do you?"

"It's my first dead body."

"And you didn't scream like a girl." Laying a bolstering hand on Griff's shoulder, Forrest gave it a friendly pat. "Plus, I happen to know you didn't kill her since you were inside with me."

"Yay."

"She's still warm, so she hasn't been dead long. I got some things I need in my truck, and I need you to stay here. Right here."

"I can do that." Because, he thought, as Forrest walked off to his truck, what else could he do?

He tried to think it through. The woman had been inside, then she'd gone out, gotten in her car. The driver's-side window was down.

Warm enough night. Had she put it down for the air, or because somebody had walked up to the car? Did a woman alone in a parking lot outside a bar roll down the window for a stranger?

Maybe, but it seemed less likely than rolling it down for someone she knew.

But . . .

"Why's her window down?" he asked Forrest. "From what you told me, she doesn't know anybody around here. She's got to have some basic street smarts, so who'd she roll the window down for?"

"Deputized two minutes and already thinking like a cop. Makes me proud of my own character assessment. Put these on."

Griff looked at the gloves. "Oh, man."

"Don't want you to handle anything—probably—but just in case. Use your phone, take some notes for me."

"Why? Don't you have backup coming or something?"

"They'll be coming. This woman came at my sister. I want a leg up. Get the make, model, license plate. Go on and get a picture of the plate. She's got a high-end rental here. We'll find out where she got it."

He shone his light in the car. "Purse is still in here, sitting on the passenger seat. Closed. Keys in the ignition, engine off."

"She'd have had to turn the key to get the window down. Strange town, she'd've locked the car up, right?"

"Son, if you ever give up carpentry and such, I'd take you on." Forrest opened the passenger door, crouched, opened the purse. "She's got herself a pretty little Baby Glock here."

Now Griff leaned over Forrest's shoulder. "She had a gun in her purse?"

"It's Tennessee, Griff. Half the women in that bar are carrying. Loaded, clean. I'd say it hasn't been fired recently. Got a Florida driver's license under the name Madeline Elizabeth Proctor, and that's not the name she gave Shelby. Miami address. Got her DOB as eight twenty-two 'eighty-five. Got some lipstick—looks pretty new—got herself a folding combat knife."

"Jesus."

"Nice one, too. Blackhawk. Visa and American Express cards, same name. We got two hundred and . . . thirty-two dollars in cash. And a key card for a room at the Lodge at Buckberry Creek in Gatlinburg. Fancy."

"Didn't want to get rousted." When Forrest glanced over, Griff shrugged. "She had to know Shelby had a cop for a brother. Go at Shelby, she's going to have a cop rousting her. Plus plenty of family circling the wagons. So she doesn't stay at the local hotel, which is pretty fancy, too. She puts some distance between herself and the Ridge, gives Shelby a phony name."

"See why I deputized you? So, what do you figure happened here?"

"Seriously?"

"Dead woman in the car, Griff." Curious, Forrest straightened up, rolled his shoulders. "It's pretty serious, all in all."

"Well, I'd guess she came tonight to mess with Shelby's head. Keep herself right in the front of Shelby's mind. Once Shelby spotted her, she could go. She came out, got in her car, most likely to drive back to Gatlinburg. Somebody came over to the car, to the driver's side. I'm leaning toward she recognized whoever it was, and felt easy enough to lower the window instead of driving off or getting her own gun. After she rolled down the window . . ."

Griff mimed putting a gun to his forehead, made a trigger with his thumb.

"That's my way of thinking, too. If I didn't know my mama would call you instead of me when the porches need scraping and painting, I'd talk you into joining the sheriff's department."

"Not on a bet. I don't like guns."

"You'd get over it." He looked over as a cruiser pulled in. "Shit, should've known he'd send Barrow first off. Guy's affable enough, but slow as a lame turtle. Go on back in, Griff, round up Derrick and fill him in."

"You want me to fill Derrick in?"

"Save some time. He's a competent individual himself, and he's been working the bar most of the night. Could be he saw somebody who didn't strike him quite right."

"Whoever did this is long gone."

"Yeah, for right now, anyway. You're a lot quicker than Barrow, Griff. 'Course, that doesn't take much."

"What we got here, Forrest? Hey, Griff, how's it going? Sheriff said— Holy shitfire!" Barrow said when he saw the body. "Is she dead?"

"I'd say that's affirmative, Woody." Forrest rolled his eyes at Griff.

Griff went inside to find Derrick and fill him in.

14

S helby sat in the tiny office holding the Coke Tansy had pushed on her with both hands. She didn't think she could actually swallow.

O. C. Hardigan had been sheriff for as long as she could remember. He'd always scared her a little, but she figured that was the badge more than the man. Not that she'd ever been in any trouble—any real trouble. He'd gone full gray since she'd left the Ridge, so his buzz cut looked like a shorn-off Brillo Pad. His square-jawed face was fleshier than it had been, and he carried a more generous paunch.

He smelled of peppermint over tobacco.

She knew he was being gentle with her, and appreciated it.

He'd said Forrest had given him a full report on her encounter with the victim—he called the woman "the victim"—but had Shelby go through it all again.

"And you'd never seen her, been contacted by her, talked to her before this morning?"

"No, sir."

"And your . . . The man you knew as Richard Foxworth, he never mentioned anyone named Natalie Sinclair or Madeline Proctor?"

"No, sir, not that I remember."

"And this private investigator—this Ted Privet. He never said her name to you?"

"No, Sheriff, I'm sure of that."

"How about this Mickey O'Hara she talked about?"

"I never heard about him before, either. Not until she talked about him."

"All righty, then. What time was it would you say when you saw her tonight?"

"I think it had to be about ten-thirty. Maybe ten twenty-five. I was more than halfway through the third set, and I started right about ten. She was all the way in the back, the far right corner." She held her hand up to demonstrate. "My right, that is. I didn't see her before that, but the light's dim back there."

She made herself take a drink. "After I saw her, she got up. Not in a hurry. It was like, all right, now you've seen me, now I made my point and I can go. She had a martini glass, but I don't know who was working that table. It had to be at least fifteen more minutes before I finished the set and could tell Forrest. Might've been a few minutes more, but no more than twenty. I had four songs left after the one I was doing when I saw her. And the talk between songs, well, I keep that short. So fifteen minutes, likely no more than seventeen."

"Did you see anyone follow her out?"

"I didn't, but I was looking for Forrest once she got up and started out. I wasn't watching the door."

"I bet you saw a lot of familiar faces in the crowd tonight."

"I did. It was so nice to see everyone." She thought of Arlo. "Mostly."

"A lot of unfamiliar ones, too."

"Tansy did a lot of marketing. She had flyers all over. I heard we had a lot of people in tonight who're staying at the hotel and the lodge and so on, even campers who came in tonight. Something new, you know?"

"Wish I could've been here myself. We're going to make a point of it, the wife and me, next time. Now, did anybody strike you, Shelby? Somebody who just didn't look right?"

"I didn't notice. Arlo Kattery was here with the two he always hung around with, but they left at the start of the second set."

"Arlo's mostly for Shady's, or one of the roadhouses."

"He didn't do anything but sit, have a few beers, then go on. I'm just thinking of him because he never looked right to me."

"Never has been."

"I guess for most of it I was pulling on the familiar faces more, and the couples. A lot of the songs I did tonight, well, they're romantic, so I played to that. It couldn't have been anybody from the Ridge, Sheriff. Nobody even knew her."

He patted her hand. "Don't you worry now. We'll figure it out. If you think of anything else, anything at all, you tell me about it. Or you tell Forrest if that's easier for you."

"I don't know what to think. I don't know what to think about any of it."

Out in the restaurant, Griff had done about all he could do. He'd helped organize people so the deputies could take statements, or just names. He'd helped Derrick serve out coffee, soft drinks, water, as another deputy interviewed the staff in the kitchen.

He'd gone out once for air, had seen the police lights around the BMW, and timed it inadvertently so that he watched them loading the bagged body into the coroner's wagon.

An experience, he decided, he'd be happy never to repeat.

The second time he made rounds with coffee, Forrest pulled him aside.

"Shelby's going to be out in a minute or so. I need to keep my hands in this thing here. I'm trusting you with my sister, Griff, because I can."

"I'll look out for her."

"I know you will. She pushed Emma Kate to go home, and that's likely for the best. She'll get out of here quicker without another female to stroke her and ask for details. Get her home."

"You can count on it."

"I know I can. Coroner'll know for certain once he digs the bullet out of her, but eyeballing, he figures a .25."

"Do you know who she is yet? Real name?"

Distracted, Forrest shook his head. "We've got her prints now. I'll be running them myself tonight. There's Shelby now. Give me a second with her, then get her out. She argues, carry her out."

"If I do, don't shoot me."

"Not this time." Forrest walked over, took Shelby by the shoulders as he studied her face, then just drew her in, held her.

Whatever he said had her shaking her head, again and again, as she burrowed into him. Then she sagged a little, shrugged. When Forrest let her go she started toward Griff.

He met her halfway.

"Forrest says you need to drive me home. I'm sorry he's being so fussy."

"Whatever Forrest says, I'm driving you home. Men aren't fussy— that's a girlie word. We're logical and protective."

"Sounds fussy to me, but thank you."

"Let's go."

"I should find Tansy first, or Derrick, or—"

"They're busy." He didn't go as far as carrying her, but he took her hand, pulled her firmly away from the building and the hard lights. "We'll take your van."

"How are you going to get home if—"

"Don't worry about it. You'll need the van. I'll drive." He held out his hand for the keys.

"All right. My brain's too rattled to argue. Nobody knew her around here. People around here don't just walk up to a strange woman and shoot her in the head, for God's sake."

"Which should tell you whoever did isn't from around here."

She looked up at him with considerable relief. "That's what I said to the sheriff."

"She brought trouble with her, Shelby. That's how it reads to me."

"It has to be that O'Hara person." The one, Shelby remembered, the brunette had warned her about. "She said he was in prison, but she lied about her own name, so who knows what else she lied about. If it was him, and if she was telling the truth about Richard, about all those millions, it's not safe to be around me."

"A lot of ifs there. I'll add some." He shot her a glance, sorrier than he could say that the sparkle she'd emitted when she sang had dulled. "If this O'Hara's around and did this, and if he thinks maybe you know something about those millions, it would be pretty stupid to hurt you."

He waited until she got in the van, then settled behind the wheel.

"And if he's such a badass, why didn't she drive away, get the gun in her purse. Why just sit there?"

"I don't know." She let her head drop back on the seat. "I thought things couldn't get crazier. After Richard died and the roof caved in, I thought, This is as bad as it can get. Then it got worse. Then I thought, All right now, that's as bad as it gets and we'll work our way through it. Then she came here and it's worse again. And now this."

"You've had a streak of bad luck."

"I guess you could put it that way."

"Luck changes. Yours already has." At an easy speed, he followed the wind of the road. "You sold the house, you're carving away the debt. You packed the house tonight and had them in the palm of your hand."

"You think so?"

"I was in the house," he said. "And you've got a date with me coming. I'm a damn good catch."

She didn't think she had a smile in her, but he found it for her. "Are you?"

"Damn right. Just ask my mother. Hell, ask yours."

"You don't lack in the confidence department, do you, Griffin?"

"I know who I am," he told her as he pulled up at her house.

"How the hell are you getting home?" She pushed fingers against that headache spot between her eyes. "I didn't even think. You can take the van, and I could get Daddy to drive me over and pick it up in the morning."

"Don't worry about it."

He got out, came around. She'd opened the door before he got to it, but he took her hand when she got out.

"You don't have to walk me to the door."

"It's just one of the many things that make me such a good catch."

The door opened as they came up the walk.

"Oh, baby girl."

"I'm all right, Mama."

"Of course you are. Come on in here, Griffin." Ada Mae scooped Shelby up in a hug. "Your granny and grandpa came by, told us everything. Forrest, is he still over there?"

"Yeah, he's still there."

"Good. Don't you worry about Callie. I checked on her five minutes ago, and she's sound asleep. Why don't I make you something to eat?"

"I couldn't, Mama."

"Let me look at the girl." Clayton stepped up, tipped up Shelby's face. "You're pale and you're tired."

"I guess I am."

"If you can't sleep, I'll give you a little something. But you give it a try first."

"I will. I guess I'll go on up. Daddy, Griff left his truck back at the bar and grill so he could bring me home. Thank you, Griff." She turned, touched her lips to his cheek.

"I'm going to see you settled and tucked in." Ada Mae put an arm around Shelby's waist. "Thank you, Griff, for seeing to my baby girl. You're a good boy."

"But am I a good catch?"

At Shelby's tired laugh, Ada Mae gave a puzzled smile. "Best in the whole pool. Come on now, my baby."

Clayton waited until they were up the stairs. "You got time for a beer and some details, Griff?"

"If you'd make that a Coke or ginger ale, I've got time. I plan to bunk on your couch there anyway."

"I can get you back to your truck."

"I'd feel better bunking right here tonight. I don't think there's going to be any trouble, but I'd feel better right here."

"All right, then. We'll have a Coke and a talk. Then I'll get you a pillow and blanket."

An hour later, Griff stretched out on the couch—a pretty comfortable couch. God knew he'd slept on a lot worse. He stared up at the ceiling awhile, thinking of Shelby, letting some of the songs she'd sung that night replay in his head.

At some point he'd let the whole business play around, like the songs, in his head. It's how he solved most problems. Let all the pieces roll around, try fitting some together, taking them apart again until a picture formed.

Right now the only clear picture was Shelby.

She was in plenty of trouble, no doubt about it. Maybe he couldn't resist a damsel in distress. Not that he'd use that term out loud. Besides, if a woman liked the term, if she was the sort who just wanted to sit around doing nothing while he rescued her, well, she'd bore the crap out of him in short order. And that would be right before she irritated him so he never wanted to deal with her again.

So it probably wasn't the damsel-in-distress thing, now that he thought about it. Turn that around into a smart, strong woman who just needed some help. Add in the way she looked, the way she sounded. The way she was.

He'd be a moron if he didn't want the whole package.

He was no moron.

He let his eyes close, ordered his mind to go drifting. Drifting, he dropped, slept light and restless until, on the edge of dreams, he heard something that brought him to full alert again.

An old house settling? he asked himself as he strained to hear.

No. That was creaking boards and footsteps. He slid off the couch, moved quietly in the direction of the sound. And, braced to attack, slapped on the lights.

Shelby clamped a hand over her own mouth to muffle the scream.

"Sorry! Jesus, sorry," Griff began.

She waved her free hand, shook her head, then leaned back against the wall. Slowly, she dropped her other hand. "Well, what's another ten years? What are you doing here?"

"I'm bunking on the living room couch."

"Oh." Now she dragged her fingers through her hair in a way that made all those wild curls go just a bit madder—and tightened every muscle in his body. "I'm sorry. I couldn't sleep, so I came down to make some tea or something."

"Okay."

"Do you want some tea or something?" On a thoughtful frown, she cocked her head. "Do you want some scrambled eggs?"

"Oh yeah."

He followed her back to the kitchen. She wore cotton pajama bottoms—bright blue with yellow flowers all over them—and a yellow T-shirt.

He could've lapped her up like ice cream.

She put the kettle on, got out a skillet.

"I can't turn my mind off," she began. "But if I asked Daddy for a sleeping pill, Mama'd start fussing again."

"They love you a lot."

"I'm lucky they do." She put a pat of butter in the skillet, let it melt while she beat some eggs. "I thought when the woman told me all those things this morning, the client of that detective was probably the person they all stole from."

"It's a good guess."

"Now I wonder, was this woman the client? Did he find me, follow me here, all of that, for her? She said no when I asked her, but she's—she *was*—a liar. So maybe she had him follow me so she could come and push me for something I don't know."

"That's another good guess, but if you're wondering did he kill her? Why would he?"

"I can't come up with something for that except maybe she double-crossed him somewhere. He talked about finder's fees on this theft I didn't believe with Forrest. I mean, I didn't believe Richard had stolen all that."

"I know what you meant."

"I believe it now, and I think she and Richard were good at that sort of thing. Stealing and double-crossing. Or maybe they were lovers—the woman and the detective—and she betrayed him."

"I don't think so."

Frowning again, she popped some bread in the toaster. "Why not?"

"I think if you add in love or sex, or both, it's—murder—it's more personal. You've got to fight first, right?"

She considered that. "I guess I would."

"Most would," Griff decided. "You've got to want to tell the other person what they did to you. You want, I'd think, some physical contact. This struck me as pretty damn cold."

"You really found her?"

"Forrest was looking left, I was looking right. That's all."

"You stayed so calm. At least it seems you did. You looked calm when you came back in. I couldn't tell anything was wrong by the way you looked. I think most people would've panicked."

"I try to avoid panic because it leads to chaos, which leads to accidents.

You get hurt that way. That happened to me when I was seventeen, climbing back out of Annie Roebuck's bedroom window."

"Climbing out?"

His smile was quick and crooked. "Climbing in was a breeze."

"Was she expecting you?"

"Oh yeah. She was the focus of my hormonal obsession for six and a half crazed and blissful months, and I was hers. We went at it like rabbits on crack—and the fact that her parents were asleep right across the hall only enhanced the insanity. Until the night we were lying there momentarily in our postcoital coma and she reached over for her bottle of water, knocked over the lamp. It crashed like a bomb."

"Uh-oh."

"Uh-fucking-oh," he concurred. "We hear her father call her name. I'm scrambling up, trying to get into my pants, my heart's a jackhammer, I'm sweating bullets. Yeah, you laugh," he said when she did. "At the time it was a nightmare of Elm Street proportions. Annie's calling back, telling him she's all right, just knocked something over, and hissing at me to get out, get out, get out, she can't remember if she locked the door. So I'm out the window half dressed, panicked, and I lose my footing."

"Another uh-oh."

"And a big ouch with it. I fell mostly in the azaleas, but still managed to break my wrist. I *see* the pain, like this bright white light, as I'm tearing ass for cover. If I hadn't panicked, I'd've climbed on down as smooth as I had every other time, and wouldn't have had to fake falling on my way to the john once I got home so my father could take me to the ER and have my wrist set."

She set a plate of eggs with a side of toast in front of him. And had to quell the oddest urge to just wrap around him and snuggle as she did with Callie.

"I really hope you didn't make all that up just to take my mind off things."

"I didn't have to, but I'd hoped it would take your mind off things."

"What became of Annie?"

"She became a newscaster. Worked local for a while in Baltimore. She's in New York now. We e-mail now and again. She got married a couple summers back. Nice guy." He sampled the eggs. "Good eggs."

"Scrambled eggs always taste best at three in the morning. Was she your first? Annie?"

"Well, ah—"

"No, don't answer that. I put you on the spot. My first was when I was just shy of seventeen. It was his first, too. July Parker."

"July?"

"Born on the first of the month. He was a sweet boy, and we fumbled our way through it."

With the smile her eyes went a little blurry as she looked back. "It was sweet, like July, in its way, but it didn't tempt me to repeat it all again, not till the summer before college. That wasn't so much better, and he wasn't so sweet as July. I decided to concentrate on my singing, the band, college. Then Richard just bowled me over, and that was that."

"What happened to July?"

"He's a park ranger. Lives in Pigeon Forge now. Mama tells me bits and pieces. He's not married yet, but he's with a nice girl. I expect you're considering having sex with me at some point."

He didn't lose his balance on the segue. "It's more planning on it."

"Well, now you have the outline of my experience in that area. Fumbling—sweetly. Disappointment, and Richard. And with Richard none of it was real. None of it was true."

"It's no problem, Red. I'll show you the ropes."

She laughed. "You do swagger."

"Sorry?"

"You're a swaggering man, Griffin, walking and talking." She finished her eggs, took her plate to the sink to rinse. "If I ever work my way up to your plan, I can't promise it'll be good, or there'll be any postcoital comas, but it'll be true. That counts for something. 'Night."

"Good night."

And he sat a long while in the quiet kitchen wishing Richard Foxworth hadn't gone out in that boat. Wishing he'd at least lived through the squall so they'd have a chance to face each other.

So he could kick the bastard's ass.

"HER LEGAL NAME was Melinda Warren." Forrest stood in what had once been Shelby's bedroom and watched Griff sand the seams on drywall. "Age thirty-one, born Springbrook, Illinois. Did time for fraud, so that much was true. And that was her first real stint, though she did some time in juvie once upon a time, got pulled in here and there on suspicion—theft, fraud, forgery. Nothing stuck until this last one. And married sure enough to one Jake Brimley, in Las Vegas, about seven years back. No divorce on record."

"And you're sure Jake Brimley was Richard Foxworth?"

"Working on that. The coroner was right about the slug—.25 caliber. Contact shot. Something like that, it'd rattle around in her skull like a marble in a pan."

"Nice." Still sanding, Griff glanced around. "Why are you telling me all this?"

"Well, you found her, so I'm respecting your vested interest."

"You're a funny guy, Pomeroy."

"I've got knees being slapped all over the county. Other than respecting your vested interest, I came by here to tell Shelby, but she and everybody else is someplace else. You're the only one here."

"I am now," Griff confirmed. "Matt's out getting supplies for what we'll be doing here Monday. Plus, I'm better at drywall work than he is. He's not very patient at it."

"And you are."

Griff adjusted the Baltimore Orioles fielder's cap he wore to help keep the dust out of his eyes. "It just takes time, and sooner or later it's smooth as glass. Shelby's at the salon," he added. "Your mother took Callie to the flower place to buy some plants for something she's calling a fairy garden. Her friend Suzannah's coming by with Chelsea later so the girls can dig in the dirt. Your father's at the clinic."

Forrest took a slug from the bottle of Mountain Dew he carried. "You're well informed about my family, Griffin."

"I slept on the couch downstairs last night."

Forrest nodded. "Another reason I'm telling you all this. If I'm not looking out for my family, I know you are. It's appreciated."

"They matter." Griff ran his fingers down the seam and, satisfied, moved to the next.

"I had time this morning to speak to Clay about all this, and other things. We're wondering, as brothers might, if you're just looking to bang our sister."

"Jesus, Forrest." And Griff beat his head lightly against the wall.

"It's a reasonable question."

"Not when I'm standing here with a sanding block and you've got a gun."

"I won't shoot you. This time."

Griff glanced back, measured his friend's easy smile. "Comforting. I'm looking to spend some time with your sister and see what happens next. My impression is the dead fake husband messed her mind up pretty good in the area you're concerned about."

"I'm not surprised to hear it. I'm going to get back to work."

"What about the other guy? This O'Hara?"

Forrest smiled again. "And there's the final reason I'm telling you all this. You keep up. Name's not O'Hara. James—Jimmy—Harlow. He went down with the brunette, a harder knock. According to the tune she sang at the time, they'd been working a con on a rich widow name of Lydia Redd Montville. Big—real big—money there on her own side and her dead husband's. Foxworth—we'll just stick with that for now—romanced her. He had bona fides said he was a wealthy entrepreneur with interests in art and import/export."

He took another swig from his bottle, gestured with it. "The brunette posed as his assistant, Harlow as his security. They worked the mark for two months or so, defrauded her out of close to a million. But they wanted more. She was known for her jewelry, and her late husband for his stamp collection. Had a vault full of both of them. According to the brunette, this was going to be their big score. Retirement time."

"Isn't that always the way?"

"Widow's son started asking too many questions on the deals Foxworth aimed her toward, so they decided to get it done, get out. Things went wrong."

"Things always do on the last score, right? You're jinxing it right off the jump."

"Seems like it. The widow was supposed to be away for few days at a spa thing—which turned out to be she was having a little tune-up. Plastic surgery."

"Because she had a younger lover, and didn't want to tell him she was getting nipped and tucked."

"It plays true. So they're in her big house, getting into the vault. Going to clean her out and book it. The son brings her home, where she plans to sit out the bruises, I expect. And they're red-handed in the cookie jar."

"Some cookies."

"It appears either Foxworth or Harlow shoots the son, the brunette comes out of the bedroom, knocks the widow out—she claims to keep Harlow from shooting her, too, though he claims it was Foxworth doing the shooting."

"Rats ratting on rats. Duplicity," Griff decided. "It's a suitable word of the day."

"That's a fine one."

"What happened next?"

"What happened next is—and both Warren and Harlow agree on this end of it—Foxworth grabs the bag they'd put the jewelry and stamps in, and they scat, leaving the son and widow a bloody mess."

"Panic." Meticulously, Griff tested the next seam. "It's a gateway to accidents."

"The widow comes to, calls an ambulance for the son. It was touch and go there, but he pulled through. Neither of them can say for sure who fired the weapon. It all happened fast, and the son was in a coma for near to three weeks, and never did get anything but spotty memory back of the whole event."

"What about the bad guys?"

"They split up, with plans to meet at a motel on the way to the Keys where there's supposed to be a private plane waiting to take them to Saint Kitts."

"I always wanted to go there. I take it not all the bad guys made it to the tropics."

"No, they didn't. The brunette and Harlow show up at the motel. Foxworth didn't. But the cops did."

"Because Foxworth tipped them off."

"Now you're stepping on my finish. They sure did get an anonymous call from a drop phone, and it's smart money to bet it was Foxworth."

Griff snagged the Mountain Dew from Forrest, took a long gulp before handing it back. "Honor among thieves is bullshit."

"The shittiest bull in the field. To top it, Harlow had a diamond ring in his pocket worth about a hundred grand. Pretty clear Foxworth planted it on him just to sweeten the . . . duplicity."

"Nice use of the word."

"I've got some skills. He'd done time before, Harlow, but nothing violent. He swears he didn't shoot anybody, and that the brunette had a clear eye line on who did, but she made the deal first, and they stuck with it. She got four years, he got twenty-five. And Foxworth walked away with millions."

"That'd piss you off."

"Wouldn't it just?"

"But if Harlow's doing twenty-five years—"

"Should be, but he's out."

Slowly, Griff lowered the sanding block. "How the hell did that happen?"

"The prison authorities and the State of Florida wonder the same. He escaped right before Christmas."

"Happy fucking holidays." Rolling it around, Griff took off his cap, shook off the dust, settled it on again. "He's got to be the prime suspect on this murder. Why didn't you tell me straight off?"

"I wanted to see if you'd get around to asking. I already sent his mug shot to your phone, though all three of them had a hand with disguises. He's a big guy, formidable."

"Like Big Bud?"

Tickled, Forrest laughed. "No, I said big. Not massive. You take a look at the picture I sent, and if you see anybody who puts you in mind of it, stay clear and call me."

"You got that. Forrest, you said he never got busted for violent crimes, but the brunette told Shelby different. That he was violent."

"Makes you wonder, doesn't it? Keep an eye on my sister, Griff."

"Both of them."

Forrest started out. "That's tedious work you're doing there."

Griff shrugged. "It's just work," he said, and went back to sanding.

15

Shelby stood by the counter in Emma Kate's trim little kitchen and watched her friend slide a lasagna casserole into the oven. She didn't have long, but wanted to squeeze through the small window of time to see Emma Kate and her apartment.

"I'm going to get laid good and proper tonight." With a wicked grin, Emma Kate set the timer on the oven. "Spinach lasagna's Matt's favorite, and I picked up a nice wine on the way home from the clinic. Anything with spinach might not be my idea of a romantic dinner for two, but it sure is his. I'll reap the benefits."

"It's nice what you have with him. I can see how well you fit together. And I really like your place here."

"I do, too."

Turning from the stove, she could see through the doorway—Matt had taken off the door and stored it—to the old butcher block table he'd refinished, and where they'd have their romantic spinach lasagna.

"Of course, when Matt. and Griff sit around, it's how they'd take out this wall here, or do such and that with the backsplash. I guess one of these days I'm going to let Matt have his way with building a place from the ground up. He talks about it a lot."

"Do you want that?"

"He's gone native on me, Shelby. Wants a tucked-away place in the hills, in the woods, like Griff has. I guess I can see it, too. Quiet and ours. Maybe I'll learn to garden. But for right now, it's sure easy to step out the door, walk a few minutes and be at the clinic."

"Oh, but wouldn't it be fun to build a house from scratch? Deciding just where you want this room or that room, where the windows would go, and what kind?"

"The three of you could have endless conversations on that," Emma Kate decided. "I start getting nervous once it goes beyond what color paint for the walls. In an apartment like this, everything's pretty well set.

"Do you want to sample the wine?"

"Better not. I can't stay long. I just wanted to see you and your apartment. Pretty well set or not, it's really you, Emma Kate, bright and fun," she said as she wandered out of the kitchen to the living room with its deep-cushioned red sofa, crazy-patterned pillows tossed over it. The framed posters of big, bold flowers added more color, more charm.

"Some of it's Matt. That jade plant's from a cutting he got from his grandmother. He babies it like his firstborn. It's kind of sweet."

She gave Shelby a rub on the arm. "I was giving you some time, but I'm starting to see you don't want to talk about last night, or any of it."

"Not really, but I should tell you her name wasn't Natalie or Madeline. She was Melinda Warren, and the man she said I should be afraid of if he found me is James Harlow. He escaped from prison, Emma Kate, right around Christmas."

She took out her phone. "Here's the picture of him Forrest sent me, so you should be careful if you see him. Forrest said he's probably changed his hair, maybe looks some different. He's six-feet-three and weighs in at two-twenty, so he can't change much of that."

"I'll keep my eye out. This is a mug shot, isn't it?"

"I think it is."

Taking another look, Emma Kate shook her head. "Wouldn't you think he'd look threatening or hard or mean in a mug shot? What he looks is sort of affable. Like some guy who played football in high school and now he teaches social studies and coaches."

"I think being able to look affable is how they all manage to swindle and steal."

"I guess you're right. And they think he killed her?"

"Who else?" Shelby had asked herself just that—who else?—a dozen times or more. And never came up with a single alternative.

"I guess they're talking to everybody who was there last night, and asking around town. Forrest said they're trying to get in touch with the detective who talked to me, but they haven't gotten ahold of him yet."

"It's the weekend."

"I suppose. She—this Melinda Warren—was telling the truth about being married."

"To Richard?" This time Emma Kate laid a hand on Shelby's arm, left it there.

"It's most likely. They have to go through some paperwork and background and all to be certain the man she married was the same man I thought I married. But . . . Hell, Emma Kate, it's not most likely, it just is."

"Shelby . . . I'm sorry if you are."

This, too, Shelby had asked herself a dozen times. Was she hurt? Was she sad? Was she angry?

The answer had been a little bit of all, but more of simple relief.

"I'm glad of it." Comforted, she laid her hand over Emma Kate's. "As awful as that is, I'm glad of it."

"I don't think it's awful. Smart and sensible, that's what it is." And turning her hand, she linked her fingers with Shelby's. "I'm glad of it, too."

"He thought I was stupid, but what I was, was pliable."

After giving Emma Kate's hand a squeeze, Shelby dropped her own to wander around the small, bright space.

"It's infuriating to look back at it now. It's . . . and you know I use the word sparely, but it suits what's in me over this. It's fucking galling, Emma Kate."

"I bet it is."

"At the time I thought it was the right thing, the thing to keep my family together. But we weren't a family. I thought, once I swallowed hard on it, that was done now. It's not done. Not until they find this Harlow person. I don't know if they'll ever find that woman's jewelry and her stamps. I can't think what Richard might've done with them."

"That's not your problem, Shelby."

"I think it is." She walked to a window, looked out at Emma Kate's view of the Ridge. The long, steep curve of road, with buildings ticking their way down it as they hugged the sidewalk.

Flowers in barrels and pots, heading-toward-summer flowers in hot reds and bold blues replacing the pastels of spring.

Hikers with their backpacks, she noted, and some locals warming the benches outside her grandmother's salon, the barbershop.

She could just see the well, just a corner of it, and the young family who stood reading its plaque. A couple of young boys made her smile as they raced after a spotted dog who'd snapped his leash and was running, tongue out, hell for leather.

It was a good view of what was what in the Ridge.

For a minute or so more, she had to take herself beyond that curving street with its hills and shops and flowers. Take it back into what still clouded over it.

"If the police could find all that, or what Richard did with it—or most of it—I wouldn't have to worry or wonder. Then it would be good and done."

"What does worry and wonder get you?"

"Not a damn thing." She turned back, smiled at the practicality that steadied her. "So I'm not thinking about it every minute of the day. Maybe if I don't think about it, something'll pop into my head."

"That happens for me when I vacuum. I hate running the vacuum."

"You always did."

"Always did, so my mind wanders around. Things do pop in."

"I'm hoping. Now I've got to get home. Mama had Callie and her friend plant a fairy garden, and I want to see it. Remember when Mama had us plant one?"

"I do. Every spring, even when we were teenagers. I'll have to try my hand at it if we ever build that from-the-ground-up house."

"You could do a miniature windowsill fairy garden right there, using your big front window."

"Now see, I'd never have thought of that. Now you did, and I'm going to end up buying little pots and plants. Wouldn't that look sweet?"

"Guaranteed."

"I could . . . Hold on." Emma Kate picked up her phone when it signaled. "Matt's texting me he'll be home in about a half hour. Which means closer to an hour, as he must be finishing up helping Griff on the house, then they'll have to talk about it awhile. Ruminate."

"Ruminating can take some time. I've got a date with Griff Tuesday."

Emma Kate's eyebrows winged up. "Is that so? And you don't mention it until you're heading out the door?"

"I'm not sure what to think about it yet, but I want to see his house. I always wanted to see what someone with some vision could do with that place."

Those eyebrows stayed raised. "And seeing the house is your sole purpose of this date?"

"It's a factor. Honestly, truly, I don't know what I'm going to do about what's moving along between us."

"Here's a thought." Lips bowing up some, Emma Kate lifted the index finger of both hands. "Why not try something I don't think you've put up front for the last few years. What do you want to do?"

"When you put it like that?" Shelby's laugh was quick and easy. "Part of me—maybe the most part of me—just wants to jump him, and the realistic part is saying, Slow down, girl."

"Which one's going to win?"

"I just don't know. He sure wasn't on my list, and I've still got a lot to tick off there."

"I'm calling you Wednesday morning to see if you ticked off 'sex with Griff.'"

Now Shelby raised her eyebrows, shot out a finger. "That's not on the list."

"Add it on," Emma Kate suggested.

Maybe she would, for some point down the road. But for now, she was spending the rest of the weekend with her daughter.

By MONDAY THERE WAS still no word on Jimmy Harlow, no sign anyone matching his description had been around the Ridge, or asked about the brunette at her hotel in Gatlinburg.

Shelby decided to be optimistic, decided it was best to think he'd done what he'd come to do, had exacted his revenge on Melinda Warren, and moved on.

She parked outside the salon with time to spare, so walked down to the bar and grill. Optimism was her choice. It didn't have to be everyone's.

Tansy answered her knock.

"Shelby." Tansy immediately enfolded her in a hug. "I've been thinking about you all weekend."

"I'm so sorry about all this, Tansy."

"Everyone's sorry about it. Come on in and sit down."

"I have to get to work, but I wanted to see you first, and tell you I understand if you and Derrick want to cancel Friday Nights."

"Why would we do that?"

"It wasn't the sort of encore any of us had hoped for on our debut."

"It didn't have anything to do with us, with you, with the bar and grill. Derrick talked to the sheriff personally just yesterday. They're looking at it as a vengeance killing, old business that came here with her."

"I'm part of that old business."

"Not to my way of thinking. It's . . ." On a whoosh sound, she levered onto a stool. "I still get a little queasy and light-headed in the morning."

"And here I am hammering at you. Let me get you a cool cloth."

"I'd do better with a ginger ale."

Quickly, Shelby went behind the bar, poured ginger ale over a lot of crushed ice. "Sip it slow," she ordered, then got a clean bar rag, soaked it with cold water, twisted it until it held cool without dripping.

When she came back around, lifted Tansy's hair and laid the cloth on the back of her neck, Tansy made a long, long *Ahhhh.*

"That really does feel better."

"Worked for me when I was carrying Callie."

"It comes on most mornings, but usually passes before long. Every once in a while it hangs on, comes back a time or two. Just the icks, you know?"

"I do. It doesn't seem right something so wonderful should make a woman feel sick, but the prize at the end of it's worth it."

"I tell myself that every morning when I'm hanging over the toilet." She sighed again when Shelby turned the cloth over, laid the cooler side against her skin.

"It's passing already. I'm going to remember that trick."

Reaching back, she patted Shelby's arm. "Thank you."

"Do you want a couple crackers? I can get some from the kitchen."

"No, it really is passing. Now you sit down here and take my brand of cool-cloth treatment."

After tugging Shelby around, Tansy looked straight into her eyes. "That Warren person? She was an awful woman, and from what I've been told, didn't give a good damn about anybody but herself. She didn't deserve to die for it, but she was an awful woman. Whoever killed her was awful, too. You didn't even know those people, Shelby."

"I knew Richard—or thought I did."

Obviously feeling herself again, Tansy hissed and flicked that away. "And Derrick's got a cousin over in Memphis deals drugs for a living. That doesn't make us part of it. Are you too upset to sing on Friday? I understand it if you are. We lost a waitress over it."

"Damn it. I'm sorry."

"Oh, don't be. Her mama had a cat fit, said she might as well work at Shady's Bar as here with people getting shot. As if it happened every week. She was a whiner anyway," she added with a wave of her hand, "and Lorna's not sorry to see her go, so neither am I."

"I'm not upset about it, not like that. If you and Derrick want me, I'm here. I've already started the playlist."

"New flyers out today, then. We set a record on Friday."

"You did?"

"Topped our best night when we had the Rough Riders from Nashville, by fifty-three dollars and six cents. You e-mail me the playlist when you're finished, and I'll make sure the machine's set. And how's your mama and all the rest?"

"Dealing. I'd better get to work before Granny docks my pay."

She walked in right on time and went straight to work. She gave the garden patio a sweep, watered the pots, opened the umbrellas so clients could sit in the shade if they chose.

Back inside, she folded towels that hadn't been seen to while she listened to the chatter of the first customers. When she stepped out she saw her grandmother had come in, already had someone in her chair. Crystal gossiped happily with the woman she was shampooing.

And Melody Bunker and Jolene Newton sat in the pedicure chairs with their feet in bubbling water.

She hadn't run into Jolene at all since she'd been back, hadn't seen

Melody since that day in The Artful Ridge. She wouldn't have minded keeping it that way. But since she hadn't been raised to be rude, she stopped by the chairs on her way to check the front treatment rooms.

"Hey, Jolene. How're you doing?"

"Why, Shelby, I swear!" She set her glossy magazine in her lap, gave her head a toss that had her long, high ponytail bobbing. "You haven't changed one single, tiny bit, even after all you've been through. Are you getting nails today, too?"

"No, I work here."

"Is that right?" Jolene widened her hazel eyes as if this was fresh news. "Oh now, I think I did know that. You told me that, didn't you, Melody, that Shelby was working at Vi's again, just like back in high school?"

"I believe I did." Without looking up, Melody flipped a page in her own magazine. "I see you took my advice, Shelby, and found work you're suited for."

"Thank you for that. I forgot how much I enjoy being here. Y'all enjoy your pedicures." She walked to the desk to answer the phone, booked an appointment, then slipped through to check the front rooms.

Out of the corner of her eye she saw Melody and Jolene with their heads together, heard Jolene's high-pitched giggle. The same as it was in high school.

She ignored it, and them, reminding herself she had a lot more important matters to concern her.

By the time she swung through the salon again, Maybeline and Lorilee—mother and daughter—were both perched on low stools doing the scrub portion of the pedicures.

So they'd gone for the deluxe, Shelby thought, and walked down to make sure the paraffin was turned on warm. She checked the locker rooms, hauled out used robes, ran through the rest of her morning checklist.

She had a friendly conversation with a woman from Ohio, one giving herself a day off from a hiking adventure with her fiancé, and offered to take a lunch order as the woman had booked a full day.

"You could eat out in the garden if you want. It's such a pretty day."

"That would be wonderful. I don't suppose I could get a glass of wine."

"I can make that happen," Shelby told her, and produced a couple of menus. "You just let me know what you want, and one of us will go get it for you. About one-fifteen? You'll be between your Aromatherapy Wrap and your Vitamin Glo Facial."

"I feel so pampered."

"That's what we're here for."

"I love this place. Honestly, I just booked the day here so I wouldn't have to hike three days running. But it's all so terrific, and everybody's so nice. Could I get this Field Green Salad with the grilled chicken—the house dressing on the side. And a glass of Chardonnay would just make my day."

"You just consider it made."

"Is the woman out front, the owner, is that your mother? You look like her."

"My grandmother. My mama's doing your facial later."

"Your grandmother? You're kidding me."

Shelby laughed, delighted. "I'm going to tell her you said that, and you'll have made her day. Now, can I get you anything else?"

"Not a thing." The woman burrowed down in one of the chairs. "I'm just going to sit here and relax."

"You do that. Sasha will come get you in about ten minutes for your wrap."

She walked back into the salon with a smile on her face, went straight to the desk to place the order for a one-o'clock pickup. She started to turn to her grandmother when Jolene hailed her.

"That's pretty polish," Shelby said, nodding toward the toes Jolene was having painted glossy pink.

"It puts me in mind of my mama's peonies. I forgot to say before, and my goodness haven't you been busy in here, I heard you were singing on Fridays down at the bar and grill. I was sorry I couldn't make it in to hear you, then I heard about what happened and wasn't sorry I wasn't there on Friday. I think I'd have had a heart attack or something finding out some woman got shot right outside."

She patted a hand to her heart as if even now it was in danger.

"I heard you knew her, too, is that right?"

Shelby gave Melody a glance. "I know you consider Melody a reliable source of information—and that Melody's confident you'll push whatever buttons, turn whatever knobs she tells you to."

"Why, Shelby, I was just asking—"

"What Melody told you to ask. The answer is no, I can't say I knew her."

"Your *husband* did," Melody said. "But that's right, he wasn't your husband at all, was he?"

"Apparently not."

"You must feel just awful, being deceived like that." Jolene picked up the theme. "Why, I'd just about *die* if I'd lived with a man all those years, had a child with him, and found out he had another wife all along."

"I'm still breathing. I guess I'm not as sensitive as you."

She started to step back.

"You're not doing anything important," Melody began. "I'd like a glass of sparkling water, with ice."

"I'll get that for you," Maybeline began, but Melody shot her a hard look. "You're busy painting my toes. Shelby can get it, can't you, Shelby?"

"I can. Would you like something, Jolene?"

Jolene had the grace to flush. "I wouldn't mind some ice water, if it's no trouble."

"None at all."

She turned, went to the back, into the tiny kitchen. She'd stew about it later, she promised herself, but for now, she'd get the damn water.

She brought out the glasses, handed one to Jolene.

"Thank you, Shelby."

"You're welcome."

When she held out the glass to Melody, Melody knocked it with her hand so water sloshed over the rim.

"Now look what you did!"

"I'll get you a towel."

"These capri pants are silk, and now they've got water spots. What are you going to do about it?"

"I'm going to get you a towel."

"You probably did it on purpose because I didn't want the likes of you working in my store."

"Your grandmother's store, last I heard. And believe me, if I'd done it on purpose, I'd've poured the whole glass in your lap. Do you want that towel, Melody?"

"I don't want anything from your kind."

Shelby knew the place had gone quiet. Even the whirl of dryers had shut off. Every ear in the place was cocked. So she smiled. "Why, Melody, you're just as spiteful and full of self-importance as you were back in high school. It must be a burden carrying all that around inside you. I'm sorry for you."

"Sorry for me? Sorry for *me*?"

Melody flung the magazine away so it landed with a thwack on the floor. "You're the one came crawling back to the Ridge with her tail between her legs. And what did you bring with you?"

Her voice pitched louder as temper rose in hot spots on her cheeks.

"I brought my daughter and not much else. You're awful flushed, Melody. I think you need this water."

"You don't tell me what I need. I tell *you*. I'm the customer. You just work here, sweeping up. You don't even have the marginal skills to polish nails or use a curling iron."

"Marginal." Shelby heard Maybeline breathe the word, saw out of the corner of her eye the longtime employee carefully cap the coral enamel with only half of Melody's toes painted.

"Melody," Jolene began, gnawing her lip at the stony stare on Maybe-line's face.

But Melody only slapped Jolene's hand aside. "You'd better show some respect after where you've come from, and what's gone on since you came back here? Whose fault is it some woman got shot right in our town Friday night?"

"I'd say the person who pulled the trigger's at fault on that."

"It wouldn't have happened here if you weren't here, and everybody knows it. Nobody decent around here wants you around. You're the one who ran off with some *criminal*. And don't tell me you thought you were married to him. Like as not you cheated people just like he did, and when he died and left you in a fix, back here you come with your bastard child."

"Be careful there, Melody," Shelby said as Jolene let out a shocked hiss. "Be real careful there."

"I'll say what I think, and what most everybody around here thinks, too. I'll say what I like."

"Not in here you won't." Viola stepped up, gripped Shelby's arm hard, took the glass of water she still held—and had been about to heave—out of her hand. "I've just spared you from a soaking or worse, as I expect Shelby was about to do what I'd like to do myself, and that's haul you up out of that chair and slap your head clean around, you rude, ugly-minded, pitiful girl."

"You don't dare speak to me that way! Just who do you think you are?"

"I'm Viola MacNee Donahue, and this is *my* place. I'll speak to you just as you deserve, and the good Lord knows somebody should've spoken to you long before this. I'm going to tell you, tell you both, to get your lazy, spiteful asses out of my chairs and out of my place. You get up and you get out, and you don't come back in here."

"We haven't finished yet," Melody began.

"You're finished, done and finished altogether. No charge for today.

Now get the hell out of my salon. Neither of you are going to walk in that door again."

"Oh, but Miz Vi! Crystal's doing my hair for my wedding." Tears spurted into Jolene's eyes. "I've got the whole day before booked here."

"Not anymore."

"Don't worry about it, Jolene." Melody grabbed the magazine forgotten in Jolene's lap, tossed it across the room. "You can just pay Crystal to come to you."

"She couldn't pay me enough," Crystal piped up.

"Oh, but Crystal—"

"Shame on you, Jolene." Crystal bent down, picked up the magazine. "We've come to expect that kind of ugly from Melody, but shame on you."

"We don't need you," Melody snapped at Crystal as Jolene blubbered. "Barely a step up from the trailer trash in the holler. We don't need this place, either. I only come in here to be civic-minded and support local businesses. There are plenty of other places to go with more class."

"You never did learn class," Viola commented as Melody grabbed up her shoes. "That's a shame, considering your grandmother. She's going to be awful disappointed in you when I call her and tell her how you behaved in my place, what you said to my own granddaughter. What you said about my great-granddaughter. That takes you back a peg," she added when some of the angry color faded from Melody's cheeks. "You must've forgotten I've known your grandmother for over forty years. We've got a lot of respect for each other."

"Tell her what you want."

"Oh, I will. Now get your second-runner-up's ass out of my salon."

Melody sailed out while Jolene scrambled up. "Oh, Melody, wait! Oh, Miz Vi!"

"She's your choice of companion, Jolene. Maybe it's time you grew up some. Go on now, get."

She ran sobbing out the door.

After one still moment, several people—staff and customers—began to applaud.

"I swear, Vi." The woman in Viola's chair gave herself a half spin in it. "I've always said coming to Vi's is more entertaining than watching the soap operas."

Since it was there, Shelby took the water back, downed it. "I'm sorry, Granny. I wasn't going to slap her. I was going to haul her out of the chair and punch her right in the face. Nobody talks that way about my baby."

"Or mine." Viola gave Shelby a one-armed hug.

"Are you really going to call her grandmother?"

"I won't have to. You better believe she's calling Flo right now, giving her an earful. Flo loves that girl, but she knows her, too. I'll be getting a call inside the next half hour. Maybeline, Lorilee, you take your usual commission for the pedis out of the till."

"No, ma'am," they said, almost in unison.

"There's no need for it," Maybeline added. "Viola, don't you make me mad and say another word about it. That girl's lucky I didn't stab her with the cuticle scissors. Shelby, she was talking trash about you for the last half hour. I'm not sorry to see the last of her in here. She always shorts my tip."

"Jolene's not so bad when she comes in on her own," Lorilee put in. "But together they're downright mean."

"All right, then." With a glint of pride along with the dregs of temper, she nodded. "I'm treating everybody to lunch."

"Lunch!" Shelby checked the time, sighed in relief. "I've got to go down to the Pizzateria, get a customer a salad and sneak out a glass of wine. I can get the rest if y'all put an order together."

"We'll have ourselves a party," Crystal declared. "Second-runner-up's ass." She hooted out a laugh. "Miz Vi, I swear I love you to distraction and back again. Twice."

"Me, too." Shelby pressed her cheek to Viola's. "Me, too."

· · ·

THE MURDER and Melody's eviction from Viola's competed for the richest juice squeezed from the local grapevine. While it was true there hadn't been a murder in the Ridge for three years, coming up on four, when Barlow Keith shot his brother-in-law—and winged two bystanders—in a dispute over a pool game at Shady's Bar, nobody knew the woman currently in a cold drawer at the annex of the funeral parlor that served as the coroner's office.

Everybody knew Melody and Viola, so that story took the lead with most.

The incident got a fresh boost on Tuesday morning, when the word went around that Florence Piedmont had dressed her granddaughter down and ordered her to apologize to both Shelby and Viola.

The Ridge waited with bated breath to see if Melody complied.

"I don't want her apology." Shelby stacked fresh towels at the shampoo stations. "She wouldn't mean it, so what's the point?"

"Her offering, meaning it or not, and you accepting it, makes her grandmother feel better." For once Viola sat in the chair while Crystal touched up her roots.

"I guess I can pretend to accept a pretend apology, if it comes."

"It may take a few days, but it'll come. The girl knows where her bread's buttered the thickest. We're slow in here today. Why don't you let Maybeline give you a nice pedicure? It'd be nice to have pretty toes for your date with Griffin tonight."

Crystal and Maybeline, currently the only others in the salon, both slid their gazes toward Shelby.

"I don't know as he's going to notice my toes, one way or the other."

"A man who's interested in a woman notices everything at the start of it."

"That's the truth," Crystal agreed. "It's after they've got you awhile they wouldn't notice if you grew an extra set of toes and painted them every color in the rainbow. Especially if there's a game on the TV and a beer in their hand."

"We've got some really pretty spring colors," Maybeline put in. "There's Blues in the Night. It's just about the color of your eyes. I've got three manis this morning, and only one pedi scheduled all day. I'd love to do you one, Shelby."

"If there's time, that'd be nice. Thank you, Maybeline."

"What are you going to wear? On your date with Griff," Crystal asked.

"I don't know. Really, I'm mostly going over to see his house. I've always loved that old place, and wonder what he's doing with it."

"Since he's fixing you dinner, you should wear something pretty."

Shelby turned to her grandmother. "He's fixing me dinner? How do you know that?"

"Because he dropped by to see me Sunday afternoon, and asked, casual-like, if there was something you especially liked to eat, or something you didn't especially like."

"I thought he'd just pick something up." Now she didn't know whether to be flattered or nervous. "What's he making?"

"I think that ought to be his surprise. You should wear a pretty dress. Nothing fancy, just pretty. You've got good legs, girl. Good long legs. You got them from me."

"And pretty underthings."

"Crystal!" Maybeline flushed, and giggled like a girl.

"A woman ought to wear pretty underthings every day anyway, but especially on a date. It's confidence-building, I think. And it's always best to be prepared."

"If I want to get Jackson heated up, all I have to do is put on a black bra and panties."

"Oh, Granny." Undone, Shelby buried her face in her hands.

"I wasn't able to get him heated up, you wouldn't be here. Seems to me your mama says your daddy favors midnight blue when it comes to lingerie."

"I'm going in the back to check on things."

"What things?" Viola wanted to know.

"Anything that doesn't involve my parents and grandparents getting heated up."

She moved fast, but still heard the quick female laughter follow her.

SHE HAD TOENAILS painted a deep violet blue, and at Callie's insistence wore a dress the color of daffodils. And because she couldn't get it out of her mind, she wore under it a white bra with tiny yellow rosebuds worked into the edging lace, and matching panties.

Not that anyone was going to see them, but maybe they would build confidence.

Once she was dressed, Callie clung to her leg. "I want to go on a date with Griff, too."

Since she'd expected something along those lines, she had a counter-offer ready. "Why don't we take Griff on a date, maybe on Sunday after-noon? We could take him on a picnic. We could make fried chicken and lemonade."

"And cupcakes."

"Absolutely cupcakes." She hauled Callie up before she walked out of the bedroom. "Wouldn't that be fun?"

"Uh-huh. When's Sunday afternoon?"

"Just a few days away."

"Don't you look pretty!" Ada Mae exclaimed. "Doesn't your mama look pretty, Callie?"

"Uh-huh. She's going on a date with Griff, and we're going to take him on a date for a picnic on Sunday afternoon."

"Why, that sounds like the best time. I don't know if the bubble maker your granddaddy's setting up in the backyard's going to be as much fun as all that."

"Bubble maker?"

"Why don't you go out and see?"

"I'm going to make bubbles, Mama. Bye." She kissed Shelby's cheek, wiggled down and took off like a rocket, calling for her grandfather.

"I sure appreciate you watching her again, Mama."

"We love every minute of it. I think your daddy's as excited about bubbles as she is. You have a good time tonight. You got a condom in your purse?"

"Oh, Mama."

Ada Mae just pulled one out of her pants pocket. "In case. You put this in your purse, and I'll have one less thing to worry about."

"Mama, I'm just going to see his house and have dinner."

"Things happen, and a smart woman's prepared when they do. Be a smart woman now, Shelby."

"Yes, ma'am. I won't be late."

"You stay as long as you want."

With the condom tucked in her purse, Shelby started out. She'd just opened the van door when Forrest pulled up.

"Where are you off to in a yellow dress?"

"I'm just having dinner with Griff."

"Where?"

She rolled her eyes. "At his house because I want to see it, and I'll be late if you're going to give me the third degree."

"He'll wait. The sheriff cleared me to let you know. Richard wasn't Jake Brimley, either."

Her pulse jumped. She actually felt the leap in her throat. "What do you mean?"

"Jake Brimley, with the Social Security number he used, died at the age of three in 2001. Richard created the identification, or paid to have it created."

"You mean . . . he used that name, but he wasn't that person?"

"That's right."

"Who was he then? God's sake, how many names can one man have?"

"I can't say—I don't know," Forrest corrected. "We're working on it. I'll do what I can to find out, Shelby. I figure you'd want to know, one way or the other."

"I would. I don't know how I can put it all away until I know. Did you find anything else out about the murder?"

"As a matter of fact, we had someone come in today. She was in the parking lot—in the backseat of a car with another individual. An individual not her husband. While they were busy doing things that put a layer of steam on the windows, she heard a loud pop. The timing's right for it to be the shot. She surfaced from her activities long enough to notice someone get into a car, drive off just a few seconds later."

"God, she saw the killer?"

"Not really. She thinks male, but she wasn't wearing her glasses at the time, so didn't get a good look. We wouldn't have that much if her conscience hadn't gotten over on her guilt. What we've got is probably male, getting into a dark car, possibly an SUV. No make, model or license, but she thinks black or dark blue, and shiny. Struck her like a new car, but she can't say for certain."

"What about the man she was with? Didn't he see anything?"

"I didn't say she was with a man."

"Oh."

"Which is part of her problem with coming forward. We'll just say the other individual was very busy below window level at the time, and didn't see anything."

"All right. And Harlow?"

"Nothing there yet. You be careful driving over there to Griff's, Shelby. Text me when you get there."

"Oh, for heaven's sake, Forrest."

"If you don't want me calling when you might be . . . busy, text me when you get there. I'm going to see if I can mooch leftovers."

"They're out back," she called out as he strolled toward the house. "Daddy's got Callie a bubble maker."

"Yeah? I believe I'll get me a beer and get in on that. Text me."

16

She stopped at the head of the short lane that led back to the old Tripplehorn place, freshened her lip gloss, took a critical look in the visor mirror.

All right, no more dark circles, and not all the color in her face came from the little pot of cream blush her grandmother had urged her to sample.

Her hair, windblown as it was, added a casual touch. Wasn't it best to stay casual? she asked herself.

And took a breath.

She hadn't been on a date—a real one, and whatever she'd said, this was a bona fide date—since she'd flown off to Vegas with Richard, to get married.

Or so she'd believed.

She'd dated plenty before that, of course, she reminded herself, through high school and into college. But it was all so vague and blurry with the enormity of the in between the then and now.

And he was fixing her dinner, which made it a sort of *serious* date, didn't it? She made herself think through the enormity, back to the blur. She couldn't think of a single time a man had fixed her dinner.

Maybe it didn't make it serious. Maybe once you got past the high school and college years, it was just something people, adult people, did now and then.

And she was making far too much of it either way.

She made the turn, bumped her way down the narrow drive—obviously something he hadn't bothered to fix yet—then just stopped the car again and looked.

She'd always loved the charm of the old place, the way it tucked into the green, spread a bit toward a sheltered stream.

She only found it more charming now.

He'd cleaned up the exterior, and what a difference. She thought he'd likely power-washed the old stone—repointed it, too, so it stood in various shades of brown and gold on its roll of a rise among the trees.

And he put in spanking new windows, added a set of doors in place of the broken windows on what she assumed must be the master bedroom due to the addition of a covered porch with bronze-colored iron rails.

He'd left most of the wonderful old trees, the maples and oaks, their green deepening toward that deep summer shade, and put in a couple of dogwoods, bloomed off now and still tenderly green. Clearing out the scrub and weeds along the foundation had to have been hard, sweaty, even miserable work. Whatever time he'd put in had paid off as young azaleas and rhododendrons swept color at the stone's skirts, while older ones, wild ones, splashed more back in the green shadows.

He was doing some sort of terracing on the far side, following the rise of the land with partially finished stone walls that mimicked the tones of the house. She imagined it finished, and filled with native shrubs and flowers.

Too charmed to be nervous now, she left her van beside his truck, gathered the potted mountain laurel she'd picked up as a host gift and walked to the wide front porch.

She admired the set of Adirondack chairs painted deep forest green, the rough wood table—a stump he must've planed down and sealed—between them. Even as she raised a hand to knock, he opened the door.

"Heard you drive up."

"I'm already in love with the place. It must've taken you a lot of sweaty days to reclaim the land around the house, all that old scrub and the briars."

"Sort of hated to kill the briars. They added a little 'Sleeping Beauty' to the place. You look great."

He looked pretty great himself, freshly shaven, from the looks of it, with a shirt of softly faded blue rolled up to his elbows.

He took her hand to draw her in.

"I'm glad to see you're not averse to plants, so you should be able to find a spot for these."

"Thanks. I'll just—"

"Oh my God."

The shock in her tone had him looking frantically for something like one of the monstrously huge wolf spiders he'd spent weeks banishing from the house.

But when she pulled free, turned a circle, her smile simply glowed. "This is wonderful. Griffin, this is wonderful!"

He'd opened up walls so what had been a dark, narrow hallway was a wide foyer that spilled naturally into a front room with a fireplace he'd refaced in native stone. The early evening light flowed through the un-curtained windows onto a gleaming deep-toned oak floor.

"I don't use this space much yet, so I just tossed an old couch and a couple chairs into it. Haven't figured out what color to paint it, so . . . I haven't."

"It's about the space," she said, and wandered it. "I peeked in the old windows so many times, even broke in once on a dare and walked all through. Are these the original floors?"

"Yeah." Every square foot of them pleased him. "They took some work, but original's best if you can keep it. I used original trim where I could, copied it where I couldn't."

"And the ceiling medallion. I had dreams about that for weeks after I came in. The little faces around the circle."

"Nice and spooky. I haven't found the right light to go there." Like Shelby, he looked up at the plaster medallion. "It has to hit me."

"It should look old. There shouldn't be anything in here that looks shiny and new. Well, the kitchen and bathrooms, that's one thing, but the rest . . . And I'm telling you your business when you obviously know just what to do. I want to see it all."

"I haven't gotten to all of it yet. Some spaces I'd start, realize I wasn't in the right mood. Keep going and you end up doing something wrong, or at least half-assed."

He should paint this room a warm, rich gold—not bright and not too dark, but like warm, rich old gold. And leave the windows undraped to show off the gorgeous trim, and . . .

And she had to stop decorating it for him in her head.

"You're not doing all this yourself, are you?"

"No." He took her hand again, started to lead her toward the back of the house. "Matt's been a slave—will work for beer—when he has the time. Forrest, too. Clay's pitched in a couple times. My father's been down, given me a week or two when he can manage it. And my brother. My mom helped clearing the brush, and said I owe her more for that than fourteen hours of labor."

"Half bath here," he added when she laughed.

She poked inside. "Look at that sink. It's just like an old washbasin on a stand. Like it could've been here all along. And that antique bronze finish on the fixtures and the lights goes so well. You've got a nice sense, Griff, of color, too. Keeping it warm and natural. The house doesn't want bold and flashy.

"What's this over here?"

"Tools and materials, mostly." He thought, What the hell? and opened the old pocket door.

"Such wonderful high ceilings," she said, obviously not put off by stacks of tools and lumber, big tubs of drywall mud, and plenty of dust. "And another ceiling medallion. I guess you know they say the original Mr. Tripplehorn was six-feet-six, and built the place to accommodate his size. Does the fireplace work?"

"Not now. It needs work, and probably a gas insert in here, something that doesn't look like a gas insert. Refacing the brick, or maybe redoing it in slate or granite. It's crap and crumbling."

"What's it going to be?"

"Maybe a library. It feels like a house like this should have one."

Because he saw it in his head, he gestured. "Built-ins flanking the fire-place, a library ladder, that kind of thing. Big leather couch, maybe a stained glass ceiling fixture, if I find the right one. One of these days," he said with a shrug. "A couple of other rooms down here I'm still thinking about. I didn't want to open everything up. Open concept's one thing, losing all the original quirks and charm's another."

"You've got the best of both. You could do a pretty sitting room here, or first-floor office, guest room." She studied another empty room. "It's such a nice view through the windows there of the trees, and just that little bend of the creek. If you put your office here, you could float the desk in the center of the room so you could see out, but not have your back to the door. Then you could— And there I go again."

"You can keep going. It's a good idea."

"Well, I was going to be a singing sensation, but interior design was my fallback. I took a couple classes in college."

"Seriously? Why didn't I know that?"

"It was a long time ago."

"I'm going to use you. But right now, I'm going to get you some wine."

"I wouldn't mind a glass." Just one, she thought, with plenty of time to burn off before she got in the van again. "Something smells really good. I didn't expect you to—"

She broke off in wonder.

Everything just opened up. Where she remembered seeing a warren of rooms, a dingy dining room separated by walls and a door from a small and even dingier kitchen, what she'd supposed had been maids' and cooks' quarters was now one wonderful space that brought the hills, the trees, the creek inside through a wall of glass doors.

"I guess I went a little shiny and bold in here."

"No, no, not bold. Beautiful. Look at the size of that farm sink. And I love how you glass-fronted so many of the cabinets."

"Even if most of them are still empty."

"You'll fill them in time. I'd haunt the flea markets and yard sales, find me some old crockery. Maybe old teapots or cups and display them in those over there. And . . ."

She stopped herself before she decorated his house from top to bottom.

"It's such a nice flow into the dining area here and the, I guess, lounge area there. You could live in this one space. So much counter space. What is this?"

"Slate."

"It's just perfect, isn't it? So handsome. My mama would cry for that cooktop. I love the lights, that pale amber tone against the bronze. You designed all this?"

"I got input from my dad, from Matt, from a couple engineers I know. An architect. When you grow up with a contractor, you tend to make contacts."

"Still, it's your work. It feels like you. Honestly, I've never seen a more beautiful kitchen, and one that fits so well into this house. You have all the convenience, but the character's right here. You could entertain half the Ridge in here. It must be a joy to cook in."

"I don't cook much." He tugged on his ear. "Your basics mostly. But I figured if I ever had a place, did my own kitchen rehab, I'd go for the gold and see if I could reach it. Kitchen's the heart of the house."

"It is, and this one's big and beautiful."

"You haven't seen the best part."

He handed her a glass of wine, picked up his own, then walked to the wall of doors. When he opened them, they folded back like an accordion, tucked away, and brought the outside in.

"Oh, that *is* the best part. That's fantastic. Warm nights, sunny mornings, you can just leave them open. And for parties."

She stepped out, sighed.

"Still a lot to do out here yet. I've barely hit this part of the workable grounds."

"You can't beat the view."

And now with her, he looked out over the still scrubby yard to the great green domes. They rose, soft and misty, with the quieting light.

"You can't. Any season," he added. "A couple months ago I looked out at snow, and it stayed white or silver gray up in the higher elevations into April. And last fall? I've never seen color like that, and we get some pretty jazzy foliage in Maryland. But the miles of it. Just miles of it rolling up into the sky? Every day for weeks, it just dazzled."

He loved it, she realized, and more, understood it. The old Tripplehorn place was lucky he'd settled in.

"You can hear the creek bubbling," she said, and found the sound more romantic than violins. "You could have a big cutting garden out here, plant things that draw butterflies and hummingbirds. And there's enough sun you could have herbs planted right outside your kitchen—for when you do cook."

"Maybe you could help me figure that out."

"I have very strong opinions about such things." She lifted her face to the breeze. "You should plant some blooming weepers, and get yourself a big wind chime for that old oak over there. Something that gives a deep, masculine tone, and a couple bird feeders—but up off the top porch or the bears could come calling."

"I'd rather they didn't. I've seen a couple sort of lumber along in the woods—when I've looked out. That's close enough for me when it comes to bears."

"I envy you this place, Griff. The feel of it, the look of it, the potential of it and the history. I like that someone I know has it, and more, knows just what to do with it. I didn't realize you were this good."

"Is that right?"

She laughed, shook her head as she turned to him. "What I mean is, I knew you were good at your work. I've seen it, and I'm seeing what you and Matt are doing for Mama. But this isn't just changing something, or making it better, prettier or more functional. It's bringing something back to life so many others left for dead."

"I came to see the property on a whim, and fell in love at first sight."

"I think it's been sitting here pining all these years, so it must love you back.

"I don't know what smells so good, but I hope it'll hold just a bit more. I'd love to just sit out here awhile."

"It'll hold. Give me a second."

"What are we having?" she asked as he went in to turn off the burner.

"I hope it's going to be penne in a spicy tomato sauce with black olives and basil."

She smiled as he walked back out to her. "And how did you know that's one of my favorite pasta dishes?"

"I'm psychic?"

"I don't think so. It was sweet of you to find out what I like and go to the trouble."

"You can tell me I'm sweet after you eat it, in case it's terrible." Which, he could admit, was a genuine concern. "I didn't make the cannolis, so they'll be fine."

"We're having cannolis?"

"Which I didn't make, and I didn't make the loaf of Italian bread. And the salad's from a bag o' salad. I hit the wall on the pasta."

"You're the first man to make me dinner, and it sounds perfect."

"What?"

"It sounds just perfect."

"No, the other." He circled a finger in the air, signaling a rewind. "I'm the first man to make you dinner?"

"Well, my daddy, of course, and Grandpa's done some heroic grilling over the years."

"I . . . If I'd known this was a first, I'd have bought fancy plates or something."

"I don't want fancy plates. I've had fancy plates. Food tastes the same on them as it does on everyday."

He considered a moment. "I've got two reliables when I want to cook and impress a woman. One's your basic steak on the grill, massive baked potato and the ever popular bag o' salad. The other, when I seriously want to impress, is this chicken thing in wine. I'm pretty good at that one."

"Why aren't we having a chicken thing in wine?"

"Because I didn't want to go for the usual with you. And I didn't do this when you first got here because I wanted to give you time to settle in first."

He took the wineglass from her, set it down, put his own beside it, then drew her in.

He thought she smelled like the mountain sunset. Fresh, breezy, with shimmering edges. He combed his fingers through the long, luxurious length of her hair, all those tumbling curls.

And reminded himself to go slow, go easy, as he laid his lips on hers.

He drew back. "That was just in case you thought I forgot to kiss you hello."

"I didn't think—can't. Don't— Oh, damn. Damn."

The next thing he knew she surged against him. She knocked him back on his heels, kicked every rational thought out of his head, and flashed a wire in his blood in one fell swoop.

He stumbled back two steps before he regained his balance, wrapped around her to keep them both from pitching off the porch. And barely stopped himself from yanking the dress up and over her head.

She was an earthquake, an explosion of reckless heat shooting bolts of fire everywhere. His brain fogged in the ash and smoke.

He whipped her around, slapped her back to the post. Now that his hands were free, he used them, shooting them under the skirt of her dress, running them over her hips, over the heat, down again.

She quivered, moaned against his mouth, then nearly snapped the last thin thread of control by rocking her hips against him.

He had to pull back. "Wait."

She had a good grip on his hair, and pulled his mouth back to hers. "Why?"

He got lost again, for a moment, for a lifetime. "Wait," he repeated, then rested his forehead on hers. "Breathe."

"I am breathing."

"No, me. I meant me." He took that breath, then another. "Okay."

She obviously took that as a green light as she pulled him back again.

"No, I mean . . ." He solved his dilemma by gathering her up, holding her close. Jesus, did she have to be so long and soft and slim right this minute? "Okay. We'll take a breath. We'll just take a couple breaths."

He had steady hands, he thought. Rock steady. Freaking surgeon-steady hands. So why were they unsteady now?

He gripped her shoulders with them, drew back an arm's length. Just look at her, he thought, those big, dazzling eyes, nearly purple in the softening light.

He reminded himself how rough she'd had it, how rough she had it still.

"Maybe we should . . . I don't want to rush you."

Something sparked in those twilight eyes, and caused his throat to go dry as dust. "Did it feel like you were rushing me?"

"I don't know. Maybe. The thing is, if we don't take a minute, a breath, a . . . something, we're going to end up naked on the porch."

"All right."

"Okay, so . . ." He dropped his hands, took a cautious half step back. "We'll take a minute."

"I mean it's all right if we end up naked on the porch."

He lost his breath again. "You're killing me, Red."

"I know I've had what we could call a drawn-out dry spell, but I'm pretty clear on the signs and signals when a man wants me. And if I wasn't, you made it pretty clear you wanted me that one day in my mama's kitchen over a Coke."

"If I didn't want you I'd be an idiot, and my own mother's proud to say she didn't raise any."

"I want you back, so that seems good news all around."

"That's . . . yes, incredibly good news—and I got those signs and signals just fine, too. The thing is, considering the circumstances, the plan was to soften you up some with dinner here, and get you to go out with me a couple more times, then get you into bed."

She leaned back on the post, nodded. Something he recognized as amusement moved into her eyes. "And I'm guessing you like having plans, personally and professionally?"

"Things work better, usually, when you do."

"You don't like surprises?"

"I'm fine with them." Merry Christmas, Happy Birthday. Let's get naked on the porch. Oh God.

"I'm good with them," he managed.

"But maybe it takes you a minute to adjust to a surprise."

"Apparently."

Now she smiled, slow and easy.

Twilight eyes, magic mermaid hair, a long, long-stemmed rose of a body.

Yeah, she was killing him.

"Would you like to hear my plan?" she asked. "It's sort of spur of the moment, but I think it's workable."

"I'm all ears."

"My plan is we just skip over all the softening up with dinner and going out a couple more times. We come back around to that if we both want, after we get naked on the porch."

"You're nothing but a surprise. But no."

She sighed. "You're a hard nut to crack, Griffin."

"I mean no naked on the porch. We can do better this time."

"There's better than naked on the porch?"

"This time." This first time, he thought. This first surprising time. "I haven't shown you the second floor."

She angled her head, and her smile deepened. "No, you haven't."

"I'd like to." He held out a hand. "I'd really like to."

She put her hand in his. "I'd like to, but I might be a little rusty."

"Not from where I'm standing," he said as they walked back into the kitchen. "But don't worry, I'll walk you through it."

She paused, tapped the purse she'd set on the counter. "Isn't it interesting how my mama gave me a condom to tuck in here before I left tonight?"

"Oh. Man." He scrubbed his free hand over his face. "I'd thank her for the thought, but it'd be embarrassing. Anyway, I've got that covered. Ha."

"All right, then."

"We can take the back stairs."

"I forgot there were back stairs." Delighted, she turned with him. "Don't you love a house with back stairs?"

"I love this one. I'm going to update them, but they're sturdy enough." He flipped on a light—a single bare bulb. "Update that, too."

"Won't that be wonderful, but right now it's all shadowy and spooky. I like how it angles off here so you can go right or left."

"We're going left."

"How many bedrooms up here?"

"There were seven on the second floor. I'm making it five. It's down to six now, once I decided to put the master in the front."

"With that wonderful covered veranda."

"Right. And the third floor's more a maze of small rooms and odd angles. Something to deal with later."

She felt so calm. She hadn't expected to feel so calm, she realized, as they walked the wide, shadowy hallway. So easy about it all. Excited, yes, God, yes, but not jumpy. And not the least bit shy.

Something about him, she thought, just smoothed away the jitters.

"Oh! Double doors. It's elegant and still simple enough to fit the rest."

"It's not finished," he began, then opened the doors, flipped on the light.

"Oh, but it's wonderful. It's going to be wonderful. Look how the evening light pours in those doors, and the fireplace—the black granite. It's powerful. It's a statement."

"Haven't decided on the wall color." He nodded toward a wall where he'd painted wide strips of varying tones. "I found the iron chandelier at a flea market. Refinished it, rewired it. I'm looking for other lighting to complement it, but right now I'm just using some family castoffs. Bed's new though. Well, the mattress is new. I found the bed a couple weeks ago. Flea market again."

She ran her hand along the curved footboard. Smooth, she thought, sturdy and simple. "It's beautiful."

"Chestnut. Pretty wood. It just needed some work."

"Almost everything does. What did you use before?"

"Sleeping bag on an air mattress. But with my plan to get you up here, I figured I'd better get an actual bed. Glad I didn't wait on that."

"I'm glad you didn't." She turned to him. "I'm glad we didn't."

He moved over, opened the veranda doors to let in the evening air, then flicked a switch to turn on the fire before he turned off the light.

"That work for you?"

"More than works. It's perfect."

He went to her, circled her waist. "You're where you want to be?"

"Exactly." With a little bit of wonder, she brushed a hand through his hair. "You're a surprise, too, because I didn't expect to be here with any-one, not for a long time." She lifted her arms, circled his neck.

A long kiss this time, slow and long and deep. Like the first time, and like the first time, her body melted like a candle in the sun.

All these feelings, she thought, all these shivery little sensations. She'd forgotten more than she remembered, she realized, about being one of two.

She let herself flow with it, just flow and float like a dandelion puff on a summer breeze. There was a storm coming, oh, she could feel it building in her, but the soft and quiet came first.

She brought her hands to his face when he changed the angle of the kiss. And shivered with anticipation as she felt him lower the zipper on the back of her dress.

He traced a finger up her spine, down. The light touch had her arching toward him, purring in her throat before he brought his hands to the straps of the dress, brushed them off her shoulders.

The dress slid down and away.

"Pretty," he murmured, and ran that finger, erotically rough with callus, along the lacy edge of her bra.

"My heart's beating so fast."

"I can feel it."

"Yours." She laid a hand on his heart, relieved when she felt it beat fast and hard under her palm. "Yours, too."

She started to unbutton his shirt, let out a breathless laugh when her fingers didn't seem to work right. "I'm shaking inside. Outside, too."

He lifted his hands to help her, but she brushed them away.

"No, I want to do it. You'll just have to tolerate some fumbling. I want . . ." She felt him quiver as she finally managed to open his shirt, lay her hands on flesh. And look up into his eyes. "I want everything."

She broke him, snapped the last link on the chain of control. She gasped when he hefted her up, dropped her back on the bed. Covered her.

She was willow slim, and part of him fretted over hurting her. But even that dropped into the dark when she bowed up, gripping his hips, holding him against her center to center.

The sun bled away to dust, and a whippoorwill began its call for its mate.

The storm broke in her, a hot, whirling tempest. Greed rose with it, for more.

He had muscles like iron despite that rangy, swaggering build. His back rippled with them. Oh God, the feel of them under her hands. The weight of him pressing her down into the bed.

And hard hands, rough, impatient hands, all over her body. Not awakening needs—awakening seemed too tame a word.

It felt more like resurrection.

When his mouth closed over her breast, a scrape of teeth, a flick of tongue, and his hand slid between her legs, the orgasm tore through her, left her shocked and shuddering in its wake.

He didn't stop, didn't pause, but drove her up again.

And she was a pebble in a catapult, flying. Helpless and quaking. Her body was his now, open, and he took it, gave her more so sensations tangled together, needs became a single throbbing ache.

Then he was inside her, and pleasure ran through her in a flood.

She rode with him, beat for beat, her heart racing as his raced. Her sunset hair spread wild over the sheets, and her skin glowed in the smoky light of dusk.

"Shelby. Look at me." His body screamed for release, for that last leap. But he wanted to see her eyes. "Look at me."

She opened them, dark and dazed, looked into his.

"It's everything," he said, and let go.

17

Shelby's first coherent thought when the haze cleared from her mind was: So *this* is what it's like.

She felt heavy and light and limp, hulled out and filled up again all at once. She thought she could run a marathon, or sleep for a week.

Most of all she felt utterly and completely alive.

Griff lay flat-out on top of her, and that was just fine. She liked the weight of him even now, the sensation of his skin against hers, everything still hot and damp like after a strong summer storm.

In pretty contrast, the breeze fluttering through the open doors cooled her cheeks, made her smile. Everything made her smile. If she wasn't careful, she'd burst into song.

"Gonna move in a minute," he mumbled.

"You're fine. It's fine. Everything's just really, really fine."

He turned his head enough to brush his lips over the side of her throat. "I was a little rougher than I meant to be."

"To my way of thinking you were just rough enough. I can't figure if I've ever felt this used up or if I've just forgotten the feeling. You're sure thorough, Griffin. You sure do good work."

"Well, anything worth doing." He levered up to look down at her in the flickering of the fire. "You weren't rusty, by the way."

Pleased, languid with it, she touched his cheek. "I forgot to worry about it."

"I wondered what you'd look like, lying here like this. It's better, even better, than I imagined."

"Right this minute, everything's better than I imagined. That might be due to that long dry spell, but I'm giving you credit for it."

"I'll take it. It's cooling down. You're going to get cold."

"I don't feel cold."

"Yet. And I haven't fed you." He dropped a kiss on her lips. "I need to finish off dinner. But first . . ."

He rolled, and as he did, scooped her up. Her heart did a stuttering roll as he just lifted her right up as he stood.

Muscles like iron, she remembered. He was stronger than he looked.

"We should take a shower."

"We should?"

"Definitely." He grinned as he carried her. "You're going to love the bathroom."

She did. She loved the generous space, the oversized claw-foot tub, the earthy tones of the tile work. Most of all she loved the enormous shower with its multiple jets—and what could be done in all that heat and steam by two inventive and agile people.

By the time they were in the kitchen again she felt fresh and new and so happy she wished she'd learned to tap-dance.

"I need to let my parents know I'm going to be a little later than I said."

"Go ahead. Though since your mother gave you a condom on your way out the door, I don't think they'll be surprised."

She sent a quick text, asked if Callie had gone to bed without any trouble. Then as Griff had the heat going under the sauce again, and water on for the pasta, she channeled some of the giddiness into a quick additional text to Emma Kate.

Been at Griff's for two hours. We haven't eaten yet. Bet you can guess why. I'm just going to say WOW until I talk to you in person. Make that WOW twice. Shelby.

"What can I do?" she asked Griff.

"You can have that glass of wine we never really got to."

"All right." She picked up her phone at the signal. "It's just Mama saying Callie's sleeping like an angel and to have a good time. Oh, I forgot to tell you, Callie was a little put out she wasn't going on a date with you. I said we'd ask you on a date."

"Oh yeah?" He glanced back as he pulled the salad out of the refrigerator.

"Why don't I take care of that? Do you have a salad set so I can toss it?"

"Huh?"

"A couple of forks, then."

"I got those. What kind of date am I going to be asked to go on?"

"A picnic." She took the forks, the bottled Italian dressing, smiled back at him.

"Is that a cold fried chicken and potato salad picnic or an imaginary tea party picnic? That would determine the dress code."

"The first. I know a place. It's not a far drive, and a short hike after that. I was thinking Sunday afternoon, if that's all right."

"Two pretty redheads and food? I'm already there."

"She's awful fond of you, Griffin."

"It's mutual."

"I know that, it shows. I just want to say, she's had a lot of adjustments to make in a short time, and—"

"Looking for trouble, Red?"

"It kind of goes with the territory. You've got a kindness in you, Griff. That shows, too. I just want to say whatever happens with us, I hope you'll . . . well, I hope you'll still take her on a date now and again."

"I'm lucky to know four generations of Donahue/Pomeroy women. I'm crazy about every one of them, and not looking for that to change. Sass and strength, it runs right through all of you."

"I'm still hunting up pieces of mine."

"That's bullshit."

He said it so casually it took her a minute to look up, blink.

"Most people I know, and I might be one of them, would've been crushed flat finding themselves millions of dollars in debt, and through none of their own doing."

He'd have heard the details, she thought. That's how things worked. "I went along with—"

"I'm going to repeat myself. Bullshit. What you did was be young and impulsive and fall for the wrong man. As wrong as it gets, from where I'm standing."

"I can't say you're standing in the wrong place on that."

"Then instead of staying crushed when you find out fully how wrong, find yourself on your own with a kid and buried under a mountain of debt, you pushed up the weight and started hacking away at it. And that little girl? She's happy and confident because you made sure of it. I admire the hell out of you."

Staggered, she stared at him. "Well. Well, I don't know what to say to that."

"Plus you're really hot"—he dumped pasta in the boiling water— "which is no small appeal."

That made her laugh, go back to tossing the salad.

"You could answer a question for me, though, one that's bugged me awhile."

"I can try."

"Why'd you stick? You weren't happy, and it doesn't take much to deduce he wasn't much of a hands-on father with Callie. Why'd you stick?"

A fair question, she decided, under the circumstances. "I thought about divorce, more than once. And if I'd known all I know now . . . but

I didn't. And I didn't want to fail. You know my granny was just sixteen when she married my granddaddy?"

"No." It shocked the sensibilities. "I had to figure young, but that's a baby."

"They'll be married fifty years before much longer. Half a century, and you have to figure they had some rough times in there. Her mama was but fifteen, and she and my great-granddaddy were together for thirty-eight years before he was killed when a semi crashed into his truck and three others one night, the winter of 1971. My own mama was still shy of eighteen when she married Daddy."

"Women in your family stick."

"The men, too. Oh, there's been some divorces, and some of them bitter, cousins and aunts and so on scattered through. But I can trace a direct line back, seven generations of women I know of, and not one of them raised a child in a broken home. I didn't want to be the first."

She shrugged, picked up her wine again, determined to lighten the mood. "Now, it's true enough my great-great-granny on my mama's side had three husbands. The first died fighting a blood feud with the Nash clan. He was only about eighteen when—so it's said—Harlan Nash bushwhacked him and shot him in the back, leaving my great-great-granny with three children and another on the way. She married her first husband's third cousin, and had time to make two children with him before he died of a fever. Then she up and married a big Irishman named Finias O'Riley. She was about twenty-two, and bore him six more children."

"Wait, I'm doing the math. Twelve kids? She had twelve kids?"

"She did, and unlike a lot of women of her time and place, lived to the age of ninety-one. She outlived five of her children, which must have been a burden, and lost her Finias, who was sheriff around here, so Forrest comes by his tendency natural, when she was eighty-two and he eighty-eight. My great-granny, who lives in Tampa, Florida, with her oldest daughter, would say she— Her name was Loretta, but they called her Bunny always."

"Prophetic, considering."

With a snicker, Shelby lifted her glass again. "They say she might've married again, as she had a gentleman caller, a widower who'd bring her flowers every week, but he died before she'd made up her mind. I'd like to think I could draw a gentleman caller at that age."

"I'll bring you flowers."

"Then if I don't see you on my doorstep in sixty years, I'm going to be disappointed."

IT RELIEVED HIM that dinner was not only edible, but actually tasty. She entertained him with the story of Melody's eviction from the salon. He'd already heard a couple of versions, but hearing it from her, could visualize it perfectly.

"What's her problem anyway?"

"She's been a bully since I've known her. Spoiled, superior, with that mean streak you mentioned yourself. Her mama doted on her, and does still. Pushed her into all the beauty pageants, even as a little thing. And she won most of them, then sashayed all around being important."

"Sashayed. Not a word you hear every day."

"It suits. She almost always got what she wanted whenever she wanted it. Can't say she's shown any gratitude for it. She's hated me for as long as I can remember."

"Probably because she knew if you'd entered those pageants, you'd have beaten her little beauty-queen ass."

"I don't know about that, but I beat her out of some of what she wanted. Simple as that."

"Such as?"

"Oh, silly things—or they are now. A boy she wanted when we were about fourteen, and he liked me. She got Arlo Kattery to beat him up—I know she did, but Arlo wouldn't say. I made captain of our cheerleading squad—all through high school—and she wanted that. Grandpa fixed up this old clunker of a Chevy so I didn't have to walk home after practice. She spray-painted 'slut' and worse all over it. I know it was her, because when I called her on it, Jolene looked so damn guilty. Same as she looked guilty the night of the Homecoming dance when I got voted queen and the windshield of that old Chevy was busted up, and the tires slashed."

"She's sounding more pathological than annoying now."

"She's just mean. I guess some people are, and if they never pay a real price for it, they just get meaner. She doesn't worry me, especially since she's banned from the salon and day spa.

"You made a wonderful meal, Griffin. Maybe you are a good catch."

"I'm telling you."

"I'm going to help you put this kitchen back to rights, then I need to get on."

He traced a finger down her arm. "No way you could stay?"

He had those wonderful green eyes, those rough, skilled, thorough hands, and a way of kissing her that just put sparkles into her blood.

"It's tempting, because that porch is still out there. It's a lot more tempting than I thought it would be. But I wouldn't feel right, not going home tonight to Callie."

"Maybe I could have a pizza date with Callie between now and the picnic."

"Oh, that'd be nice, but I've got such a busy week. I need to rehearse, and—"

"I wasn't asking you." Still he leaned over, kissed her. "Any problem with me taking Little Red for pizza?"

"I . . . I guess not. She'd really like it." She rose, carried the plates to the sink. "Are you sure you want to take this on, Griffin?"

"Callie, or you?"

"We're a set."

"Nice set."

He distracted her with talk of plans for the house while they loaded the dishwasher. He liked running his ideas and plans by someone who understood them, saw the potential.

"The one thing you need, and before much longer, is a porch swing. You can't have a beautiful front porch like that and not have a front porch swing."

"Front porch swing, check. Back porch?"

"An old bench, maybe a rocking chair. You could sit and rock and look out at the gardens you worked so hard planting."

"I'm planting gardens?"

"With a wisteria arbor in my imagination, those pretty weepers." She dried her hands after wiping up his cooktop. "I had a wonderful time. I don't just mean . . . well, I wouldn't want to leave out the tour of the second floor."

He slid his arms around her waist. "I've still got a lot to show you."

She let herself melt in, just sink into the kiss. And pulled back with real regret. "I really have to go."

"Okay, but you're going to come back for the rest of that tour."

"I don't think I could resist it."

She picked up her purse; he plucked keys out of a dish on the counter.

"Oh, are you going out?" she asked as they walked to the front door.

"Sure. I'm following you home."

"Don't be silly."

"I'm not being silly. I'm following you home. Argue if you want, I'm still doing it. The woman who threatened you was shot less than a week ago right outside where you were working. You're not driving home alone after dark."

"I can't stop you from trailing me all the way home, then doubling back, but it's silly."

"Either way." He tugged her back for a kiss, then walked to his truck while she walked to her van.

Silly, she thought again, but sweet, too. He was just racking up all sorts of points.

Lord, she hadn't thought of the point system in years. She and Emma Kate had devised it in high school. Amusing herself, she began counting up Griff's.

Good-looking, scale of one to ten. She'd definitely give him a ten, she decided, and didn't think she was pushing the mark.

Conversation skills. Another ten there. He knew how to talk, how to listen.

Humor. Another winner. She made the turn onto the road, watched his headlights follow.

Considerate. Maybe even a little too much, such as wasting his time following her home on roads she'd traveled all her life.

Good kisser. Right off the scale. She rolled her window down, let the air cool the heat just thinking of it brought on. She could honestly say she'd never been kissed better.

What were the rest of the requirements for the perfect boyfriend? She must have them written down somewhere. They'd made them up before either one of them had had sex, so that hadn't been on the list.

The adult Shelby list would include it, and he'd top that scale, too.

She took the back roads, automatically skirting the town, taking the winding path, with Griff's headlights not far behind.

And all right, they made her smile. It wasn't such a bad thing to let someone look after her, just a little. As long as she remembered she needed to be in charge of her own life, and Callie's.

She pulled into the drive, noted her parents' bedroom lights were still on. When she got out, she thought she'd wave Griff off, but he was already getting out of his truck.

"You don't have to walk me to the door."

"Sure I do. That's how it's done. And if I don't walk you to the door, how am I going to kiss you good night?"

"I like the second part. The first time I was kissed at this front door, I was fifteen, and Silas Nash—a descendant of the infamous Nash clan— gave me one that had me floating through the door and dreaming of him half the night."

"I can beat that," Griff said after a moment. "I can beat some teenager named Silas."

"He's getting his law degree from the University of Tennessee College of Law."

"I can definitely beat a lawyer," Griff claimed, and to Shelby's mind, proved it.

"I guess I'm going to float upstairs and dream about you."

"All night." He gathered her hair into his fist, kissed her again until the world spun around her. "I'm not settling for half."

"Good night, Griffin."

"'Night."

He waited until the door shut, walked back to the truck. He'd do some dreaming of his own tonight, he thought. The woman had him wrapped. Everything about her struck home for him.

He glanced up, imagined her going in to check on Callie. And thinking of him, she'd better be thinking of him, when she undressed for bed.

He'd sure as hell be thinking of her.

He pulled out, and as she had, took the back roads.

No hurry, a lot to think about. Plans to make.

He had a pizza date with a pretty little girl to think about, and a picnic with her and her mother to look forward to.

Maybe he'd pick up a bottle of champagne, give the picnic a classy, unexpected edge.

He glanced in the rearview at the headlights behind him, and since he'd been dawdling, picked up the speed a little.

Apparently not enough, he thought, as the headlights beamed closer.

He waited for the truck—he could see it was a truck now—to pass since it was in such a damn hurry.

Instead it rammed him from behind hard enough to slap him against the steering wheel and back.

Instinctively he hit the gas. He thought of the phone he'd put, as always, in the cup holder, but didn't want to risk taking a hand off the wheel.

And the truck rammed him again faster, harder, sending him into a skid that had his tires smoking over the rough shoulder. Griff fought his truck back, but the next hit, right at the curve, sent him careening off the road, skidding over the shoulder and into the oak tree green with spring.

He heard the crunch, had a moment to think, Shit! Shit! before the airbag deployed. Still the impact slammed his head against the side window. He saw stars, and the red eyes of the truck's taillights as it stopped, idled, then punched it to round the curve.

"Not hurt," he mumbled, but the stars, and they had jagged, pointy edges, circled his vision. "Not too bad, nothing broken."

Except his truck.

He groped for the phone, watched his vision waver like he'd stuck his head underwater.

Don't pass out, he ordered himself.

In the dash light he managed to find the name he wanted, and pressed Dial.

"Where's my sister?" Forrest asked.

"Home. I'm not. I've got trouble. In case I pass out, I'm on Black Bear Road, about two miles from my place. You know that turn where the big oak stands?"

"Yeah."

"My truck's in that tree. Somebody ran me off the road. I could use a cop."

"Sounds like you could use a tow truck. You hurt?"

"I don't know." Jagged, pointy stars circling. "Hit my head. Bleeding some."

"Stay there. I'm on my way."

"Truck's in the tree. Where am I going?"

But Forrest had already hung up.

He sat for a moment, trying to get a fix in his mind on the truck that had run him off the road.

Chevy, yeah a Chevy, he thought. Half-ton pickup. Older model. Maybe four, five years. Something fixed on the front grille, like a . . . plow?

It hurt his head to think, so he stopped, fumbled off his seat belt, and discovered when he fought open the door and shifted, everything hurt a little.

The best he could do right now was sit on the side of the seat, breathe in the cool night air. He swiped at the wet on his face, saw blood smeared on his hand.

Fuck.

He'd have a bandanna in the glove box, but he wasn't going to try to get to it, not right at the moment.

Nothing broken, he reminded himself. He'd broken his arm once when he was eight and the tree branch he'd been swinging on snapped. And his wrist at seventeen jumping out of Annie's window.

So he knew what a broken bone felt like.

Just banged up, shook up and rattled around some.

But his truck—and goddamn he loved his truck—was a different matter.

He made himself stand to make sure he could. A little bit dizzy, but not bad. Bracing himself, he walked around to check out the damage.

"Shit! Fuck. Fucking shit!" Furious it was as bad as he feared, he shoved a hand through his hair. And saw stars again as he smacked against the wound.

The grille was toast, and the way the hood had accordioned, he thought the same there. And Christ knew what that meant for essentials under the damn hood.

He was no mechanic, but he was pretty sure he had a bent axle to top it off.

He'd hit hard, hard enough to spiderweb the windshield.

His feet crunched on broken glass as he circled around to get both the bandanna and a flashlight out of the cab. Flares, he thought. He should've pulled out the emergency flares straight off.

Before he could get anything, headlights cut through the dark.

Forrest pulled a police cruiser behind the wrecked truck. He got out, sized up Griff with one long look, then looked over to study the truck.

"Your head's bleeding, son."

"I know it. Son of a bitch." He kicked the rear tire, which he regretted as the quick violence pinged something in the back of his neck.

He did *not* have whiplash. He would *not* have whiplash.

"You been drinking, Griff?"

"I had two glasses of wine all night, and the second one a good hour before this. I got run off the damn road, Forrest. Fucker came up behind me, rammed me, kept doing it until he caught me on this curve and sent me into the tree."

"What fucker?"

"I don't know what the hell fucker." He pressed the heel of his hand— ouch!—to the throbbing wound because he was tired of blood running into his eye. "Half-ton Chevy, four, maybe five years old. Some sort of plow or farm tool—something hooked to the grille. Red, I think it was red. The truck. Plow was yellow, mostly. I think."

"Okay, why don't we sit you down a minute? I've got a first aid kit in the cruiser. Be best to stop that bleeding."

"I'll just lean here." And he leaned back against the tipped back of his truck. "Ah, something else . . ." He dug for it as Forrest went back to the cruiser. "He slowed down after I crashed. Just for a couple seconds, like he wanted to make sure I hit good and proper. Saw his taillights, and . . .

bumper sticker! Some kind of bumper sticker on the— What hand is this?"

He lifted his left, studied it for a moment before he could remember right from left.

"Left, the left side of the tailgate."

Griff closed his eyes, found that eased a degree or two of the throbbing. "He wasn't drunk. It was purposeful. I'm not sure when he pulled up behind me, but it wasn't long after I left Shelby at your parents' front door."

"You followed her home?"

"Yeah. I wasn't going to have her driving around after dark with what happened."

"Um-hm." Forrest set up flares; Griff closed his eyes again.

"I think the truck's totaled, or nearly. I've only had it three years. I've put a lot of miles on it, sure, but it had plenty more in it."

"We'll have my granddaddy take a look once it's towed in. You're lucid," Forrest added as he walked over with the first aid kit. "You haven't puked yet."

"I'm not going to puke."

"If that changes, aim away from me. How's the vision?"

"It wavered some at first. Steady now. Ow, fuck!"

"Don't be a pussy," Forrest said mildly, and continued to clean the laceration with an alcohol swab.

"You'd be a pussy, too, if I was being sadistic Nurse Sally."

"I can't see how bad it is until it's cleaned up some. Nurse Emma Kate's on her way."

"What? No. Why?"

"Because if she says you're going to the ER in Gatlinburg, that's where you're going. And since I have to deal with this mess you're in, she and Matt can haul you there."

"You called them."

"I did. I'll call for the tow after I have a look at what's what myself. Anything else you can tell me about the truck?"

"Other than whoever was driving it was—is—a lunatic?"

"You didn't see the lunatic, at all?"

"An impression—I'd say a guy—but I was pretty busy trying not to end up like I ended up. Or worse." Griff said nothing for a moment, studied his friend as Forrest fixed a couple butterfly bandages along the gash. "You know who it is, from what I gave you already."

"I've got an impression. That's for me to deal with, Griff."

"The hell it is. It's my truck, my head."

"My job. I expect that's Matt and Emma Kate coming now. You piss anybody off lately?"

"You're the closest I've come to pissing anyone off lately, since I'm sleeping with your sister."

Forrest stopped what he was doing, eyes sharply narrowed. "Is that so?"

"I figure it's a good time to let you know since you're being all official and I'm already bleeding. I'm crazy about her. Flat-out."

"It's a fast leap from nice to meet you to crazy about."

"She's a lightning bolt." Griff stabbed a thumb at his own heart. "Bam."

Before Forrest could speak again, Emma Kate was running from the car, a medical bag in her hand. "What happened? Let me look at you."

She pulled out a penlight, shined it. "Follow the light with your eyes."

"I'm okay."

"Shut up. Tell me your full name and today's date."

"Franklin Delano Roosevelt. December seven, 1941. A day that'll live in infamy."

"Smart-ass. How many fingers?"

"Eleven minus nine. I'm okay, Emma Kate."

"I'll tell you if you're okay after I go over you in an exam room at the clinic."

"I don't need—"

"Shut up," she said again, then hugged him. "Nothing against your triage, Forrest, but I'm going to take those bandages off at the clinic, get a look at that cut myself. It might need stitches."

"Nuh-uh," Griff said.

Matt stood, hands on hips, studying the truck. "Fucker trashed your ride, man. Forrest just said somebody ran you off the road. Who was it?"

"Ask Forrest. I think he knows from what I saw of the other truck."

"I'll be looking into it. For now, take him on into the clinic, look him over. I'll have it towed to my granddaddy's shop. You can come get what you need from it in the morning."

"My tools—"

"Are still going to be there in the morning. I need to call this in, but I've got your statement clear enough, and I'll call you if I need anything else. Nothing for you to do here, Griff, but be pissed off."

He argued but, outnumbered, ended up dragged to Matt's truck.

"He knows who did it and won't say." Bitterness coated Griff's throat.

"Because he knows you might be an easy guy most of the time, in this case you'd go straight for the ass-kicking." Matt shook his head. "Wouldn't blame you. But you're banged up already—disadvantage—and it'll be almost as satisfying if whoever did this spends time in a cell."

"He could spend time in a cell after I kick his ass."

"It was deliberate?" Emma Kate asked. "You're sure?"

"Oh, hell yeah."

"What were you doing on that road?"

"Coming back from seeing Shelby got home." Griff suddenly sat straight up. "Heading back from Shelby's house, and the other truck pulled up behind me—not long after I started back home. Because he was either sitting on her house or mine. Either sitting on hers or followed us from mine, waited his chance."

"You're thinking they came after you because they couldn't get to her?" Matt said.

"I'm thinking whoever did it isn't just a lunatic. I'm thinking worse. A lot worse."

18

Shelby started out the morning singing in the shower. She felt the spring to her step and didn't care who saw it or guessed the reason why.

She got dressed, helped Callie dress.

"You get to go to Granny's today."

"To Granny's house?"

"That's right. It's her day off, and she asked especially if you'd come over and stay with her. Won't that be fun?"

"Granny has cookies, and Bear."

Bear was the big yellow dog who'd race and play with a little girl all day—and sleep in the sun when nobody was around to play with.

"I know. And Grandpa's going to be there for a while, too. Your Gamma's going to take you over on her way to work. I've got some paperwork of my own to get to this morning. Then I'll come get you when I'm finished work today."

With Callie babbling about everything she had to take to Granny's, everything she had to do at Granny's, they walked into the kitchen.

Shelby's parents broke off their conversation immediately, and the quick look they exchanged set off Shelby's radar.

"Is something wrong?"

"What could be wrong?" Ada Mae said brightly. "Callie Rose, it's such a pretty morning, I decided we're going to have our breakfast on the back porch, like a picnic."

"I like picnics. I'm taking Griff on a picnic date."

"I heard about that. This can be like practice. I've got these pretty strawberries all cut up, and some cheesy eggs already scrambled. Let's take this on outside."

"Mama wants a picnic, too."

"She'll be right along."

Shelby stood where she was while Ada Mae scooted Callie out onto the porch.

"Something's wrong. Oh God, Daddy, did someone else get shot?"

"No. It's nothing like that. And I want to tell you right off, he's all right."

"He— Griff? It's Griffin." As her heart took a hard bump, she grabbed her father's hands. He'd stay steady, she knew, no matter what. "If it was Clay or Forrest, Mama'd be a mess. What happened to Griff?"

"He got a little banged up, is all. It's nothing serious, Shelby, you know I'd tell you if it were. Somebody ran his truck off the road, and into the big oak on Black Bear Road last night."

"Banged up how? Who did it? Why?"

"Sit down, take a breath." Turning, Clayton opened the refrigerator, took out a Coke. "He's got some abrasions from the seat belt, the air bag. And got a pretty good knock on the head. Emma Kate took him into the clinic last night, gave him a going-over, and I'm going to do the same myself later this morning. But if Emma Kate said he didn't need a doctor or the hospital, we can trust that."

"All right, I will, but I want to see for myself, too."

"You can do that," he continued in his calm way, "after you take that breath."

"It must've happened when he was driving home from here. He

wouldn't have been on the road if he hadn't insisted on following me back here, making sure I got home all right. I want to go over and see for myself, if you could keep Callie."

"Don't worry about Callie. He's not out at the house. He stayed the night at Emma Kate's as she wouldn't have him stay on his own."

"Good." She did manage that breath now. "That's good."

"But I expect he's on his way to the police station by now. Forrest and Nobby—you remember my second cousin Nobby—they went down the holler last night, and brought Arlo Kattery in."

"Arlo? He ran Griff off the road?" She pressed her fingers to her eyes. "Drunk, I expect, and driving crazy."

"I don't know as that's the way it was. You go on down. It's best you hear it straight-out, than the bits and pieces I have. And you tell Griffin he's got an exam at ten o'clock or he's not clear to drive or so much as touch a power tool."

"I will. Callie—"

"She's just fine. Go on."

"Thank you, Daddy."

When she ran out, leaving the Coke unopened on the counter, Clayton knew his little girl was at least halfway in love. With a sigh, he picked up the can, opened it for himself. It was smarter than a shot of whiskey at seven-thirty in the morning.

GRIFF STRODE INTO the station house, eyes—including the left one, where angry bruising had come to the surface overnight—hot. He arrowed straight to Forrest.

"I want to talk to the son of a bitch."

Forrest stopped tapping at his keyboard, pulled the phone from between his shoulder and ear. "I'll get back to you," he said, and clicked off.

"You'd best simmer down some first."

"I'm not in a simmer-down mood. I don't even know Arlo Kattery, never spoke a word to him in my life. I want to know why he deliberately ran me off the road."

"Forrest?" The sheriff spoke up from his office doorway. "Why don't you go ahead, let Griff go back and have his say," he said when Forrest hesitated. "In his place, I'd want mine."

"All right, thanks. Nobby, you think you could call back that fella at the lab, finish that conversation?"

"I sure can. That eye doesn't look too bad there, Griff." Nobby, a twenty-year vet, gave Griff's face a considering look. "Seen a lot worse. You get some raw red meat on it, won't be so bad."

"I'll do that."

As Griff turned toward the back, Shelby came flying in.

"Oh, Griff!"

"Now, Shelby honey, I was just telling him it wasn't that bad."

"It's not." Griff picked up Nobby's theme and ran with it. "I'm okay. It doesn't hurt." Ached like a son of a bitch, but didn't hurt.

"Daddy said it was Arlo Kattery. I don't know why the man has a license if he's still driving drunk like he did when we were teenagers."

"We don't know as he was drunk when he ran Griff off the road."

"He must've been. Why else would he do something like this?"

Forrest exchanged a look with the sheriff, nodded slightly.

"Why don't we go back and ask him? He was half drunk when Nobby and I went and got him, and tried to say he'd been home all night. The plow was still on his truck. Arlo gets paid to plow some of the private roads outside of town," he explained to Griff. "Hardly much reason for a snowplow on his truck in May. White paint on it, too. And yellow paint, like the plow, on the back of Griff's truck. Nobby and I informed him of those facts, so he claimed somebody stole his truck, put the plow on it."

"Bullshit."

"Knee deep in it," Forrest said with a nod to Griff. "Not too much use arguing with a man half drunk, and chasing his tequila with a joint, so we just hauled him in. And we left him last night to sleep on the fact we'd be charging him with attempted murder this morning."

"Oh my God." Shelby shut her eyes.

"That's the reaction we want from him. Attempted murder's a stretch," Forrest commented, hooking his thumbs in his belt. "But he'll surely go down for hit-and-run, reckless endangerment and so on."

"We can tie quite a few and-so-ons onto the package," Hardigan said.

"Yeah, I expect so. He's going to do a few years however it slices out. We've just been letting it sink in. The sheriff here, if I'm reading him correctly, thinks what's sunk in may come rising up if he's faced with the pair of you."

"That's a fine read, Deputy."

"All right, then. Let's see what we see. Y'all don't mention lawyer, all right? He hasn't gotten there yet in his pea brain."

Forrest led the way back through a steel door and the three cells.

In the center one, Arlo Kattery sprawled on a bunk.

She'd gotten a look at him that night at Bootlegger's—him and his pale-eyed stare. What she saw now didn't look much different than the last time she'd seen him in full light years before. Straw-colored hair shorn short, face grizzly with the pale blond scruff. Those small snake eyes— closed now—long neck with a tattoo of barbed wire circling it.

On the short side, and stocky, with scarred knuckles from countless fights—most of which he'd instigated.

Forrest let out a shrill whistle that made her jump, and had Arlo's eyes popping open.

"Wake up, darling. You've got company."

Eyes so pale blue they seemed almost colorless, skimmed over Griff, landed on her, slanted away again.

"Didn't ask for no company. You best let me out of here, Pomeroy, or your ass is in the fire."

"Looks to me like it's your ass smoking, Arlo. All Griff wants to know—and it's a reasonable request—is why you rammed his truck and forced him into that old oak tree."

"Wasn't me. Told you that already."

"Half-ton Chevy pickup, dark red, yellow plow on the front, bumper sticker on the bottom left of the tailgate." Griff stared at him while he spoke, saw Arlo's jaw twitch.

"Plenty fit that bill around here."

"Nope, not with the details. Funny bumper sticker, too. It's got a target on it full of bullet holes, and it says: 'If you can read this, you're in range.'" Forrest shook his head. "That's sure a knee-slapper, Arlo. Add that paint transfer, and it's all wrapped up. Nobby's out there right now talking to those forensic people over in the lab. Might take a little time, but they can match that yellow paint to your plow, that white paint to Griff's truck."

"That lab stuff is bullshit. More bullshit like all the rest of this."

"Juries set store by it, especially in capital cases, like attempted murder."

"I didn't kill nobody." Arlo surged up now. "He's standing right there, isn't he?"

"That's where 'attempted' comes in, Arlo. Tried and failed."

"I wasn't trying to kill nobody."

"Huh." Forrest nodded as if considering that, then shook his head. "Nope. Don't see a jury buying that one. See, we do what we call 'accident reconstructions.' And it's going to show that you deliberately and repeatedly rammed Griff's truck. Took some skill, so you won't be able to try for diminished capacity, saying you were drunk. That wouldn't buy you much time off anyway. I figure you're going down for about twenty here."

"No fucking way."

"Every fucking way," Griff disagreed. "Forrest, hum a tune and close your ears while I tell this asshole I'll swear on a mountain of Bibles in front of God and country that I saw him behind the wheel. I'll swear I counted the bullet holes in that idiotic bumper sticker and got his license plate."

"That's a fucking lie. I had the plates covered with burlap."

"You truly are a moron, Arlo," Forrest murmured.

"He's a fucking liar." Incensed, Arlo jabbed a finger between the bars. "He's fucking lying."

"You tried to kill me," Griff reminded him.

"I didn't try to kill nobody. It wasn't even supposed to be you. Was supposed to be her."

"You want to say that again, son?" Forrest's voice was quiet as the hiss of a snake, but Griff had already shoved forward, reached through the bars to grab Arlo's shirt, yanked him so his head smacked the bars.

"Now, Griff, I can't let you do that."

But Forrest made no move to stop him as Griff repeated the action.

"All right, that'll do. For now." Forrest gripped Griff's shoulder. "We don't want him getting off on some technicality, do we? Step back now."

"Why?" Shelby hadn't moved, not at the words, not at the vicious look Arlo had given her when he said them, not at the sudden violence. "Why would you want to hurt me? I've never done anything to you."

"Always thought you were too good for me, looking down your nose and turning your back to me. Ran off with the first rich guy you could rope in, didn't you? Heard that didn't work out so well."

"You'd've hurt me because I wouldn't go out with you back in high school? I've got a child. I've got a little girl, and I'm her only parent now. You'd have risked making my baby an orphan because I wouldn't go out with you?"

"Wasn't going to make nobody no orphan. Just going to scare you, is all. I was only going to teach you a lesson, put a scare into you. Wasn't my idea, anyway."

"Whose idea was it, Arlo?"

For the first time a hint of canniness came into Arlo's eyes. He shifted them from Forrest, back to Shelby, back to Forrest. "I got things I could say, but I want that immunization thing. I don't do no twenty years for what wasn't my idea."

"You give me a name, I'll consider that. You don't, I'm going to push for twenty-five. That's my sister, you idiot fuck. One thing you should know about right enough, is family. You tell me who started this ball rolling, or I'll make sure you go down for all of it, and hard."

"I gotta have some guarantee—"

"You get nothing."

"He'll get more than nothing," Griff said. "I'll find a way to get to you. I'll find a way. And when I do, you'll wish you'd had a chance to do twenty years."

"I never touched her, did I? Never laid a goddamn hand on her. Just going to scare her some anyway. She gave me a thousand dollars, said she'd give me a thousand more after I gave you a good scare, taught you a good lesson. Just going to give you a nudge off the road, is all, but you passed me going the other way. By the time I got turned around and going, I seen you head down to the old Tripplehorn place."

"You followed me."

"I had to wait, figured, fine, I'd teach you that lesson you had coming when you drove out again. Better when it was dark, right? But then he drives out behind you and I couldn't get to you. Didn't see why I should've wasted my whole night for nothing. Figured pushing him off would give you a scare.

"Northern boys, they're good enough for you, looks like. You jumped right in the sack with this one, but you never would give me so much as a long look. I seen him take your clothes off."

"You were watching." Too angry to be sickened, Shelby stepped closer. She knew, she knew just who'd paid him. "Did Melody Bunker tell you to spy on me, too?"

"She gave me a thousand dollars, said I'd get another. Didn't tell me how to go about it, just to get it done. Miss High-and-Mighty's real peeved at you, real peeved. She come right to my trailer in the holler, give me cash money. That's how peeved she is you got her kicked out of the beauty salon."

"I hope you got a good look, Arlo, and you take that with you to Bledsoe County and the cell you'll be occupying there. And when you do, you think about this, Arlo. I never thought along the lines of being too good for you. I just didn't like you."

She turned, started out. Forrest signaled for Griff to go with her.

"Hold on, Red."

"I can't hold on. I can barely breathe. I swear, if you hadn't rapped his head I'd have done it myself. He went after you because he couldn't get to me quick enough. He could've killed you."

"He didn't."

"If you hadn't followed me home—"

"I did." He took her by the shoulders. He didn't want the what-ifs playing in her mind, or his, not then and there. "He's locked up, Shelby. He'll stay that way."

"All this because Melody got her pride handed to her, and got it handed to her because she earned it. She knows full well what he might've done. She gave him money and an excuse to do it."

"I'd lay odds before the morning's up, she's in a cell right along with him."

"Those are good odds," Forrest said as he came out. "Just hold on a minute. Nobby, you think you could sit with that moron Arlo for a bit? I got him writing it all out."

"Sure can. He confess?"

"And then some. Sheriff, I need to run this by you, and then we're going to need a warrant. That's going to be pretty sticky as we're going to need it for Melody Bunker, for soliciting a crime, conspiracy to do bodily harm."

"Well, hell, Forrest." On a long, windy sigh, Hardigan rubbed the back of his neck. "Are you damn sure on it?"

"I'll tell you how Arlo says it went."

"He wasn't lying," Griff put in. "He didn't pull her name out of his ass. She gave him money for it, and he probably didn't have a chance to spend it yet."

"We'll be going out to his trailer," Forrest began, then glanced around. "Where's Shelby?"

"She . . . she was right here. Oh hell. Oh hell no."

"Melody. My sister's got a hell of a temper if you flip the right switch. Sheriff?" Forrest said as Griff was already bolting out the door.

"Yeah, go on with him. Just what we need to tie a ribbon on this day. Your sister tossing Florence Piedmont's granddaughter out some window."

SHE DIDN'T PLAN on tossing Melody out a window, primarily because she hadn't thought of it. She didn't have a clear idea what she intended to do, but the one thing she was clear on, she didn't intend to do nothing.

Ignoring the *bitch* hadn't worked, sarcasm hadn't worked, straight talk hadn't worked.

So she'd find something that did, and finish this off once and for all.

The Piedmont house sat on a long, sloping rise of lush green with terraced walls of white brick showing off a bounty of graceful trees, perfectly trimmed shrubs.

From its vantage it could look down at the Ridge, out at the hills, down into folds of valleys. It stood elegantly, as it had since before the War Between the States, laced with verandas flowing out from the snow-white facade. Gardens swept along its feet in rivers of color.

It was a house she'd always admired. Now she shot toward it like an arrow from a bow.

She knew Melody lived in the carriage house, aimed for it once she'd crested the rise. Ears buzzing with temper, she slammed out of the van, strode past Melody's car, and would have marched straight to the door if someone hadn't hailed her.

"Why, it's Shelby Anne Pomeroy!"

She recognized the housekeeper, a longtime member of the big house—and Maybeline's sister—and struggled to rein in her fury enough to smile in return.

"It's wonderful to see you, Miz Pattie. How is everything for you?"

"It's just fine." The woman, tall, thin, her salt-and-pepper hair in a tidy and tight cap of curls, walked over. She carried a basket half full of early roses. "Such a pretty spring we're having this year, even if the heat's already starting to rise. I'm so glad you're back home to enjoy it. I am sorry about your husband."

"Thank you. Miz Pattie, I really need to speak to Melody."

"Why, she's having breakfast on the back veranda with Mrs. Piedmont and Miz Jolene. I expect this has something to do with the trouble at Miz Vi's. I got an earful on it from Maybeline, and Lorilee, too."

"Yes, it's something like that."

"Then you go right around. I hope you girls can settle this."

"Settling it's why I'm here. Thank you."

She let the fury come back, bubble up as she took the walkway, crossed the velvety green lawn, as she heard female voices and smelled those early roses.

And there was Melody, sitting at a table draped with white, decked with pretty china and juices sparkling in glass pitchers.

"I am *not* going to apologize, Grandmama, so there's no point hounding me on it. I didn't say a thing that wasn't true, and I won't lower myself to crawling to *those* people just so Jolene can have her trashy hairdresser back."

"Crystal isn't trashy, Melody, and we shouldn't have—"

"You just stop it, Jolene, and stop that whining, too. I'm sick to death of it. If anything, that little slut and her interfering grandmother should—"

She spotted Shelby, pushed to her feet as Shelby came up the slope like a highballing train. Melody's eyes widened as she saw Forrest and Griff running full out behind her.

"You get out of here. You're not welcome here!"

"I say who's welcome here," Florence said in a snap.

"If she is, I'm not."

Melody started to turn away, but Shelby grabbed her arm, spun her around. "You paid him. You paid Arlo Kattery to try to hurt me."

"Get your hand off me. I don't know what you're talking about."

"You're a liar on top of it." Before she knew it was her clear intention, Shelby bunched a hand into a fist, and used it.

She heard shouting through the buzzing in her ears, saw through the red mist that blurred her vision Melody's eyes go glassy.

The next thing she knew someone clamped her arms down from the back, lifted her off her feet. She kicked out, because she wasn't done. She wasn't nearly done, but the arms only tightened.

"Stop it. Come on, Red, pull it in now. You gave her a good shot."

"It's not enough. It's not enough for what she did."

Melody sat on her ass, where she'd gone down on the graceful veranda. "She hit me! Y'all saw how she attacked me." Sobbing, she held a hand to her jaw. "I want to press charges."

"Fine," Forrest told her. "I think the ones against you are going to be a lot weightier."

"I didn't do anything. I don't know what she's talking about. Grand-mama, it hurts."

"Jolene, stop waving your hands around like you're going to take flight and go get an ice pack." Florence, who'd gotten to her feet, sat again, heavily. "I need an explanation. I need to know why this girl would come here, with these wild accusations, and strike my granddaughter."

"I'll say it," Shelby said before Forrest could. "Let me go, Griffin. I won't do anything. I apologize to you, Mrs. Piedmont. Not to her, but to you, I apologize. This is your home, and I should never have come here this way. I was too mad to think straight."

"Grandmama, make her go away. She belongs in *jail*."

"Be quiet now, Melody. It'll only hurt to talk. Why did you come here like this?"

"Because she went a lot further than saying ugly things, or slashing tires or making up lies. This time, she paid Arlo Kattery a thousand dollars, and promised a thousand more, if he put a scare into me, if he taught me a lesson."

"I never did any such thing. Why, I wouldn't lower myself to speak to Arlo Kattery or any of his kin. He's a liar and so are you."

"I said be quiet, Melody Louisa! Why would you say Melody did this?"

"Because Arlo ran Griffin off the road last night, wrecked his truck. Look at him, Mrs. Piedmont. He's hurt because he made sure I got home safe, and because he did, Arlo couldn't get to me and do what she'd paid him to do. He got to Griff instead. She went down to the holler, down to Arlo's trailer, and paid him to do it."

"She's crazy. A liar."

"Oh my God." Jolene stood just outside the French doors, a blue ice pack in her hand. "Oh my God, Melody, I didn't think you meant it. I never thought you meant it."

"You shut up, you hear! Don't you dare say another word, Jolene, not one more word."

"I won't shut up. I won't. My God, Melody, this isn't just playing, just gossip or poking some fun. I didn't think she meant it, I swear to God, I never thought she meant it."

"You hold your tongue, Melody. Meant what, Jolene?" Florence demanded. "Stop blubbering now and say it straight-out."

"She said, after Miz Vi banned us, she said she knew how to get back at Shelby. She knew how to teach her a lesson she wouldn't forget, and how Arlo would likely do it for free, but she'd sweeten that pot."

"Liar!" Scrambling up, Melody launched herself at Jolene, fingers curled to scratch.

She might've done considerable damage if Jolene, in shocked defense, hadn't thrown the ice bag at her.

The lucky shot knocked Melody back a step, and gave Forrest time to pull her back.

"You'd best listen to your grandmama, and hold your tongue. Jolene, let's hear the rest."

"What is *wrong* with you? What is the matter with you, Melody? I just don't know."

"You'd better shut your mouth, Jolene, or you'll be sorry."

"Jolene!" Florence's voice cut through Jolene's fresh weeping. "You tell Deputy Pomeroy the rest of what you know, and right now. If you don't be quiet, Melody, I swear to God Almighty, I'll slap you myself."

"Oh, Miz Florence. I told what she said, and I promise, I *swear*, I didn't believe she meant to do anything. I was so upset, and crying, and I just said to stop it, stop it, Melody, and went on about who was going to do my hair for the wedding because Crystal, she knows just how I want it done, and it's my wedding day, Miz Florence. I just was so upset, and Melody didn't say any more. But she'd said what I told you. I didn't think she could—"

"You traitorous bitch. She was part of it." Melody threw out a hand, pointed. "She was part of it."

"I wasn't, but maybe you can't believe that, Shelby, since I've been part of things. But never to really hurt somebody. I'm tired of it. I'm so tired of all of it."

She sat, began to weep into her hands.

"I'm sorry, Mrs. Piedmont, but I'm going to have to take these ladies into the station house and sort this out."

Her back straight as a poker, Florence nodded. "Yes, I can see that. Jolene, you stop that crying now and go on with Deputy Pomeroy. Melody, go with the deputy."

"I don't want to go with him. It's all just some story that lowlife made up, and Jolene's lying. She's just lying."

"I'm not lying!"

And that started the two of them shouting at each other until Forrest broke in. "I'd advise the two of you to be quiet. Melody, you can come along on your own, or I'm going to haul you."

"You take your hands off me this minute!" The threat had her struggling against his hold. "I don't go anywhere I don't want to go."

And her grandmother surged to her feet.

"Melody Louisa Bunker, if you don't go along with Deputy Pomeroy and stop resisting, you have my oath I'll do nothing to help you. I'll make certain your mama doesn't do a thing to help you."

"You don't mean that."

"By God, I do. You go with Forrest, and you go now, or I wash my hands of it, and you."

"I'll go. But now I know you're just as hateful as the rest."

"I'll take Melody," Forrest said to Griff. "Best if you take Shelby and Jolene. You're still deputized."

"Hell. All right. Jolene?"

"I'm coming. I won't give you any trouble. Shelby, I'm so sorry about all this. I'm just—"

"It's probably best, too, if everybody stays quiet on the ride in," Griff suggested, and got an easy smile from Forrest.

"Like I said, you ever want a career change. Melody, you walk to my cruiser under your own power, or I'll cuff you."

"Oh, I'm coming. You'll be out of a job before this day's over. I'm going to make sure of it."

Before he led Melody away, Forrest glanced at Florence. "I'm sorry about this, Mrs. Piedmont. I'm sorry for this trouble for you and your family."

"I know it." When she looked at Griff there might have been a gleam of tears in her eyes, but her back remained poker straight. "I'm more sorry about this than I can say."

19

Jolene wasn't quiet on the ride in, but cried in wild, gulping sobs all the way. With ears ringing, Griff decided all he really wanted in the world at that moment was to get back to work and sanity.

The only route he saw there was herding Shelby and Jolene into the station house.

Sheriff Hardigan looked at Griff, at the two women—Shelby, eyes hot, Jolene, eyes spewing tears. Stepping forward, he dug a large white handkerchief out of his pocket, pushed it into Jolene's hands.

He said, in a tone that miraculously blended cheer and sympathy, "Well now, what's all this?"

"Forrest is right behind us," Griff began.

"I'm probably under arrest." After slapping her hands on her hips, Shelby looked directly, defiantly into Hardigan's eyes. "I punched Melody Bunker in the face."

"Hmm," was Hardigan's response before he focused on Jolene.

"I didn't know she meant to do it!" Hysteria bubbled up through the hitching sobs. "I swear, I didn't. I thought she was just being mad and saying things. I didn't think she meant to really get Arlo to scare Shelby or hurt her. I swear I'm that upset about all of it."

"I can see that. Why don't you come on in and tell me about it. You got her?" he said to Griff, arched his eyebrows at Shelby.

"I guess."

"Deputized?" Shelby gave him one hard look as Hardigan led Jolene into his office.

"That's just Forrest being Forrest." But he was relieved when Forrest himself walked in with a cold-eyed Melody.

"Jolene?"

"Sheriff's talking to her."

"Good enough. You got her?"

At the repeated question, Griff winced. "Yeah, yeah."

Forrest escorted Melody into the back break room, walked out again. "Nobby, I need you to sit on her for a couple minutes while I sort some of this out."

"No problem there."

When Forrest turned to his sister, she held out her hands, wrists together.

"Stop that shit."

"Maybe you want your deputy to do it." When she turned with the same gesture to Griff, he just took her face in his hands.

"Cut it out. Now."

She bristled a moment, but he didn't let go, kept his eyes level on hers until she hissed out a breath. "I'm not mad at either of you—too much— and I'm sick about what happened to you, Griff. I'm just all-around mad. Am I under arrest?"

"It's not going to come to that," Forrest said. "Even if she pushes it, she's in a hell of a lot more trouble. She earned the punch."

"She surely did."

"Hell of a right cross you got there, Red."

"Thank you. Clay taught me, but it's the first time I actually put it into practice. What do I do now?"

"You leave this to me and the sheriff—like you should have before you stormed the damn castle. Not that I'm ever going to blame you for the punch—and go on to work, or home, or whatever business you got going."

"I can just go?"

"That's right. And if she pushes the assault charge, we'll deal with it. But I believe she's going to be persuaded to let that alone."

"All right." She could hardly stay mad at her brother if he wasn't going to arrest her. "I'm sorry for my part in this morning."

"No, you're not."

"No, I'm not. Not yet. But I might work around to it."

She walked out, paused when Griff walked out with her.

"None of this was my fault, and I'm pretty sick of taking responsibility for what I didn't do. But—"

"There's no but," he interrupted.

She shook her head. "But, there's no question I brought you trouble. I wouldn't blame you for stepping back. I'll be sorry and disappointed if you do, but I wouldn't blame you."

His answer was to take her face in his hands again, and this time to take her mouth as well. Long, serious and slow.

"That should settle that. I'm going to go see your dad now so I can get cleared and get the hell back to work."

She smiled a little. "The black eye looks kind of rakish."

"Just what I was going for. I'll see you later. It's been a hell of an interesting morning so far."

She supposed he could put it that way, she thought as she walked to the salon. But she'd dearly love a couple of boring mornings.

She figured word of some of the interesting morning—and the incident the night before that had generated it—would have reached the salon by now.

The way conversation stopped, eyes turned to her when she walked in told her she'd gauged correctly.

"How is that boy? How bad's he hurt?" Viola demanded.

"He's going to see Daddy now, but I don't think it's too awful. He's got cuts and bruises."

"I heard they hauled Arlo Kattery in for hit-and-run," Crystal put in. "And Lorilee here saw you driving hell-bent toward the big house a little while ago."

"You might as well say what Melody's got to do with all this," Viola told her. "Everybody's going to find out anyway."

"She paid him, she paid Arlo to do it."

After the collective gasp, Shelby dropped into a chair. She was early for work anyway, and God, interesting mornings were exhausting.

"Wait one minute." Eyes narrowed, Viola swiveled the chair so Shelby faced her. "You're saying Melody paid that Kattery boy to run Griffin Lott off the road? Why in hell would she do that?"

"She paid him to go after me, but Griff was in the way, so he went for him."

"After . . . after *you*? But that . . . Why—" Realization struck, chilled her blood so some of it drained out of her face. "Because I kicked her out of here."

"It's not on you, Granny, and it's not on me. It's not on either of us. Any of us."

"God knows she's spoiled as rotten fruit, and always had a bright streak of mean in her, but I'd never have expected her to try something like this."

"She gave Arlo a thousand down, with a thousand more when it was done."

Viola nodded. The color that came back into her face was high and hot. "Is she arrested?"

"They've got her at the station house, talking about it."

"They don't lock her up, I'm going to know why."

"I don't know what's going to happen, but it's going to be ugly, that's certain. And everybody might as well know the rest. I went up to the big house and I punched her in the face. I just saw red and punched her, knocked her flat. I'd do it again if I could."

More gasps even as Viola grinned. She leaned over, gave Shelby a hard hug. "That's my girl."

"I wish I'd seen you do it." Maybeline folded her arms. "It's not Christian to say so, but I wish I'd seen you do it, and taken a picture with my phone."

"Aunt Pattie says she gets hoity-toity and orders her around something fierce when Miz Piedmont's not around." Lorilee nodded sagely. "So I wish I'd seen it, too, but I'd've taken a video."

She walked over, gave Shelby a hug. "So don't you fret about it, Shelby. I know more people than I can count who'd've paid good money to see you knock that girl on . . . on her second-runner-up's ass. Right, Miz Vi?"

"Couldn't be righter, Lorilee."

"I won't fret." She patted Lorilee's hand. "But I'm going to start work early, if that's okay. Deal with towels and supplies and such. Clear my head some."

"You go on."

Crystal waited until Shelby went in the back. "What do you suppose Mrs. Piedmont's going to do about all this?"

"I guess we'll wait and see."

They didn't have to wait long.

In the mid-afternoon lull—when stay-at-home mothers picked up their kids from school, or greeted them at the door, before those who worked outside the home could run in for an after-work cut and color or massage—Florence Piedmont stepped into Vi's.

Once again, the salon hushed like a church. Florence, all dignity in a navy blue dress and sensible shoes, nodded at Shelby, who manned the front counter, then Viola.

"Viola, do you have a few minutes to speak with me? Privately. You and Shelby."

"Of course we do. Shelby, do we have anyone in the Relaxation Room?"

"Ah . . . we shouldn't have. We have three coming in for treatments in about an hour, and two in treatments right now."

"That's fine, then. We'll go on back here, Florence, where it's nice and quiet. Crystal, when my three-thirty comes in, you set her up with a magazine."

"I appreciate the time, Viola."

"You'd make it for me." Viola led the way back, through the locker area. "We've known each other a lot of years."

"We have, a lot of years. How is your mama, Vi?"

"Feisty as ever. And how's yours?"

"Slowing down some. But she dearly loves living in Florida. My brother Samuel looks in on her every day."

"He always had a sweet heart. You have a seat now."

"Thank you, Vi, I could use one. I'll tell the truth and say I'm tired to the bone."

"We have some nice peach tea, Mrs. Piedmont. Hot or cold," Shelby added. "Could I get you some?"

"I would love some hot peach tea, thank you, if it's no trouble."

"Not a bit. Granny?"

"That'd be nice, darling, thank you."

"This is a lovely room, Viola. So peaceful and calming. You always had a clever mind, and a way of turning what worked in it into something fine."

"That's a nice thing to hear. Everybody needs somewhere peaceful and calming now and again."

"We could all use more of it, to my mind. What color paint have you got on these walls?"

"It's called Twilight Gold. Pretty name."

"It is. Peaceful," she said again, like a sigh. "Viola, Shelby, I'm going to start by saying I'm going to speak to Griffin Lott when I leave here. But I wanted to speak to the two of you first. I should've asked if Ada Mae could take a minute."

"She's doing a facial. It's all right, Flo. We'll tell her what you want to say to her."

"I want to apologize to all of you. To your daddy, too, Shelby, your daughter, your brothers. To Jackson, Viola."

"Mrs. Piedmont, ma'am, you don't have anything to apologize for."

"I ask you to accept an apology from me."

"Of course." Shelby carried over the tea, in its pretty cups.

"Thank you. Would you sit, too? I've just come from the police station. Melody has admitted to going to Arlo Kattery, to giving him money to cause you trouble, Shelby. I'm not sure she'd have admitted it this soon, but they had three people already who saw her driving up to his trailer in the holler. And though it pains me to say it, I wouldn't get her a lawyer until she told the truth."

Saying nothing, Viola just reached out, took Florence's hand.

"I don't know what she thought would happen, or why she'd do something so mean, so reckless. I don't know why she's always been so jealous of you, Shelby. When you were voted head cheerleader back in high school, she had hysterics, begged me to make a big donation to the athletic department if they'd take you down, put her up. And when you were Homecoming queen over her, she came home and cut her dress to ribbons."

Florence sighed. "She's angry most of the time, it seems. I'd hoped by putting her in charge of The Artful Ridge, having her live in the carriage house, she'd be happier, start being more responsible. But I know, I see now, I indulged her too much all along. And her mama did even more."

"She's my grandchild, my first granddaughter, and I love her."

"Of course you do."

"I overlooked too much over the years, but I won't overlook this. She caused someone true harm, and it could have been much worse. She did it for spite. She'll pay a price for that spite. I have no right to ask, and none to expect, but she's my granddaughter, so I will ask. The sheriff indicated, if you and Griffin Lott are amenable, if you agree, instead of going to jail . . ."

For the first time Florence's hand shook, so she set the teacup down carefully in its saucer.

"She could serve six months in a rehabilitation center, a private one, where she would have therapy for her various issues. She would be required to work there—chores, I suppose. Cleaning, gardening, laundry, that sort of thing. Then, if deemed ready, she would serve another six months' community service in a halfway house, with a year's probation to follow that.

"I won't pretend it's prison," Florence continued. "But she would be restricted, get therapy I feel she desperately needs, and be required to follow set rules. She would lose her freedom, and that's a kind of prison. And if she refuses to abide by the terms, the rules, then she would face prison. Her mother will try to fight me on this, but her father . . . I've already spoken to my son-in-law. We spoke at some length, and he will back me on this."

Steadier, Florence picked up her tea again. "It's your granddaughter and mine, Vi. Who would have thought we'd come here?"

Once again Viola took her hand. "Life's full of hard bumps and slick twists. We do the best we can to drive it, start to finish."

"Some days, best isn't near to good enough. You'll want time to think about this, Shelby."

"It's not that . . . it's Griff she hurt, or hurt through what Arlo did."

"It's you she meant to."

"All I want, I swear to you, Mrs. Piedmont, is for her to leave me and mine alone. I have a child to think of. I have a life to try to rebuild with my little girl, and I just want Melody to leave us be. If Griffin's all right with what you said, I would be. He's the one who ended up being hurt, whatever she meant."

"I'll speak to him, and we'll all abide by his decision. I'm sick at heart he was hurt this way, that someone in my family would have caused it. I wonder, Viola, if you know from Jackson how much damage there is to the boy's truck."

"What Jackson told me just a bit ago on the phone, it's a loss."

"Oh, Granny."

"Well, most anything can be fixed, but Jack says it wouldn't be fixed right enough, and expects the insurance company to agree and total it out."

"I'll make it right. You have my word on it."

"I never had any doubt on that, Flo."

"I know you're both busy, and I thank you so much for taking this time, and for your understanding. For your kindness."

"I'm going to walk you out," Viola said, sliding an arm around Florence's waist as they both rose. "And I'm going to give you a brochure so you can think about coming back for a nice hot stone massage or a Restore Youth Facial."

Shelby heard Florence laugh as they walked out. "It's a late hour for restoring youth, isn't it, Viola?"

"It's never too late an hour, Flo. Never too late an hour."

IT SEEMED TO Shelby the best thing to do was keep her head down and take each day as it came. She'd been far too much front and center on the gossip stage since her return to the Ridge. Experience told her some other news or interest would come along soon enough.

She felt just fine being front and center Friday night, performing doo-wop and rock and fifties ballads. The crowd seemed to feel just fine about it, too, and nobody got shot.

And since Callie was having a sleepover at Granny's, topping Friday night off in Griff's bed felt even more than fine.

Before and after her Saturday job, she hit her spreadsheet hard, meticulously paying bills, doing careful math.

And shaking her clasped hands at the ceiling when she paid off another credit card.

Three down, nine to go.

Straight after Sunday breakfast, she stood at the stove frying up chicken and listening to Callie squeal with delight while she played with the much-loved bubble maker.

Ada Mae came in, hugged Shelby from behind. "That's the best sound in the world."

"I know it. She's so happy, Mama, it turns my heart inside out."

"And how about you?"

"I'm about as happy as a little girl with a bubble machine."

"You were in fine voice Friday night, baby girl. And so pretty up there in that blue dress."

"I'm going to have fun with the sixties. I've been playing around some for next week. Tansy told me they're going ahead for sure with that expansion. That'll be exciting."

"Good thing Griff and Matt are all but done here. I love my new bathroom like Callie loves her bubble maker."

To demonstrate, Ada Mae did a neat pirouette and had Shelby grinning.

"They're handy men. A handy man's worth his weight in gold. You must've had a nice time after."

Heat rose up the back of Shelby's neck. "I did. Mama, you didn't wait up, did you?"

"It's not a matter of waiting up. You have a child under your roof—whether she's fourteen or forty—you hear that car pull up the drive. And don't even think about saying you're sorry. It put a smile on my face thinking about you being with a good man. He puts a smile on your face, too."

She knew just where her mother was going. "He does. I can admit I didn't see myself having a nice time with *any* man for a long time yet. As it is, it's a pretty surprise. Still, I can't think past next week, not yet."

"That's all right. You take your time, give him a good test-drive."

"Mama!"

"You think your generation invented sex? And you're doing the sixties next week? That generation likely figured the same. Speaking of test-driving, I heard Florence Piedmont bought Griff a new truck."

"He said she wouldn't take no, turned it around so it felt like he'd be insulting her if he refused. Grandpa's going to strip the wrecked one for parts, and Griff's having the new truck painted with the logo."

She paused as she drained some of the chicken.

"Did we do the right thing, Mama? Letting Melody get off with going to that rehabilitation center, anger management therapy and the like?"

"Next thing to a country club, I expect, and that just chafes my thighs. But down under it, I think it was the right thing. I don't know as she'll be coming back here, at least not for some time. I do know Miz Florence isn't holding her job."

"Oh."

"And I expect you could have that job, if you wanted it."

"I . . . No. I think I like just how things are. I like working at Granny's, I like the girls and the work and the customers. I like knowing if something came up, nobody'd be upset if I had to take off to deal with it. And I do know, for certain, I wouldn't want Melody's old office, her old job, her old anything. Just . . . bad juju. You know what I mean, Mama?"

"I do. You've got your granny's hand with fried chicken, girl. If you don't want to look past next week yet, you'd better be careful. Chicken like that could drive a man to propose marriage."

"I think I'm safe there."

And safe, Shelby thought, was where she needed to be.

At noon when Griff pulled up in his rental truck, she had the hamper loaded and ready, and Callie in her yellow dress with a ribbon in her hair. She'd opted for jeans and her old hiking boots.

Callie rushed out before Griff got to the door, and launched herself at him.

"You look like a picnic, Little Red."

"I got a bow." Callie reached back to where the yellow ribbon trailed.

"I see that. Pretty as they come, and so's your mom. Here, let me take that."

"You've already got her. We'll take my van since I know where we're going. I've got the blankets in there already."

"I've just got to get a couple things out of the truck."

He strapped Callie in her car seat—expertly, Shelby noted. You didn't have to show the man something twice. He walked to his rental truck, came back with a tote bag. "Contributions," he said, and put them in the van with the hamper.

"I'm hoping this spot is as pretty as I remember. It's been a while."

She drove toward town, then veered off on a back road, just skimming by the holler while Callie chattered like a magpie. As she took the rise, navigated the switchbacks, it all came back to her. The sights, the smells.

The color.

Winding through the greens, the browns, yellow trillium and crested iris splashed, while the delicate trumpets of columbine played in dappled sunlight. There, or there, mountain laurel brightened the shadows, and lady's slippers danced.

"Pretty. It's pretty country," Griff said when Callie shifted to conversation with the ever-present Fifi.

"It won't be long till the wild rhododendrons pop out. I just love the green of it. The endless, rising green of it, and how the color from wildflowers comes and goes."

She passed a little farmhouse where a boy about Callie's age rolled on the scrubby grass with a yellow dog.

"See the puppy! Mama, when can I have a puppy?"

"Her newest obsession," Shelby said under her breath. "Once we get our own house, we'll think about that. We're almost to our picnic spot," she added, hoping to block the litany of follow-up questions.

She turned onto a narrow dirt road, bumped carefully along it. "This belongs to that little farm we just passed. Daddy's delivered three babies in that house—might be more now since I've been gone—and made house calls for the grandmother until she passed. The family lets us use this road, and have picnics or hike back here. They set great store by my daddy."

"So do I, since he cleared me to work."

"Your eye's looking some better."

"I kissed it better, Mama, when I had my pizza date with Griff. Are we there yet?"

"We're as far as we can drive." She angled into the pull-off. "It's not very far to walk. About a quarter-mile. It's a little steep, though, and likely a little rough."

"We're up for it."

He settled the logistics by hauling Callie up on his shoulders, taking the hamper. "Bag and blankets for you," he told Shelby. "It's so quiet here."

He spotted a bold red cardinal watching them from a perch on a hawthorn tree.

"That's not even the best part."

"Nobody's going to come out with a shotgun?"

"I asked Daddy to check if it was okay, and the family's fine about it. We leave the land as we found it, that's all. Though they might have discouraged revenuers that way, back in the Prohibition days. Plenty ran whiskey out of the hills and the hollers. My people among them—both sides."

"Bootleggers." It made him grin.

"It'd be hard to find a handful of people with native roots who didn't have bootleggers on the family tree."

"It was a dumbass law."

"Dumbass," Callie repeated, predictably.

"Sorry."

"It's not the first time. That's a grown-up word, Callie."

"I like grown-up words." When she screamed, Griff shoved the hamper at Shelby, started to whip Callie down.

"A bunny! I saw a bunny rabbit!"

"Jesus—jeez," Griff corrected. "You scared the . . . heck out of me, Little Red."

"Catch the bunny rabbit, Griff! Catch it."

"I didn't bring my bunny rabbit catching tools." With his heart still hammering, he took the hamper back, continued the climb.

When he topped the rise, he saw every step of the climb had been worth it.

"Okay, wow."

"It's just like I remembered. The stream, the trees, especially that big old black walnut. And just enough opening up so you can see some of the hills and valleys."

"You're in charge of all the picnic spots, from this day forward."

"Hard to top this one, unless it's at your place."

When he put Callie down, she bulleted straight for the stream.

"Callie, don't go close to the edge," Shelby began, but Griff grabbed her hand and pulled her to the stream.

"Cool." He crouched down beside Callie. "Look at all the little waterfalls. The shiny rocks."

"I wanna go swimming!"

"It's not deep enough for swimming, baby, but you can take your shoes and socks off, put your feet in. You can go wading."

"'Kay. I can go wading, Griff!"

Callie plopped down, attacked her shoes while Shelby spread blankets beside the stream with its tumbling water, mossy logs, thickening ferns.

"Not worried about her getting the dress wet?" Griff asked.

"I've got a change for her in the bag. I'd like to know a little girl who wouldn't want to splash in this stream."

"You're a pretty cool mom."

While Callie stepped in to splash and squeal, Griff pulled the bottle, wrapped in its frozen cozy, out of his bag.

"Champagne?" After a surprised laugh, Shelby shook her head. "That's going to put my fried chicken to shame."

"I'll be the judge of that."

She drank champagne, had the satisfaction of seeing Griff devour her chicken. She let Callie run off some energy chasing butterflies or going back for another splash.

And relaxed, as she realized she hadn't, not really, since the morning she'd faced Arlo Kattery with bars between them.

And he'd have that view, she thought, through bars, for a long, long time.

But she had this—the green and the blue, the chirp and twitter of birds, the sun streaming through the trees to play shadows on the ground as her little girl played in the stream.

"You're definitely hired," Griff told her when he went back for another piece of chicken, another scoop of potato salad.

"Sitting here, it seems like nothing's wrong in the world."

"That's why we need places like this."

She reached out, trailed her fingers over the healing cut on his forehead. "Forrest said they still haven't caught that Harlow person, and it makes me think he did what he came to do, and he's long gone from here."

"Makes the most sense."

"Then why'd you follow me home at two in the morning on Friday night?"

"Because that makes sense to me, too. When are you going to let me follow you home again?"

Oh, she'd just been hoping he'd ask. "I guess I could see if Mama's okay watching Callie one night this week."

"Why don't we go to the movies, then back to my place for a while?"

She smiled, thinking she had this, too. A movie date with a man who made her belly flutter. "Why don't we? Callie, if you don't eat your picnic lunch, there won't be a cupcake in your future."

Shelby marked it as a perfect Sunday afternoon, and driving back with Callie fighting sleep in the back, wondered how she could prolong it.

Maybe she'd see if Griff wanted to sit out on the porch while Callie napped. Or she could see if Emma Kate and Matt wanted to come over, and they could do up some burgers on the grill for supper later.

"I guess you've got things to do at your house."

"There's never a lack of things to do at my place. Why? Do you have something else in mind?"

"I was thinking, if you wanted to stay awhile, I'd see if Emma Kate and Matt wanted to come by later on. Have some wine, and grill some burgers."

"More food? How could I say no?"

"I'll see if it's all right with Mama and Daddy, then . . ."

She trailed off as she pulled up to the house, saw her mother already running out.

"Oh God, what could've happened now?" She shoved out of the van. "Mama."

"I was just about to text you. Gilly went into labor."

"Oh, just now?"

"It's been a few hours, but they didn't say until they were heading in to the hospital. Daddy—my daddy's got Jackson already. Daddy—your daddy—and I are heading into Gatlinburg to the hospital right now, and Forrest is bringing your granny. Clay says she's moving fast. Oh, I don't know why babies always put me in a tailspin."

"It's exciting, and it's happy."

"You should go," Griff said. "You should be there."

"Oh, I don't want to put two preschoolers on my grandfather on his own."

"I'll take her. I've got Callie."

"Oh, well, I—"

"I wanna go with Griff! Please, Mama, please. Griff, I wanna go to your house. Can I go to your house and play?"

"That would be the nicest thing," Ada Mae said. "Shelby couldn't be here when Jackson was born. It would sure mean a lot to us, Griff."

"Done."

"Yay! Yay!"

Shelby looked at her daughter's shining face. "But it could be hours."

"Not if Clay's any judge. Clayton, you come on now!" Ada Mae shouted. "I'm not going to miss my grandbaby's birth because you're dawdling. Griff, thank you so much. Callie, you be good for Griff now, or I'll know the reason why. Clayton Zachariah Pomeroy!" Ada Mae marched back toward the house.

"Are you sure? Because—"

"We're sure, right, Callie?"

"Right! Let's go, Griff." Thrilled, she rubbed both her hands over his cheeks. "Let's go to your house now."

"Let me just . . ." Think what to do, Shelby mused. "I'll just run in, get some things for her to play with."

"I've got scissors and sticks for her to run with, and all those matches."

"Aren't you the funny one? Give me two minutes. And, well, you'd best just take my van in case you have to go somewhere with her. If I can borrow this truck."

"It's a rental. What do I care?"

"All right, then, all right. Two minutes. No, it'll take me five. Five minutes."

She raced toward the house as her mother came out dragging her father.

"Ada Mae, I'm a doctor, and I'm telling you, there's plenty of time."

"Oh, don't doctor me. You tell me about plenty of time when you've given birth. We're going, Shelby!"

"I'll be behind you in five minutes. I know how to get there."

Griff leaned back against the van beside Callie's window. "We're going to have some fun, Little Red."

20

They did have fun.

Griff fashioned a monster face out of cardboard and, donning it, chased a thrilled Callie around the front yard. She brought him down with the magic wand he cobbled together from some tubing and more cardboard.

As the restored prince, he answered the first text from Shelby.

At the hospital now—everything's going well. Okay there?

He considered for a moment.

We're great. We're heading out now to find some traffic to play in.

He took Callie in for a Coke, and judged by her wide, shiny eyes Coke wasn't something on her usual beverage menu. It took a solid half hour to run off her Coke high. Breathless and wiser, he loaded the kid back in the van and took her for a quick drive for a pack of juice boxes.

That had to be a better option.

He spotted the sign **Pups For Sale**, decided a stop there would entertain her for a while, and pulled up in front of the compact rancher next to the little market.

Following the arrow on the sign, he took the gravel path around the back.

In a kennel, clean and dry, three cream-colored pups and one brown pup came instantly to life, yipping, racing toward the fencing, wagging chubby bodies.

Callie didn't squeal and rush toward them as he'd expected.

She gasped, then pressed both hands to her mouth.

Then she turned her head, tipped her face up to Griff's. And her eyes were full of wonder and love and immeasurable joy.

He thought, Oh shit, what have I done?

Then she threw her arms around his legs, squeezed. "Puppies! I *love* you, Griff. Thank you, thank you."

"Well, ah, listen . . . I thought we'd just—"

While he fumbled, she tipped her face up again, all but blinded him with her shining joy before she broke off to, at last, rush the fence.

A woman, a baby on her hip, a red kerchief tied around her hair, stepped out of the back door of the rancher.

"Afternoon," she said while the baby eyed him suspiciously.

"Hey. We were just at the market, and I thought she'd get a kick out of seeing the pups."

"Why, sure. You want to go in, honey? They're as friendly as they can be. Three months old now," she continued as she opened the gate for Callie. "Had a litter of eight. Mama's our Lab-retriever mix Georgie, and the daddy's my cousin's chocolate Lab."

Callie ran in, dropped, and was immediately buried in puppies.

"That's a happy sound, isn't it?" the woman said as Callie's giggles mixed with the yips and fake growls.

"Yeah . . . but—"

"They're a good mix with kids, Daddy," she said with a smile as she juggled the baby. "Gentle and loyal and playful."

"Oh, I'm not her father. Her mother's sister-in-law's having a baby, pretty much now, so I'm watching Callie for a while."

"Griff! Griff, come see. Come see the puppies."

"Yeah, okay."

"You go on, take your time. She's got a good way with them. Lot of kids her age want to pull tails and ears or cart a pup around in a choke hold, but it looks like she knows how to be gentle and playful. They're going to go fast now," she added, as the baby decided Griff passed muster and offered a wide, drooling grin. "I just put the sign up this morning. The first four were already spoken for. I don't sell them till they're full weaned, had their shots and the vet clears them."

"I'm not really . . . I mean, I thought about getting a dog. Later. Once I've got my place more under control."

The woman narrowed her eyes. "You're the one bought the old Tripplehorn place. The one who works with Emma Kate's boyfriend. Emma Kate and Doc Pomeroy delivered Lucas here right in the exam room at the clinic. I went in for my checkup, and he got in a powerful hurry then and there. Wasn't time to head to the hospital. Is that Shelby Pomeroy's little girl?"

"Yeah."

"I should've figured from the hair. You decide you want one of the pups, I'll do half price, seeing as the little girl's granddaddy and your partner's lady helped bring my boy into the world."

"Oh, well . . . that's—"

"Griff, come play with the puppies!"

"You go on. I'll be around."

He took the brown dog.

He drew the line at Callie's helpful name suggestions. He would not name his dog Fifi in honor of her best stuffed friend. Or Donkey in honor of Shrek's best pal.

He hit on Snickers because of the chocolate, then had to go back to the market and buy one so Callie got the connection. He had to buy puppy food, a dish, a leash, a collar, dog treats.

By the time they loaded up again, with the puppy exploring the inside of the van, Griff's ears were ringing.

Shelby's next text came through as he lifted Callie out of the van, and she and the pup took off running.

Gilly's doing great. She'll be pushing soon. Nearly there. Let me know how it's going if you're done playing in traffic.

He started to text about the puppy, even though it all felt a little bit like a dream, then opted against.

Playing in traffic made us hungry. We want a snack so we're going to hunt up strangers with candy. Go Gilly.

Babies come in their own time, and Beau Sawyer Pomeroy came into the world at seven-eleven—a lucky hour, according to his daddy—at a healthy seven pounds and twelve ounces. Shelby took time to admire him—the spitting image of her brother—dig out more tissues for her mother, and hug the proud parents.

She sent another quick text: *It's a boy! Beau Sawyer's beautiful, Mama and Daddy happy and well. On my way back soon.*

By the time she managed to say all her goodbyes and navigate traffic out of Gatlinburg, the sun sat low. She considered stopping to text again, see if Griff wanted her to pick up any food, but decided surely they'd eaten something by now.

She pulled up beside her van, thought, What a day.

When no one answered her knock, she had a moment of concern, ordered it away. Easing the door open, she called out, then cocked her ear at the familiar sounds.

Shrek.

Shaking her head, she started back toward the great room.

Shrek and Donkey argued on the big screen. On the sofa, her little girl lay sprawled over Griff. Both of them were sound asleep.

She nearly screamed when something wet and cold hit her ankle. Looking down, she saw a fat brown puppy who immediately attached its teeth and interest to the laces of her hiking boots.

"Oh, no you don't." She picked up the pup, gave it a long look. "Just where did you come from?"

"Right down the road," Griff said, opening sleepy eyes.

"Whose dog is it?"

"I guess it's my dog. It just sort of happened. Snickers."

"I'm sorry, what?"

"His name. Snickers. Chocolate Lab–golden retriever mix."

"He couldn't be cuter." Amused, charmed, she cuddled the pup in while he lapped lovingly at her chin. "Did you look at the size of his feet?"

"No. Not especially."

"You're going to have one big dog here." She smiled as Snickers switched to her cheek, wiggled happily in her arms. "Which one wore you out? Callie or the dog?"

"I think we wore each other out. Baby world okay?"

"It's perfect. Beau Sawyer, if you didn't get my last text. Healthy, beautiful, and the family's all beaming. I can't thank you enough, Griff, for keeping Callie so I could be there. It meant the world to me."

"We had fun. What time is it?"

"It's about eight-thirty."

"Okay, we probably crashed about twenty minutes ago."

"Did you get something to eat? I should've—"

"There was chicken left from the picnic," he interrupted. "And I did some mac and cheese because you can't go wrong. Had some frozen peas I mostly use as an ice bag, but they worked."

He stroked Callie's back as he spoke, as he shifted. She rolled over like a bundle of rags.

"She's out."

"It's been a happy day for her. Me, too." She set the dog down, and he bounced to Griff, went for the laces. Griff scooped the pup up in one arm, looked around and found the chew rope he'd made out of old cord. "Try this," he suggested, and set the dog down with it.

"Did she talk you into that dog?"

"She didn't have to say a word." He glanced back where Callie slept, butt hiked in the air, one arm wrapped around Fifi. "It's all in the eyes. I planned to get one, more like in the fall. Get a little more done around here first. So I just shifted up the timeline. Plus, he was on sale. Do you want some food? There's still some mac and cheese. The chicken's just a fond memory."

"No, thanks. We ate here and there at the hospital. I need to get her home and in bed."

"Maybe you could stay."

Tempting, so tempting when his arms slid around her.

"I'd like that, and suspect Callie would, too. But not yet, Griff. Not quite yet."

She could prolong the moment, her mouth on his. Then her head on his shoulder. "It's been a good day."

"Red letter."

He picked Callie up. She lay boneless over his shoulder while Shelby gathered the hamper, the bag. The dog raced out the door ahead of them, ran circles around the yard while Griff fixed Callie in her seat.

He watched them drive off with the western sky taking on the color of her hair. Then there was quiet.

He liked the quiet, he reminded himself, or he'd never have bought a place so far out of town. But it felt *seriously* quiet after hours of a little girl's chatter.

He looked down to where Snickers was busy attacking his laces.

"Cut that out." He had only to shake his foot. "Let's make the rounds."

They made the rounds again twice more before midnight. He'd worked too hard on the floors he'd refinished to have them ruined by a puppy.

Considering sleeping arrangements, he fashioned a temporary dog bed out of a box, some old towels, and tied another towel into a puppy-like shape. Snickers wasn't immediately sold, but the excitement of the day did its work. With the pup as conked as Callie had been, Griff considered it a job well done, and dropped into bed himself.

He didn't know what woke him. The clock read two-twelve, and when he checked by the flashlight app of his phone, Snickers remained curled in a ball in his box.

Though he opted to let sleeping dogs lie, something felt off. Off enough for him to walk quietly out of the bedroom. Listen.

Old houses groaned and creaked, he thought—he knew it well. And still he eased open a door, picked up a pipe wrench. Flipping on lights as he went, he started downstairs.

And there, just that . . . a faint click. A door closing.

He moved quickly now, straight toward the back and the glass doors.

He hit the lights, hit the outside floods.

He'd be spotlighted, but if anyone was out there, so would they.

He saw nothing, no movement.

Had he locked the back doors? He didn't think so, as he rarely thought to. And with taking the pup in and out, he likely hadn't.

He stepped out on the back porch, filtering out the night sounds, the breeze, the mournful call of an owl, the faint echo of a dog barking somewhere across the ridge.

He heard an engine turn over, the crunch of tires on gravel.

He stood for a while, looking out into the dark.

Someone had been in his house, he was damn sure of it.

He went in, locked the door—though it occurred to him since it was all glass, it wouldn't take much if someone wanted in.

He scanned the area, looking for anything out of place.

His gaze passed over the laptop he'd left on the kitchen island, tracked back.

He'd left the top up—almost always did. But it was down now.

And when he walked over, put a hand on it, it felt slightly warm.

He lifted the lid, began to poke around. He was no computer geek, but he knew enough to get by.

It didn't take long to discover someone had hacked in, downloaded his files. Bank, bills, e-mails, the works.

"What the fuck?"

He spent the next twenty minutes cursing and changing all his passwords, all his codes and user names. Anything he could think of.

What he couldn't think of was what someone would want with his data.

He spent more time sending out an e-mail blast—friends, family, business contacts, anyone on his list—telling them his data had been compromised and not to respond to anything from his old e-mail address.

After checking every door and window, he took the laptop with him upstairs.

Better security, he thought, on his data, on his house, had just bumped up to top priority.

An hour after he'd woken, he tried to settle down again, listening to every creak, every rattle of wind. Just as he started to drift off, the dog woke and began to whimper.

"Yeah, it figures." He shoved up, pulled on pants again. "Might as well make the rounds, Snickers."

When he did, the beam of his flashlight picked up a clear footprint in the soft ground beside the gravel of his drive.

"YOUR BLACK EYE'S just fading, and you had a break-in?"

Matt dealt with touching up the paint while Griff installed the last of the trim in Ada Mae's new master bath.

"More of a walk-in. Pain in the ass having to change passwords, send out notifications, then spend damn near an hour in the police station this morning with the report. Doesn't make sense, and I'd've put it down to house-settling noises if it hadn't been for the laptop being closed."

"You're sure you left it open?"

"Sure enough. Plus it was warm, and I hadn't used it in hours. Then the footprint. It wasn't mine, Matt. Size twelve here, but this was bigger. And I heard a car."

"What did the cops say?"

"That's another reason I'm late getting here. I went back with Forrest, and he took a look around, took pictures of the footprint, for all the good that'll do. It wasn't straight vandalism. I'd already figured if it had been, to look for someone in Arlo Kattery's family or one of his pals."

"Well, it's not like you're rolling in it, but you're pretty well set. Somebody figured, hey, this guy bought this big old place, and he's driving a new truck."

"Because that asshole wrecked my old one."

"Still." Matt shook Snickers from his boot laces, gave the tennis ball Griff had dug up a little kick to send the pup chasing it. "It sounds like somebody figured they could siphon off from your accounts, something like that."

"They're out of luck on that now. Pisses me off, somebody walking into my house like that. Looks like getting a dog was . . . fortuitous. Word of the day."

"Fortuitous my ass." Matt grinned, gave the ball another gentle kick. "How many times have you cleaned up after him so far?"

"A couple." Maybe five or six. "But he's getting it. He's going to be a good job dog. He doesn't freak at the nail gun. And he's going to get big. A big dog puts off people who want to walk into your house at two in the fucking morning. You ought to get one, then he'd have a pal."

"Living in an apartment, remember?" Matt climbed onto the stepladder with brush and bucket. "I'm thinking about maybe starting a house, though."

"You've been thinking about maybe starting a house since we got here."

"I'm thinking more since I'm going to ask Emma Kate to marry me."

"If you're going to do that, you should . . . What?" Griff nearly bobbled the nail gun as he came straight up on his knees. "When? Wow."

"Yeah, I know." With a slightly dazed look in his eyes, Matt grinned. "While you were dealing with the cops this morning, I was watching Emma Kate get ready for work. She's making green smoothies, and—"

"Don't mention your famous green smoothies."

"If you'd drink one every morning, you'd reap the benefits."

"I don't understand people who eat kale, much less drink it. You decided you wanted to marry her because of green smoothies?"

Matt pushed up the brim of his ball cap, and now dazed became dreamy. "I looked at her. She's barefoot, and a little grumpy, hadn't done her makeup yet. She's wearing khakis and a blue top, and the sun's shining through the window. I thought, This is what I want, every morning."

"Grumpy Emma Kate and green smoothies?"

"Every morning. I can't see past a time I don't want just that. So I thought you'd go with me after work to buy a ring. I'm going to ask her tonight."

"Tonight?" That was enough to bring Griff fully to his feet. "You're serious? Don't you want a setup?"

"I'll get some flowers. The ring's the setup. I don't know her size, but—"

"Make a template. Go back home, dig out one of her rings, make a template to take to the ring place."

"I should've thought of that."

"What are you going to say?"

"I don't know." Matt shifted on the ladder. "I love you, will you marry me?"

"You gotta do better than that, man."

"You're making me nervous."

"We'll think about it. Go make the template."

"Now?"

"Yeah, now. I've got to take the dog out anyway before he pees on the new tile. We're taking a break." All in with the plan, Griff gave his partner a punch on the shoulder. "Jesus, Matt, you're getting married."

"If she says yes."

"Why wouldn't she?"

"Maybe she doesn't want me and green smoothies every day." Matt stepped down from the ladder. "I feel a little sick."

"Knock it off. Go, make the template." Griff grabbed the dog, who'd begun to sniff in a way that warned Griff peeing was imminent. "I've got to take him out. Take action. It's the only way to get what you want."

"I'm taking action."

SHELBY SQUEEZED IN A REHEARSAL. She felt good about her mix of music—from the Beatles to Johnny Cash to Motown. Of course, if she had an actual accompanist, she'd have slowed down the pace of "Ring of Fire," done it as a sexy, aching ballad.

Maybe down the road, she thought as she finished up her morning stint at the salon. She took lunch orders from some of the spa patrons, then rounded up some from the staff.

As she tucked away her list, grabbed her bag, Jolene stepped cautiously inside.

"I'm sorry. Miz Vi? Miz Vi, can I come in for just a quick minute? Not for service or anything. I— I talked to Reverend Beardsly, and he said I should come, and speak to you, if you'd let me."

"All right, Jolene." Giving Jolene a nod, Viola pulled the last of the foil from her customer's hair. "Dottie, will you shampoo Sherrilyn for me?"

"Sure will, Miss Vi." Dottie and Sherrilyn exchanged wide-eyed looks. Neither of them wanted to miss the show.

"Do you want to go in my office, Jolene?"

"No, ma'am, Miz Vi. I'd like to say what I need to say right out here, in front of everybody." Her face went pink as she spoke, her eyes damp, but to the relief of some, the disappointment of others, she didn't blubber.

"I want to say to you, Miz Vi, and to you, too, Shelby . . . I— I want to say first I'm so awfully sorry. I want to apologize, to say I'm so sorry for how I acted here the last time. And . . ."

Her voice trembled, tears brimmed, but she held up a hand as she took a couple of deep breaths. "I'm sorry for the other times I was rude or mean to your face or behind your back. All of them, Shelby, right back to fifth grade. I want to say, I'm ashamed of it, all of it, looking at it now in the clear. I so wanted Melody to be my friend, and I did things I've got no excuse for."

A couple of tears spilled over, but Jolene twisted her fingers together and kept going. "I knew about what she did to your car, Shelby, back in high school? I didn't know before she did it, and I didn't do it. I swear I'd tell you now if I had."

"I believe you."

"But I knew after, and I didn't say anything. I knew and I pretended I thought it was funny, and how you deserved it. I just wanted her to be my friend, but I know she never was, not really. I know that now, and it makes it worse. What she said that day in here, to you, Shelby, about you, about your baby girl, I should've stood up. It made me sick inside what she said, but I didn't stand up and say that was wrong. I hope saying it now is a start to what Reverend Beardsly says is making amends. I was only thinking of me, and I'm sorry."

She sniffled, heeled away tears from her cheeks. "I didn't know she went to Arlo that way. I should've known, and I can't say, not for sure, if somewhere deep down I did. I didn't look deep down because I didn't want to. And I don't know, not for sure, if I'd have stood up even then. That's shameful, not to know if I would have stood up."

"You did stand up," Shelby reminded her. "When you found out what happened to Griff."

"I was that shocked and upset. Seeing Griff's face all cut and bruised, hearing what happened. I couldn't . . . I couldn't be quiet, not then."

"Jolene, I'm going to ask you something, and I want you to look me in the eye." Viola waited for Jolene to blink her eyes clear. "Do you know anything about somebody going into Griffin's house last night, middle of the night?"

"Oh my gosh! Oh no, ma'am, Miz Vi."

"What happened?" Shelby demanded. "What—" And broke off when Viola held up a finger.

"I promise, Miz Vi. I *swear*." Jolene crossed her hands over her heart. "It couldn't have been Melody. She's already in that place, in Memphis. I went to see Miz Florence just this morning, to make my amends to her, and she told me. Did somebody hurt him again? Did somebody rob him?"

"No." Viola looked over at Shelby. "No. Looks to be not much of anything, and I expect all of us here know if it was one of the Kattery clan, they'd have busted the place up if they could."

Viola fisted a hand on her hip. "Is there anything else you have to say, Jolene?"

"I guess not. Just I'm sorry. I'm going to try to be a better person."

"You never had much gumption," Viola observed. "Here's the first time I've seen you show any, and you did a good job of it. I'm going to say, I'm lifting my ban on you, and you're free to come in here when you like."

"Oh, Miz Vi. Thank you, Miz Vi. I . . . I won't come in if you'd rather I didn't, Shelby."

"I hope I can accept an apology the same as my grandmother."

"I want to give one to your mama, too. She wasn't here, but . . . I want to just the same."

"She's busy right now, but you can tell her later on."

"Then I will."

"It's up to Crystal if she wants to do your hair for your wedding," Viola added.

"Oh, Miz Vi. Oh, Crystal, would you? Losing you's almost as bad as losing my fiancé. And I really do love him."

"Of course I will. You made me real proud today, Jolene."

On a sob, Jolene rushed over, flung herself at Crystal.

"There you are now. I'm going to take you back, get you a nice cold drink."

"I was so scared to come in. I was so scared."

"That just makes me even prouder." Crystal beamed a smile at Viola, and led Jolene into the back.

"Dottie, get that shampoo done now. Show's over."

Shelby turned straight to her grandmother. "Granny, what happened at Griff's?"

"What I said. Somebody went in there. He says, what I got he says," she corrected, "is they went into his laptop computer. That's all I know. You oughta ask him."

"I will. I've got to get these lunch orders in." She glanced toward the back. "Some of us have to get knocked hard to come back. I know how that is. This might be the making of her."

"She's a flighty one, and likely always will be. But I respect a well-given apology. You go on now, or those customers will be shouting us down for their lunch order. I ought to think about putting in a little café."

It wouldn't have surprised Shelby in the least. But for now, she dashed out.

She wanted to call Griff, but couldn't spare the time as she rushed to Sid and Sadie, gathered up the orders, made a beeline for the Pizzateria, did the same. Loaded, she hurried back toward the salon.

And nearly slammed into a man studying one of the area maps.

"I'm so sorry! I wasn't looking where I was going."

He smiled down at her. "Neither was I. You've got a healthy appetite."

It took her a moment, then she laughed. "Delivery service."

"Then you must know the area."

"Born and bred here, so, yes, I do. Are you lost?"

"Not exactly. I'm visiting the area for a few days. I wanted to try the Rendezvous Trail, hit Miller's Waterfall, Bonnie Jean Overlook, Dob's Creek. I came into town thinking I'd get a takeaway lunch, and I've gotten turned around."

"I can help you with that." She angled around to look at the map. "If you take this road, the one we're on, straight out of town, go on past the big hotel and take the left fork. See that?"

"Yeah." Peering down, he nodded slowly. "Okay."

She guided him through, suggested Sid and Sadie for his packed lunch.

"I sure do appreciate it."

"You're welcome, and you enjoy your time here in the Ridge."

"I will."

When she hurried off again, he folded the map and slid it into his pocket, along with the keys he'd lifted neatly out of her purse.

PART III

THE REAL

They do not love that do not
show their love.

WILLIAM SHAKESPEARE

21

At the end of the day, Shelby dumped her purse out for the second time.

"I swear they were in here. I always put them in this side pocket so I don't have to hunt for them."

"Crystal's checking the back again," Viola told her as she herself hunted under mani tables and around pedi chairs. "You ought to go look in the van again. You may have dropped them this morning."

"All right, I will. But I can *see* myself tucking them in the pocket this morning. But I do it every time, so maybe I'm seeing another time."

"I'll call Sid and the Pizzateria again. You had such a bunch of bags, honey, you might've tipped them out while you were gathering them all up."

"Thanks, Granny. I've got a spare key to the van at home, but it worries me to lose that set. It's got keys to the van, to Mama's, to the bar and grill, to here. If they don't turn up, everybody's going to have to change locks. I don't know how I could've been so careless."

She shoved her hair back as the phone on the counter with the contents of her purse rang. "It's the Pizzateria. Hi, it's Shelby. Did you— Oh, thank you! Yes, I'll run right up and get them. Thanks so much."

"Now you can stop worrying about people changing out their locks," Vi said.

"It's such a relief." With it, the tight band around her chest loosened. "I must've dropped them picking up lunch, just like you said. Johnny said one of the waiters found them under the front counter. I guess I dropped them, and they got kicked under without anyone noticing. I'm sorry for all this trouble."

"Don't you worry. I'll let the girls know."

"I'm going to be late picking up Callie." Shelby dumped everything back into her bag. She'd sort it out later. "I'm taking Jackson tomorrow—did I tell you? It'll give Clay a full free day to visit with Gilly and the new baby, get the house ready for them to come home. He mentioned Jackson could use a haircut, so I'll bring him and Callie in, if that's all right."

"I love seeing my babies. You come on in anytime. We'll work them in—and maybe give Callie a princess mani if there's time."

"I'll see you then." She kissed Viola on the cheek, and once again dashed out.

She picked Callie up, then, knowing her parents were having a date night—and wasn't that sweet?—decided on impulse to drive to Griff's. Callie could play with the pup for a bit, and Griff could give her the details on the trouble he'd had.

It didn't occur to her until she'd made the turn into his drive that she should've texted or called ahead. Drop-bys were risky, and potentially rude.

She couldn't change her mind, not with Callie so excited, but she had an apology ready when she stopped beside Griff's truck.

He was out with the dog, turned, grinned, even as Snickers raced toward the van.

"How's that for timing? I just got home."

She lifted Callie out, had no more than set her down when her girl dropped to the ground to hug the wildly wiggling dog.

"Hey. I've dropped to second place pretty quick." Griff crouched down. "None of that for me?"

"Griff." With a flirty smile, Callie lifted her arms. She kissed his cheek, giggled, rubbed his stubble. "Tickly."

"I didn't know pretty ladies were coming."

"I should've called. Just coming by, it's presumptuous."

"Presume." With Callie on his hip, he leaned in before Shelby could think if she wanted to avoid, and kissed her. "Anytime."

"Shrek kisses Fiona, and then she's her real self."

"That's right. Are you your real self, Red?"

"Last I checked. How's this going?" A little unnerved, she lowered to give Snickers her attention.

"Not bad today. He handled the job. We finished it."

"Finished?" She looked up as the dog licked everywhere he could reach. "At Mama's? Oh my goodness, she's just going to go crazy. Daddy was getting her straight from the salon and taking her into Gatlinburg to visit Gilly and the baby, then for dinner and a movie. She doesn't know you finished."

"She'll know when she gets home." He set Callie down. "Do me a favor, Little Red. Run around with Snickers some. He needs the exercise."

"Come on, Snickers! You need cersize."

"I'm thinking cold beer. You want in?"

"I better not, but you go ahead. You've earned it working so late getting that bathroom done."

He thought about the trip to Gatlinburg, the ring. But he'd given his blood oath not to say a thing until the deed was done. "Ah, well . . ."

"I only came by for a minute, to give Callie the treat, and to ask you what happened last night. I heard something about it at the salon."

"Word doesn't travel around here, it just hangs in the air at all times. I don't know exactly." He glanced toward the house, found the anger still wanted to rise. "Somebody was in the house, downloaded my files from my laptop."

"Why in the world— Oh, I bet you do your banking and all that online."

"You win. It's all good. Everything's changed up, secured. But it's weird. Easier, right, to break in during the day, strip the damn place. But to sneak in one night with a flash drive? It's just weird. Talked myself into a real security system, though. In addition to the fierce and deadly guard dog."

Shelby looked over to where Snickers stumbled and rolled. "He is all that. It's probably smart getting one out here, though we just don't have much trouble. Except we have had recently, haven't we? Sometimes I feel like I brought trouble with me."

"Don't."

She tried to shake it off. "You go get your beer. I'm going to let her run off some energy with Snickers, if that's all right, then I have to get her home, get her fed."

"We can throw together something here."

"I'd like to, so would Callie, but I have a dozen things to do yet. And I'm running late myself as I lost my keys and spent near to an hour hunting for them."

"You put them in that side pocket of the purse thing."

She lifted her eyebrows. "You're observant."

"You do it every time."

"Well, I guess I missed, as they ended up under the counter at the Pizzateria. I don't know how they did. I know I didn't get them out when I was in there, but that's where they were."

"Did you have your purse with you all day?"

"Of course—well, not *with* me," she amended. "I can't cart it around while I'm working."

"Let's go check your laptop."

"What? Why?" She nearly laughed but sudden nerves got in the way. "You can't think somebody stole my keys right out of my bag, then put them under the pizza counter."

"Let's just go check your laptop. It's probably nothing. Callie can run around the backyard with Snickers. I'll stop and pick up some dinner."

"I was going to do up some of Mama's leftover ham from their Sunday dinner with some mashed potatoes and butter beans."

"Yeah? I'm all in for that if there's enough."

"There's always enough." A smart cook knew how to make sure of it, and she'd enjoy spending time with him. But . . . "You don't really think somebody got my keys. That's just crazy."

"We'll just check it out."

Because crazy or not, he did think it.

He locked up first, for what good it did, and followed them around the winding back roads—gave the oak tree a narrow stare as he rounded the curve.

He thought of Matt, wondered if his friend had done the deed yet. He decided not quite, because once he had, Shelby would surely get a call or text from Emma Kate.

He hoped it was soon. He could keep a secret, but they made him itchy.

He glanced over at Snickers, riding as any self-respecting dog would, with his head out the window, his tongue happily lolling. As impulses went, the dog was a good one.

It didn't take long to establish Callie in the backyard. Her kid heaven included her prized bubble maker, a puppy and the old family dog.

"Just look at Clancy, running around like a puppy himself. I think Snickers has taken five years off him with this visit."

"She's still got a couple more pups over there."

"I think the one's enough right now. I'll go get my laptop so you can relax. Why don't I get you that beer first?"

"I'll take it."

While he waited, Griff considered the what-ifs. If her computer had been compromised, as his had, it could mean the Ridge had some sort of cyber thief trolling. That might make the most sense.

But it struck him as odd that both his and hers would be targets, and pretty much back-to-back. That played as more personal, more direct, to his mind.

He let the possibilities roll around in his head as he stood at the kitchen door, watching the two dogs play tug-of-war with his homemade toy while Callie danced around them in a flood of bubbles.

Moving to the Ridge hadn't been an impulse like the puppy. He'd thought long and hard about it, considered the angles, the pros, the cons. But the decision had been, like the pup, a good one.

It was a good life here. Quieter than Baltimore, but he liked the quiet. Some culture shock here and there, but he knew how to adapt and adjust.

And wasn't it interesting—or fortuitous—that months after he'd settled in down here, Shelby had come home? He might just make tomorrow's word "serendipity."

"Oh, Griffin!"

"What?" He spun around. "Somebody was in your comp, too?"

"I don't know. I didn't look. The Master Suite." She said it with a flourish, with capital letters. "It's wonderful, it's *gorgeous*. I knew it would be. I saw it happening, but finished, it's— I'm going to have a whole box of tissues handy because Mama's going to cry buckets of joy and delight when she sees it. It's all just perfect, just what she wanted. And you left it sparkling clean."

"Just part of the service."

"You put flowers in there."

"Also part of the service for exceptional clients."

"Your exceptional client's going to cry happy tears and take a soak in that big tub the minute she gets home. When I can afford a house, you're hired."

"I'll put you on the list. Let's have a look at that."

"All right."

She put the laptop on the counter, booted it up.

"Have you downloaded or uploaded anything today?"

"Clay sent a couple more pictures of the baby this morning in an e-mail, but that's all."

"Let's see." He tapped a few keys, brought up her history first. "Did you go into any of these documents, go to any of these places this afternoon?"

"No." She lifted a hand, rubbed at her throat. "No, I haven't touched it since this morning, and then only to check my mail."

"Shelby, somebody went to these places and into these docs. And you can see here, the data's been uploaded onto another drive. Copied to another drive."

"Just like yours was."

"Yeah, just like mine." Those clever green eyes sharpened with temper. "You should call your brother."

"Yes. God. Would you do that? I need to see if— I have to check my banking."

"You do that now. I'll make the call." He stepped back, put in a call to Forrest.

"Everything's still there." Her voice trembled with relief. "It's all still there."

"Forrest is on his way. You're going to want to change your passwords. But . . ."

She looked up from doing just that. "But what?"

"It just seems to me if somebody was going to pull money out of your account, he'd have done it. I changed mine minutes after whoever this was hit my comp, but he's had hours to wipe you out, if that's the reason."

"What other reason is there?"

"Information, maybe. E-mails, accounts, sites we frequent, calendars. Most of my life's on my computer. We're . . . involved, right, you and me?"

"I— I guess we are." It felt strange to say it out loud.

"And both our computers are hacked into, about twelve hours apart. Maybe you should take a look around your room, check if anything's out of place or missing. I've got my eye on Callie."

With a nod, she hurried off.

He glanced out the back door again. All was right with that world. A pretty little girl, rainbow bubbles, a couple of happy dogs, all backdropped by the smoky green hills.

But outside that picture, something was very wrong.

IT TOOK A LITTLE TIME; she wanted to be thorough. But she found nothing out of place.

"Nothing." She came back in, waited for Griff to turn from his station at the door. "Everything's just as it should be. But I checked the computer in Daddy's office here, and I think someone was on there, too. It doesn't look like they took anything, but there were searches on it when I know no one was home."

"Okay. Why don't you sit down a minute?"

"I've got to get dinner going. Callie needs to eat."

"How about a beer?"

She shook her head, then sighed. "I wouldn't mind a glass of wine. My nerves are shot. I can't begin to say how tired I am of my nerves being shot."

"It doesn't show. This work?" He picked up a bottle of red from the counter with a blue glass stopper.

"It would."

"I'll get it."

He reached up for a wineglass while she dug out potatoes for peeling.

"Something more personal, you said." She let the homey task soothe her, tried to think objectively. "My first thought goes to Melody, but I honestly can't see her thinking of something like this. It's too complicated."

"Not Melody. She goes for violence or vandalism."

She peeled a potato, quickly. "You're thinking of the murder, but that's violence. That's as violent as it gets."

"I'm thinking connections, and how one thing fits with another."

"Richard." Her hands stilled briefly as she looked up. "Richard's been the root of about all the trouble I've had, and the trouble you've had comes through me."

"Not through you, Red."

"Through me," she corrected. "I'm not taking blame. I spent too much time taking blame for things I didn't do, things I couldn't stop, but facts are facts. Connections," she repeated, and started on the next potato.

"Okay. If we look at connections—" Griff broke off as he heard the front door open. "That'll be Forrest. Let's leave it to the professional."

"I couldn't be happier to do just that."

Forrest walked in, took a beer from the fridge. "Spell it out for me."

"Somebody got to my keys, and used them to get into the house, then into my laptop like they did Griff's. I can't find anything else taken, and I keep some cash money, just a little, in my top drawer."

"Which is the first place a burglar's going to look. Move it. Tampon box is a pretty safe place."

"I'll keep that in mind, but he obviously wasn't after cash or valuables."

"Information's valuable. Where were your keys?"

"In my purse."

"Come on, Shelby, don't be a jerk about it."

"All right, all right." She drew in a breath, picked up the wine. Settled down a bit, she went back to peeling as she related the key hunt.

"I know I had them when I got to rehearsal. I took them out of the ignition. I used the key Derrick gave me, because I can rehearse early sometimes, before anyone gets in. That's what I did today. I was in and out before anyone came in, so I used them to lock up again when I left, put them in the side pocket of my purse, like always. I always put them there. I'm not careless."

"Never were. She's always been an organized soul," Forrest said to Griff. "You may not get the rhyme or reason why she puts something where she puts it, but she knows where she put it."

"Saves time. I went into the salon, and I put my purse behind the counter. Nobody would go after my keys who works there, Forrest. I know all the girls there, and most of the customers now. I mean, the regulars. We get tourists and such, but it would be next to impossible for one of them to go behind the counter, dig in my purse, come up with my keys without somebody noticing. We weren't all that busy today."

"So it stayed there, behind the counter, until you got it back out to go home, and couldn't find the keys?"

"Yes. I mean, no. I took it with me to get the lunch orders. So I had it with me when I went to Sid and Sadie, then to the Pizzateria, where they somehow ended up under the front counter. I just figured I'd dropped them out somehow."

"Which is what you were supposed to think, and would have kept thinking if our honorary deputy wasn't on the ball."

"It wasn't hard to figure it out," Griff put in.

"I wouldn't have," Shelby corrected. "I wouldn't have given it another thought."

"Did you bump into anybody, get bumped into, while you were picking up the orders?" Forrest asked her.

"No." Brow furrowed, she took herself back through the route, as she had over and over again while she'd searched for the keys.

"I hit the lunch places just after the rush, because Jolene came in to apologize, and that took some time. I guess somebody could've gotten their hand in my bag, but it seems like I'd've known it. I did nearly bump into somebody," she remembered. "I was hurrying back because I was running behind, and nearly bumped into this man looking for the best route up Rendezvous Trail."

"Mmm-hmm. He asked you about that, asked for directions?"

"Yes. He was visiting the area and wanted . . ." She shut her eyes. "Oh my God, I'm an idiot. Yes, he asked me for directions, and I showed him on his map, and I had my hands full with the lunch bags. I went right in after, set down the orders, put my purse away, then went around handing them out. It's the only time somebody could've gotten in my purse. When it was hanging right on my own damn shoulder."

"What did he look like?" Griff demanded, then glanced at Forrest. "Sorry."

"No need. That's the next question."

"He was tall. I had to look up. Ah . . . give me a second." She carted the potatoes to the sink, washed them off, laid them on the cutting board to quarter them. "White, maybe early forties. He had sunglasses on. So did I—it was a bright day. He had on a baseball cap."

"Color? Logo?"

"I think it was tan. I don't remember if it had a logo or anything. He had dark hair—not black, but dark brown, longish. Kind of curled up over his ears. A little gray in the mustache and beard. Very trim, short beard. He looked . . . like a college professor who played football."

"Big guy, then?"

"Yeah. Big, solid build. Not fat or flabby." She put the potatoes on to boil.

Nodding, Forrest took out his phone, scrolled through. "How about this?"

She looked at the phone, and the photo of James Harlow. "No, he was a little older than this."

"Gray in the beard?"

"That, and . . . He had that professor look to him."

"Take another look, try to see him with the beard, the longer hair. Do a Wooly Willy."

"I used to have one of those," Griff commented, and studied the image over Shelby's shoulder.

"I just don't . . . He had thicker eyebrows—dark like his hair, and . . . Oh God, I *am* an idiot."

"I'm happy to call my sister an idiot at any time. It's part of my job, but you're not on this."

"I was standing on the sidewalk, talking to Jimmy Harlow, close as I am to you now, and I didn't even think, never had a twinge about it. Even when he was stealing the keys out of my purse."

"It's what he does," Forrest reminded her. "He changed his appearance, and he caught you when you were distracted, asked a common type of question. Got you going over the map so he could pick your pocket, and when he was done with the keys, he made sure you'd find them in a logical place. You'd have put it down to rush and accident, and never checked your laptop."

"What was he after? What's he looking for?"

Forrest cocked a brow at Griff. "What do you think, son?"

"I think he was looking to see if between us we've got millions of dollars tucked away, or know where to find it."

"Why you?" Shelby demanded. "I understand why he'd think I might know. Even believe I had to know."

"We've been spending a lot of time together since you got back."

"I know you're sleeping with my sister," Forrest commented. "Your euphemisms are wasted on me. You move back to the Ridge, and pretty quick you hook up with this one," he said to Shelby, "who relocated here not that many months ago. A person, especially one who lives on the grift, is bound to wonder if the two of you don't go back a ways further."

"He killed Melinda Warren, so it's just him now." Griff considered. "He'd get it all, but he has to find the jewelry, the stamps first. You're his only link to it, Red."

"I don't know where it is, or if Richard sold it and blew the money, buried it or put it in some Swiss bank account. And this Jimmy Harlow wouldn't find anything otherwise on my computer. Or yours, Griffin."

"We can hope that'll be enough for him," Forrest said, "but we're not going to count on it. I'm going to contact the sheriff, run all this by him. What's for supper?"

"Ham, mashed potatoes, butter beans."

"Sounds good. That your dog out there, Griff? The pup you got from Rachel Bell over your way?"

"Yeah. Snickers."

"He's starting to dig in my mama's delphiniums. She'll skin you both for it."

"Oh shit." Griff bulleted outside, calling for the dog.

Forrest grinned, leaned back on the counter. "I don't much like thinking about my sister having sex."

"Then I advise you not to think about it."

"Doing my best not to. Some people," he continued, "it takes you a while to warm up to, then maybe you make a friendship, or maybe you don't. Other people, something just clicks, almost like you think, Hey, I remember you. From where, who the hell knows, but there's that click. You know what I'm saying?"

"I guess I do."

"With Griff, something clicked. Took a little while with Matt, but I think we'd have gotten around to it. It was Griff who shortened the time it took."

Taking his phone off his belt, Forrest keyed in a number. "What I'm saying is, he's a friend, and a good one, and knowing the kind of man he is, I'm adding on he's a lot more what you deserve than the last one.

"Yeah, Sheriff, hope I'm not disturbing your supper," Forrest began, and wandered away as he made his report.

AFTER DINNER, which turned out just fine despite the fact that her mind hadn't been on the cooking, she shooed Griff out with Callie to chase the lightning bugs. The early ones blinked their yellow lights against the dark, setting the stage for the multitudes who'd light up the hills and forests in June.

Summer was surely on the way, and the snow-caked winter of the North faded until it became distant and almost otherworldly. Something over nearly as soon as it began.

She thought how much she wanted it to be over, but despite lightning bugs, a sweet fairy garden, the deepening green of the hills, something cold had followed her home. Her little girl might be dancing with the lights out in the yard, safe under the eye of the man she was . . . involved with. Her brother would be off now, looking into that something cold. So it was here, a shadow dogging her, and she couldn't pretend otherwise.

She had run off looking for adventure, love, an exciting future, and had come home disillusioned and riddled with debt. But there was more, and worse, and she'd have to face that down, too.

She wished she had the damn millions. She'd wrap them up in shiny paper, tie them with a bow and hand them over to this Jimmy Harlow without a single regret.

Just go away, she thought. Just leave me to take a good hold on the life I can see having now.

She couldn't think what Richard had done with all those jewels and stamps, or the money he'd gotten from them if he liquidated them. How could she know when she'd never known him? He'd worn a disguise throughout their marriage just as truly as Jimmy Harlow had worn one that afternoon.

She'd never seen through it. Maybe a shadow, a shape now and then, but never the whole man.

She knew what Richard had seen now when he'd looked at her. A dupe—a mark, that's what they called people like her. Something useful, maybe valuable for a time, and once used, once the value had been mined, something carelessly discarded.

She was working her way out of debt, wasn't she? She'd taken control, taken action. She'd figure out a way to take control, to take action in what was happening now.

She wouldn't live her life being haunted by the actions of a man who'd used her, who'd lied to her, who'd been a stranger to her.

She put away the last of the dishes, decided, hell yes, she'd have another glass of wine. She'd let Callie have a little longer before bath and bed, a little longer to dance with the lights. And tomorrow she'd start working on a way to clear her life of the past, all of it, once and for all.

She poured the wine, started for the door when her phone signaled.

She pulled it out, checked the text from Emma Kate.

I'm getting married! Holy crap! Didn't know I wanted to until he asked. I've got a ring on my finger, and I'm crazy happy. I need to talk to you tomorrow—too busy now. Sending this from the bathroom before I get busy again. OMG and WTF! I'm getting married. Gotta go.

Shelby read it a second time, felt her smile getting bigger, brighter. Her best friend was dancing in the light, too.

So happy for you! she texted back. *Crazy happy for you. Stay busy—I can be jealous there as I don't know the next time I'll be able to get busy. We'll talk tomorrow. I want every detail. I love you—tell Matt he's the luckiest man in the world.*

She sent the text, then stepped out to do a little dancing of her own.

22

She met Emma Kate at the park so she could let Callie and Jackson play.

"Doc gave me an hour, bless his heart. He knew how much I wanted to talk to you. Look!"

Emma Kate shot out her hand, and the princess-cut diamond winked in the sun.

"It's beautiful. It's perfect."

"He got channel set—see how it's set in some, instead of poking out?"

"Yes. I just love it, Emma Kate."

"He said he did that so I wouldn't get it caught on things, working with patients. I love that he thought of that. And he got my exact size, too. He made a template from one of my rings—that was Griff's idea."

"I got a little of that when I told Griff after I got your text. He never gave me the tiniest hint that he'd gone with Matt to buy you a ring."

"Matt says Griff's a vault when you ask him to be."

"I want to hear all of it. Oops, wait." She hurried over to Jackson, who'd taken a little spill. After she brushed him off, kissed his knee, she dug out one of the trucks in her bag so he could roll it around in the sandbox.

"He'll do all right for a while. Callie likes to boss him around some, but that's the way it is when you're the oldest."

"We talked about kids, having them. We want to wait a little, but in another year or two . . . God, married, kids." Laughing, she pressed both hands to her heart, bumped her shoulders up and down. "I can't believe it."

"You want it."

"With Matt, I do. Yesterday he texted me how he had to work a little late, but he'd stop and get dinner to bring home. He brought wine, too, and flowers. I guess I should've known something was coming, but it was just nice not having to think about either of us cooking anything, and having a nice bottle of wine, and flowers on the table. I'm babbling on about needing to get into the salon, do something with my hair, and he says how I'm beautiful. How everything about me is beautiful."

"I figured he just wanted to get lucky."

"Emma Kate."

"It's not like he never tells me, but it was the *way*. I'm thinking, I had such a long day, but it was so nice not to have to think about fixing any-thing, and I felt good, after a couple glasses of wine. So maybe we'd both get lucky."

Pressing her hand to her heart again, she sighed. "That surely hap-pened, but before . . . Before, he reached over for my hand, and he just looked at me. I swear, Shelby, we've been together for nearly three years now, but my heart skipped a beat. It really did, and it skipped another when he said how he loves me. How I make everything in his life make sense, and being with me, having a life with me, is all he wants.

"He actually got down on one knee."

"That's so sweet. Emma Kate, you got a storybook."

"It feels like it right now, and I never expected it, and never thought I'd feel the way I did when he took out that ring."

"Tell me what he said. How did he ask?"

"He said—he said just this: 'Marry me, Emma Kate. Spend your life with me.'" Emma Kate's eyes filled; her voice broke. "'Build a life with me.'"

"Oh." Shelby pulled out tissues for both of them. "That's just right."

"I know. Just right. So I said yes. Yes, I'll marry you. Yes, I'll spend my life with you. Yes, I'll build a life with you. And he put the ring on, and it fit. I started crying I was so happy, like right now."

She sighed, laid her head on Shelby's shoulder. "I wanted to talk to you last night, but—"

"You were busy."

"Really, really busy."

Callie walked up, patted Emma Kate's wet cheeks with both hands. "Happy tears?"

"Yes, they are, darling. Happy, happy tears. I'm going to marry Matt, and it makes me really happy."

"I'm going to marry Griff."

"Are you?"

"Uh-huh. I *love* him."

"I know just how you feel." Swaying side to side, she cuddled Callie. "Just exactly how. You know what, Callie? I think you should be my flower girl."

Callie's eyes popped wide. In a reverent whisper, she said, "Mama!"

Afraid she'd start tearing up again, Shelby popped Jackson and his sandy truck onto her lap. "My goodness, Callie, that's such an honor. You've never been a flower girl."

"I've never been a bride, so it's perfect," Emma Kate decided.

"Can I get a new dress and sparkly shoes?"

"We're *both* going to get a new dress and sparkly shoes. And your mama, too. You'll be my maid of honor, won't you, Shelby?"

"You know I will." Beyond happy, Shelby threw her arms around Emma Kate, sandwiched the kids between them. "You know I will. And I'm going to give you the best bridal shower ever seen in the entire state of Tennessee—just like we planned when we were girls. Have you picked a date?"

"If my mama had her way it would be tomorrow, or two years from tomorrow so she could fuss me into insanity while she devises a scheme to hold the wedding in the governor's mansion, at the very least."

"You're her only girl." As she was her own mother's, Shelby thought with a pang. "A mother's bound to be excited over her only girl's wedding."

"Mama was born excited. She's already talking dresses and colors and venues and guest lists. Matt and I talked about having a small, civilized wedding in the fall, but now that Mama's got the bit between her teeth, we've surrendered to a big wedding, and next April. So I'll be a spring bride."

"What could be prettier? Oh, let's have an engagement party, Emma Kate. Everybody likes a party."

"I wanna party," Callie chimed in.

"Of course you do. You want a party, right, Jackson?"

"I get presents?"

"It's not a party without presents."

"Mama's ahead of you. I couldn't hold her to a backyard barbecue. She wants a dress-up party, so she's already wrangling to use the hotel. I'm letting her have her way because I'm getting mine on everything else. I'm firm on it. And I'm counting on you to help me rein her in."

"I'm your girl. How about we give y'all a push on the swings?" she asked the kids.

"I want to go high!" Callie made a beeline for the swing.

"No point in swinging unless you go high." Shelby hefted Jackson onto her hip. "We'll give them a push, bride-to-be, and we can talk wedding dresses."

"One of my current favorite subjects."

SHELBY DIDN'T TELL Emma Kate about the keys, the laptop. She wouldn't spoil the brightness of the moment. But she gnawed on it.

Once she had the kids fed and down for a nap—say hallelujah—she sat down with her laptop. Business first, she ordered herself, meticulously paid bills, adjusted her spreadsheet, calculated how close she'd come to paying off the next credit card.

Considerable to go on that yet.

The sales from the consignment shop had started to dwindle—not unexpected—and she reminded herself just how big a hole they'd helped fill in.

And she tried not to think just how mortifying it was to know some stranger had copied all her troubles—the e-mails, the lawyer and tax correspondence, the spreadsheet, the painful chipping away at bills.

Couldn't let it matter, she told herself. She'd think of the upside there. Poring over her personal miseries ought to tell Jimmy Harlow if she had access to millions, she wouldn't be squeezing out nickels and dimes to pay off debt.

He'd go away, wouldn't he? Surely he knew he risked capture and being tossed back in prison if he stayed too close.

But then, millions of dollars made a shiny incentive.

Payback made a darker one. She understood that. She'd felt that ugly tug herself over the past months.

Take action, she thought, and began to make a list.

She culled through pictures she kept in a file. Would Harlow do the same? Was he studying her years with Richard through her photographs? And why hadn't she deleted them—those images of Richard, of the two of them, in Paris, in Trinidad, in New York and Madrid? All those places.

All those places, she thought again.

Had he taken the property he'd stolen, stashed it on those travels with her? Another bank box, an airport locker, holding onto it or selling it off a piece at a time?

She had the photographs to tell her where they'd gone, when they'd gone.

Then Atlanta, where they'd settled. Or she had, she thought now. He'd still had all those "business trips." And she'd packed the baby up from time to time when he insisted they fly off somewhere for a holiday.

"Where did he go when I wasn't with him?" she wondered. "And why did he take a wife and baby he had no real interest in along other times?"

She got up, walked around the kitchen, opened the door for air, walked around again.

As cover, of course. That's all they'd ever been to him. Just another disguise. How much had he scammed or stolen on those trips with her and Callie? She could barely think of it.

But she would think of it.

She sat again, using the photographs to add to her list. Tried to put herself back in time, in those places. But God, sometimes she'd been so tired, so stressed, trying to deal with an infant in a strange place, a place where she didn't know the language or the geography.

She pored over what she had, making notes, trying to remember people he'd introduced her to, or had her arrange cocktail parties for. Wealthy people, she thought now. But then, she'd thought they were wealthy.

Had they been marks? Had they been associates?

Likely some of both.

She jumped up when she heard footsteps and, heart pounding, swung around to pull the chef's knife from the block.

"Shelby? Shelby Anne?"

"Mama." On an unsteady breath, she shoved the knife back in the block, put on a smile as her mother walked in.

"There you are. Where are my babies?"

"They're napping, after a hard day at the park. They'll be up soon, though, probably wanting a snack."

"I'm going to take care of that. Look here, I got new pictures when I went in to the hospital to see the baby this morning." She took out her phone, cuddled close to Shelby as they scrolled through. "He's just handsome as a prince. Got his daddy's chin, you see that? I went by Clay's and made sure everything's as it should be, because they're letting Gilly bring Beau home tomorrow."

"That's wonderful. She'll love being home with Jackson and the baby."

"She'd walk out of there now if we'd let her, but she's settled for to-morrow. I found the cutest stuffed hound dog and put it in Beau's crib, got some nice fresh flowers for the bedroom for Gilly. That nursery's as sweet as an ice cream cone. And I got two facials in at the salon. Later on I'm going to make up some spaghetti—Gilly favors my spaghetti—and get it over there so nobody has to think about dinner tomorrow."

"You're not just the best mama, you're the best mama-in-law."

"Gilly's one of the lights of my life. Right now I'm going to spend the rest of the day with my two other grandbabies. And you go on, go on out and do something fun."

"Mama, you've driven over to Gatlinburg and back I don't know how many times the last two days, fussed over at Clay's, and plan to cook them a meal so they don't have to. And you went in to work."

"That's right." All but sparkling with joy, Ada Mae got the pitcher of tea from the fridge. "And now I'm going to enjoy the rest of my day. Oh, I also went shopping. I got the sweetest little baby clothes for that boy. And picked up a big brother toy for Jackson, and a little something for Callie."

"The best Gamma, too. Mama, you spoil them all."

"I do a fine job of it." She poured two glasses of tea over ice, snipped some mint from the pot on her windowsill. "I don't know when I've ever felt so good. Nothing like a brand-new baby. And I've got a master suite straight out of a magazine. I swear I'd've slept in that big tub last night if I could. I've got my own baby girl and hers home with me. My chicks are happy and home, my husband still takes me on dates. I've got everything I could want."

She handed Shelby a glass, kissed her cheek. "Now you go get yours."

"Get my what?"

"Your everything. I'd start that off by asking that clever and hand-some young man out on a date. Then I'd go buy myself something pretty to wear on it."

Shelby thought of her spreadsheet. "I've got plenty to wear."

"Something new now and then perks a girl up. You work hard, Shelby.

I know you've got bills, and I know you've been sitting there at that computer worrying about them. I raised you to be smart and responsible, but I'm telling you—" Ada Mae fisted her hands on her hips, just as her own mother was wont to do. "Your mama's telling you to go out and buy yourself a new dress. Something you're buying yourself with money you earned. See if that doesn't lift you up some. And then let Griff lift you a little more. I'm going to have Suzannah bring Chelsea over later, and those girls are having themselves a slumber party here tonight. You do the same."

"I should have a slumber party?"

After a hooting laugh, Ada Mae drank some tea. "That's what we'll call it in polite company. Go on, buy a dress, go over to the salon and get prettied up, and go take Griffin's breath away."

"You know I love you, Mama."

"You'd better."

"But I don't think I tell you often enough what a wonderful woman you are. Even beyond Mama, Mama-in-law and Gamma."

"Now, that's just put the sprinkles on the icing of the chocolate cupcake of my day." She gave Shelby a squeeze.

"Let me put things away. I wasn't just paying bills, and I'm doing all right with that, so don't worry. I was trying to figure things out, I guess, looking at pictures of my time with Richard. Trying to remember all the places we went, and when and why."

"You sure did travel, so that's something you have that can't be taken away. I loved getting postcards or letters or e-mails from you when you were in those foreign places."

"I don't suppose you saved any of them."

"For heaven's sake, of course I did. I have them all in a box."

"Mama, you are wonderful. Can I have them? I'll give them back to you once I've looked through."

"There on the shelf in my sitting room closet. Blue box with white tulips on it. It's labeled."

"Thank you, Mama." She added another squeeze. "Thank you."

. . .

SHE DID BUY A DRESS, just a simple summer dress the color of the mint her mother added to tea. And Ada Mae was right. It gave her incredible satisfaction to know she bought the dress with money she'd earned.

It only took a couple of questions to find out where Griff was working that day, and she found both him and Matt, sweaty and stripped to the waist (oh my!), building a deck on a house just outside the town proper.

"Hey." Griff swiped at his face with an already damp bandanna. "Don't touch me, I'm past disgusting. In fact, you ought to stay downwind."

"I have brothers," she said simply, and bent to greet the happy Snickers. "Congratulations, Matt. Consider yourself hugged."

"Thanks. Emma Kate said you guys met in the park this morning, and you're maid of honor. Meet the best man."

"Well, Best Man, you and I have a lot of consulting to do. Meanwhile, I have a favor to ask."

"Name it." Griff grabbed a jug, gulped down straight from it whatever was inside.

"Mama's got plans for the children, and I have some . . . research I want to do. I was wondering if I could do it at your place. I'd fix you dinner as payment for the quiet spot to work."

"Sure. I get the best of that deal. I've been locking up since . . . so . . ." He dug in his pocket for his keys, pulled one off the ring. "This'll get you in."

"I really appreciate this. Matt, the four of us are going to need to get together soon. Weddings require considerable strategy. I know Miz Bitsy's leading the charge on the engagement party—"

"Don't scare me when I'm working with power tools."

"We'll handle Miz Bitsy," Shelby assured him. "Emma Kate and I have been planning our weddings since we were ten. Of course, what she wants now may not include a silver princess carriage pulled by six white horses."

"Really scaring me."

"But, I have the basics, and I can help work Miz Bitsy around."

"Will you put that in writing?" he asked, and took the jug from Griff. "Maybe in blood. I don't care whose blood."

"It's a solemn promise. But I need to hear what you want, too. I'm awful good at coordinating things."

"Emma Kate said the same. I'm counting on you."

"You can, so we'll get together soon, all right?"

"How about my place, Saturday night?" Griff asked. "We'll throw something on the grill and strategize. If you don't want to ask your parents to watch Little Red, bring her along," he added, anticipating. "We can always hang her in a closet, stick her in a drawer."

"Let me work on that. I'd better get going, and let you get back to work. Pretend I gave you another hug, Matt. You've made my very best friend happier than I've ever seen her. So I'm inclined to love you a lot."

"I'm getting married," Matt said when Shelby left.

"That's right, pal. Hold on a minute." He set down the nail gun he'd just picked up, jogged after Shelby. "Hey. I didn't get a pretend hug."

"No, you didn't, but that's because I'm going to give you a lot more than that later. No pretending."

"Oh yeah?"

"On the instructions of my mama."

"I really like your mama."

"So do I. Bye now."

"We'll probably knock off around four, four-thirty," he called out.

"I'll be there."

"Nice to know," Griff said quietly, then grinned down at Snickers, who'd followed him and his boot laces. "Really nice to know."

SHE WENT BY THE MARKET FIRST, as she'd decided on what she'd fix for dinner when she'd seen Griff at his job site.

She settled down in his kitchen, angling herself so she could see out those wonderful glass doors to the view whenever she looked up.

But once she opened her mother's keepsake box and began reading, she didn't look up often.

She broke to work on dinner, get it in the oven. And think.

It was odd and fascinating to see herself, to review her own perspective through the prism of time. Only a handful of years, really, but a lifetime altogether.

She could see it now, the naiveté, the nearly blank slate she'd been. Richard had seen that, too, and used it very well.

Callie had changed her—she could read that, too, in photographs and letters. What she'd written, how she'd written it, had shifted after Callie was born.

Had her mother been fooled by the bright tone of the letters, the e-mails, the quickly dashed postcards once the daughter had become a mother herself? Shelby doubted it. Even now she could hear the tinny tone under the brightness.

She'd been so unhappy so quickly, all the fierce self-confidence gradually, carefully, she saw now, wiped away. The only true happiness broke through when she wrote of Callie.

No, her mother wouldn't have been fooled. Her mother would have seen, very well, how she'd written less and less of Richard.

But in the first year or so, there had been plenty, and minute details of where they'd traveled, the people she met, the things she saw.

She could follow herself easily from her own words, and begin to see.

She'd think a great deal more, she promised herself. She might never have the answers, but she'd found a bank box from a key in the pocket of a jacket.

So she'd think a great deal more.

She had the counter set for dinner, the wine she'd bought—she'd have to hope for good tips on Friday night—ready when she heard Griff's truck.

She got out a beer, opened it and walked out to meet him.

He looked hot, sweaty and all but edible when he smiled over at her, leaned on his truck, tipped his sunglasses down to look at her over them while the dog ran in circles over the front lawn.

"Now, that's what's been missing from the front porch. A beautiful redhead with a cold beer."

"I figured you'd be ready for one." She walked down the steps. "I have brothers."

"I'm more than ready for one. I'm still not touching you. May turned to August today."

"It often does."

"You should brace yourself for after I get a shower. How's Callie doing?"

"About to have hot dogs on the grill for supper with her cousin and her best friend, and that's after they were all stripped down so they could run around in the sprinkler."

"Sprinkler sounds pretty good. Hot dogs don't sound bad."

"Those'll have to wait for next time."

"When I have a beautiful redhead with a cold beer fixing dinner, I'm not picky."

He walked in the house with her, with the pup rushing to keep up. Griff sniffed the air. "What's cooking? It smells great."

"Meat loaf with baby potatoes and carrots."

"Meat loaf?" He sniffed again. "Seriously?"

"It's a warm day for it, but a manly meal. You looked like meat loaf for supper when I saw you today."

"I haven't had homemade meat loaf since the last time I was in Baltimore and sweet-talked my mother into it. Why don't most women appreciate the loaf of meat?"

"You just answered your own question. I'm just going to go check on it."

"I'll grab that shower. Then brace yourself, Red."

Amused, stirred, she went back to the stove, judged she'd timed it well. Then reconsidered.

Self-confidence, she thought. She remembered what it was like to be confident and bold.

She turned the oven down and went up the back stairs.

Griff chugged the cold beer while cool water rained blissfully down on his head. It felt like pounds of sweat and grime sliding away. It was going to be a nice deck, he thought, but he hadn't been ready for the change in the weather.

Spring had come in so soft and benign, he'd forgotten what a hot, wet hammer summer could pound with in the Smokies.

And today had been just a quick preview of coming attractions.

Once it hit full, he and Matt would start earlier in the day, knock off earlier in the afternoon. And that would give him time to work inside on his own projects. Then there were the plans for the bar and grill once the permits came through.

Then, of course, there was Shelby. He wanted as much time as he could steal with her.

Even as he thought of her, the glass door opened.

She stood, her hair curling wildly over her shoulders, wearing nothing but a knowing smile. With her eyes on his, she took the beer out of his hand, set it on the counter behind her.

"You're going to need both hands," she told him.

"It's a day of miracles," he said, and reached for her.

"It's cool." Tipping her head back, she traced her fingertips up his back. "The water's cool."

"Too cool?"

"No, it's nice. And this is even better." She rose up to her toes, fixed her mouth on his. And there was nothing cool in the kiss.

He thought it a wonder the water didn't go to steam the way she heated his blood. Instant and fierce. Every sweaty hour he'd put in that day, every restless hour of the night he'd spent wanting her, worried for her, spilled away.

Soft skin, eager mouth, greedy hands—in that moment, she gave him everything he needed.

"I've been wanting you since I had you." He couldn't take fast enough. "Going crazy just to touch you again."

"I go crazy when you touch me. Don't stop touching me."

Heat and need and pleasure mixed to hammer in her heart, to shimmer under her skin. The more he gave her, the more she wanted, and reveled in her own appetite.

For him, just him, the hard hands, the tough, workingman's body. His mouth, patient and demanding at once, made her head spin.

He hiked her up by the hips, bringing her off the shower floor. That surprising strength, the hard grip with rough-palmed hands, combined to make her feel vulnerable, desirable, powerful.

Eyes on his, she wrapped her legs around his waist, dug her fingers into his shoulders for purchase.

Then she was crying out as he plunged into her. Shocked and thrilled and quivering for the next mad thrust.

Water striking, seeming to sizzle and spark against tile. Wet flesh slipping, sliding under her hands. And her own breathless gasps.

She felt weightless, wondrous, clinging to him as he whipped them both higher. Clung still as they tumbled into the blissful dark.

"Hold on," he managed, and groped to turn off the water. "Just hold on."

"Mmmm. I feel like I might slide right down the drain."

She sensed movement, stayed wrapped around him even when he dropped them both on the bed.

"I need a minute," he told her.

"Take your time."

"I meant to. But you were all wet and naked. I'll get towels in a minute."

"I bought a new dress."

"Did you?"

"Yeah, and I was going to put it on for dinner, then let you take it off me after. I didn't take my time, either."

The image brought on a small but definite surge of fresh energy. "Do you still have the dress?"

"Hanging in your laundry room."

He trailed a finger down her side. "You could go with your plan, and we'll both take our time."

"I like that idea. What I didn't think to bring was a hair dryer. I don't suppose you have one."

"Nope, sorry."

"Well, between the shower and the humidity and no hair tools, my hair's going to be as big as the moon. I must have bands and clips in my purse."

"I like your hair."

She curled into him. "I like yours. I like how the sun's starting to streak it. You'd pay good money for highlights like that at my granny's."

"Men who eat meat loaf don't have highlights."

She kissed his shoulder. "You do, and I'm getting those towels, and turning dinner back up."

"You turned it down?"

She gave him the slow, flirtatious, under-the-lashes smile Callie often did. "I wanted you in the shower, so dinner's going to take just a little longer than I'd planned."

"I like that you turned it down. I'll get the towels."

He rose, walked back into the bathroom. "What were you researching— or was that a ploy to get me wet and naked?"

"It wasn't a ploy, just a bonus." She smiled, took the towel he offered. "Griffin, my hair's like another person, and that other person also needs a towel."

"Right." He went in for another, and the beer she'd taken and set on the counter.

"So what were you researching?"

"Oh." She'd wrapped the first towel around her body, and now bent from the waist to gather her hair in the second. "You don't want to talk about that. It's all the other things. The Richard things."

"You don't want to talk about it?"

"I do." She straightened, somehow tucking parts of the towel into the whole in a way that fascinated him. "I want to talk to somebody about it who'd have some perspective on it. I thought I'd run all of it by Forrest, maybe tomorrow, even though he's probably thought of half of what I just thought of already, but . . ."

"Put on the new dress, and we'll talk about it while the loaf of meat is cooking."

23

She turned up the oven, put on the dress, banded back her hair so it wouldn't explode as it dried.

She joined him on the back porch, with wine, and just sat a moment, looking out at the mountains with their soft peaks and ridges rolling up into the sky.

"I was paying bills today when the kids were napping, and I thought about how Jimmy Harlow—it has to be him—would be looking at all my business. The lawyer stuff, the creditors, the accounts I've kept of what I was able to sell. I thought how embarrassing that is, a stranger poking around in all that, and told myself it was worth the embarrassment if it made him realize I don't have anything he wants."

"That's good thinking. Smart, positive."

"Then I was thinking more. He'd see all the photos I have on the laptop. I keep them all in files on there—I transferred them from my old one once I got it back from the authorities. I never got around to going through them all, deleting any from . . . from the time I was with Richard because there was just so much else to do. It occurred to me he'd—Harlow—he'd seen, especially from that first year or so, all the places we went. He could follow right along, like a map."

Griff nodded. "And so could you."

"Yes! That's what I realized. So could I. Griff, I think Richard took me all those places for a reason—I understand now he never did anything without an angle to play. I was like his disguise. I—and then when Callie came along, we—made him a family man. What if he stashed the jewelry or the stamps, or both, in one of those places, or sold some of it off as we went? And I started thinking more, once I started looking through the pictures, he was probably doing his work, too. On his honeymoon—or so I thought—then with his pregnant wife. Such a handy disguise, the pregnant wife."

"I'm going to agree with you, even though I know it has to burn some."

"I'm past the burning. Looking through the pictures, the letters I sent home, I started remembering what he'd always say to me—at least for the first months or year. Whenever we were going to meet somebody, he'd say, 'Just be yourself, Shelby.' How that would charm them. Not to worry, I didn't know anything about art or wine or fashion, that sort of thing. I was never nervous about meeting new people, but I started to be."

"He made you feel awkward, and . . . less."

"He did, and as the 'be yourself' started changing to how I shouldn't try to impress whoever it was because they'd just see through that. I guess I didn't have a lot to say, and that made a good disguise for him."

She sipped the wine, set that part aside for now.

"I thought maybe I could look at articles online, matching them with the time we were in a certain place. Was there a robbery? A fraud? Even worse? And I had more to use because Mama saved all my letters and postcards. Every one. So I could read through, remind myself what we did, where we went in Paris or Madrid, who we met. I was full of details at first, so swept up in it all."

"Does anything stick out now, when you look at it from what you know now?"

"A couple of things. Why was he in Memphis? I don't believe he just stuck a pin in a map. But there he was, and only four days from when he robbed that woman—Lydia Redd Montville—and shot her son."

"Four days after, according to the brunette, he double-crossed her and Harlow, ran off with the take."

"That's right. I think he must have had that take with him, or he'd stashed it. A bank box, maybe. He had his new identity, and he had a fat roll of cash. Or it seemed like it to me. And there I was, just primed to be dazzled and swept up."

"Do you want my angle on that?"

She drew in a breath. "I guess I do."

"The cops were looking for Jake Brimley, a man on his own. He had to know his partners would rat him out. He didn't go into it without a plan in place. The new ID, the seed money, a change in looks. But he needed one more thing. He needed to be a couple."

"I think that's true."

"He wouldn't want someone like the brunette, someone who could play his game. He'd want innocence, youth, someone malleable and trusting. And ready to be dazzled."

On that she could only nod, let out a long breath. "I sure fit the bill, right down to the ground."

"He was a professional manipulator, Shelby. You didn't stand a chance once he zeroed in on you. He ends up with a young, striking redhead, so he's not only not traveling alone, he has someone people notice. Notice first, remember last. Where did he take you first?"

"He spent four days in Memphis. I'd never met anyone so charming, and exciting, too, the way he talked about all his travels. Our gig was over, and I planned to come home for a week or so before the next one. But when he said he had to go to New York, for business, and asked me to go with him, I went."

She let out a half-laugh. "Just like that. It was just going to be a few days—an adventure, I thought. And it was thrilling."

"Why wouldn't it be?" Griff countered.

"We flew on a private plane. I'd never known anyone who'd been on a private plane."

"No security, no luggage check. You can take anything you want on private, right?"

"I hadn't thought of that. He almost always flew private. At the time it was just one more thrill. I'd never been anywhere like New York, and he was so sweet and charming and . . . well, he seemed dazzled by me. It wasn't the money, Griff, though I can't say I didn't love that he'd buy me nice clothes and take me to restaurants. It was the sparkle of it, all of it. It was blinding."

"He made sure of it."

"Even now it's hard to believe he didn't mean the things he said back then. How I was what had been missing from his life. I wanted to be that—I wanted to be what had been missing from his life. So when he asked me not to go back, but to go with him to Dallas—more business—I went. I threw everything away and went with him."

"Another major city."

Closing her eyes, she nodded. "Yes. You see that pattern already? We always went to a big city, always stayed for only a few days. Sometimes he'd give me a wad of cash, tell me to go out shopping because he had meetings. Then he'd come back with flowers—white roses. He said how he lived on the road or in the air right then, but how he was ready—now that he had me—to settle down somewhere."

"Exactly what you'd want to hear. It was his business to read people, to be what they wanted or expected."

She sat silent for a moment, appreciating the softening light, the whisper of air in the trees, the bubble of the stream.

"If I'd built a man I'd fall for, at that point in my life, it would have been Richard. The thing is, Griff, in those first few weeks, we crisscrossed the country."

"Covering his tracks."

"I think so, and I wonder, did he have places along the way where he left part of the take from that Florida robbery? If he had a bank box in Philadelphia, maybe he had others. Melinda Warren indicated that. He never seemed to run out of cash, so I think maybe he had those boxes to pull from, or he was stealing along the way."

"Probably both."

She shifted toward him, angling so they were face-to-face. "I think it was both. Looking through the pictures and letters, I remembered when we were in St. Louis, and I woke up to find him gone. He'd go out for walks—that's what he said. Thinking time. He didn't get back until nearly dawn, and he was excited. Just quivering with it. We left that morning. He rented a car and we drove to Kansas City. Just a quick stop, he said. He had a business associate to meet up with. And he pulled this Cartier watch out of his pocket, said he'd picked up a little something for me. A couple years later, I went to put it on, and it was gone. He got angry, said I'd been careless and lost it, but I hadn't been careless. Anyway, I went on the Internet and I looked back, matching up the dates, and found there'd been a burglary that night in St. Louis. Jewelry again, about a quarter of a million in jewelry. And watches."

"Steals them in St. Louis, fences them in Kansas City."

"I guess he figured the watch was my cut—for a while. There were other times. I'm going to see if I can match them up like St. Louis."

He reached over, gave her arm a rub. "What'll that tell you?"

"I know I can't change any of it." She dropped her gaze to her hands, thought of her notes, her stacks of photos and postcards. "But maybe he did steal in those places, and at least I can give what I know, or think I might know, to the police. It feels like I'd be doing something."

"You are doing something."

"Right now I should be putting dinner on the table." She rose. "I appreciate you listening."

"Why wouldn't I?" He walked in with her. "I've got a list of my own started."

"What kind of list?"

"I don't have the information you do." He glanced at the memory box, the laptop. "I wouldn't mind having a look at it. Mine's pretty much a list of names, events, times. Warren, Harlow and Brimley—as he was known then. Miami robbery, the shooting, the double-cross. You come next. I didn't realize it was only days after Miami, but had to figure it wasn't long."

"It's like I was as tailor-made for him as I thought he was for me." She put the meat loaf on a trivet, got out his only platter. Transferring the meat and vegetables, she glanced around as he'd gone quiet.

"What is it?"

"I don't want to upset you more than all this already does, but I don't think he just walked into the club where you were playing that night and decided, okay, she's my cover."

"What do you think?"

"I think he spent a couple days checking you out. You're a looker, Red, and I bet you were a looker at nineteen, on stage. Your name's right there, so he could look you up, ask a few questions. You're single, unattached."

Thoughtfully, she garnished the platter with curly parsley and rings of red and green peppers. "A bumpkin from a little mountain town in Tennessee."

"You've never been a bumpkin. But there you are—young, fresh, inexperienced, but game. It takes game to get on stage. He checks you out, then he moves in, feels you out. By then he's got a good sense what you're like, what you like. And he makes himself exactly what you like."

"What if I'd said no, no, I can't just run off to New York City with you?"

"He'd have moved on, found somebody who would. I'm sorry."

"No need to be. It's a relief in its way to feel like it was never really about me. It was never really personal. It makes it more of a puzzle to solve."

"Okay. Wow, that looks great."

Pleased, she set the completed platter on the eating counter. "My mama would tell you presentation counts. So even if it doesn't taste good, at least it looks good. Let's hope we have both. Sit down. I'll serve it up, and you can tell me what's next on your list."

"Houston, right?"

"It was Houston for about six months."

"Then Atlanta, Philadelphia, then Hilton Head. You said Richard never did anything without a reason. Why did he want you and Callie to go with him to Hilton Head?"

"You think he might have had some sort of deal going there, and we'd have been cover again." She plated a hefty slice of meat loaf with generous portions of potatoes and carrots. "Oh God, Griff, what if it wasn't an accident? What if the deal went bad, and he was killed? Dumped in the ocean?"

"You're probably never going to know the answer to that one. He put out an SOS, didn't he?"

"Somebody did, but . . . Griff, Forrest said Harlow escaped around Christmas. Richard—that was just a couple days after Christmas."

"Killing Richard wouldn't be a smart way to get to the millions."

"No, you're right. But there could've been a fight, an accident, and you're still right. I'm probably never going to know, at least unless they catch Harlow."

She put a smaller portion on her plate, sat. "It probably happened just the way the police think. He liked taking risks. Driving fast, skiing the fastest slopes, scuba diving, rock climbing, skydiving. He wouldn't have let a squall stop him. But it did. What else?"

"The PI. Maybe he's just what he claimed, but—" After the first bite of meat loaf, Griff stopped. "Wow." Sampled another bite. "Okay, that seals it. I'm keeping you. This meat loaf's better than my mom's—and if you tell her I said that, I'll swear you're a liar."

"I'd never insult another woman's meat loaf. You really like it?"

"Ask me again after I've licked the plate."

"Must be the beer. In the meat loaf."

"There's beer in the meat loaf?"

"An old family recipe."

"Definitely keeping you." He stopped eating long enough to cup a hand at the back of her neck, pull her over for a kiss.

"I haven't made meat loaf in years, so I'm glad it turned out."

"Prizewinning."

"Tell me what you think about that detective."

"Right. I fell into an altered state due to beer-laced meat loaf. So the PI, he tracks you to Philly, follows you down here. He's either dedicated or he has an agenda. He's licensed and all that, and he swears the brunette wasn't his client. Forrest says he won't name the client."

"I didn't get that much out of Forrest."

Griff shrugged. "We were talking. He's alibied for the night of the murder, so there's no legit cause to hassle him. Yet."

Head cocked, she stabbed a bite of carrot. "You know more."

"Bits and pieces. I know Forrest says the widow and her son both deny hiring the PI. The insurance paid out, and they've put the whole ugly business behind them. The Miami police talked to them, and it looks like they're alibied for the murder, too."

"You're just a well of information."

"He's worried about you—Forrest. Mostly it's negative information, so I guess he didn't want to dump it on you."

"Knowing's better than not."

"Now you know. Most of the rest is pure speculation. We can speculate pretty confidently Harlow's been in the Ridge. It's no big leap to speculate he killed the brunette, if for no other reason than who else, and he had motive since she'd claimed he shot the widow's son—and maybe he did—but since the gun you found in Philadelphia in Richard's safe-deposit box was the one used, it's more logical to—"

"What? What did you say? The gun I found—Richard's gun?"

Griff decided he needed a long drink of wine. "Okay, listen, he—Forrest—just got the information on that today. The Miami cops did the ballistics, verified the gun you found in the bank fired the bullet that wounded the son. I happened to run into him this afternoon, and he told me."

"Richard. Richard shot someone."

"Maybe. Maybe he just grabbed the gun after, but . . . logical speculation. His gun, his shot. Harlow always denied it, and he'd never taken a hit on weapons charges before this."

"She lied. She was in love with Richard—Jake to her. At least in her way she loved him. She lied, even after he betrayed her. It wasn't just the money, the take, that had her tracking me here. She was jealous, angry and jealous that he'd spent those years with me. Had a child with me."

"Most likely." Since he'd come to the same conclusion, Griff nodded. "And more, a lot of people project. You know what I'm saying? She couldn't imagine you being with him and being uninvolved in the rest. She was a liar, a cheat, so by her reasoning, you had to be the same."

"And Jimmy Harlow would think that, too."

"I don't know."

"You're hedging back now," Shelby said when Griff went quiet. "Because you're worried all this upsets me."

"It does upset you."

"It does, but I want to hear what you think. I don't need to be protected against upset, Griffin. I've gotten through worse. Tell me what you think."

"All right. I think it's a pretty sure bet Harlow wasn't in love with Richard, so his thought pattern might be clearer on it than the brunette's. But he's on the list I'm making, in several columns. I'm guessing he's been staying somewhere close. Not as far out as Gatlinburg, like the brunette. Probably not the hotel. One of the campgrounds or cabins, one of the motels."

"So he can watch me."

He paused a minute, but he agreed with her. Knowing was better than not.

"Think about this. He didn't confront you, get in your face, make threats like the woman. He's playing a longer game, I think, so he wanted information. He wants to know who you are. It's more likely he'll cut his losses once he does. Better to stay free than to be rich—especially when the rich part doesn't look promising."

"I hope you're right."

"Playing that longer game, he'd be smarter to take a good look at all the information, just like we are. He'd know Richard better, and it seems like he'd follow the lines if he can connect the dots."

Just as Griff's thoughts and conclusions helped her connect dots. "We stayed the longest in Atlanta. But he planned to get out, and fast. I think he had a job there, a mark there, and wanted to pull out as soon as that job was done. I barely had time to pack once he told me. He went on ahead."

"I didn't know that. He went north without you and Callie?"

"About ten days before. I was supposed to pack, and turn over the keys. I thought we'd bought that condo in Atlanta, but we'd rented, so it was just turn over the keys, and fly north. I almost didn't. I almost came home instead, but I thought maybe that's what we needed—that change. Maybe that would help set things right between us again, and he talked about how we'd have a big yard for Callie. And . . . how we'd have another child."

"Playing you."

"I see that now. Clear," she added. "I found in his papers he had a vasectomy right after Callie was born. He made sure there wouldn't be another child."

"I'm going to say I'm sorry, because that hurt you, and it's a beyond crappy thing to do. But—"

"For the best," she finished. "I have to be grateful I didn't have another child with him. Playing me is what he did, all along, and in that lightning move to Philadelphia when he must have known I was thinking about leaving. Making it sound like the best thing for Callie nudged me into trying it, going, wanting to make it work."

"A fresh start."

"Yes, that's how he made it seem. I said we stayed longest in Atlanta, but I don't think he'd have left anything important there. I can see, looking back, he planned to get out well before he told me, so I think he'd plan to take whatever he had stowed away with him."

He noted she only pretended to eat now, and wanted to erase it all, all the thoughts, the speculations, the points of view. But that wasn't what she wanted.

"You said he traveled a lot, without you."

"More and more, especially after we settled in Atlanta. I just wanted to nest a bit, find a routine. It got so he didn't ask, just told me he had a business trip. Sometimes he didn't bother to tell me. I don't know for sure where he went. He may have told me the truth, he may not. But I know where I went with him, so that's a start."

"You could dump all this on the cops."

"I suppose I will, but I want to work my way through it first, try to understand it."

"Good. So do I."

"Why?"

"You," he said immediately. "Callie. If you don't get that, I haven't been doing a good job."

"You like fixing things."

"I do. People ought to like doing what they're good at. And I like your face. I like your hair."

He reached out for it, really wanted to take it out of the band she'd pulled it into.

"I like your meat loaf," he added, polishing off the last of it on his plate. "I like taking Little Red on pizza dates. And I'm sunk when she gives me that flirty smile. So it's more than fixing things, Shelby. You're more than something to fix."

Saying nothing, she rose to clear the plates.

"I've got those. You cooked. You cooked great."

While he cleared, she opened her laptop, did a search for a photo. "Tell me what you think."

She turned the computer around.

With a considering frown, Griff crossed back, leaned over and studied the photo of her.

Taken at one of the last functions she'd attended in Atlanta, it showed her and Richard in formal dress.

"You look gorgeous, and sad—I thought that the first time I saw you. You're smiling, but there's no light in it. And what happened to your hair? You look gorgeous, like I said, but not so much like Shelby. Where are the curls? Did you sell them?"

She gave him a long look, then tipped her head to his shoulder. "You know what I want to do?"

"What?"

"I want to take a walk around your backyard, watch the sun set, give you all sorts of unasked-for advice about where you should plant things, and put that arbor. Then I want you to take my new dress off me. That'll be easy as I'm not wearing a thing under it."

"Can we do that first?"

She laughed, shook her head. "Let me drive you a little crazy first."

"Already there," he told her as she took his hand to lead him out.

HE FOLLOWED HER HOME AGAIN, used the drive back for thinking time. Added to thinking time by taking Snickers on a long patrol, then putting a good hour into framing out a closet in one of the other demo'd bedrooms.

One step at a time, he told himself as he put his tools away, cleaned up.

He took the next step by sitting down at his computer and doing his own search for unsolved burglaries and fraud cases in Atlanta during the years Shelby had lived there.

A puzzle to solve, he thought. Never did anything without a reason, Griff reminded himself. So why had the fucker pulled up stakes in Atlanta, and so abruptly?

It might be interesting to find out.

WHILE GRIFF RAN HIS SEARCHES, Jimmy Harlow worked on a laptop he'd lifted from a trade show in Tampa. The busy hotel and half-drunk conventioneers in the hotel bars had been prime picking.

He'd walked out with the laptop—fully loaded and in a nicely padded travel bag—just over two thousand in cash, two iPhones and the keys to a Chevy Suburban he drove directly to a chop shop.

He bought a new ID—it paid to have contacts—and stole a piece-of-shit Ford he drove over the Georgia border to an acquaintance who bought it for five hundred flat.

He lay low for a while, growing a beard, growing out his hair, dying both, building up his cash the old-fashioned way. He picked pockets, pulled some minor burglaries, moved on.

He made his way to Atlanta, taking a winding route, staying in flea-bag motels, stealing the occasional car—a skill learned and honed in his youth. In a side trip to New Orleans, he mugged and beat the crap out of a drug dealer who procured for a high school in the Ninth Ward.

He strongly disapproved of selling drugs to minors.

He also picked up a solid Toyota 4Runner outside a bar in Baton Rouge, which he drove to yet another chop shop.

He paid to have it reVINed, repainted, and with the help of another contact, forged the paperwork to match his new ID.

He watched the news obsessively, used the laptop to scan for the manhunt.

He trimmed his beard, bought easy, casual clothes—and broke them in so none of them looked new. He used self-tanner religiously to rid himself of prison pallor.

He bought maps, even sprang for a decent Canon digital camera, and slapped a few stickers on the truck from state parks, as any tourist might do.

He ate what he wanted, when he wanted. Slept when he was tired, got up and going when he wasn't.

Every day of the years he'd spent in prison he'd dreamed of just that. Freedom. But he'd dreamed of what he'd do with that freedom.

He had no illusion of honor among thieves—he'd been one too long. But betrayals required payback. And payback drove him.

It drove him to Atlanta, where inquiries in the right ears, grease in the right palms, gave him information.

He stole the .25 from a split-level in Marietta, where some idiot had it unsecured in the nightstand, and took the 9mm from a desk drawer in the home office.

Kids in the house, too, he'd thought at the time as he'd done a sweep of a boy's room, a girl's room. Hell, he was saving lives here.

He'd left the kids the Xbox, but had taken the iPads, another laptop, the cash in the freezer, a diamond tennis bracelet, diamond studs, the cash rolled up in the jewelry box and, because they fit, a pair of sturdy hiking boots.

By the time he arrived in Villanova, the woman who'd hooked up with Jake was gone.

He picked the lockbox, took himself on a tour. Jake had done real well for himself, and that burned bitter in his throat.

He contacted the realtor using his drop phone, discovered it was a short sale. So maybe not so well after all.

He spent a few days in the area to get a better sense of things, then worked his way down to Tennessee.

He'd rented a cabin a good ten miles from Rendezvous Ridge—a three-month, under-the-table cash deal with the owner. He was Milo Kestlering here, out of Tallahassee, where he'd been middle management for a wholesale food company. Divorced, no kids.

He had plenty of filler to his new background if he needed it, but the landlord had been happy to take his money.

He had no contacts here, and had to be careful. More careful with cops sniffing around since Melinda's murder.

Stupidity had killed her, in Harlow's opinion. Maybe prison had dulled her edge, but either way, she wasn't a factor anymore.

The redhead now, that was another matter. But he had what he wanted, for now. Enough to keep him busy, for now.

Cut it close at the boyfriend's place, he thought. Pushed it, he admitted. Always better to go in an empty house—but the door was unlocked, and the laptop right there.

Still, he'd gotten the data.

He'd taken a risk walking right up to the redhead on the street, but he'd gotten what he wanted there, too. More, he'd seen no recognition in her eyes when she looked at him.

He wouldn't have figured her for Jake's type, but maybe that had been the point.

Plenty to think about there, but for tonight, he had the numbers right in front of him. He had pictures, he had e-mails. He had lives spread out on the screen.

He'd figure out what to do with them.

He'd figure out what to do about them.

24

The wild rhododendrons burst into bloom along the banks of streams, flashed and flamed their way up the slopes. In the high country the starry yellow blossoms of bluebeard lily peeked out from fanning ferns going thick and green.

She took Callie on hikes and hunts to find them when she could, or just to sit and listen to the music of bluebirds and juncos. Once, from a safe distance, she let her girl share the wonder of watching a bear fish in a tumbling stream before he lumbered off into the green.

Callie celebrated her fourth birthday in the backyard of the house where her mother had grown up, with friends her own age, with family, with people who cared about her.

For Shelby it was the shiniest gift in the pile.

There was a chocolate cake shaped like a castle with all the characters from *Shrek* scattered around it, and games, and gifts, balloons and streamers.

"It's the happiest birthday she's ever had."

Viola sat, her great-grandson in her arms, and watched the kids play on one of Callie's treasured gifts. A Slip 'n Slide.

"She's getting old enough to know what's what about a birthday now."

"It's more than that, Granny."

Viola nodded. "It's more than that. Does she ever ask about her father?"

"She doesn't. She hasn't said a word about him since we came home. It's like she's forgotten him, and I don't know if that's right or wrong."

"She's happy. She'll have questions one day, and you'll have to answer them, but she's happy. She sure has a love affair going on with Griff."

Shelby smiled over to where a soaking wet Callie clung to Griff's legs. "She does."

"How about you?"

"I can't deny we've got something going, and since where we are makes *me* happy, I'm not thinking too much where we're going to end up."

"You've lost most of the sad, worried look behind your eyes. You've got my eyes—through me, to Ada Mae, to you, and on to Callie," Viola pointed out. "Don't think I can't read them."

"I'd say the sad's gone, and the worry's lessened. Are you going to give up that baby and give somebody else a chance?"

Viola laid a kiss on Beau's forehead. "Here you go. Sleeping like an angel right through all this noise. Go ahead and take him out in the sun for a few minutes. Not too long now, but I expect some vitamin D's good for him."

It felt wonderful to have a baby in her arms again, to feel the weight and the warmth, to smell the down of his hair. She looked over at her daughter. Such a big girl now, sprouting like a weed. And the yearning pulled and tugged inside her as Beau waved a hand in the air in his sleep.

When Clay, nearly as wet as the kids, walked over, she shook her head. "Don't you even think about stealing this baby from me. You're too wet to take him. Besides, I've barely had my turn."

"I figured I wouldn't get much chance to hold him today."

"He favors you, Clay."

"That's what Mama says."

"She's right."

"I'm after a beer—Gilly's driving. You want one?"

"I'm sticking with lemonade until this is over."

Still he put an arm around her shoulders, turned her so they walked to the big tub holding the beer. "Forrest filled me in on what's going on with you."

"I don't want you to worry about any of that. You have a new baby to think about, not to mention Gilly and Jackson."

He kept his arm around her. He had a way of hugging you in, and always had, Shelby thought, that made her feel cherished. "I've got plenty of room for my sister in my thinking-about book. Nobody who looks like this Harlow character's come by work. I haven't seen anybody like that around the neighborhood. I know the police are still looking—that's what they have to do. But he's most likely gone. Even so."

He pulled out a beer, popped off the cap. "You be careful, Shelby. I feel better knowing Griff's looking out for you."

Instantly the shoulders he'd soothed tightened. "I've done a pretty good job looking out for myself."

After a gulp of beer, Clay tapped a finger to her nose—another lifelong habit. "Don't get your nose out of joint. I like knowing you can take care of yourself. I like it better Griff's looking out for you, too, so there's no point getting pissy about it."

"I'm not getting—" The baby stirred, let out a plaintive cry.

Clay glanced at his watch. "Like clockwork. Feeding time."

"I'll take him to Gilly."

She *wasn't* pissy, Shelby thought. A little annoyed, yes, and entitled to be. She'd gotten herself into a mess, no question about it, but she'd also put considerable time, effort and creativity into pulling herself and her child out of that mess.

She didn't want to be "looked after." It slid too close to what she'd let happen before. Hadn't she allowed Richard to "look after" her? To make all the decisions, run the show, lead her where he wanted her to go?

It wouldn't happen again. And she was going to make damn sure she showed her now four-year-old daughter what a woman could do if she worked hard enough, stood straight enough.

If she looked after herself.

Later, she dealt with party debris, carting in leftovers, bagging up trash. In the kitchen her mother and grandmother put the kitchen to rights.

"I'm making up a big batch of frozen margaritas," Ada Mae announced. "Mama and I have a yen for some."

"I could have a yen for a frozen margarita."

"Forrest and your daddy will probably stick with beer." While she worked, Ada Mae peered out the window, nodded. "Looks like they've about got the extra chairs and picnic tables put away. I don't know what Matt and Griff have a yen for, but expect Emma Kate might join our margarita party. You ought to ask what they'd like to have."

"I will."

"Or maybe the four of you want to go on out for a while. Oh, look how sweet Griff is with Callie." Ada Mae stopped to beam out the window now. "He's tying balloons on her wrists."

"She thinks if there's enough of them on her, she'll lift right off the ground."

"And see there? He's lifting her up, letting her pretend she's flying. That man's born to be a daddy. Some are," she said as she got out her big blender. "Your brother Clay, for one. He's so good with his babies. I wish they could've stayed awhile longer, but little Beau needed to go home, and Jackson was ready to fall asleep standing up. Callie, now, she's still got energy enough."

"Chocolate cake, and the excitement. She'll be spinning until bedtime."

"She sure does dote on Griff, and he right back on her. You can tell a man's character by the way he treats children and animals, I say. You've got a winner there, Shelby. One who's going to look after you right."

"Ada Mae," Viola said under her breath, casting her eyes heavenward even as Shelby spoke up.

"I'm looking after me."

"Of course you are, honey! Just look what a bright, sweet child you've raised, and on your own, too. It sure eases my worries seeing you with such a good man—fine-looking, too. We met some of his people when they came down to visit and help him with the old Tripplehorn place. Fine, good people. You should go on out and ask him to Sunday dinner."

Shelby's heart began to throb. She knew what it meant when a southern woman talked about lineage and Sunday dinners.

"Mama, I've only been seeing Griff for a couple months."

"He puts a light in you." Cheerful, oblivious, Ada Mae dumped generous scoops of ice in the blender with the tequila and margarita mix. "Puts one in your baby girl, too. And Lord knows he looks at you like you're the double chocolate cream in the candy box. He's got an easy way with friends and family, *and* has his own business. You don't want to let a man like that slip away."

"Let me help you with that, Ada Mae," Viola said, and hit the switch on the blender to drown out any more words.

Shelby didn't ask him to Sunday dinner, or suggest they go out with Matt and Emma Kate. She told herself she wasn't avoiding him over the next several days—just that she had a lot to see to. Just that she had a point to make that she *could* see to her own.

She did just that with Callie off on a playdate with a new friend, and the afternoon free.

She took time to work on her next playlist—circling back to the second round of the fifties. And with the raise she'd gotten the week before at both jobs, she opted to funnel that extra into a single credit card payment.

If she kept being careful—didn't buy any more new dresses no matter what her mama said—she should have another paid off by her own birthday in November.

That would be the best gift she could ask for.

At the knock on the front door, she closed the laptop, went down to answer.

Griff stood on the porch, smiled at her. "Hey."

"Hey back." She tried to fight off the flutter in her belly, and politely stepped back to let him in—stepped back just enough to avoid a hello kiss.

"Your mother wants shelves in the laundry room."

"She has shelves in the laundry room."

"She wants more."

"That sounds like Mama. I'll show you."

"How's it going?"

"Good. Busy, like I said before. I was just working on the next playlist, and dealing with paperwork. I never seem to dig out from under paperwork. Here you go. See? Shelves."

"Uh-huh." He stepped into the room off the kitchen, scanned the setup. "Decent size. Not much natural light. Plenty of shelves, but— She'd do better with cabinets over the washer and dryer. It's half a mudroom, isn't it?"

Drawn in, despite herself, on the idea of redesign, she frowned at the space. "I guess you could say it is. She and Daddy keep their gardening shoes and such in here, and winter boots, that kind of thing."

"She'd do better taking out those shelves there, putting in a bench with open cubbies under it for shoes and boots. Sit down, take your shoes off. Sit down, put your shoes on."

"It's a better use of it, isn't it? She'd probably like that idea."

"Shelves over that—high enough you wouldn't rap your head on them. A longer folding counter under the window. If it were mine, I'd widen that window, bring in more light. Anyway, longer counter with the sink on the far side instead of the middle, keep the hanging rod over it, but put base cabinets with pull-out shelves under it."

He shrugged. "Or she could just get open corner shelves over there and be done with it. I'll do some measuring."

"All right. I'll leave you to that."

"Do we have a problem?" he asked as he took his tape measure and pencil out of his tool belt, pulled out his notebook.

"A problem? No. Why?"

"Because this is the first time I've seen you since Callie's birthday party, and you're being pretty careful to keep at least a foot away from me."

"I've just had a lot to see to—like I said."

He took some measurements, wrote down some figures. "Don't bull-shit me, Shelby. It's insulting."

"I'm not. I really have had a lot to deal with." But he was right, it was insulting. "And maybe I needed to take a breath along with it. That's all."

"Okay." He wrote down something else, then those canny green eyes lifted, zeroed in on hers. "Did I do something that felt like I was putting pressure on you?"

"No, you didn't—you haven't. I just needed to . . . Are you looking out for me, Griffin?"

He wrote down more numbers, did a quick sketch, then lowered the pad to look at her again. "Sure I am."

"I can look after myself." Since it was true, she didn't care how snippy or defensive it sounded. "I need to look after myself. I can't—just won't—get caught up again so I let somebody take over."

She saw it in his eyes, the flash of temper, a surprising spark of heat.

"You know, I'm all about accurate measurements. You screw up there, you screw up everything. If you want to measure yourself by Richard, by what was, that's your baggage, Shelby. I hope you work that out. But if you're going to measure me by him, that's going to piss me off."

"I'm not. Exactly. What the hell else do I have to measure with? Six months ago I thought I was married."

"Well, you weren't."

He said it so flatly she couldn't say why the words made her wince.

"And it seems to me you've done a good job tearing down those walls, starting to build things in the way it works for you now. If this doesn't work for you, this you and me? That's going to be tough to take because I'm in love with you. But being in love with you doesn't mean I'll stand here and let you compare me to the son of a bitch who lied to you, who used you, who broke your trust and your spirit. I won't stand for that. And I won't be pushed away so you can fucking breathe because I'm looking out for you the same way anybody who gave a rat's ass would."

He shoved the measuring tape back in the pocket of his tool belt. "Work out what you need to work out. I'll get back to your mother."

He walked right by her and away before she could begin to gather herself. He'd never raised his voice—in fact his tone had been so calm it chilled her, and she felt thoroughly thrashed.

He couldn't say those things, couldn't talk to her that way, then just leave. He'd started a fight, that's what he'd done, and then left before she could block or toss a punch of her own.

She didn't have to put up with that.

She marched out of the laundry room—and oh, she intended to have a few choice words for her mama because if this didn't smack of an Ada Mae setup so she'd have time alone with her mama's choice of the man of her daughter's dreams, she didn't know Ada Mae Donahue Pomeroy.

And she damn well did.

Frustratingly, she'd been too slow or Griff had been too quick, because she heard his truck drive off before she made it to the front door.

That was fine, she told herself, pacing back and forth, then stomping up the stairs. That was likely for the best. She'd just get herself calm again before she said her piece. Whatever that piece might be.

Because her cheeks felt hot, she went into the bathroom, splashed cool water on her face. Her brain still felt hot, but that would simmer down, too.

She'd made him seriously angry, and she'd never seen him seriously angry.

Because they'd only been seeing each other a couple of months, she reminded herself. She'd been right to slow things down; she'd been right to take a step or two back.

Then she pressed her face into the towel.

He'd said he was in love with her. And that just filled her up and emptied her out again. It made her want to shake, it made her want to weep. It made her want to hold onto him as if her life depended on it.

She couldn't think about that now, just couldn't. She was too worked up to think about that. And he was too mad to think straight anyway.

She'd go for a walk, that's what she'd do. Go for a walk and clear her hot head. And she'd talk to Emma Kate. She really needed to talk to Emma Kate.

She started downstairs again, a little desperate to get out of the house. When she saw the front door open, she all but ran.

"Now you listen," she began, then stopped dead when she saw Forrest, and the two black-suited men behind him.

"Somebody got your red up," he said easily. And since he'd seen Griff's truck heading into town from this direction, he could deduce who'd gotten her red up.

"I was just . . . going for a walk."

"That's going to have to wait. What we have here is the FBI special agents Boxwood and Landry. They need a conversation."

"Oh. All right. I—"

"Could use something cold," Forrest continued.

"Of course. Y'all go ahead and sit down. I'll be right back."

He'd sent her off to give her a chance to compose herself, so she did her best to follow through. It had to be bad, she thought while she filled glasses with ice and tea, added out of habit sprigs of her mother's mint. It had to be bad to bring the FBI to the house. She set the glasses on a tray, added the little pale blue napkins, started to get out a plate for the frosted cookies her mother served to unexpected company.

The FBI wasn't company, she thought, and picked up the tray as it was.

She heard Forrest talking, something about white-water rafting and how his brother Clay would give them a hell of a ride if they had time for one.

The tall agent rose when she came in, took the tray from her.

"Appreciate it," he said, and she heard Georgia in his voice.

Tall, she noted, lean to the point of gangly, dark skin and eyes, and dark hair cropped close to the scalp.

He set the tray down, held out a hand. "Special Agent Martin Landry. My partner Special Agent Roland Boxwood. We appreciate you speaking with us."

"It's about Richard. It has to be about Richard." She looked from Landry to the other agent.

Boxwood had more girth, more muscle. He was as light as Landry was dark, with Scandinavian blond hair, blue-ice eyes.

"Sit down, Shelby." Forrest took her hand, drew her down on the couch with him. "Our federal friends here flew in from Atlanta today."

"Atlanta," she murmured.

"They've given me the go-ahead to bring you up to date." He gave her leg a quick rub. "I sent what you put together, what Griff put together, what I put together. I boiled that all down and sent it to the police in Miami, in Atlanta, in Philadelphia—and so on. And as the so-ons made a lot of sending, I sent the boiled-down to the FBI."

"You said you were . . . you said that's what you'd do."

"That's right. Now, their boss sent these agents down to talk to you directly."

When she nodded, Landry leaned forward. "Ms. Foxworth—"

"I wasn't ever, I only thought . . . It's Pomeroy. Please."

"Ms. Pomeroy, you sold some watches last February. To Easterfield on Liberty, in Philadelphia."

"Yes. Richard had several watches, so I . . ." She closed her eyes. "They were stolen, weren't they? I should've known, I should've realized. The man who helped me, at the store, he wouldn't have known. He was just helping me. I'll pay back the money. I don't . . ." She didn't have the money. Even if she wiped out the savings she'd kept—the house fund— she didn't have enough. "If I could have a little time, I'll pay back the money."

"Don't worry about that, Shelby."

Fiercely, she shook her head at Forrest. "He stole them, and I sold them. I used the money. It's not right."

"There are other items." Boxwood spoke. He had a gravelly voice that struck Shelby as threatening. "Cuff links, earrings, an antique hair clip."

"I have the hair clip! I didn't think it was worth anything, so I didn't try to sell it. I'll get it."

"Just sit, Shelby." Forrest pressed a hand on her leg. "Just sit for now."

"All of these items—the ones you sold in Pennsylvania," Boxwood continued, "match items reported stolen in burglaries in the Atlanta area from May of 2011 to September of 2014."

"More than one," she said softly. "More than one burglary."

"Numerous other items were reported stolen from these cases. We'd like you to look at photographs."

"Yes, I'll look. Of course. We didn't move to Atlanta until the fall of 2011. We didn't live there in May, but . . . He took trips. I don't know . . ."

"You lived there in April of 2012," Boxwood added.

"Yes. We lived there."

"Can you tell us where you were on April thirteenth of that year?"

"I . . . No. I'm sorry, I don't know. That was over three years ago."

"Think about it," Forrest said easily, though his hand stayed light on her thigh. "That was just a couple days before Easter. It was Good Friday."

"Oh. Easter, and Callie would have been nearly a year old. I got her an outfit, a bonnet and everything. I took her for photographs that Friday. I have them in her album. They had props—little chicks and stuffed bunnies. Baskets and colored eggs. I sent copies to Mama, and to Granny."

"I remember those pictures."

"That was Friday afternoon. I don't remember what time, exactly. It was at this place called Kidography. It was such a clever name. I remember because I took Callie back for other pictures, the photographer—her name was Tate . . . Tate—oh God—Tate Mitchell. I'm sure of it, I'm sure that's the right name. And after, that first time on the Friday before Easter, I changed Callie into play clothes and took her for ice cream as a treat. I'd bribed her with that, told her if she was a good girl I'd take her for ice cream—even that young she knew the word 'ice cream.' We went to Morelli's."

"Best ice cream in Atlanta," Landry said.

"You've been there? Callie loved going there. We went to Morelli's, and I let her spoil her dinner. I remember that, I remember thinking, Oh well, she's not going to want a good dinner now, so it had to be late afternoon."

"What about that evening, that night?" Boxwood prompted.

"Let me think." She pressed her fingers to her eyes. "Let me try to go back and see it. There was traffic—I remember that—and how Callie fell asleep in the car. I was worried, a little, that I wouldn't get home before Richard. He didn't like if he didn't know where I was. I thought about texting him, but I didn't. He didn't like me to call or text him when he was working."

Lowering her hands, she took a settling breath. "We got home, I think it must have been around six or so. Charlene—she did some cooking and light housekeeping for us—but she had the long weekend off. So Charlene wasn't there, and I was glad to have the condo to myself. I liked Charlene fine, I don't mean to say I didn't like her."

"But the place was quiet, just you and your daughter."

She nodded at Landry. "Yes, that's it. Callie was a little cranky, what with the photos, the ice cream, the nap in the car, but I settled her down with Fifi—her stuffed dog—and some blocks. She liked these blocks that made noise. I hurried to put dinner together. I swear I can't remember what I fixed, but I had it together by seven or seven-thirty, and I was relieved. But he was late. Richard. I put it in the warmer, and I got Callie her meal, coaxed her to eat a little, and she did since I'd waited until she'd worked off that ice cream. I gave her a bath, and read her a story, and put her to bed.

"I did text Richard then, just to say his dinner was in the refrigerator, and if I was in bed already, he could heat it up. I was angry, I guess, but tired, too."

She rubbed at her temple, rubbed and rubbed as she tried to see it all again.

"I went to bed not long after Callie was down. I never heard him come in. I saw him in the morning. I looked in, and saw he'd slept in the guest room."

It seemed so personal, where he'd slept, she had to fight off a blush.

"He, ah, used the guest room sometimes if he got in late. I fixed breakfast for Callie, and I put eggs on to boil. We'd dye eggs for Easter later that day. He didn't get up till close to noon, and he was in a fine mood. I remember that, too, clear now, as he was in such a fine mood, all jokey and excited. He made Callie laugh, I remember. I guess he could see I was a little put out, and he said something—I don't remember what because he always had some excuse. Late meetings, couldn't get away. Whatever it was, then he . . ."

Trailing off, she gripped her hands together, tight, tight. "Oh God, the hair clip. He said, here was a little something for Easter, and he gave me the clip. He said I should go fix my hair, and get Callie dressed up. He was taking his ladies out for lunch. He hardly ever wanted to take Callie anywhere, and she was so happy about it, I set being put out aside. I did exactly what he wanted. I'd gotten used to doing what he wanted. The hair clip." She pressed her lips together. "He'd stolen it, then he gave it to me, like you give a Milk-Bone to a dog."

She took a long breath. "I guess you can check on the time of the photos and all, but I can't prove the rest. Somebody probably saw me come in with Callie, but I don't see why they'd remember after so much time.

And no one was home. If you think I was with Richard, if you think I was part of what he did, I can't prove I wasn't."

"That's a lot of detail on a day that long ago," Boxwood pointed out.

"It was Callie's first Easter, and the first professional photographs. I'd wanted a family photo done, after she was born, but Richard never had time. So this was special. She—Tate—she took one of the two of us, and I sent it to my parents, special. She'd taken her bonnet off—Callie—and her hair'd gone everywhere, like mine would. I hadn't gotten to the salon to have mine straightened the way Richard liked it. It's a favorite photograph of mine."

She rose, took it from the mantel. "This is the one we had taken that Friday before Easter."

"She sure looks like her mama," Landry commented.

"When it comes to Callie," Forrest put in, "Shelby remembers."

"I guess that's true. Especially the firsts." She set the photo on the mantel again, sat back beside Forrest.

"Oh!" Struck, she came half off the sofa before Forrest nudged her back again. "I wrote it in her baby book. I wrote about the photographs, and put one of them in there. I can get it."

"I don't think that's necessary, for now, Ms. Pomeroy."

"It's not easy to admit you were stupid," she said carefully, "that you were duped. I never knew he was stealing, he was cheating people, and I was living in that fancy condo, I had all those clothes, and someone to help with the work because he stole and he cheated. I can't go back and change it. Should I get the hair clip? I know just where it is. You could give it back to whoever he stole it from."

"We believe he stole the hair clip, one of the watches you sold, and other items valued at approximately sixty-five thousand dollars from Amanda Lucern Bryce, of Buckhead. Her daughter found her on Saturday afternoon, April 14, 2012."

"Found her?"

"She'd fallen—or been pushed—down the stairs of her home. Her neck was broken in the fall."

The blood drained out of Shelby's face as she stared at Boxwood. "She's dead? She was killed? Richard . . . He was in such a good mood. He made Callie laugh. I'm sorry, I need a minute." She rose abruptly on legs that shook. "Excuse me."

She rushed to the powder room, just leaned over the sink. Her stomach pitched and roiled, but she wouldn't be sick. She would not be sick.

She would fight that off. She only had to breathe. Only had to take a few minutes and breathe, then she could deal with what came next.

"Shelby." Forrest rapped on the door.

"I just need a minute."

"I'm coming in."

"I need a damn minute," she snapped when he opened the door, then she just walked into his arms. "Oh God, oh God, Forrest. He took us out to lunch. He left that woman lying there, the one he stole from, and he came home and went to bed. Then he took us out to lunch. He ordered champagne. He was *celebrating*. He was celebrating, and he'd left that woman lying there for her daughter to find."

"I know it. I know it, Shelby." He stroked her hair, swayed with her a little. "One day it would've been you. I know that, too."

"How could I have not seen what he was?"

"You didn't. And you're not the only one who didn't. Nobody thinks you were part of this."

"You're my brother, of course you don't think so."

"Nobody," he repeated, and drew her back to look in her eyes. "They have to do what they do. You're going to look at pictures of stolen articles, of people he stole from. You'll tell them whatever you know. That's all you can do so that's what you'll do."

"I want to help. The clothes on my back, Forrest, the clothes I put on my baby. It makes me sick knowing where they came from."

"Tell me where the hair clip is. I'll get it."

"The top right drawer of the vanity in the bathroom I share with Callie. I have a box in there. All my hair clips are in it. It's mother-of-pearl with little blue and white stones. I thought it was fake, Forrest. I never thought—it's a hair clip, so I never gave it a thought."

"Don't worry about it. If you don't want to talk to them anymore now, I'll tell them you're done."

"No, I want to tell them whatever I know. Whatever I know I didn't know. I'll go back in now."

"When you've had enough, you just say."

"I want it over."

She went back, and once again Landry stood.

"I'm sorry," she began.

"Don't apologize. We appreciate your cooperation, Ms. Pomeroy."

She sat, picked up the tea. Too much of the ice had melted, but it was cool enough, and wet enough. "Did he kill other people? Do you know?"

"It's possible."

"He was never violent with me or Callie. If he had been . . . that would have been different. He didn't pay much mind to her at all, and less and less to me. He'd say things, cruel things sometimes, to me, but he was never violent."

Carefully, she set the glass down again. "I never saw what he was. If I had I would never have let him near my baby. I hope you can believe that. Callie's going to be home in about an hour. If we're not done, I need us to go somewhere else, or wait until tomorrow. I don't want her to hear any of this. She just turned four."

"That's not a problem."

"If you could give me another date. If I could figure out something around it, a holiday or a doctor's appointment, something that sticks out, I might be able to tell you what I was doing. What he was doing. I don't know what else I can do to help. I want to help."

"Let's stick with Atlanta for now, work forward." Landry nodded at Boxwood.

"August eighth, same year," Boxwood said.

"My daddy's birthday is August ninth, and Forrest was born on August fifth. We always had a double birthday party, the Saturday or Sunday closest. I wanted to come. I hadn't been home in a while, and I wanted Callie to visit her family. Richard said no. We had a charity gala to attend on that Saturday, and I couldn't go running off to Daddy. I was his wife, and expected to attend, and act like I belonged. It was at the Ritz-Carlton, in Buckhead."

"Saturday, August eighth, 2012, six figures' worth of jewelry and rare stamps were stolen from the home of Ira and Gloria Hamburg. They had attended a gala at the Ritz that night."

"Like in Florida," Shelby added. "Jewelry and stamps. It must've been like a . . . specialty of his."

"You could say that." Landry sat back. "Tell us about that evening."

25

She'd known the Hamburgs, a little, had attended a dinner party in their home. Richard had played golf with Ira Hamburg a few times, and she and Richard had hosted them at the country club. They'd socialized at other galas or fund-raisers now and then.

It wasn't hard to remember some of the details of that particular night as she'd pictured her family here, in this house, celebrating birthdays—and had missed them.

She remembered Richard bringing her a glass of champagne at one point and telling her, impatiently, to mingle, for God's sake, and stop sulking. He was going outside for a bit to have a cigar and talk some business with a couple of potential clients.

She couldn't say how long she'd mingled, wandered, put bids on a couple of items in the silent auction as he'd instructed her to do. It could've been as much as an hour, she supposed.

"He was in a good mood when he found me—said he'd been hunting for me, and why didn't we go check on our bids before the auction closed. I thought he'd gotten some business because he was in a better mood, and then he put a big bid on this wine package."

"The Hamburgs live less than a mile from the hotel," Boxwood pointed out.

"I know it."

They asked her about other nights, days, times. Some she could remember, others were lost in a fog. From the photographs, she recognized cuff links, the diamond studs, a three-strand diamond and emerald bracelet Richard had given her once, then accused her of losing when it disappeared from her jewelry box.

Forrest lingered after the FBI stepped out.

"Do you want me to stay?"

"No, no, I'm all right. Mama will be back with Callie soon. Just . . . do they believe me? Don't answer as my brother, but as a police officer."

"They believe you. They played a version of good cop/bad cop with Boxwood trying to trip you up here and there, giving you the hard eye. But they both believed you. You were helpful, Shelby. The best thing now is to put it aside. Let the FBI do what they do."

"I sold stolen property."

"You didn't know it was stolen, had no reason to think it had been. We'll work that out."

"How could I not see—how can they believe I didn't know? I swear, if I didn't know I didn't know, I wouldn't believe me."

"The BTK killer had a wife and raised two children, lived in a community, went to church. None of them knew what he was. Some people wear masks well, Shelby, know how to compartmentalize beyond what's normal."

"He wasn't right, was he? I mean, Richard couldn't have been right inside to be able to do all he did."

"The police officer's telling you he was a sociopath, and a shrink would likely have a lot of fancy terms for what he was. But no, he wasn't right. That's done—you're never going back to that. You're going to have to deal with some of it, but mostly? You need to look at the here and now, and the future."

"I've been trying to. What was just won't let go. I keep finding out more."

"You're a Pomeroy with MacNee in your blood. You'll stand up to it. You call me, you hear, if you need me."

"I will. I don't know what I'd've done if you hadn't been with me today."

"That's just one more thing you never have to worry about again."

Shelby thought if the whole of the Ridge didn't know about the FBI, then they soon would. So she told her parents everything as soon as she could.

The very next morning before the first customer came into the salon, she told her grandmother and the rest of the staff.

"I thought y'all should know."

"Ada Mae called me last night, told me all this," Viola began. "I'll tell you what I told her. None of this is your fault, not a bit. And we can look at that storm as the right hand of God making sure you and Callie were well rid of the son of a bitch."

"I'd rather he wasn't dead," Shelby said after a minute. "I'd rather he was alive so I could tell him what I think of him. I hate that he died believing I was nothing. I hate that he died knowing I never had an inkling what he'd done."

"My sister's ex kept a woman over in Sweetwater for six years," Vonnie piped up. "Had an apartment there with her and everything. None of us knew a thing about it—and that man went to the Lutheran church every Sunday he was in town. Coached Little League and belonged to the Elks Club. Lydia might never have known if the woman in Sweetwater hadn't called her up and told her all of it after *she* found out Lorne had taken up with a third woman."

Vonnie shrugged. "I guess it's not the same thing, but I'm just saying, we all thought the world of Lorne until we knew to think different."

"Thank you, Vonnie. I'm sorry for your sister, but I guess that makes me feel better."

"We don't always know somebody the way we think we know them." Crystal readied her station for her first appointment. "My good friend

Bernadette's cousin down in Fayetteville? Why, her husband embezzled twelve thousand dollars from her daddy's hardware business before they found out. Bernadette's cousin stayed with him after, too. And if you ask me, anybody who'd steal from family isn't worth spit."

"Hell, that ain't nothing." Lorilee fisted her hands on her hips. "I almost married Lucas John Babbott—y'all remember. About ten years back I was ready to walk down the aisle with that man. Something just said, Don't do it, Lorilee, so I didn't, but it was close. And I found out he'd inherited his granddaddy's cabin over by Elkmont. You know what he was doing in it? That man was cooking meth, and now he's in jail."

Others picked up the theme, ran with it. Viola stepped over, put an arm around Shelby's waist. "People ask me, don't you want to retire, Vi? You and Jack could go traveling, or you could sit on the porch and sip lemonade all day. And I think, Why, I wouldn't step away from this place for all the tea in China. Where else are you going to get such entertainment—and add to the till while you do?"

She kissed Shelby's cheek. "You did right telling everybody straight-out."

"It's the same as family."

"It's just the same. Crystal! I see your nine-o'clock crossing the street. You girls get on to work now."

The next day she met Emma Kate for a drink after work—and after she'd spent a solid hour with Bitsy.

"I'm buying. I owe you."

"I won't say no." Shelby pulled out her notebook, opened it. "All right, the engagement party first. It's all set—time, place, date. I did talk her down on the flowers, and the food. Just gentle suggestions about saving the big guns for the wedding. Why didn't we make this pretty and elegant, but sometimes elegance is simple. Since you're going with yellow and orchid for your wedding colors, I steered her away from that, too. Said why didn't we go for bride white—that's like you wanted, right?"

"Yes. All white flowers. You got her to agree?"

"I showed her pictures I'd found in magazines and online, and she got so excited. Then, since I'd already talked to the florist and we'd figured it all, I said let's order these right now! Got her when her enthusiasm was high."

Pleased and proud, Shelby brushed her palms together. "It's done."

"I owe you two drinks."

"Emma Kate, you owe me so many drinks we can't count them. We're down from that orchestra she wanted to hire out of Nashville, to booking Red Hot and Blue—which Tansy suggested, and you liked."

"Oh my God, we're not going to have men in white tuxedos playing waltzes? Matt and I both really liked Red Hot and Blue when they've played at Bootlegger's."

"It'll rock some, and be a good chance for you and Matt to see if you want them for the wedding, want something else or want to go with a DJ, since you haven't decided on that."

Meticulously, Shelby ticked it off her list. "Then I said to your mama how I'd work with the hotel as she needed to be fresh and be mother-of-the-bride-to-be and got her talking about what she'd be wearing, how she wanted her hair. And I'd made up these poster boards of table decorations and flowers and all that."

Shelby gave her nails an exaggerated buff on her sleeve. "I bowled her over, is what I did, then didn't give her much chance to waffle on it."

"Poster boards!"

"I also decided I'm not showing you. You're going to trust me, and be surprised. The wedding, you're in on every little detail, but this is going to be a surprise, and I promise you'll be happy with it."

"I don't have to think about it?"

"You don't have to think about it."

"If I didn't love Matt, I might change my mind and marry you. But then he has certain attributes you lack, not to mention between him and Griff they can fix anything. He's over at Griff's right now, helping out for a couple hours. I expect it'll run to three as Matt's got a head of steam working up on finding the right property and building a house, or doing what Griff's doing and finding an old place to rehab."

"Are you ready for all that?"

"Like I trust you to make everything look beautiful, I trust him to figure that out. I'll have plenty to say about it, but I'll let him get going on it first."

"All right, then." Shelby wiggled her butt back, leaned forward. "Let's talk weddings."

They plotted, planned, with Shelby taking notes.

"Put that down for now." After twenty minutes, Emma Kate waved at the notebook. "It's starting to make my head spin."

"We got a good start here."

"More than a good start, and it's time to change the channel. I want to know about you. Have you heard any more from the FBI?"

"No. I keep expecting them to come to the door again, with a warrant for my arrest as accessory after the fact, or something. But they haven't."

"If they think you had any part of all that, they don't deserve to be special agents."

Forrest said the same, Shelby thought, but it steadied her ground to hear it from her best friend.

"I'm going to go over all the pictures and letters again. I needed to put it away for a couple of days so I could start fresh. Maybe I'll remember something else, or find something else."

"What's the point now, Shelby?"

"Knowing. Just knowing. I don't expect I'm going to find a treasure map to what he stole in Miami, or any of the others that are still unfound. I'm supposing there are others still unfound. But knowing feels important."

"I wish you'd let it go, but the girl I grew up with wasn't ever good at letting things go if they mattered to her."

"This matters to me. What if I did find something that led to something, that took the police to somewhere else and they found them? At least that woman and her son in Miami would have that."

"Shelby." Emma Kate took her hand, squeezed it. "You're looking for a way to pay them back somehow, like you're paying off all that debt. And none of it's yours, none of it. And that's one of the reasons—I know you—you slapped the brakes on with Griff."

Shifting, Shelby got busy tidying her notes. "That's not exactly so."

"It's close enough. You looked happy together. You looked good together."

"I just wanted to slow things down some."

"You've got to move at your own speed, and I'd never say different."

"I guess he had some things to say about it."

"Not much, not to me. Not to Matt, either, or I'd've gotten it out of Matt. He's not the vault Griff is, and I know the combination anyway. I expect he might say more tonight, working on the house, having a beer, that sort of thing. I'll get that out of Matt easy enough."

"He was awful mad. It's hard to know how to deal with a man who gets mad so . . . reasonably."

"I'd hate that!" Emma Kate laughed, sat back. "You can't win against reasonable, not really."

"And what makes it harder? He went by the house when I was working—he'd know I was working and Mama had Callie. Mama said how he went out back with Callie and spent nearly an hour with her on the swings, with the puppy."

"Well! That shows you what kind of dastardly individual you're dealing with."

"All right, Emma Kate." Shelby let out a sigh. "I don't know what to do about it, exactly. I've got a right to be mad about some of the things he said."

Sipping wine, Emma Kate lifted her eyebrows. "Reasonable things?"

"I guess from where he's standing, but that doesn't make them less awful for me."

"I'm trusting you on this engagement party, and you haven't let me down yet."

"And I won't."

"That's why I trust you. Why don't you trust me?"

"I— Of course I do. I do trust you."

"Good. Go over there and talk to Griff."

"Oh, but—"

"Did I say 'but' on the party? I did not," Emma Kate said definitely. "So you trust what I'm saying to you, and go over and talk to Griff. Matt says he's been stewing for days. I can see you are, too, maybe needed to, but stewing time's over. Go talk it out. One way or the other, both of you are bound to feel better, or at least know where you both stand."

She wasn't going to do it—wasn't it better to just let things sit awhile? But the idea sat in the back of her head, nagging, through dinner, through the bedtime ritual with Callie.

She told herself to settle down, spend the rest of the evening going over the photos and letters again. But she couldn't settle.

She went down where her parents held their own evening ritual of TV and needlework.

"Callie's all tucked in. I wonder if you'd mind if I went out awhile? There's something I'd like to do."

"You go on." Her father gave her an absent smile before he zeroed back in on the ball game. "We're not going anywhere."

"I'm dragging your daddy as far as the front porch when the game's over. We're going to sit and have ourselves a glass of tea and smell the roses rambling up the trellis."

"You enjoy that, and thank you. I won't be very long."

"You take your time," her mother said. "And you put some lipstick on, fluff your hair some. You can't go over to Griff's without your lipstick."

"I didn't say I was going to Griff's."

"A mama knows. You put some lipstick on."

"I won't be long," Shelby repeated, and got out before her mother suggested she change her clothes.

GRIFF HADN'T SHOWERED off the day, because he'd decided the day wasn't done. Even after Matt left, he kept at it. He broke briefly—let the dog out, fixed a sandwich, let the dog in, but kept focused on the work.

He'd finished the closet, and thanks to Matt, the interior was drywalled, had its second coat of mud. So he focused on the window seat he'd designed for the double windows looking over the backyard. It'd be a nice place to sit—with convenient storage beneath.

He saw the room, finished, pretty clearly. And even if that image irritated him half the time, he would damn well stick with it.

He made a habit of sticking.

Once he had the closet sanded, the window seat finished, the trim finished, all the room really needed was paint and a good clean. Well, some punch out—outlet covers, light switch covers, and he figured—and had wired for—a ceiling fan with a light kit.

Had to find the right one, one that worked with his image of the room.

Maybe he'd play around online tonight, see what he found.

Then there was the small en suite. That he'd tackle next, and probably within the next evening or two as he had the time.

He had music going, heard nothing else until Snickers began to bark. When the dog scrambled out of the room, raced downstairs, Griff pulled out his earbuds.

He picked up his hammer, tested its weight, and started out with it. He heard the knock then—he really needed to do a doorbell—and though he doubted the laptop invader would bother with a knock, he glanced out the landing window.

And saw Shelby's van.

Emotions rolled up, conflicting, contrasting. Pleasure—God, he'd missed just looking at her face. Annoyance. Whose fault was it he hadn't seen her face? Puzzlement, as it wasn't like her to drop by after nine at night. Relief, tremendous, that she had.

He set the hammer down on the steps, walked the rest of the way down, where the dog barked and wagged at the door.

He opened the door and wondered how he managed to keep his heart from just falling at her feet.

"I hope it's all right I came by," she began. "I wanted to talk to you."

And he wanted to pluck her right off the ground, feel her hang onto him while he kissed them both brainless.

"Sure."

"Hey, Snickers. There's a good dog," she soothed as she bent over to rub him. "Look how he's grown already. Maybe we could sit outside. It's such a nice night."

"We can do that. You want a drink or anything?"

"No, don't bother. You're working—you smell like sawdust and sweat, in a good way."

"Just fiddling with a couple things. I could use a break."

He stepped outside, gestured to one of the chairs.

"I know you're mad at me," she began as she sat, and kept rubbing the dog, who plopped his forefeet on her knees. "And you were clear as to why."

"Okay."

"I tried to explain my reasons to you, but I don't think you understand."

"I understand," he countered. "I just don't agree with your reasons."

"You haven't lived my life, Griffin. One that brought federal agents to the door."

"I heard about that, and I heard they were grateful for your cooperation."

"Forrest."

"He wasn't passing on state secrets. Plus, they talked to me."

"They . . ." Her hands stilled; her head whipped around. "They came here?"

"Just for a chat. It's also not a state secret you and I have spent time together since you got back. It wasn't a problem."

Her eyes sparked, flashed. Temper, resentment, frustration—he saw the mix clearly enough.

"Why can't you see it's a problem for me that they'd come here, ask you questions about something you didn't have anything to do with?"

"You haven't lived my life, either, Shelby. They knew about the laptop business, so they followed through. The way I look at it, having the locals and the feds involved in this is only a good thing."

"He killed someone."

"What?"

"They didn't tell you that, and Forrest didn't choose to impart that information in his reports to you?"

"No, and don't be so snotty about it. Your brother's my friend," he continued before she could toss something else at him. "He doesn't report to me. He talks to me."

She *had* been snotty about it, she admitted, but . . . Put it aside, she ordered herself, and say what needed saying.

"Richard killed a woman, in Atlanta. Or she fell down the stairs, it's not altogether clear, while he was stealing from her. He left her there, just left her dead or dying on the floor and walked away. That's who I thought I married, that's who I had a child with, that's who I lived with for nearly five years."

"That's hard on you, and I'm sorry about it. But what he did, who he was, what he was? It doesn't have anything to do with me. It doesn't have anything to do with you and me."

"It has everything to do with me, so that means it has to do with you and me. Why can't you see that?"

"Because this is now." He said it simply. "Because I'm in love with you.

Because I can see you have feelings for me. Maybe you're not where I am, and I can't argue about that, but you have feelings. What I see is you pushing them away, and me with them, because a sociopath, a con man, a thief, and apparently a murdering son of a bitch, used you, deceived you, and you're letting yourself feel guilty and responsible for it."

"I have to be responsible for my own choices, my actions and the consequences of them."

"Okay," he said after a moment. "You're right about that. Now, when are you going to stop beating yourself up for them?"

"I can't make another mistake."

"I'm not a mistake." He shoved up at that, had to stride away, pull his control back, grip it. "Don't hang that on me."

"No, no, it's me. It's—"

"It's not you, it's me? That's a classic."

"Oh, just shut up a minute. Just shut up! I do have feelings for you, and they're scaring me. I can't just run with my feelings again because, yes, this is now. Now I have a little girl. I have a life to make for her, for us. I have to know I'm doing right, not just taking what I want for me. I need to take a breath, damn it. I need to settle down and think, not just feel. I hurt people. I hurt my family, and I'm never, never going to do that again. I hurt myself in the long run."

She rose as well, walked to the rail on the other side of the steps from him. Across the lawn, into the trees, scores of lightning bugs put on a show, countless pulses of warm light against the dark.

"I'm not beating myself up, or not much anymore. Or feeling sorry for myself. I'm done with that. I came home, and I brought my girl home, and I'm building that life for us. That feels right. I feel good about that. It would've been enough, Griffin, it would've been more than enough for me. Then you . . . I just . . . There were—are—feelings."

"I planned to go slower. I figured to get you to go out with me and Emma Kate and Matt a few times, over a couple months, maybe. Get used to being around me. Then I'd ask you out. I didn't follow the blueprint."

"You have a blueprint?"

"I always have a blueprint. But the thing about them is, sometimes you see how to improve the whole with a change, or some changes. So you do. I planned to go slower, but . . . Did I push you?"

"No." It was wrong, she admitted, it was unfair and wrong to let him think so. "No, you didn't push me, Griff. You . . . appealed, and you . . ."

She looked out, all those pulses of warm yellow. He'd put a light in her, she thought. Pulses of light against the dark she'd carried.

"How much you appealed caught me off guard. I wanted—want—to be with you. You're the opposite of Richard. And I asked myself if that was why you appealed so much. You're so different from him. Not flashy or showy, just—"

"Dull?"

She glanced over quickly, relieved when she saw him smile. "No, not dull. Real. I needed real more than I can say, and there you were. I have feelings, and they scare me."

"I don't mind that. You take the time you need to work that out. Don't make excuses not to see me—be straight about it."

"I didn't know how. I hadn't figured out how because I didn't want to stop seeing you. I felt I should, for a while, but I didn't want to."

"Has it been a while yet?"

"It feels like it's been a lot longer than a while."

"There's a point of agreement. I've missed the hell out of you, Red."

"You came by to see Callie when I was at work."

"I missed the hell out of her, too. And Callie and I didn't have a fight."

With a nod, Shelby stared out at the dark, the light. "I kept thinking you'd come by to see me, too. You came to Friday Nights, but you stayed away from me."

"You hurt me."

She turned to him quickly. "Oh, Griff—"

"I'm telling you, Shelby, don't stack me up against him, not in any way. It hurts me, and it really pisses me off."

"I'm sorry for that. I can't promise it won't happen again, but I'll work on it."

"That's good enough."

"You hurt me, too, and really pissed me off."

"I'm sorry for that. I can't promise it won't happen again, but I'll work on it."

That made her laugh, and mean it. "I really have missed you something awful. I don't just mean the sex, though I've missed that. I just missed talking to you. But . . ."

"Uh-oh."

"I thought I was in love once before, so fast it was like being swept under a wave. But I wasn't in love, not the way it should count. Maybe you need a little time, too."

"If he'd been who he pretended to be when he took you under that wave, would it have counted?"

"I . . ." She could only lift her hands, let them fall.

"You can't say because he wasn't. He wasn't who you thought he was, so you can't know. Here's what I know. I wanted you the first second I saw you. That was more a holy shit moment than what they'd call love at first sight. Look at her. That's the most beautiful woman I've seen in my life."

She wanted to laugh again, but his words clogged her throat. "Wet and miserable, as I recall."

"And sad and beautiful. Then you and Callie, and you walking home with her, pushing that stroller and all those groceries up those hills. You're so mad—at yourself—so worn out. And she's so sweet. So I wanted you, then I wanted to help you. I fell for Callie first, I'll tell you that straight-out. She had me wrapped up in about two minutes."

"She has a way."

"She's got your way. I'm surprised you don't see it. Anyway, then I heard you sing, and I started falling. I watched you sing, and I fell harder. Then I had you, and that put the cap on it. But what twisted the cap, secured it tight, was—" He stuck his hands in his pockets as he studied her. "Hell, you might not like what twisted the cap tight."

"I want to know. There isn't a woman in the world who wouldn't."

"All right. What twisted the cap tight? You punching Melody. I don't think I'm a particularly violent man, but when you did that, all I could think was, Well, hell, Griff, you're in love with her. You'd be a fool not to be."

"You're making that up."

"I'm not." He stepped toward her, laid his hands on her shoulders. "I had to pull you off—sort of wished I didn't have to—but I realized, yeah, I want her. I want to help her. I can fix some things for her. But god-*damn*, a woman who throws a punch like that? She can fix some things, too. She can do whatever she needs to do."

She'd thought hearing that he was in love with her rattled her. But that last sentence, the tone of admiration, just stunned. "You thought that?"

"I know that. I've seen it. I admire the hell out of it. And I love you. So I don't mind scaring you a little because you'll handle it. But when you look at me, Shelby, you'd better see me. Just me. When you think of me, just me."

"I don't think of anyone but you when you kiss me, when you touch me."

"Then I should do more of that."

"Oh God, I wish you would."

She wrapped herself around him, pressed her mouth to his.

And he did a lot more of it.

"Come inside." He couldn't get enough. "Come to bed."

"Yes." She ran her hands up his back, thrilled to feel hard muscle again. "Yes." Drew in his scent—sweat and sawdust. "Yes."

They circled toward the door, and she said, "Oh. Wait."

"Please God, don't turn that into a no."

"No—I mean yes." Still wrapped around him, she managed a breathless laugh. "I mean, I need to text Mama. I told her I wouldn't be long, and I'm going to be longer."

"Okay. Text and walk."

"I can do that." She took out her phone, worked to keep her hands steady enough to write the quick text. "She knew I was coming to see you, so I don't think she'll be surprised to— She's sure quick to answer."

They'd made it inside, to the stairs, had started up. Shelby stopped halfway.

"Problem?"

"No. No, not a problem. She says—" Shelby let out another quick laugh. "She says you'll follow me home, so why don't I save you the trouble of that, stay the night here. Then she says—I guess you could say she knows me—don't worry about Callie wondering where I am in the morning. We should get up early enough for me to bring you home for breakfast. She'll make pancakes."

"I like pancakes."

"Yes, but—"

"Text: Thank you, Mama. We'll see you in the morning."

He nudged her up another step so they were eye level, then laid his lips on hers. "Stay. Sleep with me tonight. Wake up with me in the morning."

How could she resist? Why would she? She trailed her fingers over his cheeks. "I wasn't expecting to. I don't have a thing to sleep in."

"If that's an issue, I won't sleep in anything, either. We'll be even."

"That's fair." She laughed again, a little giddy, when he swept her up, carried her the rest of the way with the puppy running to catch up.

26

Shelby wound her way into the fifties, mixed up the playlist with bluegrass.

She slipped in early to rehearse, thought it wonderful and amazing that she already had more than half a dozen Friday Nights in her pocket.

Tansy applauded when she finished "Rolling in My Sweet Baby's Arms."

"Love it!"

"I didn't see you over there. I thought I'd punch in some bluegrass, mix in the folk and traditional with the standards. I thought I'd weave in a lot of Patsy Cline. Like a featured artist?"

"I love that, too. It's going to be even better when we bring in some musicians, have a real stage. Which we will by September—October latest, according to Matt. The permits came in this morning!"

"Tansy, that's such good news."

"I can't wait to get started. I'm scared, too, as we're pouring a lot of money into this expansion. But . . . the last few weeks sure show people like coming in on the weekend, hearing live music."

"You talked Derrick into trying every Saturday night for a band, didn't you?"

Raising her joined hands over her head, Tansy turned a victory circle. "We're going to try it for the rest of the summer, then see if the take justifies the outlay. You're a big part of why we can do all this, Shelby. I don't know how long it would've taken me to talk Derrick into the expansion if you hadn't hit it with Friday Nights."

"I love doing it, and you gave me a chance. I guess it's worked out pretty damn perfect for both of us." She stepped off the little stage. "How're you feeling?"

"Just a little queasy first thing in the morning still, but Derrick brings me saltines and ginger ale, and that usually settles it down. And look!" She turned to the side, cupped her hands on her belly. "I'm showing!"

"My goodness." Shelby widened her eyes at the tiny, tiny bulge. "You're enormous."

"Maybe not yet," Tansy said with a laugh, "but"—she lifted her shirt— "I had to jury-rig my pants with a carabiner. Can't button them anymore. I'm going to move into yoga pants, and buy myself some maternity clothes first chance I get."

Shelby remembered well that feeling, that glow. "They make such cute ones, so you don't feel like you're wearing a tent or your granny's tablecloth."

"I've already got some in a shopping basket online. I just want to make one more pass before I order. Now I know you want to get back to rehearsing, but I want to know how you're doing."

It couldn't be avoided, Shelby thought. The past dogged her like a shadow at high noon. "I'm so sorry you had to talk to those agents."

"Derrick and I were fine with that, don't you worry."

"Forrest said they've gone back to Atlanta. There wasn't much I could do to help them find all Richard stole. I know it's silly, but I feel like if I could remember something, or tell them something that leads them to finding even one more thing, I'd be better about it all. When it comes down to it, they told me more than I could tell them."

"It's hard, what they told you."

"It taught me something. If I want Callie to grow up to be a smart, strong woman, someone who values family and friends, and respects herself, I have to show her. If I want her to know the satisfaction of making something of herself with effort and work, I have to show her. That's what I'm trying to do."

"It's what you are doing."

"I feel like I have to counterbalance—you know what I mean—all she's going to hear one day about her father."

"When she does, she'll have you, and your family. She'll have us, your friends."

"Seems like Richard never learned, never understood that's more than all the jewels he stole, all the money he swindled. If the years with him had any good to them, it was putting that bone deep in me. I took too much for granted before that."

SHE TOOK NOTHING for granted now, not the laughter inside the salon or the sighs of pleasure in the Relaxation Room.

She gave her grandmother a quick, impulsive hug after she set more towels at the shampoo stations.

"What's that one for?"

"Just for you. I'm happy being here with you. I'm just happy."

"I'd be happy, too, if I had a man like Griffin Lott looking at me like I was the Venus de Milo, Charlize Theron and Taylor Swift all at once." Crystal paused in her work, snapped her scissors. "I swear, I want a man for sex, but if Charlize Theron walked in and said, 'Hey there, Crystal, how about we go on over to your place and roll around in the sheets?' I believe I'd take her straight home and give that a go."

Amused, Viola rinsed off her customer's hair. "Charlize Theron. Is she the only one who'd tempt you to switch over from a man?"

"I believe she is. Now, that Jennifer Lawrence. She's as pretty as they come, and I do believe she'd be nothing but fun to sit around and have a drink with. But she's no Charlize Theron. Who'd you switch with, Shelby?"

"What?"

"Who's your fantasy lesbian lover?"

"I never thought about it."

Crystal just circled a finger in the air. "Give it a minute."

No, Shelby thought again, she'd never take these crazy fun conversations for granted.

"I'd try Mystique," she decided, and had Crystal frowning at her.

"Who?"

"She's a super villain—from the X-Men. Forrest and Clay were just crazy for the X-Men, remember, Granny? Jennifer Lawrence, the one you'd like to have a drink with, plays her in the movies now. Mystique can change into anybody, any shape, anything. So it seems to me a roll in the sheets with her would cover about anything you were after."

"I believe we have a winner," Viola decreed, and sat her client down in the chair.

A couple of hours later, she cuddled baby Beau and watched Callie and Jackson play on the swing set. She thought it would rain by nightfall, she could scent it, see it. But for this moment, it was about as perfect a late spring evening as she could ask for.

Her father was delayed at the clinic, so Clay saw to a few little gardening chores, and Gilly sat in the porch rocker, banished from the kitchen by her mother-in-law.

"It ought to be illegal to feel this happy," Gilly said.

"I'm awful glad it's not. Today, I'd be sharing a cell with you."

"I saw Griff today."

She'd have to get used to people equating her happiness with Griff. And they weren't altogether wrong. "You did?"

"I took the boys for a walk this morning, before the heat set in, and he was down the road a bit, fixing Miz Hardigan's gate—the sheriff's mama."

"She was in the salon today."

"I stopped for a while. It's nice of him to go by and see to little things like that for her. They don't charge her for those little things. I know, 'cause she told me herself. She gives them baked goods, and she knitted them both caps and gloves for Christmas.

"Look how big Jackson is! It wasn't so long ago he couldn't get up on that swing unless one of us lifted him onto it."

And Gilly's eyes filled.

She waved a hand in the air as Shelby patted her arm. "I've still got too many hormones, I guess. But . . . I don't think I'm going back to work, Shelby, when my maternity leave runs out."

"I didn't know you were thinking about that. I know you love your job at the hotel."

"I do, and I wasn't thinking about it, not really, until . . ." She reached over, stroked a finger over Beau's cheek. "I just don't think I can stand to leave them both. I just want to stay home with them for a while. A year maybe. Clay and I have talked about it. We know things'll be a little tight, but—"

"It's hard. It's hard to choose, it's hard to have to choose."

"I love my work, I really do. I'm good at it, too, but I want this year, that's all. I want this year for myself and my family. One year out of all the rest doesn't seem like too much, but it would be everything to me."

"Then you should take it. You've worked at the hotel since college. I bet they'd give you like a sabbatical. Maybe they can't hold your job, I don't know, but I bet you could go back when you're ready. And you won't have any regrets."

"It's putting a lot on Clay."

"He's got strong shoulders, Gilly."

"I never thought I'd want to stay home full-time, but I want this year. What about you? What do you want?"

"It feels like I've got it."

"For tomorrow."

Shelby glanced at the kitchen door. "I was thinking, just thinking. I haven't told anybody but Emma Kate as yet."

"I know how to keep quiet."

"You do. Once I get my head all the way above water, if I can find my own place, and I can find one I can work out of? I was thinking maybe I could start up some kind of decorating business. Designing and co-ordinating."

"You've always been good at it."

"I've been taking some classes online to get more experience and education. Just a couple to start," she added. "Ones I've been able to fit in."

"You fit in more than anyone I know—except Granny."

"Maybe I'm making up for not having enough to do for so long. I thought, well, if I could prove myself, Griff and Matt might use me some, or talk me up to their clients."

"Sure they would. They have to redo rooms and areas up at the hotel regularly, Shelby. I'd put in a word for you."

"Oh, I don't know if—"

"Think big."

"I guess I might as well. It's just thinking right now anyway. I know I could run a business—still, I'd take more classes. But I sure know how to juggle money, keep accounts. It's a ways off, but I've started tucking some money away for business classes."

"Anytime I start toying around with the idea of starting up a cake and pastry business, that's what stops me dead in my tracks, backs me up and turns me around the other way. The business," Gilly said with an eye roll. "But you've got that MacNee in you. You know what else?"

"What else?"

"I've been wanting to give our bedroom a makeover. Between Jackson, then Beau, doing up the nursery fresh and getting Jackson in his big-boy room, our bedroom hasn't been touched in five years. It shows."

"Makeover can be a lot of fun, but . . ."

"Yes, there's the MacNee," Gilly said with a laugh. "Clay's the same. Doing it over costs. If I'm going to stay home, I'll have to be frugal about it, I know that, but God, Shelby, how I'd love to have a grown-up bedroom, a place for me and Clay to be me and Clay now and then. I can be frugal, especially if you'd help me out. You could practice on us."

Gilly shifted, wrapped a hand around Shelby's arm for emphasis. "Shelby, we've still got that mix of his old bedroom furniture and mine in there, and that awful, ugly lamp my aunt Lucy gave us as a wedding present."

"That is an awful, ugly lamp."

"If she didn't claim it was an heirloom, I'd have accidentally knocked it over and made sure it broke in a dozen pieces. I don't want fancy. I just want fresh and peaceful. Help me."

"I'd love to help."

The lamp had to go, but the furniture . . . refinish or paint, new hardware. It could work.

"And I've got plenty of being-frugal-about-it ideas. Sometimes it's no more than switching things around and repurposing. Using what you've already got in a new way, adding some touches. And paint. Paint'll change a lot for a little."

"Now I'm getting fired up instead of teary. Do you have any time this week?"

"I could come by tomorrow morning, after I take Callie to Chelsea's, before I head to the salon. About eight-thirty? Is that too early?"

"Nothing's too early when you've got a toddler and a newborn. I was wondering if I could— Well, hey, Forrest."

"Hey, Gilly." He walked out from the kitchen, bent over the baby. "When's he going to do something besides sleep?"

"Come on over and pay us a visit about two a.m."

She caught the look in his eyes and, understanding, pushed up. "I'm going to take him in awhile—and pass him off to his grandmother. That'll give me some time in the kitchen whether she wants me there or not."

She took the baby from Shelby, slipped inside.

"I need a minute," Forrest told Shelby.

"Sure. Sit down."

"Kids all right out here for a minute? Clay's right over there in the vegetable patch playing farmer."

"He's got Daddy's knack for it, and the kids are fine."

"Then let's take a walk around front."

"What is it?"

"Around front," he repeated, took her arm.

"You're making me nervous, Forrest, and damn it, I was having a really good day."

"I'm sorry for that, and sorry to drop this on you on a really good day."

"Am I in trouble? Does the FBI think—"

"No, it's nothing like that." He guided her around the side of the house toward the front yard. Out of sight of the kids, out of earshot. "It's Privet, the Florida PI."

"I remember who Privet is," she said testily. "Did he tell you who his client is, finally?"

"No, and he won't. He was found dead early this morning, by his secretary."

"Oh my God. What happened?"

"It looks like he was killed between ten and midnight, and it looks like he was shot with the same gun that killed Warren."

It shouldn't come as a shock, she thought, and still it did. "He was murdered?"

"That's right. Looks like a break-in, or made to look like it. Like a sloppy one. But then you figure—from the report we got from the investigating officers—he was shot at his desk. He had a nine-millimeter in the drawer. There wasn't any sign he went for it, or put up a fight. Head shot, like Warren, too. Not a contact shot, but close range."

"Let me take a breath." She took it bending over, hands on her thighs. "I didn't like him. He scared me some coming into the house up North the way he did, and following me here. Just . . . lurking. But he left me alone when you told him to."

"They found pictures he'd taken of you and of Callie in his office, in his files."

"Callie."

"Some notes he'd made, an expense account. Not yet paid, and over-due, according to the file. They don't have the name of the person who hired him to shadow you. The locals are talking to the secretary, and to his associate, but so far nobody seems to know who hired him for this particular job. And there's no record."

"Maybe he didn't have a client. Maybe he lied."

"Maybe."

"But . . . you said it looked like a break-in, but wasn't."

"The door was forced from the outside, some electronic equipment was missing. His watch, his wallet, the petty cash. Things tossed around some. You might think it was a sloppy break-in. But his personal tablet and laptop, they were gone, too. And it seems the ones at his house aren't turning up."

"Someone was in his house, you think?"

"Slicker job there as there's no sign of forced entry at all. But anything to do with this case of his, except for those pictures, some notes and ex-penses, they're gone."

She straightened. Her face still felt too hot, her head too light, but she knew how to follow basic logic. "You think what happened to him goes back to that damn robbery in Florida."

"I do, as he brought it and the finder's fee up to me when I advised him to move on."

"So back to Richard—or to Harlow, now. Harlow escaped from prison, and he probably had a new identity somewhere. He hired the detective to help him find Richard. But he found me and Callie. Only me and Callie because Richard was already gone. He came here, and he saw his other partner. She'd turned on him, so he killed her."

"We know he was here. You saw him yourself."

"The detective either thought Harlow was really a client, or was working with him. Doesn't matter much, I guess, which it was now. But he probably let Harlow into the office, sat there talking to him."

"And either Harlow didn't like what he heard, or he figured Privet as a loose end. He cut it off, staged a break-in, took what he needed—whatever he felt might link him—took a few valuables, some cash, and took off."

"He can't think I'm a loose end, Forrest. He stole all that information so he knows I'm not just broke but in debt. If he's still looking for those millions, he knows I can't tell him where they are."

"I don't know why he'd come back here, but I want you to keep being careful. He's killed two people now. Miami's going to keep us updated—professional courtesy. The feds will put an oar in, I expect. The damn thing is, Shelby, they can't find anybody who's seen hide nor hair of this guy except you."

"He let me see him."

"That's right."

She glanced toward the backyard, where the children played and her older brother tended the vegetable garden. "I can't run, Forrest. I've got nowhere to go, and it has to be safer for Callie here than anywhere else. I've got nothing for this man. I have to believe he was just—like you said—taking care of a loose end. It's horrible, but that's what he did."

"That's what it looks like. Don't go anywhere without your phone."

"I never do." She patted her pocket, and the phone in it, but Forrest shook his head.

"Anywhere. You take a shower, it goes in the bathroom with you. And." He pulled a small canister out of his pocket.

"What's this?"

"Pepper spray. You've got your Second Amendment rights, but you never could shoot worth shit."

Because he wasn't far off in that assessment, she bristled. "I wasn't that bad."

"Worth shit," he repeated. "And you don't want a gun around Callie. Neither do I. So you leave the gun to me, but you take this. You carry this with you. You have trouble, aim for the eyes. Put it in your pocket for now," he advised when she studied the canister.

"I'll take it, I'll be careful if doing that and saying that puts your mind at ease. He's no reason to come after me, especially now. I want to put this aside—that doesn't mean I'll be stupid—but I'm not going to keep it at the center of my life anymore. Now, Mama made her party potatoes and she's doing up some collard greens. I marinated the chicken myself, and Daddy's going to grill that up once he gets home. Why don't you come on in and eat?"

"I hate to say no. I love those damn potatoes. But I've got some things to do. Tell Mama I'll come by later if I can, scrounge up any leftovers."

"I will. I need to get back, check on the kids."

"You go on, then. I'll see you later."

He watched her walk back around the house. Things to do, he thought. The first was to go by Griff's. It wouldn't hurt to give his friend the information. He wanted as many eyes on his sister as he could get.

ON HIS HANDS AND KNEES, Griff set the next tile on the bathroom floor. The golden sand color made him think of the beach, so he thought the little en suite would be both pretty and cheerful.

While he listened to Forrest, he sat back on his heels.

"It can't be random. Breaking into a PI's office—*that* PI's office, killing him. You guys with the badges can't think that's random."

"It's being looked into. No," Forrest added, leaning on the doorjamb while Griff worked. "We don't think it's random. The trick is connecting Privet to Harlow, to Warren, to that fucker Foxworth, to the Miami case back five years ago. Odds are Harlow killed him, but you gotta ask why. What did the PI know, or who did he know, 'cause maybe those odds don't play. Maybe there's somebody else we don't know about."

"That's not a comfort."

"Nothing comfortable about any of this."

"What happened in Miami five years ago isn't over."

"Nope."

"If Harlow had the take from that job, he'd be gone. Maybe the PI was the last thing he had to cross off, and now he is. Gone."

Griff set the spacers, moved to the next tile. "Then again, if the PI knew where the take was, it seems like he'd have been gone."

"It's a puzzle."

"You're worried this Jimmy Harlow may be missing some pieces yet, and may still think Shelby's got them."

Forrest hunkered down. "There's not a lot we can do here but keep hunting for him locally, asking questions, showing his picture around. The federals, they're sniffing out leads, but what I get is there isn't a lot to sniff at this point. They've dug up some of Foxworth's past associates— same on Harlow and Warren. But nothing's shaken out of that. Not that they're telling us local badges, anyway."

"Do you think they're holding back?"

"Can't say for sure, and don't see why they would. But you never know. What I know is we've got an unsolved murder in the Ridge, and that doesn't sit well with any of us. My sister's in the middle of it, and that doesn't sit well with me, or with anybody in the department. We're keeping an eye out for her, extra patrols and the like. But she's not inclined to have dinner with the sheriff or spend the night with Nobby."

"If she was, I'd end up in jail for assaulting an officer. I'm looking out for her, Forrest. She doesn't much like that terminology, but she's going to have to live with it. It'll be easier when she moves in here."

Now Forrest sat back on his heels. "Is that so?"

"Sure it is. I've got that new security system in—pain in the ass, but it's done. I've got this fierce guard dog."

They both glanced over to where Snickers lay, snoring on his back, feet in the air.

"Vicious son of a bitch, that dog."

"He's just resting between patrols."

"Uh-huh. I think you know I meant 'Is that so?' about Shelby moving in here, not about the safety of it."

Griff continued to work. Laying a row of tile was methodical. So for him that made it soothing.

"I can't push that button yet. She'd balk. The fucker did a number on her, and she's working her way through it or out of it faster than most people would. But she's not there yet, so the word of the day is 'tenacity' with a side of patience. Because yeah, that's so. I want her here, with me. I want her and Callie here with me."

"If you go there and with your patient tenacity, son, talk her into moving in out here, my mama's going to start planning a wedding."

"That's fine, just the next step in the plan. But it's going to take Shelby longer to get there."

Forrest said nothing as Griff set the next spacers, carefully applied more adhesive to the subfloor.

"Is it my understanding you're planning to marry my sister?"

Griff sat back again, rolled his shoulders, circled his neck. "What do you think of this room?"

Obliging, Forrest straightened up, took a turn around the bedroom area. "Nice space, windows ought to give nice light, good views. Damn big closet for a secondary sort of bedroom. Window seat's a nice touch, like having its own bathroom. That tile you're laying ought to give it some glow."

"I'm thinking of a slipper tub for in here, and a vanity with an under-counter oval sink. I'm after plenty of storage with a small footprint. Recessed medicine cabinet over the vanity—more storage there, but frame it in to give it some style. And some bling with the lighting."

"Slipper tub and bling? Sounds female."

"Yeah. Pale, warm green for the bedroom walls, echo off the bathroom lighting for the ceiling fan with light kit."

"The bling."

"That's right. I'm going to do a small built-in for the closet, along with the rods and shelves."

Nodding, Forrest took another turn around, began to see it.

"You're putting this room together for Callie."

"Green's her favorite color, she tells me. That *Shrek* obsession of hers, that's bound to pass eventually. But it's a good color for her, and for a bedroom. A few years down the road, having her own bathroom's going to matter to her."

"And you're a man who looks down the road."

"I am. I'm in love with both of them, and being a trained observer, you know that already. Callie's there with me; Shelby's just gotta catch up. She'll catch up quicker, I think, if we can put this shitstorm the fucker left her in behind her."

"What if she doesn't catch up?"

"I wait. She's the one, so that's that. And Callie? The kid just lights me up. She deserves me. They both do. I'm a hell of a catch."

"Shit, Griff, if you had tits, I'd marry you myself."

"There you go." Seeing he'd reached the point where he'd have to measure and cut tile, Griff pushed to his feet. "I'm taking a break, tossing a sandwich together. You want one?"

"Thanks, but I've got a couple more things to do, and a hell of a lot better waiting in leftovers at my mama's once I do them."

"We'll walk down with you. Come on, Snick. Time for patrol."

The dog waved his feet in the air, did an ungainly rollover, then scrambled up.

"One of these days I'm going to get me a dog," Forrest said as they started down with Snickers racing down the steps, halfway up, down again.

"Snick's litter mates are gone, but I saw a sign for beagle pups on the turn at Black Bear and Dry Creek."

"It's not one of these days yet. I'm not home enough, and I don't think the sheriff would approve of me taking a dog for ride-alongs." Forrest glanced at the security panel as they passed it. "What do you figure on doing if this fancy new security system goes off?"

Griff shrugged as he opened the front door. "Call you—and get my pipe wrench. It's got weight."

"A shotgun's going to carry more weight than a pipe wrench, son."

"Don't have one, don't want one."

"City boy."

Griff breathed in the night while the dog ran over the patch of grass to the verge of the woods where the stream bubbled.

"Not anymore, but I still don't want a gun."

He looked west to the faint blush of pink the setting sun painted on the clouds that smoked over the mountains. "I never had any trouble here. Worried about it some when I had all that copper for rewiring and plumbing. That stuff's like gold and easy to transport. But nothing but that once, and that's direct to the fucker and the shitstorm."

Like his friend, Forrest looked west, toward color and cloud. "You've got a good spot here, Griff. It's got a feel to it, appealing, settled. But it's a fact it'd take a solid ten minutes for us to respond to that nine-one-one should you call for it. You can load a shotgun with rock salt if you're feeling dainty about things."

"I'll leave the firearms to you, Deputy. I'm damn good with a pipe wrench."

"Suit yourself."

He would, Griff thought as he stood in the quiet, letting the dog run and sniff, watching the first star wink to life in a sky gone the color of pale purple velvet.

Suiting himself was just what he was doing. So he'd go fix that sandwich, then finish the tile in Callie's bathroom.

"Front porch swing," he said, and bent to rub the dog when Snickers raced back to him. "Maybe I'll build one. Things mean more when you build them. Let's eat and think about that."

If he'd known while he sat in the kitchen eating a sandwich and doing some rough sketches of swings that someone was watching through field glasses, he might have changed his mind about the shotgun.

27

It took time to finish the room he wanted for Callie, to build a front porch swing. But he had plenty on his hands as Shelby was wrapped up in the plans for the engagement party.

Or more, from what she said, in keeping Bitsy under control.

He filled evenings and nights he couldn't be with her chipping away at projects on the house, and planning for down the road.

When they finally managed an evening together, she vetoed his suggestion of dinner out for a casual one at his place.

That was fine with him.

He was out in the yard when she arrived, just hanging the tire swing he'd made on a sturdy branch of an old hickory.

"Look at that!" she called out. "There's something Callie will make a beeline for."

"Pretty cool, huh? Got the tire from your grandfather."

He'd built it horizontally, choosing a mid-size tire that would suit a little girl's butt, and had fed the chain through a garden hose to protect the branch.

"It's so sweet."

"Wanna try it out?"

"Of course I do." She handed him a large insulated jug, leaned in when he slid an arm around her for a kiss.

"What's in here?"

"Hard lemonade. My granddaddy's recipe, and it's a winner." She scooted onto the tire, gave the chains a tug. "It's sturdy."

"Fun can be safe," he said, gave her a push.

She leaned back, hair flying, gave a laugh. "And it is fun. What made you think of such a thing?"

He didn't want to say—yet—that he'd been looking at plans for back-yard swing sets, and had stumbled across the idea. "Just came to me. I had this friend—what was his name? Tim McNaulty—when I was about Callie's age. He had one of these in his yard—set vertical. This way makes more sense."

"I love it. So will she."

As if hypnotized, the dog sat on the ground, his head tilting this way, then that, following Shelby's rhythm. "I swear, that dog's bigger than he was when I saw him a few days ago."

"Next outdoor project's a doghouse. A big one."

"He'll need big."

She jumped off the swing. "I'm sorry I've been so tied up lately. I feel like I've had barely a minute without something that needed doing."

"I know the feeling. It's no problem, Red. Our best pals are getting married. It's a lot."

"It'd be a Macy's Day Parade if I couldn't keep Miz Bitsy down, and that's taken every bit of creativity and energy I have. She's jumping so fast from this party to the wedding and back again, my head's on a constant revolution. She got it into her head Emma Kate should arrive at the ceremony—venue yet to be determined—in a princess carriage. White horses and a carriage, as Emma Kate had that on her wedding list when she was about twelve. It took some doing to nudge her off that one."

"Emma Kate's going to owe you for the rest of her life."

"That's a benefit. Why don't we— Oh, Griff, you got a porch swing!"

Speaking of beelines, she made one herself, twirled a circle, the full skirt of her grass-green sundress billowing. "I just love it! How'd you find one this wonderful blue?"

"Like your eyes." He followed her onto the porch. "I painted it. I made it."

"You made it yourself? Of course you did." She sat down, pushed off gently with her feet. "And it's perfect, just perfect for sitting here on a lazy afternoon or a quiet evening. It'd be extra perfect if you got us a couple of tall glasses, and sat down here with me so we could sample that hard lemonade."

"Be right back."

When the dog tried to climb up with her, she hefted him up—no easy task now. "You're almost too big." But she hooked an arm around him, swinging and thinking she'd rarely seen a prettier spot.

All so green and private with the sky a blue dome dashed with white clouds. She could hear the stream, fast and lively from the last rains, and the insistent, echoing *rat-a-tat-tat* of a woodpecker busy somewhere beyond the green, setting up the percussion section for the chorus of birds.

"He's got my spot," Griff said when he brought out the drinks.

"He didn't want to be left out."

Resigned, Griff sat on the other side of the dog, who wiggled with absolute joy.

"There couldn't be a better spot for a porch swing." She sampled the drink. "I think I did Grandpa proud."

"I'll say."

"It goes down easy, but it's got a kick. It's made for sipping. And sipping on a warm evening, on a porch swing, is even better. You've got your own little Eden here, Griffin."

"Eden needs considerable work yet."

"If Adam and Eve had put some time into working the garden instead of picking apples, they might still be there. Gardens, houses, lives, they're a continual work in progress, aren't they? I stopped progress on mine for a while, but I'm making up for it. It's peaceful here. The light, the swing, this very fine lemonade. You, this sweet dog. I'm going to get what's not peaceful out of the way, then we won't have to think about it again."

"Something happened."

"I don't know for certain, but I know now you didn't talk to Forrest this afternoon."

"No, not today."

"I'm guessing he knew I was coming over, and I'd tell you. The police think they might have a kind of witness. On the detective. The FBI agents are going in to talk to him."

"What did he see?"

"They're not altogether convinced he saw much of anything, or anything useful. But the man—a boy, really—was in the building the night Privet was killed. He said how he heard this pop. Just one pop, like a muffled firecracker, he said. He didn't think much of it. The timing's right, and more, he saw who they think is the killer leave."

"Harlow?"

"They can't say for sure, but he's claiming the person he saw wasn't that big—tall or broad. No beard, either. He says blond hair—very blond—and glasses with thick, dark rims. Wearing a dark suit. He says how he can't be sure of much, it was only a quick glimpse—saw him leaving the building when he was looking out the window. Saw him walk across the street and get into a big SUV."

"Wig, glasses, shave." Griff shrugged. "At a glance, in the dark, it's hard to say if it was Harlow or not."

"More, he was a little high at the time, and where he shouldn't have been. That's why he didn't say anything until he was picked up for possession, and not the first time on that. He'd been working as a photographer's assistant in that building, and he'd gone in late because he was setting up to shoot some porn on the side. He's trying to make a deal so he doesn't have to go to jail."

"So he could be making it up trying to save his ass."

"He could, but he has the time, and that single pop. Just one. The police didn't say how many times Privet was shot, how many shots fired. So that's something to consider."

Griff considered it while they glided on the swing and sipped. "It's a stretch to think somebody else shot the PI. Same gun, that's what they said, as the one used to kill Warren. And we know Harlow was in the area. But let's stretch it. Somebody else is involved, somebody else hired the detective. Maybe somebody connected to the Miami Montvilles, or the insurance company, or somebody Richard worked with at some point."

"It makes me wonder if maybe that somebody killed Richard and staged the boating accident."

"Bigger stretch."

"I know it, but he was so determined to go, so I'm wondering now if it was to meet somebody, to finally deal with the jewelry he'd stolen. Another double cross, but on him this time."

"What would you do if you'd just gotten your hands on millions in jewelry—not hot anymore—and had killed to get your hands on it?"

"I'd run fast and far, but . . ."

"There are still two people who want what you have," Griff finished. "So you hire a detective, and you put him on it. And on you, Red, in case you knew something."

"Griff, it's made me think about how many people I let into that house up North in those weeks after Richard's death. I might have let his killer—if there was one—inside to give me an appraisal, to take something away. Or all the times I was out of the house for hours at a go. Someone who knew how could've gotten in, looked around all they wanted. If Richard left something behind that mattered in all this.

"I don't know. Maybe I'm making it more complicated than it already is."

"It's pretty risky to try to stage a boating accident in the middle of a storm. Why not just dump the body—or leave it like the others?"

"I don't know." But she'd chewed it over endlessly. "I was thinking to buy time. Or maybe it was an accident—killing Richard, I mean. And the rest happened from there. And the simplest is usually right," she finished. "Richard died in an accident. Harlow killed the woman and the detective. And this witness was coked up, got no more than a glimpse out a window. I'm going to stop worrying about it as of right this minute.

"We've got this beautiful evening, and a few hours to enjoy it."

"Maybe you could stay, just stay again. I could get another invitation to breakfast."

She smiled, sipped. "It happens I have an overnight bag in the car, in case I got an invitation."

"I'll get it."

"Thank you. It's on the floor of the passenger seat. Oh, and there's a blanket on the seat. Would you bring that, too?"

"Are you cold?" he asked as he headed for the car. "It must be eighty, at least."

"I do love a warm evening. Makes me feel like I'll never want to go inside, just stay out, watch the sky change, the light change, hear the first night birds when twilight comes."

"We can stay out as long as you want." He started back with bag and blanket. "I fell back on the old reliable of steaks on the grill."

"That sounds perfect. For later."

She took the blanket from him, gave it a quick whip in the air to open it.

"Where'd the dog go?"

"Oh, I put him inside, with the rawhide bone I had in my pocket. I think we'll all be happier this way." She laid the blanket on the porch, straightened, shook her hair back. Smiled. "Because I think it's time you got me naked on the porch."

She staggered him. Aroused him. Delighted him. "Is that what time it is?"

"I think it's past time, but I know you'll make up for it."

"I can do that." He set her bag aside, pulled her into his arms.

He took his time so the kiss alone left her limp—all watery knees and misty thoughts. He had a way of making that meeting of lips into a long, slow shimmer. A kindling rather than an explosion.

Wrapped in him, seduced when she had thought to seduce, she let herself be guided, let herself be glided along the river of sensation. Swaying to him, with him, on the old front porch with the sunlight like shattered gold and the world too still for a single leaf to stir.

He eased the zipper down at the back of her dress, enjoying, lingering over every inch of skin he exposed. Soft as silk, smooth as lake water.

His to touch.

He nudged the straps from her shoulders, gave himself the pleasure of laying his lips there. Stronger than she looked, he thought. Shoulders that didn't shirk from lifting a load.

He wanted—needed—to help her with the weight.

For now, he gave the dress a little brush so it flowed like air to her feet. The pretty bits of lace she wore echoed the tender green of the dress.

"I bought them special." She laid fingertips between her breasts when he looked down at her. "I shouldn't've spent the money, but—"

"Worth every penny. I'll pay you back."

"I'm counting on it," she said before his mouth took hers again.

A little stronger, a little deeper now so her head fell back to accept all he offered, to give all he asked.

He drew her down with him so they knelt on the blanket. Their lips broke apart long enough for her to tug the T-shirt he wore over his head; met again as she tossed it aside. Hot flesh under her hands, the water and soap of his shower teasing her senses as she played kisses over the curve of his shoulder.

And still that faint, lingering scent of sawdust, reminding her as the calloused palms reminded her, he worked with his hands.

A quick shiver ran over her skin, ran into her blood when he flicked the clasp of her bra open. Those working hands cupped her breasts, the rough pads of his thumbs stroked across her nipples, waking new needs, churning up a storm in her belly.

Everything in her so full now, so tender and already yearning. But his hands continued to play over her, finding more, stirring more.

He laid her back, ran his finger along the edge of the panties, along that vulnerable line between thigh and center.

That sound in her throat, not quite moan, not quite sigh. It could undo him. His own needs gathered, but he held them, held them, floating his palm over the lace, building the heat under the thin barrier until her hands lost their grip on him.

Her breath quickened, deepened; the lids lowered over the magic blue of her eyes.

His to touch, he thought again. His to have.

He slipped that thin barrier away and took her up, took her over with his hands.

It burst through her, lightning through the storm, slashing pleasure, a new flash of deep, driving need. She dragged at his belt, impatient now for all, to take, be taken.

He drew her up again to help her, then took her hands in his to still them when she yanked at his jeans.

"No rush."

Her breath in rags, desire a single mad ache, she looked at him—and saw that same need, that same aching.

"Maybe I'm in more of a hurry than you."

"Let's just take a minute." He kept her hands trapped in his, took her mouth again. "I love you."

"Oh, God, Griff."

"I need to say it, need you to hear it. While I've got you naked on the porch. I love you. I don't have to rush it."

"I can't get a handle on what I feel, on what you do inside me even when you're not there. It's so much." She pressed her face into his shoulder. "It's all so much."

"That works for now." He eased her back so he could bring up her hands, kiss them before he let them go. "It all works."

He shifted, lowering to the blanket again so she lay over him. He threaded his fingers through her hair, loving the mass of it, the wild curls and color.

She didn't have his patience, but she tried to find some, guiding him now through the kiss, letting her hands stroke and stir, feeling his heart kick under her lips.

When at last there was nothing between them, she rose over him, took him in.

Filled. Surrounded. Joined.

She pressed his hands to her heart so he could feel it drumming while she set the rhythm.

Slow, she fought to keep it all slow, and found the staggering pleasure of that easy pace. Rolls of it flowing in like a sea, building layer by layer like clouds.

With the air thick as honey, the sunlight streaming, she rode him over that sea, higher into those clouds. She clung, clung, clung to that breathless peak. Then let herself be swept away.

She could hear the birds again, little trills and whistles through the circling woods. She could even hear the faintest rustle of the faintest breeze through the trees, like quiet breath, now that her heart wasn't hammering in her ears.

And she knew the pure, sated joy of lying limp on the porch, a thoroughly satisfied woman, beside the man she in turn had thoroughly satisfied.

"I wonder what the UPS guy would've thought if he'd come driving up to the house."

Shelby managed a sigh. "Are you expecting a delivery?"

"You never know. I didn't even think about it. Who could think?"

"It's nice not to think. It seems I spend most every hour of my day having to do just that. I don't think when I'm singing, and I don't have to think when you start kissing me. I guess it's like a song."

"I was thinking."

"Mmmm."

"I was thinking you looked like some sort of mountain goddess."

She choked out a laugh. "Goddess. Do go on."

"All that crazy red hair, the moon-white skin. So slim and strong, and eyes like blue shadows."

"Well, that is like a song." Moved, and a little nervous with it, she rolled over again, propped on his chest. "You've got some poetry, Griffin."

"That's about it."

"It's more than enough." She traced a finger down his cheek. "You could be a god, all these hollows here." And down the other cheek. "The sun-streaked hair, all those fine, fine muscles."

"We're a set."

She laughed, lowered her forehead to his. "How deep is that stream of yours these days, Griff?"

"I guess about to mid-thigh—your thigh."

"That'll do it. Let's go splash in the stream."

He opened one eye, one cat-green eye. "You want to splash in the stream?"

"With you, I do. We can finish working up an appetite, and have another glass of that lemonade while we put dinner together."

Before he could think of a reason against, she got up, tugged on his hand.

"We're still naked," he pointed out.

"No point getting our clothes wet, is there? Let the dog out," she suggested, then dashed away.

A goddess, he thought. Or what was that thing . . . a sprite. But he didn't imagine sprites had such long legs. He let the dog out as Shelby ran over his lawn, then, thinking of the more practical, ducked into the house, grabbed a couple of towels.

He wasn't a prude—and would have been insulted to be termed one. But it felt pretty damn weird to rush over his own front yard wearing nothing but skin.

Before he got through the flanking trees, he heard the splash, the laugh, and the joyful yip of the dog.

She made rainbows, he thought, the way she tossed water up so the drops caught the dappled light and shone into quick color. The dog lapped, barked, swam some in the deeper water, then shook himself in the shallows.

Griff hung the towels over a branch.

"It's so wonderfully cool. You could drop a line in here, maybe catch something. You follow the stream down a ways where it widens, deepens, you could catch your supper most any evening."

"I've never fished."

She straightened, naked and obviously stunned. "In your life?"

"I grew up in the 'burbs, Red, spent a lot of time with urban activities."

"We have to fix that the very first chance we get. Fishing's good for you. It's relaxing, and you're a patient man so it should suit you. What kind of urban activities?"

"Me?" He stepped into the water, and she was right, it was cool. "Sports mostly. Basketball in the winter, baseball in the summer. I never went out for football. I had a pretty skinny build."

"I like baseball." She sat down in the water, let it bubble over her. "I believe my daddy might have traded me for another model otherwise. What position did you play?"

"Did some pitching, covered second. Liked playing second better, I guess."

"How come you're not playing on the Raiders softball team? The Ridge has a pretty good team."

"I might try it next year. This year, free time's for the house. Aren't you worried about rocks under your ass, or some fish swimming up . . . where I just was?"

She laughed, lay back enough to dip her hair in the water. "You really are citified yet. I know a couple of good swimming holes. We ought to try one some night."

"Maybe I'll put in a pond. I thought about a swimming pool, but that's a lot of maintenance, plus, it doesn't fit here. But a pond would."

"You could do that?"

"Maybe. Something to think about down the road."

"I love to swim." Relaxed, even a little dreamy, she trailed her fingers back and forth to ripple the water. "I started teaching Callie before she could walk. And we had a pool in the condo in Atlanta, so we could swim all year-round. When she's a little older, I'll take her rafting with one of Clay's groups. She's fearless, and she'd like that. But I want another year or so on her first."

She cocked her head. "Have you tried that?"

"The white water? Yeah. It's a rush. I figured on going again when my parents come down in August."

Her trailing fingers stilled. "Oh, they're coming for a visit?"

"Working vacation—they'll give me about a week on the place in early August. I've got some work I want to get done before they do. And I want them to meet you."

That had nerves dancing in her stomach.

"I want them to see for themselves I'm not exaggerating."

"You've told them about me?"

He gave her a long look. "What do you think?"

"Well." She sat up again. Those nerves were doing an enthusiastic clog dance now. "Um. Well, my family has a big backyard party early in August. If the timing's right, and you think your parents would like to come, they'd be welcome."

"I was hoping you'd say that. Are you cold?"

"No." More than nerves, she thought, and glanced—suddenly uneasy—over her shoulder. "A goose walked over my grave, I guess. But I'm glad you brought the towels." She rose, water sluicing off her skin, reached for one. "I didn't think about drying off."

He tipped her face up. "Do you have a problem meeting my parents?"

"No. It makes me a little nervous, but that's natural, isn't it? It's . . ." She hunched, shivered. "Something between my shoulder blades, and now I've got the willies for no reason I can name."

She wrapped the towel around herself, felt marginally better. So she leaned into him. "I'm nervous about meeting your parents, but I'm glad I will. I think it's nice they'd come down here to help you with the house, spend time with you. And I think they must be good people to have made someone like you."

"You'll like them."

"I bet I will. Let's go in, all right? I can't settle this itch between my shoulder blades."

He took the other towel, then her hand.

Field glasses followed them through the trees, across the lawn.

28

S helby let her mother talk her into a facial. She should've known
better as being next to naked on the reclining chair under a blanket was kin to being in a closed box when dealing with Ada Mae.

"It's nice Griffin's people are coming down this summer. I told you
how we met them last fall." Having done the cleansing, the toning, the
gentle exfoliation, Ada Mae used her truly skilled fingers to apply a thick
layer of energizing mask.

"They couldn't have been nicer. I took over a basket of tomatoes from
my garden, and we sat down and had some sweet tea on the front porch
where his mama'd been working on some of the garden. Why, she'd
hacked and cut and dug away at that scrub and tangle like a woman on a
mission from God. Poison ivy in there, too. I showed her how you pull up
some jewel weed, use the juice of it when you get poison ivy on you. Being
from Baltimore, she didn't know about that.

"We had a good chat."

"You took tomatoes over so you'd get invited to sit on the porch."

"Neighborly is, neighborly does. I'm saying Natalie—that's his mama's
name—is a good woman. And his daddy—that's Brennan—he's a fine
man, fine-looking, too. Griff favors him to the life, I swear. You know
what else?"

"What else, Mama?"

"They're just as fond of Matt, just like he was one of their own, and Emma Kate right along, too. That tells me something about a person, that they can embrace somebody into the family, blood or not. This mask's just going to set awhile. I'm going to do your hands and feet while it does."

Shelby might have said not to trouble, but no one in the world gave a foot rub like Ada Mae Pomeroy.

"You need a fresh pedicure, baby girl. And don't say you don't have time. Everybody who works here has to show off the products and services—you know how your granny feels about that. You need some pretty summer toes, that's what. We got that Wistful Wisteria. It's a good match for your eyes."

"All right, Mama." She'd see if Maybeline or Lorilee could squeeze her in for a quick one.

"Your skin's looking just beautiful, and so are you. It does my heart a world of good."

"Home cooking, steady work and seeing my own baby girl thrive."

"And regular sex."

Shelby had to laugh. "I guess I can't say that's not a factor."

"I know you still have worries, but they're going to pass. That Jimmy Harlow person, he's thousands of miles away doing God knows what to who. But I say if the FBI hasn't found him, he's taken himself off to somewhere foreign. Gone to France."

Eyes closed, her feet already in bliss, Shelby smiled. "France?"

"First place popped into my head. But he's gone."

She slipped booties onto Shelby's rubbed, creamed and very happy feet. And started on her hands.

"Just like that no-good Arlo Kattery's gone, maybe for five years in jail, I hear. And Melody Bunker, too. Word I get is when she gets out of that fancy rehab place, she might be moving up to Knoxville, where Miz Florence's brother lives."

"I don't care where she goes or what she does. I swear, all that trouble from her seems years ago. It's hard to believe it was only weeks. I wonder at someone like her, Mama, who thinks so much of herself she can't see she doesn't leave much of a mark on anyone's life."

"She tried leaving one on yours."

"Well, she didn't."

"You're doing something with your life, Shelby, and we're proud of you."

"I know you are. You show me every day."

"Tell me what you want, baby. I know you've got something going on in your head. I can see it."

Relaxed, drifting, Shelby sighed. "I've started taking some classes on-line."

"I knew it was something! What classes?"

"On interior decorating. It's just a couple little courses, but I'm doing pretty well, and I like it. I thought I'd take another when it's done and I can afford it, and a business course, too. Get the experience and education."

"You've got a talent for it. You sign up for those other courses, Shelby Anne. Your daddy and I will pay for them."

"I'm paying, Mama."

"You listen to me now. We worked hard, your daddy and I, to send your brothers to college. They had to work, too, but we bore the brunt because that's what parents do. We do what we can. We'd have seen you through college just the same. You took another path for a while. But if you're looking to get more education, we're paying. You'd do it for Callie, and don't tell me different."

"I wasn't going to tell you because I knew this is what you'd say."

"You ask your daddy what he thinks, and you'll get the same answer you're getting from me. You're not sitting around looking for us to pay your way through life. You're working, you're tending your own child, and striving to . . . to hone a God-given talent. If I can't give my own daughter a hand up, well, what kind of mother would I be?"

Opening her eyes, Shelby saw what she'd imagined in her head. Her tall, occasionally fierce mother, standing over her, face set. "I love you so much, Mama."

"You'd better. You can pay me back helping me freshen up the living room. Now that we've done so much new upstairs, it's looking tired to me."

"You'll get around Daddy on that telling him I need the experience."

"And you'll get it, while I'll get a fresh look in that room."

She slipped mittens on Shelby's hands, went around, began a slow, glorious neck rub. "Now that I've got you where I want you, I'm going to say when Griff's people come visiting, you should go over there one night, cook them dinner. Show them what a good cook you are."

"Mama—"

"I know most women don't like another woman in their kitchen." In her cheerful way, Ada Mae rolled right over objections. "But she'll be visiting, and working while she is. I know I'd appreciate somebody setting a good meal in front of me after a long workday. Don't I appreciate when you do it for me?"

"You do, but—"

"You ought to make that pasta salad like you made for your daddy and me the other night, with those fancy chicken breasts and good fresh peas."

"Mama, that's weeks away yet."

"Time moves whether we're watching the clock or not."

"I know it, and that's why I've got Emma Kate's engagement party this week when it seems like two minutes ago Matt put the ring on her finger. I've got so much to do yet, to think about doing."

"I wish you'd let me treat you to a new formal for it."

They'd been this round, Shelby thought, and she was grateful, but she'd rather spend the money on design classes and continuing her education. "I love that you'd want to, but I just don't have call for that kind of dress now, so it'd be wasted on just one wearing. And I'm going to be running around all night, making sure everything goes just as it's supposed to—and keeping Miz Bitsy in line, more or less."

"Bless her heart, she needs someone to."

"And that's me this Saturday night. It'll be easier for me doing all that if I'm not wearing a long dress." She'd had enough long, fancy dresses over the last few years, and selling them had put some black ink in her ledger. "You think I ought to wear my hair up or down?" she asked, knowing that would carve a new avenue for her mother to travel.

"Oh! Mama could give you a wonderful updo, one that makes the most of your curls instead of hiding them."

Since Ada Mae was off and running, Shelby just closed her eyes and enjoyed the rest of her facial.

She did have a lot to do, and a short time to get it done. Exchanging e-mails, calls, texts with the event manager at the hotel ate up considerable as the manager was grateful to deal with her rather than the bride-to-be's "enthusiastic and creative mother."

Shelby read that subtext clearly.

She had what she hoped would be the final conversation with the florist before the actual event setup, and yet another with Bitsy.

But she took a moment—with her new Winsome Wisteria toes—to sit on the little back patio with her grandmother at the end of the workday.

"You're glowing, girl."

Shelby took a sip of sweet tea. "Mama's a genius."

"She's got a talent, but she had fine material to work with. You're looking happy these days, and there's no better beauty treatment. It's hard to bring a glow out without the happy."

"I am happy. Callie's just thriving, we've got a new baby in the family to spoil and my best friend's getting married. Working here's brought back to me how much I love the Ridge. Then there's the big bonus of my Friday Nights at the bar and grill."

She took another sip. "And last but far from least, I've got myself a boyfriend who makes me glow even when he's not around. I got awful lucky, Granny. Some second chances come too late."

"You're working for yours."

"I won't be stopping that anytime soon. Now that I've got my glow on, and my nails all pretty, I wanted to see if you'd have time Saturday to do up my hair before the party."

Viola eyed Shelby over the rim of her glass. "And you're going to let me have my way with it?"

"I'd never question the expert."

"Good. I've got ideas there. Now tell me what's really on your mind."

Granny always had read her like a book. "The party's the main focus right now. Do you know I just talked Miz Bitsy—and it took some doing—out of the last-minute hiring of a small string orchestra to play in the ballroom? God knows what she's going to cook up that we have to toss out again for the wedding when it comes."

"She does love her girl, but bless her heart, she's always had fancy ideas that don't fit Emma Kate any more than Bitsy's size-five shoes would. There's another focus in there, Shelby. I can see it."

"I really do want your opinion and advice. I just . . . I'm so grateful to be able to work here, Granny, not just because I needed a job, but because it helped me come back. Helped me feel part of things here again. I want you to know how grateful I am."

"If you've got another job lined up, Shelby, I'm not going to be upset about it. I never figured this situation here was permanent for you. Running this place wouldn't fit you any more than Bitsy's shoes, either. What are you looking at?"

"It's not yet. Probably not for six months. Maybe longer—probably longer," she amended. "I'm taking a couples classes online, on decorating."

"You've got a knack for that like Ada Mae does for skin. I used to think you'd make your fame and fortune from your voice—then use your talent for decorating on the big houses you'd have."

"I'm not willing to do all the work a music career needs. The nights, the touring, the . . . well, the focus again. That's just not for me anymore, for who I am now. I don't get a second chance there—I threw that away, and I'm not looking to find it again."

"Life's just a continual stream of choices. You're making another choice now."

"I think I could build something for me and Callie, Granny."

Lips curved, eyes sharp, Viola nodded. "You're looking forward toward a career. Not a job, a vocation."

"I am. I'm doing really well with these classes, and I'm going to add in others—one on business management, too."

As she nodded again, Viola's smile spread. "You've got that in the blood, but education adds to it."

"I'm not going to rush it. I helped Gilly with her bedroom, and Emma Kate with some ideas for her apartment, just to see if I could work with somebody's space, and their needs. Now Mama wants me to help her freshen up her living room. I can't say how Daddy's going to feel about that."

Viola returned Shelby's grin. "Men don't like change as a rule, but they get used to it."

Revved up now—no one knew starting a business from the ground up like Viola MacNee Donahue—Shelby edged forward in her chair.

"I've got such ideas for over at Griff's. Sometimes I bite my tongue because it's his place, and he's so smart and clever about it already."

"Anyone smart and clever values another eye, another perspective on things."

"Well, sometimes I don't bite my tongue in time, and he hasn't gotten put out by it. Anyway, I'm going to take these classes, get the credentials, then I'm going to try to start up a small business. I'll need to keep working to support myself and Callie, and get this damn debt paid in full. Starting small's the idea, like you did—and Grandpa, too. Building steady. Do you think I've got the right direction?"

"Does it make you happy?" Viola held up a finger, then tapped it on the table. "Don't go discounting being happy in your work, Shelby. It's hard enough going to a job every day and dealing with a boss if you're not happy with your work. But when it's your own, everything's on you. If it doesn't make you happy, you're better off drawing that paycheck and leaving the worry to somebody else."

"This is just why I wanted to talk to you before I took too many more steps. It does make me happy, Granny. It made me so happy just doing those little bits for Gilly and Emma Kate, seeing how pleased they were, knowing I could see what they'd like and how they'd like it. And I felt so silly happy when Griff used the paint color I picked for the front room, and how he bought this painted chest I saw over at The Artful Ridge— it's sure nice being able to go in there now—and just mentioned how it would look good at the foot of his bed. And it does."

"Then you do it. Do what makes you happy."

On a long breath, Shelby sat back. "I take a step forward, like with the classes, then I take two back. At least in my head. I thought Richard would make me happy."

"You made a mistake," Viola said flatly. "It won't be the last you'll make before you're done with the world. Not if you're lucky enough to live a long, full, interesting life."

"I can hope it's the biggest one I'll ever make." She reached for Viola's hand. "Will you help me? I don't mean with the money I'll need to get going. I mean, when I'm ready to start things up, can I ask you the half a million questions I'm bound to have?"

"I'd be insulted if you didn't. I've got a head for business, and your grandfather does, too. Who do you think helped your daddy get the business side of his practice going?"

"I should've figured. I'm counting on you."

"I'll count on you right back. Well, look here, we've got us a handsome man come to call."

"Miz Vi." Matt walked over to the table, bent down to kiss her cheek. "Excuse the grunge. We just finished up for the day over at Bootlegger's."

"And how's that coming?"

"We've got the footers in, ready for the inspector tomorrow. How are you, Shelby?"

"I'm good, thanks. Why don't I go get you a cold drink?"

He lifted the bottle he carried. "Have Gatorade, will travel."

"A glass with ice, then."

"Real men don't need glasses." With a wink, he chugged straight from the bottle. "Emma Kate mentioned you wanted to talk to me. Just me." Now he wiggled his eyebrows, made her laugh.

"I did, but I didn't expect you to make time so soon. You've got a lot going on."

"So do you. I heard you just headed off a string orchestra. Consider your feet kissed."

"You sit on down," Viola told him. "Take my chair," she added as she rose. "I'm shuffling my tired feet home, and having myself a drink with more kick than tea. You behave yourself with my girl, Matthew."

"Yes, ma'am."

"I'll see you tomorrow, Granny. Love to Grandpa."

"You have his," Viola said as she went back inside.

"Is there anything else I should know about—now that we've avoided the cello?" Matt took a seat, stretched out his legs. Sighed. "God, that feels really good."

"A man who works as hard as you ought to have Vonnie for a massage every week. Keep yourself loose and healthy."

"Emma Kate's always saying the same thing about yoga. I'd rather the massage than trying to twist myself into a pretzel."

And he'd very likely rather be home now than sitting here waiting for her to get to the point.

"I didn't expect to talk to you about this until after the party or I'd've had my thoughts more together on it. I was just talking to Granny about it. She and my mama are the only ones I've said anything to."

"Not about the party, then."

"No, not about that. That's going to be just perfect, don't worry. It's . . ." She blew out a breath. "It's that I've started to take some classes," she began, and took him through it.

"Griff said you had an eye. You can't always believe a man who's got stars in his own, but I got a sample myself with what you did at our place. And it cost under two hundred to do it."

"It was mostly just using what you already had in a different way."

"It looks better. Fresher. And the idea of matting and framing her great-grandmother's crocheted doilies? I wasn't big on that—seemed too girly, too fussy, when she told me. But they look great."

"Oh, they're done?"

"She picked them up last night, and we hung them where you said. Even if I didn't like it—and I do—the look on Emma Kate's face once they were up would've been more than enough."

"I'm so glad the idea worked, for both of you."

"She's itching to do something with the rest of the place now—I'd thank you for that, but it would be a lie. I'm trying to get her to hold off since we're going to look at a piece of land Sunday afternoon."

"You found something? Where?"

"Hardly more than a stone's throw from Griff's. Just under three acres, so not as much land as he's got, but the same stream runs through it."

"I bet it's pretty. I didn't think y'all wanted to move that far out of town."

"Emma Kate's a little nervous about it, but I think she'll come around when she sees it. Maybe you could save your ideas for her until I start building."

"Actually . . . I wanted to ask you—just you, Matt, not Griff, not Emma Kate—if you think, once I get my credentials, you could see your way clear to using me, if I seemed right and the job called for it. Or just mentioning my name to a client who maybe was thinking about using a decorator. I have two of my class projects right here on my phone."

She pulled it out of her pocket. "It's hard to see the details on the phone, but you'd see if you thought it worked overall."

"You haven't said anything to Griff?"

"No." Once she'd found the projects, she handed Matt the phone. "He'd say yes because he wouldn't want to tell me no, and so would Emma Kate. That's not what I'm looking for, that's not how I want to start out. I give you my word, if this doesn't seem like something that you'd feel comfortable doing, I won't say a thing to him or Emma Kate about it. I don't want you to feel like I'm putting you in the middle of something."

She took a breath while he studied her project, then flipped the screen to the second one.

"Your work, yours and Griff's, is so good. And your reputation, even though you haven't been around here all that long—not by Ridge standards—is already so solid. I think I could contribute to that. As an outside consultant."

He flicked a glance up at her, then looked at the phone again. "You did these?"

"I did. There are written projects, too, but—"

"They're good, Shelby. Really good."

"Honestly?"

"Honestly and seriously. Griff does most of our design work, and he'll step a toe into decorating if the client wants some guidance. You should show these to him."

"I will, but I don't want to show him with the idea he'd feel obliged to—"

"Show him," Matt interrupted. "We're a team, and when we make a decision, we both have to be in on it, have to agree. It's how we work. So I can't tell you yes until he's seen them. What I can tell you is when I talk to him about it, after he has, my weight's on yes."

"It is? You mean it? You— Wait." She leaned in. "Look right here," she said, and pointed to her eyes. "Is this a favor to me?"

"Yeah. I think it's going to be a favor to all of us."

"All of us." She sat back again. "Thank you. I'll show him. It's going to take some time for me to get those credentials, work up a business plan, but knowing you'd recommend me takes a weight off."

"Is there any way you can do a little freelancing now?"

"I haven't finished the first class yet."

"Tansy's driving Derrick around the bend already. Paint samples, cut sheets of light fixtures, flooring samples, more cut sheets. And we just got the footers put in. If you'd work with her, it would give her some direction—she's got good ideas, but they're scattershot right now, and mixed in with her ideas for the nursery. And it would give him a breather. He'd owe you."

"I'd be glad to help her out if she wants."

"Done. You and Derrick can work out your fee."

"Oh, I'm not going to charge them for—"

With a shake of his head, he handed her back the phone. "That's not a good business plan."

She huffed out a breath. "It's not, is it?"

"Do you know how many friends, relatives, casual acquaintances and complete strangers wanted me and/or Griff to build their deck, paint their house, re-lay tile, gut their kitchen when we were starting out?"

"No."

"Me either because there were too many to count. Take the advice of someone who's been there, done that, and don't go down that road. If Tansy wants to get your opinion on cribs or paint for the nursery, pal-to-pal, that's one thing. This is expanding their business. You'll earn your fee."

"All right, if they want me."

"I'll give Derrick a call. If he's interested, he'll let you know. I've got to get going."

"Me, too." She rose with him. "Mama picked up Callie, but they're going to be wondering where I am by now. Thank you, Matt." She hugged him, gave him an extra squeeze. "You save a dance for me Saturday night."

"Absolutely. Show Griff those class projects," he repeated.

"I will, first chance."

She went back in. There were some customers still—a couple of women using the Relaxation Room after their treatment, a couple more who'd come in for hair after their own workday.

But Shelby's workday was done.

She got her purse, said her goodbyes, then stepped out the door.

And unexpectedly into Griff's arms.

The kiss caught her off guard, which may have accounted for her head going giddy.

"Hi," he said.

"Hi."

"I saw your van, so I was coming in to hunt you up."

"I was just . . ." The giddiness cleared when she spotted Crystal, her customer and the shampoo girl who'd stayed late to sweep up, all with their faces pressed to the front window.

Crystal just flapped a hand at her heart when Shelby made shooing motions.

"We're this evening's first performance."

Griff only grinned, waved to the women as Shelby tugged him toward her van. "Working late?"

"Actually, I needed to talk to Granny, then I had a little rendezvous with Matt."

"A rendezvous in the Ridge. Do I have to go punch him?"

"Not this time. You know, there's something I'd like to talk to you about, and some things I'd like to show you."

"About the big party?"

"Not altogether. Why don't you come home with me, come on to supper? Mama and Daddy would be pleased to see you. And Callie would be thrilled."

"Three redheads, a doctor and a free meal. I'd be crazy to say no." Still he looked down at his grubby T-shirt, dusty jeans. "But there was dirty work to be done today, and I haven't gotten home to clean up."

"You can wash up at the house, and we'll eat outside. We tend to in this kind of weather."

"Then I'm right behind you."

"I'll just let Mama know you're coming, so she doesn't get caught without her lipstick." Even as she reached for her phone, it signaled a text.

"Your mama?" Griff asked as she read.

"No. From Derrick."

It said only: *Yes, please yes. Save me from decorating hell.*

"Something we'll talk about." She walked to the driver's door. "What're you still doing in town?"

"It looks like I was waiting for you."

It made her smile. The whole damn day made her smile.

THE BURLY SUV drove slowly by as she got into the van. She didn't so much as glance over, but probably wouldn't have recognized the driver.

He'd changed his look again.

As she drove toward home, he drove up into the hills.

He knew what he planned to do, and when, and it pleased him to know what had started in Miami was nearly over.

29

When Griff walked into Vi's place on Saturday, Snickers rocked the house. Women—stylists, customers, technicians—hunkered down to *oooh* over him, to rub his belly, stroke his ears, and generally to send the dog into an apoplexy of joy.

He thought back to his early twenties when he'd routinely looked for ways to meet women.

He should've rented a puppy.

He'd come in—under protest, and under Emma Kate's orders—to get his hair trimmed up. He hated getting his hair trimmed up, but she'd been a little bit scary in the intensity of the order.

"You need yourself a trim," Viola stated, and made his shoulders hunch.

"Emma Kate said I had to, but you're busy, so—"

"Nobody's in my chair this minute. You come over here, Griffin, and sit."

The pup immediately plunked his butt down and looked pleased with himself. And the women chorused an *awwww!*

"A man should look well-groomed for his best friend's engagement party." Viola pointed a finger at her chair. "Be good like your dog."

"Just, you know, a little." Wishing himself pretty much anywhere else, Griff sat.

"Have I ever taken whacks at it?"

"No, ma'am."

She whipped a cape around him, picked up her spray bottle to dampen it down.

"You've got a fine head of hair, Griffin. I'll see you keep it. I suspect you were traumatized at the barbershop as a young boy."

"They brought in a clown—one of those crazy-wigged clowns. It was bad. Really bad. Did you ever read *It*? Stephen King's book? That kind of clown."

"No clowns around here of any kind." Enjoying herself, she gave his cheek a rub. "Boy, you need a shave."

"Yeah, I'll take care of it later."

"I'll give you a shave." When his eyes went a little wild, she just smiled. "Have you ever had a woman give you a good, close shave with a straight razor?"

"No."

"You're in for a treat." She adjusted the chair, picked up her scissors. "You haven't asked where Shelby is."

"I was counting on you to tell me."

"She's in the back. We got a group of six women, friends since college. They're taking a long weekend together, staying up at the big hotel. It's nice having forever friends. You've got that with Matt."

"Yeah, I do."

She kept up an easy conversation while she drew small sections of his hair up between her fingers, snipped. To relax him, he knew. Every couple of months, when he talked himself into going in for a trim—or got pushed there—she did the same.

He liked to watch her work—the quick, competent, precise moves, the way her eyes measured the cut even as she talked to him or tossed out orders, answered questions.

She could keep up with half a dozen conversations at once. He considered it a rare skill.

"She's going to be beautiful all her life."

"Shelby?"

Viola met his eyes in the mirror, smiled. "Wait till you see her tonight. She's got to get out of here soon, get Callie settled, then come back here so I can do her hair up. I see it in my head already."

"You're not going to straighten it, are you?"

"Not a bit. She says she's got to get up to the hotel early, so you won't be able to take her, and that's a shame because I believe the pair of you would make quite the entrance.

"Lorilee, I'm about done here. Would you go heat me up a towel for Griff's shave?"

"Sure thing, Miz Vi."

"You really don't have to—"

"Griffin Lott, how are you going to talk me into leaving my husband of near to fifty years and running off with you if you don't trust me not to cut your throat?"

So he ended up cocked back in the chair, a moist hot towel covering his face—but for the nose. He had to admit, it felt great—until he heard the sounds of her stropping the razor.

"I still use my great-granddaddy's razor," she said conversationally. "That's for sentiment mostly. He passed it to my granddaddy, and he's the one taught me how to shave a man."

He actually felt his Adam's apple try to shrink.

"When's the last time you did?"

"I shave Jackson most every week." She leaned down close. "We think of it as foreplay."

As he choked, she removed the towel. "We won't think of that as you're thinking of that with my grandbaby. Added to it, I used to shave Mayor Haggerty every Saturday morning—before he retired and moved to Tampa, Florida. We've got a woman mayor now."

She poured oil into her hands, rubbed them together, then smoothed it over his face.

"This is going to soften your beard up, and give you a nice cushion between your face, the cream and the blade. Smells nice, too."

"That doesn't sound like your grandfather's shave."

"You've got to move with the times." Busily she laid a thick layer of shaving cream over his face, his throat, using a wide, stubby brush to whirl it. "So to go back, I don't shave the mayor these days. But there are one or two around who like a good barbershop shave regular who come in. Others go to Lester's Barbershop. He's always talking about retiring, and if he ever does, I'll be expanding my services for gentlemen."

"Always thinking."

"Oh, I am, Griffin."

His gaze slid toward the straight razor with its pearl handle, then away.

"What you do," she continued, "is work in short strokes, with the grain of the hair. Then, if you want a good, close shave like I'm giving you today, you go back again, against the grain." Gently, with her thumb, she pulled the skin under his sideburn tight. "Don't feel much pressure, right? Gotta let the blade do the work. If you need pressure, you need a sharper blade."

She worked methodically, keeping up a flow of words. He relaxed, mostly, even when he felt the blade against his throat.

"Are you aiming to marry my girl, Griffin?"

He opened his eyes, looked up into hers. He saw amusement in hers. "As soon as she's ready."

"That's a fine answer. I taught her to shave a man."

"Really?"

"She might be out of practice, but she had a good hand with it. And speaking of that, here she comes."

He was afraid to move, could only shift his eyes. He heard the dog scramble up, heard her voice. Heard her laugh.

"Fathoms deep," Viola murmured. "That's what the poets say. You're fathoms deep, Griffin."

"And still sinking."

"Well, look at this! I didn't know you went for the barbershop shave, Griff."

"It's my first."

Shelby stroked two fingers over his left cheek. "Mmmm. Smooth as it gets."

"Foreplay," Viola said again, and had Shelby snickering.

"It does make you think, doesn't it? Granny, I'm sorry, but I have to go. I got an SOS from the hotel as it seems Miz Bitsy took herself up there even after she promised she wouldn't. Now I have to put out a couple little fires before she gets them blazing."

"You go right on. I told you to take the day off."

"I thought she'd be busy right in here. She's got appointments, for hair and nails. I've got to get her out of the way, smooth things down and be back here in less than a half hour to get the girls. I promised I'd take them to Story Time, and Tracey's got plans. Miz Suzannah's got a dentist appointment. I can't let Miz Bitsy have her head up there right now, and I don't want to disappoint Callie and Chelsea."

"I'll do it."

Shelby gave Griff's shoulder a pat before she hurried to the front counter for her purse. "I don't doubt you're good at putting out fires, but—"

"No, not Miz Bitsy. I'll pick up the kids, take them to Story Time."

As with the puppy, this generated a chorus of *aww*s from bystanders.

"Griff, I'm talking about two four-year-olds."

"I got that."

"And don't you have work?"

"Matt took off—he and Emma Kate were able to grab an appointment to look at this place for the wedding."

"What place?"

"I don't know. Some wedding place. I've done about all I can do on my own till about three, when we've got some more material coming in."

"I'm supposed to have the girls over at Miz Suzannah's at around three. They're having a sleepover."

"There you go. I'll pick them up, take them to Story Time. We can kick around in the park or something for an hour, whatever, if you're not back. I'll drop them off, and be back when the material gets here."

"You can take my truck. I'll take your van."

"I'm not sure if Tracey would feel right about you taking the girls."

"Oh, she'll be fine, Shelby." Viola flicked that idea away. "She's a sensible girl, she knows Griff, and she knows you've got your plate full today."

"You're right. My head's already spinning." She dug her keys out of her purse pocket. "Thank you, Griff. I'll be back as soon as I can."

"Take your time. If you're not back by three, I'll just give Callie a nail gun, give Chelsea a skill saw. It'll keep them busy."

"You're a comfort to me."

"Keys are in my right front pocket."

She arched her eyebrows. "You just want my hand in your pocket."

"Didn't know it was an option when I put the keys there, but it's a nice one."

She slid her hand in, hooked the keys. "Thank you," she said again, kissed him, said *mmmm* again. "Y'all pray for me," she called out as she hurried for the door.

GRIFF SETTLED DOWN at Rendezvous Books, where apparently Story Time for the preschool set happened once a month. And who didn't like Story Time? he asked himself, leaning against one of the stacks with a glass of iced coffee while about a dozen pint-sizers sat in a circle, listening to a story about a young boy and a young dragon with an injured wing.

He knew Miz Darlene—a retired schoolteacher who worked part-time at the bookstore. He and Matt had put a small addition on her house the previous fall, giving her a cozy reading room.

She deserved one, he thought. She read really, really well, doing voices, adding just the right elements of sorrow, joy, surprise and wonder.

She had the kids in the palm of her hand. And he was pretty interested in what was happening with Thaddeus and his dragon Grommel himself.

From somewhere deeper in the store, a baby began to cry. He could hear a woman's voice softly soothing, then the sound of her steps as she walked, back and forth, back and forth, and the crying stopped.

Sunlight streamed in the front window, through the glass panes of the front door, falling in square patterns of light on the old wood floor.

The pattern changed when the door opened; the bell jingled, then the pattern fell back into place. Changed again when a shadow crossed over it. He barely noted the man as more than that—a shadow that changed the pattern briefly.

Then the story ended, and Callie ran straight to him.

"Did you hear? Did you? Grommel's wing got better, and Thaddeus got to keep him! I wish I had a dragon."

"Me, too." He reached down for Chelsea's hand.

"Can we get a book?" Callie wanted to know. "About Thaddeus and Grommel?"

"Sure. Then I say we get ice cream cones and head to the park."

They got the book, and since it turned out there was already a second adventure written, he bought each girl the new one, then ice cream that dripped in strawberry streams faster than the kids could eat them.

He used the water fountain in the park to deal with sticky hands before he worked off the ice cream high by chasing the girls around, up and down the big play station.

When he dropped down, feigning defeat, the girls ran circles around him.

Callie tugged Chelsea's hand so they moved a few steps away, and began to whisper.

"What's the secret?"

"Chelsea says boys are supposed to ask."

He sat up cross-legged. "Ask what?"

More whispering, then Callie gave an innately female head toss and marched to him. "I can ask if I want."

"Okay."

"Can we get married? We can live in your house, and Mama can come, too. 'Cause I love you."

"Wow. I love you, too."

"So we can get married like Emma Kate and Matt, and we can all live in your house with Snickers. For happy ever after."

Undone, he drew her in. "Let me work on that."

"No tickles," she said, rubbing his cheek.

"Not today."

"I like tickles."

He drew her in again. Fathoms deep, he thought. "They'll be back."

He took out his phone at the signal.

Sorry it took so long—fires all out. On my way back.

He kept an arm around Callie as he answered.

In the park, smoking cigarettes and having a couple beers. We can switch off from here.

Her answer came moments later. *Don't litter. I'll be there in ten minutes.*

He slipped the phone back in his pocket. "Your mom's on the way, Callie."

"But we want to play with you!"

"I have to go to work. But before I do . . ." He shoved up, grabbed up both girls like footballs and had them squealing as he raced around the play set with Snickers running after them.

He caught sight of the man who'd come into the bookstore—or he thought it was him—at the far end of the park. Found himself holding the girls just a little closer.

Then the man glanced to the left, grinned, waved and strolled off toward someone Griff couldn't see.

Kids, he thought, setting the girls down so they could chase him. They made you suspicious of everything and everyone.

. . .

SHELBY ZIPPED THROUGH the rest of the day, doing the switch—kids and cars—with Griff, dropping the girls off at Miz Suzannah's. She gave Callie an extra hug, thinking it was her first genuine sleepover—one outside family.

Back to the salon for hair, and at Crystal's insistence, makeup. While she'd have preferred seeing to her own face, she couldn't find a way to say no without insulting Crystal. But her nerves showed enough for Crystal to vow not to "tart her up."

It certainly saved time, having herself fussed over like a celebrity, while she sent and answered texts from hotel catering, from the florist, from Emma Kate.

And too many to count from Miz Bitsy.

They kept her faced away from the mirror while they worked in tandem, then swung the chair around with a flourish for the big reveal.

All doubts vanished.

"Why, I look *amazing*!"

"Played up your eyes more than you usually do," Crystal began, "but kept it subtle. So it's elegant, like your hair."

"I'll say I'm elegant. And I look like me with a boost—not like the two of you fussed over me for near to an hour. I love it, Crystal, and I'll never doubt you again. And Granny, my hair is just wonderful. That thin band for just a little sparkle sets off the curls you've got tumbling out the bun in the back."

"A few loose tendrils around your face," Viola added, fussing with them a little more, "so it doesn't look like you spent five minutes on it— just spent the right five."

"I don't know if the rest of me can live up to what y'all have done, but I'll try my best. Thank you, thank you so much!" She hugged them both. "I've got to go. I'm determined to be at the hotel before Miz Bitsy. I'll see you both there."

She calculated she'd have the house to herself for an hour before her mother got home—two if Ada Mae opted to get her hair and face done up at the salon first.

She wouldn't need two.

She grabbed a Coke out of the kitchen, took a breath. She'd planned on wearing her simple black dress, but with the Grecian style Granny had come up with, she reassessed as she went upstairs.

The black dress would work for anything, no question—and had already done service at three Friday Nights. She'd yet to wear the silver gray one she'd brought with her from her closet up North. It just didn't suit Friday Nights. But for this . . .

Taking it out, she held it up in front of her, turned to the mirror. The lines were a little more fluid, more flowy, and would play up the hair. Not the black shoes now, she decided. They'd be too stark. But she had those blue sandals with the low heels—low heels would be more practical anyway when she'd likely be running around half the night.

And the dress had slit pockets, so she could slip her phone right in, have it handy.

Decision made, she dressed, added long dangling earrings and a trio of thin, sparkly bracelets from Callie's dress-up box.

She packed toiletries, a change of clothes since she was having her own overnight at Griff's after the party.

In an hour flat, and feeling pretty damn good about herself, she got back in her car and drove to the hotel.

Shelby figured she'd spent more time there in the past three weeks than she had in the whole of her life, but it still made her smile to make that turn up the rising road and see the spread of the big stone building through the trees.

She parked, took the slate path toward the wide front veranda, where two big white pots held red and white begonias with some trailing blue lobelia.

If Emma Kate and Matt decided to have their wedding here, she imagined those pots spilling with yellow and lavender flowers.

Some of the staff greeted her as she crossed over the wide-planked floor of the lobby, headed straight for the ballroom.

Decorating was well under way, and she saw, happily, that she'd been right. The deep purple cloths over the white added casual elegance, the perfect canvas for the bowls of white hydrangeas and clear, square holders holding white tea lights.

A mix of high- and low-tops, of chairs and stools.

She planned to echo that on the terrace, add some freestanding urns with white calla lilies and roses, some peonies and airy, trailing greenery.

It was all so Emma Kate.

Spotting the florist, Shelby moved to her. "Point me where you want me."

By the time the future bride and groom arrived, everything was in place—and she saw from the look on her friend's face, every hour of work, every drive up and back, every banging Bitsy headache had been worth it.

"Oh, Shelby."

"Don't start watering up! You'll have me doing it, and we'll ruin our makeup. We both look amazing."

"It's so beautiful. Everything I wanted, and more I didn't know I wanted. It's like a dream."

"It was our dream." She took Emma Kate's hand, and Matt's, joined them. "Now it's your dream. I now pronounce you engaged."

"We have one more favor."

Shelby reached in her pocket, pulled out her fist. "I happen to have one favor left over, right here. What can I do?"

"Matt and I decided on our song—at least for now. 'Stand by Me.' You know it, don't you?"

"Of course I do."

"We want you to sing it tonight."

"But you've got a band."

"We really want you to sing it." Emma Kate took Shelby's hand between both of hers. "Would you please, Shelby? Just that one song. For us."

"I'd be happy to. I'll speak to the band about it. Right now we're going to get you a drink, and I'm going to show you around before people start getting here and you don't have a minute."

"Griff's right behind us," Matt said. "In fact, here he is now."

"Oh, well, my! Look at you." She brushed a hand down the lapel of his dark gray suit, and thought how lucky it was she'd worn the pale gray dress. "You're so dashing."

"Goddess of the mountain," he murmured. "You take my breath."

He lifted her hand, kissed it. She flushed—something she'd taught herself not to do—as a redhead—while still in her teens. "Thank you, sir. The four of us do look nearly as wonderful as the room. I think we should have the first glasses of champagne. And Emma Kate, I want to show you the terrace. We've strung little white lights in the potted trees. It's a fairyland."

"Flowers and candles and fairy lights," Griff commented as they toured the space. "All the sparkle, none of the fuss."

"I cut miles of frills out of Miz Bitsy's vision, but I really do think she's going to be pleased with how it all turned out. We might have a storm coming in, but not until after midnight."

She tapped her pocket and her phone. "I keep checking my weather app, and so far, so good. There's Miz Bitsy now. And doesn't she look pretty in her long red dress? I'd better go talk to her."

"Want backup?"

She grabbed his hand. "Do I ever."

SHE DANCED WITH HIM. It didn't occur to her until later that not once did a memory of other formal parties and elegant dress intrude. She never thought of Richard, who'd worn a tux as if he were born in one.

Everything centered on the moment.

Dancing with her father, who pulled out some of the ballroom moves he'd retained from when Ada Mae had nagged him into lessons. And her grandfather, who swung her into some clogging—and there her muscle memory wasn't as keen as his—when the band kicked it up a few licks. With Clay, who hadn't inherited any rhythm at all, and with Forrest, who'd taken Clay's share of it.

"How'd you get in here?" she asked Forrest. "You're not wearing a tux or even a suit and tie."

"It's the badge." He circled her in a smooth two-step. "I told Miz Bitsy I was on duty."

"Are you?"

He only grinned. "I consider myself always on duty, and I haven't worn a monkey suit since senior prom. I hope to continue that winning streak."

"Nobby's wearing one."

"He is, but he swore to back me up on the on-duty excuse."

"What'd you bribe him with?"

"A fancy coffee and a couple bear claws fresh from the bakery."

She laughed, circled with him.

"You look as good as it gets tonight, little sister."

"I feel as good as it gets tonight, big brother. Look how happy everybody is. Emma Kate could light the place up all on her own."

"Stealing her back," Griff said as he cut in.

"I could arrest you for that, but I'll let it go. There's a blonde over there who looks like she could use some company."

Shelby glanced over. "Her name's Heather. She worked with Emma Kate at the hospital in Baltimore. She's single."

"That works."

Griff drew Shelby in as Forrest wandered toward the blonde. "You've got a hit on your hands, Red."

"I know it." She slid her hands up his back, pressed her cheek to his.

"It feels so good—just like you. I was just saying how happy everybody is. It's so nice knowing people are happy for Emma Kate and Matt. And Miz Bitsy— Oh, there she goes, tearing up again, and bolting toward the ladies'. I'll just go take care of that."

Shelby turned her head, brushed a kiss over his cheek. "It shouldn't take long—or it could take twenty minutes if it's a genuine crying jag. I'll probably appreciate another glass of champagne once I handle this."

"I'll make sure it's waiting."

She started for the doors, and the restrooms beyond them. And pulled out her phone when it rang.

"Miz Suzannah? Is everything all right?"

"It's nothing much, honey. It's just Callie forgot Fifi, and she's heart-broken. We didn't realize it until we were getting them into bed. I've tried substitutes, but she's just set on her Fifi."

"I don't know how I could've sent her off to you without Fifi. We don't want her first overnight spoiled. I'll just run to the house and get Fifi, drop her off. It won't take fifteen minutes for me to get there."

"I'm so sorry to interrupt and cause you that trouble. My Bill would go get the dog, but I know your mama's been locking up."

"Don't worry about it. I'm on my way now. Tell Callie I'm bring-ing Fifi."

She spotted Crystal on her way to the ladies'. "I've got a favor to ask. Miz Bitsy's in there, crying a little, just happy, you know how it is, and emotional. I've got to run get Fifi for Callie. Could you just soothe Miz Bitsy—or ask Granny to—and let Griff know, if you see him, I'll be back in under a half hour."

"Sure, I will. You want me to go get Fifi?"

"Thank you, but I'll be quick."

"Oh, here! I meant to give you this at the salon. The lipstick I used on you."

"Thank you, Crystal. Keep this party going!"

"You can count on me."

Hurrying off, Shelby shoved the lipstick in her right pocket, the phone in her left. She cast her mind back to packing for Callie. She *knew* she'd had Fifi right there, but . . .

She saw it now, Callie picking up the stuffed dog to talk to it about their sleepover.

And carting the dog with her when she'd followed her mama into the other bedroom.

"On the windowsill," she remembered. How she'd overlooked that, she'd never know.

That was all right—she'd be back again before anyone missed her. And Callie and Fifi would be reunited.

She cut around town as a Saturday night in the summer could be busy, and made it to the house in under ten minutes. Grateful for the low heels, she ran for the door. They'd scheduled her song for midway through the evening, so she had thirty minutes to spare. But no more.

She dashed straight upstairs, into her bedroom.

"There you are, Fifi. I'm so sorry you got left behind." She plucked the much-loved dog off the windowsill, turned to rush right back out again.

And he stepped into the doorway. The dog slipped out of her numb fingers as he moved toward her.

"Hello, Shelby. Long time, no see."

"Richard."

His hair was dark, a deep, unfamiliar brown, and fell in careless waves well over his collar. Thick scruff covered the lower half of his face. He wore a camo T-shirt and rough khaki pants with scarred army boots. A combination he wouldn't have been caught dead in.

Oh God.

"They—they said you were dead."

"They said what I wanted them to say. It didn't take you long to go running back home, and spreading your legs for some carpenter. Did you cry for me, Shelby?"

"I don't understand."

"You never did understand much of anything. I guess we've got to have a long talk, you and I. Let's go."

"I'm not going anywhere with you."

He reached casually behind his back, drew out a gun. "Yes, you are."

The gun in his hand struck her just as unbelievable as all the rest. "Are you going to shoot me? For what? I don't have anything you could want."

"Did have." He nodded toward the photo on her dresser. She saw now he'd taken it apart.

"I know you, Shelby. You're so damn simple. One thing you'd never get rid of—that picture you gave me of you and the kid. If they picked me up, they'd still have nothing. I kept what I needed with my lovely wife and daughter."

"Behind our picture," she murmured. "What did you hide there?"

"Key to the kingdom. We'll talk. Let's go."

"I'm not—"

"I know where she is," he said quietly. "Spending the night with her little friend Chelsea. At the grandmother's. Maybe I'll just go over there, pay Callie a visit."

Fear sliced through her, a knife to the bone. "No. No, you stay away from her. You leave her be."

"I'll kill you right here where your family will find you. If I have to handle it that way, the kid's my next stop. Your choice, Shelby."

"I'll go. Just leave Callie alone, and I'll go with you."

"Damn right you will." He gestured her out of the room with the gun. "So predictable—always were, always will be. I knew you were a born mark the first time I saw you."

"Why don't you just take what you came for and go? We don't mean anything to you."

"And how far would I get before you called your cop brother?" As they stepped out of the house, he put an arm tight around her waist, pressed the gun into her side. "We're going to walk down a little bit, take my car. A minivan, Shelby? You're an embarrassment to me."

That tone, that pitying tone. How often had she heard it? "I'm nothing to you, never was."

"Oh, you were so useful." He pressed a kiss to her temple, made her shudder. "And at first, hell, you were even fun. God knows you were eager in the sack. This one. Get in, climb over. You're going to drive."

"Where are we going?"

"A little place I know. Quiet. Private. It's just what we need for a heart-to-heart."

"Why aren't you dead?"

"You'd like that."

"I swear on all that's in me, I would."

He shoved her into the car, forcing her to crawl over to the driver's seat.

"I never did anything to you. I did what you wanted, went where you wanted. I gave you a child."

"And bored the crap out of me. Drive, and keep it to the speed limit. You go over, you go under, I'll shoot you in the gut. It's a painful way to die."

"I can't drive if I don't know where I'm going."

"Take the back roads around that hole-in-the-wall you call a town. Try anything, Shelby, I'll take you out, then I go after the kid. I've got too much at stake, and I've worked and waited for it too long to let you fuck it up."

"You think I care about the jewelry, the money? Take it and go."

"Oh, I will. First thing Monday morning. If you hadn't come into the bedroom, you'd never have known I was there. As it is, we'll have a reunion weekend, then I'm gone. Just do what you're told, like always, and you'll be fine."

"They'll look for me."

"And they won't find you." Sneering, he pressed the barrel of the gun into her side. "Jesus, you stupid bitch, do you think I've outwitted the cops all this time and can't keep ahead of a bunch of Barney Fifes for a day? Take this turn coming up, to the right. Nice and easy."

"Your partner's been around. Jimmy Harlow. Maybe he'll have better luck finding you."

"I don't think so."

His tone froze her blood.

"What did you do?"

"Found him first. Steady on these switchbacks. I wouldn't want this gun to go off."

Her insides quaked, but she kept her hands steady as she negotiated the tight wind of the climb.

"Why did you marry me?"

"It served my purpose at the time. I never could smooth you out, though, never could make anything out of you. Listen to you, look at you, I gave you plenty of money, taught you how to buy the right clothes, how to give a decent dinner party, and you're still the ignorant hick from the Tennessee hills. It's amazing I haven't bashed what brains you have out before now."

"You're a thief and a swindler."

"That's right, honey." His sneer shifted to a cheerful grin. "And I'm damn good at it. You? You've never been good at anything. Take this excuse for a road on the left. Nice and slow now."

He might've thought her ignorant, useless, malleable, but she knew the hills. And had a reasonable idea where they were going.

"What happened in Miami? All those years ago," she asked, wanting to keep him talking, distract him as she slid her left hand into her pocket.

"Oh, we'll talk about that. We've got a lot of things to talk about."

Texting while driving, she thought, struggling not to give way to hysteria, was dangerous.

She hoped to God she managed to do it right.

Because while she knew the hills, she thought she knew the man beside her now. And she believed he meant to kill her before he was done.

30

The country-dark road twisted like a snake as it climbed, and gave her an excuse to ease off the gas. She let the fear show—no point in pride—and the show of fear could be another weapon. Or at least a shield, she thought, as she slipped her hand into her pocket, and prayed she could manage a coherent message.

"Why didn't you just run?"

"I don't run," he said with that same self-satisfied smile on his face. "I navigate. You were just what I needed to make my new ID solid after the Miami job. It didn't take me long to realize you'd be useless on the grift, but you made for a good temporary cover."

"Nearly five years, Richard?"

"I never figured to keep you around that long, then you got knocked up. I think on my feet," he reminded her. "Who's going to look for a family man, a man with a hick wife and a baby? And I had to wait for the take to cool down. And for Melinda to get out. She made a hell of a deal—you have to give her credit. I'd thought she'd get double what they gave her, and that would've been plenty of time for cooling off and covering my tracks. But she always could surprise me."

"You killed her."

"How could I? I'm dead, remember? Make this right. Nearly there."

Nothing back here, she thought, but a couple of cabins—at least that's all there'd been when she'd left the Ridge.

She hit Send—she hoped—because she had to put her left hand back on the wheel.

"But you're not dead, and you killed her."

"And who are the assholes looking for over it? Jimmy. I'm in the clear. I'm going to stay in the clear. And when I pick up what's mine Monday morning, I'll be in the clear with millions. Long-range plans, Shelby, take a lot of patience. This one cost me a little more than a year for each five million. That's a damn good deal in the world of big pictures. Pull up right beside that truck."

"Who else is here?"

"Nobody now."

"My God, Richard, whose place is this? Who did you kill?"

"An old friend. Turn off the car, hand me the keys." Once again, he jabbed with the barrel of the gun. "You're going to sit where you are until I come around for you. Try anything—anything—I'll put a bullet in you. Then I'll go get Callie. I know people who'd pay a premium for a pretty girl her age."

She hadn't known he could sicken her even more. "She's your child. She's your blood."

"Do you actually think I care?"

"No." Her hand was back in her pocket, frantically tapping. "I don't think you care about anything or anyone. And there's nothing I wouldn't do to keep Callie safe."

"Then what's left of the weekend should be easy on both of us."

She considered locking the doors when he got out, just to give herself more time to send the next message. But it would only spike his temper. It had to be better to make him believe she was utterly helpless.

It wasn't too far from the truth.

When he came around, opened her door, she got out compliantly.

"Here's our little home away from home." He used a penlight to shine a thin beam, showing the way to a small cabin, roughly built.

Her shoes crunched on the short gravel walk leading to a sagging front porch. A couple of old chairs, a rickety table. Nothing she could see that could be used as a weapon.

He dropped the penlight back in his pocket, handed her a key.

"Unlock the door."

She did what she was told, and at the prod of the gun, stepped off the dark porch into the dark cabin. She jolted when he turned on the light—couldn't help herself. It came yellow and dull from the globes on a wagon wheel dropped from the pitched ceiling.

"I call it the Hickville Dump. It's not much, but it's ours. Sit down."

When she didn't move fast enough he shoved her toward a chair of red-and-green plaid. She caught herself, turned to sit, and saw the blood on the floor, smears of it leading to a closed door.

"Yeah, you're going to clean that up, then I've got a shovel with your name on it. You're going to bury Jimmy, save me the sweat."

"All of this for money?"

"It's always the money." The excitement, the light that had first drawn her to him, beamed out. But she saw it now for what it was. Hard and false.

"It's always the money," he repeated, "but it's the ride, too. It's knowing you're the smartest one in the room, no matter what fucking room. It's knowing if you want it, you can take it."

"Even if it belongs to someone else."

"Especially, you moron, if it belongs to someone else. That's the ride. I'm going to grab a beer." He sent her a wide smile "Get you something, honey?"

He backed into the tiny open kitchen when she said nothing.

So sure she was paralyzed, she thought, he didn't even bother to restrain her. She kept her hands clenched together in her lap, the knuckles white. But it was as much a rising fury as fear now.

The lamp, she thought, the one on the table with the black bear hunched by the trunk of a tree. It might be heavy enough if she could get her hands on it.

There'd be knives in the kitchen.

She imagined the Winchester rifle over the fireplace was unloaded. But maybe not.

And there was an engraved plate on the stock that read "William C. Bounty."

She relaxed her fingers, started to slide her hand toward her pocket, let it lie still again when Richard walked back, sat across from her.

"Isn't this cozy?"

"How did you do it? How did you survive the boating accident?"

"Surviving's what I do. Melinda was getting out. I didn't count on Jimmy busting out, complicated things a bit. I didn't think he had that in him. But Melinda, I knew she'd be a problem. She always was a dog with a bone, just never let go, so she'd need to be dealt with before I cashed in."

He settled back, obviously relaxed. "I always figured on the five years— and it was close enough. So . . . a little vacation with the fam, tragedy strikes, and I'd be off the grid again."

"We'd have been with you if Callie hadn't gotten sick." When his eyes gleamed, understanding struck her with true horror. "You were going to kill us. You were going to kill your own baby."

"Young family's holiday vacation ends in tragedy. It happens."

"You couldn't have gotten away with it. If the authorities hadn't hunted you down, my family would have."

"Not if I died trying to save you. It should've played out that way. I'd have spent a couple days painting us as a happy little family—people tend to believe what they see. Good-looking couple, pretty little girl. Then we'd make a day of it on the boat. Go out far enough, get some wine in you, wait until dusk."

He took a slow sip of beer, smiled at her. "I toss the kid over, and it's easy money you'd go right over after her. I wouldn't have to put a mark on either one of you."

"You're a monster."

"I'm a winner. I'd scuttle the boat, get my scuba gear. With my new ID and a change of clothes in a waterproof pouch, I'd have made it to Hilton Head in a few hours. Which is what I did—without you along."

"The squall."

"Unexpected bonus."

"You could've died out there. Why risk dying?"

"You don't get it, never will." He leaned toward her, that light glowing again. "That's the *point*, that's the rush. All I had to do was dump the tanks, catch a cab and pick up the car I had waiting in long-term parking at the airport. Drive to Savannah and my drop box there. Wouldn't have needed that if I damn could have found the key for my box in Philly."

He watched her while he took another sip of beer. "You got into that. Where was the key?"

"In the pocket of your leather jacket, the bronze one I gave you for your birthday two years back. It had gone through a little hole and into the lining of the jacket."

"Well, son of a bitch." He gave a half-laugh, shook his head as he might over a missed putt on the green. "That key would have saved me some time and trouble. Either way, I'm dead. The way it turned out, you got to play the grieving widow for a while. How did that suit you?"

"I wish it had been true."

He laughed, toasted her with his beer. "Coming back to the boonies brought some of that sass back. Let's see if a little housework knocks it back out of you." He rose, went back in the kitchen.

When he picked up a bottle of bleach and a scrub brush, she got to her feet.

"You want me to clean up the blood?"

"You're going to clean up the blood, unless you want to clean up your own along with it."

"I can't—"

He swung out with the back of his left hand, quick as a snake, striking her across the cheekbone hard enough to send her stumbling back and into the chair again.

She didn't know why the blow shocked her, now that she knew him. Really knew him. But he'd never hit her before.

"God! I've wanted to do that for *years*!" The furious pleasure on his face iced her blood. He could, and would, do more than knock her down if she bucked him. Even as he stepped toward her, she held up a trembling hand.

And again it was more rage than fear.

But she let only the fear show. "I just meant I need a bucket. I need a bucket of water and—and a mop. I can't get it cleaned up with just the bleach and a brush. That's all I meant. Please, don't hurt me."

"Why the fuck didn't you say so?"

She let her head hang, and thinking of never seeing Callie again, her family, never seeing Griff, let tears come.

Let him see the tears, she thought, let him think that's all that's in me.

"You start sniveling, I'll give you worse than a love tap. Go find a damn bucket. Make a move I don't like, you *will* be mopping up your own blood."

She went into the kitchen, scanning, scanning. No knife block, but surely there was a knife in a drawer. And there was a good cast iron skillet still on the stove, and a coffeepot. Filled with hot coffee that would make a weapon.

She looked under the sink, considered her options there, then in a skinny closet. There she found a broom, mop, bucket. Some old cord, some rusty chain, butane lighter fluid, bug spray.

She considered grabbing the bug spray, aiming for his eyes with that as the pepper spray was in the purse she'd left in her car. But he was nearly on top of her.

She took out the mop, the bucket, filled the bucket with hot soapy water.

She carted it over to the largest smear of blood.

"I need to use the bathroom."

"Hold it," he advised.

"I'll do what you tell me to do. I just want to get through this, Richard, but I need to use the bathroom."

He narrowed his eyes. She kept her gaze downcast, her shoulders slumped.

"Right there. Door stays open."

"If you won't give me privacy, at least don't look at me."

She walked to the tiny bathroom—razors maybe in the old medicine cabinet? A window too small for her to wiggle through if she had the chance.

She put the seat down on the toilet while he hovered in the doorway.

"Just don't look at me!" She let out a choked sob. "The door's open, you're standing right there. I'm just asking you not to watch me. For God's sake."

He leaned against the jamb, cast his eyes up to the ceiling. "Awful dainty for someone one step up from an outhouse."

She smothered her sensibilities, lifted her skirt, pulled down her panties. And shot her hand in her pocket.

Please God, if you're listening, let this make sense. Let this go through.

When she was done, heat flushed her face.

"Jesus, look at you, sweaty, splotchy, your hair like something a rat wouldn't nest in. I don't know how I ever got it up with you."

She dipped the mop in the bucket, wrung it out, began to wash up the blood.

"And what's your pithy comeback? Hurt feelings." He made crying noises. "God, you're weak. You think that asshole you're fucking now's going to stick?"

"He loves me." Saying it, knowing it, steadied her.

"Love? You're a handy piece of ass. It's all you ever were, all you'd ever be. A handy piece of ass who'll splash around in some backwoods creek."

She froze, and slowly lifted her gaze. "You spied on us, on me?"

"I could've taken you both out." He lifted the gun, pointed it at her head. Said, "Pow, pow. But I wanted to lay it on Jimmy's plate. A nice, tidy circle."

"But you killed Jimmy."

"Unavoidable alteration in plans. Don't worry, I've got it covered. I always do. Put your back into it, Shelby."

She went back to mopping, and began to make plans of her own.

GRIFF GOT HUNG UP talking construction with Derrick, lost track of some time. He had Shelby's champagne, but he didn't have Shelby. A glance around showed him Bitsy was back—a little damp-eyed as she danced with her future son-in-law.

Shelby was probably dealing with some other small crisis, he thought, but set out to look for her.

"Hey, Griff, hey!" Crystal came over, pointed at the glass of champagne. "Is that up for grabs?" She took it, drank deep. "I need it after drying Miz Bitsy up. She was watering like a leaky pipe."

"Looks like you and Shelby got it done."

"Oh, it was just me—that's why I was looking for you, but I got waylaid a couple times. It's a hell of a party! Shelby had to run home for a minute. Get Fifi for Callie. She should be back by now, I guess."

"When did she go?"

"Oh, I don't know exactly since I was dealing with the leaky pipe, then Miz Bitsy's sister—they call her Sugar?—she came in so the two of them were leaking together. I guess it's been about twenty minutes or so. She should be back or on her way."

Maybe it was the dregs of all that had happened, but the dread just dropped over him like a shroud. He yanked out his phone, intended to call her, and it signaled an incoming text in his hand.

"It's Shelby."

"There you go." Crystal patted his arm. "She's just letting you know she's on her way back, I expect. No call to look so worried, honey."

But when he brought up the text the bottom dropped out of his world.

"Where's Forrest?"

"Forrest? I just saw him over that-a-way flirting with a pretty blonde. I—"

But Griff was already moving, and fast. He cut across the dance floor, ignoring those who called out a greeting. He spotted Forrest, and what he felt must have showed on his face. After a casual glance in his direction, Forrest's eyes went cold.

He turned away from the blonde without a word.

"What happened?"

"She's in trouble." Griff held out the phone.

richard live hs gun mking me drive black drango wst on bb rd ky license 529kpe

"Christ."

"What's BB Road?"

"Black Bear Road. Wait." Forrest clamped a hand on Griff's arm before his friend could take off. "You're not going to find her driving hell-bent all over the hills."

"I'm not going to find her standing here."

"We're not going to be. Nobby's over by the bar there. Get him. I'm calling it in."

"I'm going after her, Forrest."

"Not saying different, but we're going to go with the best chance of finding her. Get Nobby."

They pulled Nobby outside, and Clay and Matt with them.

"We're going to do this smart," Forrest began. "Two men to a team. The sheriff's putting more together right now. We're going to blanket the area west of town. Odds are he'll keep to the back roads. Clay, you look here."

Clay clamped a hand on Forrest's shoulder, leaned in to look at the map on his phone. "You and Nobby are going to cover this section here. You keep your eyes peeled for that vehicle, that license plate. Matt, you sure about this?"

"Hell yes."

"I'm going to have you go into town, hook up with the sheriff, he'll—"

"What's going on here?" Viola stepped outside. "What's happened? Where's Shelby?"

Griff only waited a beat. "You're wasting time figuring out what you should say or not, Pomeroy. Richard's alive—I don't know how—and he has her. We're going after her."

The color drained out of her face, made her eyes blaze like blue fire. "Boy, if you're putting a posse together, your granddaddy and I are going to be part of it."

"Granny—"

"Don't Granny me," she snapped at Forrest. "Who taught you to shoot?"

"I'm going now," Griff said.

"Nobby, set it up from here, will you? Griff and I are going."

"Callie," Viola called out.

"She's fine, Griff checked, and we've got a man there sitting on the house right now." Forrest kept going, opened the lockbox on the side of his truck, took out a Remington rimfire rifle, a box of ammo.

"I've seen you shoot so I know you can handle it."

Target shooting was as far as Griff had gone, ever, but he didn't argue.

Forrest got in the truck, took his favored Colt out of the glove box. "We're going to get her back, Griff."

"Not sitting here, we won't."

"I'm counting on you to keep a cool head." Even as he spoke, Forrest punched the gas and they were flying. "We're going to keep your phone open, in case she's able to send you another message. Use mine to coordinate with the other teams as they come along. The sheriff's already pulled in the federals. They got equipment we don't run to in the Ridge, and better techs. Shelby keeps her head, keeps her phone on, they're going to track it."

"He had to be watching her, or be in the house when she went back."

"We'll find out when we get her back."

"He's going to be the one who killed the woman."

Forrest's face was stone as the speedometer inched higher. "I wouldn't bet against it."

"I saw him, I think. I got a bad feeling about the guy I saw—when I took Callie to the bookstore, then to the park. He played me."

"Let's worry about now."

The now had fear tearing through his heart, his head, his belly. "He has to have somewhere to go. Shelby said he never did anything without a reason."

"We'll find him, and we'll get her back. Safe."

Before Griff could respond, his phone signaled. "It's Shelby. Jesus, she's got nerves of steel." He struggled to read the jumbled text as they flew around switchbacks. "Old Hester Road, I think she means Hester."

"I know where she means. It's Odd Hester. Scatter of cabins and old campsites, deer stands up that way. Remote. You relay that, Griff, to Nobby, and he'll take it from there."

"What the hell does he want with her?"

"Whatever he wants, he's not going to get it."

Ice, sharp and jagged, poured in through the tearing fear. "How far away are we?"

"A ways, but we're traveling a hell of a lot faster than they are. Bring the others along now, Griff."

He made the relay, yanked off his formal tie.

He wouldn't lose her. He would not lose her. Callie would not lose her mother. Whatever had to be done, he'd do it. He looked at the rifle across his lap.

Whatever had to be done.

"She's sending another. *Right hardpack track past mulberry stand. Single cabin. Truck.* There's a truck already at the cabin."

"Might have more hostages. Or it might be his old partner. Let the others know."

Griff couldn't say how Forrest kept the truck on the road, not at this speed, not around turns so sharp they could cut bone. More than once they fishtailed or the tires kissed the narrow shoulder.

And still it wasn't fast enough.

"She's sending . . . it says . . . William, she means William. William Bunty."

"Bounty," Forrest corrected. "I know where it is. She's guiding us in faster than the fucking feds ever could."

"How far?"

"Ten minutes."

"Make it less." With hands cold as steel, Griff began to load the rifle.

SHELBY EMPTIED the bucket twice, refilled it.

Stalling, as nothing was going to remove the stains from the old wood floor.

But she poured a puddle of bleach from the bucket on the stain, got down on her hands and knees to scrub at it.

"Now that's the kind of job you're suited for."

"Scrubbing floors is honest work."

"Loser work. You lived the high life for a while. I gave you that." He gave her a nudge in the ass with his foot. "I gave you a good taste of the high life. You should be grateful."

"You gave me Callie, so I'm grateful. You always meant to kill them, didn't you, the people you ran with, the woman who you lived with—she said you married her. Did you?"

"Not any more than I married you. Thinking I did was about the only really stupid moment she had when we were together. Women, what can you do? They're wired to be suckers. But she wouldn't have given up, even thinking I was dead. She'd want the score. She was getting too close. I walked right out behind her, out of that dive where you were singing to a bunch of rubes."

He shook his head, circled her while she worked. "I saved you from a life of embarrassment thinking you could ever make anything with that mediocre voice. And Mel's face when she saw me? Priceless. I take back what I said—that was her second really stupid moment. She rolled the window down, said, 'Jake. I should've known.'

"Those were the last words she said, and yeah, she should've."

"She loved you."

"See what love gets you?" He gave her another little kick. "It's just another con."

She sat back on her heels, then rose slowly, bucket in hand. "I'm going to need more than this to bleach out that stain. Is there more?"

"You've got plenty, right there."

"Yes, but I need it to—"

She heaved it up, straight bleach with a faint tinge of blood, into his face.

When he screamed, she had a choice. Go for the gun or run for the door. And she was too fired up to run.

She kicked, aiming for his groin. The floor was just wet enough that she slipped a little, and it took the leading edge off the kick. But she made contact. Even as she tried to grab for the gun, he fired it—wild and blind.

Her ears rang. She ducked, snatching at the mop, hoping to make better contact with his balls with the handle. But his flailing hand got a fistful of her hair, firing stupefying pain into her skull.

She jabbed her elbow into the same tender area, and knew she hurt him, knew she gave him pain. But he was as wild as she was now, and flung her across the room like a rag.

"Bitch, you bitch."

She rolled. She wasn't sure how well he could see, hoped he was blind. Desperate, she wrenched off a shoe, flung it across the room, praying he'd follow the sound.

But he walked slowly toward her, the whites of his eyes shattered and red.

"I'm not just going to kill you now. I'm going to hurt you first." He rubbed his left eye with his free hand.

Making it worse, she knew. Please, please make it worse.

"Let's start with a kneecap."

She braced for the pain, then scrambled back in shock as the door where the bloodstains ended burst open.

Richard whirled, blinking his burning, blurry eyes as the bloody mountain of a man rammed him.

Horrible sounds, the grunts, snarls, the crack of fist against bone. But the only sound that mattered was the clatter of the gun as it leaped out of Richard's hand on impact and hit the floor.

She bolted after it, nearly dropped it again out of hands soap slick with her own sweat.

She swayed up to her knees, bit down, gripped the gun in both hands.

The big man was bleeding, and whatever force had driven him into the room and at the man who'd shot him was eaten away now. Richard had his hands around the man's throat. Squeezing, squeezing.

"Dead. Thought you were dead, Jimmy."

I thought the same about you, she thought, and said calmly, coldly, "Richard."

His head whipped around. She wondered what she looked like through those burning eyes. She hoped she looked like Vengeance.

He bared his teeth, let out a short laugh. "You haven't got the spine."

He lunged at her.

. . .

THEY HEARD the first shots as Forrest spun the truck onto the dirt track. All plans to go in quiet, one in front, one in back, while backup poured in behind them, dissolved.

He floored it, fishtailed over the gravel walk as the next shots rang out.

"Go in fast," Forrest shouted as they leaped out of either side of the truck. "If he's standing, drop him."

They hit the door together. Griff swung the rifle up.

But Richard was already down.

She knelt on the floor, holding the gun out, gripped in both hands. There was blood and bruising on her face. Her dress was torn at the shoulder where more bruises bloomed.

Her eyes were cold and fierce, her hair a wild, tumbling tangle of flame.

She never had and never would look more beautiful to Griff's eyes.

She swung the gun toward them, and he saw her arms tremble. Then she dropped those trembling arms.

"I think he's dead this time. I think I killed him. I think he's dead now."

Griff shoved the rifle at Forrest. His heart started beating again when he had his arms around her.

"I've got you. You're all right. I've got you."

"Don't let go."

"I won't." He eased back only to pry the gun out of her stiff fingers. "He hurt you."

"Not as bad as he wanted. Callie."

"She's fine. She's safe. She's asleep."

"He said he'd kill her if I didn't go with him. He said he'd go after her." She looked over at her brother, who pressed fingers against Richard's throat. "I had to protect her."

"You did what you had to do," Forrest told her.

"Is he dead now?"

"He's breathing. They both are, but they sure are a mess. It'll be up to the doctors and God whether they make it."

"He shot him, shot the big one—Jimmy—and thought he was dead, but he wasn't. I threw bleach in his eyes, but it wasn't enough. I slipped on it, I think, when I went to kick him in the balls, and he got me by the hair. He was going to shoot me, but the other one came out like a demon from hell. I got the gun. I got the gun, and the big one, he couldn't fight anymore he was bleeding so bad. Richard was choking him. I said his name. I said, 'Richard,' so he looked at me. I don't know why I thought that would make him stop. He thought less than nothing of me. He thought I was weak and stupid and spineless. He said that. He said I didn't have the spine, and he came at me. I had the spine to shoot him three times. I think it was three times. He didn't go down until the third time."

Forrest shifted, crouched eye-to-eye with her. "You did what you had to do."

Her eyes lost the fierceness, went glassy with tears. "You have to take it back."

"Take what back, baby?"

"That I can't shoot worth shit."

Weak-kneed, Forrest rested his brow to hers a moment. "I take it back. Get her out of here, Griff. I got this."

"I'm all right."

Rather than argue, Griff just picked her up.

"You came." She touched his cheek. "I knew you would, somehow. I didn't know if the texts were going through, or who I was texting for sure. I've got them alphabetical, so it was going to be you or Forrest or Granny, maybe Grandpa. I knew if they got through, you'd come. You'd fix it."

"You fixed it yourself before I got the chance."

"I had to— Someone's coming." Her fingers dug into his shoulder. "The lights. Someone—"

"Backup. You're safe now." He turned his face into her hair. "You've got the whole damn Rendezvous Ridge Sheriff's Department and God knows who else coming."

"Oh, that's all right, then. Will you take me to see Callie? I don't want to wake her up. I don't want her to see me until I've cleaned up, but I need to see her. Well, my God, that's Grandpa's date-night car. Set me down. Set me down so they're not scared."

He put her on her feet, but kept an arm around her. When he felt her shivering, he stripped off his jacket, draped it over her shoulders as her grandparents got out of the car.

"I'm all right. I'm not hurt. I'm—" The rest was muffled against her grandfather's shoulder. She felt him shaking, knew he wept. Wept with him a little as others drove up.

"Where is the bastard?" Jack demanded.

"Inside. I shot him, Grandpa. He's not dead—again—but I shot him."

Jack took her face in his hands, kissed her wet cheeks.

"Let me see the girl." Viola pulled her away, studied her face. "You were born to take care of yourself and yours. You did what you were born to do. Now we're going to take you home and . . ."

She paused, steadied herself. "Griff's going to take you home," Viola corrected. "Your mama and daddy are at Suzannah's with Callie. Just staying there while she sleeps. They need to hear your voice."

"I'll call right away. I had my phone in my pocket. He never knew I had it. He never knew much about me, I guess. Sheriff."

Her head felt too light, and the dark circled for a few seconds as Hardigan strode up to her.

"I shot him. He was going to kill me so I shot him."

"I want you to tell me everything that happened."

"She gave Forrest the outline," Griff interrupted. "She needs to get away from here. She needs to see her daughter."

Sheriff Hardigan tapped his cheek where Shelby's was bruised. "He do that?"

"Yes, sir. It was the first time he ever hit me. I guess it's going to be the last time."

"You go on home now, darling. I'll be around to talk to you tomorrow."

It took some time. Clay rushed up, picked her up off her feet, held her suspended as if he'd never let her go. There was Matt, who thrust his phone out to her after he'd hugged her so she could speak to Emma Kate.

"Tell Forrest I'm taking his truck."

Griff drove away from the cabin, from the blood, from the lights, then just stopped at the turn onto the road.

He drew her over against him, held on.

"I need a minute."

"You can take all the minutes you want." She started to relax against him. "Oh hell, Griffin, I forgot to tell them. Richard has a key in his pocket—or I guess that's where it is. It was in that picture frame, the one holding the picture of me and Callie I gave him. He said he was going Monday morning to the bank, and I think he means one of the banks right in the Ridge. It's where he put the jewelry, the stamps, too, I guess. He put it right in the bank in Rendezvous Ridge."

Keeping his eyes closed, Griff just breathed in the scent of her hair. "Who'd have figured to look for it there?"

"I guess he was canny in that way. I have to tell them."

"You will. Tomorrow's soon enough. They've waited five years. They can wait one more night."

"One more night. I want a hot shower and a gallon of water, and I want to burn this dress. But I want to see Callie more than anything."

"That's first on the list."

"Do you know the way to get back to the Ridge from here?"

"I haven't got a clue."

"That's all right." She took his hand in hers. "I do. I know how to get us home again."

Epilogue

S helby slept long and deep, comforted by the sight of her sleeping child, and her own mother's fussing, her father's gentle, if insistent, exam.

The sun beamed high and bright when she woke, turned the hills she loved into a glimmering green, bathed to shining by the storm that blew through while she slept.

She might have winced when she looked at her face in the mirror, at the purpling bruise on her cheekbone. And winced again, with an added hiss, when she pressed testing fingers against it.

But she reminded herself it would heal and fade.

She wouldn't allow Richard to leave a mark on her. Or on hers.

She heard voices as she went downstairs, followed them into the kitchen.

She saw Griff leaning on the counter smiling at her grandmother, and her grandfather giving Matt some instructions over a hitch in his truck. Her mother put a pretty tray together; her father drank coffee in a splash of sunlight. Emma Kate and Forrest with their heads together, and Clay, Gilly and the baby huddled together.

"This looks like a party."

All conversation stopped; all eyes turned to her.

"Oh, baby girl, I was just fixing you breakfast in bed. You need rest."

"I slept just fine, Mama, and I feel just fine now." She went to kiss her mother's cheek, snatched a piece of bacon off the plate she didn't really want to make her mother smile. "Party. Oh, Emma Kate, your party."

"Don't even start to go there." Jumping up, Emma Kate hugged her hard. "You scared me, Shelby. Don't ever scare me like that again."

"I'm happy to promise that."

"Come over here and sit," her father ordered. "I want a look at you."

"Yes, sir, Daddy. But where's Callie?"

"We took Jack over to Miz Suzannah's so she'd have more company." Gilly smiled but gripped Shelby's hand tight. "We all thought you'd sleep longer."

"I'm so glad you're all here. I'm so glad I woke up to all of you." She looked at Griff. "All of you."

She sat so her father could turn her face this way and that, shine his little light in her eyes. "Headache?"

"No. Not a bit, I promise."

"Do you hurt anywhere?"

"No—well, my cheek's a little sore. Tender."

"That's what this is for." Viola gave her an ice pack, and a kiss on the top of her head.

"Feels good." Like bliss, Shelby thought. "He backhanded me because he could, and he pulled my hair like a girl in a catfight. Mostly he just tried to hurt me with words, like always. But he couldn't. Nothing he could say could— Oh, good Lord, I forgot again. Forrest, I have to tell you why he was here, in the house when I came to get Fifi. He was after—"

"A key? Safe-deposit box he's been paying for under the name of Charles Jakes for about five years now?"

Deflated, she shifted the angle of the ice bag. "Yes, that's what I forgot to tell you."

"Griff filled me in last night when I came by. You slept late, Shelby.

We found what the feds have been after right in the First Bank of Tennessee on High Street."

"All of it? Here?"

"Most of it. The owners and their insurance company'll be notified. That's for the federals."

"Tell her the rest, Forrest." His mother poked him. "I still can't believe it."

"What rest?" Her stomach pitched so she reached for the Coke her mother had put in front of her. "Is he dead? Did I kill him?"

"Not that part of the rest. He made it through the night, and they give him a decent shot of making it altogether."

Closing her eyes, she let out a breath. She'd done what she'd had to do, just as Forrest had said, but dear God, she didn't want a killing on her hands. Even Richard's.

"He's going to live?"

"They say he is. Then he can spend the rest of his life behind bars. The other one, he's one tough son of a bitch. They're giving him a better than decent shot."

"I didn't kill him. I don't have to live with having killed him." She closed her eyes again. "But he'll go to prison. He won't get out again."

"He's going to spend what's left of his life in a cell. He's never going to touch you or Callie."

"Tell her the good part," Ada Mae insisted. "We've had enough talk of that man in this house."

"Spending his life in prison's a pretty good part," Forrest said, but shrugged. Then grinned. "There's a finder's fee for the property stolen in Miami. Standard ten percent. There's going to be some paperwork and some hoops to jump through, but Special Agent Landry figures you'll get about two million out of it."

"Two million what?"

"Dollars, Shelby. Pay attention."

"But . . . he stole it."

"And the information you gave us found it."

"We need to have mimosas." When Ada Mae wept into her hands, Jack put his arms around her. "Oh, Daddy, why don't we have any champagne?"

"They're going to give me all that money." Shelby held up her hands, struggled to take it in. "Enough I can pay off the rest of the debt?"

"Don't see how it's your debt to begin with," Viola said, "but you'll be free and clear. The man's not dead, Shelby Ann, and you were never his wife. Unless you've got fools for lawyers, some of that debt's already going to be gone. You'll have enough left, if I have any say about it, to give you a good start."

"I can't imagine it. I have to let it settle in. I just can't believe I'd be free of that weight. Free of him, altogether."

"I want you to eat now, and rest some more."

"I need to see Callie, Mama."

"What are you going to tell her?"

"I'm going to tell her as much of the truth as I can."

"She's got MacNee, Donahue and Pomeroy in her," Viola said. "She'll stand up to it."

LATER SHE TOOK Callie to Griff's. She thought both of them could use some time around a man who'd never hurt them. And she wanted some quiet time of her own with him.

She sat on the porch with him while Callie raced around with the dog in a shower of bubbles.

"I can't believe you bought her another bubble machine."

"It's not another. It's one for here."

"I'm so glad you said it was all right to bring her here for a while."

"It's always all right, Red."

"I guess I know that, too. So much went through my mind last night, on that awful drive, in that cabin. I'm only going to bring him up to say Daddy's checked in with the hospital. They both came out of it. Richard, he's trying to work a deal, but they're not giving him room for one. And the other one, he's giving them chapter and verse. I think Forrest had the right of it. He's never going to get out of prison. I don't have to worry for Callie on that score."

"I'd never let him near her."

She heard it in his voice—the fierceness and the love.

"I believe that, too. Everything from last night's a little jumbled today. I don't know if I told you everything straight."

"It doesn't matter. You're here."

"I'd like to fix us a nice supper later, the three of us."

"I'll fix it."

Smiling, she tipped her head to his shoulder. "You're not a bad cook as cooks go, but I'm better. And I'd like to do something normal. That's how I feel when I'm here. I feel normal."

"Then stay. Stay for supper, stay the night, stay for breakfast. Stay."

"I have Callie."

He said nothing for a moment, then rose. "Would you come in for a minute? I want to show you something." When she looked out in the yard, he turned.

"Hey, Little Red, will you watch Snickers for me, make sure he stays right in the yard? We need to go in for a minute."

"I will. I will. He likes the bubbles! See, Mama, they make rainbows."

"I see them. You stay right in the yard with Snickers. I'm just inside."

"Where's she going to go?" Griff asked as he drew Shelby in. "And you'll be able to see her out the window anyway."

"Did you start on another room?"

"Mostly finished one." He led her upstairs. She could hear Callie laughing through the open windows, hear the dog's joyful barks.

Normal, she thought again. Safe and real.

On the second floor he opened a door.

The light spilled in through the windows, splashed on the pretty green of the walls. He'd hung a crystal light catcher in one of those windows, and more rainbows shimmered.

"Oh, it's a wonderful space. The color's like bringing the hills right inside. You did a window seat!"

"Thinking about doing some shelves over there, but haven't decided. Plenty of closet space."

He opened double doors and made her eyes go wide. "This is amazing. It's all set up, all painted and pretty. Even the light in here. Is that . . ." She opened another door. "A bathroom, so pretty and fresh. And . . ."

She spotted it then, the little soap dish. A grinning Shrek.

It felt like arms hugged her heart.

"You did this for Callie."

"Well, I thought she needed her own space, one she could grow into. You know Callie and I are getting married. Can't have your bride bunking in an unfinished room."

Her eyes stung. "She mentioned that. How you're getting married."

"Want in on that?"

She turned to him. "What?"

"Bad timing." Flustered, frustrated, he scrubbed a hand over his hair. "I usually ace the timing angle. Might still be a little off balance. I want her to have her own space, that makes her happy. I want her to be comfortable here. Sometimes you might want to stay, and she'd have this for herself. Like the office you'd have on the third floor."

"Office?"

"I haven't started on it yet because you might want it somewhere else, but I think it's a good space. It'd be across from where I'm going to put mine. First-floor-office idea was good," he added, "but the third floor takes work away from the living space."

She hadn't quite caught up. "You're going to build me an office?"

"How are you going to run a business if you don't have an office?"

She walked to the window, watched Callie and the dog. "I never talked to you about any of that."

"Miz Vi did."

"Of course she did. You believe I can do that? Start up and run my own business?"

"I think you can do anything. You have already. What's going to stop you? Anyway, you'd both have space, and you could spend more time here. See how it works for you."

"How about you, Griffin? How's it work for you?"

"I love you. I can wait awhile. You've had a hell of a time, Shelby. I can wait awhile, but I want the two of you here as much as I can get. I want you to be mine. I want—"

When he cut himself off, she shook her head. "Say it. You've earned it."

"I want Callie to be mine. Damn it, she deserves me. I'm good for her, and I'm going to keep being good for her. I love her, and she should be mine. That's the second part of this, I guess, but it's just as important as the first part, just as important as you and me."

She sat on the window seat, took a breath.

"I'm going to be there for the two of you. That's where I draw the line. You know what fear is—you do, because you went through it. The kind of fear where you don't think you've got any blood left in your body. Where everything's drained out of you, but fear. That's what it was when he had you. I can be patient, Shelby, but you're going to know what you are to me. What you and Callie are."

"I know fear. I know fear like what you spoke of. I felt it, too, and with it a terrible, blinding rage. Both so tangled they were one thing in me. That fear and rage that if he did what he planned to do, I'd never see my baby again, or tuck her in at night, or watch her play and learn. Never dry her tears. And a fear and rage I'd never see you again, or have you hold onto me or take my hand the way you do. So many things, I can't say all of them. It would take a lifetime.

"But I knew you'd come. And you did."

She drew another breath. "I've never said I love you."

"You'll get around to it."

"How about now?"

She watched the change, so subtle in his face, in his eyes. And her heart just smiled inside her.

"Now works for me."

"I've never said I love you because I didn't trust. Not you, Griffin, I came to trust you so easily, and that scared me a little so I didn't trust me."

Crossing her hands over her heart, she swore she could feel it swell. "It's all been so fast, so I'd think, I can't get carried away with all this. I can't let myself go, just ride this wave. But I did. I am. I love you, I love who you are with me, with Callie. I love who you are. It might've been fear and rage that made it come so clear. But it is clear. You made Callie this room—for her. She's already yours. So am I."

He stepped to her, took her hands. "Was there a yes in there?"

"There was a whole bunch of them. Weren't you paying attention?"

"I got a little lost after 'I love you.'" He drew her in, took her under, took them both under with the light splashing and rainbows circling.

"I do love you," she murmured. "It fills me up, lights me up. Like Callie does. I didn't know anyone else could make me feel that way. But you do."

Overcome, he rocked her, rocked them both. "I'm never going to stop."

"I believe you. I believe you and I . . . we're going to build wonderful things together. With you, I can look past today and tomorrow into weeks and months and years."

"I've got to get you a ring. I should get Callie a ring."

Her heart just melted. "You're right. She does deserve you. I'm going to keep you filled up and lit up, too." She eased back, framed his face. "I want more children."

"Right now?"

"Pretty much right now. I don't want to wait. We're good with children, you and me, and Callie should have a big, noisy, messy family."

He was grinning, and those clever eyes shining with it. "How big?"

"Three more, that'll make four."

"Four's doable. It's a big house."

"I have such ideas about this house—I've held back."

"Really?"

"Really. And I'm going to be ferocious on some of them." She threw her arms around him. "I'm going to work with you on this house, on this family, on this life. And we *are* going to build something strong and real and beautiful together."

"I think we've already started. If you're going to have all these ideas and give me all this help when it comes to the house, you should move in pretty soon."

"How's tomorrow?"

She loved seeing the surprise, then the joy.

"Tomorrow's also doable. Word of the day. 'Doable.' It's all doable."

"Why don't we go talk to Callie about it?"

"Let's do that. Stay for supper," he said again as they started downstairs. "Stay the night, stay for breakfast. I know I don't have a bed set up for her yet, but I'll fix something up."

"I know you will."

They walked outside the old house they'd make theirs. Walked to where a little girl and an ungainly puppy raced around in a whirl of glistening bubbles, where the hills rose green and the clouds smoked over them in a bold blue sky. And the water bubbled musically over rocks in dappled light and shadow.

She'd found her way home, Shelby thought.

All the way home.

CHASE BRANCH LIBRARY
17731 W. SEVEN MILE RD.
DETROIT, MI 48235
313-481-1580

CHASE BRANCH LIBRARY
17731 W. SEVEN MILE RD.
DETROIT, MI 48235
313-481-1580